STAR TREK® CHRONOLOGY

The History of the Future

MICHAEL OKUDA

DENISE OKUDA

POCKET BOOKS

NEW YORK   LONDON   TORONTO   SYDNEY   TOKYO   SINGAPORE

An Original Publication of POCKET BOOKS

POCKET BOOKS, a division of Simon & Schuster Inc.
1230 Avenue of the Americas, New York, NY 10020

STAR TREK is a Registered Trademark
of Paramount Pictures.

This book is published by Pocket Books,
a division of Simon & Schuster Inc., under exclusive license
from Paramount Pictures.

ISBN: 0-671-53610-9

First Pocket Books trade paperback printing November 1996

10 9 8 7 6 5 4 3 2

POCKET and colophon are registered trademarks
of Simon & Schuster Inc.

Printed in the U.S.A.

CONTENTS

For Gene

INTRODUCTION

Do you remember when you first watched *Star Trek?* Even though it was a lot of fun, it was probably a little confusing at first. You had to figure out what was special about the guy with pointed ears, who were the Klingons, how did transporters work, what was the Federation, and a host of other details. This learning process became part of the fun of watching *Star Trek:* studying the show carefully to learn more about the elaborate background developed for the series. What was especially delightful was that there was so much material being constantly revealed — a wonderful future society, complete with a history spanning the time between our present day and *Star Trek*'s future. Even better, the details of this scenario seemed to have a pretty good degree of internal consistency from episode to episode. (Sure, when you watched *very* closely, you began to notice that some things didn't *quite* add up, but by that time you were hooked. Or at least, we were.)

This project started when Michael wanted to do a simple timeline to show the interrelationship of the first two *Star Trek* series, for use by the writers of *Star Trek: The Next Generation.* Mike was well aware of the inconsistencies and contradictions that can creep into a complex show like *Star Trek,* and he was afraid of going into too much detail for fear of running into too many such errors. Several hours and many pages of notes later, he discovered, to his surprise, that the *Star Trek* timeline held together pretty well. Former *Star Trek* research consultant Richard Arnold proved to be a tremendous help at this stage, providing for us (as he had for some of *Star Trek: The Next Generation*'s writers) many of the basic assumptions that form the framework on which this chronology is built.

At about the same time, *Star Trek* creator Gene Roddenberry coincidentally expressed his concern with the difficulties involved in keeping *Star Trek* books and other projects consistent with the show itself. He was especially concerned because it was so difficult for an outside writer to be aware of all the intricate back story for *Star Trek* that has accumulated over the years. Gene admitted that this was even a problem for *Star Trek* staff writers and for himself, simply because there were so many *Star Trek* episodes and movies to keep track of. (Of course, the more successful the show becomes, the worse the problem gets.) At a meeting called to discuss the issue, Gene realized that the solution was to compile a chronology to serve as a reference for writers. Gene suggested that *Star Trek* designer Mike Okuda might be interested in undertaking such a project, not knowing that Mike had already started preliminary work on this document! Encouraged by Gene's confidence, Mike and Denise compiled the book you now hold in your hands.

We choose, in this volume, to treat *Star Trek*'s invented universe as if it were both complete and internally consistent. In effect, we are pretending that the *Star Trek* saga has unfolded according to a master plan, and that there is a logical, consistent timeline in those episodes, even though we (and you) know very well that this is not entirely true. In fact, the producers of the *Star Trek* television series and the feature films made things up as they went along. The truth is that it is virtually impossible to invent everything for a show like *Star Trek* in advance. Producers usually want to leave many things somewhat vague, so as much room as possible is left for writers to explore and "discover" nifty new things; and quite frankly, time pressures work very strongly

against too much preplanning. This is not to demean their impressive efforts to maintain consistency despite the nearly-impossible schedules of television and film production.

Indeed, this book celebrates the fact that they were amazingly successful in this endeavor, and we hope this volume will be of use to future *Star Trek* writers who wish to continue in this tradition. Nevertheless, one of the challenges in compiling this chronology was to deal with the inevitable gaps and inconsistencies that have cropped up over *Star Trek's* three decades of existence. Where things added up in a logical manner, we have documented it here. But where things didn't quite make sense, we noted the apparent errors. In some such cases, we have offered what we think are plausible-sounding explanations, but we leave it up to the reader to accept or reject the rationalization. In our eyes, the fact that the show's writers and producers were quite capable of mistakes in no way diminishes their extraordinary achievements under the often-brutal pressures of weekly television production.

SOME SPECIFIC NOTES:

Following are some of the guidelines we used in compiling this chronology.

Basic assumptions: This chronology is built on a number of basic assumptions. The first is that the original *Star Trek* series was set 300 years in the future of the first airings of the episodes, meaning that the first season (which aired in 1966-1967) was set in 2266-2267. Although some episodic references suggest the producers of that show vacillated between 200 to 800 years, the 300-year figure seems to be the most internally consistent. (This assumption has also been used by writers of the *Star Trek* feature films and the various spin-off series when determining dates referring back to the original series.) The second basic assumption is that the first season of *Star Trek: The Next Generation* was set in 2364, as established in "The Neutral Zone" (TNG). These dates have been used by the producers of the *Star Trek* spin-off shows and some of the writers of the *Star Trek* features, so many ages and dates mentioned in the show have been consistent with these assumptions. Most of the dates set forth in this chronology were derived from these two reference points.

Conjectural dates: In some cases, an event may not have a specific date established, but other contextual information may limit the "window" in which the event could have occurred. In cases where this window is fairly narrow, we have sometimes arbitrarily picked a date for these events. An example is the date for *Star Trek: The Motion Picture*, which we conjecture took place in 2271. This is based on Decker's line that Kirk hadn't seen active duty in two and a half years. If the original *Enterprise* returned to spacedock for refitting shortly after the end of the third season of the original *Star Trek* series, it seems to make sense that the movie was set about that long after that point. (We believe that the third season ended in mid 2369). However, it is pos-

sible that Kirk and the *Enterprise* might have had other assignments after the original series, but before the refit. There's no evidence that they *didn't* have such assignments, but in the absence of any specific evidence to support such a theory, we felt it reasonable to put the refit start immediately after the third season. Nevertheless, there is a window of several years after the original series during which the *Enterprise* could have begun the refit process and still remain reasonably consistent with data points from the movies. In cases like this, we tried to be careful about which dates we conjectured, trying to remain faithful to the source material. Where we have arbitrarily chosen a date, we have noted that the dating is conjectural, and we have included some indication of the basis for the conjecture. The reader is, of course, free to agree or disagree with our interpretations.

Academy graduation dates: In several cases, we have conjectured that our characters entered Starfleet Academy when they were 18 years old and that they graduated four years later at the age of 22. We also assume that medical school is an eight-year program. These conjectural dates help us see what was probably happening in those characters' lives at those times, but they should probably be taken with a grain or two of salt. (We have been fairly liberal about conjecturing graduation dates for characters from the original *Star Trek* series and *Star Trek: The Next Generation*, but we have been more cautious about doing so for the two current shows, *Star Trek: Deep Space Nine* and *Star Trek: Voyager*, since they are still in production.)

Undated events: The above notwithstanding, there were many events for which there were insufficient data to even guess at a date. In such cases, we have generally omitted the reference from the main chronology, even though some of these are of significant importance to the *Star Trek* scenario. In other words, just because a particular event isn't listed in this document doesn't mean it didn't happen or that it's not considered to be important. It means only that we didn't feel we could derive a reasonably credible date for that event. Some of these undated events are listed in Appendices A through G.

Scripts: We tried to use only data from aired versions of episodes and the finished versions of movies. Although we cross-checked the spellings of names with scripts, for virtually all other information we regarded the aired version as authoritative. It was our goal to create as authentic a reference as possible, derived almost totally from the show itself.

Filling in the blanks: Certain events, such as the fates of original series characters, are obviously very important to the *Star Trek* universe, but have not (yet) been depicted in any episode or film. In the vast majority of cases, we resisted the temptation to fill in these blanks because we did not want to step on the toes of future *Star Trek* writers. We wanted to document where the show has been, but not to limit the places where future writers might want to go.

Again, see Appendices A–G. On the other hand, there are a surprising number of data points, left blank in the first edition of this Chronology, that have since been filled in by episodes or movies, and these have been incorporated into this revised edition.

Chronological order of episodes: *Star Trek* episodes (especially those of the original series and early in *The Next Generation*) were usually produced so that they could be viewed in almost any order without significant continuity problems. This may have been a conscious financial decision designed to make it easier to syndicate the show on independent television stations. Nevertheless, for the first edition of this Chronology, we arbitrarily chose to assume that the events in the episodes happened pretty much in the order in which the episodes were produced. The original network air sequence seemed inappropriate, since it would put "Where No Man Has Gone Before" (TOS) after "The Corbomite Maneuver" (TOS). Specific exceptions were made in cases like "Unification, Parts I and II" (TNG), which were filmed in reverse order (because of Leonard Nimoy's schedule), or "Symbiosis" (TNG), in which Denise Crosby plays Tasha Yar, but which was filmed after "Skin of Evil" (TNG) in which that character is killed. We adopted a different rule after the beginning of *Star Trek: Deep Space Nine*, when we had two *Star Trek* television shows on the air simultaneously. From that point, we have listed episodes in approximate air sequence (allowing for scheduling variations in some local markets).

Dating conventions: Most past events in *Star Trek* history are described not in terms of specific dates, but in relative terms. For example, it is common for something to be described as having happened "four months ago" or "two centuries in the past." In such cases, there are often significant ambiguities as to the exact time of such events. We found, however, that by applying some simple general rules, we were able to derive a significant number of usable data points. Using such rules enables us to paint a far more detailed picture of *Star Trek* history, but it is important to remember that these dating conventions introduce a certain margin for error.

Years: When a particular event is described as having taken place "about a century" before a given episode, we are in most cases arbitrarily assuming that it was exactly one hundred years ago. We realize that most people tend to round such expressions off in everyday speech, but we wanted a general rule. When we assumed that a given event happened exactly one hundred years ago, we generally find it would not really have made a significant difference if it had been 97 years or 103 years. In a similar fashion, we arbitrarily assumed that all references to numbers of years have been converted to Earth-standard years. In other words, when Worf says something happened to him ten years ago, we assume he is speaking of Earth years rather than Klingon years. We realize that this assumption is probably unrealistic, but we felt that it was no more so than the *Star Trek* convention of having so many aliens breathe oxygen and speak English.

Episode time spans: We generally assume that episodes span an average of approximately two weeks. If an event is described as having occurred two months before a given episode, we will typically put the event about four episodes earlier. There are certainly many specific cases where a given episode clearly takes only a day or two, but we are assuming in such cases that there are twelve or so days that we didn't see on television before the next episode. There are also episodes, like "The Paradise Syndrome" (TOS) or "Resolutions" (VGR), which take much more than two weeks, but we're assuming that over the course of an entire season, things average out.

Early draft scripts: In our research, we reviewed many early drafts of *Star Trek* scripts. Many of these scripts contained fascinating background information that never made it to film. Even revised final draft scripts often contain lines of dialog and other tidbits that were not shot or somehow ended up on the cutting room floor. Unfortunately, one problem with using material from early drafts is that many times such drafts will contain information that is inconsistent with other drafts or the actual aired version. Choosing which version is "authoritative" would be difficult. Our solution was to stick fairly strictly with the actual episodes and films as produced and aired. (One of the very few exceptions to this was some material from an early draft of "Journey to Babel" [TOS], which made it possible to conjecture the year in which Spock was born. We broke our rule here because Spock's birth is of such importance to the *Star Trek* universe.)

The animated *Star Trek*: This show, produced several years after the network run of the first series, is considered controversial in that there is significant question as to whether these episodes are part of the "official" *Star Trek* saga. Convincing arguments can be made for both sides of this issue, especially since Gene Roddenberry and Dorothy Fontana were both very actively involved with its planning and production. On the other hand, in later years Gene expressed regret at some elements of the show and instructed Paramount not to consider this series as part of the "official" *Star Trek* universe. For this reason, we have not included material from the animated series, despite our fondness for many of these stories. The only exception to this is some events in Spock's childhood as depicted in "Yesteryear," written by Fontana. We want to make it clear, however, that we feel the ultimate decision as to the "authenticity" of the animated *Star Trek* episodes — as with everything in the *Star Trek* universe — must be up to each individual viewer.

Star Trek V and VI: Gene indicated that he considered some of the events in *Star Trek V: The Final Frontier* and *Star Trek VI: The Undiscovered Country* to be apocryphal. Among these events was the birth of Spock's long-lost half-brother, Sybok. We did not want simply to pretend that the films did not exist, but wanted to respect Gene's feelings. Our compromise was to mention Gene's discomfort with the material, leaving it up to the reader to judge its "authenticity."

Star Trek **novels:** Many fine and imaginative novels, comic books, and other stories based on *Star Trek* have been published over the years. Some of these are adaptations of episodes and movies, while others are original works of fiction. We considered including key elements of some of these works in this chronology, since many such stories detail fascinating events not depicted in the episodes or movies. We finally chose not to do so, not out of dislike for these stories, but because it became too difficult to choose which books and events to include. Additionally, some events in some novels are even contradicted when later episodes and films are produced. For example, one of our favorite *Star Trek* novels is Judith and Gar Reeves-Stevens' *Federation*, even though their account of the events surrounding Cochrane's first warp flight is substantially different from what was later revealed in *Star Trek: First Contact*. We have therefore fallen back on our original purpose, to provide a reference to the show itself. We hope this way the Chronology will be of use to fans, as well as to *Star Trek* writers of both scripts and novels.

Eugenics Wars and other present-day events: Some late 20th-century events suggested in the first *Star Trek* series probably seemed comfortably far in the future to the producers of that show. Little did they know that their creation would survive long enough to see a number of their "predictions" proven wrong. Such events include the launch of an orbital nuclear platform in 1968 ("Assignment Earth" [TOS]) and the rise of Khan Noonien Singh to power in the early 1990s ("Space Seed" [TOS]). While we are grateful these events have not come to pass, we are including them in this chronology because of our desire to make this a complete record of the *Star Trek* universe as established to date.

The second edition: This revised and expanded edition of the *Star Trek Chronology* includes material through the fourth year of *Star Trek: Deep Space Nine* and the second year of *Star Trek: Voyager*. Portions of this update material were previously published in Simon and Schuster Interactive's *Star Trek: Omnipedia* CD-ROM. We've snuck in a small number of data points from the eighth *Star Trek* feature, *Star Trek: First Contact*, even though this was scheduled for release after our cutoff date for this book. We did this because of the pivotal importance of Zefram Cochrane's flight to the *Star Trek* timeline. (We included the 21st-century material from the film, but did not include the 24th-century events.) We have also included a few data points from "Flashback" (VGR), which was filmed during *Voyager*'s second season, but scheduled for airing during the third season, and a couple of episodes from that season that were in preproduction as this book was being completed. Because of publishing deadlines, our writeups for the last few episodes of *Star Trek: Deep Space Nine* and *Star Trek: Voyager* had to be done before the episodes were completed and aired. It is therefore possible that some information from those episodes may have been changed or deleted between the script and the aired versions. Similarly, our *Star Trek: First Contact* data points are also from the script, and are therefore subject to change when the final, edited film is released.

News from the Delta Quadrant: Under the conventions we used for most of the Chronology, we probably shouldn't include any information from the *Starship Voyager* in the Delta Quadrant, since the Federation presumably knows nothing of *Voyager*'s adventures. (Starfleet, after all, probably believes that *Voyager* was destroyed in the Badlands.) Nevertheless, we took the license of including these data since it seemed inappropriate to omit such an important part of the *Star Trek* saga.

Finally: We hope the chronology will make it easier for *Star Trek* writers to remain consistent with what's been established to date and for fans to keep track of *Star Trek*'s elaborate back story. We do not, however, want this to intimidate our writer friends or to inhibit the imaginations of fans who may have differing interpretations of the *Star Trek* timeline. As such, we encourage both fans and writers to take this material with a grain of salt and to enjoy it in the spirit intended, as a fun way to explore the *Star Trek* universe.

ACKNOWLEDGMENTS

ACKNOWLEDGMENTS FOR THE SECOND EDITION (1996)

This book was an enormous project and we could not have completed it without the help and support of our friends, family, and colleagues.

Our thanks to the researchers who worked with us on this revised edition and on the *Star Trek Omnipedia* CD-ROM project, portions of which were incorporated into this work: Curt Danhauser, Casey Bernay, Josh Schroeder, Alan Kobayashi, Penny Juday, Mark Bernay, Anthony Fredrickson, James Van Over, Jackie Edwards, Judy Saul, Richard Barnett, Matthew F. Lyons, and Debbie Mirek. Thanks to Susie Miller for proofreading and for compiling the index.

At Paramount Pictures, our gratitude to Rick Berman, Paula Block, Harry Lang, Gary Hutzel, Dave Rossi, Eddie Williams, Steve Elkin, and Mary Mandebach. At the *Star Trek* art departments, our appreciation to Anthony Fredrickson, Doug Drexler, Wendy Drapanas, Rick Sternbach, Laura Richarz, John Eaves, and James Van Over. At Industrial Light and Magic, thanks to John Knoll and Bill George.

At Pocket Books, we salute our editor, Kevin Ryan, for being a keeper of the flame. Margaret Clark spearheaded the massive job of photo editing and clearances, no small task since the all-color format of this edition required her to start from scratch. Thanks also to John Ordover, Scott Shannon, Tyya Turner, Kara Welsh, Donna O'Neill, Donna Ruvituso, Gina Centrello, and David Stern. Art direction by Murphy Foglenest. Copy editing by Arthur Harvaty.

At Simon and Schuster Interactive, our gratitude to Keith Halper and Elizabeth Braswell, who were responsible for the *Star Trek Omnipedia* CD-ROM, which included an intermediate update of this Chronology. Also thanks to Peter Mackey, Marshall Lefferts, and the good people at Imergy who were our developers on the project.

Many photographs in this volume were directly taken from film and video frames of the actual episodes and movies. As a result, the directors of photography of the shows should be credited: Jerry Finnerman and Al Francis (original *Star Trek* series), William E. Snyder ("The Cage" [TOS]), Ernest Haller ("Where No Man Has Gone Before" [TOS]), Richard H. Kline (*Star Trek: The Motion Picture*), Gayne Rescher (*Star Trek II: The Wrath of Khan*), Charles Correll (*Star Trek III: The Search for Spock*), Don Peterman (*Star Trek IV: The Voyage Home*), Andrew Laszlo (*Star Trek V: The Final Frontier*), Hiro Narita (*Star Trek VI: The Undiscovered Country*), John Alonzo (*Star Trek Generations*), and Matt Leonetti (*Star Trek: First Contact*). Ed Brown, Jr., Marvin Rush, and Jonathan West were direc-tors of photography for *Star Trek: The Next Generation, Star Trek: Deep Space Nine,* and *Star Trek: Voyager.* Production stills by: Mel Traxel (*Star Trek I*), Bruce Birmelin (*Star Trek II, IV,* and *V*), John Shannon (*Star Trek III*), Gregory Schwartz (*Star Trek VI*), and Elliott Marks (*Star Trek Generations* and *Star Trek: First Contact*). *Star Trek: The Next Generation, Star Trek: Deep Space Nine,* and *Star Trek: Voyager* still photographers have included Carin Baer, Byron J. Colten, Julie Dennis, Danny Feld, Kim Gottlieb-Walker, Michael Leshnov, Dianna Lynn, Brian D. McLaughlin, Michael Paris, Robbie Robinson, Fred Sabine, Gregory Schwartz, Barry Slobin, and Joseph Viles. ILM effects stills by Terry Chostner and Kerry Nordquist. *Enterprise*-A and *Enterprise*-D photography and composites by Gary Hutzel. CGI renderings of the original *Enterprise* by John Knoll. Photos of the original *Enterprise* model by Ed Miarecki. Some photos are from the collections of Doug Drexler, Greg Jein, and Richard Barnett. Eighth-dimension images courtesy of John Whorfin, Yoyodyne Propulsion Systems. Photo laboratory and digital services by RGB Laboratory, Composite Image Systems, and at The Photo Lab, Patrick Donahue and Rik Thomas. Archive photos courtesy of the Bettman Archive; our thanks to Jocelyn Clapp.

This book was produced on Apple Macintosh comput-ers using Microsoft Word software. Other resources includ-ed Adobe Photoshop, Adobe Illustrator, Quark Xpress, Adobe PageMaker, Microsoft Excel, Radius VideoVision, and Electric Image. We salute everyone who helped cre-ate these wonderful tools for the rest of us.

Special thanks to Russ Galen, Allan Rinkus, Barry Friedman, Helen Cohen, Paul Brodsky, Bob Levinson, Bob Greenberger, Stephen Poe, Jay Roth, and Adam Lebowitz. Inspiration by: Saul Bass, Louis Grant, Susan Ivanova, Claude Lacombe, J.J. Adams, John Drake, Alexander Waverly, Dorothy Gale, Jim McCarthy, Duncan Idaho, Dr. Henry Jones, Jr., Dr. Jeremy Stone, Dr. Sidney Zwibel, and Dr. Ted Geisel.

ADDITIONAL ACKNOWLEDGMENTS FROM THE FIRST EDITION (1993)

We are immensely grateful to Dorothy Fontana, story editor and associate producer on the original *Star Trek* series and associate producer on *Star Trek: The Next Generation* for reviewing this manuscript in great detail and for offering many fascinating insights into both shows. Dorothy's comments were especially valuable because of her pivotal role in helping to establish and maintain such an extraordinary degree of continuity in the first *Star Trek* series, and because of her role in helping to get the second series started on the right foot. Her notes helped us steer clear of many misconceptions that have crept into Trek lore.

We also want to thank Bob Justman, producer on the first *Star Trek* series and supervising producer on *Star Trek: The Next Generation,* for reviewing this text and for offering his veteran's perspective into the making of both shows.

We want to acknowledge Richard Arnold for serving as a valuable resource in helping us pin down dozens of obscure references that served as the framework for this chronology. Richard also lent a significant hand with research and proofreading. His encyclopedic knowledge of *Star Trek* did much to help keep this book on track.

Our appreciation to *Star Trek: The Next Generation* producer Ronald D. Moore, for giving us a lot of nifty behind-the-scenes insights into the show. Ron is also very knowledgeable about all the *Star Trek* series, and his comments helped us catch quite a number of errors.

Much assistance with research and proofreading was provided by Debbie Mirek, Mike Rosen, Kurt Hanson, Guy Vardaman, Nancy Ohlson, Richard Barnett, Carole Lyne Ross, Tim DeHaas, Diane Lee Baron, Greg and Mary Varley, Jeff and Kiku Annon, Shelly Perron, and John Tuttle. Thank you, all.

Greg Jein built several original spacecraft models used in some of the photographs in this volume. We're very pleased and grateful to have had his talent and energy on this project. Those familiar with Trek history might recognize Greg's conjectural *Daedalus*-class starship model, which is based on an early concept for the *U.S.S. Enterprise*, designed in 1964 by original series art director Matt Jefferies. (That model has since been used for set dressing on *Star Trek: Deep Space Nine*. It can occasionally be glimpsed on a shelf in Ben Sisko's office.) Greg also built an old Romulan ship based on descriptions in an early draft of "Balance of Terror" (TOS), as well as a conjectural design for the *S.S. Valiant* (mentioned but not seen in "Where No Man Has Gone Before" [TOS]).

At Paramount Pictures, we want to recognize the assistance, support, and enthusiasm of Rick Berman, Michael Piller, Ralph Winter, Jeri Taylor, David Livingston, Peter Lauritson, Merri Howard, Brad Yacobian, Bobby della Santina, Brannon Braga, Ira Steven Behr, Peter Allan Fields, Wendy Neuss, Gary Hutzel, Heidi Smothers, Steve Frank, Susan Sackett, Denny Martin Flinn, and Ralph Johnson. Our colleagues and friends at the *Star Trek* art departments: Tom Betts, Nathan Crowley, Ricardo Delgado, Wendy Drapanas, Doug Drexler, Bill Hawkins, Joseph Hodges, Richard James, Alan Kobayashi, Jim Magdaleno, Randy McIlvain, Jim Martin, Andy Neskoromny, Louise Dorton, Andrew Probert, Gary Speckman, Rick Sternbach, and Herman Zimmerman. At Paramount's Licensing department: Paula Block, Brooks Branch, Suzie Domnick, Bonnie Foley, Andrea Hein, Terri Helton, Carla Mason, Christin Miller, Tammy Moore, Helene Nielsen, Neil Newman, Pamela Newton, Debbi Petrasek, David Rosenbaum, and Valerie Shavers.

We want in particular to recognize the pioneering work of Bjo Trimble, whose *Star Trek Concordance* was a valuable resource in compiling this chronology, as it has been in the production of all *Star Trek* films and episodes since the original series. Bjo's concordance is even more amazing when you consider that it was originally written in the days before videocassette recorders. (Bjo, in turn, has acknowledged the work of Dorothy Jones Heydt, whose research was the basis of the original fan version of the concordance.)

We also want to acknowledge the *Star Trek* enthusiasts who have shared us with their own versions of the *Star Trek* timeline. Their considerable ingenuity and detailed research served as helpful references for this volume. Alex Rozensweig, Erik Pflueger, Gary Wallace, David B. Dornburg, Terry Jones, Melvin H. Schuetz, and Ronald M. Roden, Jr., all came up with differing but credible alternate versions of this history. Thanks also to Bjo Trimble for providing us with timeline material that she's compiled. The fact that some of our key dates differ from those in some of these fan-developed histories is not a reflection on their work and doesn't necessarily mean they're wrong; it merely shows that we used some different basic assumptions. We hope they'll like what we've come up with.

Special thanks to Charlie and Beverly Kurts, Diane Sternbach, Naren Shanker, Marc Okrand, David Gerrold, Jackie Edwards, Carmen Carter, Jeanne Dillard, George Kalogridis, Bob Greenberger, Larry Yaeger, Peter Kavanagh, Carl Done, Diane Castro, Jim and Barbara Van Over, Scott Leyes, Ira C. Neuss, Anthony Fredrickson, Donna Drexler, "Microbe" York, Tom Servo (space hero), Liz Radley, Terry Erdmann, Dennis Bailey, Michael J. Lim, Gerald Kawaoka, Wayne Momii, Mary van de Ven, Bob Abraham, Glee and Tom Stormont, Lillian Holt, Ed Miarecki, Larry Nemecek, Roy Cameron, Steve Horch, K. M. "Killer" Fish, Ken and Trish Yoshida, Dr. Chris Hill, M.D., Tom Mirek, Kathy Leprich, Pat Repalone, James Arakaki, Craig Nagoshi, Judy Saul, Tamara Haack, Todd Tathwell, Craig Okuda, and Annette Yokoyama.

We want to thank our parents, Hiromi and Patsy Okuda, and Jack and Carolyn Tathwell. Without their support, encouragement, and love, we wouldn't be where we are, and this book wouldn't be in your hands.

Finally, our love and thanks to Gene Roddenberry, who brought so many people together to produce a television show that has brought so much enjoyment to audiences for over three decades. This book is a celebration of his work.

— Michael Okuda

— Denise Okuda

1.0 THE DISTANT PAST

*God-machine
Vaal of planet
Gamma Trianguli VI,
approximately
10,000 years ago*

Many of the dates or ages of the items in this section are conjectural. It is entirely possible that many individual events took place in a sequence considerably different from that shown here, but these estimates should convey a sense of the overall flow of history.

We have included a few non-Star Trek data points in this and the following section in order to lend some perspective as to what was happening in "real" history.

15 BILLION YEARS AGO

The universe was formed in a massive explosion known as the Big Bang. In the aftermath of the explosion, matter and energy gradually condensed into the universe we know today. At least two members of the Q Continuum, traveling back from the future, took refuge in the first moments of the cosmos. One, the individual later known as Quinn, also briefly tried to conceal the *Starship Voyager* in the maelstrom of creation.

Scientific theory. The Qs' visits were established in "Death Wish" (VGR).

6 BILLION YEARS AGO

The Guardian of Forever

The Guardian of Forever was a time portal created billions of years ago. It remains functional until at least the 23rd century, and it may be the last surviving artifact of an incredibly ancient civilization, although its origin and purpose are still a total mystery.

"The City on the Edge of Forever" (TOS). The Guardian said it had been awaiting a question "since before your sun burned hot in space and before your race was born," suggesting it was at least five billion years old. Interestingly, the ruins surrounding the Guardian registered on Spock's tricorder as being on the order of 10,000 centuries old, which is "only" a million years. One might speculate that the Guardian was not an artifact of that civilization, or that the civilization in question somehow spanned billions of years, perhaps with the help of the Guardian itself.

5 BILLION YEARS AGO

The star that would one day be known as Sol began to condense out of nebular material, forming the sun and our solar system.

Scientific theory.

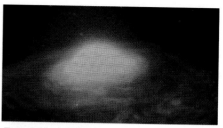

Formation of a solar system

4 BILLION YEARS AGO

A humanoid civilization, the first to evolve in our galaxy, explored the cosmos, but found themselves alone. Knowing the life span of a single race to be finite, these humanoids perpetuated themselves by seeding the oceans of many Class-M planets with genetic material. Several humanoid species on planets across the galaxy evolved over the next few billion years from these seeds, resulting in a remarkable commonality of genetic makeup between humanoids from widely seperated planets including Earth, Vulcan, Qo'noS, and Cardassia. The ancient humanoids encoded the genetic seeds with a message that would reveal itself only when their offspring reached a high level of technology and cooperation. Other planets seeded by these humanoids included Ruah IV, Indri VIII, and Vilmor II.

"The Chase" (TNG), according to the scientific work of Professor Galen.

Ancient humanoid

3.5 BILLION YEARS AGO

The chemical building blocks of life on Earth are formed as amino acids combine to form the first proteins in a muddy puddle in what will one day be known as France.

"All Good Things..." (TNG). Q showed Picard the first moment of primordial life on Earth. "The Chase" (TNG) suggests that those first building blocks of life may have had help.

Earth

2 BILLION YEARS AGO

The civilization on planet Tagus III flourished two billion years ago. By the 24th century, much still remains a mystery about this ancient culture, at least partially because the ruins on the planet have been sealed off since Earth's 23rd century. Nevertheless, Tagus remains a subject of interest to many archaeologists and enthusiasts, including Captain Jean-Luc Picard.

"Qpid" (TNG). Q told Picard that the folks on Tagus "really knew how to have fun" two billion years ago.

First single-celled organisms evolved on Earth.

Scientific theory.

100 MILLION YEARS AGO

A civilization in the D'Arsay system launched a robotic interstellar craft containing an archive of their culture, religion, and politics. The D'Arsay civilization perished, but the archive survived, preserving some part of its makers.

"Masks" (TNG). Eighty-seven million years ago.

D'Arsay archive

MILLIONS OF YEARS AGO

The inhabitants of planet Organia underwent a transformation from humanoid bodies to beings of pure energy.

"Errand of Mercy" (TOS). Ayelborne said that his people had evolved beyond the need for physical bodies millions of years ago.

Organians in their form of pure energy

Portal of the Tkon Empire

ONE MILLION YEARS AGO

The Tkon Empire became extinct about 600,000 years ago when their sun went supernova during a period of time known to the Tkons as the Age of Makto. According to legend, the Tkons were once enormously powerful, even capable of moving stars. Prior to the Age of Makto, other Tkon eras included the Ages of Fendor, Ozari, Xora, Cimi, and Bastu. The population of the Tkon had numbered in the trillions.

"The Last Outpost" (TNG). Data described the history of the Tkon Empire from computer records.

Sargon's people, a technologically advanced civilization, explored the galaxy aboard space vessels and planted colonies on many planets.

"Return to Tomorrow" (TOS). Sargon told Kirk that his people had established colonies 600,000 years ago.

Editors' Note: Spock speculated that Sargon's account of such colonization might explain certain elements of Vulcan prehistory, suggesting that Spock's people may have originally been from Sargon's planet. It is possible that Spock was mistaken, since "The Chase" (TNG) establishes that Vulcan had been "seeded" by ancient humanoids some four billion years ago. Of course, it is also possible that Sargon's people and the Vulcans were both beneficiaries of the ancient humanoids from "The Chase."

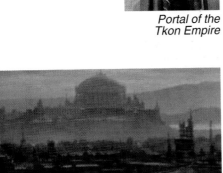

Bajor

500,000 YEARS AGO

Civilization flourished on the planet Bajor many millennia ago. The culture boasted architects, artists, builders, and philosophers. By Earth's 24th century, the Bajoran culture was all but destroyed by the Cardassians, who forced the Bajorans to resettle on neighboring planets.

"Ensign Ro" (TNG). Picard noted he'd studied ancient Bajoran civilization in the fifth grade, and that the ancient Bajorans had flourished "when humans were not yet standing erect," suggesting a time frame of about 500,000 years ago. This corresponds to the emergence of Homo Erectus, generally accepted by anthropologists as the first humans.

Ruk

The star Exo, which had at one time been bright enough to support life on its planet, Exo III, began to fade about 500,000 years ago, eventually rendering the planet's surface uninhabitable, with temperatures of 100 degrees below zero. Dr. Roger Korby's research discovered that as the sun dimmed, the civilization moved underground for survival, becoming more mechanized and less human. The android Ruk had been built by the ancient civilization that he called "the Old Ones." At the time of Korby's arrival on Exo III, Ruk had been tending the Old Ones' machinery for many centuries. Androids had apparently been commonplace in the now-vanished culture, but at some point the Old Ones began to fear their creations, and tried to deactivate them. The androids eventually learned to defend themselves, killing the Old Ones.

"What Are Little Girls Made Of?" (TOS). Spock noted that the star had been fading for a half million years.

A terrible cataclysm on Sargon's planet totally ripped the atmosphere away about 500,000 years ago. The planet was left almost totally dead, the only survivors suspended in special protected canisters stored deep below the surface. Millennia later, Sargon would describe the cataclysm as the result of a crisis faced whenever a civilization becomes so powerful that its inhabitants dare think of themselves as "gods." Prior to this disaster, Sargon's people roamed the galaxy aboard starships.

Survival canisters stored beneath the surface of Sargon's planet

"Return to Tomorrow" (TOS). Spock noted the planet's atmosphere had been destroyed about a half million years ago.

The technologically advanced inhabitants of planet Talos IV were nearly wiped out by a terrible war thousands of centuries ago. The war made the surface of the planet uninhabitable, and the few remaining Talosians survived by living underground. They found this life limiting, so they devoted themselves to developing their mental powers, while their technical skills atrophied. They developed a practice of telepathically sharing illusory experiences with specimens in their menagerie of alien life-forms, gathered prior to the war, when the Talosians were a spacefaring people. The Talosians eventually found such illusions to be a dangerous narcotic that very nearly destroyed what was left of their civilization.

Talosian

"The Menagerie" (TOS) and "The Cage" (TOS). Vina told Pike about the war "thousands of centuries ago" and its consequences. This would seem to imply that the Talosian war had happened somewhere between 100,000 to 900,000 years ago.

200,000 YEARS AGO

The civilization of the planet Iconia flourished many millennia ago, becoming a strong influence on many ancient cultures, as evidenced by linguistic similarities between Iconian, Dewan, Iccobar, and Dinasian. The Iconians were known as "demons of air and darkness," because of their ability to use interdimensional "gateways" that allowed them to transport instantaneously across interstellar distances. The Iconians used this technology to maintain control of their vast interstellar empire. The Iconian civilization was destroyed some 200,000 years ago when all major cities on Iconia were heavily damaged by large-scale orbital bombardment.

Surface of planet Iconia, nearly all signs of civilization eradicated by orbital bombardment

"Contagion" (TNG). Some 200,000 years ago, per Captain Donald Varley's interpretation of archaeological evidence from Denius III. We also saw an Iconian gateway in "To the Death" (DS9).

50,000 YEARS AGO

The Horta of planet Janus VI began their most recent cycle of rebirth about 50,000 years ago. At that time, their entire species died, except for one individual who guarded their Vault of Tomorrow which contained the eggs for the next generation of Horta. This individual became the "mother" of her race.

"The Devil in the Dark" (TOS). Spock learned the history of the Horta during his mind-meld.

Mother Horta tends her children in the Vault of Tomorrow

Lokai of the planet Cheron attempted to lead a revolution against that planet's government, fighting against what he saw as racial injustice and oppression of his people. Although the Cheron government claimed to have been making reforms, these were deemed inadequate by Lokai and his followers. Lokai was convicted of treason, but managed to flee from the planet. He was followed by Commissioner Bele on a pursuit that would last some 50,000 years, ending only after racial hatred had destroyed their entire civilization.

"Let That Be Your Last Battlefield" (TOS). Bele explained that he'd been chasing Lokai across the galaxy for 50,000 years.

Two unknown adversaries outside of our galaxy fought a terrible war, culminating in the use of a "doomsday machine." Intended as a bluff, the device was so powerful, it would destroy both sides. Unfortunately, the planet-killing weapon apparently did exactly that, and subsequently wandered through intergalactic space for unknown millennia before attacking at least six solar systems near L-374 in our own galaxy.

"The Doomsday Machine" (TOS). Conjecture. Date for the ancient war is unknown, but it would likely have been many millennia ago during which the weapon apparently crossed an intergalactic distance prior to the episode.

Planet killer

Sky Spirit

Trill homeworld

Kurlan naiskos

Vaal

45,000 YEARS AGO

A group of extraterrestrials from the Delta Quadrant voyaged for over two generations across the galaxy to the planet Earth, making contact with indigenous humans living as nomadic hunters in the Siberian Peninsula region. The space travelers gave these humans, whom they called "Inheritors," a genetic bonding to help them — and their world — survive. Subsequently the extraterrestrials, known as "Sky Spirits" to the humans, found that the Inheritors had gained a sense of curiosity and adventure that caused them to migrate across their planet, settling on the American continents. In later generations, some Inheritors would even find homes on distant worlds.

"Tattoo" (VGR). The Sky Person related the story to Chakotay.

30,000 YEARS AGO

The Verathan civilization, originally from the Verath system in the Gamma Quadrant, reached its height, spanning some two dozen star systems.

"Q-Less" (DS9). Vash said the Verathan civilization reached its height 30,000 years ago.

25,000 YEARS AGO

The first of at least 947 archaeological expeditions was conducted at the ancient ruins on planet Tagus III, about 22,000 years ago. Among these studies were a number of Vulcan expeditions that concentrated on the northeastern part of the city.

"Qpid" (TNG). Picard described the history of Tagus archaeological research in his speech to the Archaeology Council's annual symposium.

The Trill began living as a "joined species," a pairing of intelligent but helpless creatures who live in humanoid host bodies. So complete is the symbiotic relationship that most outside observers deal with the joined Trill as single entities.

"The Host" (TNG). Odan noted his people have lived in this fashion for "millennia."

12,000 YEARS AGO

An artisan on the planet Kurl, during that world's Fifth Dynasty, earned recognition for creation of small ceramic figurines, called *naiskos*, that embody that culture's belief that within each person is a community of individuals, each with its own desires, views, and voices. The name of this artisan was lost when the Kurlan civilization died, but he remains known as the Master of Tarquin Hill.

"The Chase" (TNG). Picard explained the history of the master when Professor Galen gave him the naiskos that later adorned the captain's ready room.

10,000 YEARS AGO

The machine-god Vaal on planet Gamma Trianguli VI was built at least 10,000 years ago in order to protect the inhabitants of that planet by providing food and climate control.

"The Apple" (TOS). Spock described Vaal as being "very ancient, very high order of workmanship." McCoy noted that the people had apparently had "no change or progress in at least ten thousand years," suggesting that Vaal was constructed at least that long ago.

A species of intelligent spacefaring organisms became nearly extinct some millennia ago. These organisms formed symbiotic relationships with humanoid life-forms that lived within their bodies, providing life support and effectively becoming "living spaceships" to their humanoid companions. The last surviving specimen, an individual that called itself Gomtuu (and would eventually be known as Tin Man to the Federation), suffered injury when radiation from an explosion penetrated its outer layers, killing its crew. Gomtuu wandered alone through space for millennia, looking unsuccessfully for others of its kind, eventually becoming despondent because it was dependent on its humanoid crew for emotional sustenance.

Gomtuu, a spaceborne organism

"Tin Man" (TNG). Tam Elbrun noted that Tin Man had been wandering in space for millennia.

The sun of the Fabrini system went nova about 10,000 years ago, destroying the planets in that system. Before this happened, the inhabitants of the planet Fabrina created a giant space ark to insure the survival of their species. The ark, fashioned from a 200-mile-diameter asteroid, was known as *Yonada* to its inhabitants, and was designed to simulate perfectly the surface of their home world for a ten-millennium voyage to a planet near Daran V.

Fabrini asteroid ship

"For the World Is Hollow and I Have Touched the Sky" (TOS). Spock noted Yonada had been in transit for 10,000 years.

The Q Continuum begins a new era of discovery, celebrating learning, dialog, and even humor from all across the universe.

"Death Wish" (VGR). Ten millenia before the episode.

The Kalandans constructed a small planet, about the size of Earth's moon, for colonization. Despite the planet's small size, it had a Class-M environment and supported a Kalandan outpost until a deadly disease organism, accidentally created in the planet's formation, killed all the inhabitants. This left the automated defense systems to protect the now-vacant outpost.

Quark's vision of Gint, the first Grand Nagus

"That Which Survives" (TOS). The Kalandan planetoid was described as being just a few thousand years old.

The Ferengi people began following a path of capitalism that became the foundation of their civilization. Gint, the first Grand Nagus, codifies Ferengi cultural values in a book he calls the Rules of Acquisition.

"Bar Association" (DS9). Ten thousand years before the episode. Gint established in "Body Parts" (DS9).

The first "Tear of the Prophets" was discovered by the Bajorans in the sky above their planet. Over the next ten millennia, a total of nine of these extraordinary objects were discovered, inspiring revelations that shaped Bajoran theology. Bajoran religious faith holds that the tears have come from the Prophets, who reside in the Celestial Temple.

A Tear of the Prophets

"Emissary" (DS9). Ten thousand years before the episode, according to Kai Opaka.

6,000 YEARS AGO

The great leader Landru of planet Beta III in star system C-111 chose to provide for his people's future after his death by creating a powerful computer system that would run the planet's society. Prior to Landru's rise to power, the planet had been wracked by war. Landru changed his society, returning to a simple time of peace and tranquillity. The computer, which was made operational about 6,000 years ago, was programmed with the sum of Landru's knowledge and was given the prime directive of always acting for the good of the people. The knowledge that Landru had been replaced after his death with a computer was kept from the people.

Landru of Beta III

Gary Seven, a descendant of humans raised by an unknown civilization

"Return of the Archons" (TOS). Reger described a high-tech lighting panel as being very old, before the time of Landru, then added that some had speculated that this made the artifact as old as 6,000 years. Spock noted that Landru had built and programmed the machine 6,000 years ago.

Unknown aliens took several humans from Earth to be raised on a distant planet some 6,000 years ago. The descendants of these humans were trained for generations so that they could secretly be returned to Earth as part of an effort to prevent Earth from destroying itself before it could mature into a peaceful society.

"Assignment: Earth" (TOS). Gary Seven described his mission to the Beta Five computer.

An ice age began on planet Sigma Draconis VI, triggering a remarkable regression in the civilization there. Once technologically advanced beyond the Federation's 23rd-century level, the society regressed to a virtual Stone Age. Although some elements of their past technological achievements remained, the inhabitants no longer possessed any understanding of the technology in the 23rd century.

"Spock's Brain" (TOS). Spock described the planet's history.

5,000 YEARS AGO

Greek god Apollo

Planet Earth was visited by a group of extraterrestrials who settled the Mediterranean area some five thousand years ago. The visitors, who possessed powerful psychokinetic abilities, were worshipped by the ancient Greeks as gods and were apparently the origin of many Greek myths. The humans eventually outgrew the cultural need for these gods, who departed Earth for planet Pollux IV. Many years later, the last visitor—who was once known as the god Apollo—attempted to persuade members of the *Enterprise* crew to worship him as did the ancient Greeks.

"Who Mourns for Adonais" (TOS). Apollo described the history of his people, mentioning their visit with the ancient Greeks 5,000 years ago.

Zarabeth

Planet Sarpeidon experienced an ice age some 5,000 years ago. A woman from Sarpeidon's present, Zarabeth, was exiled into this past by the tyrant Zor Khan, after two of Zarabeth's kinsmen conspired to kill the dictator. Zarabeth lived completely alone in this past, except for a brief visit from Spock and McCoy, who accidentally traveled into the past thorough Sarpeidon's atavachron time portal.

"All Our Yesterdays" (TOS). Spock and McCoy went 5,000 years into Sarpeidon's past.

4,000—3,000 B.C. First large-scale human civilizations developed in Sumer region of the Nile river valley on Earth. The Sumerians were responsible for the earliest known form of writing, known as cuneiform. The civilization also had the first known records of the use of wheeled vehicles. The first epic tales of Gilgamesh began in this period.

Historical accounts.

Corbis-Bettman

Sumerian cuneiform writing

The Progenitors of planet Aldea in the Epsilon Mynos star system install a powerful cloaking shield around their entire planet, controlled by a sophisticated computer called the Custodian. The Aldeans, who sought anonymity to avoid marauders and other hostile passersby, eventually faded into mythology until the cloaking shield began to cause major environmental damage on Aldea, forcing the Aldeans to seek outside help in 2364.

"When the Bough Breaks" (TNG). Rashella noted that their shield "has confused outsiders for millennia." Duana noted that their main computer, the Custodian, had been built by the Progenitors many centuries ago.

3834 B.C. The (nearly) immortal Flint was born in Mesopotamia on Earth. Flint described his early self as a bully who didn't die, despite serious injuries in an ancient war. Flint lived under a variety of assumed names, including Merlin, Leonardo da Vinci, and Johannes Brahms, finally settling on a small planet he purchased under the name of Mr. Brack.

"Requiem for Methuselah" (TOS). Flint described his history.

The star known as Sahndara went nova, presumably destroying the planets in that system over 2,500 years ago. At least a few of the natives of one of the planets were able to escape. They spent some time on planet Earth, circa 400 B.C., where their leader, Parmen, became a great admirer of the philosopher Plato. After leaving Earth, circa 200 B.C., they settled on a planet that they named Platonius, and attempted to pattern their world after Plato's Republic. About six months after their arrival on this planet, the Platonians began to develop powerful telekinetic abilities, the result of having absorbed trace quantities of kironide from the planet's environment.

"Plato's Stepchildren" (TOS). Parman noted his people had arrived on their planet some 2,500 years ago. Philana, Parmen's wife, said she was 2,300 years old, but may have been lying about her age.

Planet Vulcan

630 B.C. Bajoran prophet Trakor encountered the Orb of Change for the first time. Afterwards he predicted that "when the river wakes, stirred once more to Janir's side, three vipers will return to their nest in the sky." Trakor added that "when the vipers try to peer through the temple gates, a sword will appear in the heavens, the temple will burn, and the gates will be cast open."

"Destiny" (DS9). Three thousand years before the episode (2371).

500–600 B.C. First records of parts of the Old Testament. Birth of Confucianism and Buddhism. Height of the Greek age of philosophy and the influence of the Greek oracle at Delphi.

Historical accounts.

Spock's ancestors adopted a ceremonial ground that remains in their family at least until the 23rd century. These ceremonial grounds, used for the mating rituals, embodied the Vulcan heart and soul, reflecting Vulcan culture from the "time of the beginning."

"Amok Time" (TOS). Spock noted the grounds had been held by his family for over 2,000 years. T'Pau's comments about the ceremonies suggest that these grounds predate the Vulcan Time of Awakening.

Spock's family ceremonial grounds

4 B.C. Jesus Christ was born. Christ's teachings were the basis of Earth's Christian religion.

Historical accounts.

A.D. 1ST–10TH CENTURIES

The inhabitants of planet Vulcan engaged in terrible and destructive wars, a result of the violent passions and emotions that governed the Vulcan people. It was a savage time, even by Earth standards. Myths from this period describe a terrifying weapon of war called the Stone of Gol, that killed with the power of the mind.

In the midst of this turmoil, the great philosopher Surak led the Vulcan people on the path toward logic and peace, demonstrating enormous courage by working for peace in the face of war. It was a new beginning for the Vulcan people, known as the Time of Awakening. Later generations revered Surak as the father of Vulcan civilization.

The Stone of Gol

Not all of Vulcan adopted Surak's teachings, however. Vulcan dissidents who still clung to their warrior ways left their homeworld to found what became the Romulan Star Empire.

"The Savage Curtain" (TOS). Spock described Surak's role in Vulcan history. "Balance of Terror" (TOS), "The Enterprise Incident" (TOS), and "Unification, Parts I and II" (TNG) allude to the common Vulcan-Romulan ancestry. "Amok Time" (TOS) (see previous item) implied that the reformation (referred to in "Gambit, Part II" [TNG] as the "Time of Awakening") was about 2,000 years ago. In "All Our Yesterdays," McCoy noted that the primitive Spock had reverted to what Vulcans were like some 5,000 years before he was born, implying that the reformation was less than 5,000 years ago. "Gambit, Part II" (TNG) established the Time of Awakening as 2,000 years ago, and also established the Stone of Gol. That episode also established the ancient Debrune as being Romulan offshoots about 2,000 years ago, reinforcing the theory that the Vulcan-Romulan split occurred at about the time of Surak.

Editors' Note: It is interesting to note that the Vulcans and the Romulans apparently had significant interstellar spaceflight capabilities perhaps two millennia before Earth did.

Vidiian victim of the phage

The society on planet 892-IV, evolving on a path similar to that of Earth, developed a culture similar to Earth's ancient Rome, a remarkable example of Hodgkins' Law of parallel planet development.

"Bread and Circuses" (TOS). Kirk noted the planet was ruled by leaders who could trace their line back 2,000 years.

A.D. 370. The humanoid citizens of the Vidiian Sodality in the Delta Quadrant fell victim to a deadly viral disease that they called the phage. The phage consumed their bodies, destroying their genetic codes and cellular structures. The Vidiians survived only by harvesting organs from non-Vidiians to replace their own tissues as they were consumed by the virus.

"Phage" (VGR). Over two millenia before the episode (2371).

The ancient Debrune established an outpost on planet Barradas III. The Debrune were believed to be an offshoot of the ancient Romulans. Other planets in the same sector settled by Romulans or Romulan offshoots included Calder II, Yadalla Prime, and Draken IV.

"Gambit, Part I" (TNG). About 2,000 years ago, but presumably after the Vulcan-Romulan schism. This apparently means that the Romulans had to have existed by this point.

A Founder of the Dominion

A.D. 372. A civilization of shape-shifters in the Gamma Quadrant, weary of being hunted and killed by non-shape-shifters, retreated to an obscure planet in the Omarion nebula. There, they founded a vast interstellar empire that eventually became known as the Dominion. The Founders, as they became known, exercised firm control over numerous other civilizations, using the efficient Vorta as their administrators, and the fearsome Jem'Hadar as their enforcers. So complete was the Founders' control that the inhabitants of many of their client planets regarded them as gods.

"To the Death" (DS9). Weyoun said the Dominion had endured for 2,000 years.

A.D. 625. Mohammed began writing the Koran. This work would become the cornerstone of the Muslim religion.

Historical accounts.

Kahless the Unforgettable united the Klingon Homeworld by defeating the tyrant Molor in battle and defeating the Fek'Ihri. The charismatic Kahless provided his people with the laws of honor that continue to shape modern Klingon society to this day. Kahless's strict sense of honor once pitted him in hand-to-hand combat with his own brother, Morath. Legend has it that the two brothers fought for twelve days and twelve nights when Morath brought dishonor to his family by telling a lie.

Kahless the Unforgettable

At the end of his worldly life, Kahless pointed to a star in the sky and said, "Look for me there, on that point of light." Later, Klingon clerics would go to planet Boreth, orbiting the star designated by Kahless, to await his return. Succeeding generations of Klingons celebrated Kahless's great victory in the Kot'baval festival, even in modern times.

"The Savage Curtain" (TOS) first established Kahless. "Rightful Heir" (TNG) establishes that Kahless went to Sto-Vo-Kor some fifteen centuries prior to the episode (2369), during Earth's ninth century. Parts of his legend were also told in "Reunion" (TNG) and "Birthright, Part II" (TNG). The Kot'baval festival established in "Firstborn" (TNG). "The Sword of Kahless" (DS9) suggests that the shroud of Kahless's bat'leth was 1,400 years old, although this discrepency could be the result of inaccuracies in Dax's dating techniques (or the shroud was made a hundred years after the sword was). That episode also established the fact that Kahless defeated not only Molor, but the Fek'Ihri as well. The legend of Morath established in "New Ground" (TNG).

A terrible war broke out on planet Solais V. The conflict lasts into the 24th century, by which time the historic enemies are on the verge of extinction.

"Loud as a Whisper" (TNG). The Solais war had lasted for fifteen centuries prior to the episode.

The people of planet Kaelon II adopted the custom of the Resolution, a ceremony in which individuals commit suicide at the age of 60 to avoid being a burden to their society. This practice, still observed in modern times, is considered to be a celebration of life, allowing it to end in dignity.

"Half a Life" (TNG). Timicin said the Resolution was instituted "fifteen or twenty centuries ago."

An individual of the Metron civilization was born about 1,500 years ago. In the year 2266, this individual was responsible for incapacitating the *Starship Enterprise* and a Gorn space vehicle, attempting to end a conflict between the two by allowing the commanders of the two spacecraft to engage in physical combat. Little else is known of the Metrons, as they have chosen to remain undetectable to Federation science.

"Arena" (TOS). The Metron said he (or she) was about 1,500 years old.

A Metron

11TH–18TH CENTURIES

Nearly all life on the planet Zetar was destroyed about a thousand years ago by some terrible cataclysm. Only a hundred individuals from that planet survived, in the form of energy patterns representing their thoughts and their will. These individuals searched for a millennium to find a suitable physical body through which they could live.

"The Lights of Zetar" (TOS). The Zetarians described their plight to Kirk.

A.D. 1014. Irish warriors defeat Viking forces at the battle of Clontarf on Earth, a conflict fought with ancient bladed weapons. Ironically, victorious Irish king Brian Boru is killed by retreating Vikings in the aftermath of the battle.

Historical accounts and "Bar Association" (DS9). Miles O'Brien claimed to be a direct descendent of King Brian Boru, and played the part of Boru in a holographic re-creation of the historic battle.

A.D. 1367. The technologically advanced civilization on planet Ventax II was suffering from overcrowding, environmental pollution, and terrible wars a thousand years ago. The Ventaxians, according to historical record, entered into a pact with a supernatural being called Ardra. The agreement called for Ardra to grant the planet a millennium of peace and prosperity. At the end of this span, Ardra would be entitled to claim the planet and its inhabitants.

"Devil's Due" (TNG). Ventaxian leader Jared described their agreement with Ardra, noting it had been signed ten centuries ago.

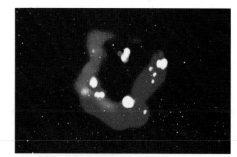

The lights of Zetar

Ventaxian city after Ardra

Promellians and Menthars fought a devastating war near planet Orelious IX at least 1,000 years ago. The war was so fierce that it resulted in the destruction of the planet as well as both cultures. Space near the former Orelious IX became occupied by an asteroid field, the remains of the planet.

"Booby Trap" (TNG). The war was at least a millennium ago.

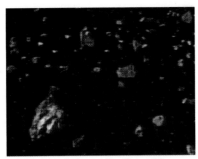

Remains of planet Orelious IX

A.D. 1368. The planet Kataan in the Silarian sector experienced a severe drought, found by the planet's inhabitants to be due to a gradual increase in solar radiation. Over a number of years the increase culminated in the star going nova, destroying all life in the system. Prior to the explosion, the Kataans were successful in launching a small space probe containing a memory record of life on that planet. The probe travels for a thousand years before encountering the *Starship Enterprise*-D commanded by Captain Picard.

Also launched aboard the probe was a single artifact from the Kataan civilization, a simple flute that was once played by an iron-weaver named Kamin, who lived in the town of Ressik on Kataan.

"The Inner Light" (TNG). Data noted the star had exploded a thousand years prior to the episode, set in the year 2368.

A.D. 1371. A group of humanoid space travelers were stranded in the Gamma Quadrant, on a planet they called Meridian. The planet existed on two intersecting dimensional planes.

"Meridian" (DS9). One thousand years before the episode (2371).

Ressik, a village on planet Kataan

A.D. 1371. A group of explorers from another galaxy visited the Ocampa homeworld in the Delta Quadrant. The explorers, noncorporeal sporocystian lifeforms who called themselves the Nacene, were unaware that their technology would be incompatible with a Class-M environment. The result was an ecological catastrophe for the planet's inhabitants, leaving the world completely dry. Realizing this to be a debt that could never be repaid, two of the explorers, a male and a female, remained behind to care for the Ocampa. They created an underground city for the Ocampa, as well as a massive spaceborne array to supply power to the city. This artificial environment was designed to provide for the inhabitants' every need, to the point where the Ocampas' powerful intellectual and psionic abilities begin to atrophy. Many years later, the female explorer set off to explore more of the galaxy, leaving only one, who called himself the Caretaker, to watch over the Ocampa.

"Caretaker" (VGR). A thousand years before the episode (2371). The Ocampa doctor said that his people had lived underground for 500 generations, suggesting that an Ocampa generation is about two Earth years long. "Cold Fire" (VGR) later established that the female caretaker left the Ocampa homeworld around the year 2072, and also established that they were noncorporeal sporocystians called the Nacene.

The Caretaker's array

A.D. 1372. The Klingon Homeworld was invaded by raiders that the Klingons called the Hur'q, or Outsiders. The Hur'q pillaged the Homeworld, destroying much, and looted many cultural artifacts including the revered Sword of Kahless. It was believed that the Hur'q removed the sword from the planet. Later generations believe that the return of the sword would bring about a new era of glory to the Klingon Empire.

"The Sword of Kahless" (DS9). About a millenium before the episode (2372).

A.D. 1372. The Vulcan holiday of Rumarie ceased to be observed on that planet. The Rumarie was an ancient pagan festival involving hedonistic feasting, orgies, and other celebrations.

"Meld" (VGR). A millenium before the episode (2372). The fact that the Rumarie apparently survived over a thousand years after the time of Surak would seem to imply that the adoption of total logic by the Vulcan people did not happen overnight.

Surface of the Ocampa homeworld, devastated by an ecological catastrophe

The inhabitants of the planet Thasus once had corporeal bodies of solid matter, but have long since evolved into forms of pure energy.

"Charlie X" (TOS). The Thasian, in communicating with Kirk, said he was reverting to his form of "centuries ago," implying that his people had corporeal bodies that long ago.

The ruling family of the Ramatis star system was discovered centuries ago to lack the gene required for the sense of hearing. A system was developed whereby a "chorus" of interpreters both hear and speak for members of the ruling family. This ingenious arrangement continued for centuries, with each succeeding generation of chorus family members continuing to provide services to the ruling family members.

"Loud as a Whisper" (TNG). Riva's chorus noted that the arrangement had lasted for centuries.

An interpretive "chorus" serves as a medium of communication to the rulers of the Ramatis system

The people of planet Ardana built a magnificent city in the clouds. The city, named Stratos, was built centuries ago and was described as the finest example of sustained antigravity elevation in the galaxy. The leaders of the cloud city promised the people of Ardana that all would be able to dwell in Stratos, but after construction was completed, the members of the working class were not allowed to live there.

"The Cloud Minders" (TOS). Vanna described Stratos as having been built "centuries" ago.

Cloud city Stratos

A civil war began centuries ago on planet Daled IV. The planet, which rotates only once per year, has one hemisphere in perpetual light and the other in eternal darkness. As a result, two disparate civilizations had evolved on the world, so different that they fought each other for many centuries. A young woman, whose parents each came from a different side, is later raised on a neutral planet in the hope she can bring peace to her world.

"The Dauphin" (TNG). Data described the planet's history, noting the war had lasted for centuries.

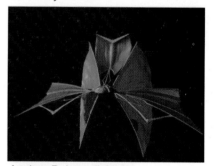

Ancient Bajoran lightship

A.D. 1570. The Skrreean people, living in the Gamma Quadrant, were enslaved by the T-Rogorans, who forced the Skrreeans for centuries to live as laborers and servants.

"Sanctuary" (DS9). Eight hundred years prior to the episode (2370).

Ancient Bajoran explorers used solar sailing spacecraft to voyage to the far reaches of their star system. Some may even have reached the neighboring Cardassian system using their lightships.

"Explorers" (DS9). Eight hundred years before the episode (2371).

A.D. 1609. Galileo Galilei constructed Earth's first astronomical telescope. Galileo would later become known as the father of modern science for his work supporting the Copernican view of the universe.

Historical accounts.

Galileo

A.D. 1647. A man named Ronin was born in Glasgow on planet Earth. Ronin became infused with an anaphasic life-form, effectively granting him eternal youth, as long as he had the company of a woman whose biochemistry was compatible with his energy matrix. He found such a woman in the person of Jessel Howard. Ronin's powers made him powerfully seductive, and he filled Jessel's life with great love and passion. Upon Jessel's death, Ronin became her daughter's lover, and continues for generation after generation for nearly eight centuries.

"Sub Rosa" (TNG). Ronin told the story to Beverly.

A.D. 1665. Earth mathemetician Pierre de Fermat died, leaving behind a written note claiming to have discovered a "remarkable proof" to the theorem that there is no whole number N, greater than 2, for which X to the Nth power,

Fermat

Corbis-Bettman

Newton

*Asteroid deflector mechanism
provided by the Preservers*

Neural parasite creature

plus Y to the Nth equals Z to the Nth, for any whole numbers X, Y, and Z. Fermat's "proof" was never discovered, and Earth's scientists toiled until 1993 to validate Fermat's last theorem.

Historical accounts , "The Royale" (TNG) , and "Facets" (DS9).

A.D. 1666. Noted Earth scientist Isaac Newton formulated three laws of motion and gravitation that formed the basis for much of his planet's understanding of celestial mechanics. Newton developed his theory of universal gravitation after an apple fell from a tree in his garden and hit his head. In later years, Newton would fail to recall that the tree had been jostled by a man, a member of the Q Continuum later known as Quinn, who caused the apple to fall, thereby bringing about a new era in Earth science.

Historical accounts and "Death Wish" (VGR). Although 20th-century historians regard the apple story as apocryphal, we're not inclined to argue with a member of the Q Continuum. Newton also could not remember that he was briefly brought into the 24th century by another member of the Q Continuum. Newton (or at least a holographic re-creation) was also seen in "Descent, Part I" (TNG) along with the real Dr. Stephen Hawking.

A.D. 1669. Guinan's father is born.

"Rascals" (TNG). Guinan said her father was 700 years old. (She seemed to imply that her father was still alive at the time of the episode, 2369).

A.D. 1680. Several Native American tribes rose up against Spanish overlords, freeing the region of Earth known as New Mexico. The uprising was later known as the Pueblo Revolt.

Historical accounts and "Journey's End" (TNG).

A.D. 1692. Spanish forces returned to New Mexico and recaptured much of the territory lost in the Pueblo Revolt. Hundreds of Native Americans were killed in the battle. One of the soldiers fighting against the Native Americans was Javier Maribona-Picard, ancestor of *Enterprise*-D captain Jean-Luc Picard.

Historical accounts, except for Javier Maribona-Picard, who was established in "Journey's End" (TNG).

18TH CENTURY

A group of interstellar anthropologists called the Preservers visited planet Earth. They judged Earth's Native Americans to be in danger of extinction, and transplanted a small group of Delaware, Navajo, and Mohicans to a distant Class-M planet, where they were encouraged to live in a manner that preserved their culture. Since this planet was near a potentially dangerous asteroid belt, the Preservers provided a powerful deflector beam mechanism to protect the settlement from asteroid impacts. The transplanted Native Americans referred to their alien benefactors as The Wise Ones.

"The Paradise Syndrome" (TOS). Judging from the Native American culture seen in the episode, the colony would probably have been established at least 500 years prior to the episode, about 200 years in our past.

The T'Lani and Kellerun people declared war on each other. The interstellar hostilities would last until the 24th century.

"Armageddon Game" (DS9). Date is conjecture, based on Bashir's log that the war had lasted for "centuries."

The population of the Beta Portolan system was overcome by mass insanity. Beta Portolan may have been the original source of the insanity that also affected planets Levinius V in 2067, Ingraham B in 2265, and Deneva in 2267.

"Operation: Annihilate!" (TOS). Date is pure conjecture; Spock's research suggested their knowledge of Beta Portolan was based on archaeological data, suggesting the mass insanity was centuries old.

The two inhabited planets of the Eminiar star system began a bitter war. The planets, known as Eminiar VII and Vendikar, were in danger of destroying each other, when an agreement was reached in which the war would be conducted by computer simulations, with the computers determining casualties on each side. Once casualties were calculated, the appropriate individuals would report to disintegration chambers so that their deaths could be recorded. Representatives of Eminiar VII supported the arrangement as one that permitted both societies to survive despite a devastating war.

"A Taste of Armageddon" (TOS). Anan 7 noted that the war had lasted for 500 years.

Colonists from planet Peliar Zel migrated to that world's two moons. Relations between the two offworld colonies were strained at best, and Peliar Zel Governor Leka would one day describe them as "two squabbling children." Hostilities extend into the 24th century, when the services of Trill Ambassador Odan are instrumental in maintaining peace in the system.

"The Host" (TNG). Governor Leka described the planets' history, noting that the two moons had been settled five centuries ago.

Lord Nelson

Hundreds of condemned criminals from a star system called Ux-Mal were imprisoned on a moon of the planet Mab-Bu VI. The criminals were somehow separated from their bodies and their life entities were left to drift in the electromagnetic storms in the moon's atmosphere.

"Power Play" (TNG). The entity occupying Troi's body said they'd been imprisoned for five centuries.

A small bar was opened in the seaport city of Marseilles in southeastern France on Earth. The descendents of the bar's founder kept the place in operation into the twenty-fourth century.

"The Cloud" (VGR). Tom Paris said that Sandrine's family had owned the bar for over 600 years before the episode (2371). "Non Sequitur" (VGR) established that there was a real bar on which Paris's holodeck simulation was based, and that the bar survived at least until 2371.

19TH CENTURY

A.D. 1805. Earth's British navy, under the command of Lord Horatio Nelson, engaged French and Spanish forces in the battle of Trafalgar. Nelson won a brilliant victory, preventing an invasion of Britain, but he was killed in the conflict. Among the combatants in the battle of Trafalgar was an ancestor of *Enterprise*-D captain Jean-Luc Picard. Many years later, the Federation Starfleet honored Nelson's memory by naming the *Constellation*-class *U.S.S. Victory* after Nelson's flagship.

Battle of Trafalgar

Historical accounts. Picard recalled Nelson's sacrifice in "The Best of Both Worlds, Part I" (TNG). Picard's ancestor established in Star Trek Generations. *The Starship Victory established in "Elementary, Dear Data" (TNG) and "Identity Crisis" (TNG).*

A.D. 1821. Writer John Keats died in Rome on planet Earth. He was one of his planet's greatest poets. It is not known that Keats had been inspired by a noncorporeal extraterrestrial entity named Onaya, who helped Keats find his creative voice because she needed the neural energy of creativity for her own sustenance. While Onaya inspired Keats, she also caused his premature death at age 30.

Historical accounts. Keats's association with Onaya from "The Muse" (DS9).

A.D. 1864. The American nation on Earth was nearly destroyed by a terrible internal conflict known as the Civil War. Among the thousands of combatants in the war was Colonel Thaddius Riker, a Union soldier. Riker, known as "Old Iron Boots," was in command of the 102nd New York unit during General Sherman's march to Atlanta. Riker was badly injured in that campaign, but

Quinn and Thaddius Riker

The Orient Express

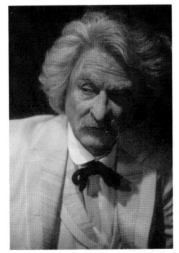

Data and future Enterprise
crew member Guinan

Writer Samuel Clemens

he was rescued by an unidentified individual who was later known as Quinn. Riker survived the war and raised a family. His descendents would later include William Riker of the *Starship Enterprise*-D.

Historical accounts and "Death Wish" (VGR).

A.D. 1871. The Cardassian Union was established, uniting the Cardassian people under the Detapa Council. The Council had direct control of both the Central Command (the military, which handled external affairs), and the Obsidian Order (security, which handled internal affairs).

"Defiant" (DS9). Dukat noted that the Cardassian system of government was established five centuries before the episode. It is not clear if the Cardassians had spaceflight capabilities at this point, or if the Cardassian Union was limited to the Cardassian homeworld.

A.D. 1883. The Orient Express, a transcontinental fixed-rail transport service on planet Earth, began regular service between Paris and Istanbul. At its peak, the Orient Express carried some 10,000 passengers a year.

"Emergence" (TNG) and historical accounts.

Guinan took up residence on planet Earth in the city of San Francisco. Because Earth's inhabitants had not yet made official first contact with extraterrestrial life, Guinan was careful to conceal her El-Aurian origin, and she integrated herself into the native culture, becoming known as an author and a socialite.

Intelligent life-forms from planet Devidia II in the 24th century invaded the city of San Francisco on planet Earth. The Devidians killed humans in order to steal neural energy. They traveled into the past so they could make it appear that their victims had been killed by a cholera epidemic.

"Time's Arrow, Parts I and II" (TNG). Prior to the 1893 scenes in the episodes.

A.D. 1893. Lieutenant Commander Data, in Earth's past, investigated evidence of the Devidian invasion. While in 19th-century San Francisco, Data encountered writer Samuel Clemens, who became suspicious of Data's activities.

"Time's Arrow, Part I" (TNG). Date established in newspaper headline. (The date is about 500 years prior to Star Trek: The Next Generation.*)*

While conducting further investigation of the Devidian invasion, Data's head was accidentally severed, and buried at the Presidio near San Francisco. His body was sent back to the future, where both parts of Data were reunited in 2369. *Enterprise*-D personnel were successful in preventing further Devidian activity in Earth's past. During the investigation, Data and Picard met future *Enterprise*-D bartender Guinan, learning that she had visited Earth some 472 years prior to her service aboard the starship.

"Time's Arrow, Part II" (TNG). After the events in "Time's Arrow, Part I" (TNG).

Samuel Clemens paid for past-due rent owed to Mrs. Carmichael, a boarding house owner, by a mysterious "Mr. Pickerd" and his associates, who had apparently hoped to stage a presentation of Shakespeare's *A Midsummer Night's Dream*.

Jack London, heeding the advice of Samuel Clemens, traveled from San Francisco to Alaska, where adventures in the Yukon inspired London's novels.

After "Time's Arrow, Part II" (TNG). We're confident that Clemens kept his word to Picard about paying the rent.

2.0 THE TWENTIETH CENTURY

"We came in peace for all mankind."

1902

The coal mines in the state of Pennsylvania on planet Earth are shut down by a labor dispute. The strike ends after eleven bitter months when all the miners' demands are met. Union leader Sean Aloysius O'Brien is murdered a week before the end of the strike. The martyred O'Brien, ancestor of Starfleet engineer Miles Edward O'Brien, is given a hero's funeral.

> *"Bar Association" (DS9). There was a real Pennsylvania coal strike in 1902 led by United Mine Workers' president John Mitchell. This dispute lasted five months.*

1905

Albert Einstein publishes his special theory of relativity. Einstein is later honored with the Nobel Prize for his work.

> *Contemporary accounts.*

Einstein

1930

Dr. Leonard McCoy in Earth's past, having gone through the Guardian of Forever's time portal while under influence of accidental overdose of cordrazine, causes major damage to the flow of history by preventing the death of social worker Edith Keeler. Kirk and Spock, on a mission to prevent this from happening, are able to reverse the damage by permitting the death to occur. It is reported that failure to permit Keeler's death would have triggered a chain of events in which Nazi Germany was able to develop atomic weapons, resulting in Hitler's winning of World War II, and a new dark age for planet Earth.

> *"City on the Edge of Forever" (TOS). Edith Keeler told McCoy the year.*

Social worker Edith Keeler

Kira and O'Brien in 1930

Miles O'Brien and Kira Nerys materialize in the city of San Francisco for less than a minute. They are searching for Benjamin Sisko, Julian Bashir, and Jadzia Dax, who were lost somewhere in time because of a transporter malfunction in the year 2371. O'Brien and Kira find no evidence of their friends in this time period.

"Past Tense, Part II" (DS9). The couple seen in the alleyway appeared to be emerging from a speakeasy, suggesting that Kira and O'Brien had appeared sometime during the Prohibition, between 1920 and 1933. We're arbitrarily pegging it as 1930 because Star Trek: Deep Space 9 *graphic designer Doug Drexler, having done some careful study of "City on the Edge of Forever" (TOS), noticed a poster in that episode's New York city alley promoting a boxing match to be held at Madison Square Gardens. Doug created a copy of that poster for "Past Tense, Part II," headlining the same boxers, adding a line that this was their "first rematch since Madison Square Gardens." While this is admittedly a stretch, one could argue that this suggests O'Brien and Kira's visit was sometime after the events of "City on the Edge of Forever."*

1932

Analytical psychiatrist Carl Jung of Earth develops his active imagination technique to help explore the human psyche. Some Native American observers note a similarity between this technique and the Native American use of an animal guide who helps a person focus his or her thoughts.

Contemporary accounts and "The Cloud" (VGR).

Corbis-Bettman

Carl Jung

Seven women are knifed to death in Shanghai, China, on planet Earth. The murders remain unsolved until 2267, when new information suggests they had been committed by an energy being that thrives on fear.

"Wolf in the Fold" (TOS). Computer research revealed the account.

1934

The first short story featuring fictional detective Dixon Hill is published in *Amazing Detective Stories Magazine*. Many years later, *Enterprise*-D captain Jean-Luc Picard becomes an avid fan of the Dixon Hill mysteries.

"The Big Goodbye" (TNG). Data reads bibliography of Dixon Hill stories from ship's computer records.

Editors' Note: The computer readout screen that Data reads when studying Dixon Hill stories lists episode writer Tracy Tormé as the author of those stories!

1936

Another Dixon Hill detective story, "The Long Dark Tunnel," is published in *Amazing Detective Stories Magazine.*

"The Big Goodbye" (TNG). Date from Data's computer research.

1937

Amelia Earhart

July 2. Noted aviator Amelia Earhart vanishes in an aircraft somewhere above Earth's Pacific Ocean. Earhart and her navigator, Fred Noonan, had been attempting a flight around their planet. Earhart and Noonan's disappearance remains unsolved by Earth authorities for centuries, although it is believed that she crashed. It is not generally known that Earhart's expedition had been financed by the American government in a covert effort to gather military information about the Japanese government.

Over 300 humans from planet Earth are abducted by extraterrestrials who call themselves the Briori. The humans are transported across the galaxy to a planet in the Delta Quadrant, where they are made to work as slaves.

Later, the human slaves revolt and manage to kill their Briori captors and to destroy the Briori ship. The surviving humans, with no way to return home, are eventually successful in making a new home on the distant planet.

Contemporary accounts relate Earhart's disappearance. "The 37's" (VGR) establishes the other disappearances, the Briori, and the "fact" that Earhart had been working for American military intelligence.

1941

December 7. Earth's nation of Japan launches an unprovoked sneak attack against the United States of America, striking a serious blow against the Pearl Harbor naval facility in Hawai'i. The attack draws the United States into a terrible world war.

Contemporary accounts and "The 37's" (VGR).

Sneak attack at Pearl Harbor

1942

Stephen Hawking is born on Earth. Hawking becomes one of his planet's foremost theoretical physicists, seeking to link quantum mechanics with the theory of relativity.

Contemporary accounts and "Descent, Part I" (TNG).

1945

The United Nations is chartered on planet Earth. The organization represents a significant effort in the quest for planetary peace.

Contemporary accounts.

1947

July. Humans near the town of Roswell, New Mexico, on the North American continent on Earth report the discovery of an extraterrestrial spacecraft. Official government investigators later announce that the report was mistaken, and that object sighted had simply been a weather balloon.

Extraterrestrial spacecraft held in Hangar 18

Authorities do not reveal that they have, in fact, captured a spacecraft of Ferengi origin that made a forced landing near Roswell. The vessel and at least three alien crew members are held for study at the Wright Field military base in Ohio. The investigation is conducted under the direct orders of American president Harry S Truman. Government personnel are successful in establishing communication with the aliens and even in opening preliminary trade discussions, but the visitors soon depart aboard their ship. The American government subsequently denies all reports that it had captured an alien spacecraft or extraterrestrial life-forms.

"Little Green Men" (DS9). A calendar on the wall established the date as July, 1947. The military facility is not directly established to be Wright Field, but this seems likely, since Quark's ship was held in Hangar 18, and popular UFO mythology holds that the Army held a flying saucer in Wright Field's Hangar 18.

Sputnik

October 14. Earth test pilot Chuck Yeager becomes the first human to fly an aircraft faster than the speed of sound in his planet's atmosphere. Yeager accomplishes the feat in a small rocket-powered vehicle called the *Glamorous Glennis.*

Contemporary accounts. Geordi La Forge mentioned Yeager's flight in "New Ground" (TNG).

1957

October 4. *Sputnik I,* Earth's first artificial satellite, is launched, marking the dawn of Earth's space age.

Contemporary accounts.

Radio telescope used in Project Ozma

Cosmonaut Yuri Gagarin

John F. Kennedy

Kira and O'Brien in the Summer of Love

Gary Seven

1960

Earth-based radio telescopes are used to listen for evidence of radio signals from Tau Ceti and Epsilon Eridani as part of Project Ozma, one of Earth's first attempts to search for extraterrestrial life.

Contemporary accounts.

1961

Yuri Gagarin, piloting space vehicle *Vostok I,* becomes the first human to travel in space.

Contemporary accounts.

American president John F. Kennedy commits his nation to an ambitious program to land a human on Earth's moon by the end of the decade.

Contemporary accounts.

1963

A Nuclear Test Ban Treaty is adopted on planet Earth. The agreement represents a significant early step toward the control of weapons of mass destruction.

Contemporary accounts.

1964

The World Series of baseball on Earth is won by the St. Louis Cardinals team, defeating the New York Yankees.

Contemporary accounts. Benjamin Sisko hoped to watch a holosuite re-creation of game seven with Kasidy Yates in 2371 ("The Adversary" [DS9]).

1966

Scientists on Miri's planet begin a "life prolongation project," creating a virus intended to halt the aging process. The project is a terrible disaster and results in the deaths of all the adults on the planet. The planet's children survive, aging at a greatly reduced rate, although the virus causes their death upon the onset of puberty.

"Miri" (TOS). Spock indicated the project began 300 years prior to the episode (2266).

1967

Miles O'Brien and Kira Nerys materialize in the city of San Francisco for less than a minute. They are continuing their search for Benjamin Sisko, Julian Bashir, and Jadzia Dax, who were lost somewhere in time because of a transporter malfunction in the year 2371. O'Brien and Kira find no evidence of their friends in this time period.

"Past Tense, Part II" (DS9). The clothing and automobiles on the San Francisco street were typical of the "Summer of Love" in the late 1960s.

1968

The *U.S.S. Enterprise,* on a historical research mission into the past, encounters Gary Seven, a human trained by unknown extraterrestrials, being returned to Earth to help the planet's inhabitants survive their critical nuclear age. Kirk accidentally interferes with this mission, but is able to restore events before a nuclear missile can cause a disastrous explosion.

"Assignment: Earth" (TOS). Year established by Kirk in captain's log. Note that from Kirk's perspective, these events occurred after the 1969 events from "Tomorrow Is Yesterday" (TOS).

Editors' Note: This episode was an unofficial pilot for a proposed television series, Assignment: Earth. *The show would have chronicled the adventures of Gary Seven and his assistant, Roberta Lincoln, defending the Earth against malevolent extraterrestrials. The series was never produced.*

1969

The *U.S.S. Enterprise*, accidentally sent into the past by near collision with a black hole, is detected as an unidentified flying object in Earth's atmosphere. In attempting to prevent further detection, Kirk accidentally captures U.S. Air Force captain John Christopher. Christopher is returned during the light-speed breakaway factor maneuver that also returns the *Enterprise* to its own time.

"Tomorrow Is Yesterday" (TOS). A radio broadcast intercepted by Uhura said the first moon landing mission would be launched "next Wednesday," which would seem to put the episode within a week before Wednesday, July 16, 1969, when Apollo 11 *was launched.*

Editors' Note: One of Star Trek*'s least-recognized prognostications about the future is the fact that writer Dorothy Fontana accurately predicted that the first moon landing mission would be launched on a Wednesday!*

The U.S.S. Enterprise in *Earth's upper atmosphere*

July 20. Neil Armstrong and Buzz Aldrin become the first humans to walk on Earth's moon. Dedication on landing ship *Eagle* proclaims: "We came in peace for all mankind." Armstrong and Aldrin's landing is the beginning of a dramatic transformation of the moon. By the 24th century, that world would be home to some 50 million people, and such developments as Lake Armstrong and New Berlin city would be clearly visible from Earth.

Contemporary accounts. Twenty-fourth century developments established in Star Trek: First Contact.

August 15. A large musical festival is held near the town of Woodstock, New York, on Earth. The event is a celebration of counterculture and becomes a symbol for a generation. The sound system fails just before the music begins, but fortunately, a spotlight operator named Maury Ginsberg happens to notice the cause of the problem is a loose cable, and the concert begins without a hitch. If Ginsberg's van hadn't broken down on the way to the show, and if he hadn't been given a ride by an individual later known as Quinn, it is very possible that Ginsberg would not have noticed the problem and there might have been no Woodstock concert. Ginsberg later marries, becomes an orthodontist living in Scarsdale, and raises four children.

"One small step..."

Contemporary accounts and "Death Wish" (VGR). For some reason, contemporary accounts have no record of Quinn or Ginsberg, or of their crucial contribution to Woodstock.

1974

Five women are brutally knifed to death in Kiev, USSR, on planet Earth. It is later discovered that these murders were probably committed by the same energy entity responsible for similar killings on planet Argelius II in 2267.

"Wolf in the Fold" (TOS). According to computer records.

1976

Viking I space probe lands on planet Mars, Earth's first major attempt to employ space flight in the search for extraterrestrial life.

Contemporary accounts.

Surface of Mars as seen by Viking

Launch of shuttle Columbia

Saving the whales

The Book

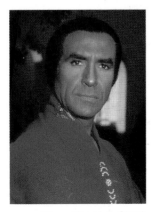

Khan Noonien Singh

1977

First spaceship *Enterprise* (Space Shuttle OV-101) undergoes flight testing.

Contemporary accounts.

Editors' Note: NASA's shuttle was, of course, named after Star Trek*'s starship. The naming was ordered by President Gerald Ford after an outpouring of support by* Star Trek *fans. It's only fitting, therefore, that the Starship* Endeavor, *a* Nebula-*class vessel mentioned (but not seen) in "Redemption, Part II" (TNG) was named after the NASA space shuttle orbiter.*

1981

Shuttle *Columbia*, Earth's first reusable spaceship, makes first orbital flight.

Contemporary accounts.

1983

Pioneer 10 spacecraft becomes first human-launched space probe to leave Earth's solar system. The craft drifts in deep space until it is destroyed in 2287 by a Klingon bird-of-prey. *Pioneer 10* had been launched from Earth on March 2, 1972.

Contemporary accounts. Pioneer 10 *was destroyed in* Star Trek V: The Final Frontier.

1986

January 28. Seven astronauts are killed when spaceship *Challenger* explodes 73 seconds after liftoff from Earth.

Contemporary accounts. Star Trek IV: The Voyage Home *was dedicated to the memory of the* Challenger *astronauts.*

A Klingon bird-of-prey piloted by Kirk and his crew lands in old San Francisco to take two humpback whales back to the future. Using the ship's cloaking device, the vessel remains undetected by terrestrial authorities, although Commander Pavel Chekov is temporarily incarcerated by military authorities while working to repair the spacecraft. Cetacean biologist Gillian Taylor leaves this time period and travels to the 23rd century with Kirk.

Dr. Nichols, a scientist and plant manager at Plexicorp in San Francisco, begins to develop the molecular matrix for transparent aluminum on his Macintosh computer.

Star Trek IV: The Voyage Home. *Date is conjecture, based on studio publicity suggesting our heroes had gone back to 1986.*

1992

The book *Chicago Mobs of the Twenties* is published in New York. A copy of this book is carried aboard the Federation starship *U.S.S. Horizon* in 2168, and is accidentally left on planet Sigma Iotia II in that year.

"A Piece of the Action" (TOS). Spock read the publication date from the Book, no doubt due in print soon from Pocket Books (which has its publication offices in New York), albeit behind schedule.

Khan Noonien Singh rises to power, assuming dictatorial control over one quarter of the planet Earth, from South Asia to the Middle East. Khan is the product of genetic engineering and eugenics experiments.

"Space Seed" (TOS). Spock reveals date and description of the Eugenics Wars from historical research.

Editors' Note: If we assume Khan was in his thirties at this point, we are left with the interesting conclusion that he would probably have been born before the original airing of the episode in 1967. Fortunately, none of this seems to have come to pass, at least the last time we checked with CNN and our local newspapers.

1993

Mathematician Andrew Wiles, a professor at Earth's Princeton University, develops a remarkable proof for Fermat's last theorem, ending a quest that has baffled human academicians for hundreds of years.

Contemporary accounts. "Facets" (DS9) establishes that over the next few centuries, other mathematicians, including Tobin Dax, later searched for other proofs of Fermat's theorem. "The Royale" (TNG) establishes that amateur scientist Jean-Luc Picard was among them.

A group of eugenically bred "superior" humans seize power simultaneously in some forty of Earth's nations. Terrible wars ensue, in part because the genetic "supermen" take to fighting among themselves. Entire populations are bombed out of existence during these Eugenics Wars, and Earth is believed to be on the verge of a new dark age.

"Space Seed" (TOS). More from Spock's historical research.

1994

Claire Raymond, a woman living on Earth, dies of an embolism. Her husband, Donald Raymond, has her cryogenically frozen and sent into space for possible revival at some future date.

"The Neutral Zone" (TOS). Dr. Crusher said Raymond had died some 370 years prior to the episode.

1996

Earth's Eugenics Wars are over, as Khan Noonien Singh is overthrown. Khan escapes from his homeworld on the DY-100 class sleeper ship *S.S. Botany Bay* along with 96 of his fellow genetic "supermen."

"Space Seed" (TOS) and Star Trek II: The Wrath of Khan. *Khan mentions the year.*

Editors' Note: It is unfortunate that neither NASA nor any other terrestrial space agency had any spacecraft as advanced as the Botany Bay *by 1996. This is one place where* Star Trek*'s technological predictions have missed by a significant margin. On the other hand, we should probably be grateful that the show was also wrong about predicting the rise to power of genetic tyrants.*

"Future's End, Parts I and II" (VGR), in preproduction as this Chronology was being completed, will suggest that certain parts of Earth (notably the city of Los Angeles) were remarkably untouched by the Eugenics Wars. (One might even speculate that Starling's time meddling caused an alternate timeline in which the Eugenics Wars never happened, or at least happened in a dramatically different form.)

Earth scientists discover signs of ancient life on Mars. Microscopic fossilized traces in meteorites are the first physical evidence that humans are not alone in the universe.

Contemporary accounts.

Claire Raymond

Launch of the Botany Bay

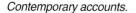

Microscopic fossilized traces of Martian lifeforms

Poet Tarbolde writes "Nightingale Woman," a love sonnet considered to be among the most passionate for the next two centuries. It is not known that Tarbolde had been inspired by a noncorporeal entity named Onaya , who helped Tarbolde find his creative voice because she needed the neural energy of creativity for her own sustenance. While Onaya inspired Tarbolde, she also hastened his death.

"Where No Man Has Gone Before" (TOS). Gary Mitchell mentions date after quoting a passage from the work. Mitchell mentions that Tarbolde is from the Canopus Planet, presumably implying that this was written prior to human contact with this world, and that Tarbolde's work was later translated into English. Tarbolde's association with Onaya from "The Muse" (DS9).

Editors' Note: The words to "Nightingale Woman" were actually written by Gene Roddenberry as a love poem from a pilot to his airplane!

Voyager 6

1999

Voyager 6 spacecraft launched from Earth. This probe eventually fell into a black hole, emerging on the other side of the galaxy, where it encountered a planet of living machines that enhanced the craft and returned it to Earth in 2271.

Date is conjecture from Star Trek: The Motion Picture. This probe was probably launched before construction of the more advanced Nomad probe in the early 2000s ("The Changeling" [TOS]). In actual fact, as of this writing NASA has launched only two spacecraft in the Voyager series, and additional probes seem unlikely due to severe cutbacks in planetary sciences programs. This is especially unfortunate since the Voyager program has been an important part of what some have termed the greatest exploratory era in human history (so far, at least).

Editors' Note: Following production of "Q Who?" (TNG), Gene Roddenberry half jokingly speculated that the planet encountered by Voyager might have been the Borg homeworld.

The machine planet

The New York Yankees baseball team has an extraordinary year, later remembered by some as the best ever.

"Past Tense, Part II" (DS9). Vin argued that the '99 Yankees was the best ball club he'd ever seen.

3.0 THE TWENTY-FIRST CENTURY

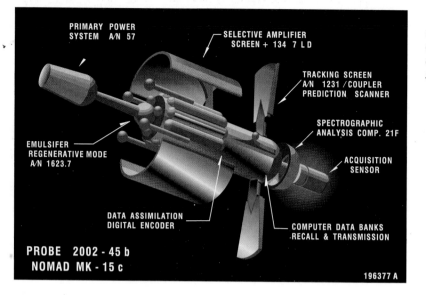

PRIMARY POWER
SYSTEM A/N 57

SELECTIVE AMPLIFIER
SCREEN + 134 7 L D

TRACKING SCREEN
A/N 1231 / COUPLER
PREDICTION SCANNER

SPECTROGRAPHIC
ANALYSIS COMP. 21F

EMULSIFER
REGENERATIVE MODE
A/N 1623.7

ACQUISITION
SENSOR

DATA ASSIMILATION
DIGITAL ENCODER

COMPUTER DATA BANKS
RECALL & TRANSMISSION

PROBE 2002 - 45 b
NOMAD MK - 15 c

196377 A

Engineering drawing of Nomad *space probe*

2002

Space probe *Nomad* launched from Earth, the first interstellar probe intended to seek out new life-forms. The probe was designed by scientist Jackson Roykirk. *Nomad* is later believed destroyed in a meteoroid collision.

"The Changeling" (TOS). Exact date is conjecture, but Kirk noted that Nomad *had been launched in the early 2000s. (The script for the episode gives the launch date as 2002, but we still consider it conjecture, since it was not mentioned in the final air version of "The Changeling.")*

2009

Captain Shaun Geoffrey Christopher commands the first successful Earth-Saturn space-probe mission.

Conjecture from "Tomorrow Is Yesterday" (TOS). Assumes 40 years from the episode (1969) during which Shaun is born and raised.

Editors' Note: Episode writer Dorothy Fontana named Shaun Geoffrey Christopher for fellow Star Trek *writer John D. F. Black's three sons, Shaun, Geoffrey, and Christopher.*

2015

The London Kings baseball team has a good year, bolstered by the performance of rookie Buck Bokai.

"Past Tense, Part II" (DS9). Sisko noted that 2015 was Bokai's rookie year.

2018

Advances in sublight propulsion technologies make "sleeper ships" obsolete.

"Space Seed" (TOS). Marla McGivers said sleeper ships were necessary prior to this date. She was apparently not referring to the invention of warp drive, since this is before Cochrane's birth.

Baseball great Buck Bokai

American city in decay

Henry Garcia

Gabriel Bell

Bell Riots of 2024

2020

The American government, reacting to serious problems of homeless and jobless people, creates special Sanctuary Districts in most cities where such people can be cared for. Unfortunately, while established with benevolent intent, the Sanctuary Districts quickly degenerate into inhumane internment camps where the unemployed, the mentally ill, and other outcasts are imprisoned.

"Past Tense, Part I" (DS9). Sisko said that every major U.S. city had a Sanctuary District by the early 2020s.

2022

Henry Garcia, a resident of San Francisco on Earth, is laid off from his job at a brewery, and is imprisoned in the city's Sanctuary District. As a result, it becomes impossible for Garcia to find another job. Garcia is only one of many thousands of people so victimized.

"Past Tense, Part II" (DS9). Garcia told his story on the Net.

2024

Student unrest in Europe makes France an undesirable tourist destination for Earth's elite. Although France's Neo-Trotskyist government tries to quell the protests, they have no more luck than the earlier Gaullist government.

Rumors of unrest are also filtering out of Sanctuary District A in San Francisco.

Prior to the 2024 scenes in "Past Tense, Part I" (DS9).

August 30. Benjamin Sisko, Julian Bashir, and Jadzia Dax materialize in the city of San Francisco, the result of a transporter malfunction in the year 2371. Without proper identification or money, Sisko and Bashir are placed in a Sanctuary District by city authorities.

August 31. Sisko and Bashir are involved in an altercation in which 21st-century civil rights leader Gabriel Bell is killed. Bell's death is a serious disruption of the timeline, since history records that he played a crucial role in abolishing the Sanctuary Districts in American cities.

"Past Tense, Part I" (DS9). Dates from Sisko and from the digital clock in the processing center.

September 1. Tensions in Sanctuary District A continue to mount, and district residents take over an administrative processing center, holding six center employees hostage. Ben Sisko, aware of the late Gabriel Bell's role in the peaceful resolution of what history will call the Bell riots, assumes Bell's identity to help protect the hostages.

September 2. Residents of Sanctuary District A manage to gain access to Earth's planetary computer network, and many residents are able to tell their stories of imprisonment to the outside world. As a result, the American public becomes aware of the great injustice that had been hidden from them.

The Bell riots end when the governor of California orders Federal troops to retake the processing center by force. Hundreds of sanctuary residents are killed, although none of the hostages are harmed. History records that Gabriel Bell sacrificed his life to save the hostages. Benjamin Sisko, Julian Bashir, and Jadzia Dax are returned to their proper time. One San Francisco resident retains knowledge that an extraterrestrial had been present on Earth.

"Past Tense, Part II" (DS9). Dates from Sisko and from the digital clock in the processing center.

In the wake of the Bell riots and the senseless death of so many people, American public opinion turns against the Sanctuary Districts. The sanctuaries are abolished as the United States finally begins to face serious social problems it has struggled with for over a century.

After the 2024 events of "Past Tense, Part II" (DS9).

2025

The reunification of Ireland is brought about by the use of violence as a tool for political reform.

"The High Ground" (TNG). Data mentioned the date to Picard.

2026

Harmon "Buck" Bokai, a shortstop from the London Kings who becomes known as one of baseball's greatest players, hits in his 57th consecutive game, breaking Joe DiMaggio's long-standing record. The hit is a squeaker that just goes under Eddie Newsom's glove.

"The Big Goodbye" (TNG). Data mentioned date to news vendor in the holodeck program. Buck Bokai established in "The Storyteller" (DS9) and "If Wishes Were Horses" (DS9).

2030

Zefram Cochrane, inventor of warp drive, is born. His work makes such an enormous contribution to space exploration that great universities and even entire planets are one day named after him.

"Metamorphosis" (TOS). Cochrane disappeared 150 years before the episode (2267) and was 87 years old at that time.

Editors' Note: Cochrane is described in "Metamorphosis" as "Zefram Cochrane of Alpha Centauri." Because interstellar travel would have taken many, many years prior to the invention of warp drive, we are assuming that Cochrane was born on Earth, and that he later moved to Alpha Centauri, presumably after the invention of warp drive.

Zefram Cochrane

A famous novelist writes a classic on the theme "Let me help." He recommends these words even over "I love you."

"The City on the Edge of Forever" (TOS). Kirk, back in 1930, told Edith Keeler that this will be written a hundred years in her future by an author living on a planet orbiting the far left star in Orion's belt.

James Kirk and Edith Keeler look toward the left star in Orion's belt

2033

July 4: Fifty-second state is admitted to the United States of America.

"The Royale" (TNG). Riker notes that a United States' flag with 52 stars would indicate a date between 2033 and 2079. This would suggest that the United States survives as a political entity until at least the latter date. Under U.S. law, new states are admitted to the Union on the Fourth of July.

Editors' Note: Star Trek: The Next Generation executive producer Rick Berman insisted that the U.S. flag seen on the Charybdis's wreckage be painted to have 52 stars, for the benefit of those watching the episode with VCRs. (On the other hand, by amazing coincidence, the mission patch on Richey's spacesuit looks a whole lot like the Apollo 17 emblem.)

2036

New United Nations rules that Earth citizens may not be held responsible for crimes committed by ancestors.

"Encounter at Farpoint" (TNG). Picard cites date to Q during trial.

American flag, circa 2033

Hovercars come into popular use on Earth.

"The 37's" (VGR). Paris noted that the first hovercars were in use about a century after 1936.

2037

NASA launches spacecraft *Charybdis* on July 23, commanded by Colonel Steven Richey. It is the third attempt to explore beyond Earth's solar system. The ship is declared missing after telemetry is lost.

"The Royale" (TNG). Data described the mission.

2040

Television no longer survives as a significant form of entertainment. *Star Trek* is no doubt an exception.

"The Neutral Zone" (TNG). Data mentioned the date to L. Q. "Sonny" Clemonds.

Symbol of the National Aeronautics and Space Administration

2042

The sport of baseball meets its demise after the last World Series is held. Baseball great Harmon "Buck" Bokai, a former shortstop for the London Kings, now playing third base, hits the winning home run. Interest in the former "national pastime" of the Americas has fallen to the point where only 300 spectators are in attendance at the final game. The disappointed Bokai feels he could have played for at least five more years.

"If Wishes Were Horses" (DS9). Year 2042 established in the episode. Note that in "Family Business" (DS9), Sisko said that baseball hadn't been played in 200 years, suggesting that baseball may have survived in some form until 2171.

Harmon "Buck" Bokai

2044

Space vehicle *Charybdis*, launched from Earth in 2037, arrives at the eighth planet in the Theta 116 system. An unknown alien intelligence on the planet discovers a book *(Hotel Royale)* in the possession of mission commander Richey and creates an environment based on the book in an effort to sustain Richey's life.

"The Royale" (TNG). Data described mission.

Editors' Note: It is probably reasonable to assume that this unknown alien intelligence was also responsible for transporting the Charybdis across interstellar distances, since Earth science had not yet developed the warp drive at the time the ship was launched. (Warp drive inventor Zefram Cochrane would have been only about six years old at the time the Charybdis was launched in 2037. Cochrane was undoubtedly smart, but not that smart.)

2048

Miles O'Brien and Kira Nerys materialize in the city of San Francisco for less than a minute. They are continuing their search for Benjamin Sisko, Julian Bashir, and Jadzia Dax, who were lost somewhere in time because of a transporter malfunction in the year 2371. O'Brien and Kira find no evidence of their friends in this time period.

"Past Tense, Part II" (DS9). O'Brien mentioned he and Kira had gone to 2048.

2053

Earth's civilization is devastated by World War III. The infamous Colonel Green is a key figure in this horrific conflict, which results in the death of untold millions of humans, and nearly returns Earth society to the stone age. The planet's climate experiences a serious "nuclear winter" caused by thousands of tons of dust and debris kicked into the atmosphere by the nuclear explosions.

Star Trek: First Contact. Date is conjecture, about a decade prior to the 21st-century scenes in the film. This is consistent with "A Matter of Time" (TNG), which establishes the holocaust to have taken place in the mid-21st century, and "Encounter at Farpoint" (TNG), which establishes that the war occurred before 2079. Colonel Green established in "The Savage Curtain" (TOS). The nuclear winter was established in "A Matter of Time." "A Piece of the Action" (TOS) gave the death toll for World War III as being 37 million, although Star Trek: First Contact gave a much larger figure.

Colonel Green

2063

Zefram Cochrane pilots Earth's first faster-than-light spaceflight. Cochrane's ship, the *Phoenix*, is a tiny vessel that, ironically, was built from an unused nuclear missile left over from the third world war. The warp signature of the *Phoenix* attracts the attention of a passing Vulcan ship, indicating that humankind now has the capacity for interstellar travel.

Within a day of the *Phoenix's* epic flight, Cochrane becomes the first human to officially make contact with extraterrestrial life, when the Vulcan ship lands at Montana on the North American continent. The event sparks a remarkable turning point in the difficult recovery from Earth's terrible nuclear war, and marks the beginning of humanity's interstellar age.

Zefram Cochrane

History does not record the fact that a Borg attack from the future nearly prevented Cochrane from making his flight, and that Cochrane had some last-minute help from the crew of the *Starship Enterprise*-E, also from the future.

Star Trek: First Contact. Date mentioned in film.

Editors' Note: The first edition of this Chronology conjectured that Cochrane broke the light barrier in 2061. Star Trek: First Contact establishes that this historic event took place in 2063. Both dates are consistent with the back story established in "Metamorphosis" (TOS). Other humans had contact with extraterrestrials prior to Cochrane, but his was the pivotal first contact that changed the course of history.

Glenn Corbett originated the role of the illustrious Zefram Cochrane in "Metamorphosis" (TOS), although Cochrane, seen making the first warp flight, was played by James Cromwell in Star Trek: First Contact. (We speculate that the differences in their appearance was because Cochrane, in Star Trek: First Contact, had suffered significant radiation poisoning, but that by the time of "Metamorphosis," the Companion had reversed the effects of the exposure.) Cochrane's ship, the Phoenix, was designed by illustrator John Eaves under the direction of production designer Herman Zimmerman. Eaves's design was based on a conjectural design for Cochrane's ship developed by modelmaker Greg Jein for the first edition of this Chronology. (Eaves made several significant changes to the design of the Phoenix, in part because the storyline for Star Trek: First Contact reveals that Cochrane's ship was launched from an uprated U.S. Air Force Titan missile, a fact unknown to Jein at the time the first Chronology was compiled.)

Phoenix, the first warp-powered spacecraft

2065

S.S. *Valiant* embarks on deep space exploration mission. Expedition is lost and is eventually swept out of the galaxy. The ship is nearly destroyed while trying to return across the energy barrier at the edge of the galaxy. Six crew members are killed, but a seventh experiences a mutation that dramatically enhances latent ESP powers, making that person a threat to the ship and its crew. The *Valiant's* captain later orders the ship destroyed to prevent the mutated crew member from escaping.

"Where No Man Has Gone Before" (TOS). Valiant expedition embarked 200 years prior to the episode (2265).

Vulcan emissary

S.S. Valiant

Neural parasite creature

Freighter carrying radioactive waste

First city of the Klingon Homeworld

Quinn

2067

British astronomer John Burke of the Royal Academy maps the area of space including Sherman's Planet. This region is later the subject of a territorial dispute between the Federation and the Klingon Empire.

"The Trouble with Tribbles" (TOS). Spock and Chekov's discussion established the date as 200 years prior to episode (2267).

Planet Levinius V is infested by the same parasite creatures that later attacked planet Deneva.

"Operation: Annihilate!" (TOS). Two hundred years prior to episode (2267).

An unknown planet launches a sublight freighter vessel carrying large quantities of unstable nuclear waste products. The ship drifts through space, unattended, for about 300 years before settling into orbit around planet Gamelan V, where radiation leakage threatens life on the planet.

"Final Mission" (TNG). Data noted the freighter's reactor core elements appeared to have been inactive for about 300 years prior to the episode (2367).

The people of planet Argelius II undergo a "great awakening," a significant cultural milestone in their hedonistic society devoted to love and pleasure.

"Wolf in the Fold" (TOS). Prefect Jarvis noted the "great awakening" had taken place 200 years prior to the episode (2267).

2069

The Klingon emperor dies. No successor ascends the throne because the Klingon High Council has grown in political power and is now in effective control of the empire.

"Rightful Heir" (TNG). Gowron noted the empire had not been ruled by an emperor in three centuries prior to the episode (2369).

2072

One of the two extragalactic travelers who had been caring for the inhabitants of the Ocampa homeworld in the Delta Quadrant leaves that planet. The female caretaker, a sporocystian life-form, who calls herself Suspiria, takes with her some 2,000 Ocampa people, establishing a new home in a spaceborne array several light-years from the Ocampa homeworld. Suspiria helps her disciples to develop their inborn psychokinetic abilities so that some of them can join her in the subspace domain she calls "Exosia."

"Cold Fire" (VGR). Approximately 300 years before the episode (2372).

A member of the Q Continuum who will one day be known as Quinn is imprisoned in a comet in the Delta Quadrant because he has asked that he be allowed to end his life. Although this individual had once been known as a great philosopher, the Continuum has judged his wish to die to be evidence of mental instability and imprisoned him to prevent him from ending his life. Ironically, this philosopher once celebrated the undeviating continuity of the Q Continuum, a condition that he now finds intolerable.

"Death Wish" (VGR). Three hundred years before the episode (2372).

Bajoran technicians construct a traditional solar-sailing lightship. This particular vessel will one day be used by noted Bajoran poet Akorem Laan.

"Accession" (DS9). Three hundred years before the episode (2372).

2079

Earth continues the difficult recovery from the third world war. In this postatomic horror, the legal system is based on the principle of "guilty until proven innocent." Lawyers have fallen into disfavor as Shakespeare's suggestion to "Kill all the lawyers" has been taken quite seriously.

"Encounter at Farpoint" (TNG). Q says that this is the year that his re-created courtroom is based on. It is unclear exactly when the nuclear conflict occurred, although Picard referred to a terrible "nuclear winter" having occurred during the middle of this century in "A Matter of Time" (TNG). This conflict is presumably the "third world war" Dr. McCoy referred to in "Bread and Circuses" (TOS), in which 37 million people were killed.

An official of a post-holocaust court

2082

Colonel Steven Richey, commander of Earth's space vehicle *Charybdis*, dies in captivity on the eighth planet in the Theta 116 system.

"The Royale" (TNG). Richey died 283 years prior to the episode (2365).

2086

The Lornak clan of the planet Acamar III begins a bitter blood feud with their rival clan, the Tralestas. The feud lasts until the year 2286, when the Lornaks massacre all but five of the Tralestas.

"The Vengeance Factor" (TNG). The massacre was described as having taken place 80 years prior to the episode (2366), and the feud had run for 200 years prior to that.

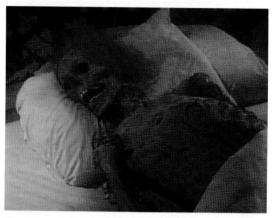

Remains of Colonel Steven Richey

4.0 THE TWENTY-SECOND CENTURY

*The Great Seal of the
United Federation of Planets*

2103

Planet Mars is colonized by humans from the planet Earth.

"The 37's" (VGR). Date mentioned by Kim.

Mars colony

2105

Eight women brutally knifed to death by an unknown assailant in the Martian Colonies. This is later found to be the same entity that committed several murders on planet Argelius II in 2267.

"Wolf in the Fold" (TOS). Date given by library computer during Scotty's trial on board the Enterprise.

2113

A united world government is finally established by the people of planet Earth.

Star Trek: First Contact. Approximately 50 years after Cochrane's first warp flight.

Zefram Cochrane

2117

Zefram Cochrane, now residing in the Alpha Centauri system, departs at the age of 87 for parts unknown. He is believed to have died, but his body is never found.

"Metamorphosis" (TOS). Cochrane disappeared 150 years prior to the episode (2267).

Editors' Note: Cochrane, of course, made it to a planetoid in the Gamma Canaris system, where he was cared for by an entity known as the Companion, who loved him. This account, as well as the Companion's merging with Commissioner Nancy Hedford, should theoretically not be part of this chronology because of Kirk's promise to Cochrane not to reveal that information.

2123

November 27. Spaceship *Mariposa* is launched for colonization of Ficus sector. The craft settles colonists on planet Bringloid V. It later crashes on planet Mariposa while attempting to settle a second group of colonists. There are only five survivors of the crash, who attempt to keep their colony viable using cloning technology.

"Up the Long Ladder" (TNG).

2132

Baseball great Harmon "Buck" Bokai dies. The man who broke Joe DiMaggio's record for hits in consecutive games was well over a century old.

"If Wishes Were Horses" (DS9). The aliens noted that Bokai had died 200 years before Ben Sisko was born, in 2332. We don't know exactly when Bokai was born, but he broke DiMaggio's record in 2026, so we can probably assume he was in his twenties at that point, and that Bokai was about 130 years old at the time of his death. Note that in the same episode another scene has Sisko telling Dax that Bokai had died 200 years before the episode (2369), which would make it 2169. We arbitrarily picked the 2132 date over 2169 since it seemed to stretch credibility less.

Harmon "Buck" Bokai

2133

Bajoran religious leader Kai Taluno, traveling in the Denorios Belt, experiences a serious malfunction of his spacecraft and is stranded for several days. Taluno reports having experienced a vision in which "the heavens opened up," nearly swallowing his ship. The Denorios Belt, located in the Bajor system, is the location where at least five of the Bajorans' revered Tears of the Prophets were found.

"Emissary" (DS9). Dax said Taluno's vision was sometime during the 22nd century, but the date is purely conjectural.

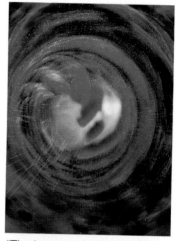

"The heavens opened up"

2150

The nation-state of Australia joins Earth's world government, an important step in unifying the people of this once war-torn planet.

"Attached" (TNG). Picard said Australia had joined the world government in 2150. Since Star Trek: First Contact suggested that a world government had been established by 2113, Picard's line would seem to imply that Australia was a holdout until this point.

2156

Romulan Wars begin between Earth forces and the Romulan Star Empire. The war is fought with primitive atomic weapons, and the Romulan fleet is not even equipped with warp drive. Among the Earth casualties are several members of the Stiles family.

Date is conjecture from "Balance of Terror" (TOS). War ended about 100 years prior to episode; this date was a few years prior to that. The conflict was described as being between Earth and the Romulans, suggesting that the United Federation of Planets did not exist at this point. "Homefront" (DS9) seemed to imply that the Romulan Wars actually reached Earth.

City on planet Romulus

Two women knifed to death at Heliopolis City on planet Alpha Eridani II. The murders remain unsolved until 2267 when it is learned that the same entity had committed several similar murders on planet Argelius II.

"Wolf in the Fold" (TOS). Date mentioned in Scotty's trial.

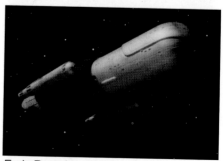

Early Romulan spacecraft

Romulan Neutral Zone

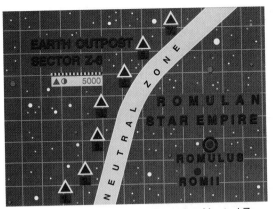

Emblem of the Romulan Star Empire

United Federation Headquarters in Paris

2160

Romulan Wars ended by the Battle of Cheron. The Romulans suffer a humiliating military defeat at the hands of Earth forces.

"The Defector" (TNG). Admiral Jarok (as Setal) mentioned the battle but not the date, although this was presumably just before the peace treaty is signed, since he associated the battle with the establishment of the Neutral Zone. (See next entry.)

Editors' Note: The Battle of Cheron may refer to the planet seen in "Let That Be Your Last Battlefield" (TOS), although Spock, in that episode (set in 2268), indicated an unfamiliarity with the inhabitants of Cheron.

Romulan peace treaty signed, establishing the Romulan Neutral Zone as a buffer between the planets Romulus and Remus and the rest of the galaxy, violation of which is considered to be an act of war. All negotiations were conducted by subspace radio, without face-to-face contact between the parties. *"Balance of Terror" (TOS). About one hundred years prior to episode.*

Editors' Note: The names of Romulan homeworlds were given as Romulus and Remus in "Balance of Terror" (TOS) although Spock's star map in that episode listed them as Romulus and Romii. See entry in 2311 for information on the Treaty of Algeron.

2161

The United Federation of Planets is incorporated. Starfleet is established with a charter "to boldly go where no man has gone before." The Federation is governed by a representative Council, located in the city of San Francisco on Earth, and the Federation council president's office is located in the city of Paris. The Constitution of the Federation includes important protections of individual rights including the Seventh Guarantee, protecting citizens against self-incrimination.

The Federation was first mentioned in "A Taste of Armageddon" (TOS). In "The Outcast" (TNG), Troi mentioned that the Federation was founded in 2161. The Starfleet Academy emblem in "The First Duty" (TNG) also gave this as the year in which the Academy was established. The Federation Council chambers were established as being in San Francisco in Star Trek IV: The Voyage Home. The Federation president's office was first seen in Star Trek VI: The Undiscovered Country, and again in "Homefront" (DS9) and "Paradise Lost" (DS9). In all three cases, the view out the window from the president's office shows the Eiffel Tower and the city of Paris. The Seventh Guarantee was established in "The Drumhead."

Editors' Note: The Romulan Wars ("Balance of Terror" [TOS]) were described as being between Earth and the Romulans, suggesting that the Federation was not established until at least that point. Starfleet was apparently responsible for the Starship Archon and Horizon missions a few years later (2167 and 2168), thereby suggesting that both Starfleet and the Federation were in existence by then. The U.S.S. Essex, also lost in 2167, was clearly a part of the Federation Starfleet. Original Series story editor Dorothy Fontana once speculated that the Federation had been founded at least partially as a means of providing a defense against the Romulans in the aftermath of the war described in "Balance of Terror."

(An early draft of this chronology, which speculated that 2161 might be the date for the Federation's founding, was used for reference when producer/writer Jeri Taylor needed information for "The Outcast" [TNG] thus making 2161 "official"!)

The term "United Federation of Planets" was not used until the 23rd episode of the original Star Trek series, "A Taste of Armageddon" (TOS). "Starfleet" did not come into use until the 15th episode, "Court Martial" (TOS) During the first few episodes, the operating authority for the Enterprise *was variously referred to as Space Command ("Court Martial" [TOS]), Space Central ("Miri" [TOS]), the Star Service ("Conscience of the King" [TOS]) and the United Earth Space Probe Agency ("Tomorrow Is Yesterday" [TOS]). The latter name was once even abbreviated as UESPA, pronounced "you-spah" in "Charlie X" (TOS) Nevertheless, later episodes imply Starfleet to have existed prior to "Court Martial" (TOS) so we are assuming that it did. Dorothy Fontana tells us that the term UESPA was suggested by story editor John D. F. Black. Fontana said she considers some of the other names listed above to be mistakes, but she also notes that present-day U.S. Navy personnel use at least as many terms when they refer to the Navy, CINCPAC, the "Silent Service," and the Pentagon.*

2164

The drug felicium is used to halt a plague on planet Ornara. It is not realized at the time, but felicium, a product of the planet Brekka, has powerfully addictive properties, making the Ornarans dependent on the substance long after the plague has been controlled.

"Symbiosis" (TNG). Two hundred years prior to episode (2364).

2165

Sarek of Vulcan is born, the son of Skon and grandson of Solkar. Sarek becomes one of the Federation's most distinguished diplomats.

Sarek of Vulcan

"Journey to Babel" (TNG) Sarek gives his age as 102.437 in the episode. He names his ancestors during the fal-tor-pan *ceremony in* Star Trek III: The Search for Spock.

Editors' Note: We assume that Skon was Sarek's father, and that Solkar was his grandfather. It seems unlikely that Solkar was Sarek's mother because Vulcan females tend to have names beginning with the letter T.

Guinan has her last encounter with Q prior to 2365. The two are not particularly fond of each other.

"Q Who?" (TNG). She said her last meeting was 200 years prior to episode.

The planet Deneva is colonized by the Federation to provide a freighting line base. The planet is held to be one of the most beautiful in the galaxy.

"Operation: Annihilate!" (TOS). Kirk noted the planet had been colonized over a century prior to the episode (2267).

Denevan colony

2167

The *Starship Archon* visits planet Beta III in star system C-111. The planet's master computer, known as Landru, destroys the ship by pulling it out of orbit. Many *Archon* crew members are killed, but many more are "absorbed" into Beta III's computer-controlled society, becoming known as "the Archons" to the planet's inhabitants.

"Return of the Archons" (TOS). One hundred years prior to episode (2267).

The *U.S.S. Essex*, (registry number NCC-173) a *Daedalus*-class starship under the command of Captain Bryce Shumar and First Officer Steven Mullen, is caught in an electromagnetic storm and destroyed above the Class-M moon of planet Mab-Bu VI. There are no survivors of the crew of 229. The fate of this ship remains a mystery until 2368. Shumar's immediate superior in the sector had been Admiral Uttan Narsu of Starbase 12.

"Power Play" (TNG) Exact date is conjecture, but the ship had crashed over 200 years prior to the episode (2368).

U.S.S. Essex

Starship Horizon

The Book

Biosphere colony on Moab IV

Kavis binary star

Editors' Note: Since the Essex *was operating at about the same time as the* Horizon *(from "A Piece of the Action" [TOS]) and the* Archon *("Return of the Archons" [TOS]), we conjecture that those two other vessels were also* Daedalus-*class starships.*

2168

The *Starship Horizon* visits planet Sigma Iotia II, about one hundred light-years beyond Federation space. The crew reports the humanoid population of the planet to be on the verge of industrialization.

At this point, Starfleet has not yet instituted the Prime Directive of noninterference, and a member of the *Horizon* crew leaves behind a copy of a book entitled *Chicago Mobs of the Twenties*. The disastrous though unintended result is that the people of Iotia adopt the book as a model for their society.

Shortly after the contact at Sigma Iotia II, the *U.S.S. Horizon* is lost along with all crew members. Because of this, Starfleet remains unaware of the contact and the cultural contamination until radio signals from the *Horizon* are received a hundred years later.

"A Piece of the Action" (TOS). Kirk noted the contact was one hundred years prior to episode (2268).

Editors' Note: Kirk mentioned that subspace radio had not yet been invented at this point.

Settlers from Earth establish a colony on planet Moab IV. They create a sealed, well-planned, genetically balanced biosphere in which they hope to forge a perfect society.

"Masterpiece Society" (TNG). Benbeck noted his people had been working for two centuries to create their paradise.

2169

A new type of impulse engine is adopted for Starfleet vessels. The basic design of this sublight propulsion system remains essentially unchanged for at least two centuries.

"Relics" (TNG). Scotty noted that impulse engine design hadn't changed much in 200 years.

Ancient burial vaults of the First Hebitian civilization on planet Cardassia are unearthed. Grave robbers remove priceless artifacts, including many made of jevonite, described as unimaginably beautiful.

"Chain of Command, Part II" (TNG). Madred said they were unearthed 200 years before the episode (2369).

2170

A group of Native Americans, seeking to preserve their cultural identity, leaves their North American home to search for a planet on which they can begin a colony. The group is led by a man named Katowa.

"Journey's End" (TNG). Two hundred years before the episode (2370).

Last detonation of Kavis Alpha neutron star prior to 2366, when Dr. Stubbs used that star's burst as part of his astrophysical research.

"Evolution" (TNG). Stubbs noted that the phenomenon occurs regularly, every 196 years, the stellar equivalent of Earth's Old Faithful.

2172

Bajoran year 9174. Bajoran poet Akorem Laan embarks upon an interplanetary voyage aboard a traditional Bajoran solar-sailing lightship. Akorem's works included "Kitara's Song," "The Call of the Prophets," and "Gaudaal's Lament."

"Accession" (DS9). About 200 years before the episode (2372). Akorem actually disappeared without a trace during his voyage, and his fate remained a mystery for two centuries until he emerged from the Bajoran wormhole in 2372. At Sisko's request, the Prophets in the wormhole sent Akorem back in time, so that from the perspective of Akorem's contemporaries, he only disappeared for a brief time before returning. Upon his return, the timeline was changed, since in the original timeline he never finished his classic, "The Call of the Prophets," but in the new timeline, he did.

Akorem Laan

A Class-M planet in the Teplan system, near Dominion space in the Gamma Quadrant, suffers orbital bombardment from the Jem'Hadar. The planet's technologically sophisticated inhabitants had attempted to resist the Dominion, and the attack was intended to make an example to other worlds. The Jem'Hadar also employ an unusually cruel form of biological warfare, infecting the planet's humanoid population with a deadly blight that takes years to kill its victims.

"The Quickening" (DS9). Two hundred years before the episode (2372).

2196

Starfleet withdraws the last *Daedalus*-class starship from service.

"Power Play" (TNG). Data explained those ships had not been in service for 172 years prior to the episode (2368).

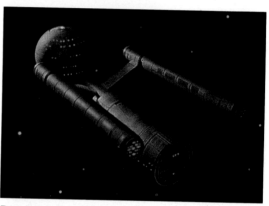

Daedalus-*class Starship*

5.0 THE TWENTY-THIRD CENTURY

*First City
of the Klingon
Empire*

2209

The first case of transporter psychosis, a rare disorder caused by a breakdown of neurochemical molecules during transport, is diagnosed by researchers on planet Delinia II.

"Realm of Fear" (TNG). The *Enterprise-D computer gave the year as 2209.*

Editors' Note: We still don't know when the transporter was invented, but it was apparently before this date.

2215

Planet Selcundi Drema begins disintegration, forming an asteroid belt in that solar system.

"Pen Pals" (TNG). One hundred fifty years prior to episode (2365).

*The first case of transporter psychosis is
diagnosed on planet Delinia II.*

2217

The *U.S.S. Valiant* contacts planet Eminiar VII in star cluster NGC 321. The ship and its crew become casualties of the ongoing war between Eminiar and Vendikar.

"A Taste of Armageddon" (TOS). Fifty years prior to the episode (2267).

Editors' Note: This was presumably another Starship Valiant, *since an earlier ship of the same name was launched in 2065 and never returned ("Where No Man Has Gone Before").*

2218

First contact with the Klingon Empire. As a result of this disastrous initial contact with the Klingons, Starfleet thereafter adopts a policy of covert surveillance of newly discovered civilizations before first contact is attempted.

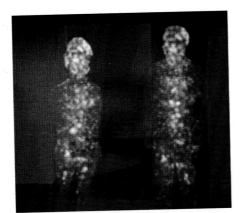

Klingon battle cruiser

"Day of the Dove" (TOS). McCoy noted that Klingons and humans had been adversaries for 50 years prior to the episode, set in 2268.

Editors' Note: "First Contact" (TNG) also described this as having happened "centuries ago," but it is only 144 years before that episode (2367).

2219

Richard Daystrom is born. He becomes a brilliant computer scientist, the inventor of duotronic systems, and winner of the Nobel and Zee-Magnees prizes.

"The Ultimate Computer" (TOS). Daystrom invented duotronics 25 years prior to the episode, and Kirk noted Daystrom was 24 years old at the time (2268).

Dr. Richard Daystrom

2222

Montgomery Scott is born. He becomes chief engineer of original U.S.S. Enterprise under the command of Captain Kirk.

"Relics" (TNG). Beverly said that Scotty was 147 years old in 2369. This would make Scotty 44 years old during the first season of the original Star Trek series, which was actor James Doohan's age at that point.

Pralor Automated Unit 3947 is activated by a Builder on the Pralor homeworld in the Delta Quadrant. Like all such automated units, 3947 has been constructed for the Pralor war against the Cravic.

"Prototype" (VGR). According to 3947, he was activated 1,314,807 hours prior to the episode (2372), which works out to about 150 years.

Scotty

2223

Relations with the Klingon Empire degenerate, giving rise to some 70 years of unremitting hostility between the Klingons and the Federation until the Khitomer Conference of 2293.

Star Trek VI: The Undiscovered Country. Spock said that there had been hostility between the two powers for 70 years prior to that film, set in 2293.

Sybok

2224

Sybok is born, son of Sarek and a Vulcan princess. The princess, Sarek's first wife, dies shortly after Sybok's birth. Sybok is Spock's elder half-brother.

Date is conjecture from Star Trek V: The Final Frontier and "Journey to Babel" (TOS). This is seven years prior to conjectural date for Spock's birth, based on the Vulcan seven-year mating cycle.

Editors' Note: Gene Roddenberry considered some events in Star Trek V to be apocryphal; however, they are included in this chronology because of our desire to be as complete as possible.

Leonard McCoy

2227

Leonard H. McCoy is born. He becomes chief medical officer of the original U.S.S. Enterprise. His father is David McCoy.

Data gave McCoy's age as 137 during "Encounter at Farpoint" (TNG). His middle initial and his father's name were established in Star Trek III.

2229

Sarek of Vulcan and Amanda Grayson of Earth are married. Sarek would later describe his decision to marry the human Amanda as a "logical thing to do."

Sarek and Amanda

Infant Spock

James T. Kirk

Vina

Spock at age 7

Date is conjecture from "Journey to Babel" (TOS). A line in an early draft of the script suggested they were married 38 years prior to the episode (2267).

Editors' Note: In virtually all cases, we did not consider material from early script drafts to be "official," preferring to accept only information from aired episodes. There were, however, a very few items from scripts that we chose to include because of their importance within the Star Trek universe. The marriage of Sarek and Amanda is one such event.

Curzon Dax attempts for the first time to solve an Altonian brain teaser. The puzzle would intrigue Dax for over a century, even when the Dax symbiont was joined with its next host.

"A Man Alone" (DS9). Dax said she'd been trying to master it for about 140 years prior to the episode (2369).

2230

Spock is born, son of Sarek and Amanda. Spock, a Vulcan-human hybrid, becomes science officer on the *Enterprise* under the command of Captain Christopher Pike and Captain James Kirk. He later plays a crucial role in negotiating peace between the Federation and the Klingon Empire, and in the effort for Vulcan/Romulan reunification.

Date is conjecture: A year after conjectural date for Sarek and Amanda's marriage. (See previous entry.) Dorothy Fontana, writer of "Journey to Babel" (TOS), notes that this birth date would make Spock about the same age as actor Leonard Nimoy at the time the episode was first aired.

T'Pring is born. When she and Spock are seven years old, they are telepathically joined by parental arrangement so that they will be married when they reach adulthood.

"Amok Time" (TOS). Spock said both he and T'Pring were seven at the time of their mind-joining, suggesting they were born in the same year.

2233

James T. Kirk is born in Iowa on Earth on March 22. He has an older brother, George Samuel Kirk.

Kirk's age was given as 34 in "The Deadly Years" (TOS). In Star Trek IV: The Voyage Home, he told Gillian he was born in Iowa. Kirk's brother described in "What Are Little Girls Made Of?" (TOS). Sam Kirk's age was not given, but in "Operation: Annihilate!" (TOS), Sam was seen briefly and appeared to be significantly older than his brother. Reliable sources from the town of Riverside, Iowa, inform us that their city will be the birthplace of the Enterprise captain. We have no reason to doubt their veracity, although the Riverside birthplace is not derived from any episode or film.

2236

S.S. Columbia crashes on planet Talos IV. Crew member Vina is the only survivor. She is listed as an adult on the ship's manifest, although she appears as a youthful woman to Captain Pike some eighteen years later. The severely injured Vina is cared for by the Talosians, although their ability to repair her body is limited by the fact that they had never seen a human before.

"The Cage" (TOS). Eighteen years prior to episode (2254).

2237

Spock, age 7, causes his parents considerable concern by disappearing overnight into the Llangon mountains near his home city of ShirKahr in an effort to test himself with the traditional *kahs-wan* survival ordeal. His pet sehlat, I-Chaya, is seriously injured by a wild animal, and Spock chooses to have his pet euthanized by a healer rather than die a lingering, painful death.

"Yesteryear" (animated) "Unification, Part I" (TNG), and "Journey to Babel" (TOS). Spock's age, the name of his hometown, and the death of his pet are established in the animated episode "Yesteryear." Sarek, in "Unification, Part I" confirms that Spock often disappeared into the mountains, apparently in reference to the "Yesteryear" back story. Spock's pet sehlat was established in "Journey to Babel."

Editors' Note: As indicated in the preface, we are not using material from the animated Star Trek series. This information from "Yesteryear," written by Dorothy Fontana, is the sole exception, partly because it is reinforced by material in "Journey to Babel" (TOS) and "Unification, Part I" (TNG), but also because of Fontana's pivotal role in developing the background for the Spock character in the original Star Trek series. Note that we are using only the back story elements of Spock's childhood from "Yesteryear," and that we are not including the framing story, which had the adult Spock journey back in time to visit his younger self.

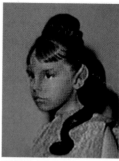

T'Pring

Young Spock is telepathically joined to T'Pring in a ritual Vulcan ceremony arranged by their parents. Less than a marriage but more than a betrothal, the mind-touch insures the two will be drawn together at the proper time once they are grown.

"Amok Time" (TOS). Spock said the joining had taken place when he was 7 years old. We are arbitrarily putting this after the events in "Yesteryear" (animated), since that episode represented a rite of passage.

Hikaru Sulu is born in San Francisco on planet Earth. He serves a distinguished career in Starfleet, first as staff physicist and helm officer on the *U.S.S. Enterprise*, and later as captain of the *U.S.S. Excelsior*.

Hikaru Sulu

Date is conjecture. Assumes Sulu was 29 during the first season of Star Trek. Sulu's birthplace is established to be San Francisco in Star Trek IV: The Voyage Home. He served as Enterprise physicist in "Where No Man Has Gone Before," prior to his duty at the helm. Sulu commanded the Excelsior (and got a first name) in Star Trek VI: The Undiscovered Country.

2239

Uhura is born in the United States of Africa on planet Earth. She becomes communications officer aboard the *U.S.S. Enterprise*, and later serves at Starfleet Command in San Francisco.

Uhura

Date is conjecture. Assumes Uhura was 27 years old during the first season of Star Trek, based on Nichelle Nichols's age. Her birthplace is also conjectural, and was suggested in the Star Trek writers' guide. Uhura's stint at Starfleet was shown in Star Trek III: The Search for Spock.

A reclusive individual known as Mr. Brack purchases the planet Holberg 917G, a Class-M world in the Omega system. Brack is later discovered to be a pseudonym for the (nearly) immortal Flint.

"Requiem for Methuselah" (TOS). Spock's research revealed that Brack had purchased the planet thirty years prior to the episode (2269).

2240

Montgomery Scott enters Starfleet Academy.

Conjecture. Assumes he was admitted at age 18.

Mr. Brack

Scotty

Dr. Richard Daystrom

Launch of the Starship Enterprise

Captain Robert April

2242

The battle of Donatu V is fought near Sherman's Planet, in a region disputed by the Klingon Empire and the United Federation of Planets.

"The Trouble with Tribbles" (TOS). Spock noted the battle was fought 23 solar years prior to the episode (2267).

2243

Montgomery Scott begins his career as a Starfleet engineer at the age of 21.

"Relics" (TNG). Scotty said he had been a Starfleet engineer for 52 years at the time of his retirement (2295). It is unclear if Scotty entered the Academy at age 21, or if he entered earlier and simply began serving aboard a cadet ship as an engineer at this point. (We're assuming that he entered the Academy at age 18).

Dr. Richard Daystrom invents duotronic computer technology and is awarded the Nobel and Zee-Magnees prizes. His revolutionary systems become the basis for the main computers used aboard the *Starship Enterprise.* Daystrom, still a relatively young man at this point, spends much of his later years trying to live up to this achievement, but is largely unsuccessful. Many years later he is recognized when the Daystrom Technological Institute is named in his honor.

"The Ultimate Computer" (TOS). Spock noted that the duotronic breakthrough had taken place twenty-five years prior to the episode (2268). Existence of Daystrom Institute established in "Measure of a Man" (TNG), "The Offspring" (TNG), "Captain's Holiday" (TNG), and "Data's Day" (TNG).

2244

Montgomery Scott graduates from Starfleet Academy.

Conjecure. Assumes he was admitted at age 18.

2245

First *Starship Enterprise*, NCC-1701, is launched from the San Francisco Yards facility in orbit around Earth. Captain Robert April assumes command of the *Constitution*-class ship and begins a five-year mission of exploration. One of the ship's designers is a young engineer named Laurence Marvick.

Assumption based on Gene Roddenberry's suggestion that the Enterprise *was twenty years old at the time of "Where No Man Has Gone Before" (TOS). Marvick established in "Is There in Truth No Beauty?"*

Editors' Note: Gene Roddenberry said he wanted the Enterprise, *as seen in the original* Star Trek *television series, to be a ship with "some history." Given a date of 2265 for "Where No Man Has Gone Before" (TOS), a 20-year-old ship would put the* Enterprise's *launch in 2245. This is inconsistent with Admiral Morrow's line in* Star Trek III: The Search for Spock, *where he says the ship was 20 years old at that point (2285), which would put the* Enterprise *launch in 2265. The problem with Morrow's date is that it would mean that the ship was launched just prior to the first season of the original series. This would contradict "The Menagerie" (TOS), which suggests that Spock served aboard the* Enterprise *with Captain Pike for over 11 years, since 2252. For this reason, we are using Gene's date of 2245 for the* Enterprise's *launch.*

Captain Robert April is not based on any direct evidence from any episode or film, but is included at Roddenberry's suggestion. The character name is from Gene's first proposal for the Star Trek series, back in 1964, which listed April as Enterprise captain and series lead. April was depicted in the animated Star Trek episode "The Counter Clock Incident," written by Fred Bronson, using the pseudonym John Culver. (An intermediate draft of the script for "The Cage" (TOS) also gave the character the name of Captain James Winter, no doubt a descendant of Star Trek feature film producer Ralph Winter.)

Pavel A. Chekov

Pavel A. Chekov born. He is an only child. Chekov later becomes navigator and tactical officer on the *Enterprise* under the command of James Kirk, and also serves as first officer aboard the *Reliant* under Captain Clark Terrell.

"Who Mourns for Adonais" (TOS). Chekov noted he was 22 years old at the time of the episode (2267). The fact that Chekov is an only child was established by Sulu in "Day of the Dove" (TOS). Chekov's Reliant stint seen in Star Trek II.

Leonard McCoy enters college, pursuing a medical degree.

Conjecture. Assumes McCoy was 18 years old at the time of admission. See note on questions regarding McCoy's past in Appendix A (Notes on Star Trek: The Original Series characters).

2246

Kodos the Executioner seizes power, declares martial law, and orders 4,000 people killed on planet Tarsus IV when a food shortage caused by an exotic fungus becomes critical. Emergency supplies arrive too late to prevent killings. Future *Enterprise* crew members James Kirk and Kevin Riley are among the nine eyewitnesses who survive the incident. Riley loses his parents in the massacre. Another surviving eyewitness is Kirk's friend Thomas Leighton. Later, a burned body is discovered and identified as Kodos. This was the last known record of Kodos prior to 2266, when it is learned the identification of the body is mistaken.

Anton Karidian, aka Kodos the Executioner

"The Conscience of the King" (TOS). Twenty years prior to episode (2266), according to the computer record.

Editors' Note: Kirk would have been about 13 years old at this point, and Kevin Riley would have been several years younger.

2247

Lenore Karidian is born. Her birth is also the first known record of actor Anton Karidian, later discovered to be the same person who was known as Kodos the Executioner.

"Conscience of the King" (TOS). Lenore was 19 years old at the time of the episode (2266).

Lenore Karidian

2249

Spock chooses to enter Starfleet instead of the Vulcan Science Academy, thereby alienating his father, Sarek, until the Babel conference of 2267.

"Journey to Babel" (TOS). Amanda said Spock and Sarek had not spoken as father and son for eighteen years prior to episode (2267). Note that this date is inconsistent with Garth's speech in "Whom Gods Destroy" (TOS), which suggests that Spock may have joined Starfleet after the Axanar peace mission. (See next page.)

Charles Evans is born. His parents are part of an unsuccessful colonization project that ends with a disastrous crash on planet Thasus.

"Charlie X" (TOS). He was 17 at the time of the episode (2266).

Spock

James T. Kirk

2250

James Kirk enrolls in Starfleet Academy. Mallory, father of a future *Enterprise* crew member, helps Kirk get into the academy. One of his most influential professors is historian John Gill. Kirk's personal hero is Fleet Captain Garth, considered to be the prototypical starship captain, whose exploits are still required reading at the Academy. Spock also studies under Gill, although Kirk and Spock were apparently not in that class together.

Date is conjecture: Assumes Kirk was seventeen years old at the time of his admission, as suggested by the Star Trek *[original series] writers' guide. This is reasonably consistent with references in "Where No Man Has Gone Before" (TOS), which establish that Kirk had been in the Academy some fifteen years prior to that episode, although Kirk seems to have been of a prior graduating class than Mitchell. (See later entry on Mitchell.) Mallory established in "The Apple" (TOS). Gill established in "Patterns of Force" (TOS), and Garth is from "Whom Gods Destroy" (TOS).*

Ben Finney

James Kirk, a midshipman at Starfleet Academy, befriends Ben Finney, an instructor. The two become so close that Ben later names his daughter, Jamie, after Kirk.

"Court Martial" (TOS). Date is conjecture, but Kirk was described as being a midshipman at the Academy when they met.

A Vulcan science mission reports an unusual subspace rupture in the Hanoli system. In an effort to control the dangerous phenomenon, expedition members detonate a pulse wave torpedo at the coordinates of the tear. Unfortunately, the attempt fails and minutes later the rupture expands radically, destroying the expedition along with the entire Hanoli system.

"If Wishes Were Horses" (DS9). Date is conjecture; the incident happened in the "mid-23rd century."

Ensign James Kirk serves on *U.S.S. Republic*, NCC-1371. He reports an error made by his friend, Ben Finney, causing Finney to be passed over for promotion. According to Kirk's report, Kirk had relieved Finney on watch and had discovered the circuits to the atomic matter piles improperly left open, endangering the safety of the ship. Years later Finney holds this against Kirk, believing the report to be the sole reason why Finney never attained the command of a starship.

"Court Martial" (TOS). Date is conjecture. Kirk's Farragut *tour of duty ("Obsession" [TOS]) in which Kirk is a lieutenant) was described as his "first assignment," suggesting the* Republic *incident may have occurred while he was still at Starfleet Academy. This is reinforced by the fact that Kirk was an ensign at the time, suggesting Kirk's service on the* Republic *occurred before Kirk met Mitchell, who was at some point a student of Kirk's at the academy.*

Editors' Note: The apparent fact that Kirk would have been an ensign (and later a lieutenant) while still at Starfleet Academy will probably raise some eyebrows among those familiar with protocol at present-day military schools, but we are told that at such institutions it is possible (though very uncommon) for a student to be accorded a rank such as ensign prior to graduation. Additionally, it's probably reasonable to assume that Starfleet, while steeped in tradition, has also changed a few things from the way its 20th-century predecessors did them.

Garth

Starfleet captain Garth wins a major victory at planet Axenar. Afterwards, James Kirk, apparently still on the *Republic*, visits Axanar on a peace mission. The operation is a major achievement for Garth, in overall charge of the mission. Starfleet awards Kirk the Palm Leaf of Axanar for his role in the assignment.

Date is conjecture. "Court Martial" (TOS) established that Kirk got the award, although the back story is established in "Whom Gods Destroy" (TOS), when Kirk notes he visited Axanar as a "new fledged cadet," implying he was still with Starfleet Academy at the time. The episode seems to suggest that Kirk was not under Garth's command during the Axanar mission. Kirk's assignment to the Republic at this point is conjecture, based on the theory that academy cadets spend part of their training on an actual starship. This would be consistent with practices at present-day Navy and Coast Guard academies, which require cadets to perform at-sea duty.

Kirk meets Gary Mitchell at Starfleet Academy. They become best friends, although Mitchell, attending classes taught by Kirk, would later describe Kirk as an instructor who forced you to "think or sink." Kirk later asks for Mitchell to serve under him on his first command. Another acquaintance of Kirk's is Finnegan, an upperclassman whom Kirk would later recall as having a penchant for practical jokes.

Gary Mitchell

"Where No Man Has Gone Before" (TOS). Fifteen years prior to the episode. Mitchell described Kirk as a lieutenant, so perhaps Kirk was an instructor or a teaching assistant after his assignment to the Republic ("Court Martial" [TOS]), in which Kirk was an ensign. On the other hand, it might be possible that Kirk was serving as an instructor at Starfleet Academy after his graduation in 2254. This would be consistent with the fact that Kirk was described as a lieutenant when he served aboard the Farragut, his first assignment after the academy, but it would be inconsistent with the reference to Kirk having met Mitchell fifteen years ago. Unfortunately, of all the original Star Trek characters, Kirk's back story seems to have the greatest number of internal contradictions. Finnegan was established in "Shore Leave" (TOS).

Starship Enterprise, under the command of Captain Robert April, returns from five-year voyage and begins refitting for the next mission. Christopher Pike assumes position of Enterprise captain.

Conjecture.

2251

Starship Enterprise, under command of Captain Christopher Pike, sets out on the ship's second five-year mission to explore the unknown.

Conjecture, see reference to Spock's beginning of service on the Enterprise in 2252.

Christopher Pike

2252

Spock, still an academy cadet, begins serving aboard the U.S.S. Enterprise under the command of Captain Pike.

"The Menagerie, Part I" (TOS). Spock said he had served with Pike for 11 years, 4 months. Pike apparently served as Enterprise captain until 2263. This date might also be interpreted as evidence that Pike had commanded two five-year missions of the Enterprise. The notion that Spock might have served aboard the Enterprise while still a cadet is consistent with the implication that Kirk was also apparently a cadet while aboard the Republic ("Court Martial" [TOS]). It is also possible that part of Spock's service with Pike was aboard some other ship, although this is not consistent with our speculation that Pike had commanded two five-year missions.

The humanoids known as the "Sky People" return to visit their "Inheritors" on planet Earth. The Sky People are disappointed when they are unable to find any significant signs of their ancient beneficiaries, unaware that a small number of Inheritors have survived by finding new homes on distant worlds.

Spock

"Tattoo" (VGR). Date is conjecture, but is approximately "twelve generations" before the episode (2372).

Ruth

*Pike and Vina in an illusory situation
created by the Talosians*

Pike held captive

Charles Evans, aged 3, is sole survivor of a spaceship crash on planet Thasus. He is cared for by the mysterious, noncorporeal Thasians, which give him extraordinary mental powers in order to insure his survival.

"Charlie X" (TOS). Fourteen years prior to episode (2266).

Kirk is romantically involved with Ruth. Kirk also becomes acquainted with R. M. Merrick, a student who is eventually dropped from Starfleet Academy when he fails a psychosimulator test.

"Shore Leave" (TOS). Fifteen years prior to episode (2267). (No last name was given for Ruth.) Merrick is from "Bread and Circuses" (TOS). Date is speculation as these could have happened at any point when Kirk was at the Academy. (See Editors' Note under "Bread and Circuses" (TOS) regarding Merrick.)

2253

Spock graduates from Starfleet Academy.

Conjecture. Assumes Spock entered the academy in 2249 (as per "Journey to Babel" [TOS]) and that he completed the standard four-year curriculum. Of course, Spock is a pretty smart guy and may well have graduated in fewer than four years, although no direct evidence exists to suggest this.

Dr. Leonard McCoy develops an impressive technique for the creation of axonal pathways between grafted neural tissue and basal ganglia. This procedure is later incorporated into the Starfleet database for Emergency Medical Holograms aboard Federation starships in the late 24th century.

"Lifesigns" (VGR). The Doctor gave the year as 2253. It is conjecture that McCoy developed the technique before graduation.

Dr. Leonard McCoy graduates from medical school.

Conjecture. Assumes McCoy began college in 2245 and that he completed an eight-year medical program. (See Appendix A [Notes on Star Trek: The Original Series characters] regarding uncertainties in McCoy's back story.)

2254

James Kirk graduates from Starfleet Academy. He is the only cadet ever to beat the "no-win scenario" of the *Kobayashi Maru* simulation. Kirk is awarded a commendation for original thinking for reprogramming the simulation to make it possible to win.

Date is conjecture, assumes Kirk was seventeen when he entered the Academy. "The Drumhead" (TNG), "Datalore" (TNG), and "The First Duty" (TNG) establish Starfleet Academy to be a four-year curriculum. Kobayashi Maru simulation established in Star Trek II: The Wrath of Khan.

Lieutenant Kirk is assigned duty aboard the *Starship Farragut* under the command of Captain Garrovick.

"Obsession" (TOS). The episode establishes that the Farragut was Kirk's first assignment after his graduation from the Academy. Kirk noted that Garrovick was "my commanding officer from the day I left the Academy."

U.S.S. *Enterprise*, under the command of Captain Pike, is involved in a violent conflict on planet Rigel VII. Three crew members, including the captain's yeoman, are killed, and seven are injured. Pike later blames the incident on his own carelessness in not anticipating hostilities by the Rigelians.

"The Cage" (TOS). Two weeks prior to the incident on Talos IV.

"The Cage" (TOS). (No stardate given in episode.) U.S.S. *Enterprise*, en route to the Vega colony, detects distress call from spaceship S.S. *Columbia*, which records indicate had disappeared near the Talos Star

Group some 18 years ago. Investigation leads to discovery of the *Columbia*'s crash site on planet Talos IV, and contact with the planet's indigenous inhabitants. The Talosians attempt to capture Pike in an effort to insure survival of their civilization, but Pike and the *Enterprise* escape by convincing the Talosians of human unsuitability for captivity.

Thirteen years prior to "The Menagerie" (TOS), according to Spock's testimony at the court-martial.

Editors' Note: José Tyler tells Dr. Haskins that space travel has become much faster in the eighteen years since the Columbia's crash because "the time barrier has been broken." This might be interpreted as a reference to the development of warp drive, but this would be inconsistent with other dating information that suggests that Zefram Cochrane invented the space warp around 2063. (Warp drive clearly had to exist prior to the Columbia's crash because the Columbia and other craft were already operating across considerable interstellar ranges.) We therefore choose to interpret Tyler's line as referring to some significant but unspecified improvement in warp drive technology.

Tyree

Captain Pike's greeting to the illusory survivors on Talos IV gives his ship's name as the "United Space Ship Enterprise," establishing what "U.S.S." stands for.

Lieutenant Kirk, commanding his first planet survey, befriends Tyree, an inhabitant of a technologically unsophisticated Class-M planet. Years later, Kirk returns to Tyree's planet when the Klingons intervene in a local dispute.

"A Private Little War" (TOS). Thirteen years prior to episode.

Editors' Note: The episode never establishes the name of Tyree's planet, although a draft of the script suggests that the planet's name may be Neural. Although the episode does not make this clear, Kirk would seem to have been serving aboard the Starship Farragut at this point.

Sheliak representative

2255

Last contact between the reclusive Sheliak Corporate and the United Federation of Planets prior to 2366. The two parties agree to the Treaty of Armens in which the Federation cedes planet Tau Cygna V to the Sheliak. The treaty contains 500,000 words and took 372 Federation legal experts to draft.

"Ensigns of Command" (TOS). Riker said the Federation and the Sheliak hadn't communicated for 111 years prior to the episode (2366).

Hikaru Sulu enters Starfleet Academy.

Conjecture. Assumes he was admitted at age 18.

2256

U.S.S. Enterprise, still under the command of Captain Christopher Pike, completes Pike's first five-year mission of exploration (the second for the ship, counting Captain April's earlier mission) and begins a year of refit work in spacedock.

Conjecture.

Leonard McCoy ends a romantic relationship with the future Mrs. Nancy Crater.

"The Man Trap" (TOS). McCoy said, "We walked out of each other's lives ten years ago." (Episode was set in 2266.)

Pike and Enterprise *command crew*

The future Nancy Crater

Enterprise *in spacedock*

Uhura

Hikaru Sulu

Commander Merrick

David Marcus

2257

Lieutenant Kirk, still serving aboard the *U.S.S. Farragut* (his first assignment after graduating from Starfleet Academy), encounters a dangerous "vampire cloud" near planet Tycho IV. When facing the creature, Kirk hesitates for a moment before firing ship's phasers, and afterward feels responsible when the creature causes the death of 200 people, including *Farragut* captain Garrovick. Years later Garrovick's son serves aboard the *Enterprise* with Kirk in command.

"Obsession" (TOS). Eleven years prior to episode (2268).

U.S.S. *Enterprise* embarks on Captain Pike's second five-year mission of exploration (the third for the ship).

Conjecture. The fact that Spock said he'd served with Pike for eleven years (as established in "The Menagerie" [TOS]) seems to support the notion that Pike commanded two five-year missions, with a year's hiatus between them for refit.

Uhura is admitted to Starfleet Academy.

Conjecture. Assumes she was 18 years old at the time she entered the Academy.

Karidian company of actors begins a tour of official installations under sponsorship of the Galactic Cultural Exchange Program. They are recognized for their performances of classic Shakespearean plays.

"Conscience of the King" (TOS). Nine years prior to episode (2266), according to Enterprise *historical computer banks.*

2259

Hikaru Sulu graduates from Starfleet Academy.

Conjecture. Assumes he was admitted at age 18.

2261

U.S.S. *Enterprise*, under the command of Captain Christopher Pike, completes its second five-year mission of exploration. The ship enters spacedock for a major refit. During this refit, the ship's crew capacity is boosted from 203 to 430.

Conjecture. Reference to increase in crew complement is based on Pike's comment in "The Cage" (TOS) that suggested the ship's capacity was 203 at that point. During the first season of the original series, Kirk indicated that the ship's crew was about 430.

Exploratory vessel *S.S. Beagle,* a small Class-IV stardrive vessel, crashes on planet 892-IV after having sustained meteor damage. The ship had been performing the first survey of the sector. The crew are captured by the planet's inhabitants and forced to fight as Roman gladiators. The ship's commander, Merrick, survives by becoming a strongman in local politics until 2267, when the *U.S.S. Enterprise* makes contact with the planet.

"Bread and Circuses" (TOS). Kirk said the Beagle *was missing for six years prior to episode (2267).*

David Marcus born to Carol Marcus and James Kirk. Carol Marcus asks Kirk not to be involved with the boy's upbringing. Kirk does not see his son again until 2285.

Star Trek II: The Wrath of Khan. *Date is conjecture. Assumes David was about 24 years old at the time of* Star Trek II.

Robert and Nancy Crater arrive at planet M-113 for archaeological research of the ancient ruins there. Nancy Crater is later killed by the last surviving native of the planet.

"The Man Trap" (TOS). Spock noted the Craters had arrived five years prior to the episode (2266).

The last message is received from Dr. Roger Korby's archaeological expedition on planet Exo III. Korby's signal describes the discovery of underground caverns. Neither Korby nor his expedition is heard from again, and two subsequent expeditions are unsuccessful in locating them on the planet. Korby, who is known as the Pasteur of archaeological medicine, is recognized for his translation of medical records from the Orion ruins, resulting in a revolution in immunization techniques.

"What Are Little Girls Made Of?" (TOS). Kirk noted it had been five years since Korby's last message. (Episode set in 2266.)

James Kirk is romantically involved with the future Janet Wallace. The relationship does not work out because of differences in career goals. Janet eventually marries a scientist, Theodore Wallace, a man 26 years her senior.

The future Janet Wallace

"The Deadly Years" (TOS). Janet reminded Kirk it had been "six years, four months, and an odd number of days" since they'd last seen each other.

Uhura graduates from Starfleet Academy.

Conjecture.

Spock meets botanist Leila Kalomi on Earth. Kalomi is romantically attracted to Spock, but Spock indicates he cannot return the feeling due to his Vulcan heritage.

"This Side of Paradise" (TOS). Leila reminded Spock that she'd told him of her love six years prior to the episode (2267).

2263

Spock visits his parents on Vulcan for the last time before the Babel conference on the Coridan admission. The visit is strained because of Sarek's disapproval of Spock's career choice.

Leila Kalomi

"Journey to Babel" (TOS). Amanda chided Spock for not having visited them for four years prior to the episode (2267).

James Kirk sees Areel Shaw for the last time before Kirk's trial at Starbase 11. The two had been romantically involved.

"Court Martial" (TOS). Areel said they hadn't seen each other for "four years, seven months, and an odd number of days" prior to the episode (2267).

Pavel Chekov enters Starfleet Academy.

Conjecture. Assumes he was admitted at age 18.

James Kirk is promoted to captain of the *Starship Enterprise* and meets Christopher Pike, who is promoted to fleet captain.

Conjecture. In "The Menagerie, Part I" (TOS), Kirk said he met Pike once prior to that episode, when the latter was promoted to fleet captain.

Areel Shaw

Miners Childress, Gossett, and Benton begin work at the lithium mining operation on planet Rigel XII.

"Mudd's Women" (TOS). Ruth noted the three miners had been there for almost three years. (Episode set in 2266.)

A group of 150 colonists under the leadership of Elias Sandoval leave Earth to settle on planet Omicron Ceti III.

"This Side of Paradise" (TOS). Kirk noted the Sandoval expedition had settled on the planet three years prior to the episode, and that the trip had taken a year, suggesting they had departed four years prior to the episode (2267).

2264

Captain James Kirk, in command of the original *U.S.S. Enterprise*, embarks on an historic five-year mission of exploration.

Date is conjecture: Assumes "Where No Man Has Gone Before" took place 13 months and 12 days into the mission, per one conjectural theory for stardates. (The episode was set on stardate 1312.) This system of determining stardates was not used in later episodes, but is at least useful for pegging the start of Kirk's mission in relation to that episode. This is also reasonably consistent with Captain Harriman's line in Star Trek Generations, that the Enterprise-B, launched in late 2293, was the first Enterprise in 30 years without Kirk in command.

Starship Enterprise

Tuvok is born on planet Vulcan.

"Flashback" (VGR). Tuvok said he was 29 years old at the time of the Khitomer conference (2293).

Joran Belar is born on the planet Trill.

"Equilibrium" (DS9). Calendar date is conjecture, but Trill computer records gave his birth as being on stardate 1024.7, which would seem to be shortly before Harry Mudd's conviction, see next item.

Harcourt Fenton Mudd is convicted of purchasing a space vessel with counterfeit currency. He is sentenced to psychiatric treatment and his master's license is revoked, effective stardate 1116.4. Mudd had previously been convicted of smuggling, although that sentence had been suspended.

"Mudd's Women" (TOS). Date is conjecture, but it was apparently prior to "Where No Man Has Gone Before" (TOS) because the stardate of his license suspension is lower than the stardate in "Where No Man."

April Wade is born on Earth. She becomes a prominent medical researcher at the University of Nairobi.

"Prophet Motive" (DS9). Wade was 106 years old at the time of the episode (2371).

The real Nancy Crater is killed by planet M-113's last surviving native. The creature later assumes Nancy's form and lives with Professor Robert Crater, an archaeologist studying M-113.

"The Man Trap" (TOS). Exact date is conjecture, but Professor Crater noted that Nancy had been killed a year or two prior to the episode (2266).

The Sandoval expedition arrives at planet Omicron Ceti III for colonization. Unfortunately, the planet is later found to have high levels of deadly Berthold rays, threatening the lives of the colonists.

"This Side of Paradise" (TOS). Kirk noted the colonists had been there for three years prior to the episode (2267).

2265

A bottle of Dom Perignon champagne of this year's vintage will be used in 2293 for the christening of the *Starship Enterprise*-B.

Star Trek Generations. The vintage, 2265, was legible on the bottle's label.

Dr. Elizabeth Dehner, a psychiatrist studying crew reactions in emergency situations, joins the *Enterprise* crew when the ship is at the Aldebaron colony.

Shortly before "Where No Man has Gone Before" (TOS).

James T. Kirk

A bottle of Dom Perignon

Dr. Elizabeth Dehner

"Where No Man Has Gone Before" (TOS). Stardate 1312.4. The *Enterprise* encounters an ancient recorder buoy near the edge of the galaxy. Investigation determines the buoy to be from *S.S. Valiant*, which had disappeared in the area some two centuries ago. Evidence from the buoy's record tapes suggest the ship was destroyed by her captain. Kirk orders the *Enterprise* to explore beyond the galaxy's rim, where the ship encounters a strange energy barrier, resulting in the deaths of nine personnel. Gary Mitchell, Kirk's friend from his Academy days, is somehow mutated by the barrier and gains tremendous psychokinetic powers. It is later learned that psychiatrist Elizabeth Dehner had been similarly mutated. An attempt to quarantine Mitchell at the Delta Vega mining facility is unsuccessful, and Kirk is forced to kill him to protect the ship. Dehner is also killed in the incident.

Delta Vega lithium cracking station

Date is conjecture: Assumes the episode was six months to a year prior to Star Trek's *first season. This is to allow sufficient time to account for the costume and set changes between this pilot episode and the series.*

Editors' Note: The tombstone created by Gary Mitchell for Kirk gives the captain's name as "James R. Kirk." The captain's name would later be changed to "James T. Kirk." Dorothy Fontana notes that Kirk's middle initial changed because Gene Roddenberry simply forgot that this episode had established it as "R," but noted that Gene was also fond of giving his characters the middle name "Tiberius." (Gary Lockwood's character in Roddenberry's series The Lieutenant *was named William Tiberius Rice.)*

Guinan

This episode (and "Mudd's Women" [TOS]) establishes that the Enterprise *uses "lithium crystals" in its engines, although later episodes changed this to "dilithium crystals." According to Fontana, RAND Corporation physicist (and* Star Trek *technical adviser) Harvey Lynn suggested the change. The reason was that lithium is real, but dilithium is not, thus giving* Star Trek's *writers more freedom to tell stories without being scientifically wrong. Fontana further suggests that the change might have been a technological upgrade to the ship's engines.*

The Borg destroy Guinan's home planet. A small number of Guinan's people, the El-Aurians, manage to survive by spreading themselves across the galaxy.

"Q Who?" (TNG). One hundred years prior to the episode (2365).

Dr. Leonard H. McCoy

Planet Ingraham B is attacked by the same parasite creatures that later decimated the population of planet Deneva.

"Operation: Annihilate!" (TOS). Two years prior to the episode (2267).

2266

Dr. Leonard H. McCoy is assigned to duty aboard the *U.S.S. Enterprise* as ship's surgeon. He replaces Dr. Mark Piper.

Date is conjecture: He was apparently assigned after "Where No Man Has Gone Before" (TOS), in which Dr. Piper was ship's surgeon, but before "The Corbomite Maneuver," which marked McCoy's first appearance.

Dr. Simon Van Gelder is assigned as associate director of the Tantalus V penal colony. He serves on the staff of colony director Tristan Adams.

"Dagger of the Mind" (TOS). Spock's computer research indicated Van Gelder had been assigned six months prior to the episode.

Lieutenant Hikaru Sulu

Lieutenant Hikaru Sulu accepts a transfer from staff physicist to helm officer aboard the *U.S.S. Enterprise.*

Date is conjecture: He was apparently transferred after "Where No Man Has Gone Before" (TOS), but before "The Corbomite Maneuver" (TOS).

The *Starship Enterprise* begins a routine star-mapping mission.

Three days prior to "The Corbomite Maneuver" (TOS).

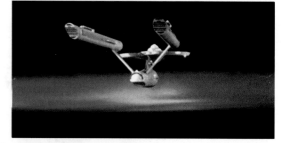

Enterprise *at the barrier*

5.1 STAR TREK: THE ORIGINAL SERIES — YEAR 1

"...to boldly go where no man has gone before."

2266 (CONTINUED)

Assumes the original Star Trek *television series was set 300 years after the first airdate of the show (September, 1966).*

Balok's false image

"The Corbomite Maneuver" (TOS). Stardate 1512.2. The *U.S.S. Enterprise*, on a routine star-mapping mission, makes first contact with the spaceship *Fesarius* of the First Federation. Although *Fesarius* commander Balok is initially wary of the *Enterprise*, presenting a false image, he eventually accepts the assurances of good intentions by *Enterprise* personnel after Kirk offers assistance when Balok's ship appears to be disabled. Kirk assigns Lieutenant Bailey to cultural exchange duty aboard the *Fesarius*.

A number of women on planet Rigel IV are brutally murdered by an unknown assailant, popularly known as *Beratas*. The killer is later discovered to be the same energy entity responsible for similar murders a year later on planet Argelius II. The entity is believed to have traveled in the body of Hengist, a native of Rigel IV, hired by the Argelian government as an administrator.

"Wolf in the Fold" (TOS). Computer records indicated the killings had taken place one year prior to the episode (2267).

"Mudd's Women" (TOS). Stardate 1329.8. The *Enterprise* attempts to rescue a small Class-J cargo ship that has strayed too close to an asteroid belt. The attempt fails, although the crew of the vessel is successfully beamed aboard the *Enterprise* before the smaller ship is destroyed. In the rescue attempt, however, the *Enterprise* lithium crystal circuits are damaged, nearly crippling the ship. The captain of the transport, Harcourt Fenton Mudd, is later coerced into assisting Kirk in dealing with lithium miners on Rigel XII to provide crystals to save the *Enterprise* from a decaying orbit.

Harcourt Fenton Mudd

Three women traveling with Mudd, who had apparently been recruited by Mudd as wives for settlers on planet Ophiucus III, elect instead to remain with the lithium miners on Rigel XII.

Harcourt Fenton Mudd is turned over to Federation authorities for illegal operation of transport vessel.

Just after "Mudd's Women" (TOS).

"The Enemy Within" (TOS). Stardate 1672.1. The *U.S.S. Enterprise* is on a routine geological survey to planet Alfa 177. Magnetic ore contamination from landing party site causes a transporter malfunction, resulting in a partial replication of Captain Kirk. The duplication is nearly perfect, but each copy has only part of the personality traits of the original, thereby threatening the survival of both copies. Science Officer Spock and Engineer Scott successfully modify the transporter to recombine Kirk to his original form.

Remaining members of the *Enterprise* landing party are trapped on the surface of Alfa 177 until the repair of the transporter, resulting in severe frostbite and exposure. Upon return to the *Enterprise,* all landing party members are treated by medical personnel and are given excellent prognoses for a full recovery.

Editors' Note: This episode marks the invention of the Vulcan nerve pinch, used to neatly (and nonviolently) render the "evil" Kirk unconscious. Star Trek production staffers (and several scripts) would later refer to the trick as FSNP, the "Famous Spock Nerve Pinch." To the question of why Spock couldn't have sent a shuttlecraft down to the planet surface after the transporter broke, the answer is that at this relatively early point in the series the show didn't yet have a shuttlecraft.

"The Man Trap" (TOS). Stardate 1513.1. The *U.S.S. Enterprise* is assigned to perform routine health examinations of archaeological personnel at planet M-113. An investigation is conducted when three members of the *Enterprise* crew are discovered dead on the planet, killed under unknown circumstances. It is learned that the killer is the last specimen of a species indigenous to M-113. The creature, which is later found to possess an unusual hypnotic ability to cause its prey to see it as someone else, is also discovered to live on sodium chloride that it extracts from its victims' bodies. Two additional casualties are discovered on board the *Enterprise,* including archaeologist Robert Crater, before the creature is killed while it is attempting to attack Captain Kirk.

Editors' Note: Spock tells Uhura that his home planet of Vulcan has no moon, although we see several moons around that planet in Star Trek: The Motion Picture. Curiously, none of these satellites were seen when the Starships Enterprise visited that planet in "Amok Time" (TOS) or "Sarek" (TNG). "The Man Trap" (TOS) is also the source of the fannish blessing, "May the Great Bird of the Galaxy bless your planet," spoken by Sulu, which was itself derived from Star Trek associate producer Bob Justman's gag nickname for producer Gene Roddenberry.

Dr. McCoy spills a small amount of acid on a table in his medical laboratory, scarring the table. A year later he notices an identical scar on the same table on the alternate universe version of the *Enterprise*.

"Mirror, Mirror" (TOS). McCoy noted that he'd spilled acid there a year ago.

"The Naked Time" (TOS). Stardate 1704.2. *U.S.S. Enterprise* assigned to pick up science team from planet Psi 2000. Landing party discovers all researchers to be dead under unusual circumstances, later determined to have been caused by an unknown virus. The landing party accidentally brings back the virus to the ship, infecting most of the crew and threatening the *Enterprise* when the virus causes personnel to lose emotional control. Among those most seriously affected is Lieutenant Kevin Riley, who commandeers the ship's engine room. McCoy develops a serum that enables personnel to regain emotional stability. An emergency restart of ship's engines using a theoretical intermix formula results in the accidental regression of the *Enterprise* and all ship's personnel through time, some 71 hours into the past.

Editors' Note: This episode marks the first appearance of Christine Chapel, played by Majel Barrett, the future Mrs. Gene Roddenberry. Chapel appeared in the original series and in several of the movies. Barrett had pre-

Incompletely duplicated replica of Captain Kirk, embodying aggressive personality traits

The stranded landing party on Alfa 117

The last M-133 creature

Discovery of frozen members of the Psi 2000 science team

Christine Chapel

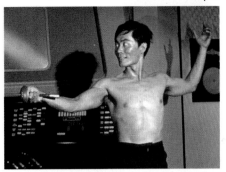

Sulu under influence of Psi 2000 virus

Romulan Bird-of-Prey

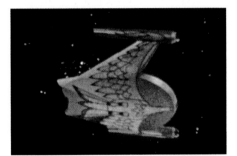

Romulan commander

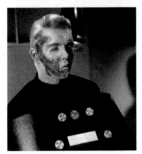

*Captain Pike wheelchair-bound
following the accident*

viously portrayed the mysterious "Number One," second in command of the Enterprise *in the pilot episode, "The Cage." Barrett also lent her voice to the* Enterprise *computer in the original* Star Trek *series as well as in* Star Trek: The Next Generation, Star Trek: Deep Space Nine, *and* Star Trek: Voyager. *Barrett also played Lwaxana Troi.*

"The Naked Time" (TOS) was originally planned to be the first part of a two-part story. According to Dorothy Fontana, episode writer John D. F. Black left the series without doing the second part, so Fontana eventually did that story as a separate episode, "Tomorrow Is Yesterday" (TOS), "The Naked Time" does not clearly describe the nature of the Psi 2000 infection, but it is established to be a virus when the same malady strikes the crew of the Tsiolkovsky *and the* Enterprise-D *in "The Naked Now" (TNG). This episode establishes the* Enterprise *warp drive to be powered by antimatter reactions. Prior to this point, the motive power of the ship's engines was not specifically described.*

Charles Evans is rescued from the planet Thasus by the crew of the science probe vessel *Antares*, under the command of Captain Ramart. Evans, a 17-year-old human boy, is the only survivor of a spaceship crash on Thasus some 14 years ago.

Prior to "Charlie X" (TOS).

"Charlie X" (TOS). Stardate 1533.6. First contact with mythical Thasians. *U.S.S. Enterprise* assigned to rendezvous with the spaceship *Antares* to transport the orphaned Charles Evans to his nearest living relatives on Colony Alpha 5. Evans is found to exhibit unusual telekinetic powers, evidence of the existence of the Thasians, previously believed to be purely mythical. Evans eventually returns to Thasus, where his powers, given to him to aid his survival, would not be a threat as they would be in normal human society. Evans is believed to have been responsible for the destruction of the science vessel *Antares* shortly after its rendezvous with the *Enterprise*.

Editors' Note: The term "Starfleet Command" had not yet been decided on when this episode was filmed. In these early episodes, various terms were used to describe the operating authority for the Enterprise, *including "United Earth Space Probe Agency." In this episode, Kirk referred to this as UESPA Headquarters, which he pronounced as "you-spah."*

"Balance of Terror" (TOS). Stardate 1709.2. Neutral Zone outposts 2, 3, 4, and 8 are reported destroyed in apparent Romulan attack. The *Enterprise* responds, determining the Romulan action to be a measure of Federation resolve, untested by the Romulans since the establishment of the Neutral Zone a century ago. The Romulan spacecraft, while capable of sublight speeds only, is discovered to be equipped with a cloaking device that can render a ship nearly invisible to sensors, as well as a powerful new plasma energy weapon used to destroy the Neutral Zone outposts. The *Enterprise*, acting in direct violation of Starfleet orders, enters the Neutral Zone under the authority of Captain Kirk and successfully destroys the Romulan ship, thereby repelling a potential Romulan incursion.

The sole casualty aboard the *Enterprise* is phaser specialist Robert Tomlinson. He is survived by his fiancée, Angela. Their wedding ceremony had been in progress when interrupted by news of the Romulan attack.

An accident aboard an old Class-J starship causes the death of several Starfleet cadets. The toll would have been higher if not for Fleet Captain Christopher Pike, who dragged several cadets to safety. Pike is seriously injured in the incident and is later confined to a wheelchair due to severe delta-ray exposure.

"The Menagerie, Part I" (TOS). Exact date is conjecture, but Commodore Mendez describes the accident as having happened "months" before the episode.

"What Are Little Girls Made Of?" (TOS). Stardate 2712.4. *U.S.S. Enterprise* at planet Exo III on a search mission for missing scientist Dr. Roger Korby, fiancé of *Enterprise* nurse Christine Chapel. Korby is discovered alive, but it is learned he had imprinted his personality into an android body, using ancient alien technology he had discovered on the planet. Also transferred to an android body is Korby's assistant, Dr. Brown. Korby ultimately discovers that the process somehow diminishes his human emotions, and he destroys himself.

Nurse Christine Chapel elects to remain on board the *Enterprise.* Chapel had given up a promising career in bioresearch to sign aboard a starship in the hopes of someday finding her lost fiancé.

"Dagger of the Mind" (TOS). Stardate 2715.1. The *Enterprise,* on a resupply mission to Tantalus V penal colony, accidentally takes on an inmate attempting to escape. The inmate is later discovered to be Dr. Simon Van Gelder, associate director of the rehab colony. Investigation by Kirk and psychiatrist Helen Noel reveals Van Gelder to be suffering from adverse effects of an experimental neural neutralizer device developed by colony director Dr. Tristan Adams. The device, intended for treatment of violent patients, had induced temporary mental disorders in Van Gelder. The device is destroyed, and Van Gelder is apparently promoted to colony director. Dr. Adams is reported to have died as a result of overexposure to the neural neutralizer.

Spock uses Vulcan mind-meld to obtain information from Dr. Van Gelder

Editors' Note: This episode is the first time we've seen Spock perform the Vulcan mind-meld.

The *U.S.S. Enterprise*, on a star-charting mission, reports finding seven planets in star system L-370.

"The Doomsday Machine" (TOS). Exact date is conjecture, but Spock said they'd charted seven planets in the system a year prior to the episode.

"Miri" (TOS). Stardate 2713.5. The *Enterprise* responds to a distress call, discovered to be from a Class-M planet virtually identical to Earth. Indigenous humanoid inhabitants determined to be nearly all dead, found to be victims of a disastrous research project whose goal, ironically, was to prolong life. Investigation reveals the only survivors are a group of children, who are discovered to be aging at a rate equivalent to one month for every century of real time. A native child, a young woman named Miri, provides information from which *Enterprise* personnel determine that these children die upon reaching puberty. The *Enterprise* landing party, infected with the same disease, is quarantined on planet surface until a viable antitoxin can be developed by Dr. Leonard McCoy.

Miri

Federation authorities dispatch a sociological team to help the children on Miri's planet.

Just after "Miri" (TOS).

Klingon operatives attempt to influence local politics on Tyree's planet by providing firearms to the technologically unsophisticated inhabitants.

"A Private Little War" (TOS). Exact date is conjecture, but Tyree noted that the "firesticks" had appeared nearly a year before the episode.

Enterprise summoned by scientist Dr. Thomas Leighton to Planet Q to investigate reports of a new synthetic food process. Because of the hope that this development will end the threat of famine at the Earth colony on planet Cygnia Minor, Kirk orders the *Enterprise* to divert three light-years off course to meet with Leighton.

Just prior to "The Conscience of the King" (TOS).

The villagers with "fire sticks"

*Lenore and Anton Karidian
face Captain Kirk*

"The Conscience of the King" (TOS). Stardate 2817.6. Kirk learns that Dr. Thomas Leighton's report was an effort to inform Kirk covertly of a suspicion that actor Anton Karidian, currently performing on Planet Q, is in fact the infamous Kodos the Executioner. These allegations are eventually borne out, but not before Karidian's daughter is found to be responsible for a series of murders, an attempt to eliminate all remaining witnesses of Karidian's crimes 20 years ago. Among Lenore Karidian's victims is Dr. Thomas Leighton, killed shortly after he revealed his suspicions to Kirk. Attempts are also made against James Kirk and Kevin Riley, the last surviving eyewitnesses to Kodos's killings.

The people of planet Acamar III, having endured generations of clan wars, finally establish peace for nearly all concerned. A significant exception is the outcast nomadic Gatherers, who continue to be a source of violence for a century, raiding many nearby planets and star systems.

"The Vengeance Factor" (TNG). Sovereign Marouk said her people have had peace for a century prior to the episode (2366).

A space vessel carrying visitors from planet Ingraham B to planet Deneva carries a deadly parasitic life-form that has already caused mass insanity on Ingraham B over a year ago.

"Operation: Annihilate!" (TOS). Aurelan Kirk noted the parasites had arrived eight months prior to the episode.

A serious plague threatens the inhabitants of the New Paris colonies. The *U.S.S. Enterprise* is assigned to transport emergency medical supplies to planet Makus III for transfer to New Paris under the direction of Galactic High Commissioner Ferris.

Prior to "The Galileo Seven" (TOS).

2267

Shuttlecraft Galileo

"The Galileo Seven" (TOS). Stardate 2821.5. The *Enterprise* is on an emergency medical supply mission to Makus III. Mission is delayed when *Shuttlecraft Galileo* is lost investigating Murasaki 312, a quasar-like phenomenon. *Galileo*, under command of Science Officer Spock, is later discovered to have crash-landed on planet Taurus II, but attains a suborbital trajectory sufficient for detection by *Enterprise* sensors before criticality of New Paris mission forces ship to leave the system. *Galileo* crew members Latimer and Gaetano are reported killed by indigenous life-forms on Taurus II.

The *U.S.S. Enterprise* proceeds at warp speed to Makus III to deliver emergency medical supplies for the New Paris colonies.

Just after "The Galileo Seven" (TOS).

Pavel Chekov graduates from Starfleet Academy.

Conjecture. Assumes he was admitted in 2263 at age 18.

Stardate 2945.7. The *Starship Enterprise* encounters ion storm, Records Officer Benjamin Finney is reported killed when a sensor pod is ejected.

Just prior to "Court Martial" (TOS).

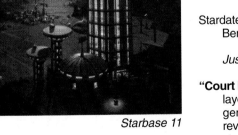

Starbase 11

"Court Martial" (TOS). Stardate 2947.3. The *Enterprise* makes an unscheduled layover at Starbase 11 for repairs from ion storm. Kirk is accused of negligent homicide in the death of Ben Finney, but court-martial investigation reveals Finney to be still alive. Kirk, who becomes the first starship captain to stand trial, is exonerated of all charges when it is revealed that Finney had tampered with *Enterprise* computer records. Kirk's case is prosecuted by Areel Shaw, with Samuel T. Cogley serving for the defense and Commodore Stone presiding. The *Enterprise* departs Starbase 11.

Editors' Note: The term "Starfleet Command" was used for the first time in "Court Martial," during the computer records of Kirk, Spock, and McCoy. Kirk refers to his former assignment, the U.S.S. Republic, as being a "United Star Ship," offering a second possible meaning to the letters "U.S.S." Kirk repeats the term United Star Ship in "Squire of Gothos" (TOS) as well. (Captain Pike, in "The Cage" [TOS], said the Enterprise *was a United Space Ship.)*

Spock receives a promotion from lieutenant commander to the rank of full commander.

His rank was given as lieutenant commander in "Court Martial" (TOS) but he's a full commander in "The Menagerie" (TOS).

Commodore Stone steps down as commanding officer of Starbase 11 and is succeeded by Commodore José Mendez.

Between "Court Martial" (TOS) and "The Menagerie" (TOS).

U.S.S. Enterprise First Officer Spock reports orders for the ship to return to Starbase 11, although no computer record is found of the message.

Just prior to "The Menagerie, Part I" (TOS).

Spock uses computer voice to falsify orders for the Enterprise

"The Menagerie, Part I" (TOS). Stardate 3012.4. The *Enterprise* arrives at Starbase 11, but investigation by Commodore Mendez fails to reveal source of orders to return to starbase. Further investigation shows the orders to have been falsified by Commander Spock, who kidnaps Fleet Captain Pike, then commandeers the *Enterprise* to planet Talos IV in violation of General Order 7, which prohibits such contact. Pike had been seriously injured several months prior in an accident aboard a training vessel. Kirk and Mendez, who had been left behind at Starbase 11 when the *Enterprise* departed, are successful in pursuing the ship aboard a shuttlecraft. Once Kirk and Mendez are aboard the *Enterprise*, Spock submits himself for arrest, and Mendez orders a general court-martial convened against Spock.

"The Menagerie, Part II" (TOS). Stardate 3013.1. The *Enterprise*, en route to Talos IV, is site of court-martial proceedings against Commander Spock on charges of commandeering the *Enterprise*, sabotage, abduction of Fleet Captain Pike, and attempted violation of General Order 7. All charges are dropped when it is determined that Spock had been acting on behalf of the Talosians in the best interest of Captain Pike. Captain Kirk, under special authority from Starfleet Command, permits Captain Pike to accept an offer from the Talosians to live the remainder of his life on their planet, where he need not suffer the infirmities of his injured body.

Court-martial of Spock

"Shore Leave" (TOS). Stardate 3025.3. The *U.S.S. Enterprise* surveys a newly discovered planet in the Omicron Delta region for possible shore leave. Initial studies suggest a near-idyllic environment, but later reports indicate some highly unusual phenomena. The ship is briefly incapacitated due to crew unfamiliarity with the planet's technology, which is determined to have been built as a vast amusement park.

Enterprise crew personnel (except for Spock) enjoy R&R on the "amusement park planet."

Just after "Shore Leave" (TOS).

U.S.S. Enterprise on resupply mission to colony on planet Beta VI.

Just prior to "The Squire of Gothos" (TOS).

Creation of the amusement park planet

Trelane, the Squire of Gothos

Remains of outpost on Cestus III

The Vault of Tomorrow

"The Squire of Gothos" (TOS). Stardate 2124.5. *U.S.S. Enterprise* bridge personnel are abducted by an unknown alien agency to Gothos, a newly discovered "rogue planet" in a star desert. Investigation reveals the force to be an entity named Trelane, who is learned to be a child member of an extremely advanced and powerful civilization who possess the ability to create and manipulate planets.

Editors' Note: Trelane indicated that he had observed Earth history of nine centuries ago, but described events in the early nineteenth century. If Trelane is correct, then this episode (and Star Trek's *first season) would be set in the early twenty-eighth century. Since this is inconsistent with the preponderance of other dating information, we assume that it was an error, perhaps another example of Trelane's fallibility and youth.*

A Federation outpost on planet Cestus III is destroyed by a Gorn spacecraft. The Gorn ship reportedly approached at sublight speeds along standard Federation approach lanes before knocking out the outpost's phaser batteries with their first salvo.

One day prior to "Arena" (TOS). This was apparently the first contact between the Gorns and the Federation.

Commodore Travers of Cestus III base apparently invites Captain Kirk and senior *Enterprise* staff to dinner. It is not discovered until later that the message had been falsified by the Gorns, and that the Cestus III outpost had already been destroyed at the time the messages were sent.

Just prior to "Arena" (TOS).

"Arena" (TOS). Stardate 3045.6. The *U.S.S. Enterprise* arrives at planet Cestus III, discovering the base destroyed by an apparently unprovoked Gorn attack. The *Enterprise* pursues the attacking vessel, but chase is interrupted by intervention and first contact with the Metrons. The *Enterprise* crew learns that Gorn hostilities may have been due to Federation ignorance of boundaries of Gorn space. Ultimately, the Metrons decline to establish diplomatic relations with the Federation.

Editors' Note: This episode established for the first time that warp factor six was the normal maximum cruising speed of the Enterprise, *and that things get really hairy when you reach warp eight. This was also the first time it was shown that the transporter can't work when shields are in place. The Federation evidently ironed out its differences with the Gorns at some point between this episode and the year 2371, when "Family Business" (DS9) established that there was a Federation colony on that planet.*

The *Starship Enterprise* returns to Cestus III.

After "Arena" (TOS).

Federation miners on planet Janus VI open a new underground level in search of mineral pergium deposits.

"The Devil in the Dark" (TOS). Vanderberg noted that their troubles began about three months before the episode, when the new level was opened.

"The Alternative Factor" (TOS). Stardate 3087.6. The *U.S.S. Enterprise* detects a violent time/space discontinuity while surveying an uncharted planet. Investigation suggests the time/space phenomenon was triggered by Lazarus, a being from our universe, and his mentally unstable counterpart from a parallel continuum composed of antimatter. Their conflict threatens the existence of both universes, but the Lazarus from the alternate universe succeeds in sealing himself and his counterpart in an isolated time pocket.

The *U.S.S. Enterprise* puts in for general repair and maintenance at Cygnet XIV. The technicians at Cygnet XIV, a society dominated by women, reportedly felt the *Enterprise* computer lacked character, and gave it a stereotypically female personality.

"Tomorrow Is Yesterday" (TOS). Date is conjecture, but Kirk explained to Captain Christopher about the repair stopover at Cygnet XIV. We speculate that it was after "The Alternative Factor" (TOS) because the giggling computer didn't seem to be a problem in that episode. Dorothy Fontana insists the computer wasn't so much giggling as it was sexually teasing the good captain.

U.S.S. Enterprise heads toward Starbase 9, but suffers near collision with a black hole. Full reverse warp power is successful in pulling the ship away, but the resulting whiplash effect propels the *Enterprise* across space and backward in time.

Just prior to "Tomorrow Is Yesterday" (TOS).

The Enterprise *in Earth's upper atmosphere*

"Tomorrow Is Yesterday" (TOS). Stardate 3113.2. The *Enterprise* is accidentally thrown back in time to 1969 after near collision with black hole, where the starship's appearance results in potential disruption of Earth history. This potential disruption is in the form of U.S. Air Force Captain John Christopher, accidentally taken aboard the *Enterprise* when the ship is sighted as a UFO in Earth's atmosphere. Research suggests Christopher's inadvertent abduction would prevent him from fathering a child who, according to records, will lead the first successful Earth-Saturn probe. Kirk leads a landing party to Earth's surface to avoid altering history before the *Enterprise* can employ the light-speed breakaway factor to return to present day.

Editors' Note: When Air Force colonel Fellini threatens to lock Kirk up "for two hundred years," Kirk wryly responds, "That ought to be just about right." If taken literally, this conflicts with the basic assumption that the original Star Trek series is set 300 years in the future. One might, on the other hand, grant Kirk a bit of poetic license in what seemed to be a pretty tough situation. (See also the Editors' Note after "Space Seed" [TOS]).

Kirk's line to Captain Christopher establishes that there were only twelve Constitution-class starships in the Starfleet at this point. Despite the fact that the term "Starfleet Command" had been established several episodes earlier, the operating authority for the Enterprise *is described in this episode as being either Starfleet Control (heard in a Starfleet comm voice over the radio) or the United Earth Space Probe Agency (mentioned by Kirk to Christopher). See also the Editors' Note following "The Naked Time" (TOS).*

U.S. Air Force Captain John Christopher

"Return of the Archons" (TOS). Stardate 3156.2. The *U.S.S. Enterprise* investigates the loss of the *Starship Archon*, which disappeared near planet Beta III in 2167. Landing party discovers the *Archon* had been destroyed by a sophisticated computer that acts to protect and provide for the planet's inhabitants. The self-aware computer system, known as "Landru" to the planet's inhabitants, self-destructs when it realizes it has become harmful to the society it was designed to protect.

Enterprise sociologist Lindstrom and a team of experts remain on planet Beta III to help the native inhabitants, now free of Landru's control, guide their culture back to a more normal form.

After "Return of the Archons" (TOS).

The *Enterprise* heads for star cluster NGC 321 under orders from Federation Ambassador Robert Fox. Thousands of Federation lives have been lost in the region over the past twenty years, and it is hoped that a treaty port can be established at planet Eminiar VII to help avoid future loss of life.

Just prior to "A Taste of Armageddon" (TOS).

Lawgivers enforce the will of Landru

Capital city on Eminiar VII

Eminiar offical Anan Seven

Khan Noonien Singh

Spore-producing plants

*Colony leader
Elias Sandoval*

"A Taste of Armageddon" (TOS). Stardate 3192.1. The *U.S.S. Enterprise* is warned to remain away from planet Eminiar VII, where the *Starship Valiant* had disappeared in 2217. Despite a Code 710 forbidding contact, Ambassador Fox orders the *Enterprise* to make contact with the local planetary government. The ship's crew is declared a casualty in a computerized war with neighboring planet Vendikar, according to Eminiar official Anan 7. Kirk, acting to protect his ship, causes the war agreement to be abrogated, resulting in both sides suing for peace rather than facing actual armed combat.

"Space Seed" (TOS). Stardate 3141.9. The *Starship Enterprise* detects a distress signal from old DY-100 interplanetary space vehicle, adrift near the Mutara sector. Investigation determines the craft to be the *S.S. Botany Bay*, a sleeper ship carrying refugees from Earth's Eugenics Wars.

One surviving passenger on the ship is identified as Khan Noonien Singh, former dictator of one-quarter of planet Earth. Captain Kirk renders an administrative ruling permitting Khan and his shipmates to settle on planet Ceti Alpha V. Also choosing to settle on Ceti Alpha V is *Enterprise* historian Marla McGivers, charged with acting improperly in rendering aid to Khan during an unsuccessful bid to take control of the ship.

Editors' Note: There is a possible inconsistency in Kirk's mention to Khan that the Botany Bay *had been in transit for about two centuries. Given a 1996 launch, this would put the episode at about 2196, instead of 2267. One might rationalize that Kirk was not giving an exact figure, or that he was making a deliberate effort to avoid giving Khan accurate information. It is likely that the producers of the original* Star Trek *series had not yet tied down a specific date for the* Enterprise*'s adventures at this relatively early point in the show's production. Another point: If the first season of the original* Star Trek *series was indeed two hundred years in the future, it would mean that the S.S. Valiant (from "Where No Man Has Gone Before"), which was lost 200 years prior to the episode, would have been launched around 1965. The notion that the* Botany Bay *was found near the Mutara Sector is, of course, purely based on circumstantial evidence from* Star Trek II: The Wrath of Khan.

Another inconsistency is the fact that the character of Chekov was not yet part of the Star Trek *cast when "Space Seed" was filmed, although Khan claimed to remember him in* Star Trek II. *Writer Ron Moore speculates that Kirk may have been breaking the rules in releasing Khan, and that he therefore never told Starfleet about the settlement on Ceti Alpha V. This could explain why the* Reliant*'s crew knew nothing about Khan.*

"This Side of Paradise" (TOS). Stardate 3417.3. The *U.S.S. Enterprise* investigates the Omicron Ceti III colony, believed to be seriously endangered by prolonged exposure to lethal Berthold rays. Medical tests show all colonists to be in perfect health, a phenomenon later found to be due to the effects of a symbiotic spore which also protected the colonists from the Berthold rays. The spores also had unusual psychological effects upon their hosts. *Enterprise* personnel are also affected by these spores, but exposure to intense subsonic energy is found to nullify their effects.

Fifty mining personnel on planet Janus VI are killed by a mysterious subterranean entity. The *Starship Enterprise* is summoned by colony administrator Vanderberg to help investigate the deaths.

Prior to "The Devil in the Dark" (TOS).

"The Devil in the Dark" (TOS). Stardate 3196.1. The *U.S.S. Enterprise* arrives at Janus VI pergium mining colony to probe mysterious deaths. Investigation determines the deaths to have been caused by a silicon-based indigenous life-form known as a Horta. Further investigation reveals the Horta to be intelligent and the killings to have occurred in self-defense after miners inadvertently damaged the Horta's underground egg chamber when opening a new level three months ago. Peaceful relations are established with the newly discovered life-form.

Negotiations with the Klingon Empire over disputed areas of space are reported in danger of breaking down. Starfleet Command anticipates a possible surprise attack by the Klingons, who have just issued an ultimatum to withdraw from disputed areas. Starfleet learns the Klingons have invaded the planet Organia, and orders the *Enterprise* to intervene.

Prior to "Errand of Mercy" (TOS), according to Kirk.

Editors' Note: This back story was also alluded to in Star Trek VI: The Undiscovered Country, *which suggested that hostilities with the Klingons had extended back as far as 2223, 70 years prior to that film, and in "Day of the Dove"; together they suggest that first contact with the Klingons had taken place in 2218.*

Janus VI pergium processing facility

"Errand of Mercy" (TOS). Stardate 3198.4. The *Starship Enterprise* is assigned to prevent an anticipated Klingon incursion at Organia, a planet believed to be inhabited by an agrarian humanoid culture of relatively low technical sophistication. This incursion becomes the focal point of the long-simmering dispute between the Federation and the Klingon Empire, threatening to erupt into interstellar war.

Local planetary government declines offer of Starfleet assistance, at which time the true noncorporeal form of the Organians is discovered. The immensely powerful Organians announce the imposition of the Organian Peace Treaty on both the Klingons and the Federation, predicting that the two adversaries would become friends.

Klingon Commander Kor, military governor of planet Organia

Editors' Note: This episode marks the first appearance of the Klingons in Star Trek. *It is interesting to note how the Klingons evolved over the years from being relatively simplistic villains into a complex, aggressive, yet highly honorable and tradition-bound society. Similarly, it is interesting to note how the look of the Klingons continually evolved as makeup and costuming techniques (and budgets) improved over the years. Dorothy Fontana tells us that the Klingons were used more often than the Romulans in the original series because their makeup was simpler, and therefore less expensive. Fontana notes that she felt the Romulans offered more interesting elements as adversaries, but that the tightly budgeted show just couldn't afford all those pointed ears! Nearly three decades after "Errand of Mercy" (TOS) was filmed, actor John Colicos reprised his role of Kor in "Blood Oath" (DS9) and "The Sword of Kahless" (DS9).*

The Guardian of Forever

"The City on the Edge of Forever" (TOS). (No stardate given in episode.) The *U.S.S. Enterprise* investigates a time/space distortion phenomenon, later discovered to be a time portal, an artifact of an ancient dead civilization. While treating helmsman Sulu for injuries suffered during a shipboard mishap, ship's surgeon Leonard McCoy is accidentally injected with an overdose of cordrazine. Suffering from the resulting paranoid delusions, McCoy flees through the time portal, effecting disastrous changes in Earth's history. Kirk and Spock follow in an attempt to undo the damage. While searching for McCoy in the past, Kirk falls in love with a social worker named Edith Keeler. Although Kirk and Spock are ultimately successful in restoring the time continuum, the mission is made infinitely more difficult when Kirk learns that to repair the damage, he must permit the death of Keeler.

"Operation: Annihilate!" (TOS). Stardate 3287.2. The *Starship Enterprise* makes an unsuccessful attempt to save the pilot of a small spacecraft on a course directly into the sun of the planet Deneva. Further investigation

Kirk stops McCoy from saving Edith Keeler

reveals that the entire population of the Deneva colony (approximately 1,000,000 individuals) had been infected by a parasite that dominates its host through control of the nervous system.

Among the victims are Kirk's brother, George Samuel Kirk, and his sister-in-law, Aurelan Kirk. They are survived by their son Peter Kirk.

This same parasite, which was apparently of extragalactic origin, was also believed responsible for planetwide infestations in the Beta Portolan system, on planet Levinius V, and on Ingraham B. McCoy develops a means of eradicating the parasites by exposing them to high levels of ultraviolet radiation. Planetwide treatment of Deneva is effected through the use of 210 ultraviolet satellites placed into orbit around the planet.

Editors' Note: In "What Are Little Girls Made Of?" (TOS), James Kirk said his brother Sam has three sons. This seems to suggest that Sam had two other surviving sons besides Peter. That episode also indicated that Sam had wanted to transfer to the Earth Colony Two research station. Since Sam was apparently older than James, these other two sons may have been old enough to have been away at college, or pursuing careers of their own. The reason why Sam Kirk's body bears such a family resemblance to his brother is that the part was "played" by William Shatner!

Neural parasite creature undergoing analysis in Enterprise *science lab*

5.2 STAR TREK: THE ORIGINAL SERIES — YEAR 2

Diplomatic reception preceding the Babel conference of 2267

2267 (CONTINUED)

"Catspaw" (TOS). Stardate 3018.2. The *U.S.S. Enterprise* explores planet Pyris VII, making first contact with entities of unknown origin. These life-forms are found to possess technology permitting transmutation of matter.

The *Enterprise* is assigned to treat Assistant Federation Commissioner Nancy Hedford for Sakuro's disease. An *Enterprise* shuttlecraft is dispatched to pick up Commissioner Hedford from Epsilon Canaris III for transport to the ship. Hedford had been assigned to Epsilon Canaris III to prevent a war.

Just prior to "Metamorphosis" (TOS).

"Metamorphosis" (TOS). Stardate 3219.8. The *Shuttlecraft Galileo*, carrying Kirk, Spock, McCoy, and Commissioner Hedford, loses control and makes an emergency landing on a planetoid in the Gamma Canaris region. The shuttlecraft is successfully recovered, along with the missing *Enterprise* personnel, but the terminally ill Commissioner Hedford chooses to remain behind and is presumed to have died.

Editors' Note: In the episode, Kirk and company met Zefram Cochrane and his mysterious friend, the Companion, but later promised not to reveal Cochrane's whereabouts. We therefore assume that historical records based on Kirk's logs would not include any mention of Cochrane, Hedford's recovery, or the Companion on the planetoid.

"Friday's Child" (TOS). Stardate 3497.2. The *U.S.S. Enterprise* is assigned to negotiate a mining treaty with inhabitants of planet Capella IV. Also bidding for rights is a Klingon agent. Negotiations are complicated by local power struggle, resulting in selection of a new leader, whose regent agrees to a treaty with the Federation. The new leader, an infant chosen according to Capellan law, is named Leonard James Akaar, in recognition of the assistance of Leonard McCoy and James Kirk in maintaining Capellan independence.

Unknown alien creatures discovered on planet Pyris VII

Commissioner Nancy Hedford

Leonard James Akaar

Apollo and Lieutenant Palamas

"Who Mourns for Adonais?" (TOS). Stardate 3468.1. The *Enterprise*, collecting data on planets in the Beta Geminorum system, discovers a previously unknown life-form near planet Pollux IV. This life-form, identifying itself as Apollo, was apparently the last of a group of entities that resided on ancient Earth, and claimed to be the basis of the Greeks' myths of the gods.

Spock, under the influence of *pon farr,* the Vulcan mating drive, ceases eating and becomes severely withdrawn. Dr. McCoy later examines Spock and expresses the opinion that Spock must return to his home world within a week or die.

Three days prior to "Amok Time" (TOS).

Spock with traditional Vulcan lirpa *weapon*

"Amok Time" (TOS). Stardate 3372.7. The *U.S.S. Enterprise* is on a diplomatic mission to planet Altair VI. Kirk, acting against Starfleet orders, diverts the ship instead to planet Vulcan so that Science Officer Spock may return to his native world to fulfill the normal Vulcan seven-year mating cycle.

On Vulcan, T'Pring, Spock's betrothed, demands a *Koon-ut-kal-if-fee* challenge for the right of marriage. T'Pring later chooses instead to marry Stonn, thus freeing Spock.

The *U.S.S. Enterprise* proceeds to planet Altair VI on its diplomatic mission, albeit a bit late. The mission entails participation in a presidential inauguration ceremony, expected to stabilize the entire Altair system after a long interplanetary conflict.

Just after "Amok Time" (TOS).

Commodore Matt Decker

Stardate 4202.1. The *Starship Constellation*, under the command of Commodore Matt Decker, encounters several destroyed solar systems, presumably including system L-370. Science officer Masada reports the fourth planet of system L-374 seems to be breaking up, but heavy subspace interference prevents notification of Starfleet Command.

Prior to "The Doomsday Machine" (TOS).

The *Starship Constellation* is nearly destroyed by an automated weapon of unknown origin. In an effort to save his crew, Commodore Matt Decker transports the ship's company to the third planet of system L-374, but all are subsequently killed when the robot weapon destroys that world as well.

Just prior to "The Doomsday Machine" (TOS).

Derelict U.S.S. Constellation

"The Doomsday Machine" (TOS). (No stardate given.) The *U.S.S. Enterprise,* responding to a distress call from *Starship Constellation*, discovers widespread destruction in solar systems L-370 and L-374, and other systems in the sector. The *Constellation* is discovered to be derelict, apparently attacked by an immensely powerful force. Commodore Matt Decker, in command of the *Constellation*, is found to be the sole surviving crew member. Decker reports his findings on the nature of the automated planet killer, theorizing that it is of ancient extragalactic origin. Tactical projections suggest that if unchecked, this device will pass through the most densely populated portion of the galaxy near the Rigel colonies. In an effort to prevent this, Decker pilots a shuttlecraft on a suicide mission into the "doomsday machine." Decker is unsuccessful, but data from his attempt are used to conduct a second effort, using the more powerful reactors from the derelict *Constellation*. The second attempt is successful, resulting in the destruction of the *Constellation* and the deactivation of the planet killer.

Spock, Sulu, and Decker struggle to maintain control while under attack by the planet-killer

Engineering Officer Montgomery Scott is injured in an explosion aboard the *U.S.S. Enterprise*.

Prior to "Wolf in the Fold" (TOS).

"Wolf in the Fold" (TOS). Stardate 3614.9. Engineering Officer Scott, on thera-
peutic shore leave on planet Argelius II, is accused of the brutal murder of a
native woman. Inquiry by local authorities supports the accusation, and
diplomatic relations between Argelius and the Federation are strained by two
additional murders for which Scott is also accused. Further investigation
reveals the presence of a previously undiscovered energy entity that feeds
on the emotion fear in humanoids. It is further discovered that this life-form
was the actual cause of the murders, as well as numerous other previously
unsolved crimes.

The four planets of the Malurian system are attacked by an unknown agency.
More than four billion people are wiped out, including members of a
Federation science team headed by Dr. Manway.

Prior to "The Changeling" (TOS).

*Scott confronted with evidence of
murder on planet Argelius II*

"The Changeling" (TOS). Stardate 3451.9. The *U.S.S. Enterprise* investigates
the recent unexplained attack on the Malurian system, and discovers the
cause of the destruction to be an ancient space probe. The probe, known as
Nomad, had been launched from Earth in the early 21st century on a mission to search for extraterrestrial life. It is determined that a freak accident
involving an alien space probe called *Tan Ru* caused *Nomad* to execute a
mission of "sterilizing" all life-forms. It is believed that *Tan Ru* had been programmed to sterilize soil samples, possibly as a prelude to colonization, and
that the control programs of the two probes had somehow merged in the collision. Kirk succeeds in destroying the errant *Nomad* with a minimum of further damage to the ship.

Planet Ceti Alpha VI explodes, disrupting the orbit of Ceti Alpha V. The resulting
climatic changes are devastating to the colony there, headed by Khan
Noonien Singh. Starfleet remains unaware of the explosion and of its consequences until 2285, when the *Starship Reliant* investigates the planet as
a possible site for Project Genesis testing.

*Star Trek II: The Wrath of Khan. Exact date is conjecture, but Khan said Ceti
Alpha VI had exploded six months after the events in "Space Seed" (TOS).*

*Spock, McCoy, and Kirk on survey mission
to planet Gamma Trianguli VI*

"The Apple" (TOS). Stardate 3715.3. The *Enterprise* conducts a routine survey
of planet Gamma Trianguli VI. Survey party reports discovery of a primitive
humanoid culture, but further investigation yields evidence of an immensely
powerful and ancient computer system that controls the planet's climate. It
is determined that the computer, known to the planet's inhabitants as Vaal,
has become the central object of the planet's religion, as the native civilization apparently exists primarily to provide fuel for the computer system. Upon
detection of *Enterprise* personnel on the planet, Vaal attempts to discourage
the investigation by causing the death of two *Enterprise* crew members and
attempting to destroy the starship in orbit. Arguing that Vaal has served to
stagnate the planet's culture, Kirk orders ship's phasers to destroy the computer, thus permitting the inhabitants of Gamma Trianguli VI to return to a
normal course of cultural development.

Mirror-universe Spock

"Mirror, Mirror" (TOS). (No stardate given.) The *Enterprise* is on a diplomatic
mission to the Halkan system to secure dilithium mining rights. The assignment is impeded by a severe ion storm that nearly results in the loss of the
Enterprise landing party due to the storm's disruption of transporter func-
tions. It is later learned that transport disruption resulted in exchange of landing party members with corresponding individuals from a parallel dimension,
and both parties are returned to their original universes.

Upon their return, landing party members report the alternate universe to be
remarkably similar to their own, but much more violent, controlled by a
repressive empire. They also report that the alternate Spock, understanding
the inevitability of change and the accompanying potential for loss of life, may
be willing to help guide his society in a more humane direction.

Mirror Spock and McCoy

Editors' Note: The story of the mirror universe was later continued in "Crossover" (DS9), "Through the Looking Glass" (DS9), and "Shattered Mirror" (DS9).

In the mirror universe, the mirror Spock replaces the mirror James Kirk as captain of the *I.S.S. Enterprise*. Using the starship as his initial power base, Spock rises to commander in chief of the Terran Empire, bringing about a remarkable turnaround by preaching the radical concepts of peace and disarmament. Unfortunately, Spock's reforms leave the empire defenseless, and it is later conquered by an alliance of the Klingons and the Cardassians. Shortly thereafter, the Bajoran government joins the Alliance. Terrans suffer greatly in this new order, becoming slave workers under Alliance rule.

"Crossover" (DS9). These events in the mirror universe happened after "Mirror, Mirror" (TOS). They did not necessarily happen immediately afterward, but occurred before 2370, probably over a number of years.

Starfleet loses contact with Federation cultural observer John Gill, stationed on planet Ekos.

About six months prior to "Patterns of Force" (TOS).

U.S.S. *Enterprise* assigned to transport Commodore Stocker to Starbase 10.

Just before "The Deadly Years" (TOS).

Dr. McCoy afflicted with hyperaccelerated aging disease

"The Deadly Years" (TOS). Stardate 3478.2. U.S.S. *Enterprise* on resupply mission to Gamma Hydra IV research colony. Landing party reports all colonists dead or dying, victims of an unusual hyperaccelerated aging disease. Shortly thereafter, nearly all landing party personnel are discovered to have similar symptoms. Commodore Stocker orders the *Enterprise* on a direct course to Starbase 10 so that the starbase's medical facilities can be employed to help cure the hyper-aging disease. The course takes the *Enterprise* across the Romulan Neutral Zone, resulting in a confrontation with a Romulan spacecraft. Medical Officer McCoy develops a cure for the disease, based on old adrenaline-based therapies for radiation exposure.

Crew member Norman, recently assigned to duty aboard the U.S.S. *Enterprise*, evades several attempts by Dr. McCoy to schedule a routine physical examination.

Three days prior to "I, Mudd" (TOS).

Deep Space Station K-7

"I, Mudd" (TOS). Stardate 4513.3. The U.S.S. *Enterprise* is hijacked by an android masquerading as *Enterprise* crew member Norman, who takes the ship to a previously unknown Class-K planetoid. The perpetrator of the hijacking is discovered to be known criminal Harcourt Fenton Mudd. The android population of the planet, which attempts to assume control of both Mudd and the *Enterprise*, is disabled by Kirk and his staff. It is learned that the androids were originally from the Andromeda galaxy and had been stranded when their home sun went nova. Mudd is released into custody of the android population.

The U.S.S. *Enterprise* is summoned to Deep Space Station K-7 by a Priority-1 distress call, indicating near or total disaster. Accordingly, the entire quadrant is placed on defense alert.

Just prior to "The Trouble with Tribbles" (TOS).

Kirk discovers the tribbles in the quadrotriticale

"The Trouble with Tribbles" (TOS). Stardate 4523.3. The *Enterprise*, at Deep Space Station K-7, determines Priority-1 distress call was initiated to protect agricultural supplies of quadrotriticale, a special hybrid wheat deemed strategically essential to the development of Sherman's Planet. The planet had been claimed by both the Federation and the Klingon Empire. The concern for security is proven justified when a Klingon operative attempts to sabotage the Federation development claim by poisoning supplies of quadrotriticale.

The sabotage is accidentally discovered when some pet tribbles are learned to have been poisoned by the tainted grain. Klingon captain Koloth nevertheless threatens to file a protest with Federation authorities.

Editors' Note: Koloth, played by William Campbell, reappeared in "Blood Oath" (DS9), which establishes that Koloth later became a tough negotiator for the Klingon Empire. Benjamin Sisko and company revisited the original Enterprise *and Station K-7 in a fifth-season episode of* Star Trek: Deep Space Nine *that was in planning as this Chronology was being completed.*

"Bread and Circuses" (TOS). Stardate 4040.7. The *Enterprise* discovers wreckage of space vehicle *Beagle*, reported missing in the area some six years ago on planet 892-IV. *Enterprise* landing party, investigating the wreckage, is captured by planet's inhabitants. Engineering Officer Scott is successful in rescuing the landing party without violating Prime Directive protection of indigenous life-forms by causing a brief failure of local power utilities.

Postmission analysis suggests a variation of Earth's Christian religion may be evolving on planet 892-IV, potentially reforming the planet's Roman culture into a more humane form.

A magazine published on planet 892-IV

Editors' Note: Kirk said he had known Beagle *captain R. M. Merrick at Starfleet Academy, noting that Merrick had been dropped in his fifth year after failing a psycho-simulator test. This would seem to contradict other references which establish Starfleet Academy to be a four-year institution. On the other hand, "The First Duty" (TNG) establishes that Wesley Crusher had to repeat his sophomore year (meaning it would have taken him five years to graduate) and perhaps something similar happened to Merrick.*

The *Starship Enterprise* picks up 114 Federation dignitaries, including 32 ambassadors, for transport to a conference on the neutral planetoid Babel.

About two weeks prior to "Journey to Babel" (TOS). McCoy complained that the dignitaries had been on the ship for that long.

Ambassador Sarek of Vulcan suffers a mild heart attack, his second. Benjisidrine medication is prescribed for the condition.

Shortly prior to "Journey to Babel" (TOS).

"Journey to Babel" (TOS). Stardate 3842.3. The *U.S.S. Enterprise* is en route to planetoid Babel, providing transport of dignitaries for talks to consider the question of planet Coridan's admission to the Federation. The conference is disrupted by apparent Andorian terrorism, later discovered to be the work of the Orion government, which opposes Coridan's admission.

Ambassador Sarek's party arrived on board the Enterprise

Ambassador Sarek suffers another heart attack, and is treated by Dr. Leonard McCoy, using blood donated by Commander Spock. The operation is a success, although Sarek's wife, Amanda, opposes the procedure on the grounds of risk to both patients. This is McCoy's first actual surgical experience with a Vulcan patient.

Editors' Note: Although Spock's parents had been referred to in previous episodes, "Journey to Babel" (TOS) is the first time they were seen and referred to by name. Sarek and Amanda became recurring characters in the Star Trek *features, and Sarek even made two appearances in* Star Trek: The Next Generation.

Coridan is admitted to the Federation.

After "Journey to Babel" (TOS). The episode "Sarek" (TNG) establishes that the issue was decided in favor of admission.

Tellarite Ambassador Gav

Dr. M'Benga

Colony on Nimbus III

Kirk confronts the gamesters of Triskelion

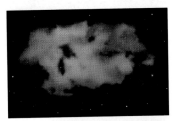

Spacefaring cloud

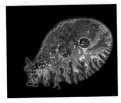

Space amoeba

"A Private Little War" (TOS). Stardate 4211.4. An *Enterprise* landing party conducts botanical study of a technologically unsophisticated Class-M planet, but becomes embroiled in a local dispute. Spock is seriously injured in this dispute, exposing evidence that the indigenous population has been provided access to relatively advanced weaponry. Further investigation reveals Klingon operatives to be responsible for this cultural contamination. Captain Kirk, who had surveyed the planet some 13 years ago, determines measured provision of similar weaponry to all local groups to be the only means of maintaining survival of all.

Editors' Note: Dr. M'Benga, who cared for Spock after his injury on the planet's surface, is established as having interned in a Vulcan ward. M'Benga appeared again in "That Which Survives" (TOS).

The Romulan, Klingon, and Federation governments, in a joint venture, establish a colony on planet Nimbus III, dubbing it the Planet of Galactic Peace. The experiment is a failure, although the colony survives for at least 20 years.

Star Trek V: The Final Frontier. Romulan ambassador Caithlin Dar said the settlement had been established 20 years prior to the film (2287).

The *U.S.S. Enterprise* is assigned to perform a routine check of the automated communications and astrogation facilities on planetoid Gamma II.

Just prior to "The Gamesters of Triskelion" (TOS).

2268

"The Gamesters of Triskelion" (TOS). Stardate 3211.7. The *U.S.S. Enterprise* at planet Gamma II for routine inspection of automatic communications and astrogation equipment. During beam-down, landing party personnel are abducted by a previously unknown, technically advanced civilization of planet Triskelion in the M24 Alpha system. Captain Kirk learns the inhabitants of Triskelion practice a form of slavery, using captured beings known as "thralls" as expendable participants in athletic competition. Faced with an untenable situation, Kirk successfully gambles and wins freedom for both the *Enterprise* crew and the thralls.

Starfleet Command receives a message from the *U.S.S. Horizon*, lost a century ago. The message, sent via conventional radio, suggests the ship had caused cultural contamination at planet Sigma Iotia II.

"A Piece of the Action" (TOS). Kirk noted the message had been received a month prior to the episode.

"Obsession" (TOS). Stardate 3619.2. The *U.S.S. Enterprise* encounters a cloud creature believed responsible for deaths aboard the *Starship Farragut* eleven years ago. The creature kills two *Enterprise* crew members. Kirk pursues the creature back to its home planet, Tycho IV, where it is killed by a small antimatter charge.

The *U.S.S. Enterprise* proceeds to rendezvous with *U.S.S. Yorktown* for transfer of vaccines, which the *Enterprise* then transports to the colony on planet Theta VII, where they are urgently needed.

After "Obsession" (TOS). This is somewhat conjectural, but McCoy and Spock reminded Kirk of the critical situation on Theta VII, suggesting that the Enterprise would deal with the crisis immediately after leaving Tycho IV.

"The Immunity Syndrome" (TOS). Stardate 4307.1. *U.S.S. Enterprise* on course to Starbase 6 for R&R, receives orders to divert for priority rescue mission to Gamma 7A system. En route, it is learned that the *Starship Intrepid* has been destroyed, and that the same agency has apparently attacked the Gamma 7A system, killing billions of people there. Investigation reveals the destruction to have been caused by a vast spaceborne organism that creates negative particles and consumes energy from planetary systems and space vehicles. Although nonsentient, the creature is deemed a serious threat to the galaxy and is destroyed.

The crew of the *U.S.S. Intrepid* had been entirely composed of individuals native to the planet Vulcan.

The source of the culture contamination

"A Piece of the Action" (TOS). (No stardate given.) The *U.S.S. Enterprise* makes a follow-up visit to planet Sigma Iotia II (previously visited a century ago by the *Starship Horizon*), and discovers severe cultural contamination caused by a single book left behind by the previous expedition. In an effort to minimize further cultural damage, Kirk assists local leaders in unifying the planet under a common government.

Enterprise personnel express concern that a Starfleet personal communicator had been accidentally left behind on Sigma Iotia II. It is feared that the highly intelligent Iotians might disassemble the unit and thereby learn the operating principles of the transtator, a basic component of Federation technology.

"By Any Other Name" (TOS). Stardate 4657.5. The *U.S.S. Enterprise* answers a distress call, and a landing party is captured by individuals later learned to be advance agents for the Kelvan Empire in the Andromeda galaxy. It is learned that the Kelvans hope to establish a colony in this galaxy and that they believe invasion is the only means by which this can be accomplished.

Kelvan leader Rojan and Captain Kirk

Captain Kirk negotiates an agreement with the Kelvans whereby a suitable planet can be peaceably set aside for their use. A messenger drone is sent to the Kelvan Empire to inform them of the agreement.

A Federation research station is established on planet Minara II to study a nearby star predicted to go nova in about six months. Among the station personnel are Drs. Linke and Ozaba. The star had exhibited signs of imminent collapse for some time.

"The Empath" (TOS). The station had been established six months prior to the episode.

"Return to Tomorrow" (TOS). Stardate 4768.3. The *Starship Enterprise*, venturing light-years beyond explored territory, uncovers evidence of a catastrophic war a half million years ago on a previously uncharted planet. Further investigation results in discovery of canisters containing the intellects of three surviving members of the now-dead civilization. An attempt is made to provide these survivors with android bodies, but one survivor, Henoch, is destroyed when he tries to steal a living body. The remaining two survivors, Sargon and Thalassa, choose to "depart into oblivion."

Kirk reveals the "alien" to the Ekosians

"Patterns of Force" (TOS). (No stardate given.) The *U.S.S. Enterprise* investigates apparent disappearance of cultural observer John Gill, stationed on planet Ekos. During orbital approach the ship is attacked by a thermonuclear weapon, the first of several discoveries that suggest severe cultural contamination. Investigation reveals that Gill, acting in violation of the Prime Directive, had engaged in a cultural experiment attempting to eliminate the planet's dangerous anarchy by imposing a government modeled after old Earth's Nazi Germany. Unfortunately, in imposing the efficiency of the Nazis, Gill created an environment in which the abuse of power also flourished. Kirk assists local inhabitants in overthrowing the Nazi government.

"The Ultimate Computer" (TOS). Stardate 4729.4. The *U.S.S. Enterprise* is assigned to perform field testing of the experimental M-5 multitronic computer designed by Dr. Richard Daystrom. Although initial exercises are very promising, later tests in simulated combat reveal M-5 to be unpredictable, resulting in the destruction of the *Starship Excalibur* and its crew.

Dr. Richard Daystrom

Commodore Robert Wesley

U.S.S. Exeter
*crew member,
a victim of
the Omega IV
bacteriological
war*

Enterprise captain Kirk and task force commander Commodore Wesley aboard the *U.S.S. Lexington* are credited with quick thinking, allowing disconnection of the M-5 unit before further deaths can result. Postmission analysis suggests that despite the M-5's design goal of rendering human participation unnecessary in space exploration, it was human thinking that saved the situation.

Editors' Note: Commodore Bob Wesley was named for the pseudonym that Gene Roddenberry used when he wrote for Have Gun, Will Travel, *while still working as a police officer.*

"The Omega Glory" (TOS). (No stardate given.) The *U.S.S. Enterprise* discovers the *Starship Exeter* floating derelict in orbit at planet Omega IV, all crew personnel dead. The boarding party discovers deaths to have been caused by exposure to an alien biologic agent, apparently brought to the ship from the planet surface. Evidence suggests the planet also contains biologic agents that provide immunity to the disease, so *Enterprise* boarding party personnel are transported to the surface.

Investigation on the surface of Omega IV suggests both the disease and the population's immunity are results of ancient bacteriologic warfare, perhaps over a millennium ago. Also discovered is *Exeter* captain Ronald Tracey, who survived the disease by chance because he had remained on the surface of the planet. Tracey is found to have interfered in local government, in violation of the Prime Directive, and is taken into custody.

"Assignment: Earth" (TOS). (No stardate given.) The *U.S.S. Enterprise*, on historical research mission into Earth's past, encounters evidence that Earth had extraterrestrial assistance in surviving its critical nuclear age, circa 1968.

5.3 STAR TREK: THE ORIGINAL SERIES — YEAR 3

Captain James Kirk
surgically altered for
a covert Starfleet mission
to a Romulan ship

2268 (CONTINUED)

"Spectre of the Gun" (TOS). Stardate 4385.3. The *U.S.S. Enterprise* makes first contact with the Melkot, a noncorporeal civilization possessing unusual telepathic powers. After an initial period of uneasiness, Kirk persuades the Melkot of the Federation's peaceful intentions. The Melkot agree to diplomatic relations with the Federation.

Melkot

"Elaan of Troyius" (TOS). Stardate 4372.5. The *Enterprise* is on a diplomatic mission to the Tellun system. Assignment is to transport Elaan, the Dohlman of planet Elas, to planet Troyius as part of a peace agreement between the two warring planets. The mission is complicated by interference from Klingon interests, apparently trying to protect Klingon access to rich dilithium deposits on Troyius.

Editors' Note: This episode marks the first time the Klingon battle cruiser was actually used. Earlier episodes referred to this vessel, but this is the first episode that actually showed it onscreen. (In the original network airings of these episodes, "The Enterprise *Incident" [TOS] actually aired before "Elaan of Troyius" [TOS], so the first time the audience saw the Klingon battle cruiser, it was flown by Romulans.)*

Elaan of Troyius

"The Paradise Syndrome" (TOS). Stardate 4842.6. Captain Kirk is missing from a landing party investigating the inhabitants of a Class-M planet threatened with collision from an asteroid. Search for Kirk is cut short so that *U.S.S. Enterprise* can intercept asteroid to divert it from collision. This attempt fails, resulting in severe damage to *Enterprise* warp drive systems. *Enterprise* returns to search for Kirk, who has suffered an injury resulting in memory loss. Eventually Spock discovers evidence of an ancient deflector device which is successfully employed to divert the asteroid. It is learned that Kirk, while suffering from amnesia, had married a native woman named Miramanee, who was subsequently killed in a local power struggle.

Kirk, living
among
the Indians

Romulan Commander

"The *Enterprise* Incident" (TOS). Stardate 5027.3. The *U.S.S. Enterprise* crosses the Romulan Neutral Zone in violation of treaty, and is captured by three Romulan battle cruisers. Captain Kirk and Commander Spock are taken into Romulan custody and accused of criminal espionage by a Romulan commander. They later escape, stealing an improved Romulan cloaking device. The *Enterprise* flees from Romulan space, and it is learned that Kirk and Spock have been conducting a covert Starfleet mission intended to gain military intelligence about the improved cloaking device. During their escape, the Romulan commander is taken prisoner aboard the *Enterprise*.

Editors' Note: The original reason for the Klingon-Romulan alliance in Star Trek's *third season was to "explain" why the Romulans were using Klingon battle cruisers. The real reason for this was that the show had just made a major investment in designing and building the new Klingon ship. Establishing an alliance between the two adversaries created a reason to show more of the nifty new model. That ship was seen three times during the run of the original series, and the basic design was also used in the* Star Trek *features and in* Star Trek: The Next Generation.

This episode suggests Spock had been in Starfleet for 18 years, implying that he had joined in 2250, although "Journey to Babel" (TOS) puts his entry into Starfleet at 2249.

Romulan battle cruiser

The capture of the Romulan cloaking device at this relatively early point in Star Trek *history raises the question of why the* Enterprise *and other Starfleet vessels have never incorporated the invisibility screen into their standard equipment. One theory advanced by Gene Roddenberry suggested that the men and women of the Federation Starfleet are explorers and scientists, so they "don't sneak around." One could therefore assume that Federation policy prohibits the use of cloaking devices in what is primarily a nonmilitary fleet. The matter was eventually resolved by the episode "The* Pegasus" *(TNG) which established that under the Treaty of Algeron, the Federation agreed not to develop or use cloaking technologies.*

The Romulan commander is turned over to Federation authorities.

After "The Enterprise *Incident" (TOS).*

The Polaric Test Ban Treaty is signed following the near-destruction of a Romulan research colony on planet Chaltok IV. A chain reaction in subspace, ignited by the detonation of a polaric ion device, had nearly obliterated all organic material on the planet.

"Time and Again" (VGR). Tuvok said that the treaty was signed in 2268. We're arbitrarily putting the signing after "The Enterprise Incident" (TOS) since it seems a little more likely that the Federation and the Romulans would have done so after the episode than before. Tuvok didn't make it clear, but it seems that the treaty was between the Federation and the Romulans.

Gorgan

"And the Children Shall Lead" (TOS). Stardate 5029.5. The *Enterprise,* at planet Triacus, discovers all adult members of Starnes expedition to be dead. Surviving children show uncharacteristically little emotional impact from the tragedy. They are later discovered to be under the telepathic influence of a noncorporeal being which calls itself the "Gorgan," apparently the source of legends of ancient marauders from Triacus. This entity attempts to gain control of the *Enterprise*, using the children as agents. *Enterprise* personnel help the children face their grief, thus freeing them from the Gorgan.

The survivors of the Starnes expedition tragedy on planet Triacus are taken to Starbase 4.

After "And the Children Shall Lead" (TOS).

"Spock's Brain" (TOS). Stardate 5431.4. *U.S.S. Enterprise*, traveling near the Sigma Draconis system, is attacked by a spacecraft from a previously unknown civilization in that system. The only casualty is Commander Spock, whose brain is surgically removed by the attacker. The *Enterprise* pursues the spacecraft to Sigma Draconis VI, where it is discovered that Spock's brain is being used as a vital component in a massive computer system that provides for the planet's inhabitants. Captain Kirk leads a landing party to the planet and is successful in retrieving the brain. Dr. McCoy makes use of the planetary computer's advanced knowledge to learn surgical techniques necessary to restore the brain to Spock's body. Finally, *Enterprise* personnel encourage the planet's inhabitants to learn survival without dependence on the computer system.

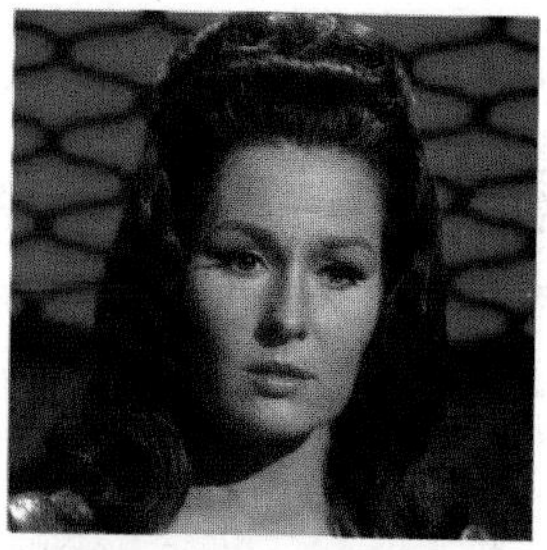

Kara

"Is There in Truth No Beauty?" (TOS). Stardate 5630.7. The *U.S.S. Enterprise* is assigned to transport diplomatic and cultural exchange party to rendezvous with Medusan spacecraft. Among the party is Medusan Ambassador Kollos, Dr. Miranda Jones, and technical specialist Laurence Marvick. Emotional stress, exacerbated by direct visual contact with Kollos, causes Marvick to exhibit irrational behavior, at which time he pilots the *Enterprise* across the energy barrier at the edge of the galaxy. The hazardous return trip is made possible by the navigational expertise of Ambassador Kollos. Shortly thereafter, Jones establishes a mind-link with Kollos.

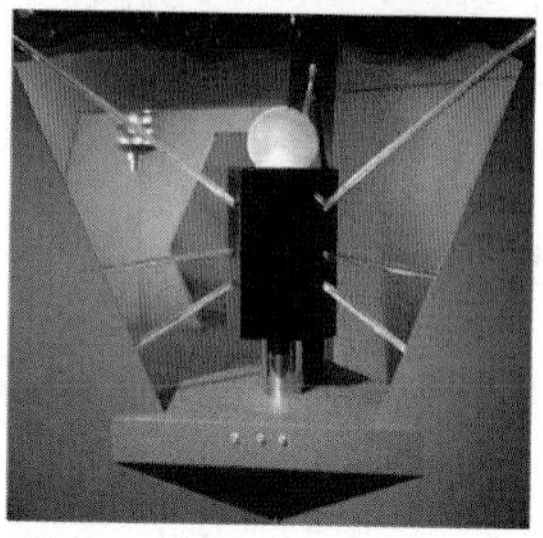

Sigma Draconis VI planetary computer device

Editors' Note: Laurence Marvick is described as being one of the designers of the Enterprise.

The *Starship Defiant*, in unsurveyed territory near the Tholian border, disappears without a trace.

"The Tholian Web" (TOS). Kirk's log said the Defiant *had disappeared three weeks prior to the episode.*

"The Empath" (TOS). Stardate 5121.5. The *U.S.S. Enterprise* on a mission to rescue personnel at the research station on planet Minara II before that planet's star goes nova. *Enterprise* landing party discovers all station personnel missing. Further investigation reveals station personnel to be dead, part of a bizarre experiment by beings called Vians, who are attempting to determine the worthiness of the planet's inhabitants to be rescued.

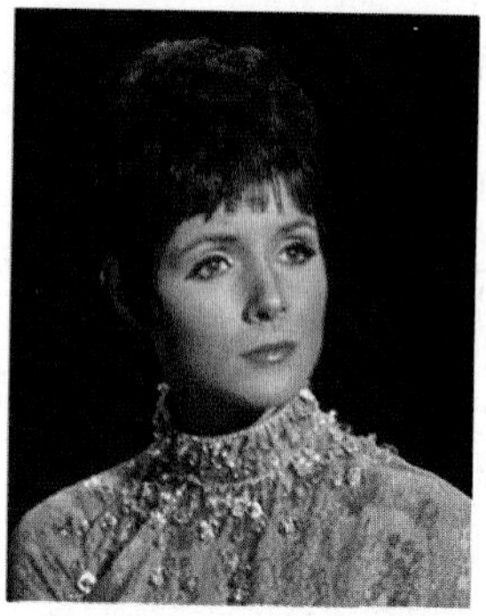

Gem, a member of one of the races inhabiting the Minara system

The star Minara explodes.

Just after "The Empath" (TOS).

"The Tholian Web" (TOS). Stardate 5693.2. The *U.S.S. Enterprise* investigates the disappearance of the *Starship Defiant* in uncharted territory, locates the *Defiant,* and discovers evidence of severe violence that resulted in the death of all *Defiant* personnel. This behavior is determined to be the result of distortions to the central nervous system caused by a spatial phenomenon called interphase, a temporary overlap of two universes. The interphase phenomenon is also found responsible for the literal disappearance of the *Defiant* and for the loss of *Enterprise* captain James Kirk.

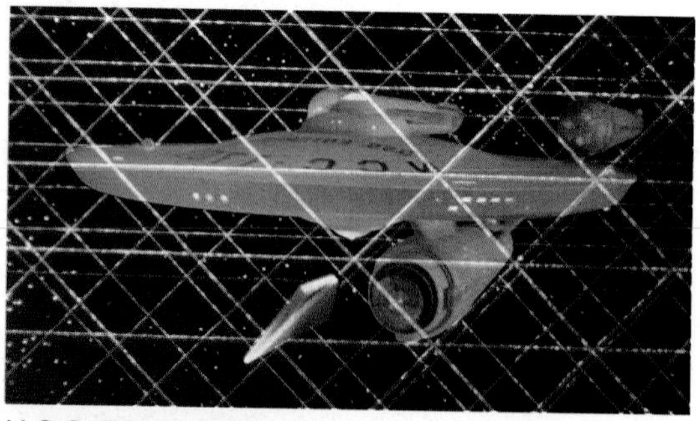

U.S.S. Enterprise *caught in Tholian web*

Efforts to rescue Kirk from interspace are hampered by a severe energy drain on *Enterprise* systems by the interphase phenomenon, and by mental and behavioral disorders in *Enterprise* personnel, also caused by interphase. The rescue is further complicated by a previously unknown territorial claim on the area by Commander Loskene, representing the Tholian Assembly, although Kirk is successfully recovered before the Tholians can take decisive action against the *Enterprise*.

Editors' Note: This is the only encounter we've seen with the Tholians, although several episodes of Star Trek: The Next Generation *and* Star Trek: Deep Space Nine *have made references to them. See Appendix G (Notes on planets and societies). Spock's line about "the renowned Tholian punctuality" suggests the Federation had prior contact with the Tholians. Spock also*

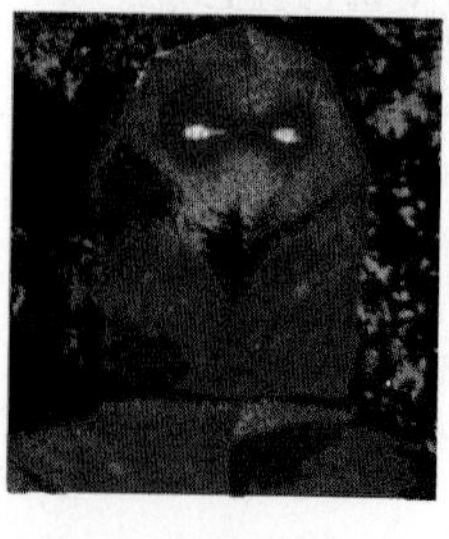

Tholian Commander Loskene

*Dr. Leonard McCoy and
Fabrini High Priestess Natira*

Klingon Commander Kang

Parmen

Alexander

notes that there is no record of a starship's crew ever having mutinied, although the episode "Whom Gods Destroy" (filmed after "The Tholian Web") establishes that Garth's crew mutinied some time ago when he ordered them to kill the inhabitants of planet Antos IV. Garth may have been exaggerating, of course.

Dr. Leonard McCoy is diagnosed as having xenopolycythemia, a rare blood disorder for which there is no known cure. His condition is terminal.

Just prior to "For the World Is Hollow and I Have Touched the Sky" (TOS).

"For the World Is Hollow and I Have Touched the Sky" (TOS). Stardate 5476.3. The *Enterprise* successfully deflects an attack by technically unsophisticated missile weapons. Investigation reveals the origin of the attack to be an asteroid traveling under power as an inhabited sublight space vehicle. Course projections indicate the asteroid will impact planet Daran V in a little over a year, threatening the lives of the 3.7 million people on that world.

Transporting to the asteroid ship, Captain James Kirk, Mr. Spock, and Dr. McCoy determine the ship, called *Yonada*, to have been built by inhabitants of the Fabrina system just prior to the explosion of their sun some 10,000 years ago. The boarding party is unsuccessful in gaining the cooperation of local authorities, but Dr. McCoy, suffering from terminal xenopolycythemia, elects to remain behind for personal reasons when Kirk and Spock return to the *Enterprise*. McCoy, having married Yonadan high priestess Natira, discovers documentation revealing technical schematics for the vehicle. Using this information, *Enterprise* personnel are successful in restoring Yonada to its intended flight path, averting the feared collision with Daran V. Also discovered among the Yonadan records is a cure for xenopolycythemia, permitting Dr. McCoy to return to duty aboard the *Enterprise*.

The *U.S.S. Enterprise* receives a distress call from a colony on planet Beta XII-A. It is not realized at the time that the signal has been fabricated by an alien life-form, and that a Klingon battle cruiser under the command of Kang has received a similarly falsified distress call.

Just prior to "Day of the Dove" (TOS).

"Day of the Dove" (TOS). (No stardate given.) A *U.S.S. Enterprise* landing party at planet Beta XII-A discovers the distress call to have been a ruse, apparently a trick by a Klingon battle cruiser also orbiting the planet. *Enterprise* personnel, avoiding capture by a Klingon landing party, are successful in taking the Klingons captive aboard the *Enterprise*. Dangerous radiation emissions are detected aboard the Klingon vessel, and the ship is destroyed by the *Enterprise* to avoid further hazard.

Aboard the *Enterprise*, intense fighting breaks out between *Enterprise* and Klingon personnel. The situation (including the falsified distress calls) is eventually learned to have been engineered by a previously unknown energy-based life-form that thrives on the emotions of hatred and anger. *Enterprise* and Klingon personnel cooperate to drive this life-form away by generating positive emotions.

Editors' Note: Actor Michael Ansara returned to Star Trek *nearly 30 years after "Day of the Dove" (TOS), reprising his role of Kang in "Blood Oath" (DS9).*

"Plato's Stepchildren" (TOS). Stardate 5784.2. The *Enterprise* responds to a distress call from a previously unknown civilization. The inhabitants of this planet are discovered to have escaped nearly three millennia ago from the Sahndara star system, just before Sahndara went nova. They had stopped for a time on ancient Earth, where their leader, Parmen, had developed a great admiration for the philosopher Plato. Later, having settled on a planet they named Platonius, these unusually long-lived humanoids had attempted to recreate Plato's Republic.

At Platonius, *Enterprise* Chief Medical Officer Dr. Leonard McCoy declines an invitation to remain behind with the Platonians. Although the Platonians attempt to coerce McCoy to stay by using their unusual telekinetic powers, McCoy is successful in making use of local kironide chemical deposits to create similar telekinetic powers in *Enterprise* personnel, permitting their escape. One Platonian, Alexander, who had helped the *Enterprise* people, expresses a desire to leave Platonius, and is welcomed as a guest aboard the *Enterprise*.

Captain Kirk informs Starfleet Command of the Platonians and of their unusual telekinetic powers, advising other starships to take appropriate precautions before making contact with that planet.

Just after "Plato's Stepchildren" (TOS).

"Wink of an Eye" (TOS). Stardate 5710.5. The *U.S.S. Enterprise* responds to distress calls from planet Scalos. A landing party discovers evidence of a technically advanced humanoid civilization, but no immediately apparent life-forms. Upon the landing party's return to the *Enterprise*, a number of unexplained malfunctions are traced to the presence of previously undetected humanoid life-forms from the planet.

Scalosian Queen Deela

It is learned that these humanoids are the victims of a terrible volcanic disaster which hyperaccelerated the Scalosians so that they live their lives at a much faster rate than normal. Scalosian queen Deela further reveals that their purpose in attempting to control the *Enterprise* crew is to provide breeding stock for the genetically damaged Scalosians, although the acceleration process is learned to be fatal to humans. *Enterprise* personnel are successful in preventing the takeover, in the process developing a counteragent to reverse the hyperacceleration effect.

"That Which Survives" (TOS). (No stardate given.) The *Starship Enterprise* investigates an anomalous planet whose apparent geologic age is much less than the indigenous vegetation would indicate. Landing party discovers evidence of significant geologic instability, although this investigation is interrupted when the *Enterprise* is discovered to be missing from planet orbit. The ship is later found to have been transposed across some 990.7 light-years from the planet, apparently by the same agency responsible for the geologic instability.

Losira

This agency is found to be the image of a woman named Losira, who was the last surviving member of a Kalandan colony there. The planet itself is learned to be an artificial construct, the product of Kalandan technology. The image of Losira was used by the colony's still-functioning computer to defend the installation despite the fact that all colonists had been killed some years prior by disease.

Editors' Note: This episode featured the second appearance of Dr. M'Benga to the Enterprise *sickbay. M'Benga had been previously seen in "A Private Little War" (TOS).*

A shuttlecraft is stolen from Starbase 4. It is later learned that the vehicle was taken by Lokai, a fugitive from the planet Cheron.

Two weeks prior to "Let That Be Your Last Battlefield" (TOS).

A planetwide bacterial infection threatens life on planet Ariannus, a vital transfer point on commercial space lanes. The *U.S.S. Enterprise* is assigned to perform decontamination employing an orbital spraying technique.

Just prior to "Let That Be Your Last Battlefield" (TOS).

"Let That Be Your Last Battlefield" (TOS). Stardate 5730.2. En route for planet Ariannus for decontamination mission, the *U.S.S. Enterprise* intercepts and recovers a shuttlecraft that had been stolen from Starbase 4, found to be piloted by Lokai from the planet Cheron. Shortly thereafter, a second ship

Commissioner Bele of the planet Cheron

intercepts the *Enterprise*. The pilot of the second ship, Commissioner Bele of the planet Cheron, reports that he has been in pursuit of Lokai for crimes against the Cheron government, and requests extradition of Lokai from Federation custody. *Enterprise* captain Kirk declines the request, citing the absence of an extradition treaty.

Upon completion of decontamination at Ariannus, the *Enterprise* is coerced to return both Lokai and Bele to Cheron, where it is discovered that their home civilization had been completely destroyed by racial hatred.

Editors' Note: The U.S.S. Enterprise destruct command sequence, used when Kirk tries to prevent Bele's takeover of his ship, was repeated almost word for word in the film Star Trek III: The Search for Spock. However, the destruct sequence for the Enterprise-D, first seen in "11001001," was different.

Garth and an inmate of the Elba II penal colony

"Whom Gods Destroy" (TOS). Stardate 5718.3. The *U.S.S. Enterprise* is assigned to deliver new medication to the penal colony on planet Elba II. One of the inmates, the former Captain Garth of Izar, is discovered to have taken over the colony, taking advantage of a cellular metamorphosis technique he had learned at Antos IV. In the process, Garth captures *Enterprise* captain Kirk and first officer Spock, and causes the death of an Orion inmate named Marta. Kirk and Spock are successful in restoring control to colony administrator Donald Cory, and early indications suggest that new treatment may be able to reverse the course of Garth's mental illness.

The government of the planet Gideon agrees to limited diplomatic contact with Federation representatives. Previous attempts at establishing diplomatic relations had been stymied by Gideon's fierce tradition of isolationism. Gideon, reported to be a near paradise, is being considered for admission into the Federation.

Prior to "The Mark of Gideon" (TOS).

Odona of Gideon

"The Mark of Gideon" (TOS). Stardate 5423.4. The *Starship Enterprise*, on a diplomatic mission to planet Gideon, reports Captain James Kirk missing while in transit to the planet's surface. Investigation determines Kirk to have been abducted by the Gideon council, an attempt by Gideon prime minister Hodin to use disease organisms in Kirk's bloodstream to help solve a serious overpopulation problem. Although Kirk declines to remain on Gideon to provide the disease organism, Hodin's daughter, Odona, becomes similarly infected and thus is able to fill the planet's needs.

A Federation vessel makes first contact with a spacecraft from a civilization calling itself "The Children of Tama." Attempts to establish communications are unsuccessful due to the unusually great difference between language types, although their behavior suggests a peaceable people. This is the first of seven such incidents over the next century, including contact by the *Shiku Maru,* whose commander, Captain Silvestri, described the Tamarians as "incomprehensible." Accounts from the other contacts are similar. As a result, no formal relations are established between the Tamarians and the Federation.

"Darmok" (TNG). Data noted that Federation vessels had first encountered Tamarian ships a hundred years prior to the episode (2368).

2269

Lieutenant Mira Romaine

"The Lights of Zetar" (TOS). Stardate 5725.3. The *U.S.S. Enterprise* is assigned to transport Lieutenant Mira Romaine to planetoid Memory Alpha, a massive archive for Federation cultural history and scientific knowledge. On final orbital approach to Memory Alpha, an energy phenomenon of unknown origin intercepts the *Enterprise*, resulting in serious neural impact on Romaine. This phenomenon subsequently attacks the Memory Alpha installation, resulting in the death of all station personnel. *Enterprise* personnel later determine that the energy is the embodiment of the survivors of the planet Zetar, destroyed many years ago. The survivors found Romaine to be a compatible life-form to serve as their corporeal body, but *Enterprise* personnel are successful in expelling the Zetar life-forms when it is found that they threaten Romaine's identity.

Lieutenant Mira Romaine returns to Memory Alpha to help rebuild the facility.

After "The Lights of Zetar" (TOS).

A botanical plague threatens the vegetation on planet Merak II. The plague's devastation is expected to leave the planet's surface uninhabitable. The only known treatment requires quantities of the rare mineral zenite.

Prior to "The Cloud Minders" (TOS).

Spock and Stratos dweller Droxine

"The Cloud Minders" (TOS). Stardate 5818.4. The *U.S.S. Enterprise* is on an emergency assignment to obtain mineral zenite from miners on planet Ardana. Delivery of the zenite is delayed by terrorist activity. Investigation reveals the terrorists to be driven by severe social inequities between the working class, living in the underground mines, and the upper class, living in Stratos, a cloud city. Stratos authorities defend the arrangement, citing evidence that the workers exhibit lower intelligence, but it is learned this mental impairment is due to environmental conditions. *Enterprise* captain Kirk negotiates with both parties for improved working conditions in exchange for delivery of the zenite consignment.

The *Starship Enterprise* proceeds to planet Merak II to deliver the zenite for treatment of the botanical plague.

Just after "The Cloud Minders" (TOS).

Stratos
Administrator
Plasus
(Jeff Corey)

"The Way to Eden" (TOS). Stardate 5832.3. The *Enterprise* locates the space cruiser *Aurora*, reported stolen. Intercepting the *Aurora*, the *Enterprise* takes into custody several individuals led by Dr. Sevrin, a noted scientist. Sevrin reveals he is on a quest to find the mythical planet that is the source of the legends of Eden. Sevrin coerces ship's personnel to locate a planet matching his criteria, using ship's computer banks to correlate astronomical data. Sevrin then orders the *Enterprise* to those coordinates.

At Sevrin's planet it is learned that although beautiful, the planet's environment is severely toxic to humanoid life, and Sevrin is killed by exposure to the planet's flora. Captain Kirk recommends that no legal action be taken against the remaining members of Sevrin's party.

Editors' Note: An earlier version of this story was written by Dorothy Fontana under the title "Joanna." The Irina character (Chekov's love interest in the aired episode) was originally Dr. McCoy's daughter, Joanna, who caught the interest of Captain Kirk in Fontana's version.

Dr. Severin

A serious epidemic of Rigelian fever breaks out onboard the *Starship Enterprise*, causing the death of three crew members and threatening the lives of 23 others. The effects of Rigelian fever resemble those of bubonic plague, killing its victims in a day. The *Enterprise* diverts to planet Holberg 917G in the Omega system in order to obtain sufficient quantities of ryetalyn necessary for treatment of the epidemic.

Just prior to "Requiem for Methuselah" (TOS).

"Requiem for Methuselah" (TOS). Stardate 5843.7. An *Enterprise* landing party attempts to gather raw ryetalyn from the surface of Holberg 917G, a class-M planet previously believed to be uninhabited. The ryetalyn is critically needed as an antidote to Rigelian fever, now threatening the lives of the entire *Enterprise* crew. The planet is discovered to be the abode of a reclusive individual known as Flint, who is later discovered to be a nearly immortal man, originally from Earth. Flint offers assistance in obtaining and refining

The android, Rayna, and her creator Flint

Kirk encounters the image of President Abraham Lincoln

Excalbian

Mr. Atoz

Dr. Janice Lester

the ryetalyn, but is later learned to be deliberately detaining the landing party personnel to provide experience with human interaction to a sophisticated android of Flint's construction. The android, designed as a human female called Rayna Kapec, proves incapable of withstanding the stresses of human emotions and suffers a total systems failure.

Flint, who is learned to have had many identities over his lifetime, claims to have been Leonardo da Vinci, Reginald Pollack, Sten from Marcus II, Brahms, Alexander, Merlin, Solomon, Lazarus, Abramson, and other historical figures. Flint ultimately provides refined ryetalyn for the successful treatment of the *Enterprise* crew, and is further discovered to have sacrificed immortality when he left Earth's ecosystems, but indicates a desire to devote the remainder of his life to improving the human condition.

Editors' Note: Rayna Kapec was apparently named for Karel Capek, the Czechoslovakian writer who first coined the term "robot" in his stage play R.U.R. The spelling of the medication "ryetalyn" is indicated in the script as "vrietalyn."

"The Savage Curtain" (TOS). Stardate 5906.4. The *U.S.S. Enterprise* conducts scientific studies in orbit around planet Excalbia and encounters a life-form claiming to be the late President Abraham Lincoln of Earth. Captain Kirk, intrigued by the nearly perfect image of the historical figure, accepts an invitation to transport to the surface of Excalbia with Spock, where similar re-creations of numerous other historical figures are encountered. Among these re-creations are Surak of Vulcan, Colonel Green of Earth, and Kahless the Unforgettable from the Klingon Homeworld. The *Enterprise* crew discovers the entire situation to have been engineered by the inhabitants of Excalbia, so that they may observe and learn about the concepts of "good" and "evil." Upon completion of the drama, the Excalbians return Kirk and Spock to the *Enterprise*.

Editors' Note: In "Reunion" (TNG) and "New Ground" (TNG), Worf tells Alexander about Kahless the Unforgettable, the leader who united the Klingon Homeworld, describing how Kahless fought his brother Morath for twelve days and nights because Morath had broken his word. A sculpture in Worf's quarters of two figures wrestling depicts this heroic struggle. More bits of the legend of Kahless were told in "Birthright Part I and II" (TNG), and we actually met a clone of Kahless in "Rightful Heir" (TNG). Oddly enough, Kahless in "The Savage Curtain" (TOS) looked nothing like Kahless as seen in "Rightful Heir."

"All Our Yesterdays" (TOS). Stardate 5943.7. The *U.S.S. Enterprise* investigates planet Sarpeidon, hours before the predicted explosion of its star, Beta Niobe. Although earlier reports indicated Sarpeidon had been inhabited by a civilized humanoid species, sensors indicate no inhabitants remain. Investigation reveals a sophisticated time portal called the atavachron, which was used by the inhabitants to escape into their planet's past. Unfamiliarity with the atavachron results in the accidental transport of Captain Kirk, Mr. Spock, and Dr. McCoy to various points in Sarpeidon's past, although all three are recovered by Mr. Atoz, the atavachron operator. Atoz subsequently escapes into his chosen past time, and the *Enterprise* departs Sarpeidon just prior to the explosion of Beta Niobe.

The *U.S.S. Enterprise* receives a distress call from a Federation archaeological team investigating the ruins on planet Camus II. The ship, on course to rendezvous with the *Starship Potemkin* at Beta Aurigae for gravitational studies, diverts to Camus II.

Just prior to "Turnabout Intruder" (TOS).

"Turnabout Intruder" (TOS). Stardate 5928.5. The *Starship Enterprise* conducts a rescue mission at Camus II, aiding survivors of the Federation archaeological team suffering from a serious radiation exposure accident. Upon returning to the ship, *Enterprise* captain James Kirk is discovered to be exhibiting severely aberrant behavior, resulting in the convening of a hearing to evaluate Kirk's command competency. Investigation reveals the fact that Kirk, while on Camus II, had been the victim of an abduction by Dr. Janice Lester, a member of the archaeological team. Lester had evidently employed an ancient device discovered in the ruins to transfer her consciousness into the body of James Kirk, and Kirk's consciousness into Lester's body. This mental exchange by the emotionally unstable Lester is determined to be the cause of Kirk's irrational behavior, although the transference is later found to be temporary, and both Kirk and Lester revert to their original bodies. Lester is placed in the medical care of former archaeological expedition leader Dr. Coleman.

Life entity transference at Camus II

Editors' Note: Starfleet has been accused of sexism because of Janice's speech to Kirk complaining that "your world of starship captains doesn't admit women." While it is indeed possible that Starfleet did not have female captains at this point (chronologically, the first female captain we saw was the commander of the U.S.S. Saratoga in Star Trek IV: The Voyage Home), we chose to interpret Janice's line as meaning that Kirk's personal world, revolving around his career as starship captain, left no room for a lasting commitment to a woman. (Gene Roddenberry apparently disagreed with this rationalization, admitting in later years that the line was simply sexist.)

"Turnabout Intruder" (TOS) was the last episode of the original Star Trek television series.

The *U.S.S. Enterprise* goes to Starbase 2.

Just after "Turnabout Intruder" (TOS).

Editors' Note: Although this chronology does not use material from the animated Star Trek series, Dorothy Fontana suggests that she would place those stories at this point, after the end of the third season, but prior to the end of the five-year mission.

Kirk's five-year mission ends and the *Starship Enterprise* returns to spacedock.

Date is conjecture. Assumes the pilot episode "Where No Man Has Gone Before" (TOS) was about a year into the five-year mission and that the first season was about a year after that episode.

Enterprise undergoing refit at orbital dry dock

The asteroid/spaceship *Yonada* reaches its promised land, and the Fabrini, under the leadership of high priestess Natira, begin to disembark.

"For the World Is Hollow and I Have Touched the Sky" (TOS). Kirk noted that Yonada would arrive at its destination some 390 days after the episode, set in the latter half of 2268.

Editors' Note: Kirk promised McCoy that he would arrange for the Enterprise to be there when the Fabrini reached their promised land, but since this would have been after the end of Star Trek's third season, we have no way of knowing whether or not McCoy actually managed to make it. Although Yonada's arrival is, by our reckoning, after the end of Kirk's five-year mission, there is certainly enough margin for error in the timeline that the arrival could have been before the end of that voyage. In fact, our assumption that the Enterprise returned for refitting immediately after the end of the five-year mission is conjecture, and it is conceivable that the ship had other assignments after the mission, but before the refit.

Renora is born on planet Bajor. As an adult, she will become a highly respected jurist.

"Dax" (DS9). She said she was 100 years old in 2369.

Renora

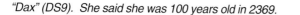

Admiral James T. Kirk

Keiko Ishikawa O'Brien's mother is born on Earth.

> *"Dax" (DS9). Keiko's mother celebrated her 100th birthday in 2369.*

James T. Kirk is promoted to admiral and becomes chief of Starfleet operations, accepting the promotion against the advice of his friend, Leonard McCoy.

> *Star Trek: The Motion Picture. Kirk said he'd been chief of Starfleet operations for two and a half years prior to the film, so this assumes that the promotion happened shortly after the end of the third season.*

> *Editors' Note: The various data points from* Star Trek: The Motion Picture *in this part of the Chronology are somewhat conjectural in that they assume that the* Enterprise*'s refit began almost immediately after the end of the third season.*

2270

Spock undergoes Kohlinar discipline on his home planet Vulcan

Spock retires from Starfleet. He returns to Vulcan to undergo the *Kohlinar* training in an effort to purge the remaining emotional influences from his intellect.

> Leonard McCoy also retires, returns to Earth, and enters private medical practice, swearing he'll never return to Starfleet.

> *Conjecture. Both left Starfleet after the original* Star Trek *series, but before* Star Trek: The Motion Picture.

Starship Enterprise, in San Francisco orbital dry dock, begins major refitting process. Will Decker is promoted to *Enterprise* captain on Kirk's recommendation.

> *Star Trek: The Motion Picture. Scotty noted he'd spent eighteen months working on the refit project, so this is that long before the movie.*

Felisa Howard is born.

> *"Sub Rosa" (TNG). She was a hundred years old at the time of her death in 2370.*

Dr. Leonard McCoy

5.4 STAR TREK (TOS) MOTION PICTURES

"Remember..."

2271

Star Trek: The Motion Picture. Stardate 7412.6. Three Klingon starships and Starfleet's Epsilon IX station are destroyed by a massive machine/organism called V'Ger. Sol sector placed on alert when V'Ger is found to be heading toward Earth at warp 7.

The refitted *U.S.S. Enterprise* is returned to service to investigate the threat. Starfleet Admiral Nogura temporarily reinstates Admiral James Kirk as *Enterprise* captain, assigning former captain Decker to serve as executive officer. Commander Spock and Dr. McCoy both return to Starfleet duty.

Kirk is successful in averting the V'Ger threat to Earth, although Commander Decker and Lieutenant Ilia are reported missing in action.

Editors' Note: The date for this film is somewhat conjectural. Decker's line about Kirk not having logged "a single star-hour in two and a half years" suggests the film is set that long after the conclusion of the first Star Trek series. We are assuming that the Enterprise underwent its refit immediately after the end of Kirk's five-year mission, although evidence from the film neither supports nor disproves this notion.

Commander Decker and Lieutenant Ilia

This film marked the first appearance of the "new and improved" Klingons, using latex makeup appliances to create their distinctive forehead ridges. Makeup artist Fred Phillips created the new designs. Phillips explained that this is what he had always wanted to do for the Klingons, but could never afford on a television budget. Phillips and Roddenberry reportedly joked that the difference was because only "southern" Klingons were seen in the original series, but those seen in the movies were "northern" Klingons.

Demora Sulu is born. Her father is Hikaru Sulu.

Conjecture, assuming she was 22 years old at the time of the Enterprise-B launch in Star Trek Generations. It is not at all clear whether she was born

Demora Sulu

U.S.S Enterprise *at spacedock in Earth orbit*

Science Officer Xon

Commander Kor

Ambassador Sarek

before or after the events in Star Trek: The Motion Picture *or the start of the conjectural post-refit five-year mission under Kirk's command.*

U.S.S. Enterprise embarks on another five-year mission of exploration under the command of James T. Kirk.

Conjecture.

Editors' Note: Paramount Pictures had at one point planned a second Star Trek *television series (entitled* Star Trek II, *not to be confused with the movie of the same name) that would have depicted a second five-year mission of the* Enterprise *under the command of Captain Kirk. Most of the original Star Trek cast had agreed to return for this series, and new additions would have included Will Decker, Ilia, and Vulcan science officer Xon, who would have been played by actor David Gautreaux. However, just before production started, Paramount decided not to go ahead with the series and the first episode was turned into* Star Trek: The Motion Picture.

Klingon forces, under the command of Kor, win a stunning victory over the Romulans in the battle of Klach D'kel Brakt.

"Blood Oath" (DS9). "Almost a century" before the episode (2370).

The terraforming project at planet Caldos is completed with the installation of weather controls and fusion systems. It is one of the Federation's first ventures into the massive engineering required to change a planet's climate. The colony that is later built on the planet employs architecture closely patterned on buildings from the Earth cities of Edinburgh, Glasgow, Aberdeen, and other parts of the Scottish Highlands.

"Sub Rosa" (TNG) Nearly a century before the episode (2370).

2273

Ambassador Sarek of Vulcan begins working on treaty with the reclusive Legarans. He does not succeed until the year 2366.

"Sarek" (TNG). At the time of the episode (2366), Sarek said he'd been working on the treaty for 93 years.

2274

Colony ship *Artemis* departs on a mission to settle planet Septimus Minor. The ship ultimately ends up at Tau Cygna V in the de Laure Belt, where one-third of the original colonists die from exposure to the hyperonic radiation in the area. Though not apparent at the time, the colony at Tau Cygna is in direct violation of the Treaty of Armens which cedes the planet to the Sheliak Corporate.

"Ensigns of Command" (TNG). The ship was launched 92 years prior to the episode, and the colony had been in place for "over ninety years."

2276

Starship *Enterprise* returns from a five-year mission of exploration commanded by James T. Kirk.

Conjecture. Kirk apparently retired from Starfleet sometime between this point and 2282, when he met Antonia at his uncle's farm in Iowa.

An individual named Tressa is born on planet Drayan II in the Delta Quadrant. Her people's biology has an aging process that appears to be the opposite of many other humanoid species.

"Innocence" (VGR). Ninety-six years before the episode (2372).

2277

Commander Spock is promoted to captain, becomes member of Starfleet Academy faculty on Earth, and accepts command of *Starship Enterprise.*

Leonard McCoy is promoted from lieutenant commander to commander.

Commander Pavel Chekov assigned as first officer of *U.S.S. Reliant.*

Starship Enterprise retired from exploratory service, becoming a training vessel assigned to Starfleet Academy at San Francisco.

Date is conjecture: These events happened after Star Trek: The Motion Picture *because we saw the new ranks in* Star Trek II: The Wrath of Khan.

Starfleet abolishes the practice of maintaining a different emblem for each starship, instead adopting the *Enterprise* symbol for the entire organization.

Conjecture. In the original series we saw different insignias for each starship, but since Star Trek: The Motion Picture, *we've seen nearly all Starfleet personnel wearing the* Enterprise *emblem.*

Colony on Septimus Minor

2278

The *Starship Bozeman*, three weeks out of starbase under the command of Captain Morgan Bateson, disappears into what is later learned to be a temporal causality loop near the Typhon Expanse. The *Soyuz*-class ship remains trapped in the causality loop until freed by the *Enterprise* in 2368.

"Cause and Effect" (TNG). Captain Bateson tells Picard the year that the Bozeman *embarked on its fateful trip.*

Editors' Note: The registry number of the U.S.S. Bozeman, *NCC-1941, was suggested by model maker Greg Jein, who did the modifications to change the* Miranda-*class* Reliant *into the* Soyuz-*class* Bozeman. *Greg's credits include miniatures for Steven Spielberg's movie* 1941. *Greg also built spaceships for Spielberg's* Close Encounters of the Third Kind *and the principal* Enterprise-D *models for* Star Trek: The Next Generation.

Starship Enterprise

Pardek becomes a member of the Romulan Senate, representing the Krocton Segment of the planet Romulus. Pardek later meets Spock at the Khitomer Conference of 2293. He is regarded as a "man of the people" and sponsors many reforms, but is considered by the Romulan leadership to be something of a radical because of his advocacy for peace.

"Unification, Part I" (TNG). Data describes Pardek's career, noting that he had served in the Romulan Senate for nine decades prior to the episode (2368).

2279

Admiral Mark Jameson is born. His celebrated Starfleet career includes a stint as commander of the *Starship Gettysburg.*

"Too Short a Season" (TNG). He was 85 years old at the time of the episode (2364).

A treaty is signed between the Navot and the Paqu groups on Bajor, settling an ancient territorial dispute. The accord defines a border between the two groups along the river Glyrhond.

"The Storyteller" (DS9). Ninety years prior to the episode (2369).

U.S.S. Bozeman *NCC-1941*

2280

The Kes and the Prytt groups of planet Kesprytt II sever diplomatic relations, entering a period of cold war.

"Attached" (TNG). "Almost a century" before the episode (2370).

Romulan Senator Pardek

Saavik

2281

Saavik enters Starfleet Academy.

> *Date is conjecture: Saavik was taking the* Kobayashi Maru *test in 2285 (Star Trek II: The Wrath of Khan), suggesting she was near the end of her studies there at that time. This is four years prior to her test date, since "The First Duty" (TNG) establishes the Academy to be a four-year curriculum.*

James Kirk meets young Demora Sulu, daughter of Hikaru Sulu.

> *Twelve years before the launch of the* Enterprise-B (2293) as seen in Star Trek Generations.

James T. Kirk retires from Starfleet.

> *Date is conjecture.* Star Trek Generations *suggests that Kirk retired from Starfleet sometime after the first* Star Trek *movie, and that he returned in 2284, prior to* Star Trek II. *His retirement could probably have been at any point between 2277 and 2282, when Kirk met Antonia.*

2282

James T. Kirk, at his uncle's farm in Idaho on Earth, meets a woman named Antonia. James and Antonia fall in love.

> *Eleven years prior to the launch of* Enterprise-B *as seen in* Star Trek Generations.

2283

McCoy's bottle of Romulan Ale, given as a birthday gift to Kirk in 2285, was of this year's vintage.

> Star Trek II: The Wrath of Khan. *Kirk read date off bottle.*

2284

Audrid Dax, a member of Trill's powerful Symbiosis Commission, dies. The Dax symbiont is transplanted to Torias.

> *"Facets" (DS9) established Audrid's name and her membership in the commission. "Babel" (DS9) establishes that Dax had not had a female host for some 80 years prior to Jadzia. Since "Babel" was set in 2369, this would put Audrid's death at 2289. We're arbitrarily moving this back to 2284, since "Equilibrium" (DS9) established that Torias Dax, Audrid's successor, died in 2285, and "Blood Oath" (DS9) established that Curzon Dax was already a noted Federation mediator by 2289.*

Torias Dax marries a woman named Nilani Kahn, a scientist who is also a joined Trill.

> *"Rejoined" (DS9). The marriage presumably occurred between Torias's joining and his death, a fairly brief period, since Torias died only six months after having been joined.*

Dr. Carol Marcus

Dr. Carol Marcus presents Project Genesis proposal to the Federation. The project is funded, and her team begins work at the Regula I Space Laboratory.

> Star Trek II: The Wrath of Khan. *Kirk said that Carol's Genesis proposal had been made a year ago.*

Commander Kyle is assigned to *U.S.S. Reliant.* He had served as a transporter chief aboard the *Enterprise* during Kirk's first assignment as captain.

Date is conjecture: This happened after the original Star Trek *series, but before* Star Trek II: The Wrath of Khan.

Nilani Kahn warns her husband, Torias Dax, about her concern that his shuttle is not ready for a full impulse test scheduled for the next day. Torias ignores Nilani's fears.

"Rejoined" (DS9). The day before Torias's shuttle accident.

Torias Dax is seriously injured in a shuttle accident and goes into a coma. When Torias Dax's isoboramine levels drop to dangerous levels, the Dax symbiont is surgically removed. The procedure will eventually result in Torias's death, but it will give the Dax symbiont a chance for life.

The Dax symbiont is joined with a musician named Joran Belar. Shortly after the joining, Joran is found to have violent tendencies that make him unsuitable as a host.

"Equilibrium" (DS9). Six months before Torias's death. The fact of Joran's joining with the Dax symbiont was later suppressed by the Symbiosis Commission, but at the time, Joran was permitted to inform his brother of the joining, so it was presumably not a secret at that point.

Stardate 8105.5. *Starship* Excelsior *commissioned at San Francisco orbital yards. The vessel serves as experimental test bed for the unsuccessful Transwarp Development Project, but later is refitted with a standard warp drive and serves successfully as a ship of the line.*

Date is conjecture: This presumably happened before Star Trek III: The Search for Spock, *because the ship was seen in that film. "Threshold" (VGR) establishes that transwarp represents a breaking of the warp 10 barrier, so that a ship could theoretically travel at an infinite velocity, occupying all points in the universe simultaneously. On the other hand, given the bizarre side effects of transwarp travel seen in "Threshold," it's probably just as well that the* Excelsior *tests didn't work.*

James T. Kirk, retired from Starfleet and now living in a mountain cabin on Earth, decides to return to Starfleet as an academy instructor. Kirk's decision is a disappointment to Antonia, Kirk's lover. The two subsequently separate, much to Kirk's regret. Kirk moves into an apartment in San Francisco.

Star Trek Generations. *Nine years prior to the launch of the* Enterprise-B *(2393).*

Editors' Note: The first edition of this Chronology speculated that Kirk had joined the academy faculty in 2277, but Star Trek Generations *reveals that Kirk had left Starfleet some time after* Star Trek: The Motion Picture, *only to return at this point, prior to* Star Trek II: The Wrath of Khan.

Commander Kyle and Captain Terrell

Trill homeworld

U.S.S. Enterprise

2285

Trill composer Joran Belar, also known as Joran Dax, writes a melody that will one day trigger a memory in Jadzia Dax.

"Equilibrium" (DS9). Eighty-six years before the episode (2371).

U.S.S. Reliant, *assigned to support Project Genesis, conducts search for a lifeless planetoid for third-stage experiment in the Mutara Sector. This stage would involve testing the Genesis device on a planetary scale.*

Shortly before Star Trek II: The Wrath of Khan.

According to Trill Symbiosis Commission records, Torias Dax dies after six months in a coma. The Dax symbiont is joined with a new host named Curzon. Also according to Symbiosis Commission records, a host candi-

Khan

date named Joran Belar, having been recommended for rejection from the initiate program, is killed after reportedly murdering the doctor who recommended his expulsion.

"Equilibrium" (DS9). Eighty-six years prior to the episode (2371), according to Ben Sisko. Note that the Symbiosis Commission's records gave the date Joran's death as stardate 8615, which would seem to be after Star Trek VI *(2287), but we're using Sisko's date because of the ambiguities inherent in stardates.*

Editors' Note: In fact, the Dax symbiont had spent the last six months in Joran, an unsuitable host candidate who died when his body rejected the Dax symbiont. However, the Symbiosis Commission subsequently altered its files and suppressed all records that the Joran Dax joining had occurred at all. The commission had maintained for generations that only one in a thousand Trills could serve as a host to a symbiont. The fact that an unsuitable joining could survive for so long called this belief into question, and the commission proved willing to do almost anything to maintain its control over the host selection process. Note that the commission was largely successful in keeping its secret, and that Sisko (and presumably Jadzia Dax) also promised not to reveal this information in 2371.

Detonation of the Genesis device

Star Trek II: The Wrath of Khan. Stardate 8130.3. Admiral James Kirk celebrates his 52nd birthday. Kirk and Spock, now serving as Academy instructors, later shuttle up to the *Enterprise* to participate in an inspection and cadet training exercise.

Lieutenant Saavik takes *Kobayashi Maru* test at Starfleet Academy on Earth. Saavik later pilots *Enterprise* out of spacedock on training exercise.

Federation starship *Reliant* continues survey mission to find a lifeless planet to serve as test site for Project Genesis. While surveying planet Ceti Alpha V, the *Reliant* landing party accidentally discovers the encampment of Khan Noonien Singh, the former tyrant of Earth's Eugenics Wars. Khan commandeers the *Reliant* and uses the ship to gain control of space station Regula I and the Genesis project being developed there. It is later learned that this was an effort to win vengeance on Captain James Kirk for his role in exiling Khan to Ceti Alpha V in 2267

Although Khan is ultimately thwarted, Captain Clark Terrell is killed and his ship, the *Reliant*, is destroyed when Khan attempts to steal the Genesis device.

The death of Captain Spock

Captain Spock dies of severe radiation exposure during the Genesis crisis, but his heroic actions permit the *Enterprise* to escape the detonation of the device. Khan and his followers are also reported killed in the explosion. Spock's coffin is consigned to the depths of space.

Editors' Note: The fact that Saavik was a lieutenant while still apparently an Academy cadet is consistent with the notion that Kirk apparently also held the rank of lieutenant while at the Academy.

Lieutenant Saavik and David Marcus assigned to *U.S.S. Grissom* for further study of the Genesis Planet in the Mutara Sector.

Between Star Trek II *and* Star Trek III.

The destruction of the U.S.S. Enterprise

Star Trek III: The Search for Spock. Stardate 8210.3. *U.S.S. Enterprise* returns to Spacedock in Earth orbit for repairs following battle in the Mutara Sector. Upon arrival, *Enterprise* captain James Kirk is informed by Admiral Morrow that rather than being refit, the *Enterprise* is due to be scrapped.

U.S.S. Grissom science team consisting of Saavik and Marcus, investigating the Genesis Planet in the Mutara Sector, discovers an extraordinary range of life-forms, including the regenerated, living body of Captain

Spock. It is speculated that the torpedo serving as his coffin somehow soft-landed on the planet. During the investigation, the *Grissom* is attacked by a Klingon vessel, resulting in the loss of all hands except for Saavik and Marcus, who are stranded on the planet's surface. Marcus is later killed by a Klingon landing party.

Admiral James Kirk commandeers the *Starship Enterprise*, taking it to the Mutara Sector in an effort to recover the body of Spock from the Genesis Planet so that it can be returned to planet Vulcan. During the unauthorized mission, Kirk orders the destruction of the *Enterprise* to prevent the ship from falling into Klingon hands. Kirk gains control of the Klingon vessel, using it to return Spock's now-living body to Vulcan.

Genesis Planet disintegrates due to protomatter used in its creation matrix.

Vulcan High Priestess T'Lar presides over the ancient *fal-tor-pan* ceremony, re-fusing Spock's *katra*, residing in the mind of Dr. McCoy, with Spock's body, recovered from the Genesis Planet.

Editors' Note: The Enterprise *flight data recorder played for Sarek indicated the stardate of Spock's death as being 8128.7. This would seem to be inconsistent with the stardate of 8130.3 given by Saavik during her* Kobayashi Maru *exercise. One might rationalize that this is due to relativistic effects of spaceflight, or other peculiarities of stardate computation.*

This film established Dr. Leonard McCoy's middle initial to be "H," and the name of his father to be David.

Starship *U.S.S. Hathaway* is launched. When retired eighty years later, this *Constellation*-class ship is part of a Starfleet strategic simulation exercise under the command of Captain Picard and Commander Riker.

"Peak Performance" (TNG). The Hathaway *was 80 years old at the time of the episode (2365).*

Spock undergoes reeducation and retraining process at his parents' home on planet Vulcan. He rapidly assimilates his technical and scientific education, taught in the Vulcan way, but has difficulty with humanistic concepts taught by his mother, Amanda.

Between Star Trek III *and* IV. *Kirk's log in* Star Trek IV *established the total length of their stay (and of Spock's reeducation) was about three months.*

Ferengi grand nagus Zek takes a vacation. It's the last vacation he'll take for 85 years.

"The Nagus" (DS9). Eighty-five years before the episode (2370).

2286

Star Trek IV: The Voyage Home. Stardate 8390.0. The Klingon Ambassador demands extradition of Admiral Kirk for alleged crimes against the Klingon nation. The Federation Council declines the request, citing pending Federation action against Kirk for violation of nine Starfleet regulations.

An alien space probe of unknown origin damages several spacecraft and wreaks environmental havoc on Earth. The probe returns to deep space after communicating with two humpback whales brought to this century by Admiral Kirk.

Cetacean biologist Gillian Taylor, originally from Earth's 20th century, becomes a scientist on a Federation science vessel.

Admiral James Kirk and his shipmates vote to return to Earth to face charges stemming from acts committed during the rescue of Captain Spock. Kirk is found guilty of disobeying direct orders and is demoted to captain, and assigned command of the *Starship Enterprise*, NCC-1701-A.

T'Lar

U.S.S. Hathaway

Zek

The Klingon ambassador

The new U.S.S. Enterprise, *NCC-1701-A*

Butler

U.S.S. Enterprise, NCC-1701-A, the second starship to bear the name, enters service under the command of Captain James Kirk.

Editors' Note: In "Homefront" (DS9), the Federation president said that, with the exception of the Borg incident ("Best of Both Worlds, Parts I and II" [TNG]), a state of emergency hadn't been declared on Earth in a century. This would appear to be a reference to the state of emergency in Star Trek IV, although this was 86 years prior to "Homefront" (which was set in 2372).

The Lornak clan of the planet Acamar III massacre all but five members of the clan Tralesta, ending a blood feud that had lasted for 200 years. Yuta of the clan Tralesta is one of the survivors. Her cells are altered to slow her aging so that she may have enough time to exact vengeance upon all members of the clan Lornak.

"The Vengeance Factor" (TNG). Eighty years prior to the episode (2366).

James Kirk's pet dog, a Great Dane named Butler, dies.

Star Trek Generations. Seven years before the launch of the Enterprise-B *(2293).*

2287

Sybok takes control of the Enterprise

Star Trek V: The Final Frontier. Stardate 8454.1. *U.S.S. Enterprise*-A undergoes final testing and preparation for service under the direction of Engineering Officer Montgomery Scott.

Romulan, Federation, and Klingon diplomatic representatives on planet Nimbus III are seized by Sybok, Spock's half brother. The *Starship Enterprise*-A is dispatched to parlay for their release. Negotiations are unsuccessful, and an attempt is made to free the hostages by force. The attempt is also unsuccessful, resulting in the capture of the *Enterprise*-A by Sybok and his followers.

Sybok commandeers the *Enterprise*-A in a search for the mythical planet Sha Ka Ree, located at the center of the galaxy. The planet is eventually located, but Sybok is killed by a malevolent entity living there.

The ancient *Pioneer X* space probe, drifting in interstellar space, is destroyed by a Klingon bird-of-prey under the command of Captain Klaa

Editors' Note: Gene Roddenberry reportedly said he considered some of the events in Star Trek V *to be apocryphal. The film is included in this chronology, however, because of our desire to be as complete as possible.*

Transwarp Development Project deemed unsuccessful by Starfleet Command. *U.S.S. Excelsior* is refitted with a standard warp drive and is assigned Starfleet duty. The ship, previously classified as an experimental vessel with an NX registry prefix, is redesignated as NCC-2000.

Date is conjecture, but presumably happened between Star Trek IV *and* Star Trek VI. *The date is arbitrarily biased more toward* Star Trek VI *to allow Starfleet time to have adequately conducted its experiments and tests, while allowing enough time for the ship to have spent three years cataloging planetary atmospheres. "Threshold" (VGR) establishes more about the nature of transwarp drive.*

A Federation starship suffers a systemwide technological failure. This is the last such occurrence prior to the Nanites' takeover of the *Enterprise*-D's main computers in 2366.

"Evolution" (TNG). Data noted that such a failure had not happened in the past 79 years. One wonders if this incident refers to the failure of transwarp drive.

Starship Enterprise pursued by the Klingons

2288

Starfleet retires *Soyuz* class of starships.

> *"Cause and Effect" (TNG). Geordi notes that* Soyuz-*class ships haven't been in service for 80 years prior to the episode (2368).*

> *Editors' Note: The* Soyuz-*class U.S.S. Bozeman in "Cause and Effect" was, of course, a modification of the* Miranda-*class U.S.S. Reliant model built for* Star Trek II: The Wrath of Khan. *It was originally hoped that a new model could be built for the* Bozeman, *but practical considerations necessitated the use of the* Reliant *model, so model-maker Greg Jein added some nifty outboard "sensor pods" to turn it into a different class of starship.*

2289

Federation negotiator Curzon Dax conducts difficult talks with Klingon representative Kang at the Korvat colony. On the first day of negotiations, Dax walks out on Kang's speech, angering the Klingon, but winning his respect. Dax gives Koloth, another member of the Klingon contingent, the nickname D'akturak, meaning "ice man," because of Koloth's cold, tough demeanor. Kang comes to believe that Dax, unlike other Federation representatives, does understand the Klingon psyche.

> *"Blood Oath" (DS9). Eighty-one years prior to the episode (2370).*

Captain Hikaru Sulu

2290

Hikaru Sulu is promoted to captain and placed in command of the *Starship Excelsior.* The ship is assigned to scientific research in Beta quadrant, near the Klingon neutral zone.

> Star Trek VI: The Undiscovered Country. *This was three years prior to* Star Trek VI, *set in 2293, since Sulu mentioned in his log that he'd just finished his first mission as captain of* Excelsior, *and that the mission had lasted three years.*

Three Klingon warships under the command of captains Kor, Koloth, and Kang attempt to apprehend a criminal known as the Albino. Although most of the Albino's crew is captured, the Albino himself escapes and sends the three captains a message that he will take revenge by murdering their firstborn children. The Albino eventually makes good on the threat, using a genetic virus. Kang's son, one of the victims of the Albino, was the godson of, and named for, Curzon Dax. The three warriors and Dax take a blood oath to avenge the death of the three children.

> *"Blood Oath" (DS9). The Albino was nearly captured 80 years before the episode, although the murders of the children and the blood oath took place a few years later.*

The Albino

Janice Rand is assigned as *Excelsior* communications officer.

> *Date is conjecture, but she served as* Excelsior *communications officer during* Star Trek VI, *although this would have been after her stint at Starfleet Command, seen in* Star Trek IV.

U.S.S. Enterprise, *U.S.S. Excelsior*, and other Federation starships are outfitted with improved sensors to support a scientific project cataloging planetary atmospheric anomalies.

> Star Trek VI: The Undiscovered Country. *The project had been under way for three years prior to the film (2393).*

Klingon sleeper ship *T'Ong* is launched on an extended mission of exploration under the command of Captain K'Temok. They return in the year 2365, when there is peace between the Federation and the Klingon Empire.

Communications Officer Janice Rand

Uprated Klingon Bird-of-Prey

Ensign Tuvok

Klingon Chancellor Gorkon

Camp Khitomer

"The Emissary" (TNG). The ship was launched 75 years prior to the episode. K'Ehleyr said the ship was from an era when the Federation and the Klingons were still at war. This is consistent with the 2290 date, which is before the Khitomer Conference in Star Trek VI: The Undiscovered Country.

2292

The Klingon Defense Force develops an improved bird-of-prey spacecraft capable of maintaining limited invisibility cloak while firing torpedo weapons.

Date is conjecture. This was presumably soon before Star Trek VI: The Undiscovered Country.

Editors' Note: This development raises the question of why Klingon space-craft are still generally unable to use their weapons while cloaked in Star Trek: The Next Generation-*era episodes. The real reason, of course, is that* Next Generation *writers were not aware of this new "development" during the first four seasons of that show, before* Star Trek VI *was written. We imagine that cloaking technology, like present day "stealth" technology, is a constantly evolving race between the designers of cloaking devices and the folks who design sensors. Even though this "improved" ship could evade detection while firing, one might assume that improved sensor designs would later render this development ineffective, at least until the next advance in cloaking technology. In fact, Kirk's use of plasma sensors on photon torpedoes in* Star Trek VI *would seem to do just that.*

The alliance between the Klingon Empire and the Romulan Star Empire collapses. The two former allies become bitter enemies for at least 75 years.

"Reunion" (TNG). Geordi expressed surprise at evidence of Klingon-Romulan cooperation, noting that the two powers had been blood enemies for 75 years prior to the episode (2367). The battle of Klach D'kel Brakt, set in 2271, probably had something to do with it, as well.

2293

Tuvok, a recent Starfleet Academy graduate, is assigned as a junior science officer to the *U.S.S. Excelsior* under the command of Captain Sulu.

"Flashback" (VGR). Two months before Star Trek VI: The Undiscovered Country.

Montgomery Scott buys a boat. Uhura agrees to chair a seminar at Starfleet Academy.

Just prior to Star Trek VI: The Undiscovered Country.

Star Trek VI: The Undiscovered Country. Stardate 9521.6. Klingon moon Praxis explodes, causing severe damage to the Klingon Homeworld of Qo'noS. Federation starship *Excelsior* also damaged by subspace shock wave from explosion.

Klingons launch major peace initiative, during which Captain Spock agrees to serve as a special envoy at the request of Ambassador Sarek. Initial talks appear encouraging, but Klingon chancellor Gorkon is assassinated while en route to Earth for a peace conference. *Enterprise* captain James T. Kirk and Dr. Leonard H. McCoy are convicted of the murder by a Klingon court, and are sentenced to life imprisonment at the Rura Penthe dilithium mines. The peace conference is rescheduled to take place at Camp Khitomer.

Kirk and McCoy are later found to be innocent of Gorkon's murder when the crime is found to be the work of Starfleet admiral Cartwright and other Federation and Klingon forces opposed to the change in the status quo. Kirk, commanding *Enterprise*, and Captain Sulu, commanding the

Starship Excelsior, are successful in preventing another attempt by these forces to disrupt the peace conference. The Khitomer Conference becomes a major turning point in galactic politics, representing the beginning of rapprochement between the two adversaries.

Stardate 9523.1. Last mission of the *Starship Enterprise*-A under the command of Captain James T. Kirk. The *Enterprise*-A is retired shortly thereafter.

Editors' Note: Exact date of the retirement of the Enterprise-*A is conjecture, but it had to happen sometime after* Star Trek VI *and the launching of the* Enterprise-*B in* Star Trek Generations.

Date of Star Trek VI *determined from Dr. McCoy's testimony that he had served aboard the* Enterprise *for 27 years. McCoy was apparently assigned to the ship in early 2266 (between "Where No Man Has Gone Before" and "The Corbomite Maneuver"). This film established James T. Kirk's middle name to be Tiberius, and Sulu's first name to be Hikaru. This was also the first time the Klingon Homeworld has been referred to by name, Qo'noS (pronounced "kronos.") In "Flashback" (VGR), we learn that Tuvok had been a member of the* Excelsior *crew during the Khitomer incident.*

James Tiberius Kirk

Spock meets Romulan senator Pardek during the Khitomer Conference. They remain in contact, pursuing the goal of Romulan/Vulcan reunification, until the year 2368, when Pardek is exposed as an undercover agent for the conservative Romulan government.

"Unification, Part I" (TNG). Sarek said this is where Spock and Pardek met.

As part of the Khitomer accords, the Klingon Empire relinquishes claim to planet Archanis IV and the Archanis sector.

"Broken Link" (DS9). Conjecture. Kira said the Klingons gave up Archanis IV a hundred years before the episode (2372), but it seems likely the event was tied to the Khitomer accords, which were within ten years.

Captain James T. Kirk retires from Starfleet.

Between Star Trek VI *and the launch of the* Enterprise-*B as seen in* Star Trek Generations.

U.S.S. Enterprise, NCC-1701-B, the third starship to bear the name, enters service under the command of Captain John Harriman. Ensign Demora Sulu is the ship's helm officer. Former *Enterprise* captain James T. Kirk, as well as Montgomery Scott and Pavel Chekov are honored guests for the christening ceremony.

Captain John Harriman

Shortly after launch, the *Enterprise*-B responds to a distress call from two El-Aurian refugee ships. All passengers and crew from one ship are killed when the El-Aurian transport encounters a temporal flux energy ribbon known as the nexus. *Enterprise*-B personnel are successful in rescuing 47 refugees from the second ship, including Dr. Tolian Soran, who was momentarily absorbed by the nexus prior to being rescued. Also rescued is an El-Aurian refugee named Guinan

Former *Enterprise* captain James T. Kirk is believed killed shortly after the rescue, when energy from the nexus impacts the *Enterprise*-B. Kirk had been making emergency modifications to the ship's deflector system that made it possible for the *Enterprise*-B to escape the energy ribbon.

Both Guinan and Soran suffer severe disorientation from their removal from the nexus. Guinan gradually recovers, but Soran becomes obsessed with returning to the nexus.

Seventy-eight years before the Star Trek: The Next Generation-*era portion of* Star Trek Generations.

U.S.S. Enterprise *NCC-1701-B*

Captain Montgomery Scott

2294

Captain Montgomery Scott retires from Starfleet and books passage to the Norpin V retirement colony aboard the transport ship *Jenolen*. While en route to Norpin V, the *Jenolen* disappears, with the apparent loss of all crew and passengers.

"Relics" (TNG). The Jenolen *had been reported missing 75 years prior to the episode (2369).*

Editors' Note: Scotty, of course, survived the Jenolen's *crash, but Starfleet had no way of knowing this until 2369 when the* Enterprise-D *discovered the Dyson Sphere.*

Scotty's comment in "Relics" (TNG) in which he wonders if James Kirk had come to his rescue is inconsistent with the fact that Scotty believed that Kirk was killed on the Enterprise-B's *first voyage. The real reason for this, of course, is that "Relics" was written and filmed before* Star Trek Generations *was written, so everyone involved was unaware of Kirk's impending fate. Of the inconsistency, episode writer (and* Star Trek Generations *co-writer) Ronald D. Moore has noted that Scotty was included in the film, despite the inconsistency, simply out of affection for the character.*

2295

An outbreak of deadly plasma plague on planet Obi VI. Dr. Susan Nuress, a researcher investigating the disease, conducts at least 58 tests resulting in at least one highly virulent mutated strain.

"The Child" (TNG). Pulaski noted the outbreak had taken place 70 years prior to the episode (2365).

2296

The Eastern Continental government of planet Rutia IV denies a bid for independence by the Ansata, a separatist organization. Members of the Ansata begin a long terrorist war in an attempt to force the government to grant their demands.

"The High Ground" (TNG). Alexana told Riker that the Ansata had been fighting for 70 years prior to the episode (2366).

2297

First contact with the inhabitants of planet Ventax II by a Klingon expedition. The planet's culture is reported to be a peaceful agrarian economy, despite evidence of a technologically advanced society in centuries past.

"Devil's Due" (TNG). Dr. Clark said the contact had taken place 70 years prior to episode (2267).

6.0 THE TWENTY-FOURTH CENTURY

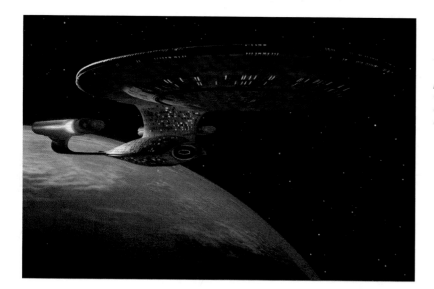

The fifth Federation starship to bear the name U.S.S. Enterprise *played a key role in both exploration and diplomacy during the latter half of the 24th century*

2302

Last Federation contact with planet Angel I prior to 2364. The contact is by a Federation vessel that reports the planet to have a technological development level similar to mid-20th-century Earth.

"Angel One" (TNG). Data noted that the contact had taken place 62 years prior to episode (2364).

Jaresh-Inyo enters the world of politics. Over the next seven decades, his career leads him to represent his people on the Federation Council, and he eventually is elected to the office of Federation President.

"Paradise Lost" (DS9). Seventy years before the episode (2372).

Jaresh-Inyo

2304

Tuvok undergoes *pon farr* and marries T'Pel, abandoning his *Kohlinar* training. Tuvok and T'Pel raise a family together.

"Ex Post Facto" (VGR). Sixty-seven years prior to the episode (2371), also six years after Tuvok resigned from Starfleet as established in "Flashback" (VGR). His wife's name established in "Persistence of Vision" (VGR).

2305

Jean-Luc Picard is born to Maurice and Yvette Picard in LaBarre, France, on Earth. He becomes captain of the fifth and sixth Federation starships to bear the name *Enterprise*. Picard's family can trace its roots in western Europe back to the time of Charlemagne.

Jean-Luc Picard

Timicin

Cardassian homeworld

Bajor

Settlement on the planet Meridian

Conjecture: This date is consistent with a Starfleet Academy graduation in 2327, as established in "The First Duty" (TNG), assuming that Picard had applied unsuccessfully for the Academy at age 17, and that he was accepted when he was 18 (as suggested in "Coming of Age" [TNG]). Picard's parents and place of birth were first established in his computer dossier file in "Conundrum" (TNG), then later in "Chain of Command, Part I" (TNG) .

2307

Timicin is born on planet Kaelon II. He becomes a scientist and plays a key role in that planet's effort to extend the life of the star Kaelon by a helium fusion ignition process.

"Half a Life" (TNG). Timicin was 60 years old at the time of the episode (2367).

2309

Representatives of the Cardassian Union offer assistance to planet Bajor. The Cardassian presence is initially seen as benign, even constructive, but over the next two decades it becomes increasingly oppressive.

"Emissary" (DS9). Kira noted that the Cardassians had offered help 60 years prior to the episode (2369).

Federation starships first explore the Indri system near Caere. The eighth planet of the Indri system is Class-L, supporting deciduous vegetation, but no animal life.

"The Chase" (TNG). Sixty years before the episode (2369).

2311

The Tomed Incident. Thousands of Federation lives are lost to Romulan forces. Afterwards, the Treaty of Algeron is signed, reaffirming the Romulan Neutral Zone. As part of the pact, the Federation promises not to develop or use cloaking technology in its spacecraft. The treaty is instrumental in keeping peace between the two powers for decades, although some elements of the Federation Starfleet oppose the renunciation of cloaking technology, which some regard as vital to maintaining the Federation's defenses. The Romulans subsequently enter an extended period of isolationism.

"The Neutral Zone" (TNG). Fifty-three years prior to episode. The Treaty of Algeron established in "The Defector" (TNG).

Editors' Note: "The Neutral Zone" (TNG) makes it clear that the Federation and the Romulans had no contact at all during the years between this incident and "The Neutral Zone" (TNG) (2364), but other episodes have suggested that there was some contact between the Romulans and the Klingons during this period, in that the Romulans apparently had been trying to destabilize the Klingon government for two decades prior to Star Trek: The Next Generation's fourth season ("Redemption, Part I" [TNG], set in 2367). "The Defector" (TNG) established the Treaty of Algeron and seemed to imply that it had been established at the conclusion of the Romulan war in 2160, as is indicated in the first edition of the Chronology. "The Pegasus" (TNG), however, clarifies the matter, making it clear that the treaty was signed after the Tomed Incident. (Ah, the joys of backpedaling....)

The planet Meridian, existing on two intersecting dimensional planes, materializes briefly in this universe in the Trialus system. These appearances in our dimension occur every 60 years.

"Meridian" (DS9). Sixty years prior to the episode (2371).

2312

A life-form known as a Douwd, an "immortal being of disguise and false surroundings," who has lived in this galaxy for thousands of years, assumes the form of a human named Kevin Uxbridge. On Earth in the New Martim Vaz aquatic city in Earth's Atlantic Ocean, he falls in love with and marries a human woman named Rishon. They eventually join the 11,000 colonists in the ill-fated Delta Rana IV colony in 2361.

"The Survivors" (TNG). Kevin said he'd lived in human form for about 50 years prior to the episode but he and Rishon had been married for 53 years, so we are arbitrarily pegging the date he became human as 54 years prior to the episode. The Rana IV colony had existed for five years prior to the episode (2366).

Kevin Uxbridge

2313

Gatherer Penthor Mull of planet Acamar III is accused of leading a raid on the Tralesta clan. He is killed by a microvirus carried by Yuta as part of her quest to avenge the 2286 massacre of her clan.

"The Vengeance Factor (TNG). Fifty-three years prior to episode (2366).

2314

Mark and Anne Jameson are married. The future Admiral Mark Jameson's celebrated Starfleet career includes a stint as commander of the *Starship Gettysburg.*

"Too Short a Season" (TNG). Anne Jameson said they had been married for 50 years at the time of the episode (2364).

2319

The father of Mordan IV leader Karnas is assassinated by a rival tribe. Karnas seizes 65 passengers of a starliner, demanding that Starfleet provide weapons in exchange for the lives of the hostages. Two Federation mediators are killed in unsuccessful attempts to resolve the situation. Federation hostages, held by revolutionaries on planet Mordan IV, are freed thanks to negotiations conducted by Captain Jameson of *U.S.S. Gettysburg.* Although Jameson is credited with the peaceful resolution of the situation, it is later learned that this intervention included a weapons-for-hostages deal that resulted in a bloody 40-year civil war.

Mark Jameson

"Too Short a Season" (TNG). Forty-five years prior to episode (2364).

The invention of the multiplex pattern buffer, used in transporter systems, eradicates transporter psychosis, a rare disorder caused by breakdown of neurochemical molecules during transport.

"Realm of Fear" (TNG). Fifty years prior to the episode (2369).

2320

Miranda Vigo is born on New Gaul.

"Bloodlines" (TNG). About fifty years prior to the episode (2370).

2322

Jean-Luc Picard applies to Starfleet Academy, but is rejected. However, his admission test score is sufficient to allow him to reapply the following year. His application is made over the strong objections of his father, Maurice Picard.

Date is conjecture, assumes he was 17 years old at the time, that he was 18 years old when admitted next year, and that he graduated in 2327, as men-

Picard

Starfleet Headquarters at San Francisco

Beverly Crusher

Dr. Richard Galen

Picard fights the Nausicaans

tioned in "The First Duty" (TNG). Picard confesses his early failure to gain academy entrance to Wesley in "Coming of Age" (TNG). Maurice's feelings about his son's entry into Starfleet were made known in "Tapestry" (TNG).

The Bajoran wormhole undergoes a brief subspace inversion. The spectacular natural phenomenon occurs once every fifty years.

"The Visitor" (DS9). Fifty years before the episode (2372).

2323

Editors' Note: The year 2323 works out as the zero point for the system of stardates developed for Star Trek: The Next Generation, assuming that the beginning of year 2364 (the first season of Star Trek: The Next Generation) was stardate 41000, and that stardates progress at 1000 units per year. In other words, under the Next Generation system of stardates, January 1, 2323 would seem to correspond to stardate 0. This probably shouldn't be taken too seriously, because Star Trek's stardates have never been too internally consistent, but we're mentioning it here because it's kinda fun. (No, we don't know how these stardates relate to the stardates used in the original Star Trek series or the movies, nor do we know what stardates would have been for years between the movies and this point. See the Appendix I [Regarding stardates] for more information on stardates.)

Jean-Luc Picard enters Starfleet Academy on his second application. The superintendent of the academy is a full Betazoid. As a freshman cadet, Picard passes four upperclassmen on the last hill of the 40-kilometer run on Danula II, becoming the only freshman ever to win the academy marathon. One of Picard's interests is archaeology, and he studies the legendary Iconians.

Date is conjecture. Assumes Picard was 18 years old when he was admitted to the academy, and that he graduated in 2327, as established in "The First Duty" (TNG). Picard's academy marathon win described by Admiral Hanson in "The Best of Both Worlds, Part II" (TNG). Picard's interest in the Iconians was established in "Contagion" (TNG).

2324

Beverly Howard, the future Beverly Crusher, is born in Copernicus City, Luna, to Paul and Isabel Howard. Beverly's mother dies while she is still a child, and young Beverly is raised by her grandmother, Felisa Howard.

"Conundrum" (TNG). Date and parents' names given in computer bio screen. This is consistent with Beverly being about 40 years old during the first season, as suggested by the writers'/directors' guide. Felisa Howard established in "Sub Rosa" (TNG).

Starfleet Academy team wins a parrises squares tournament over the heavily favored team from Minsk. The academy team scores a dramatic victory in the last 40 seconds of the final game of the series.

"The First Duty" (TNG). Boothby reminds Picard of the "parrises squares tournament in '24."

Jean-Luc Picard, a Starfleet Academy sophomore, has a run-in with "a couple of surly Nausicaans" while on a training assignment at Morikin VII. At the academy, Picard is particularly close to his archaeology professor, Dr. Richard Galen, who regards Picard as his most promising student. Galen is bitterly disappointed when Picard chooses starship command over archaeology, although Picard retains an interest in that science throughout his life, even publishing an occasional academic paper.

"Tapestry" (TNG). Picard told the tall tale to Riker. Galen is from "The Chase" (TNG), although the date is conjecture. We're assuming that Galen was Picard's professor at the academy.

2325

Devinoni Ral is born on Earth, in Brussels, the European Alliance. He is one-fourth Betazoid, which Ral uses to his advantage as an adult in his career as a professional negotiator.

"The Price" (TNG). Ral's age is given as 41 in the episode.

2327

Jean-Luc Picard graduates from Starfleet Academy. He is class valedictorian. In later years, Picard would credit Academy groundskeeper Boothby for helping him to find the strength to make it through some difficult times.

"The First Duty" (TNG). Picard reminds Boothby that he graduated in the class of '27. Robert Picard noted in "Family" (TNG) that Jean-Luc had been valedictorian.

Awaiting his first assignment at Starbase Earhart shortly after graduation, Picard (known as "Johnny" to his friends) picks a fight with three very large Nausicaans, one of whom thrusts a sword through Picard's heart. Picard's injuries are severe enough to require the implanting of a bionic replacement heart into his body. In later years, Picard would regret his youthful brashness, although in truth the incident helped shape his character by helping him to realize the fragility of life and the importance of each moment.

"Tapestry" (TNG). Note that the episode establishes that the incident at Starbase Earhart happened 30 years prior to the episode (2369), but this was a mistake, since the episode also pegs the incident has having in 2327, shortly after Picard's graduation. Unfortunately, the mistake was not caught until after the episode was filmed.

William Patrick Samuels is born in Bergan, Norway, on Earth.

"The Maquis, Part I" (DS9). Samuels was 43 years old at the time of his death in 2370.

2328

Ian Andrew Troi of Earth and Lwaxana Troi of Betazed are married. They live in a house near Lake El'nar on Betazed.

"Dark Page" (TNG). About seven years before Deanna Troi's birth in 2336.

Editors' confession: In "Dark Page" (TNG), an entry in Lwaxana's journal dated stardate 30620.1 is established to be during the year in which she got married, 2328. Unfortunately, under the Star Trek: The Next Generation system of stardates (which allocates 1,000 stardate units per year, and puts the beginning of year 2364 at stardate 41000) the beginning of the year 2328 should be around stardate 5000. Star Trek technical consultant (and Chronology co-author) Mike Okuda decided that a four-digit stardate would be confusing since this sounds like an Original Series number, so he arbitrarily picked 30620, even though it is not consistent with stardates used elsewhere in the show.

The Cardassian Empire formally annexes the Bajoran homeworld, forcing much of the native population of Bajor to resettle elsewhere, including three planets in the Valo system on the outskirts of Cardassian territory. Those who remained on Bajor are tortured and otherwise mistreated. The Cardassians also proceed to strip the planet of its natural resources, causing severe environmental damage.

An underground of Bajoran nationals conducts a terrorist campaign against the Cardassians for the next 40 years. The United Federation of Planets,

Devinoni Ral

*Starfleet Academy
groundskeeper Boothby*

Ian Troi

Bajor under Cardassian rule

Isolinear chips

Kestra Troi

Benjamin Lafayette Sisko

Noonien Soong

considering this to be an internal Cardassian affair, expresses sympathy for the Bajoran people, but declines involvement in the issue until 2368. So determined are the Bajorans to drive out their oppressors that they abolish their caste system, called D'jarras, so that all may become soldiers in the fight for freedom.

"Ensign Ro" (TNG). Admiral Kennelly noted the Cardassians had annexed Bajor 40 years prior to the episode (2368). The Cardassians' "scorched earth" policy described by Sisko in "Emissary" (DS9). Abolition of the D'jarras established in "Accession" (DS9).

2329

Isolinear optical chip technology replaces duotronic enhancer systems aboard Starfleet vessels. Duotronic technology had originally been developed by Dr. Richard Daystrom in 2243.

"Relics" (TNG). Geordi said that duotronic enhancers had been replaced about 40 years prior to the episode (2369).

Kestra Troi is born on Betazed to Ian Andrew and Lwaxana Troi.

"Dark Page" (TNG). About a year after their marriage in 2328.

Mullibok, a Bajoran national, escapes from a Cardassian labor camp on Bajor after the death of his wife at Cardassian hands. He flees to Jeraddo, a Bajoran moon, by stowing away on a Cardassian survey vessel. Mullibok is the first settler on Jeraddo, where he survives by becoming a farmer.

"Progress" (DS9). Forty years prior to the episode (2369).

2331

United Federation of Planets establishes an outpost on planet Boradis III. It is the first Federation settlement in the system. This colony is among the thirteen settlements in the Boradis sector within potential striking range of the Klingon sleeper ship *T'Ong* when it returns to the area in 2365.

"The Emissary" (TNG). Thirty-four years prior to episode (2365).

2332

Benjamin Lafayette Sisko is born in New Orleans on planet Earth.

Conjecture from "The Emissary" (TNG). Assumes that Sisko graduated from Starfleet Academy in 2354, which is 15 years prior to the episode, that previously Sisko had attended for four years, and that he entered the academy at age 18. Sisko's middle name established in "Homefront" (DS9).

The temporal energy phenomenon known as the nexus passes through Federation space. Its last transit across this part of the galaxy was in 2293, some 39.1 years ago.

Star Trek Generations. Thirty-nine years after the launch of Enterprise-B *(2293), and 39 years before the movie (2371).*

Scientists Noonien Soong and Juliana O'Donnell are secretly married while on a four-day trip to planet Mavala IV. Both are residents of the science colony at Omicron Theta. No record of their marriage is made at the colony because Juliana's mother disapproved of her involvement with the older scientist.

"Inheritance" (TNG). Date is conjecture, but it was before the construction of Data and Lore and before the destruction of the Omicron Theta colony in 2336.

2333

Jean-Luc Picard takes command of the *U.S.S. Stargazer* when the ship's captain is killed. Picard is subsequently promoted to captain. At age 28, Picard is among the youngest Starfleet officers ever to command a starship.

Date is conjecture, based on a reference in the Star Trek: The Next Generation Writers'/Directors' Guide *that Picard had commanded the Stargazer for 22 years. Also based on a reference in "The Battle" (TNG) which suggests the Battle of Maxia had taken place nine years prior to that episode. Boothby, in "The First Duty" (TNG), commented that Locarno would have been even younger than Picard, had he made the captaincy at age 25. The circumstances of Picard's promotion were described by Q in "Tapestry" (TNG).*

U.S.S. Stargazer, *NCC-2893*

2335

William T. Riker is born in Valdez, Alaska, on planet Earth. He is the son of Kyle Riker.

"The Icarus Factor" (TNG). Riker was apparently 30 years old at the time of the episode (2365) because he was 15 years old when his father left him 15 years earlier. "Future Imperfect" (TNG) establishes that his birthday in 2367 fell on stardate 44286. If we assume that there are 1,000 units in a calendar year and that they are evenly spread out, this works out to a calendar date of approximately April 15th. (Please see Appendix I [Regarding stardates] for a few words on how many grains of salt this date should be taken with.)

Chakotay is born at a Federation colony near the Cardassian border. His father is Kolopak.

"Tattoo" (VGR). Conjecture. Assumes that Chakotay was about the same age as actor Robert Beltran at the time of the episode (2372).

Noted cyberneticist Dr. Noonien Soong and his wife, Juliana Soong, make their fourth attempt to create a positronic-based humanoid android. Their first three tries had been failures because of positronic matrix failures, but this effort is successfully made operational. They name their new creation Lore, but Lore exhibits dangerously antisocial behavior and the Soongs are forced to deactivate him. Prior to his deactivation, Lore had evidently been in contact with the Crystalline Entity, urging it to destroy the Omicron Theta colony.

The Soongs subsequently fabricate another android, nearly identical in structure to Lore, but with different programming and without the capacity for emotions. They name this second android Data, who, like Lore, has been built in Noonian Soong's own image. Juliana Soong gives Data the capacity for creativity to help compensate for his lack of emotions.

"Inheritance" (TNG). Date is conjecture, but it was before the destruction of the Omicron Theta colony in 2336. Crystalline Entity and Lore's involvement established in "Datalore" (TNG).

Geordi La Forge is born in the African Confederation on planet Earth. He is the son of Dr. Edward M. and Captain Silva La Forge.

"Cause and Effect" (TNG). Year and place of birth given in Geordi's medical records screen. Note that this screen gives Geordi's mother's name as Alvera K. La Forge. Although the name Alvera had been chosen by the producers, Geordi's mother became Silva in "Interface" (TNG).

William Thomas Riker

Lore

Geordi La Forge

Deanna Troi

2336

Deanna Troi is born on Betazed. She is the second child of Lwaxana Troi and Starfleet officer Ian Andrew Troi.

"Conundrum" (TNG). Year given in computer bio screen. The name of Troi's father was established in "The Child" (TNG). The existence of her older sister, Kestra, was revealed in "Dark Page" (TNG).

Noonien and Juliana Soong continue their efforts to train Data to function in human society. As with their previous creations, they regard Data as their child, but their efforts are less than successful. The Soongs are forced to deactivate Data. In an effort to give him more understanding of humanity, they program into him all the records of the colonists at Omicron Theta. Unfortunately, before Data can be reactivated, the science colony at Omicron Theta is destroyed by what is later known as the Crystalline Entity. All lifeforms on the planet are absorbed or destroyed by the Entity. The still-dormant Data remains unharmed in storage underground, near the Soongs' laboratory.

"Datalore" (TNG) and "Inheritance" (TNG). Date is conjecture, but this is prior to Data's discovery by the Tripoli crew in 2338. Data said that when he was discovered, he was covered by a layer of dust, suggesting some time had passed.

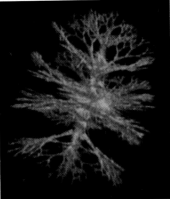

Crystalline Entity

Noonien and Juliana Soong both flee the Omicron Theta colony aboard an escape pod, although Juliana had been seriously injured in the attack. Noonien and Juliana are believed killed by the Crystalline Entity, although they both manage to make it to planet Terlina III.

Juliana Soong slips into a terminal comatose state shortly after arriving at Terlina III. Just prior to her death, Noonien uses a synaptic scanning technique to transfer her memories into the positronic matrix of a new android. This new android, even more sophisticated than Data, is not only indistinguishable from the original Juliana, but she in fact believes that she is her. Noonien lives in seclusion with the new Juliana, but she later tires of the solitude and eventually leaves Noonien. She subsequently remarries, and Noonien would regret her departure for the rest of his life. Much later, Juliana would admit that she had pressured her husband into leaving Data behind at Omicron Theta because she feared that Data might develop a personality similar to that of Lore.

"Brothers" (TNG) establishes Noonien's escape to the Terlina system after the destruction of Omicron Theta. "Inheritance" (TNG) establishes Juliana Soong and her backstory.

Kestra Troi, the older daughter of Ian and Lwaxana Troi, accidentally drowns during a family picnic at Lake El'nar on Betazed. Kestra's mother, Lwaxana, is so overcome with grief and guilt over her child's death that she erases her personal journal for the entire period of Kestra's life and even suppresses all memories of Kestra from her conscious memory.

"Dark Page" (TNG). Deanna was still an infant at the time of her sister's death.

2337

Natasha Yar is born at the Federation colony on planet Turkana IV. She eventually leaves the planet, joins Starfleet, and becomes chief of security aboard the *U.S.S. Enterprise*-D.

Natasha Yar

"The Naked Now" (TNG) establishes that Tasha was 15 at the time she escaped from the Turkana colony, and "Legacy" (TNG) is set 15 years after her escape, meaning that Tasha would have been 30 had she been alive in 2367 (when "Legacy" is set). Tasha was 27 when she died in "Skin of Evil" (TNG).

Beverly Howard colors her hair brunette. She is displeased with the results and later recalls that she "couldn't change it back fast enough."

"The Quality of Life" (TNG). Beverly said she was thirteen when she dyed her hair.

Will Riker's mother dies, leaving him to be raised by his father, Starfleet civilian adviser Kyle Riker.

"The Icarus Factor" (TNG). Riker was two years old when his mother died.

Trill ambassador Odan successfully mediates a dispute between the two moons of planet Peliar Zel, although the entity later known as Odan is at the time known as Odan's father. Odan bridges the differences between the two adversaries by persuading their representatives to trade places for a week so that they can more clearly understand each other's position. During the negotiations, Alpha moon representative Kalin Trose quells a plot by radicals to assassinate the Beta moon's delegation.

"The Host" (TNG). Odan, in Riker's body, describes the negotiations as having taken place 30 years prior to the episode (2367).

The government of the Federation colony on planet Turkana IV begins to fall apart, eventually resulting in the destruction of all the cities above ground.

"Legacy" (TNG). Ishara Yar says the colony started collapsing almost 30 years prior to the episode (2367).

Kyle Riker

A spacecraft of unknown origin reports encountering a single life-form of a previously unknown type in the Denorios Belt in the Bajor system.

"Emissary" (DS9). Thirty-two years before the episode (2369), according to Dax.

2338

Data is discovered at the remains of the colony on planet Omicron Theta by crew of the Federation starship *U.S.S. Tripoli*. The *Tripoli* crew reports all colonists missing and all plant life dead. It is later discovered that the deaths had been caused by what will become known as the Crystalline Entity.

"Datalore" (TNG). Data had been found 26 years prior to episode (2364). Additional attacks established in "Silicon Avatar" (TNG).

Data finds the first few months after his activation to be a difficult and disorienting learning experience. As his systems grow in complexity, it becomes increasingly difficult to integrate new pathways into his neural net. Data even considers having his positronic matrix wiped so that he can start again, but realizes that this is tantamount to committing suicide, so he instead chooses to treat his problems as challenges to be overcome.

"Eye of the Beholder" (TNG). The first few months after his activation.

Data

Noted archaeologist Richard Galen and Captain Jean-Luc Picard see each other for the last time for over thirty years. Picard had been Galen's most promising student, and Galen had been bitterly disappointed when Picard chose to pursue Starfleet instead of archaeology.

"The Chase" (TNG). In 2369, Picard said it had been over 30 years since he had last seen Galen.

Worf, son of Mogh

2339

A bitter civil war rages on planet Klaestron IV. The war is ended when Klaestron general Ardelon Tandro is murdered, so angering his troops that they win a decisive battle. It is not known at the time that Tandro had betrayed his people, and he is posthumously honored as a national hero. Tandro had been good friends with Federation mediator Curzon Dax, who was assigned to the planet to help resolve the war.

"Dax" (DS9). Thirty years prior to the episode (2369).

2340

Worf is born on the Klingon Homeworld of Qo'noS.

"The Bonding" (TNG). He was six years old at the time of the Khitomer massacre (2346). For whatever it might be worth, "Parallels" (TNG) establishes that his birthday in 2370 fell on stardate 47391. If we assume that there are 1,000 units in a calendar year and that they are evenly spread out, this works out to a calendar date of approximately May 23rd, if you don't correct for relativistic time dilation, subspace compression, and/or any of the other peculiarities of stardate computation.

Editors' Note: The name of the Klingon Homeworld was established as Qo'noS (pronounced "kronos") in Star Trek VI: The Undiscovered Country.

Ilon Tandro is born on planet Klaestron IV to General Ardelon Tandro and his wife, Enina Tandro. Ardelon Tandro had been murdered months earlier by parties unknown.

"Dax" (DS9). A few months after General Tandro's murder.

Ro Laren

Ro Laren is born on the planet Bajor. As an adult she serves a tour of duty aboard the *Starship Wellington*, and is court-martialed after a disastrous incident at Garon II. She later serves aboard the *U.S.S. Enterprise*-D under the command of Captain Jean-Luc Picard.

"Conundrum" (TNG). Year of birth given in computer screen bio. Ro's back story established in "Ensign Ro" (TNG).

Medical researcher Nathaniel Teros conducts groundbreaking work with neuromuscular adaptation for low-gravity species. Although his work finds no practical success, his principles are sound.

"Melora" (DS9). Thirty years prior to the episode (2370).

Rurigan

Planet Yadera Prime, located in the Gamma Quadrant, is conquered by the Dominion. One Yaderan, a man named Rurigan, escapes his homeworld and settles on planet Yadera II. There, he uses a hologenerator to create a duplicate of the village where he lived. So sophisticated is Rurigan's programming of this replica that the holographic "people" have actual sentience, arguably qualifying as bona fide life-forms.

"Shadowplay" (DS9). Thirty years before the episode (2370).

Geordi La Forge, aged five, is caught in a fire. His parents rescue him after a couple of minutes. Although he is not hurt, Geordi would later recall that these were the longest couple of minutes of his life, and that it was some time before he would allow his parents out of earshot.

"Hero Worship" (TNG). Geordi said he was five years old at the time of the fire. He also noted that he did not yet have a VISOR at this point.

2341

Jadzia is born on the planet Trill.

"Emissary" (DS9). Dax said she was 28 years old (as of 2369); we're assuming she was speaking of the age of Jadzia, her humanoid host.

Data enters Starfleet Academy. The Academy had ruled that Data is a sentient life-form and thus was eligible for consideration for entry.

"Conundrum" (TNG). Information from Data's bio screen. "Redemption, Part II" (TNG) establishes Data had been in Starfleet for about 26 years (which should mean he joined the service around 2342). Starfleet Academy ruling on Data's sentience established in "Encounter at Farpoint" (TNG).

Julian Subatoi Bashir is born. He becomes a Starfleet physician and serves on Deep Space 9.

"Distant Voices" (DS9). Bashir celebrated his 30th birthday during that episode, set in 2371. Note that in "Emissary" (DS9), Dax suggested that he was 27 at the time of the episode (2369), which would make his birthdate 2342. We're using the "Distant Voices" birthdate since it seems more definitive, although we did use the 2342 date in the first CD-ROM edition of the Chronology. Bashir's middle name was established in "The Wire" (DS9).

Jadzia

Mila begins employment as housekeeper to Enabran Tain.

"Improbable Cause" (DS9). Thirty years before the episode (2371). It is not clear if Tain was head of the Obsidian order at this point.

2342

Ishara Yar is born on planet Turkana IV. Her older sister is Natasha Yar.

"Legacy" (TNG). Ishara described her parents as having been killed "just after" she was born. (See next entry.)

Julian Subatoi Bashir

Natasha Yar, a five-year-old child living in the collapsing colony on Turkana IV, is orphaned when her parents are killed by crossfire between rival gangs. She is left to care for her younger sister, Ishara.

"The Naked Now" (TNG). Tasha said she was five when she was orphaned. Turkana IV established in "Legacy" (TNG).

April 9. Jean-Luc Picard stands up the future Jenice Manheim in the Café des Artistes in Paris. Years later the two re-create the event in the *Enterprise*-D holodeck, this time with Picard keeping the rendezvous.

"We'll Always Have Paris" (TNG). Twenty-two years prior to episode (2364).

Editors' Note: The futuristic Paris cityscape seen from the Café des Artistes was the same backdrop used by production designer Herman Zimmerman for the Federation president's office in Star Trek VI: The Undiscovered Country.

Ishara Yar

Beverly Howard (the future Dr. Beverly Crusher) enters the Starfleet Academy medical school.

"Conundrum" (TNG). Year given in computer bio screen.

2343

Starfleet officer Ian Andrew Troi dies. He was the husband of Lwaxana Troi and the father of Kestra and Deanna Troi.

"Dark Page" (TNG). Deanna was seven years old at the time of her father's death.

Starfleet approves early design work on *Galaxy*-class starship development project. The third ship of this class will eventually become the fifth Federation starship to bear the name *Enterprise*.

Conjecture.

Jenice Manheim

Geordi La Forge, aged eight, gets his first pet, a Circassian cat. Years later Geordi would recall his pet as "funny-looking."

"Violations" (TNG). Geordi said he was eight when he got his pet.

Kira Nerys is born in the Dahkur Province of Bajor. Like all of her people, she lives in the shadow of the Cardassian occupation of Bajor.

"The Maquis, Part I" (DS9). Kira said she had lived under Cardassian rule for 26 years before the liberation, which took place in 2369. Her birthplace established in "Second Skin" (DS9).

Kira Nerys

2344

Starship Enterprise-C, under the command of Captain Rachel Garrett, is nearly destroyed defending a Klingon outpost on Narendra III from a Romulan attack. The rendering of assistance by a Federation starship is a key development in maintaining the path to friendly relations between the Federation and the Klingons.

"Yesterday's Enterprise*" (TNG). Twenty-two years prior to episode (2366).*

Editors' Note: Although the Khitomer Conference of 2293 (Star Trek VI: The Undiscovered Country) was depicted as a turning point in Federation-Klingon relations, it seems clear from this incident at Narendra and the Khitomer massacre of 2346 ("Sins of the Father" [TNG]) that peace between the two powers was gradually achieved over a period of time, involving many attempts and many breakthroughs over a number of years.

Captain Rachel Garrett

A few members of the *Enterprise*-C crew are reported to have been captured by the Romulans following the battle at Narendra III. Years later evidence is uncovered indicating that among those captured crew members was, inexplicably, a 29-year-old woman named Natasha Yar—apparently the same woman who served on the *Enterprise*-D as security chief prior to her death in 2364 at the age of 27. It is later suggested that the lives of these Starfleet personnel were spared when Natasha Yar agreed to become the consort of a Romulan official. For years, reports of the capture of *Enterprise*-C personnel are regarded only as unconfirmed rumors until the attempted Romulan hegemony into Klingon politics in 2367—68. It has been speculated that the woman captured by the Romulans had actually originated in an alternate timeline.

"Redemption, Part II" (TNG). Sela described the fate of Tasha Yar to Captain Picard. We are assuming her account was substantially truthful.

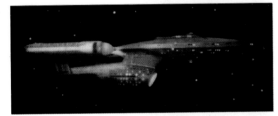

U.S.S. Enterprise NCC-1701-C

U.S.S. Stargazer captain Jean-Luc Picard meets medical student Beverly Howard. Although the two are attracted to each other, Howard has already met her future husband, *Stargazer* officer Jack Crusher.

"Attached" (TNG). Jean-Luc and Beverly knew each other for 20 years prior to her assignment to the Enterprise-D (2364).

Last attempt to make diplomatic contact with the Jarada prior to 2364. The attempt is dramatically unsuccessful because of mispronunciation of a single word.

"The Big Goodbye" (TNG). Twenty years prior to episode (2364).

Young William Riker goes fishing with his father, Kyle Riker, near their home in Valdez, Alaska. The younger Riker is able to hook a big fish, but his father insists on reeling it in. The incident would bother Will for many years.

"The Icarus Factor" (TNG). Riker told Worf he was nine at the time.

Lieutenant Yar

Will and Kyle Riker

2345

Data graduates from Starfleet Academy with honors in exobiology and probability mechanics.

> *"Encounter at Farpoint" (TNG). Starfleet Academy was established to be a four-year institution in "The First Duty" (TNG), but the 2345 graduation date disregards Data's mention of his having been part of the "class of '78." The latter date reference was written prior to the establishment of the calendar year of* Star Trek: The Next Generation *late in the first season and is being ignored because it is inconsistent with the preponderance of other established dating information.*

Kurn is born, son of Mogh, and brother to Worf.

> *"Sins of the Father" (TNG). Date is conjecture, but Kurn said he was "barely a year old" when Worf left for Khitomer with their parents. Further assumes the Khitomer massacre of 2346 happened fairly shortly after their arrival.*

The criminal known as the Albino finds sanctuary on planet Secarus IV, hiding from Klingon warriors Kang, Kor, and Koloth, and Federation official Curzon Dax. Years ago, the Albino had murdered the firstborn child of each of the three warriors, and they, along with Dax, had subsequently sworn a blood oath to kill the Albino to avenge the deaths.

> *"Blood Oath" (DS9). Twenty-five years before the episode (2370).*

The Albino's sanctuary on Secarus IV

Sela is born on Romulus. She later claims to be the child of former *Enterprise*-D crew member Tasha Yar and a Romulan official.

> *"Redemption, Part II" (TNG). A year after the past events in "Yesterday's Enterprise."*

2346

Mogh suspects Ja'rod, a member of the powerful Duras family, of plotting with the Romulans against the Klingon emperor. He follows Ja'rod to the Khitomer outpost. Mogh expects the trip to Khitomer to be relatively short, so he arranges for family friend Lorgh to care for his younger son, the infant Kurn. Mogh's wife and elder son, Worf, accompany Mogh to Khitomer.

Sela

> *"Sins of the Father" (TNG). Date is conjecture, but this presumably took place between the birth of Kurn (who was "barely a year old" when Mogh left) and the Khitomer massacre. Worf's former nursemaid, Kahlest, described Mogh's suspicions to Picard.*

Kira Nerys's mother, an icon painter from the Dahkur Province on Bajor, dies of malnutrition in the Singha refugee camp.

> *"Second Skin" (DS9). Kira was three at the time of her mother's death.*

The Kazon people, living as second-class citizens on the Trabe homeworld in the Delta Quadrant, overthrow their oppressors in a bloody revolt. During the uprising, Kazon forces capture several Trabe spacecraft, which later become the Kazon fleet. The revolution is engineered by Jal Sankur, who united all the Kazon sects to fight against their common enemy. The average Trabe citizen was unaware that the Trabe government had subjected the Kazon to brutal conditions, and that they had encouraged the Kazon to fight among themselves as a means of making them easier to control. Prior to the revolt, the Trabe had been among the most culturally and technologically advanced people in the Delta Quadrant.

A Kazon

> *"Initiations" (VGR). Twenty-six years before the episode (2372), although "Alliances" (VGR) suggests that it was 30 years prior to 2372. Jal Sankur was established in "Maneuvers" (VGR). The fact that the Kazon used ships stolen from the Trabe was established in "Alliances" (VGR).*

Khitomer

Sergey Rozhenko

Prison camp in the Carraya system

Romulan forces attack the Klingon outpost at Khitomer. The attack is successful because a Romulan collaborator had given the attackers access to secret Klingon defense codes. Four thousand Klingons are killed in the massacre. Twenty years later, Worf's father, Mogh, is posthumously accused of providing the defense codes to the Romulans, but it is ultimately learned that Ja'rod, the father of council member Duras, is guilty of the crime.

Federation starship *U.S.S. Intrepid,* responding to a distress call from Khitomer, is one of the first ships on the scene to offer aid.

One of the survivors is a six-year-old Klingon child, Worf, who is rescued by *Intrepid* warp field specialist Sergey Rozhenko. Rozhenko finds the child buried under a pile of rubble and left for dead. He adopts Worf as his son to be raised on the farm world of Gault with his wife, Helena, and their biological son, Nikolai. The only other survivor, Worf's nursemaid, Kahlest, is treated on Starbase 24 and later returned to the Klingon Homeworld. The Klingon High Command, unaware that Worf's brother, Kurn, is living with a family friend, informs Rozhenko that Worf has no living relatives, and Worf remains unaware that he does have a living biological brother.

"Sins of the Father" (TNG). Twenty years prior to the episode. References to Worf's adoptive parents are from "Family" (TNG). References to Worf's having been raised on Gault and having an adoptive brother are from "Heart of Glory" (TNG), although Nikolai's name was not established until "Homeward" (TNG). Worf also mentioned that his parents were killed when he was six years old in "The Bonding" (TNG). In "Birthright, Part I" (TNG), Worf said that his father died 25 years prior to the episode (2369), which would put the Khitomer Massacre at 2344. We're assuming that the "Sins of the Father" date (2346) is correct and that Worf was rounding off in "Birthright."

Unknown to Klingon authorities, nearly a hundred Klingon warriors from a perimeter outpost near Khitomer are taken prisoner after the battle. Rather than execute all of these people as his government demands, Romulan officer Tokath establishes a secret prison camp in the Carraya system, an extraordinary humanitarian gesture toward his enemies that costs Tokath his career in the Romulan Guard. Tokath's Klingon prisoners believe themselves to have suffered a great dishonor in having been captured in battle, and thus willingly accept the fact that their families believe all of them to have died at Khitomer.

"Birthright, Parts I and II" (TNG). The Carraya camp was established several months after the Khitomer Massacre.

Captain Jean-Luc Picard becomes romantically involved with Miranda Vigo while he spends two weeks on Earth for shore leave. Miranda is a botanist. The two stay in touch for a short while afterward, but somehow never get together again.

"Bloodlines" (TNG). Twenty-four years prior to the episode (2370).

Astrophysicist Dr. Paul Stubbs begins a project to study the decay of neutronium expelled at relativistic speeds in a stellar explosion. He chooses a binary star system in the Kavis Alpha sector, desirable because of the predictability of its stellar bursts. He prepares and begins to test an instrumented probe for launch into the star, whose next predicted burst will occur in 2366.

"Evolution" (TNG). Stubbs said he'd been working on the "egg" probe for 20 years.

At the age of five, young Julian Bashir performs his first "surgery," sewing a leg back on Kukalaka, his beloved stuffed teddy bear. Julian keeps Kukalaka with him, even after he becomes an adult.

"The Quickening" (DS9). Julian said he was five when he fixed his teddy bear.

Jason Vigo is born. The boy's mother, Miranda Vigo, had been involved with Jean-Luc Picard, but years later, genetic tests would show that Picard was not the boy's father.

"Bloodlines" (TNG). Jason was 23 years old at the time of the episode (2370). Miranda evidently told Jason that his father was a Starfleet officer.

War breaks out between the Talaxians and the Haakonians in the Delta Quadrant.

"Jetrel" (VGR). Date is conjecture; Neelix said the war had lasted the "better part of a decade," and that the war had ended 15 years prior to the episode (2371).

Jason Vigo

2347

Worf at seven years of age gets into trouble at school on planet Gault for beating up several teenaged human boys.

"Family" (TNG). Age of seven mentioned by Worf's adoptive father, Sergey Rozhenko.

Ro Laren witnesses her father's brutal torture and murder at the hands of Cardassian forces.

"Ensign Ro" (TNG). Ro said she was seven at the time of this incident. Assumes Ro was born in 2340, as suggested in computer bio screens in "Conundrum" (TNG) and "The Next Phase" (TNG).

A bottle of Chateau Picard from this year's vintage is given to Jean-Luc by Robert in 2367. Captain Picard later shares this bottle with Chancellor Durken of the planet Malcor III.

"Family" (TNG). Robert Picard mentioned the date. Picard and Durken shared the drink in "First Contact" (TNG).

Cardassian forces, fearing a massive attack will be launched from planet Setlik III, launch a preemptive strike against the Federation colony there. The *Starship Rutledge*, commanded by Captain Benjamin Maxwell, responds to the attack, but is too late to prevent the massacre of nearly a hundred civilians, including Maxwell's wife and children. Miles O'Brien operates a transporter for the first time, successfully jury-rigging the unit so that he and thirteen other Starfleet personnel are able to avoid Cardassian capture. Afterwards, O'Brien is promoted to *Rutledge* tactical officer.

Rutledge crew member Raymond Boone is taken prisoner by the Cardassians, but is apparently released. It is not realized at the time that Boone had been killed in captivity, and that he had been replaced by a Cardassian agent, surgically altered to resemble Boone.

"The Wounded" (TNG). Date determined from "Realm of Fear" (TNG), in which O'Brien said he'd been operating transporters for 22 years prior to the episode (2369), and from ""Paradise" (DS9), where O'Brien said he had first operated a transporter at Setlik III. Raymond Boone's back story from "Tribunal" (DS9). Note that this is inconsistent with "Rules of Engagement" (DS9), in which O'Brien testified that he'd been in Starfleet for 22 years at that point, set in the year 2372. This would put O'Brien's entry into Starfleet at 2250. The previous data points would seem to indicate that O'Brien joined Starfleet prior to 2347.

Starfleet Command orders a change in the design of the Starfleet emblem. The new, simplified design features an elliptical background field and a slightly redrawn arrowhead.

Date is conjecture, but we saw the older, feature-film version of the emblem in use on board the Enterprise-C *in 2344 ("Yesterday's* Enterprise*" [TNG]) and the newer version on Jack Crusher's uniform in 2349 ("Family" [TNG]).*

Editors Note: Producer Ronald Moore (writer of "Family" [TNG]) tells us that Jack Crusher's wearing of the newer insignia in that episode was purely an accident. Moore happened to be visiting the set when Jack's holographic

Ro Laren

Captain Benjamin Maxwell

The Picard vineyards

Miles Edward O'Brien

The former Beverely Howard

Picard's family home in
Labarre, France

Wesley Crusher

Jack Crusher

message to Wesley was being filmed, and noticed that Jack was not wearing a Starfleet emblem on his uniform. When he pointed this out to our costumers, the only badge they could find was the Next Generation version, so that's the one they used.

2348

Starfleet officer Jack Crusher marries medical student Beverly Howard. Jack proposes to Beverly with a joke by giving her a book entitled *How to Advance Your Career Through Marriage*. Jack and Beverly had been introduced by Walker Keel, a close friend of Jean-Luc Picard and Jack Crusher. Picard had been strongly attracted to Beverly, but suppressed his feelings after she married his friend, Jack.

"Family" (TNG). Date is conjecture, a year before their son Wesley's birth. Walker Keel established in "Conspiracy" (TNG). Beverly learned of Picard's love for her in "Attached" (TNG).

The Caldos colony's weather control system experiences a problem that is dealt with by the colony's engineers. This is the last problem that the system would have for the next 22 years.

"Sub Rosa" (TNG). Twenty-two years prior to the episode (2370).

Marouk, the sovereign of planet Acamar III, makes an effort to reconcile her differences with her people's Gatherers. The nomadic Gatherers refuse to accept the peace that has existed on the planet for 82 years.

"The Vengeance Factor" (TNG). Marouk said the last attempt to make peace with the Gatherers was 18 years prior to the episode.

Jean-Luc Picard visits his family in his hometown of Labarre, France. It is his last trip home prior to his convalescence after the Borg encounter of 2367.

"Family" (TNG). Picard hadn't been home in almost twenty years.

2349

Wesley Crusher is born to Jack and Beverly Crusher. When Wesley is ten weeks old, Jack records a holographic message that he hopes Wesley will play when he reaches his 18th birthday. Although the elder Crusher hopes to record a series of messages to his son, this is the only one he will make.

"Evolution" (TNG). Beverly noted Wesley was 17 during that episode (2366). Jack's holographic message was seen in "Family" (TNG).

Tuvok returns to Starfleet after an absence of over five decades. Although in his youth he had found it difficult to accept Starfleet's multicultural environment, the experience of having raised a family has helped him realize that there are still many things he can learn from other species. His first assignment is aboard the *Starship Wyoming*.

"Flashback" (VGR). Tuvok resigned from Starfleet in 2298, and decided to return over 50 years later.

Dr. Paul Manheim's time-gravity work begins to gain acceptance in the Federation scientific community.

"We'll Always Have Paris" (TNG). Fifteen years prior to episode (2364).

Harry Kim is born.

"Eye of the Needle" (VGR). According to Paris, Harry was two years old in 2351.

Ensign Stefan DeSeve, a Starfleet officer, renounces his Federation citizenship to live on Romulus.

"Face of the Enemy" (TNG). Twenty years prior to the episode (2369).

Kobliad security officer Ty Kajada begins tracking Rao Vantika, who is accused of causing the death of others to keep himself alive.

"The Passenger" (DS9). Kajada said he'd been tracking Vantika for 20 years prior to the episode (2369).

Former *Enterprise*-D security officer Tasha Yar is reportedly executed following an attempted escape from Romulus with her daughter, Sela. The attempt fails when the child cries out for fear of being taken from her home.

"Redemption, Part II" (TNG). Sela told Picard that she was four years old at the time her mother was killed.

Tasha Yar

Curzon Dax and Benjamin Sisko meet for the first time. Curzon takes young Ben Sisko under his wing and teaches him to appreciate life, guiding his education and values.

"Dax" (DS9). Dax said they'd known each other for 20 years prior to the episode.

2350

Beverly Crusher graduates with a medical degree from Starfleet Academy.

"Conundrum" (TNG). Year given in computer screen bio. Assumes that a medical degree is an eight-year program.

Benjamin Sisko enters Starfleet Academy.

"Emissary" (DS9). Four years prior to his graduation in 2354. In "Defiant" (DS9), Sisko said he had been with Starfleet for 20 years prior to that episode (2371), which would put Sisko's entry into the academy in 2351.

Benjamin Sisko

Chakotay, a young man living at a Federation settlement near the Cardassian border, applies for acceptance to the Starfleet Academy. Chakotay's application is sponsored by Captain Sulu, a Starfleet officer patrolling the Cardassian border.

"Tattoo" (VGR). Date is conjecture, but is presumably before Chakotay's trip with his father to Earth. It is not clear if "Captain Sulu" refers to Hikaru Sulu, although this seems to be the implication. (This Captain Sulu is clearly not Demora Sulu, since Chakotay referred to Sulu as "him.") Chakotay's tribe is apparently not the same as the group that settled planet Dorvan V in "Journey's End" (TNG), since Dorvan V was established to have been settled in 2350, while Chakotay, in "Tattoo" (VGR), notes that his tribe had inhabited their home colony for "a few hundred years."

Chakotay

The Romulan science vessel *Talvath* departs Romulus on a mission to sector 1385. The ship is commanded by Telek R'Mor of the Romulan Astrophysical Academy.

"Eye of the Needle" (VGR). About a year before the Talvath *made contact across time with the Voyager (2351).*

Kolopak, father of Chakotay, embarks on an expedition to seek his ancestral roots in the Central American region of planet Earth. Kolopak takes his son with him on his expedition, in hopes that young Chakotay will gain a respect for their ancient Native American culture and traditions. During the trip, Kolopak is deeply disappointed when his son informs him of his decision to leave their tribe and to instead join the Federation Starfleet.

Romulan scientist
Telek R'Mor

Settlement on Dorvan V

Marta

Dekon Elig

Terok Nor

"Tattoo" (VGR). Date is conjecture. If Chakotay was the same age as actor Robert Beltran, Chakotay would have been about 37 years old at the time of "Tattoo," which was set in the year 2372. This would suggest a birth year of 2335. Chakotay was 15 at the time of Kolopak's expedition, suggesting a date of 2350.

A Federation citizen named William Samuels settles at the colony on Volan II, near the Cardassian border. He becomes a farmer and raises two daughters with his wife, Louise.

"The Maquis, Part I" (DS9). Twenty years prior to the episode (2370).

Kyle Riker leaves his son, William, at age 15. Will's mother had died some years earlier. The younger Riker bitterly resents being "abandoned," and the two do not speak again until 2365.

"Icarus Factor" (TNG). Fifteen years prior to episode (2365).

A group of Native American humans settles on planet Dorvan V, near the Cardassian border. These humans had originally left Earth in the 22nd century in an attempt to preserve their cultural identity. Federation authorities warn the settlers that ownership of the planet is disputed by the Cardassians, but the colonists have searched for over a century for a new home, and have finally found one on Dorvan V.

"Journey's End" (TNG). Twenty years prior to the episode (2370).

A daughter is born to Romulan officer Telek.

"Eye of the Needle" (VGR). Seven months before the Talvath *made contact with the* Voyager *(2351).*

2351

Marta is born on the planet Bajor. Her parents are later killed by the Cardassians, and she is raised by neighbors. Mardah has a brother and a sister, Sarjeno and Koran.

"The Abandoned" (DS9). Mardah was 20 years old at the time of the episode (2371).

Amanda Rogers is born to two members of the Q Continuum, living in human form on planet Earth. When the Continuum becomes displeased with their decision to live among mortals, the Continuum causes a tornado to destroy their home in Topeka, Kansas, killing both parents. Amanda is subsequently raised by foster parents, unaware of her heritage as a Q.

"True-Q" (TNG). She was 18 years old at the time of the episode (2369).

Young Julian Bashir, aged ten, is trapped along with his father in a remote region of planet Ivernia II by a severe ionic storm. Also trapped by the storm is a young Ivernian girl who suffers from a deadly illness. The storm makes it impossible to send for medical help, and the girl dies. Later, Julian learns that a common Ivernian herb could have saved her. The incident inspires Julian to aspire to the medical profession.

"Melora" (DS9). Bashir said he was ten years old at the time.

The Cardassian military constructs a mining station, designated Terok Nor, in orbit of the planet Bajor. Unknown to the Cardassians, the Bajoran underground smuggles a small booby trap, an aphasia device, aboard the station. The aphasia device had been developed by brilliant geneticist Dekon Elig.

"Babel" (DS9). Eighteen years prior to the episode (2369). The name Terok Nor, first mentioned in "Cardassians" (DS9) is the Cardassian name for what later became Deep Space 9.

The Romulan science vessel *Talvath*, investigating a microscopic wormhole, makes contact with the Federation starship *Voyager*, some 70,000 light-years distant and 20 years in the future. *Talvath* commander Telek R'Mor briefly transports through the wormhole to the *Voyager*. He returns with a computer chip containing messages intended to be delivered in 20 years to the families of the *Voyager* crew.

"Eye of the Needle" (VGR). Twenty years before the episode (2371).

Sergey and Helen Rozhenko

Sergey and Helena Rozhenko, along with their adopted son, Worf, and their biological son, Nikolai, move from the farm world of Gault to Earth.

Date is conjecture. The fact of the move is based on Worf's line in "Heart of Glory" (TNG) that he spent his formative years on Gault, but in "Family" (TNG) Guinan indicated that Worf looked toward his adoptive parents on Earth as his home. Worf spoke of a foster brother in "Heart of Glory" (TNG), who was named Nikolai in "Homeward" (TNG).

Quark reaches his Age of Ascension and leaves his homeworld of Ferenginar, to seek fortune on his own. His brother, Rom, remains home for ten more years.

"Family Business" (DS9). Twenty years before the episode (2371). He didn't return home for a visit until 2371.

Two Bajoran nationals, Baltrim and Keena, escape from Cardassian imprisonment. They flee to the Bajoran moon, Jeraddo, where they start a new life on a farm owned by Mullibok. Baltrim and Keena had been the victims of Cardassian torture and were made unable to speak.

"Progress" (DS9). They escaped 18 years prior to the episode (2369).

2352

A new era of peace begins between the Klingon Empire and the United Federation of Planets.

"Way of the Warrior" (DS9). Two decades before the episode (2372). One might speculate that this was an result of the Narendra III incident in 2344 and the Khitomer incident of 2346, and presumably a further evolution of the Khitomer accords of 2393.

Varria

Fifteen-year-old Natasha Yar escapes from the failed colony at Turkana IV. Her younger sister, Ishara, who has joined one of the gangs on the planet, declines to leave with her. Tasha eventually joins Starfleet and becomes *Enterprise*-D security chief. Shortly after Tasha's departure, the colony breaks off contact with the United Federation of Planets.

"Legacy" (TNG). Ishara Yar said her sister left the colony 15 years prior to the episode (2367). Her age at the time of her escape was established to be 15 in "The Naked Now" (TNG).

Varria, an idealistic young woman, begins a 14-year association with unscrupulous collector Kivas Fajo, a Zibalian trader of the Stacius Trade Guild. They remain together until 2366, when she is killed by Fajo after she attempts to help Data escape from Fajo's captivity.

"The Most Toys" (TNG). Varria told Data she'd been with Fajo for 14 years.

Joseph Sisko's physician moves to New Orleans on planet Earth.

"Homefront" (DS9). Twenty years before the episode (2372).

Dr. Dalen Quaice

Beverly Crusher serves a residency on planet Delos IV under Dr. Dalen Quaice.

"Remember Me" (TNG). Beverly told Data she'd known Quaice for 15 years prior to the episode (2367).

Tora Ziyal

Editors' Note: This would appear to be inconsistent with the date of 2350 established in "Conundrum" (TNG) for Beverly's graduation from Starfleet medical school. Maybe she had really known Quaice 17 years, and she was just rounding it off?

Scientists at the Darwin research station on planet Gagarin IV conduct an ambitious genetic experiment designed to give their children extraordinarily powerful immune systems.

"Unnatural Selection" (TNG). The oldest of the superchildren was twelve at the time of the episode (2365). This is a year prior to that point.

2353

Starfleet civilian adviser Kyle Riker is the sole survivor of a Tholian attack on a starbase. Afterward, Riker recovers under the care of future *Enterprise*-D chief medical officer Katherine Pulaski. The two become romantically involved, and Pulaski later says she would have married him "in a cold minute," but Riker had other priorities in his life. Pulaski would also later theorize that the emotional scars from the Tholian attack were the reason Kyle never remarried.

"Icarus Factor" (TNG). Twelve years prior to episode (2365).

Tora Ziyal is born. She is the daughter of a Bajoran woman named Tora Naprem and Gul Dukat, a Cardassian military official. Such liaisons are not unknown, but the offspring are generally ostracized in both Bajoran and Cardassian society.

"Indiscretion" (DS9). Ziyal was 13 years old at the time of the crash of the Cardassian freighter Ravinok (2366).

Jeremiah Rossa is born to Connor and Moira Rossa at the Federation colony on Galen IV. He is the grandson of Starfleet admiral Connaught Rossa. His parents are later killed in a Talarian attack on the colony, and he is adopted by the Talarian captain Endar, who claims the right to raise Jeremiah as his own son, naming him Jono.

"Suddenly Human" (TNG). Data noted Jeremiah/Jono was 14 years old at the time of the episode (2367).

William Riker

Solar flares cause dramatic weather shifts on a Class-M planet in the Delta Quadrant, resulting in a sudden ice age. A few of the planet's technologically sophisticated inhabitants survive by placing themselves in a state of artificial hibernation. The system is designed to revive them in 15 years, when the ice age is predicted to end.

"The Thaw" (VGR). The flares occurred 19 years prior to the episode (2372).

William Riker enters Starfleet Academy. One of his friends is fellow student Paul Rice, who would eventually command the *U.S.S. Drake*, although Riker would later recall that he felt at odds with everyone during his first year. The superintendent of the Academy is a native of the planet Vulcan.

"Chain of Command, Part I" (TNG). Jellico said Riker had graduated with the "class of 'fifty-seven.'" This date is four years prior. Paul Rice established in "The Arsenal of Freedom" (TNG). Riker's feelings about his first year were mentioned in "Frame of Mind" (TNG). Riker mentioned the superintendent in "The First Duty" (TNG).

Geordi La Forge enters Starfleet Academy at age 18. His major field of study is engineering. One of his classmates is Donald Kaplan, who later serves aboard the *U.S.S. Intrepid*.

"Cause and Effect" (TNG). Year given in computer bio screen. Donald Kaplan established in "Force of Nature" (TNG).

La Forge

2354

Jeremy Aster is born to Marla Aster. Jeremy's mother later becomes a crew member aboard the *Enterprise*-D and is killed in 2366 on an archaeological research mission when an ancient artifact explodes. *Enterprise*-D security officer Worf adopts the orphaned boy into his family through the Klingon *R'uustai* ceremony.

"The Bonding" (TNG). Jeremy's age is given as 12 in the episode (2366).

Jeremy Aster

Benjamin Sisko graduates from Starfleet Academy. Also graduating is Sisko's close friend, Calvin Hudson. While awaiting his first posting, Sisko meets his future wife, Jennifer, at Gilgo Beach on Earth.

"Emissary" (DS9). About 15 years prior to the episode (2369), since Sisko recalled that he had asked Jennifer to marry him "almost 15 years ago." Hudson's graduation established in "The Maquis, Part II" (DS9).

Jennifer Sisko

Lieutenant Jack Crusher dies on a *U.S.S. Stargazer* away-team mission under the command of Captain Picard. Wesley Crusher is present when Picard brings the elder Crusher's body back to his family at a starbase. Picard accompanies Beverly as she views the body. Although Picard had been in love with Beverly before she married Jack, he makes a conscious decision not to pursue a relationship with her now, because he feels guilt about his attraction to his best friend's widow.

"True Q" (TNG). Beverly said that Jack died when Wesley was five years old. "Violations" (TNG) shows Beverly's memory of Picard and her viewing Jack's body. Beverly learned of Picard's feelings for her in "Attached" (TNG).

Beverly Crusher and Jean-Luc Picard after her husband's death

Captain Picard, aboard *U.S.S. Stargazer*, visits planet Chalna. The inhabitants call themselves the Chalnoth. Years later Picard encounters Esoqq, a native of that planet, while both are held captive by unknown aliens conducting a behavioral study.

"Allegiance" (TNG). Picard said he visited Esoqq's planet 12 years prior to the episode (2366), while commanding the Stargazer. It is unclear whether this occurred before or after Jack Crusher's death.

Dr. T'Pan, noted specialist in the field of subspace morphology, is appointed director of the Vulcan Science Academy. Her husband, Dr. Christopher, is a noted subspace theoretician.

"Suspicions" (TNG). Fifteen years prior to the episode.

Dr. T'Pan

2355

U.S.S. Stargazer, under the command of Captain Picard, is nearly destroyed in a conflict in the Maxia Zeta star system by an unknown adversary, eventually learned to be a Ferengi spacecraft. Picard would later recall that an unidentified ship suddenly appeared and fired twice on the *Stargazer* at point-blank range, disabling the *Stargazer*'s shields. Picard saves his crew by employing what is later termed the "Picard maneuver." The ship is abandoned, and the crew drifts in lifeboats and shuttlecraft for ten weeks before being rescued. It is later learned that the son of Ferengi DaiMon Bok was the commander of the attacking Ferengi vessel and was killed in what the Ferengi call "The Battle of Maxia."

"The Battle" (TNG). Nine years prior to episode (2364).

Captain Picard is routinely court-martialed for the loss of *U.S.S. Stargazer* by Starfleet prosecutor Phillipa Louvois.

"The Measure of a Man" (TNG). Ten years prior to episode (2365). The fact that Picard continued to serve in Starfleet suggests that the court-martial did not result in a conviction.

Phillipa Louvois

Shakaar Edon

Kira Nerys joins the Bajoran underground, fighting the Cardassians for the liberation of her homeworld. Her resistance cell is led by freedom fighter Shakaar Edon.

"The Circle" (DS9). Odo noted that she'd been breaking the rules for fourteen and a half years prior to the episode (2370). Shakaar established in "Shakaar" (DS9). Shakaar's first name established in "Crossfire" (DS9).

Jake Sisko is born to Benjamin and Jennifer Sisko.

"Move Along Home" (DS9). Jake said he was 14 years old in 2369.

Worf, aged 15, reaches the second Age of Ascension. This ceremony is an important step in the coming of age of a Klingon warrior.

"The Icarus Factor" (TNG). In the episode (set in 2365) Worf celebrates the tenth anniversary of his Age of Ascension ceremony.

2356

Jake Sisko

A Tarellian spacecraft, believed to carry the last survivors of the planet Tarella, is destroyed by the Alcyones. The Tarellians had tried to escape their war-devastated home, but had been hunted because they were carriers of deadly biological warfare agents. Eight years later, one more Tarellian ship is discovered, attempting to make planetfall at Haven.

"Haven" (TNG). The last Tarellian ship was destroyed eight years prior to episode (2364).

The war between the Talaxians and the Haakonians is ended when the Haakonians conquer the Talaxian homeworld. The decisive end to the decade-long war comes when a weapon of mass destruction called the metreon cascade is used against Rinax, a moon in the Talaxian system. Some 300,000 Talaxians are killed in the attack. Among the casualties is Neelix's entire family on Rinax. Neelix himself escaped death because he was on the surface of Talax. In subsequent years, many survivors suffer a fatal degenerative blood disease called metremia, caused by exposure to metreon isotopes.

"Jetrel" (VGR). Fifteen years before the episode (2371).

Ma'Bor Jetrel

In the aftermath of the metreon cascade attack on Rinax, Haakonian scientist Ma'Bor Jetrel feels terrible remorse at the death wrought by his work. In an effort to assuage his conscience, Jetrel begins developing a process he calls regenerative fusion that could theoretically restore some of the people of Rinax who were disintegrated by the metreon cascade. It is a difficult project, and one that wins little support from the Haakonian government, which is anxious to put the war behind it.

"Jetrel" (VGR). After the metreon cascade attack.

2357

William Riker graduates from Starfleet Academy. He is eighth in his class. His classmates include future *Drake* captain Paul Rice. Riker's first assignment is as helmsman aboard the *U.S.S. Pegasus* under the command of Captain Erik Pressman. One of his subsequent assignments is as a lieutenant aboard the *U.S.S. Potemkin.*

"Chain of Command, Part I" (TNG). Riker's stint aboard the Pegasus *was established in "The* Pegasus*" (TNG). His* Potemkin *assignment was established in "Peak Performance" (TNG). Riker was transferred from the* Hood *to the* Enterprise-D *in "Encounter at Farpoint" (TNG). Paul Rice established in "The Arsenal of Freedom" (TNG).*

Geordi La Forge graduates from Starfleet Academy with a major in engineering. One of his early assignments is aboard the *Starship Victory*.

> *"Conundrum" (TNG). Year was given in computer bio screen. His major is established in "The Child" (TNG) to have been engineering. Geordi's Victory assignment was established in "Elementary, Dear Data" (TNG) and "Identity Crisis" (TNG).*

La Forge

Worf enters Starfleet Academy. He is the first Klingon to serve in the Federation Starfleet. Worf's stepbrother, Nikolai Rozhenko, also enters the Academy.

> *"Heart of Glory" (TNG). Worf described his family history to Korris, noting he was the only Klingon in Starfleet at the time of the episode (2364). Date of Worf's Academy entrance from computer bio screen in "Conundrum" (TNG). Nikolai was first established in "Heart of Glory" (TNG), although he didn't get a first name until "Homeward" (TNG).*

Freighter *S.S. Odin* is disabled by an asteroid collision. Some survivors escape on lifeboats, drifting for five months before ultimately ending up on planet Angel One.

> *"Angel One" (TNG). Seven years prior to episode (2364).*

Worf

Ornaran captain T'Jon assumes command of the freighter spacecraft *Sanction*. He makes the critically important medical cargo run between the planets Ornara and Brekka some 27 times over the next seven years until the *Sanction* suffers a serious malfunction in 2364.

> *"Symbiosis" (TNG). T'Jon said he'd been in command for seven years prior to the episode (2364).*

Federation outpost at Galen IV is attacked by Talarian forces as part of an ongoing border conflict. Most of the population of the outpost is killed. Among the casualties are Connor and Moira Rossa, whose son, Jeremiah, is rescued by Talarian captain Endar. Jeremiah had been the sole survivor.

> *"Suddenly Human" (TNG). Data said the outpost was wiped out ten years and three months prior to the episode (2367). The episode also referred to a peace agreement with the Talarians, apparently reached sometime during the ten-year span between this point and the episode.*

The Shakaar resistance group is successful in liberating the notorious Gallitep labor camp, site of numerous atrocities committed against Bajorans imprisoned there. The camp had been commanded by Gul Darhe'el, known as the "Butcher of Gallitep." One member of Darhe'el's staff is a file clerk named Aamin Marritza, who had felt great remorse about his inability to prevent the atrocities. Among those freed is the brother of Bajoran militia officer Lenaris Holem. Among Shakaar's freedom fighters is young Kira Nerys.

Gul Darhe'el

> *"Duet" (DS9). Kira said it was 12 years prior to the episode (2369). Kira was about 12 years old at the time of the liberation. "Shakaar" (DS9) suggests that the resistance group was named for Bajoran resistance leader Shakaar Edon, and also established that Lenaris's brother was at Gallitep.*

Vash, an archaeologist, visits Earth before setting out to seek her fortune.

> *"Q-Less" (DS9). Vash said she hadn't been back to Earth in 12 years prior to the episode (2369).*

2358

Major system work progresses on the *Galaxy*-class *Starship Enterprise*-D, under construction at Starfleet's Utopia Planitia Fleet Yards in orbit around planet Mars. The project is under the overall supervision of Commander Quinteros. Significant contributions to the design of the warp propulsion system are

Dr. Leah Brahms

Nikolai Rozhenko

made by Dr. Leah Brahms, a junior member of engineering team 7 and a graduate of the Daystrom Institute. The dilithium crystal chamber is designed at Outpost Seran-T-One.

Date is conjecture, but Quinteros was established in "11001001" (TNG), and Brahms was seen in "Booby Trap" (TNG) and "Galaxy's Child" (TNG). Outpost Seran-T-One mentioned in "Booby Trap" (TNG).

Nikolai Rozhenko, after one year at Starfleet Academy, finds it difficult to conform to the school's rules and returns to his former home on planet Gault. Nikolai is the stepbrother of Worf, who continues his studies at the academy. Nikolai later earns a doctorate elsewhere.

"Homeward" (TNG). A year after Nikolai's and Worf's entry into the academy. The fact that Worf's adoptive brother returned to Gault established in "Heart of Glory" (TNG).

A son is born to Pa'Dar, exarch of Tozaht, a Cardassian settlement on Bajor.

"Cardassians" (DS9). Twelve years prior to the episode.

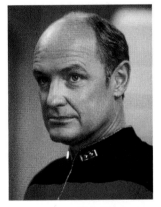

Erik Pressman

The experimental *Starship Pegasus* explodes near the Devolin system, killing nearly everyone on board. *Pegasus* captain Erik Pressman manages to escape, along with his helm officer, Ensign William T. Riker, and seven others, who report the crew had mutinied. There are no other survivors of the tragedy. It is not revealed that the *Pegasus* had been engaged in a top-secret research mission in violation of the Treaty of Algeron at the time of the mutiny.

"The Pegasus" (TNG). Seven months after Riker's graduation from Starfleet Academy (2357).

A civil war breaks out among the inhabitants of the Parada system in the Gamma Quadrant.

"Whispers" (DS9). Twelve years prior to the episode (2370).

Miranda Vigo and her son Jason leave Earth and settle on planet Camor V. Miranda, who had dreamed of running a farm someday, moved to Camor V to help care for the orphans left behind from the Cardassian war. She eventually cares for at least 40 Camorite orphans, feeding them with vegetables she grew in her garden.

"Bloodlines" (TNG). Twelve years prior to the episode (2370).

2359

A Starfleet Judge Advocate General's report on the *Pegasus* incident concludes that a mutiny did in fact take place aboard the *Pegasus* just prior to its destruction. The report also concludes that the surviving *Pegasus* crew had withheld information from the inquiry and recommends further investigation. No such follow-up is made, however.

"The Pegasus" (TNG). After the destruction of the U.S.S. Pegasus.

Starfleet officer William T. Riker, formerly of the *U.S.S. Pegasus*, is assigned to a new posting on planet Betazed.

Conjecture. This is after the Pegasus incident established in "The Pegasus" (TNG), but before Riker left Betazed for his Potemkin assignment in 2361, established in "Second Chances" (TNG). It is, of course, possible that Riker had another assignment between the Pegasus and Betazed.

Julian Bashir enters Starfleet medical school.

Conjecture. Assumes he enters medical school at age 18.

Riker and Troi

Worf and K'Ehleyr have an unresolved romantic relationship.

"The Emissary" (TNG). Six years prior to the episode (2365).

Professor Richard Galen, one of the century's most noted archaeologists, makes a discovery in micropaleontology so profound that he devotes the rest of his life to gathering evidence to support his theory.

"The Chase" (TNG). Picard noted Galen had all but disappeared during the decade before the episode (2369).

K'Ehleyr

A bitter civil war on planet Mordan IV is concluded. The conflict had lasted for 40 years and had been exacerbated by the improper intervention of Starfleet officer Mark Jameson in local affairs in 2319.

"Too Short a Season" (TNG). Data noted that Mordan IV had peace for five years prior to the episode (2364).

2360

Surmak Ren joins the Bajoran underground to fight against the Cardassian occupation of their homeworld.

"Babel" (DS9). Six months prior to Surmak's capture with Dekon Elig.

The Federation personnel transport ship *Santa Maria*, en route to deliver colonists to planet Gemulon V, develops serious life-support problems and is forced to land on a planet in the Orellius Minor system. No one aboard suspects that colony leader Alixus has engineered the crash as part of her plan to create a new society according to her technophobic philosophies.

Bajoran raider aircraft

"Paradise" (DS9). The crash was more than ten years prior to the episode (2370).

A Bajoran resistance stronghold at Lunar V is hit by Cardassian forces. Just before the attack, the resistance fighters are successful in hiding a few sub-impulse raider aircraft underground, where they escape damage.

"The Siege" (DS9). Ten years before the episode, but before the apparent death of Li Nalas, since he was there.

Caylem's wife, a member of the Alsaurian resistance movement, is killed while fighting the oppressive Mokra Order government forces on her homeworld.

Li Nalas

"Resistance" (VGR). Twelve years before the episode (2372).

Bajoran resistance leader Li Nalas is believed killed.

"The Homecoming" (DS9). Ten years before the episode.

Scientist Dekon Elig and his medical assistant, Dr. Surmak Ren, are captured by the Cardassian military and sent to the Velos VII internment camp. Both Dekon and Surmak had been active in the Higa Mentar sect of the Bajoran underground.

"Babel" (DS9). Nine years prior to the episode (2369).

Colyus begins service as the Protector at Rurigan's village on planet Yadera II in the Gamma Quadrant. Also in the village, a girl named Taya is born. Colyus, Taya, and all the inhabitants of the village (except Rurigan) do not realize that they are sentient holograms originally programmed by Rurigan.

Surmek Ren

"Shadowplay" (DS9). Ten years before the episode.

Sirah

Hovath, apprentice to the leader of a small Bajoran village, begins to learn the secrets of the leader, and his role as ceremonial storyteller for his people. The most closely held secret is the fact that the leader, known as the Sirah, uses a tiny stone, a fragment of an orb from the Bajoran celestial temple, to create the illusion of a powerful enemy. The Sirah uses this enemy to unite the people of the village, and it is this unity that holds the village together.

"The Storyteller" (DS9). Nine years prior to the episode (2369).

2361

Kevin and Rishon Uxbridge arrive at the Delta Rana IV colony. Rishon does not suspect that her husband, Kevin, is in reality an immensely powerful member of a civilization called the Douwd, traveling in disguise as a human. The colony is later destroyed and all the colonists (except for Kevin) are killed in a Husnok attack. Among the casualties is Kevin's wife, Rishon. Reacting in anger and grief, Kevin responds by using his extraordinary powers to destroy the entire Husnok race.

"The Survivors" (TNG). Five years prior to episode (2366).

Vash

Bajoran merchant Roana and her husband open a shop on the Promenade of station Terok Nor. They'd had a shop on Bajor for the past seventeen years.

"Rivals" (DS9). Nine years prior to the episode (2370).

Worf graduates from Starfleet Academy.

"Conundrum" (TNG). This is four years after his entry into the Academy in 2357.

Archaeologist Vash begins working as an assistant to Professor Samuel Estragon, who has spent much of his career searching for a device called the *Tox Uthat,* an artifact from the 27th century, sent back in time for safekeeping. Estragon never finds the *Uthat,* although Vash uses his notes after his death to locate the device on planet Risa.

"Captain's Holiday" (TNG). Vash said she had worked for Estragon for the past five years, and she implied he had died shortly before the episode (2366).

Starship *Potemkin* makes last Federation contact with the failed colony on planet Turkana IV prior to *U.S.S. Enterprise*-D visit in 2367. *Potemkin* personnel are warned that anyone transporting to the colony will be killed. Turkana IV is the birthplace of future *Enterprise*-D security chief Tasha Yar.

"Legacy" (TNG). Data described the history of the colony. (See Editors' Note regarding the relationship of the Potemkin *in "Legacy" and another ship of the same name in "Turnabout Intruder" [TOS].)*

Lidell Ren

Editors' Note: Although "Second Chances" (TNG) establishes that William Riker was a crew member on the Potemkin *in 2361, it seems likely that the Turkana IV incident took place prior to his joining the crew, since Riker seemed unfamiliar with that planet during "Legacy" (TNG).*

Tolen and Lidell Ren are married on the Banean homeworld in the Delta Quadrant.

"Ex Post Facto" (VGR). About ten years prior to the episode (2371).

Jeremy Aster's father dies of a Rushton infection. Jeremy's mother, Marla Aster, raises Jeremy alone. They take up residence on the *U.S.S. Enterprise*-D when Marla Aster becomes a staff archaeologist on the ship.

Tolen Ren

"The Bonding" (TNG). Jeremy's father died five years prior to the episode (2366).

Lieutenant William Riker, assigned to a Starfleet facility on planet Betazed, accepts a posting to the *Starship Potemkin*. The day before he leaves for the *Potemkin*, Riker spends time with his *imzadi*, Deanna Troi, at Janaran Falls on Betazed. The two agree to meet six weeks later on Risa.

> *"Second Chances" (TNG). Less than six weeks prior to the Nervala IV incident, since the Risa date was after the Nervala rescue mission.*

Starship Potemkin at Nervala IV to assist in evacuation of scientists from a research station on the planet's surface when a dangerous energy distortion field covers the planet. Lieutenant William Riker, a member of the *Potemkin* crew, is the last person to beam up from the station. It is not realized at the time that a malfunction in the *Potemkin*'s transporter, caused by the distortion field, causes an exact duplicate of Riker to be materialized at the Nervala station. Unaware of the duplicate Riker, the *Potemkin* departs Nervala IV, and the duplicate is forced to live incommunicado at the station for years. William Riker is awarded a promotion for "exceptional valor" during the Nervala IV rescue mission.

> *"Second Chances" (TNG). Eight years prior to the episode (2369).*

Rom leaves his homeworld of Ferenginar to seek his fortune.

> *"Family Business" (DS9). Ten years after Quark left home (2361).*

Lieutenant Commander William Riker breaks his date with Deanna Troi to meet on Risa because of the career opportunities presented by his recent promotion. The incident marks the end of their romantic relationship.

> *"Second Chances" (TNG). Six weeks after Riker left Betazed.*

2362

Klingon forces conduct a raid against Federation territory. Despite the treaties and accords between the two powers, the incident illustrates the fragility of the peace.

> *"Aquiel" (TNG). Beverly said that there hadn't been a Klingon raid in more than seven years prior to 2369.*

Dr. Dalen Quaice begins a tour of duty at Starbase 133. He remains at that posting until the death of his wife, Patricia, in 2367. Quaice had been a mentor to *Enterprise*-D chief medical officer Beverly Crusher during her medical residency.

> *"Remember Me" (TNG). Beverly told Picard that Quaice had been stationed there for six years prior to the episode (2368).*

Dekon Elig is killed while trying to escape from the Velos VII internment camp, where he was being held by the Cardassians for acts committed while he was a member of the Higa Metar sect of the Bajoran underground. His certificate of death is filed by Dr. Surmak Ren.

> *"Babel" (DS9). According to the station computer, Dekon was killed on stardate 39355, which would be about two years prior to the first season of* Star Trek: The Next Generation.

Quark loans latinum to his cousin Gaila to start a munitions consortium. Gaila promises that if he becomes a success, he'll repay Quark by buying him his own ship. Gaila eventually becomes so successful that he buys his own moon, on which he lives.

> *"Little Green Men" (DS9). Ten years prior to the episode (2372). Gaila's ownership of a moon established in "Civil Defense" (DS9).*

Dr. Beverly Crusher decides to undergo the Starfleet training course to qualify her for advancement to the rank of commander, despite the fact that this is not required for her to serve as chief medical officer aboard a starship.

> *"Thine Own Self" (TNG). Eight years prior to the episode (2370).*

Betazed

Starship Potemkin

William Riker

Rugal

U.S.S. Victory

Fallit Kot

Raymond Boone

A Bajoran terrorist attack against a Cardassian settlement at the Tohat Province on Bajor results in the death of a Cardassian woman, the wife of Kotan Pa'Dar (the settlement's exarch) and the destruction of their home. Pa'Dar's 4-year-old son, Rugal, is also believed killed. Pa'Dar does not realize that Rugal has been placed at an orphanage by Gul Dukat, in hopes of someday using the incident to humiliate Pa'Dar politically. Rugal is subsequently adopted by a Bajoran couple, who raise him as their own. Gul Dukat, a political enemy of Pa'Dar, is commander of station Terok Nor.

"Cardassians" (DS9). Eight years prior to the episode (2370).

Ensign Geordi La Forge serves aboard the *U.S.S. Victory* under the command of Captain Zimbata. On stardate 40164.7 he and fellow *Victory* crew member Susanna Leijten are part of an away team investigating the disappearance of 49 persons at the colony on planet Tarchannen III. Five years later all members of this away team are mysteriously compelled to return to the same planet.

"Elementary, Dear Data" (TNG). Geordi mentioned serving on that ship prior to his Enterprise-D duty. In "Identity Crisis" (TNG), Susanna described the incident at Tarchannen III as having taken place five years prior to the episode (2367) while they were both aboard the Victory.

Ferengi entrepreneur Quark, indicted in the hijacking of a shipment of Romulan ale, escapes imprisonment when he assists Romulan authorities to apprehend Fallit Kot, Quark's partner in the deal. Kot is subsequently sentenced to eight years in a Romulan labor camp.

"Melora" (DS9). Eight years prior to the episode.

A fire storm sweeps the surface of planet Bersallis III. These fire storms, which occur every seven years, are caused when solar flare radiation reacts with high energy plasma in the planet's atmosphere.

Seven years prior to "Lessons" (TNG).

Miranda Vigo dies.

"Bloodlines" (TNG). Jason was 15 years old at the time, although it is conjecture that Miranda died. Jason only said that he was "on my own since I was fifteen." We believe Miranda was dead at the time of the episode, else Picard would have tried to contact her.

The individual believed to be former *Starship Rutledge* crew member Raymond Boone takes up residence at the Volan III colony, where he runs a ladarium mining sluice. This person, actually a Cardassian agent, physically resembles the real Boone, but his family has noticed unusual behavioral changes since Boone's return from Cardassian capture during the Setlik III massacre.

"Tribunal" (DS9). Eight years prior to the episode (2370).

2363

Starfleet officer George Primmin is assigned to Security.

"Move Along Home" (DS9). Primmin said he'd been a security officer for six years prior to the episode (2369).

Federation starship *Tsiolkovsky* begins its last science mission. It is ultimately destroyed after its crew is killed by a variant of the Psi 2000 virus.

"The Naked Now" (TNG). Eight months prior to episode.

Cardassian official Gul Dukat meets Odo, a shape-shifter of unknown origin, at a reception at the Bajoran Center for Science. Dukat is impressed with Odo's potential to serve as a security investigator.

"Necessary Evil" (DS9). Seven years prior to the episode. Odo was apparently still living on Bajor at this point.

Cardassian information service correspondent Natima Lang, on assignment to station Terok Nor, falls in love with Quark, an entrepreneur on that station. Lang, whose political views are somewhat radical, is impressed that Quark is selling food to Bajorans in defiance of Cardassian rule.

"Profit and Loss" (DS9). A month before Natima's departure from the station.

Quark installs the first holosuite at his bar on the Promenade of station Terok Nor.

"Profit and Loss" (DS9). Quark said he installed his first holosuite while he and Natima were together.

Gul Dukat

Dr. Farallon begins work on a revolutionary new particle fountain mining technology on planet Tyrus VIIA.

"The Quality of Life" (TNG). Farallon said she had spent six years working on the project (2369).

Natima Lang breaks up with Quark and leaves Terok Nor after discovering that Quark has been using Lang's personal access codes to steal money from the Cardassian information service. The two had been deeply in love, and both would regret this parting for years. Lang subsequently joins the Cardassian underground, opposing military rule of the Cardassian Union.

"Profit and Loss" (DS9). Seven years prior to the episode (2370).

Quark

Klingon warrior Kang, on a decades-old quest to win revenge on a criminal called the Albino, meets a former wife of the criminal on planet Dayos IV. Kang feeds and clothes this woman who had been discarded by the Albino, and later tells her the story of how the Albino murdered his son. Kang suspects that she knows the Albino's whereabouts, but she says nothing.

"Blood Oath" (DS9). Seven years before the episode (2370).

Gul Darhe'el, known as "the Butcher of Gallitep," dies in his sleep of a massive coleibric hemorrhage. He is buried under one of the largest military monuments on planet Cardassia with full honors. Darhe'el had commanded the infamous Gallitep labor camp, where he was responsible for many atrocities against Bajoran nationals.

"Duet" (DS9). Six years before the episode (2369).

Kang

Galaxy-class starship *Enterprise*-D, Starfleet registry number NCC-1701-D, is launched from Utopia Planitia Fleet Yards orbiting the planet Mars, charged with the mission "to boldly go where no one has gone before." The ship is officially commissioned on stardate 40759.5. Captain Jean-Luc Picard will assume command of the vessel, the fifth Federation starship to bear the name *Enterprise*, on stardate 41124.

"Lonely Among Us" (TNG) establishes that the ship had been launched less than a year prior to the first season, and "Encounter at Farpoint" (TNG) seems to imply that Picard had taken command shortly prior to that episode. Stardate and ship's motto from dedication plaque on Enterprise*-D bridge. Picard's date of command established in "The Drumhead" (TNG). "All Good Things..." (TNG) suggests that Picard took command of the ship just prior to "Encounter at Farpoint" (TNG).*

Symbol of the Utopia Planitia Yards

Utopia Planitia Fleet Yards engineer Marla Finn and another engineer become romantically involved. Lieutenant Walter Pierce becomes jealous and kills both of them. Pierce disposes of the bodies by throwing them into the plasma stream in one of the *Enterprise*-D's warp drive nacelles and subsequently commits suicide by jumping into the plasma stream, as well. No bodies are ever discovered, although the subspace energy present within the nacelle causes Pierce's empathic pattern to be imprinted onto a bulkhead in the nacelle.

Marla Finn

Nick Locarno

Captain Paul Rice

"Eye of the Beholder" (TNG). Stardate 40897.2. The stardate would indicate this is after the commissioning of the ship, but the episode suggests it is before Picard took command.

2364

Nick Locarno is accepted as a cadet at Starfleet Academy on Earth. Locarno is considered one of the most promising students ever to attend that institution.

"The First Duty" (TNG). Picard noted that Locarno would have graduated with that year's graduating class (2368), suggesting he had entered four years earlier.

Commander William Riker is offered the opportunity to command the *Starship Drake*, but declines the assignment in order to serve on the *U.S.S. Enterprise*-D. Command of the *Drake* is accepted by Riker's classmate Paul Rice. The *Drake* is later destroyed at planet Minos.

"The Arsenal of Freedom" (TNG). Exact date is conjecture, but Riker told Tasha he had thought a tour aboard the Enterprise*-D was more advantageous, implying this was shortly prior to Riker's transfer to the* Enterprise*-D in "Encounter at Farpoint" (TNG). Paul Rice was apparently named for William Rice, a character in Gene Roddenberry's 1963-1964 series* The Lieutenant.

Admiral Leonard McCoy travels aboard *U.S.S. Hood* to rendezvous with the *Enterprise*-D at Farpoint Station. Also aboard the *Hood* are Commander William T. Riker (serving as first officer), Lieutenant (Junior Grade) Geordi La Forge, Dr. Beverly Crusher, and her son Wesley Crusher, all en route to assignments on the *Enterprise*-D.

Prior to "Encounter at Farpoint" (TNG).

6.1 STAR TREK: THE NEXT GENERATION — YEAR 1

Crew of the
Starship Enterprise,
NCC-1701-D

2364 (CONTINUED)

Editors' Note: The calendar date of 2364 for the first season was established in "The Neutral Zone" (TNG). This was the reference point from which most Star Trek: The Next Generation-era dates were derived.

Captain Jean-Luc Picard travels via shuttlecraft to his new command, the *Galaxy*-class *Starship Enterprise*-D. Picard's shuttle, the *Galileo*, is piloted by Lieutenant Natasha Yar, who is newly assigned as security chief for the *Enterprise*-D. Picard assumes command of the *Enterprise*-D effective stardate 41148, by order of Rear Admiral Norah Satie.

The *Starship Enterprise*-D is assigned to study unknown space in the great stellar mass beyond planet Deneb IV.

"All Good Things..." (TNG). Just prior to the events in "Encounter at Farpoint" (TNG).

Editors' Note: "Legacy" (TNG) established that Picard asked Yar to join his crew after seeing her heroism on planet Carnel during a rescue mission in which the Enterprise-D also participated. Unfortunately, this was inconsistent with the flashback scenes in "All Good Things..." (TNG), where we saw Yar piloting the shuttle that took Picard up to the Enterprise-D for the first time. Because the "Legacy" backstory was not actually seen, we are using the "All Good Things..." back story, which was indeed seen in the episode's flashback scenes. Note that this represents a revision from the first edition of this chronology, which assumed that the Carnel incident took place several weeks before the events in "Encounter at Farpoint" (TNG). Also, "The Drumhead" (TNG) gave the stardate of Picard's assuming command of the ship as 41124 .

The flashback scenes in "All Good Things" (TNG) showed an alternate version of the events in "Encounter at Farpoint" (TNG), but we're assuming that in cases where the alternate version conflicts with "Farpoint," that "Farpoint" is the "correct" version. In the "All Good Things..." version, the mission to Farpoint was not interrupted by Q, but the ship never made it to Farpoint because of the anti-time anomaly that ultimately destroyed the ship.

Starship Enterprise-D

Farpoint Station

Q

Admiral Leonard McCoy

Senator Pardek

"Encounter at Farpoint, Parts I and II" (TNG). Stardate 41153.7. *U.S.S. Enterprise*-D assigned to study Farpoint Station at planet Deneb IV. Farpoint is a new starbase recently built by the Bandi for possible use as a Starfleet facility. Investigation reveals the station to have been built with the unwilling help of a spacefaring life-form capable of assuming virtually any shape or form, in this case, that of the station itself. The creature is allowed to return to deep space.

First contact with an extradimensional life-form called the Q, a visitor from what it calls the Q continuum. This entity demonstrates extraordinary power to manipulate space and matter, and interferes with the execution of the Farpoint investigation mission, placing *Enterprise*-D personnel on trial, charged with being a "dangerous, savage, child-race."

Commander William T. Riker, previously assigned to the *U.S.S. Hood* under the command of Captain Robert DeSoto, joins *U.S.S. Enterprise*-D crew at Farpoint Station and assumes duties of executive officer. Lieutenant (Junior Grade) Geordi La Forge joins the *Enterprise*-D crew at Farpoint Station, assumes duties of flight controller (conn). Dr. Beverly Crusher also joins the *Enterprise*-D crew at Farpoint Station, assumes duties of chief medical officer, effective stardate 41154. Also taking up residence aboard the *Enterprise*-D is her 15-year-old son, Wesley. Dr. Crusher had been married to Starfleet officer Jack Crusher, who at the time of his death was serving aboard the *U.S.S. Stargazer* under the command of Captain Jean-Luc Picard.

Starfleet Admiral Leonard McCoy, traveling on starship *U.S.S. Hood,* makes inspection visit of new *U.S.S. Enterprise*-D.

Editors' Note: The stardate of Beverly Crusher's assignment to the Enterprise-D was established as 41154 in "Remember Me" (TNG). Picard's reluctance to accept Beverly as chief medical officer is learned, in "Attached" (TNG) to be because he felt guilt at his feelings of love for his best friend's widow.

During the Farpoint mission, Geordi La Forge tells a joke to Data on the bridge, but Data, lacking emotions, is unable to understand the concept of human humor.

Star Trek Generations. *Data got the punch line seven years later.*

The Q continuum does not render a verdict in its trial of humanity. Rather, it continues to observe humanity's representatives aboard the *Starship Enterprise*-D, looking for evidence that humankind have some capacity for growth.

"All Good Things..." (TNG). After the events in "Encounter at Farpoint" (TNG).

"The Naked Now" (TNG). Stardate 41209.2. *U.S.S. Enterprise*-D assigned to rendezvous with science vessel *Tsiolkovsky*, which had been monitoring the collapse of a red giant star. A strange series of messages from the *Tsiolkovsky* suggests severe psychological disorders are threatening the crew. By the time the *Enterprise*-D reaches the rendezvous, all 80 crew personnel aboard the science vessel are dead. Investigation determines *Tsiolkovsky* crew suffered from a virus similar to the Psi 2000 disease that affected the crew of an earlier *Enterprise* in 2266. Contamination from the away team causes the virus to spread among the *Enterprise*-D crew until an appropriate treatment is developed.

Romulan Senator Pardek participates in a trade negotiations conference. Among the other participants are the Barolians.

"Unification, Part I" (TNG). Data locates an archival video of Pardek in the Barolian records of the negotiations, noting that the conference had taken place four years prior to the episode (2368).

An outbreak of Anchilles fever on planet Styris IV spreads out of control, resulting in deaths estimated in the millions.

Prior to "Code of Honor" (TNG).

"Code of Honor" (TNG). Stardate 41235.25. *U.S.S. Enterprise*-D on diplomatic mission to establish treaty with planet Ligon II and acquire a rare vaccine needed to treat the plague on planet Styris IV. *Enterprise*-D security officer Yar becomes a pawn in a power struggle between Ligonian leader Lutan and his political rivals, who are ultimately successful in deposing Lutan.

U.S.S. Enterprise-D delivers critically needed vaccines to planet Styris IV.

After "Code of Honor" (TNG).

Ligonian leader Lutan

Starfleet propulsion specialist Kosinski performs warp system upgrades on *Starships Fearless* and *Ajax*. Both ships report minor performance gains.

"Where No One Has Gone Before" (TNG). Exact date is conjecture, but this was fairly soon before the episode.

"Haven" (TNG). Stardate 41294.5. *Enterprise*-D en route to planet Haven in the Beta Cassius system for shore leave, but is interrupted by urgent call for assistance. Electorine Valeda Innis of Haven, requesting Federation intervention to prevent landing of a Tarellian ship recently detected on course for Haven, explains that diplomatic efforts have failed to dissuade the Tarellians from a plan to disembark on Haven to die. Innis expresses a fear that the Tarellians, the last eight survivors of terrible biological warfare on their planet, will infect Haven with the deadly virus.

Kosinski

Enterprise-D counselor Deanna Troi is informed that she must fulfill the marriage pledge with Wyatt Miller she undertook as a child. The wedding is planned to take place on board the *Enterprise*-D, with her mother, Lwaxana Troi, and Wyatt's parents in attendance. The wedding is canceled when Miller, an aspiring physician, chooses to take up residence with the Tarellians in hope of finding a cure for their plague.

"Where No One Has Gone Before" (TNG). Stardate 41263.1. *U.S.S. Enterprise*-D rendezvous with *Starship Fearless* for transfer of Kosinski and his assistant, an inhabitant of planet Tau Alpha C.

Deanna and Lwaxana Troi

U.S.S. Enterprise-D participates in a warp experiment under the supervision of Starfleet propulsion specialist Kosinski. The tests involve modification of the ship's warp fields to gain higher engine efficiency. Initial results are extremely promising, although one test accidentally propels the ship across several million light-years, past galaxy M33. It is learned that the gains in efficiency are not due to Kosinski's modifications, but rather to the efforts of Kosinski's assistant, known as "the Traveler."

Wesley Crusher's efforts in working with the Traveler to return the *Enterprise*-D to the Milky Way galaxy are recognized by Captain Picard, who grants Crusher the rank of "acting ensign," effective stardate 41263.4.

Kosinski

The old Vulcan ship *T'Pau* is decommissioned and sent to the surplus depot Zed-15 orbiting Qualor II. The ship is later surreptitiously dismantled and smuggled out of the yard by Romulan operatives as part of a plan to place Vulcan under Romulan rule.

"Unification, Part I" (TNG). Dokachin noted the T'Pau *had been logged in on stardate 41344, which would seem to place it between "Where No One Has Gone Before" (TNG) and "The Last Outpost" (TNG).*

Ferengi agents steal a T-9 energy converter from the unmanned monitor post on planet Gamma Tauri IV. The theft is a matter of great concern because prior to this, the Federation had virtually no direct contact with or knowledge of the Ferengi.

Prior to "The Last Outpost" (TNG).

The Traveler works with Wesley Crusher

Riker confronts Portal of the last Tkon outpost

Selay delegation

Edo representatives

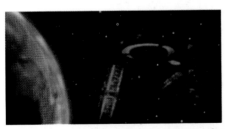

The space entity

DaiMon Bok

"The Last Outpost" (TNG). Stardate 41386.4. *U.S.S. Enterprise*-D in pursuit of Ferengi spacecraft, attempting to recover T-9 energy converter. Upon entering the Delphi Ardu star system, both ships are incapacitated by a powerful energy beam, apparently emanating from an outpost of the long-dead Tkon Empire. Diplomatic efforts are later successful in freeing both ships, with Ferengi daimon Taar agreeing to return the stolen energy converter.

First contact with Ferengi Alliance, as well as with the Tkon Empire.

"Lonely Among Us" (TNG). Stardate 41249.3. *Starship Enterprise*-D on diplomatic mission to transport delegates from planets Antica and Selay in the Beta Renner system to an interstellar conference on the neutral planetoid Parliament in hope of resolving conflicts between the two antagonistic planets, both of which have applied for membership in the Federation.

U.S.S. Enterprise-D suffers a major series of malfunctions as computer system is invaded by an energy-based life-form that inhabits various crew members, then the *Enterprise*-D itself. The entity, which is found to be a spaceborne energy cloud, is learned to be something of a kindred spirit to Picard and the crew, exploring the unknown in this manner.

U.S.S. Enterprise-D delivers the Antican and Selay delegations to Parliament for their conference to consider their petitions for admission to the Federation.

Just after "Lonely Among Us" (TNG).

U.S.S. Enterprise-D delivers a party of Earth colonists to the Strnad star system. Shortly thereafter, ship's personnel discover another Class-M planet in the adjoining Rubicun star system. This second planet is discovered to be inhabited by a peaceful humanoid species known as the Edo and is deemed suitable for shore leave by *Enterprise*-D personnel.

Just prior to "Justice" (TNG).

Editors' Note: The Strnad star system was named for former Star Trek *production staffer Janet Strnad.*

"Justice" (TNG). Stardate 41255.6. *U.S.S. Enterprise*-D personnel, on shore leave at planet Rubicun III, accidentally violate local laws. Acting Ensign Wesley Crusher commits an apparently minor transgression, but local authorities impose a death sentence for the act in accordance with planetary law. Attempts to negotiate a release for Crusher are unsuccessful because of the presence of a powerful noncorporeal spaceborne entity that the Edos worship as their god. *Enterprise*-D captain Picard violates the Prime Directive of noninterference by violating local laws to secure Crusher's release.

Ferengi vessel contacts *U.S.S. Enterprise*-D and requests a meeting in the Xendi Sabu star system. *Enterprise*-D waits at rendezvous point for three days, the Ferengi offering no response other than a signal to "stand by." In an apparently unrelated development, *Enterprise*-D captain Picard suffers from an unusually painful series of headaches.

Three days prior to "The Battle" (TNG).

"The Battle" (TNG). Stardate 41723.9. Ferengi daimon Bok, aboard a Ferengi ship at the Xendi Sabu rendezvous site, offers a gift to *Enterprise*-D captain Picard: the hulk of Picard's former command, the *U.S.S. Stargazer*. Examination of records aboard the *Stargazer* reveals apparently damning evidence suggesting Picard had attacked a Ferengi spacecraft some nine years ago in "The Battle of Maxia" in which the *Stargazer* was believed destroyed. The gift is found to be an elaborate ploy by Bok to gain revenge on Picard for the latter's involvement in the Battle of Maxia, during which Bok's son was killed. Bok is also discovered to have falsified the *Stargazer* records and to have attempted to injure Picard through the use of a Ferengi mind-control device.

U.S.S. Enterprise-D tows the hulk of the *U.S.S. Stargazer* to Xendi Starbase 9.

Just after "The Battle" (TNG).

DaiMon Bok is relieved of command, charged by Ferengi authorities with being unstable and dangerous. He is confined to Rog Prison and stripped of his title as daimon.

"Bloodlines" (TNG). After the events in "The Battle" (TNG).

Enterprise-D counselor Deanna Troi departs *U.S.S. Enterprise*-D on a shuttlecraft at Starbase G-6 for a visit to her home planet of Betazed.

Prior to "Hide and Q" (TNG).

An explosion at the Federation mining colony on planet Sigma III injures 504 persons. An urgent call for medical assistance is transmitted to the *U.S.S. Enterprise*-D.

Just prior to "Hide and Q" (TNG).

"Hide and Q" (TNG). Stardate 41590.5. *U.S.S. Enterprise*-D en route to rescue mission at Sigma III mining colony is interrupted by the reappearance of the entity known as "Q." The rescue mission is largely successful, although at least one life is lost at the colony.

Starfleet Command receives a transmission from Karnas, a leader on planet Mordan IV, reporting that terrorists have seized hostages including Federation Ambassador Hawkins. Karnas urgently requests the assistance of Starfleet Admiral Mark Jameson, noting a terrorist threat to kill the hostages if Jameson does not intervene in six days.

Two days prior to "Too Short a Season" (TNG).

"Too Short a Season" (TNG). Stardate 41309.5. *Enterprise*-D at planet Persephone V to pick up Admiral Mark Jameson and his wife, Anne, for transport to planet Mordan IV to negotiate the release of Federation hostages. Upon arrival at Mordan IV, Jameson reveals that his celebrated negotiations (which led to release of other Federation hostages by Karnas some 45 years ago) were in fact a weapons-for-hostages deal that resulted in a bloody civil war. This conflict ended only five years ago, and it is learned that Karnas has staged the entire hostage crisis as a means of exacting retribution on Jameson for his role in exacerbating the war. Jameson, suffering from the effects of a youth drug obtained on planet Cerebus III, dies at Mordan IV after convincing Karnas to release the hostages.

Starship *Enterprise*-D goes to planet Isis III.

Just after "Too Short a Season" (TNG).

"The Big Goodbye" (TNG). Stardate 41997.7. *U.S.S. Enterprise*-D assigned to make diplomatic contact with the reclusive civilization known as the Jarada. The mission is somewhat delayed when a holodeck malfunction traps Captain Picard and other *Enterprise*-D personnel in an ongoing simulation program. The contact is ultimately successful in large part because of Captain Picard's precise enunciation of a formal Jaradan greeting.

U.S.S. Enterprise-D completes an assignment in the Omicron Theta star system.

Just prior to "Datalore" (TNG).

"Datalore" (TNG). Stardate 41242.4. *U.S.S. Enterprise*-D, at Omicron Theta system, takes side trip to planet where Lieutenant Commander Data was discovered. Investigation reveals remains of a Federation colony, apparently destroyed and all inhabitants killed by a powerful spaceborne Crystalline Entity of unknown origin.

Also discovered is the preserved but abandoned underground laboratory of famed cyberneticist Dr. Noonien Soong. Dr. Soong, long assumed dead, is believed to be the designer of the android Data. Among the equipment in the facility are sufficient components to assemble a second android, nearly identical to Data. Upon return to the *Enterprise*-D, these components are assembled, then activated. The resulting android, known as Lore, is struc-

U.S.S. Stargazer

Rescue operations at Sigma III mining colony

Karnas of Mordan IV

Picard and Data in Dixon Hill holodeck simulation program

turally identical to Data, but with dramatically differing personality programming. This android exhibits aberrant behavior, threatening the *Enterprise*-D, and is eventually transported into space, where it is presumed destroyed.

Though unknown at the time, Lore drifts in space for two years and is eventually rescued by a passing Pakled ship.

"Brothers" (TNG). Lore described his adventures to Data and Dr. Soong.

Twelve students from *U.S.S. Enterprise*-D participate in Quazulu field trip, accidentally bringing a respiratory virus back to the ship.

Prior to "Angel One" (TNG).

U.S.S. Enterprise-D investigates disappearance of Federation freighter *Odin*, missing for seven years. The wreckage of the *Odin* is found with three escape pods missing, suggesting the possibility of survivors.

Just prior to "Angel One" (TNG).

Data examines the nonfunctional head of his brother, Lore

"Angel One" (TNG). Stardate 41636.9. Investigation of probable flight path of *Odin* escape pods leads to planet Angel I. Survivors of the *Odin* are found to be alive on the planet's surface, having integrated themselves into the society. Local authorities request removal of survivors on the grounds they are interfering with planetary authority, but *Enterprise*-D captain Picard rules that the survivors have become a legitimate part of the social system and are thus immune to Prime Directive constraints.

Romulan spacecraft are detected near a Federation border post. The *U.S.S. Berlin* is dispatched to investigate. Upon completion of the *Odin* investigation, *U.S.S. Enterprise*-D sets course for Romulan Neutral Zone, although no direct contact with the Romulans is made at this time.

Lore

U.S.S. Enterprise-D departs toward Romulan Neutral Zone.

Just after "Angel One" (TNG).

Starship *Enterprise*-D, at Omicron Pascal, is delayed for a week, making it late for a scheduled layover at Starbase 74.

Prior to "11001001" (TNG).

"11001001" (TNG). Stardate 41365.9. *U.S.S. Enterprise*-D at Starbase 74, orbiting Tarsas III for scheduled maintenance layover. Service and upgrades are performed by a special team from planet Bynaus. While in dock, a malfunction is reported, threatening a potentially catastrophic failure of the *Enterprise*-D's antimatter containment fields. As a result, all *Enterprise*-D personnel are evacuated, and the ship is removed from the starbase. The incident is later learned to have been engineered by the Bynars in an effort to appropriate the ship for use in restarting their home planet's main computer system in the Beta Magellan system. The Bynar planetary computer had been damaged when Beta Magellan went supernova.

Capital city on planet Angel 1

Editors' Note: At one point during the first season, "11001001" (TNG) was slated to be produced before the episode "The Big Goodbye" (TNG). Had the episodes been filmed and aired in that order, the modification by the Bynars to the holodeck in "11001001" would have served to explain what happened to Captain Picard when his favorite Dixon Hill simulation malfunctioned. This episode marks the first reference to the game "parrises squares" when Tasha, Worf, and two other Enterprise-D personnel are off to challenge a team from the starbase.

U.S.S. Enterprise-D has an appointment at planet Pelleus V.

Two days after "11001001" (TNG).

U.S.S. Enterprise-D begins mapping assignment at Pleiades cluster.

Prior to "Home Soil" (TNG).

Enterprise-D at Starbase 74

"Home Soil" (TNG). Stardate 41463.9. *U.S.S. Enterprise*-D mapping assignment at Pleiades cluster is interrupted by a Federation request to investigate a loss of communication with the Federation terraforming team on planet Velara III. The *Enterprise*-D away team discovers that terraforming activity had been inadvertently disrupting a life-form indigenous to Velara III. This inorganic life-form exists in the narrow electrically conductive zone above the planet's water table, and it was threatened by the terraforming process. The life-form is discovered to be intelligent when it responds by seizing control of the *Enterprise*-D computer. The crew believes that project director Mandl was aware of the intelligent nature of the Velara life-forms and that he authorized the continuation of the terraforming despite that knowledge.

Bynar technicians

U.S.S. Enterprise-D evacuates Velara III terraforming station personnel and returns them to starbase.

After "Home Soil" (TNG).

Benzan of the planet Straleb, and Yanar of the planet Atlec, begin a romantic relationship. Benzan gives Yanar the Jewel of Thesia, a Straleb national treasure, as a nuptial gift, this despite the fact that their respective parents are unaware of the relationship.

"The Outrageous Okona" (TNG). Okona said the two had been seeing each other for about six months prior to the episode, although the exact date is conjecture.

Terraforming team

"When the Bough Breaks" (TNG). Stardate 41509.1. *U.S.S. Enterprise*-D discovers the mythical planet of Aldea, which had been shielded from visibility in the Epsilon Mynos system. The planet's inhabitants, found to be a technologically advanced society of artisans, use their sophisticated transporter technology to abduct several children of *Enterprise*-D crew members. This is discovered to be an effort by the Aldeans to reestablish their society, rendered infertile due to radiation exposure caused by damage to their ozone layer.

Although diplomatic efforts to secure the freedom of the *Enterprise*-D children are initially unsuccessful, the Aldeans eventually agree to their release. *Enterprise*-D personnel assist with the dismantling of the Aldean shielding system and perform a reseeding of the Aldean ozone layer, a move expected to reverse the sterility of the Aldean people.

Benzan

Jadzia, a young woman on planet Trill, enters the Trill initiate program, working toward her goal of becoming a host for a Trill symbiont. She is later dropped from the program at the recommendation of Curzon Dax, although she later reapplies and is accepted.

"Equilibrium" (DS9). Dax said she'd spent three years as an initiate, and "Dax" (DS9) established that Curzon Dax had died (and therefore Jadzia Dax was joined) two years before 2369.

Trill homeworld

"Coming of Age" (TNG). Stardate 41416.2. Lieutenant Commander Dexter Remmick of the Starfleet inspector general's office conducts a thorough investigation of the *U.S.S. Enterprise*-D while the ship is at the Relva VII Starfleet facility. Remmick's assignment to uncover unspecified problems aboard the *Enterprise*-D is later explained to be a probe of Captain Picard by Admiral Gregory Quinn, a prelude to Picard's being offered the job of commandant of Starfleet Academy. Quinn's offer to Picard is coupled with a plea based on Quinn's suspicions that problems exist within the structure of Starfleet itself. Picard declines the offer, citing his belief that he can better serve the interests of the Federation as captain of the *Enterprise*-D.

Acting Ensign Wesley Crusher undergoes Starfleet Academy entrance competition tests at Relva VII. Although Crusher fails to gain admission to the Academy, his score is sufficient to allow him to resubmit his application the following year.

U.S.S. Enterprise-D travels to Algeron IV.

Just after "Coming of Age" (TNG).

Starfleet Admiral Gregory Quinn and Inspector General Dexter Remmick

Talarian freighter Batris

Renegade Klingons

Yar confronts Armus

"Heart of Glory" (TNG). Stardate 41503.7. *U.S.S. Enterprise*-D responds to a distress call from the freighter *Batris*, a damaged Talarian freighter. Three survivors, Klingon warriors, are rescued from the *Batris* before it explodes, although one warrior dies shortly thereafter. Investigation identifies the survivors, Korris and Konmel, to be militants opposing the Klingon government. They attempt to seize control of the *Enterprise*-D, but are thwarted.

"The Arsenal of Freedom" (TNG). Stardate 41798.2. *U.S.S. Enterprise*-D at Lorenze Cluster to investigate the disappearance of the *U.S.S. Drake* at planet Minos. Although the planet Minos had been inhabited in the past, recent probes indicated no intelligent life currently on the planet. Nevertheless, *Enterprise*-D personnel encounter technically sophisticated weapons systems that threaten both an away team on the planet's surface, and the *Enterprise*-D itself. Further investigation indicates these weapons systems, still functional, were responsible for the destruction of the *Drake*, as well as the entire Minosian culture.

Editors' Note: Riker mentioned to Tasha and Picard that he had been offered command of the U.S.S. Drake, *apparently just prior to his accepting the job as executive officer on the* Enterprise-D.

"Symbiosis" (TNG). (No stardate given in episode.) *U.S.S. Enterprise*-D responds to a distress call while studying solar flares at the Delos system. The distress call is found to have originated from the *Sanction*, a disabled Ornaran interplanetary freighter. Although *Enterprise*-D personnel are unable to save the freighter, the *Sanction*'s cargo and part of its crew are successfully rescued. It is learned that the *Sanction* had been transporting medical supplies of felicium from planet Brekka to Ornara in order to keep a 200-year-old plague in check.

Investigation by *Enterprise*-D personnel reveals the medication to be a narcotic substance, no longer necessary for medical reasons. Representatives of Brekka request Federation assistance to insure delivery of these medical supplies, but Captain Picard rules that Prime Directive considerations prohibit Federation intervention. Prime Directive considerations further prevent Picard from revealing to the inhabitants of planet Ornara the exploitive nature of their dealings with Brekka for the addictive medication, but Picard believes the Ornarans will learn this for themselves.

Editors' Note: "Symbiosis" (TNG) was filmed after "Skin of Evil" (TNG), but is listed first because Tasha Yar, killed in the latter episode, is shown as being alive here.

Ship's counselor Deanna Troi attends a psychology conference in the Zed Lapis sector.

Just prior to "Skin of Evil" (TNG).

"Skin of Evil" (TNG). Stardate 41601.3. Shuttlecraft 13, carrying Deanna Troi and pilot Ben Prieto on a return flight to the *Enterprise*-D, is forced to make a crash-landing on planet Vagra II. Investigation by an *Enterprise*-D away team determines the crash to have been caused by an entity that calls itself Armus. During the investigation, *Enterprise*-D security chief Tasha Yar is killed by Armus.

Later efforts are successful in rescuing Troi and other *Enterprise*-D personnel from the planet. Captain Picard assigns Worf as acting security chief.

"We'll Always Have Paris" (TNG). Stardate 41697.9. *U.S.S. Enterprise*-D is en route to planet Sarona VIII, when the ship encounters a brief temporal distortion. This phenomenon is also reported by the freighter *Lalo* and the Ilecom star system. Shortly thereafter, the *Enterprise*-D responds to a distress call from a science laboratory on planetoid Vandor IV. Investigation determines the temporal distortions to have been created by Dr. Paul

Manheim, studying the relationship between time and gravity. Manheim suffers neurochemical injury caused by the temporal distortions, until Data is successful in repairing the temporal anomaly caused by Manheim's experiments.

Starship Enterprise-D goes to planet Sarona VIII for crew shore leave.

Just after "We'll Always Have Paris" (TNG).

Admiral Norah Satie uncovers evidence of a widespread alien conspiracy infiltrating Starfleet Command. Among the evidence is a series of unusual occurrences, including strange orders, high-ranking officials backing apparently irrational decisions, the evacuation of Starbase 12 for two days, and the apparently accidental deaths of McKinney, Ryan Sipe, and Onna Karapleedeez. Satie enlists the assistance of key personnel, including captains Walker Keel, Tryla Scott, and Rixx to counter the incursion.

Prior to "Conspiracy" (TNG). Satie's role in uncovering the conspiracy is described in "The Drumhead" (TNG).

Admiral Satie

U.S.S. Enterprise-D is assigned to scientific investigation on planet Pacifica.

Just prior to "Conspiracy" (TNG).

"Conspiracy" (TNG). Stardate 41775.5. Mission to Pacifica is interrupted when Captain Picard receives an urgent request from *Starship Horatio* captain Walker Keel for a covert meeting at planetoid Dytallix B. Also present at this meeting are Captain Tryla Scott of the *U.S.S. Renegade*, and Captain Rixx of the *U.S.S. Thomas Paine*. At the planetoid, Keel informs Picard of his suspicion that unknown threat forces have infiltrated Starfleet Command and are responsible for recent unusual activity. Shortly thereafter, the *Horatio* is destroyed with the loss of all personnel, including Walker Keel.

Walker Keel

Picard pursues the investigation of Keel's report by taking the *Enterprise*-D to Earth and requesting a meeting at Starfleet Command. Keel's suspicions are borne out and Picard discovers that numerous key Starfleet personnel are being controlled by an extragalactic intelligence. Picard and Riker are successful in stopping the intelligence and neutralizing its control, but its origin and purpose remain a total mystery.

Aamin Marritza accepts a position as an instructor at the Cardassian military academy on planet Kora II. Seven years earlier, Marritza had served as a filing clerk at the notorious Gallitep labor camps under the command of Gul Darhe'el. Just prior to his arrival at Kora II, Marritza underwent cosmetic surgery to change his face to closely resemble that of Gul Darhe'el.

"Duet" (DS9). Marritza had served for five years prior to the episode (2369).

Captain Rixx

Communications are lost with Federation starbases in Sector 3-0, near the Romulan Neutral Zone. Two outposts in that area are reported destroyed.

Prior to "The Neutral Zone" (TNG); contact was reported lost on stardate 41903.2.

Captain Picard attends an emergency conference at Starbase 718 to discuss the possibility of an emerging Romulan threat in the wake of the destruction of the outposts near the Neutral Zone.

Just prior to "The Neutral Zone" (TNG).

"The Neutral Zone" (TNG). Stardate 41986.0. Awaiting Picard's return from a Starfleet conference, Lieutenant Commander Data discovers an apparently derelict spacecraft. Investigation determines the spacecraft to contain the cryogenically preserved remains of several humans who died in the late 20th century. Three of these individuals are successfully revived because medical advances in the intervening years have rendered their maladies curable.

Temporal distortion causes Data to exist simultaneously on different planes

Cryosatellite

*Enterprise-D computer records
display the face of Claire Raymond's
great-great-great-great-grandson*

These individuals, named Claire Raymond (who was a homemaker prior to her death), Sonny Clemonds (an entertainer), and Ralph Offenhouse (a business executive), are later returned to Earth aboard the *U.S.S. Charleston*.

Federation outposts at Delta Zero Five and Tarod IX near the Romulan Neutral Zone are discovered to have been destroyed not by Romulans, but by an unknown agency that literally scooped the outposts off their planetary surfaces. This agency is later believed to be the Borg, suggesting a Borg presence near Federation space significantly earlier than 2367.

Investigating these disappearances, the *Enterprise*-D encounters a Romulan spacecraft studying similar occurrences on the other side of the Neutral Zone. This is the first Federation contact with the Romulans since the Tomed incident of 2311.

Editors' Note: Data gave the current calendar year in "The Neutral Zone" (TNG) as 2364. This was used as a reference point from which most Star Trek: The Next Generation *dates were derived. The apparent reference to Borg activity near Federation and Romulan space appears to be inconsistent with Q's statements in "Q Who?" (TNG) suggesting that the Borg were still several years away from Federation space at this point. On the other hand, it is also possible that Q did not know everything going on with the Borg.*

Claire Raymond's great-great-great-great-grandson, Thomas, whom she said looked a lot like her late husband, Donald, also bore an uncanny (and purely coincidental) resemblance to Star Trek: The Next Generation *co-producer Peter Lauritson. Raymond's family tree diagram seen on Troi's desk-top viewer also contained the (hopefully illegible) names of various characters from* The Muppet Show *and* Gilligan's Island.<None>

The derelict spacecraft in which the 20th-century cryonauts had been lost in space was designed by Rick Sternbach and Mike Okuda. They inscribed the ship in very tiny letters with the name S.S. Birdseye. The satellite's reactor module was labeled with the numbers 4077, an homage to M*A*S*H, *one of Mike's favorite television shows. Inside the ship, all of the nonfunctional cryonic suspension modules (the ones containing hideously decomposed bodies) bore signs with the names of various members of the art department, as well as the name of episode director James Conway. ("The Neutral Zone" was the last episode of our very grueling first season, and the unusual number of gags described here is probably a reflection of the extraordinary level of exhaustion shared by everyone in the production company.)*

6.2 STAR TREK: THE NEXT GENERATION — YEAR 2

Starship Enterprise-*D*

2365

Geordi La Forge is promoted to the rank of full lieutenant and is assigned as *Enterprise*-D chief engineer. Lieutenant Worf is promoted to permanent chief of security, replacing the late Tasha Yar. Acting Ensign Wesley Crusher is assigned regular bridge duty, serving as flight controller (conn).

These promotions were not shown, but happened between the end of the first season and the beginning of the second.

Captain Picard recruits an old friend, Guinan, to serve as hostess of the Ten-Forward lounge. She comes on board the *Enterprise*-D at Nestoriel III.

Guinan was first seen in "The Child" (TNG). "Yesterday's Enterprise*" (TNG) and "Redemption, Part II" (TNG) established that Guinan had not been aboard the* Enterprise-D *until sometime after Tasha's death. Data mentioned Nestoriel III in "Time's Arrow, Part I."*

Dr. Katherine Pulaski

"The Child" (TNG). Stardate 42073.1. Dr. Beverly Crusher accepts a position as head of Starfleet Medical and departs the *Enterprise*-D. Dr. Katherine Pulaski arrives from the *U.S.S. Repulse* via shuttlecraft as her replacement.

U.S.S. Enterprise-D assigned to transport medical specimens of plasma plague from planet 'audet IX to Science Station Tango Sierra in hope that a cure can be found for an outbreak of the disease on planet Rachelis. The project is supervised by Lieutenant Commander Hester Dealt, medical trustee of the Federation Medical Collection Center.

Ship's counselor Deanna Troi is impregnated by an unknown alien life-form. The resulting child, which gestates and grows at a highly accelerated rate, is the product of this unknown form's desire to learn more about human life. The entity is found to be a source of eichner radiation, compromising the safety of the storage of the deadly plasma plague specimens. Seeking to avoid harm to the *Enterprise*-D crew, the entity departs the ship.

Editors' Note: This episode was originally written for Captain Kirk and his crew for the Star Trek II *television series project that was never produced.*

Deanna Troi and her son, Ian Andrew

U.S.S. Enterprise-D heads for Morgana Quadrant.

After "The Child" (TNG).

"Where Silence Has Lease" (TNG). Stardate 42193.6. The *U.S.S. Enterprise*-D is updating star charts while en route to the Morgana Quadrant. The voyage is interrupted when the *Enterprise*-D is trapped in a region of space that appears to be devoid of stars or any object other than the *Enterprise*-D itself. A second ship is eventually sighted, tentatively identified as the *Galaxy*-class *U.S.S. Yamato*, although further investigation reveals the ship to be a fabrication. The entire situation is eventually determined to be a first-contact scenario with a noncorporeal intelligence known as Nagilum, who is attempting to understand the nature of human life.

Nagilum

U.S.S. Enterprise-D continues toward the Morgana Quadrant.

Just after "Where Silence Has Lease" (TNG).

The crew of the *Starship Lantree* is subjected to routine examinations at the beginning of a duty cycle. All are found to be in perfect health.

"Unnatural Selection" (TNG). Pulaski noted the exams had taken place eight weeks prior to the episode.

Geordi La Forge builds a model of the ancient British sailing ship *H.M.S. Victory*, intended as a gift for *Starship Victory* captain Zimbata, under whose command La Forge served prior to his *Enterprise*-D assignment.

Prior to "Elementary, Dear Data" (TNG).

Editors' Note: In reality, Geordi's beautiful H.M.S. Victory *model still graces the late Gene Roddenberry's office in his home.*

Moriarty, a computer-generated life-form

"Elementary, Dear Data" (TNG). Stardate 42286.3. *U.S.S. Enterprise*-D arrives three days early for scheduled rendezvous with the *Victory*. While awaiting the *Victory*'s arrival, user error on the part of a holodeck participant results in the accidental creation of a computer software-based sentient intelligence within a simulation program. This intelligence is based on the character of Dr. James Moriarty from the Sherlock Holmes stories. To avoid the destruction of what is apparently a self-aware life-form, Captain Picard orders the Moriarty simulation program saved until a way can be found to give physical form to the synthetic intelligence.

U.S.S. Victory arrives for rendezvous with the *Enterprise*-D. Captain Zimbata receives his gift of Geordi's model.

Just after "Elementary, Dear Data" (TNG).

Quark arrives at Cardassian mining station Terok Nor, orbiting planet Bajor. Quark establishes a bar and a gambling facility on the station's Promenade. Although Quark's business dealings arouse the suspicions of station authorities, no conclusive evidence of wrongdoing emerges.

Four years prior to "Emissary" (DS9).

Starship Victory, NCC-9754

"The Outrageous Okona" (TNG). Stardate 42402.7. *U.S.S. Enterprise*-D, traveling through the Omega Sagitta system, offers assistance to space vehicle *Erstwhile*, an interplanetary vessel in need of guidance system repairs.

While in the Omega Sagitta system, Captain Picard mediates a dispute between planets Atlec and Straleb. Ruling families of both planets have filed claims against *Erstwhile* captain Thadiun Okona. The dispute is resolved when Benzan, son of Secretary Kushell (of the Legation of Unity of the planet Straleb) and Yanar, daughter of Debin (captain of an Atlec space vessel) agree to marry.

U.S.S. Enterprise-D responds to a distress call from Kareen Brianon, assistant to noted molecular cyberneticist Dr. Ira Graves on the planet Gravesworld. Dr. Graves had been a teacher to reclusive roboticist Dr. Noonien Soong.

About eight hours prior to "The Schizoid Man" (TNG).

"The Schizoid Man" (TNG). Stardate 42437.5. *U.S.S. Enterprise-D*, en route to Gravesworld, also receives distress call from *U.S.S. Constantinople*. An away team is left on Gravesworld, while the *Enterprise*-D proceeds expeditiously to a successful rescue mission to the *Constantinople*. Still on Gravesworld, Dr. Ira Graves is discovered by *Enterprise*-D staff physician Dr. Selar to be terminally ill. Before his death Graves succeeds in recording the sum of his personal knowledge into Data's brain. Data subsequently downloads Graves's memories into the *Enterprise*-D computer system.

Editors' Note: Although this has been the only appearance of the Vulcan Dr. Selar to date, we did hear Selar being paged over the PA system of the alternate timeline Enterprise-D in "Yesterday's Enterprise" (TNG), and Selar was also mentioned by Dr. Crusher in "Remember Me" (TNG), "Sub Rosa" (TNG), and "All Good Things..." (TNG).

Dr. Selar

"Loud as a Whisper" (TNG). Stardate 42477.2. *U.S.S. Enterprise-D* is unexpectedly diverted to the Ramatis star system, assigned to transport famed mediator Riva to help resolve a bitter planetary conflict on planet Solais V. Initial attempts to negotiate a cease-fire between the two combatants are unsuccessful, but Riva remains behind to continue efforts to bring the adversaries together in a quest for peace.

The first officer of the *Starship Lantree* is treated for Thelusian flu, an exotic but harmless rhinovirus.

Five days prior to "Unnatural Selection" (TNG).

Mediator Riva

U.S.S. Lantree under the command of Captain Iso Telaka visits the Darwin Genetic Research Station on planet Gagarin IV. It is not realized at the time that exposure to the genetically engineered children of Darwin station scientists results in hyperaccelerated aging of all *Lantree* personnel.

Three days prior to "Unnatural Selection" (TNG), according to Telaka's log.

Twenty *Lantree* personnel are killed by unknown causes, leaving only six crew members alive. Captain Telaka orders course set for nearest Federation outpost.

Just prior to "Unnatural Selection" (TNG), stardate 42293.1.

"Unnatural Selection" (TNG). Stardate 42494.8. *U.S.S. Enterprise-D* mission to Star Station India is interrupted by a distress call from the *U.S.S. Lantree*. Responding to the call, *Enterprise*-D discovers all *Lantree* personnel to be dead from an unknown malady strongly resembling old age.

Darwin genetic research station

The source of this affliction is learned to be the Darwin Genetic Research Station on planet Gagarin IV. Further investigation determines the aging disease to be caused by genetically engineered children at the station. These children are found to possess an unusually powerful immune system that actually attacks potential causes for infection, including other human beings. Remains of *Starship Lantree* are destroyed to eliminate risk of further contamination.

U.S.S. Enterprise-D resumes mission to rendezvous with Starfleet courier at Star Station India.

Just after "Unnatural Selection." (TNG).

Kira Nerys, a member of the Bajoran underground, arrives at space station Terok Nor. Her mission is to find the names of a number of Bajoran nationals believed to be Cardassian collaborators.

"Necessary Evil" (DS9). Two weeks prior to Vaatrik's death.

Kira Nerys

Mendon

"A Matter of Honor" (TNG). Stardate 42506.5. *U.S.S. Enterprise*-D at Starbase 179 to participate in new officer exchange program. Serving temporarily aboard the *Enterprise*-D is Ensign Mendon, a Starfleet officer from the planet Benzar. *Enterprise*-D executive officer William Riker is assigned duty aboard the Klingon vessel *Pagh*, the first Federation Starfleet officer to serve aboard a Klingon ship.

A previously unknown submicron life-form is discovered by Mendon, who reports the life-form has been detected on the hulls of the *Enterprise*-D and the *Pagh*. Mendon devises a successful means of removing the parasites from both ships, using a tunneling neutrino beam.

Odo, at Cardassian space station Terok Nor, is invited by station commander Gul Dukat to serve as a security investigator. Odo's first assignment is to investigate the murder of Vaatrik, a Bajoran national who worked at the station. Kira Nerys is a suspect in the case, but Odo's investigation finds her innocent. It is not learned until years later that Kira had indeed killed Vaatrik while trying to find a list of collaborators who were selling out their fellow Bajorans.

"Necessary Evil" (DS9) and "The Wire" (DS9). Five years prior to the episodes. Kira and Odo met for the first time at this point.

"The Measure of a Man" (TNG). Stardate 42523.7. *U.S.S. Enterprise*-D at newly established Starbase 173 for crew rotation and off-loading experiment modules. Lieutenant Commander Data is assigned to Commander Bruce Maddox for study of Data's positronic neural systems to further the goal of manufacturing additional androids for Starfleet service. Data declines to accept the transfer, and Starfleet Judge Advocate General Phillipa Louvois subsequently rules that Data is indeed a life-form with full civil rights, and that he is therefore free to make his own decisions.

Editors' Note: This episode shows for the first time the weekly poker game that became a fixture of off-duty life for our heroes.

Ensign Sonya Gomez is among the new crew members transferring aboard the *Enterprise*-D at Starbase 173.

"Q Who?" (TNG) establishes her assignment.

Judge Advocate General Phillipa Louvois

"The Dauphin" (TNG). Stardate 42568.8. *U.S.S. Enterprise*-D assigned diplomatic mission to ferry Salia, a young planetary head of state, from planet Klavdia III to her home on Daled IV. Salia, an allasomorph, is returning to her home to accept her role of leader, and will attempt to unite the warring factions of her planet.

U.S.S. Yamato at planet Denius III, where Captain Donald Varley, participating in an archaeological study, deciphers evidence from an ancient Iconian artifact, making it possible to determine the actual location of the Iconian homeworld, somewhere in the Romulan Neutral Zone. Varley, citing the potentially disastrous consequences should the Romulans gain access to Iconian weapons technology, orders the *Yamato* to proceed to Iconia. Near Iconia, the *Yamato* is scanned by an Iconian space probe.

Shortly prior to "Contagion" (TNG), according to Varley's log.

"Contagion" (TNG). Stardate 42609.1. The *Enterprise*-D responds to distress call from *Starship Yamato* in the Romulan Neutral Zone, but is unable to save the ship or its crew from destruction due to major onboard computer malfunction. Investigation determines the *Yamato* to have been the victim of a computer software weapon surviving from the long-dead planet Iconia. This weapon is believed to have been transmitted during a sensor scan from an Iconian probe. During the investigation, the Romulan warbird *Haakona* is similarly infected by the software weapon, but assistance from the *Enterprise*-D averts destruction of the Romulan craft as well as an interstellar incident.

Iconian portal

A passing Klingon cruiser reports discovering pieces of an unknown space vehicle in the upper atmosphere of the eighth planet in the Theta 116 system. *Enterprise*-D diverts from scheduled course to investigate.

Just prior to "The Royale" (TNG).

"The Royale" (TNG). Stardate 42625.4. *U.S.S. Enterprise*-D investigates report of wreckage in orbit of the eighth planet in the previously unmapped Theta 116 system. An elaborate recreation of a 20th-century Earth environment is discovered on the otherwise uninhabitable planetary surface. Investigation determines the environment to have been created by an unknown alien intelligence in an effort to create a habitat for Colonel Stephen Richey, the commander of the space vehicle *Charybdis*. That vehicle had been reported missing in 2037 after the third unsuccessful attempt to explore beyond Earth's solar system.

The remains of Charybdis *commander Steven Richey on Theta 116*

U.S.S. Enterprise-D makes layover stop at Starbase 73.

Just prior to "Time Squared" (TNG).

"Time Squared" (TNG). Stardate 42679.2. Mission to planet Endicor is interrupted by discovery of a duplicate of *Enterprise*-D shuttlepod 5, drifting in space. Discovered on board the recovered vehicle is a duplicate of Captain Jean-Luc Picard. Both the shuttle and the duplicate captain had apparently come backward in time six hours, during which the *Enterprise*-D had evidently been lost with all hands except the captain. The time loop is determined to have been caused by a temporal distortion. This distortion—and the impending destruction of the *Enterprise*-D—is disrupted when Captain Picard orders the *Enterprise*-D into the center of the phenomenon.

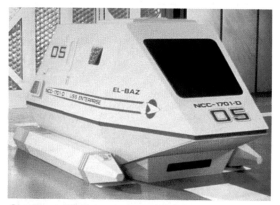

Editors' Note: The shuttlepod seen in this episode, the El-Baz, *is named for former NASA planetary geoscientist Farouk El-Baz, currently on faculty at Brown University. Several years ago, El-Baz worked on a documentary film with* Star Trek: The Next Generation *executive producer Rick Berman.*

U.S.S. Enterprise-D resumes mission to the Endicor system.

Shortly after "Time Squared."

Shuttlepod El-Baz

A Talaxian freighter is captured by operatives of the Vidiian Sodality. All 23 members of the Talaxian crew are held so that they may serve as involuntary organ donors for Vidiians suffering from a disease they call the phage.

"Faces" (VGR). Six years before the episode (2371).

Lieutenant Commander Data, while performing modifications on ship's sensors, detects a radio transmission from a previously unknown life-form in the Selcundi Drema sector. Data responds to the signal. This action is later determined to be in violation of the Starfleet Prime Directive.

"Pen Pals." Exact date is conjecture, but Data told Picard he first detected the signals about eight weeks prior to the completion of the geological survey. That survey was finished six weeks into the episode, suggesting the signals had been received about two weeks prior.

U.S.S. Enterprise-D at planet Nasreldine. A crew member contracts a flulike illness there. Afterward, minor readout anomalies require an unscheduled course change to Starbase Montgomery for engineering consultations.

Kyle Riker

Prior to "The Icarus Factor" (TNG).

"The Icarus Factor" (TNG). Stardate 42686.4. *U.S.S. Enterprise*-D at Starbase Montgomery for engineering consultations. Starfleet civilian adviser Kyle Riker, father of William Riker, is a guest aboard the *Enterprise*-D.

Commander William Riker is offered command of *Starship Aries*, a small scout ship serving in frontier areas, but he declines the promotion in favor of

Kyle and William Riker

Sarjenka, an inhabitant of Drema IV

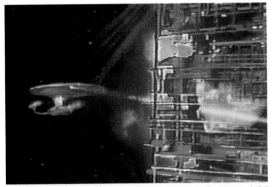

Encounter with Borg spacecraft near System J-25

Enterprise-D encounters Pakled ship

Pakled

continued service aboard the *Enterprise*-D. This is the second time Riker declines the opportunity to command a starship.

U.S.S. Enterprise-D heads for Beta Kupsic.

Just after "The Icarus Factor" (TNG).

"Pen Pals" (TNG). Stardate 42695.3. *U.S.S. Enterprise*-D on survey mission of star systems in Selcundi Drema sector. Acting Ensign Wesley Crusher is placed in charge of planetary geophysical surveys.

Lieutenant Commander Data reports receipt of a radio signal from a life-form on planet Drema IV. Data also acknowledges responding to the signal, even though such a response was in violation of Prime Directive protection. The signal is determined to be a distress call resulting from massive geologic instability on the planet. Captain Picard determines assistance to be appropriate, even though such intervention is a further violation of the Prime Directive. Picard further orders appropriate steps be taken to minimize cultural contamination from this action.

Starfleet receives a garbled message from the Ficus sector. The message is later found to be a distress call from a colony in the Bringloid system.

About a month prior to "Up the Long Ladder" (TNG).

"Q Who?" (TNG). Stardate 42761.3. *U.S.S. Enterprise* encounters the entity Q at the frontier of Federation territory. Q expresses a desire to become a member of Starfleet. When Picard declines the request, Q sends the *Enterprise*-D some 7,000 light-years across the galaxy. At the previously uncharted star system J-25, evidence is found of a Class-M planet which exhibits massive surface scarring. The phenomenon is similar to that found at outposts Delta Zero Five and Tarod IX near the Romulan Neutral Zone on stardate 41986.

At System J-25, the *Enterprise*-D shortly thereafter makes first contact with a Borg spacecraft. The Borg are determined to be a humanoid species making extensive use of cybernetic implants. Their spacecraft is extremely powerful, but highly decentralized, supporting a hivelike shared consciousness. First contact is a Borg incursion on the *Enterprise*, resulting in severe damage to the *Enterprise*-D, the loss of shuttle 06, and the death of eighteen *Enterprise*-D personnel.

Q, apparently satisfied with his demonstration of the hostile and powerful nature of the Borg, later returns the *Enterprise*-D to Federation space.

U.S.S. Enterprise-D travels to Starbase 83.

After "Q Who?" (TNG).

"Samaritan Snare" (TNG). Stardate 42779.1. Captain Jean-Luc Picard and Ensign Wesley Crusher take personal leave at Starbase 515. Crusher's leave is for the purpose of taking Starfleet Academy exams. Picard reports to the Starbase hospital for routine replacement of his bionic heart

U.S.S. Enterprise-D is en route to planet Epsilon IX for astronomical survey of Epsilon Pulsar cluster when diverted to investigate a distress call from the Rhomboid Dronegar sector. The distress call is found to have been sent from a Pakled ship, the *Mondor*. Further investigation reveals the call was a ruse, an unsuccessful attempt to gain access to Federation weapons technology by capturing *Enterprise*-D chief engineer Geordi La Forge.

U.S.S. Enterprise-D at Starbase 73. Picard has meeting with Admiral Moore to discuss a distress call received from the Ficus sector.

Just prior to "Up the Long Ladder" (TNG).

"Up the Long Ladder" (TNG). Stardate 42823.2. *U.S.S. Enterprise*-D, having departed from Starbase 73, proceeds to the planet Bringloid V in the Ficus sector. A colony on the planet had sent a distress call because of severe solar flares in that system. At Bringloid V, *Enterprise*-D personnel evacuate all colonists and discover evidence of a second, previously unknown colony, in a nearby system. Investigating further, the missing colony is discovered on a nearby planet called Mariposa. It is learned that due to a disastrous crash landing of their ship, the Mariposa colony began with only five individuals who used cloning technology in an attempt to keep their society populated. The inhabitants of the colony report, however, that replicative fading threatens to make their culture nonviable. The Bringloidi colonists and the Mariposans agree to a joint settlement in an attempt to make both groups viable.

Lwaxana Troi and her aide, Mr. Homn

Starfleet Command begins advance planning to develop a means to defend against a possible Borg attack, based on evidence that the Borg are approaching Federation space. The project is given high priority, but little of use is forthcoming due to the extraordinary power of the Borg.

"Best of Both Worlds, Part I" (TNG). Admiral Hanson said they'd been aware of the Borg and had been working on new defense technologies for more than a year prior to the episode.

Anteden assassins

"Manhunt" (TNG). Stardate 42859.2. *U.S.S. Enterprise*-D on diplomatic mission to transport Antedean and Betazoid delegates to a conference on the planet Pacifica to consider the question of admitting planet Antede III to the Federation. The telepathic assistance of Betazoid ambassador Lwaxana Troi is instrumental in exposing two Antedan delegates as assassins, intent upon disrupting the conference.

A Federation conference on planet Pacifica convenes to consider the petition of planet Antede III for admission to the United Federation of Planets.

Just after "Manhunt" (TNG).

Starbase 336 receives an automated transmission from the *T'Ong*, a Klingon sleeper ship launched in 2290, now returning to Klingon space.

"The Emissary" (TNG). Two days prior to the episode.

Emissary K'Ehleyr

"The Emissary" (TNG). Stardate 42901.3. Special Federation emissary K'Ehleyr is dispatched to the *Enterprise*-D with orders to intercept the Klingon sleeper ship *T'Ong* near the Boradis system before its crew is automatically revived. The *Enterprise*-D mission is based on fears that the *T'Ong* crew, launched prior to the Khitomer peace conference of 2293, still believes that a state of war exists between the United Federation of Planets and the Klingon Empire. K'Ehleyr's orders include the option to destroy the *T'Ong* and its crew if necessary, but Captain Picard opposes this course. Instead, he and Lieutenant Worf devise an alternate strategy in which Worf poses as *Enterprise*-D captain long enough to order the *T'Ong*'s crew to accept command of K'Ehleyr.

Sirna Kolrami

During the *T'Ong* crisis, Emissary K'Ehleyr and *Enterprise*-D security chief Worf renew an old romantic relationship, although K'Ehleyr declines to take the Klingon oath of marriage. Unknown to Worf at the time, their liaison results in the conception of a child.

The title of this episode, "The Emissary" (TNG), should not be confused with "Emissary, Parts I and II" (DS9), which was the 2-hour pilot episode for Star Trek: Deep Space Nine.

"Peak Performance" (TNG). Stardate 42923.4. *U.S.S. Enterprise*-D participates in strategic simulation exercise near the Braslota star system ordered by Starfleet in preparation for possible conflict with the Borg. Also participating

U.S.S. Hathaway, NCC-2593

William Riker undergoes therapy following an injury on planet Surata IV

in the exercise is the *U.S.S. Hathaway,* an older vessel temporarily commanded by William Riker. The entire operation is overseen by Zakdorn tactician Sirna Kolrami. The exercise is briefly interrupted by the Ferengi spacecraft *Kreechta,* whose commander misinterprets the tactical importance of the obsolete *Hathaway.*

U.S.S. Enterprise-D returns to the nearest starbase.

Just after "Peak Performance" (TNG).

Alexana Devos accepts a job as security director with the Eastern Continental government of planet Rutia IV. Two days later, a terrorist bomb destroys a shuttlebus, killing sixty schoolchildren. Operatives of the Ansata separatist movement are implicated in the incident.

"The High Ground" (TNG). Exact date is conjecture, but Alexana said she started as director six months prior to the episode. She also said the shuttlebus bombing happened two days after she took the job.

"Shades of Gray" (TNG). Stardate 42976.1. *U.S.S. Enterprise*-D on survey mission to planet Surata IV, when Commander William Riker is injured by accidental contact with indigenous plant form.

6.3 STAR TREK: THE NEXT GENERATION — YEAR 3

Worf, son of Mogh, defends his family honor before the Klingon High Council

2366

Dr. Katherine Pulaski completes her assignment on the *U.S.S. Enterprise*-D and is replaced by Dr. Beverly Crusher, who returns after a year at Starfleet Medical. Geordi La Forge is promoted to the rank of lieutenant commander. Worf is promoted to full lieutenant.

These changes occurred after the end of the second season but before the first episode of the third.

Starfleet Command studies the threat posed by the Borg and concludes that significant defensive resources will be needed when the Borg reach Federation space. Accordingly, Starfleet begins development of a new type of starship. While officially classified as an escort, the new *Defiant*-class vessels will be heavily armed and are specifically designed to meet the Borg in battle.

"The Search, Part I" (DS9). Five years before the episode (2371).

Dr. Katherine Pulaski

"Evolution" (TNG). Stardate 43125.8. *U.S.S. Enterprise*-D on astrophysical research mission for Dr. Paul Stubbs in the Kavis Alpha Sector. The mission, to deliver an instrumented probe into the Kavis Alpha neutron star, is accomplished successfully despite a systems failure aboard the *Enterprise*-D due to the activity of a newly evolved nanite lifeform. The Nanites, accidentally evolved from nanotechnologic robots developed for medical applications, now are found to be an intelligent species, and are granted colonization rights on planet Kavis Alpha IV.

Editors' Note: This episode was actually filmed after "The Ensigns of Command" (TNG) but was aired first, since "Evolution" (TNG) also dealt with Beverly Crusher returning to the Enterprise-D *after her absence in the second season.*

Dr. Paul Stubbs

Sheliak representative

Data pilots Shuttlepod Onizuka

Tau Cygna V settlement

Kevin and
Rishon
Uxbridge

Observation
post on
Mintaka III

Romulan admiral Alidar Jarok is censured for his arguments to the Romulan High Command that a war with the Federation would destroy the Romulan Star Empire. Jarok is reassigned to command a distant sector of the empire. It is later learned that this reassignment is part of a plan to provide the idealistic Jarok with false strategic information as a test of loyalty.

"The Defector" (TNG). Exact date is conjecture; Jarok said his reassignment was four months prior to the episode.

"The Ensigns of Command" (TNG). (No stardate given in episode.) *U.S.S. Enterprise*-D receives message from the Sheliak Corporate demanding the removal of Federation colonists on planet Tau Cygna V. The Sheliak claim the settlement exists in contravention of the Treaty of Armens, in which the Federation ceded the planet to the Sheliak. Captain Picard negotiates with the Sheliak to gain sufficient time to evacuate the colonists.

Lieutenant Commander Data transports to Tau Cygna V via shuttlepod and negotiates with colonists to evacuate their settlement in the time allowed by the Sheliak.

Editors' Note: The shuttlepod seen in this episode, the Onizuka, *was named for* Challenger *astronaut Ellison Onizuka. The shuttle* Onizuka *was recreated in floral form as part of a* Star Trek: The Next Generation *float in the 1992 Tournament of Roses Parade in Pasadena. Also part of that float was an enormous floral model of the U.S.S. Enterprise-D, and a second shuttlepod named in honor of* Star Trek *creator Gene Roddenberry.*

U.S.S. Enterprise-D receives a distress call from the Federation colony on planet Delta Rana IV. The transmission reports the colony is under attack from an unidentified spacecraft.

Three days prior to "The Survivors" (TNG).

"The Survivors" (TNG). Stardate 43152.4. *U.S.S. Enterprise*-D is at planet Delta Rana IV in response to distress call and for possible confrontation with a hostile force. Investigation reveals that the entire colony has been destroyed, except for a single dwelling, that of Kevin and Rishon Uxbridge. The mission is interrupted by the attack of what is apparently a Husnock spacecraft. Further investigation determines that both the attack and the image of Rishon Uxbridge are illusions created by Kevin, who the crew learns is a powerful entity known as a Douwd. Kevin reveals that the colony had been destroyed by a Husnock attack some years prior, that in anger he had used his powers to destroy utterly the entire Husnock species, and that he must now live with the guilt of that act.

U.S.S. Enterprise-D heads for Starbase 133.

Just after "The Survivors" (TNG).

D'Ghor begins a systematic financial attack on the House of Kozak, preying on Kozak's weakness for gambling. The House of D'Ghor and the House of Kozak had been sworn enemies for seven generations.

"The House of Quark" (DS9). About five years before the episode (2371).

"Who Watches the Watchers?" (TNG). Stardate 43173.5. *U.S.S. Enterprise*-D on resupply mission to Federation anthropological observation team on planet Mintaka III. The proto-Vulcan humanoid inhabitants there are at the Bronze Age level and are thus still subject to Prime Directive protection.

The mission is complicated when the observation team's holographic duck-blind briefly fails, resulting in cultural contamination when Mintakan natives see the Federation facility. The contamination is made worse when one of the natives receives medical care from *Enterprise*-D personnel and interprets the experience as a fulfillment of local religious prophesy, believing Captain Picard to be a deity. Picard employs limited exposure to Starfleet personnel and technology in order to minimize the effect of the contamination by convincing Mintakan leader Nuria that he is not their god.

Editors' Note: The Mintakan tapestry given to Picard at the end of the episode could sometimes be seen in later episodes as a decoration on the back of Picard's chair in his living quarters.

Cardassian official Gul Dukat, believing that the days of the Bajoran occupation are numbered, becomes concerned with the future for his Bajoran mistress, Tora Naprem, and their daughter, Tora Ziyal. Dukat arranges for them to be transported aboard the freighter ship *Ravinok* to planet Lissepia, where they could live out their lives away from the Bajoran-Cardassian hostilities and prejudice.

The Cardassian freighter *Ravinok,* transporting Bajoran prisoners, is reported missing. Among the Bajoran prisoners believed lost aboard the *Ravinok* is Lorit Akrem, a friend of Kira Nerys. Also missing are passengers Tora Ziyal, and her mother, Tora Naprem. The Cardassian government does not realize that the ship had been attacked by Breen forces, and that the *Ravinok's* survivors have been forced to work in Breen dilithium mines on a planet in the Dozaria system.

"Indiscretion" (DS9). Six years before the episode (2372).

"The Bonding" (TNG). Stardate 43198.7. *U.S.S. Enterprise-D* away team is on an archaeological research mission, when an explosive artifact, a bomb left over from an ancient war, kills archaeologist Marla Aster. Surviving Aster is her 12-year-old son, Jeremy. The Koinonians, a civilization of non-corporeal life-forms from the planet, offer to accept responsibility for the orphaned child's upbringing, but the offer is declined. *Enterprise-D* security officer Worf, who had commanded the mission on which Lieutenant Aster was killed, adopts Jeremy into his family through the Klingon *R'uustai* (bonding) ceremony.

Jeremy Aster and the re-created image of his mother, Marla

Editors' Note: Producer/Writer Ron Moore named the Koinonians for his fraternity at Cornell University.

Jeremy Aster is returned to Earth to be raised by his aunt and uncle, his only living biological relatives.

After "The Bonding" (TNG).

"Booby Trap" (TNG). Stardate 43205.6. *U.S.S. Enterprise-D* is at an asteroid field in the Orelious system to chart the historic battle that resulted in the extinction of both the Menthars and Promellians. A derelict Promellian ship, apparently disabled during the battle, is discovered in the asteroid field. An energy-damping field, which drained power from the Promellian ship, is found to be still active, threatening the *Enterprise-D* until a means is devised to maneuver the ship from the field using minimal thruster power.

Derelict Promellian ship

"The Enemy" (TNG). Stardate 43349.2. *U.S.S. Enterprise-D* responds to an unidentified distress signal originating at planet Galorndon Core. Investigation reveals the signal to be from the wreckage of a small Romulan vessel. The incident is of tactical significance because of Galorndon Core's location a half light-year within Federation space.

One survivor from the downed Romulan craft is found and transported back to the *Enterprise-D* for medical treatment. The patient later dies because of the unavailability of Romulan-compatible ribosomes. A second survivor, Centurion Bochra, is later reported by Geordi La Forge. A Romulan warbird arrives to participate in the rescue mission, and takes custody of Centurion Bochra. Warbird commander Tomalak denies that the incursion of Bochra's ship was a treaty violation, claiming it was the result of a navigational error.

Geordi La Forge and Centurion Bochra

The separatist Ansata of planet Rutia IV begin the use of an interdimensional transport device in their terrorist raids. Although the nature of the process

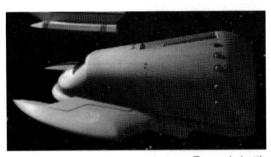

Hekran scientist Serova

Devinoni Ral

Sovereign Marouk

Yuta, of the clan Tralesta

Ferengi shuttle

results in irreversible cellular damage to the transport subject, the Ansata terrorists continue to use the device because it is virtually untraceable and can successfully transport through force fields.

"The High Ground" (TNG). Exact date is conjecture, but Alexana noted that the Ansata had begun to use the new transporter about two months prior to the episode.

Hekaran scientist Serova develops a theoretical model for the long-term effects of warp drive on the fabric of space. Her findings suggest potentially serious side effects resulting from cumulative subspace instabilities, eventually resulting in a violent subspace rift. Her findings are not widely accepted among the scientific community. Even her own brother, Rabal, is skeptical.

Four years before "Force of Nature" (TNG).

Worf sees his stepbrother, Nikolai Rozhenko, for the last time prior to their meeting on planet Boraal II in 2370.

"Homeward" (TNG). Four years prior to the episode.

The government of the planet Barzan, under the leadership of Premier Bhavani, invites bids for control of a wormhole near Barzan. The wormhole is considered a vital natural resource due to its highly unusual stability. Bhavani hopes that fees for wormhole use will be of significant economic benefit to her people.

Prior to "The Price" (TNG).

"The Price" (TNG). Stardate 43385.6. *U.S.S. Enterprise*-D serves as host for negotiations for use of the Barzan wormhole. Negotiator Devinoni Ral, acting on behalf of the Chrysalians, forms a strategic alliance with the Ferengi in an effort to discourage other bidders. During the negotiations, an expedition of shuttle vehicles from the *Enterprise*-D and the Ferengi vessel finds the wormhole to be partially unstable. The Ferengi shuttle is lost due to the instability. It is believed to have ended up somewhere in the Delta Quadrant.

Editors' Note: We ran into the two lost Ferengi again in "False Profit" (VGR).

"The Vengeance Factor" (TNG). Stardate 43421.9. *U.S.S. Enterprise*-D discovers a Federation scientific outpost near the Acamarian system has been ransacked. All station personnel are discovered to have been heavily stunned by phaser fire. Investigation suggests the attack was conducted by an Acamarian outlaw group called the Gatherers. The Gatherers had been blamed for a significant number of similar incidents in recent months.

Starship Enterprise-D travels to planet Acamar III to enlist local government support in discouraging the Gatherers' raids. With the assistance of Acamarian sovereign Marouk, a conference is convened at planet Gamma Hromi II with representatives of the Gatherers. The conference is disrupted when Marouk's personal servant, Yuta, attempts to murder Gatherer delegate Chorgan, a member of the clan Lornak. Yuta is discovered to be a member of the nearly extinct clan Tralesta. She is found to have been trying for 80 years to exact revenge upon the Lornak clan for the massacre of her people 80 years ago. A truce is later negotiated with the Gatherers, who agree to return to their original home planet, Acamar III.

Scheduled rendezvous with starship *U.S.S. Goddard* is postponed by new orders from Starfleet.

U.S.S. Enterprise-D goes to Starbase 343 to take on medical supplies for the Alpha Leonis system. Captain Picard authorizes shore leave for *Enterprise*-D personnel. A rendezvous with the *U.S.S. Goddard* is scheduled after the starbase layover.

Just after "The Vengeance Factor" (TNG).

"The Defector" (TNG). Stardate 43462.5. The *Enterprise*-D, near the Romulan Neutral Zone, detects a small Romulan scout craft within the zone in violation of treaty. Shortly thereafter, a Romulan warbird is detected in pursuit.

The pilot of the scout ship requests asylum and is taken aboard the *Enterprise*-D. The pilot is determined to be Romulan admiral Alidar Jarok, who claims to have defected to warn of a potentially destabilizing new Romulan outpost at planet Nelvana III, inside the Neutral Zone. Because of the gravity of the situation, Picard orders the *Enterprise*-D into the Neutral Zone to investigate, but determines Jarok's information to be baseless. The crew later finds that Jarok is the victim of an elaborate hoax conducted by the Romulan government, intended as a test of loyalty and an attempt to provoke an interstellar incident. The *Enterprise*-D withdraws with Klingon assistance. Jarok commits suicide by poison.

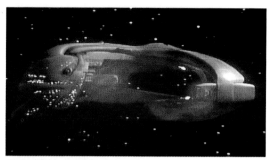
Romulan warbird

The government of the planet Angosia III petitions for membership in the United Federation of Planets.

Prior to "The Hunted" (TNG).

"The Hunted" (TNG). Stardate 43489.2. *U.S.S. Enterprise*-D at planet Angosia III on diplomatic mission in response to the Angosian application for membership to the Federation. The mission is interrupted when *Enterprise*-D captain Picard agrees to render assistance to local authorities in capturing a prisoner escaped from a high-security penal colony. The prisoner, a former Angosian soldier named Roga Danar, is successfully captured and returned to local authorities.

Enterprise-D personnel learn that Danar is the product of intense biochemical and psychological manipulation engineered for a recent Angosian war. Upon conclusion of the war, the Angosian government imprisoned the soldiers for fear of having the warriors loose in normal society. Danar's escape is discovered to be part of an uprising by prisoners to demand rehabilitation for the veterans. Captain Picard cites Prime Directive considerations in declining Starfleet interference with the uprising. Picard agrees to further consider the Angosian petition for Federation membership, pending outcome of the uprising.

Romulan Admiral Alidar Jarok

U.S.S. Enterprise-D heads for the starbase at Lya III.

Just after "The Hunted" (TNG).

The government of planet Rutia IV requests Federation medical assistance following an outbreak of terrorist activity on the planet.

Prior to "The High Ground" (TNG).

"The High Ground" (TNG). Stardate 43510.7. *U.S.S. Enterprise*-D at planet Rutia IV to deliver medical supplies following reports of local unrest on the planet. While supervising delivery of the supplies, *Enterprise*-D chief medical officer Beverly Crusher is kidnapped by members of the Ansata separatist movement. Attempts to negotiate Crusher's release with Ansata operatives are unsuccessful, and the Ansata conduct additional terrorist attacks against the *Enterprise*-D itself. Although the first attack is thwarted, the second results in the kidnapping of Captain Jean-Luc Picard.

Roga Danar

Rutian security director Alexana assists *Enterprise*-D personnel in conducting a rescue mission that succeeds in freeing both Picard and Crusher.

The United Federation of Planets signs a peace treaty with the Cardassians, concluding a long and bloody conflict with the Cardassian Union. Still to be resolved are a number of hotly-contested border disputes between the two powers.

Crusher treats bombing victim on Rutia IV

"The Wounded" (TNG). Exact date is conjecture, but Picard's log establishes the treaty had been signed "nearly a year" prior to the episode (2367).

Ansata Leader Finn

Note that "Chain of Command, Part I" (TNG) suggests that Captain Jellico had helped to negotiate this agreement, although Admiral Nechayev said it was two years prior to that episode (2369), which would put this treaty at 2367. Border disputes were established in "Journey's End" (TNG), which establishes that the disputes were settled after three years of negotiations.

A large celestial body, probably a black hole, passes through the plane of the Bre'el star system, disrupting the orbit of the moon of planet Bre'el IV. The asteroidal moon's orbit begins to decay, threatening the inhabitants of Bre'el IV.

Just prior to "Deja Q" (TNG).

Q

"Deja Q (TNG). Stardate 43539.1. *U.S.S. Enterprise*-D responds to distress call from planet Bre'el IV, and attempts to use the ship's tractor beam to alter the orbit of the descending asteroidal moon. The effort fails due to insufficient beam power. A second attempt is made with an unorthodox technique, using a low-level warp field to reduce the moon's gravitational constant. This effort is also unsuccessful.

Q once again appears on the *Enterprise*-D, this time claiming that he has been stripped of his powers. He requests asylum and is assigned to help develop a solution to the Bre'el crisis. Q meets with another member of the Q continuum and thereafter reports that his powers have been restored. Q uses those powers to circularize the Bre'el moon's orbit at a safe altitude.

Q does not realize it, but his rebellion against the order of the Continuum is of considerable interest to many in the Continuum, including a former philosopher who will one day be known as Quinn.

"Death Wish" (VGR). After Q's rebellion in "Deja Q" (TNG).

Starship Enterprise-D heads for Station Nigala IV.

Just after "Deja Q" (TNG).

Lieutenant Commander Shelby of Starfleet Tactical is placed in charge of Borg tactical analysis by Admiral J. P. Hanson. Her assignment is to develop a defense strategy against an anticipated Borg offensive.

"The Best of Both Worlds, Part I" (TNG). Admiral Hanson told Picard that Shelby had taken over the project six months before the episode.

Stardate 43587. Crewman First Class Simon Tarses is assigned to duty in the medical department aboard the *U.S.S. Enterprise*-D.

"The Drumhead" (TNG). The stardate given by Tarses places it between "Deja Q" (TNG) and "A Matter of Perspective" (TNG).

Commander Shelby

U.S.S. Enterprise-D is en route to a mission for the study of a proto-star cloud, when it is briefly diverted by a request from the Tanuga IV research station for dicosilium supplies.

Just prior to "A Matter of Perspective" (TNG).

Dr. Nel Apgar and his wife

"A Matter of Perspective" (TNG). Stardate 43610.4. The *Starship Enterprise*-D makes delivery of dicosilium to the Tanuga IV research station. Commander William Riker remains on the station while the *Enterprise*-D departs for 24 hours to conduct its original protostar survey mission. Riker gathers data to evaluate the progress of Dr. Nel Apgar, a scientist believed to be on the verge of developing a technique for the use of Krieger waves for power generation. Shortly thereafter the *Enterprise*-D returns to pick up Riker, and the space station explodes under mysterious circumstances, resulting in the death of Dr. Apgar.

Local authorities accuse Commander Riker of murder in the incident, but Captain Picard successfully negotiates a stay of extradition pending an

investigation. Research using a holodeck recreation of the events leading up to the explosion results in Riker's acquittal.

U.S.S. Enterprise-D heads for Emila II.

Just after "A Matter of Perspective" (TNG).

"Yesterday's *Enterprise*" (TNG). Stardate 43625.2. *U.S.S. Enterprise*-D personnel discover an unusual radiation anomaly in space. Investigation determines the anomaly to be a temporal rift, possibly a Kerr loop of superstring material. Initial readings suggest there may have been a spacecraft within the rift, but later indications show this reading was mistaken. A Class-1 sensor probe is launched to further investigate the phenomenon.

Tasha Yar

Several years later, evidence accumulates indicating that there was indeed a space vehicle in the anomaly. The other ship may have been the *Ambassador*-class starship *Enterprise*, NCC-1701-C, and its emergence from 22 years in the past may have triggered significant damage to the temporal continuum. Evidence suggests that in the alternate timeline, the Federation may have been embroiled in an extended war with the Klingon Empire, but the return of the *Enterprise*-C to its proper time apparently restored the original path of the continuum. It is later determined that in this alternate timeline, *Enterprise*-D security officer Tasha Yar did not die at Vagra II, and instead traveled back in time with the *Enterprise*-C into a common past, about 2344. In this past Yar was captured by Romulans, and eventually gave birth to a daughter, Sela, who grew up to become a Romulan operative.

U.S.S. Enterprise, NCC-1701-C

U.S.S. Enterprise-D travels to planet Archer IV.

Just after "Yesterday's Enterprise*" (TNG).*

Lieutenant Commander Data attends a cybernetics conference, learning of recent advances in submicron matrix transfer technology. Upon returning to the *Enterprise*-D, Data uses the new techniques to attempt the transfer of his neural net programming into a positronic brain similar to his own. Commander Riker temporarily departs the *Enterprise*-D to take personal leave while the ship conducts a routine mapping mission in sector 396. He returns to the *Enterprise*-D shortly after stardate 43657.0.

Data

Prior to "The Offspring" (TNG).

"The Offspring" (TNG). Stardate 43657.0. Lieutenant Commander Data announces that his efforts to program a positronic brain have been a result of his desire to create a child. He further reveals that he has constructed an android body for the child, and that he has activated it, giving it the name Lal, from the Hindi word meaning "beloved."

Upon being notified of the development, Starfleet Research at the Galor IV annex of the Daystrom Institute expresses an interest in Data's work, and requests the transfer of Lal to the Daystrom Institute for study. Data declines the request on grounds that he does not wish to give up custody of his child. Starfleet Admiral Anthony Haftel, citing the disastrous M-5 tests of 2268, renders an administrative ruling requiring Data to relinquish custody, but Captain Picard orders Data not to comply, citing issues of personal liberty. The question becomes moot when a malfunction in Lal's neural matrix cascades into a systemwide failure, resulting in her death.

Kova Tholl, an inhabitant of planet Mizar II, is abducted by unknown aliens as part of a behavioral study. Tholl is a public servant, assistant to the regent of Pozaron, the third-largest city on Mizar II. Tholl is replaced by a near-perfect replica.

Data's android child, Lal

"Allegiance" (TNG). Tholl said he had been kidnapped about twelve days prior to the episode.

Worf faces his accusers

Chancellor K'mpec

"Sins of the Father" (TNG). Stardate 43685.2. *U.S.S. Enterprise*-D conducts a cometary cloud and asteroid survey. Klingon commander Kurn serves aboard the *Starship Enterprise*-D as part of the continuing exchange program. Kurn informs Lieutenant Worf that the two are brothers, having been separated shortly before the Khitomer massacre of 2346. He further informs Worf that the Klingon High Council has judged their father, Mogh, to be a traitor for his alleged role in the Khitomer massacre 20 years ago.

Captain Picard orders the *Enterprise*-D to the Klingon Homeworld so that Worf can challenge the allegations against his father. Although initial evidence appears to be damning, comparison against sensor logs from the *U.S.S. Intrepid* suggests the data files had been tampered with. It is later revealed that Worf has uncovered information implicating Ja'rod, the father of council member Duras, in betrayal just prior to the Khitomer massacre. Kurn is injured in an ambush, apparently by Duras family operatives attempting to dissuade Worf from presenting these findings, but Picard agrees to fulfill the ceremonial role of *cha'DIch* so that the inquiry can continue. Chancellor K'mpec, leader of the High Council, refuses to admit the new evidence, citing the political implications of exposing the powerful Duras family. A compromise is reached in which Worf accepts discommendation from the council for his father's alleged acts, but is allowed to go free.

Editors' Note: K'mpec was not referred to as "chancellor," but since Gorkon (Star Trek VI) and Gowron ("Way of the Warrior" [DS9], et al.) both had that title, it seems reasonable that K'mpec was a chancellor as well.

U.S.S. Enterprise-D assists in eradicating an outbreak of Phyrox plague on planet Cor Caroli V. Starfleet classifies the incident as "secret."

Just prior to "Allegiance" (TNG).

"Allegiance" (TNG). Stardate 43714.1. *U.S.S. Enterprise*-D proceeds to rendezvous with *U.S.S. Hood* for terraforming project on planet Browder IV.

Captain Picard is abducted by unidentified alien scientists, who employ the captain to conduct a behavioral study into the nature of authority. Also abducted for the study is Kova Tholl of the planet Mizar II, and Esoqq of the planet Chalna. All three individuals are replaced with near-perfect replicas, who conduct additional studies in their subjects' natural environments. The study is discontinued when Captain Picard and his fellow captives refuse to participate.

Editors' Note: The fake participant in the study, Cadet Haro, was described as a "Bolian," from planet Bolarus IX. These people, first seen as Captain Rixx in "Conspiracy" (TNG), were named after director Cliff Bole, who directed that episode.

U.S.S. Enterprise-D resumes course for rendezvous with *U.S.S. Hood* for Browder IV terraforming project.

Just after "Allegiance" (TNG).

In the mirror universe, the mirror Benjamin Sisko and Jennifer Sisko are separated.

"Through the Looking Glass" (DS9). Five years before the episode (2371).

U.S.S. Enterprise-D at planet Gemaris V, where Captain Picard serves as mediator in a trade dispute between the Gemarians and their nearest neighbor, the Dachlyds.

At least two weeks before "Captain's Holiday." Riker noted that the conference had lasted for two weeks.

Esoqq of planet Chalna

"Captain's Holiday" (TNG). Stardate 43745.2. At the recommendation of Chief Medical Officer Crusher, Captain Picard takes shore leave on the resort planet of Risa while the *Enterprise*-D departs to Starbase 12 for a week of routine maintenance. While on shore leave, Picard works with archaeologist Vash in an effort to continue Dr. Samuel Estragon's search for the *Tox Uthat*, a 27th-century artifact hidden in the past. The device is believed to have enormous potential as a weapons system. Although the search for the *Uthat* is successful, the artifact is destroyed to prevent it from falling into the hands of two 27th-century Vorgon criminals who have also traveled back to this time.

U.S.S. Enterprise-D undergoes a maintenance layover at Starbase 12.

Editors' Note: In "Captain's Holiday," Riker asked Picard to bring him a souvenir, a Horga'hn *statuette. Picard does so, and in later episodes the* Horga'hn *can often be seen in Riker's quarters.*

Vorgon criminals from the 27th century

The unmanned *Vega IX* probe returns scientific data from the star Beta Stromgren, a star beyond Federation space, believed to be on the verge of exploding into a supernova. Among the data is evidence of a small object, possibly a spaceborne organic life-form. The object, believed to be of significant strategic importance, is code-named Tin Man.

Prior to "Tin Man" (TNG).

The Tox Uthat

"Tin Man" (TNG). Stardate 43779.3. *U.S.S. Enterprise*-D is en route to mission to prepare detailed exospheric charts of planets in the Hayashi system. The mission is interrupted by a priority rendezvous with *U.S.S. Hood*, relaying classified orders to investigate the newly discovered Tin Man. Also conveyed aboard the *Hood* is Tam Elbrun, a Federation specialist in communication with unknown life-forms. Elbrun, a full Betazoid, had earlier been a patient of Deanna Troi's at the University of Betazed.

Despite interference from a Romulan expedition wishing to utilize Tin Man for Romulan interests, mission specialist Elbrun is successful in establishing a symbiotic rapport with the previously unknown creature. Elbrun elects to remain with Tin Man (which refers to itself as Gomtuu) and is successful in propelling the *Enterprise*-D and a *D'Deridex*-class Romulan warbird to safety just prior to the explosion of Beta Stromgren.

Tam Ulbrun

Editors' Note: Engineer Russell, who worked with Geordi to reroute the ship's power and get the sensors working in the episode, was named for Russell Bailey, the son of "Tin Man" (TNG) cowriter Dennis Bailey.

U.S.S. Enterprise-D goes to Starbase 152 for inspection and repairs to damage resulting from the Gomtuu encounter.

Just after "Tin Man" (TNG).

Lieutenant Reginald Barclay III, a systems diagnostics engineer, transfers from the *U.S.S. Zhukov* to serve aboard the *U.S.S. Enterprise*-D. Barclay is highly recommended by *Zhukov* captain Gleason, despite Barclay's tendencies toward reclusive behavior.

Prior to "Hollow Pursuits."

Reginald Barclay

"Hollow Pursuits" (TNG). Stardate 43807.4. *U.S.S. Enterprise*-D accepts a shipment of special tissue samples donated by the Mikulaks for transport to planet Nahmi IV. It is hoped the samples will help develop a cure for an outbreak of Correllium fever on that planet. A number of serious systems malfunctions aboard the *Enterprise*-D are later traced to contamination from invidium used in the Mikulak sample containers. The invidium contamination is rendered inert by exposure to cryogenic temperatures.

Lieutenant Barclay receives an unsatisfactory performance rating for his work in the *Enterprise*-D engineering department. Barclay's rating is further jeopardized by revelations that he had been surreptitiously creating holodeck simulations of his crewmates, in violation of protocol. Counselor Troi reports

Tissue samples from Nahmi IV

this behavior to be due to Barclay's feeling of social awkwardness. Later, his performance improves when given support from his superiors. Barclay is credited with being instrumental in diagnosing and resolving the malfunctions resulting from the Mikulak invidium contamination.

U.S.S. Enterprise-D proceeds to Starbase 121 for complete systems and biode-contamination.

Just after "Hollow Pursuits" (TNG). One might assume they went to planet Nahmi IV as well.

Serious tricyanate contamination threatens the subsurface water supply for the Federation colony on planet Beta Agni II. The *U.S.S. Enterprise*-D is ordered to lend assistance.

Prior to "The Most Toys" (TNG).

Kivas Fajo

"The Most Toys" (TNG). Stardate 43872.2. *U.S.S. Enterprise-D* procures 108 kilograms of hytritium compound from the Zibalian trader Kivas Fajo. The hytritium is required to treat the tricyanate contamination at planet Beta Agni II. Because of the risks inherent in beaming such a dangerously unstable substance, the hytritium is transported via shuttlepod piloted by Data. An apparent failure in a hytritium containment vessel results in the destruction of the shuttle, along with its pilot, en route to the *Enterprise*-D.

The remaining hytritium compound is deemed sufficient to neutralize the Beta Agni II groundwater contamination, and the treatment is performed without incident. Postmission analysis suggests that the tricyanate contamination may have been deliberate sabotage, and further investigation implicates Kivas Fajo. It is later learned that Fajo was indeed responsible for the Beta Agni II contamination, and that he had staged the entire incident as a ruse to abduct Data, who was not killed in the shuttle explosion as previously believed. *U.S.S. Enterprise*-D intercepts Fajo's ship, the *Jovis*, and extracts Data from Fajo's custody with the assistance of Varria. Fajo himself is placed under arrest for kidnapping and theft.

Varria

Editors' Note: The shuttlepod piloted by Data in this episode, the Pike, *was named for the former* Enterprise *captain seen in "The Menagerie" (TOS). Fajo was named for* Star Trek *production staffer Lolita Fatjo. Varria was named for writer René Echevarria.*

"Sarek" (TNG). Stardate 43917.4. *U.S.S. Enterprise*-D on diplomatic mission to host a conference between Federation Ambassador Sarek and a delegation from Legara IV. Preparations for the conference are disrupted by outbreaks of unexplained violence among the *Enterprise*-D crew. Investigation suggests that Ambassador Sarek may be suffering from Bendii syndrome, and that the violent incidents may be the side effects of that ailment.

Sarek of Vulcan

Further investigation supports the theory that Sarek is indeed afflicted with Bendii syndrome, which causes the gradual and irreversible degeneration of intellectual capacity and emotional control. Sarek is found to have deteriorated to the point where his ability to conduct the Legaran conference is in doubt. At the suggestion of Sarek's wife, Perrin, Captain Picard agrees to a mind-meld with Sarek in hope of reinforcing the ambassador's emotional control for a brief time. The mind-meld, though painful for Picard, is successful, and the Legarans indeed agree to diplomatic relations with the Federation. This agreement is hailed as the final triumph of Sarek's distinguished career.

Editors' Note: Except for a brief cameo by DeForest Kelley as Admiral McCoy in "Encounter at Farpoint" (TNG), "Sarek" (TNG) marks the first major "crossover" involving a character from the original Star Trek *series.*

Sarek, Perrin, and the Vulcan delegation return to Vulcan on board the *Starship Merrimack.*

Perrin

After "Sarek" (TNG).

"Menage à Troi" (TNG). Stardate 43930.7. *U.S.S. Enterprise*-D is in attendance at the biennial Trade Agreements Conference on Betazed. In attendance at closing banquet held aboard ship is Betazed delegate Lwaxana Troi, along with a Ferengi delegation headed by DaiMon Tog.

U.S.S. Enterprise-D departs Betazed for a stellar mapping mission in the Gamma Erandi Nebula, during which time Counselor Troi and Commander Riker take shore leave on Betazed. Riker, Troi, and Lwaxana Troi are abducted by DaiMon Tog from the surface of Betazed to the Ferengi vessel *Krayton*. Tog offers Lwaxana Troi a partnership designed to take advantage of her Betazoid telepathic abilities in trade negotiations. Lwaxana declines the proposal.

Upon the *Enterprise*-D's return from the Gamma Erandi mapping mission, Betazed authorities inform Captain Picard of the abduction, and the *Enterprise*-D gives chase to the *Krayton*. Lwaxana Troi is successful in negotiating the release of her daughter and Riker from Ferengi custody, and Picard is able to negotiate freedom for Lwaxana.

Acting Ensign Wesley Crusher receives the results of his Starfleet Academy application. He is accepted, but misses his opportunity for transport aboard the *U.S.S. Bradbury* to Starfleet Academy due to his assistance with the search for the Ferengi vessel. Although Admiral Hahn at the Academy indicates Crusher is welcome to apply again next year, Picard recognizes Crusher's sacrifice by granting him a field promotion to full ensign.

Editors' Note: Author Ray Bradbury, for whom the unseen U.S.S. Bradbury *was named, was a friend of* Star Trek *creator Gene Roddenberry's and was a speaker at the memorial service following Gene's death in 1991. This episode was cowritten by Gene Roddenberry's longtime assistant, Susan Sackett (with Fred Bronson).*

U.S.S. Enterprise-D proceeds to Xanthras system for rendezvous with the Starship *Zapata*.

Just after "Menage à Troi" (TNG).

"Transfigurations" (TNG). Stardate 43957.2. *U.S.S. Enterprise*-D is charting an unknown star system in the Zeta Gelis cluster, when the wreckage of a small space vehicle is discovered on one of the planets in the region. One survivor is discovered in critical condition, and chief medical officer Crusher is successful in stabilizing his condition by using Geordi La Forge's neural system to regulate that of the patient.

The survivor, referred to as "John Doe," is found to possess extraordinary recuperative powers, and Doe is fully recovered in a very short time. Dr. Crusher expresses some concern over what appears to be a progressive mutation of Doe's cells, his apparent loss of memory, and his subsequent inability to recall his origin or the circumstances of his crash.

Analysis of wreckage from Doe's vehicle indicates a probable origin point. En route to that point, an alien vessel is encountered that identifies itself as Zalkonian. The captain of the Zalkonian vessel identifies himself as Sunad, and claims custody of Doe for crimes against his people. Doe, whose cellular mutation has been accelerating, is found to be undergoing a metamorphosis into an energy-based being, and it is learned that Sunad's mission is to prevent this evolution by killing all individuals undergoing the change. Once Doe's transfiguration is complete, he departs the *Enterprise*-D to live in free space, beyond Sunad's ability to harm him.

Editors' Note: Sunad (spell it backward) was named for former Star Trek *story editor Richard Danus.*

DaiMon Tog

Wesley Crusher

Crash site in the Zeta Gelis cluster

John Doe

William Riker

Remains of the New Providence colony at planet Jouret IV

Admiral Hanson

Starfleet Command offers *Enterprise*-D executive officer William Riker a promotion to captain of the *Starship Melbourne*. This is the third command offer made to Riker, who eventually declines the promotion.

Prior to "Best of Both Worlds, Part I" (TNG).

The New Providence colony on planet Jouret IV sends a distress call. The *U.S.S. Enterprise*-D proceeds to Jouret IV in response.

About twelve hours prior to "Best of Both Worlds, Part I" (TNG).

"The Best of Both Worlds, Part I" (TNG). Stardate 43989.1. *U.S.S. Enterprise*-D at Jouret IV finds the New Providence colony to have been totally destroyed, with no sign of the colony's 900 inhabitants. Surface conditions are almost identical to those found at System J-25 on stardate 42761.3, suggesting that the New Providence colony had been attacked by the Borg. Admiral J. P. Hanson of Starbase 324 assigns Lieutenant Commander Shelby to the *Enterprise-D* to assist with tactical preparations.

Hanson reports a distress signal has been received at Starbase 157 from *Starship Lalo* near Zeta Alpha II, indicating a probable Borg sighting in Federation space. Contact with the *Lalo* is subsequently lost, and the ship is believed destroyed by a Borg vessel. Further readings indicate the Borg vessel to be headed to Sector 001 at high warp speeds. Admiral Hanson orders every available Starfleet ship to rendezvous at Wolf 359 to mount a defense. A request is also made to the Klingon High Command to provide additional ships for this engagement.

Diverted to engage the Borg in advance of the fleet, efforts are made by *Enterprise*-D personnel to improvise improvements to existing defenses and weapons for the anticipated encounter. These preparations are unsuccessful in preventing the abduction of Captain Picard by the Borg. Picard is subjected to extensive surgical modification to incorporate him into the Borg collective consciousness.

Editors' Note: "Emissary" (DS9) establishes that Picard was captured by the Borg on stardate 43997.

6.4 STAR TREK: THE NEXT GENERATION — YEAR 4

*Locutus
of Borg*

2367

"The Best of Both Worlds, Part II" (TNG). Stardate 44001.4. A powerful deflector-based weapon devised by *Enterprise*-D personnel is unsuccessful in disabling the Borg vessel, which continues at high speed toward Earth. The use of the improvised deflector weapon temporarily incapacitates the *Enterprise*-D.

An armada of 40 Federation and Klingon starships is nearly annihilated at Wolf 359 by the Borg. Eleven thousand personnel (including Admiral J. P. Hanson) and 39 starships are lost. It is believed that the involuntary cooperation of Captain Jean-Luc Picard, then known as Locutus of Borg, played a significant role in this terrible defeat. The Borg ship proceeds to Earth and is met by the *Enterprise*-D, whose drive systems are once again functional. A rescue mission is successful in recovering Captain Picard, and a study of Picard's Borg implants yields information making it possible to trigger a self-destruct command on the Borg vessel.

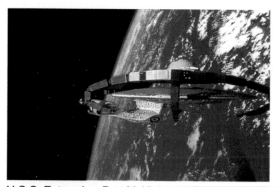

U.S.S. *Enterprise*-D at McKinley station

Editors' Note: Casualty figures from the battle of Wolf 359 are from "The Drumhead" (TNG).

Among the ships lost at the battle of Wolf 359 was the *Starship Saratoga*. One of the survivors of the *Saratoga* crew is Lieutenant Commander Benjamin Sisko, the ship's executive officer. Sisko manages to escape with his son, Jake Sisko, although Ben's wife, Jennifer, is lost in the disaster. Sisko is later assigned to Starfleet's Utopia Planitia Fleet Yards on Mars, where he will spend nearly three years. Sisko also works on the construction of orbital habitats on Earth.

"Emissary" (DS9). Established in the flashback scenes. Sisko's stint at Utopia Planitia mentioned by Picard. Sisko's work on orbital habitats established in "Way of the Warrior" (DS9).

Sisko

Jean-Luc Picard meets his nephew, René

Sergey and Helena Rozhenko

Dr. Beverly Crusher cares for young Willie Potts in medical isolation

Talarian captain Endar and his son, Jono, also known as Jeremiah Rossa

U.S.S. Enterprise-D arrives at Earth Station McKinley for an estimated six weeks of repair work. Captain Picard also undergoes extensive medical treatment and therapy for the Borg surgical modifications and implants. Unknown to anyone at the time, a defective hatch is installed on the dilithium chamber of the *Enterprise*-D warp drive system. Undetectable submicron fractures in the casing cause a near-disastrous failure several months later, shortly before stardate 44765.2.

After "Best of Both Worlds, Part II" (TNG). Failure of the dilithium chamber hatch described in "The Drumhead" (TNG).

"Family" (TNG). Stardate 44012.3. Repair work on the *Enterprise*-D at Earth Station McKinley is completed a week early. While in dock, Captain Picard takes shore leave at his family home in Labarre, France, visiting his brother and sister-in-law, Robert and Marie Picard. There, Picard declines an offer to serve as director of the Atlantis Project, choosing instead to remain with Starfleet. Sergey and Helena Rozhenko visit their adoptive son, Worf, aboard the *Enterprise*-D. Wesley Crusher views a holographic message from his late father, recorded when Wesley was only ten weeks old.

Editors' Note: Transporter chief Miles Edward O'Brien is given a first and middle name in this episode when he introduces himself to Worf's parents. O'Brien had been a recurring character since "Encounter at Farpoint" (TNG) (he was battle bridge conn, not referred to by name), but he had not been referred to by first or middle name prior to this point.

"Family" (TNG) was actually the fourth episode filmed during the fourth season. It is listed second because it is a direct continuation of the story line from "Best of Both Worlds, Part II" (TNG), and as such was the next episode aired.

U.S.S. Enterprise-D at planet Ogus II for crew shore leave. The two-day layover is cut short when a child's practical joke endangers the life of his brother, Willie Potts, necessitating an emergency medical evac to Starbase 416.

Enterprise-D chief engineer Geordi La Forge performs dilithium vector calibrations on the ship's warp propulsion system. Although the system can remain on line during the calibration, this procedure requires maximum warp velocity to be restricted during the operation.

Just prior to "Brothers" (TNG).

"Brothers" (TNG). Stardate 44085.7. En route to Starbase 416 for emergency medical treatment of Willie Potts, Lieutenant Commander Data exhibits severely aberrant behavior, commandeering the *Enterprise*-D to a distant planet. Beaming down to the planet, Data discovers he had been summoned by his creator, Dr. Noonien Soong, long thought to be dead. Also arriving is Lore, Data's android brother, who was thought destroyed in 2364 near Omicron Theta. Soong informs his two creations that he is dying, but attempts unsuccessfully to install a new circuit chip in Data, a modification which would have permitted Data to experience human emotions. An *Enterprise*-D away team investigating Soong's lab reports Soong to have died and Lore to have departed. Data, having fulfilled his creator's command, returns to normal operation.

U.S.S. Enterprise-D proceeds to Starbase 416 for emergency care of Willie Potts. The treatment is successful in restoring Potts to health.

Editors' Note: Dr. Soong's emotion chip was later featured in "Descent, Part II" (TNG) and in Star Trek Generations.

"Suddenly Human" (TNG). Stardate 44143.7. *U.S.S. Enterprise*-D is in sector 21947 in response to a distress call from a Talarian observation craft. Among the survivors is a young human, Jeremiah Rossa, found to be the grandson of Starfleet admiral Connaught Rossa. Investigation determines that Jeremiah had been raised by a Talarian captain, Endar, in keeping with a Talarian tradition permitting a warrior to claim the son of a slain enemy. Admiral Rossa requests her grandson be returned to her care, but *Enterprise*-D captain Picard rules the child's interests would be better served by returning him to his adoptive family, since Jeremiah now considers Endar to be his father.

"Remember Me" (TNG). Stardate 44161.2. *U.S.S. Enterprise*-D at Starbase 133 for crew rotation. Also on board for passage to planet Kenda II is Dr. Dalen Quaice, mentor to Dr. Beverly Crusher. Upon departing for planet Durenia IV, a freak accident in a warp field experiment causes Dr. Crusher to be trapped for several hours inside a static warp bubble. She is rescued, unharmed, by the efforts of her son, Ensign Wesley Crusher, with the assistance of the individual called the Traveler, a native of planet Tau Alpha C. The Traveler had previously participated in a warp propulsion system experiment aboard the *Enterprise*-D in 2364.

The Traveler

Editors' Note: Picard noted the ship's complement at the end of the episode was 1,014 people.

"Legacy" (TNG). Stardate 44215.2. *U.S.S. Enterprise*-D bypasses a scheduled archaeological survey of planet Camus II in response to a distress call from Federation freighter *Arcos*, in orbit around planet Turkana IV. Upon arrival at Turkana, two survivors from the *Arcos* are discovered to have landed on the planet surface. The two are discovered to have been captured by one of two rival gangs now in control of the colony. One of the gangs offers assistance in the person of Ishara Yar, sister to the late *Enterprise*-D security chief. The rescue is successful, although Yar is discovered to be using the operation to attempt to gain an advantage over her rival gang.

Ishara Yar

Editors' Note: The bypassed archaeological survey of planet Camus II referred to in Picard's opening log was intended as an "inside" joke, a salute to the original Star Trek *television series. The seventy-ninth and final episode of that show, "Turnabout Intruder" (TOS), involved an archaeological expedition on Camus II. "Legacy" (TNG) is the eightieth episode of* Star Trek: The Next Generation. *The gag was the brainchild of executive producer Rick Berman, actor Jonathan Frakes, and script coordinator Eric Stillwell. The reference to the* Starship Potemkin *(See 2361), also mentioned in the last episode of the original* Star Trek, *is another such inside joke.*

"Reunion" (TNG). Stardate 44246.3. *U.S.S. Enterprise*-D investigating radiation anomalies in the Gamma Arigulon system reported by the *Starship LaSalle*. The study is cut short when the *Enterprise*-D is met by a *Vor'cha*-class Klingon attack cruiser bearing Chancellor K'mpec, leader of the Klingon High Council, who requests a meeting with Captain Picard. Also aboard the attack cruiser is Klingon emissary K'Ehleyr, who comes aboard the *Enterprise*-D with a child, Alexander. K'Ehleyr informs Lieutenant Worf that Alexander is his son from their encounter during her previous visit to the *Enterprise*-D.

Worf and his son Alexander

K'mpec reveals that he has been fatally poisoned by political enemies, and appoints Picard to mediate the rite of succession. K'mpec explains the highly unusual request on the basis of his fears that factions within the Klingon High Council may plunge the empire into civil war. Picard accepts, and K'mpec dies shortly thereafter.

Picard hears claims from council member Duras and political newcomer Gowron as part of the *ja'chuq* (succession) process. Emissary K'Ehleyr

K'Ehleyr

Tahna Los

Riker and Barash

Barash's true form

Picard and Crusher on Pentarus III

Two-dimensional life-forms

uncovers suppressed evidence that Duras's father had betrayed the Klingon people at the Khitomer massacre of 2346. Duras murders K'Ehleyr in an attempt to prevent her from reporting these findings, but Worf later claims the right of vengeance and kills Duras. Gowron remains as the sole contender for leadership of the Klingon High Council and is subsequently installed in that position. Worf is officially reprimanded by Captain Picard for his actions in the death of Duras.

U.S.S. Enterprise-D at Starbase 73. Lieutenant Worf is met by his adoptive parents, Sergey and Helena Rozhenko, who take custody of Worf's son, Alexander. They return to Earth to raise the child.

After "Reunion" (TNG).

Bajoran Kohn-Ma terrorist Tahna Los, in Cardassian captivity, suffers a brutal, disfiguring beating. It is not his first experience with torture at the hands of the Cardassians.

"Past Prologue" (DS9). About two and a half years prior to the episode (late 2369).

"Future Imperfect" (TNG). Stardate 44286.5. *U.S.S. Enterprise*-D is conducting a security survey of the Onias sector near the Romulan Neutral Zone. Evidence of activity at planet Alpha Onias III, a barren and inhospitable Class-M world, necessitates an away mission to the planet's surface. Commander William Riker is diverted during the beam-up process, and detained by an alien called Barash. The alien eventually agrees to release Riker and to be a guest on the *Enterprise*-D.

Riker celebrates his 32nd birthday.

Captain Picard is asked to mediate a dispute among the salenite miners on planet Pentarus V.

Wesley Crusher is accepted to Starfleet Academy when a position opens up in the current year's class.

Prior to "Final Mission" (TNG).

"Final Mission" (TNG). Stardate 44307.3. *U.S.S. Enterprise*-D receives a distress call from planet Gamelan V. Gamelan chairman Songi reports an unidentified spacecraft has entered orbit around her planet, resulting in significant increases in atmospheric radiation levels. Commander Riker orders the *Enterprise*-D diverted to Gamelan V, and determines the spacecraft to be an ancient freighter carrying unstable nuclear wastes. *Enterprise*-D personnel are successful in sending the freighter through the Meltasion asteroid belt and into the Gamelan sun, although the operation entails hazardous radiation exposure to the *Enterprise*-D crew.

Captain Picard departs for Pentarus V, aboard the Pentaran mining shuttle *Nenebek*. Also aboard the shuttlecraft is pilot Dirgo and Ensign Wesley Crusher. A malfunction of the shuttle's propulsion system forces a crash landing on Lambda Paz, a moon of Pentarus III. Although no one is immediately killed in the crash, Dirgo dies in an attempt to secure water for the survivors before the *Enterprise*-D can locate them.

Wesley Crusher leaves the *Enterprise*-D to enroll in Starfleet Academy on Earth.

After "Final Mission" (TNG).

"The Loss" (TNG). Stardate 44356.9. *U.S.S. Enterprise*-D, on course for planet T'lli Beta, delays to investigate anomalous sensor readings. While studying the area, a warp drive malfunction is detected, apparently caused by a school of two-dimensional life-forms discovered nearby.

Attempts to restore engine function are unsuccessful until it is determined that the life-forms are attempting to return to a nearby cosmic string fragment. The *Enterprise*-D main deflector is used to simulate the string's natural harmonics in a successful effort to guide the life-forms to the string, apparently their natural home.

A side effect of the presence of the two-dimensional life-forms is the temporary loss of empathic powers by *Enterprise*-D counselor Deanna Troi.

Editors' Note: Planet T'lli Beta was named by episode writer Hillary Bader for her grandmother, Tillie Bader. A planet labeled T'lli Beta can be barely glimpsed on the huge stellar cartography wall display in Star Trek Generations.

U.S.S. Enterprise-D arrives at designated coordinates for rendezvous with *U.S.S. Zhukov.*

Just before "Data's Day" (TNG).

Miles and Keiko O'Brien

"Data's Day" (TNG). Stardate 44390.1. *U.S.S. Enterprise*-D rendezvouses with *U.S.S. Zhukov* to transport Vulcan ambassador T'Pel to the Romulan Neutral Zone for negotiations. T'Pel is apparently killed in a transporter accident while beaming over to the Romulan ship *Devoras*. Investigation reveals the accident to have been staged by the Romulans, and it is later revealed that T'Pel is in reality Romulan subcommander Selok, who had been an undercover agent in Federation territory. The incident had been staged in order to facilitate her return to Romulan space.

Enterprise-D crew member Francisca Juarez gives birth to a baby boy. The child's father, Alfredo Juarez, is also a member of the *Enterprise*-D crew. Chief Miles Edward O'Brien is married to botanist Keiko Ishikawa in a ceremony held in the Ten-Forward lounge. Captain Jean-Luc Picard officiates, and Lieutenant Commander Data serves as father of the bride.

Starship Enterprise, NCC-1701-D

Long-range sensors continue to gather scientific data on the Murasaki Quasar.

Lieutenant Commander Data records personal log for transmission to Commander Bruce Maddox, Cybernetics Division, Daystrom Institute. The recording is made to provide information on Data's programming.

Editors' Note: This episode marks the first appearance of Data's pet cat, whose name is later established to be Spot. Captain Picard's introduction to the O'Brien wedding ceremony is an homage by writer Ron Moore to a similar speech given by Captain Kirk at the Tomlinson wedding in "Balance of Terror" (TOS). In "Data's Day" (TNG), we also get our first glimpse of the Enterprise-D *barbershop. The Murasaki Quasar was a reference to the original series episode "The Galileo Seven" (TOS).*

Data and his pet cat, Spot

Data noted that this episode marked the 1550th day since the commissioning of the Enterprise-D. *We tried to project this back to determine when the ship was commissioned. Our theory was this: With* Next Generation *stardates, you can sometimes get a fair idea of when an episode theoretically occurs within a given year by treating the last three digits as measuring thousandths of a year. (This means that a stardate with the last three digits of 500 would be about halfway through a given year.) The resulting date is a rough estimate at best, given the number of cases where things don't line up properly. (See Appendix I [Regarding stardates] for more information.) Nevertheless, we tried it anyhow.*

Given a stardate of 44390, this yields an estimated date of late May 2367 for the episode. Subtracting 1550 days gives an approximate commissioning date of late February 2363. This might be inconsistent with the first season episode, "Lonely Among Us" (TNG), which suggests the ship was launched in the latter half of 2363 (because of Picard's line that the

Ambassador T'Pel, aka Subcommander Selok

Captain Ben Maxwell

Gul Macet

Galor-class Cardassian warship

Phoenix *pursued by* Enterprise-D

Enterprise-D is less than a year old in that episode). We rationalize that the ship was commissioned in February but officially launched several months later.

For whatever it's worth, the dedication plaque on the bridge bears a launch stardate of 40759.5, corresponding to an approximate calendar date of October 4, 2363. It's no coincidence that the launch of Sputnik I, *which many regard as the dawn of the Space Age, was on October 4, 1957.*

U.S.S. Enterprise-D travels to planet Adelphous IV.

Just after "Data's Day" (TNG).

Julian Bashir graduates from Starfleet medical school.

Conjecture. Assumes he entered Starfleet medical at age 18, and that it is an eight-year program.

A Cardassian science station in the Cuellar system is destroyed by the *U.S.S. Phoenix* under the command of Captain Benjamin Maxwell. The action is in violation of the peace treaty between the Cardassians and the Federation, although Captain Maxwell claims to have evidence that the science station was in fact a military transport facility.

Two days before "The Wounded" (TNG).

"The Wounded" (TNG). Stardate 44429.6. *U.S.S. Enterprise*-D, on mapping survey near Cardassian space, is attacked by a Cardassian *Galor*-class warship, the *Trager*. The commander of the attacking vessel informs *Enterprise*-D captain Picard that the attack is in response to the destruction of the Cardassian station in the Cuellar system two days ago. Captain Picard is instructed by Starfleet admiral Haden to investigate Maxwell's attack.

Picard determines Maxwell's actions against Cardassian forces to be due to Maxwell's theory that the Cardassians are about to launch an unprovoked military offensive against the Federation. Captain Picard, acting under direct orders from Starfleet, prevents Maxwell from taking further action against the Cardassians. Two Cardassian spacecraft are destroyed before Maxwell is relieved of his command. While Maxwell is placed in custody, Picard instructs Cardassian officer Gul Macet to inform his government that Starfleet is aware that Maxwell's charges of covert military preparations have a basis in fact.

Editors' Note: This episode marks the first appearance of the Cardassians, a group of adversaries that would recur in Star Trek: The Next Generation *episodes as well as in* Star Trek: Deep Space Nine. *(The back story established in "The Wounded" [TNG] suggests, however, that hostilities between the Federation and the Cardassians had existed for at least several years prior to the episode. Picard notes he had fled from the Cardassians while in command of the* Stargazer, *suggesting these hostilities had existed earlier than 2355, when the* Stargazer *was destroyed.)*

"The Wounded" (TNG) also marks the first appearance of the Nebula-class starship, although an earlier preliminary "study model" of the Nebula-class design might be barely spotted among the wreckage in the spaceship "graveyard" in "The Best of Both Worlds, Part II" (TNG), "Emissary, Part I" (DS9), and in the junkyard from "Unification" (TNG). A second study model of that ship graced Captain Riker's desk in his imaginary ready room in "Future Imperfect" (TNG). The same model was also seen in Sisko's office on Deep Space 9.

Starship Phoenix returns to Starbase 211.

> *Just after "The Wounded" (TNG).*

Inhabitants on planet Ventax II are terrified by visions of the mythical figure Ardra, coinciding with legends predicting Ardra would return to Ventax a thousand years after her earlier visit, a millennium ago. The visions of Ardra are accompanied by a series of geologic tremors in Ventaxian cities.

> *Several days before "Devil's Due" (TNG).*

Ventax II city

"Devil's Due" (TNG). Stardate 44474.5. *U.S.S. Enterprise*-D responds to emergency transmission from Federation science station on planet Ventax II. Station director Howard Clark reports widespread panic among the local population, due to the anticipated arrival of Ardra, a legendary supernatural being. A humanoid identifying herself as Ardra does arrive at Ventax II, but *Enterprise*-D captain Picard is able to convince local authorities that this individual is not the legendary supernatural figure and that they are therefore not bound by an ancient contract with Ardra.

> *Editors' Note: This episode was originally written back in 1978 for Kirk and company for the* Star Trek II *television series that was never produced. It is the second script from that project to have been resurrected for* Star Trek: The Next Generation. *(The first was "The Child" [TNG].)*

Ardra

U.S.S. Enterprise-D completes a mission at planet Harrakis V ahead of schedule, permitting Captain Picard to grant extra personal time for many of the crew.

> *Just prior to "Clues" (TNG).*

"Clues" (TNG). Stardate 44502.7. *Starship Enterprise*-D passing through the Ngame Nebula to a diplomatic assignment to the Evadne system. While en route, a T-tauri–type star with a single Class-M planet is discovered. While investigating this anomalous planet, the *Enterprise*-D accidentally passes through an unstable wormhole, displacing the ship approximately 0.54 parsecs from previous position. *Enterprise*-D captain Picard orders a hazard advisory issued to Starfleet regarding the wormhole, and orders course resumed for Evadne IV.

> *Editors' Note: The main story of "Clues" (TNG), the* Enterprise-D *encounter with the reclusive Paxans and their efforts to erase all human and computer memories of the incident, is not described above because we assume the second attempt at erasing the memories of* Enterprise-D *personnel was successful. A historical record that includes information based on* Enterprise-D *records would therefore have no mention of this incident. (Data does retain a memory of the encounter, but he was ordered by Captain Picard never to reveal this information, not even to Picard or the authors of this book.)*

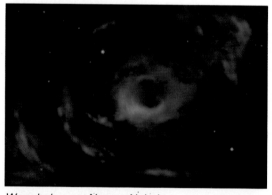

Wormhole near Ngame Nebula

U.S.S. Enterprise-D goes to planet Evadne IV.

> *After "Clues" (TNG).*

The automated Argus Subspace Telescope Array, located near the edge of Federation space, mysteriously stops relaying its information. This is later discovered to be due to a probe from the Cytherians.

> *"The Nth Degree" (TNG). Picard's log notes the array had stopped transmitting nearly two months prior to the episode.*

U.S.S. Brattain issues a distress call, the last known signal from the ship. It is later learned that the *Miranda*-class starship was trapped in a Tyken's Rift.

> *"Night Terrors" (TNG). The distress call was sent 29 days prior to the episode.*

Argus Subspace Telescope Array

Commander Riker disguised for covert surveillance on planet Malcor III

Barclay as Cyrano

Dr. Leah Brahms

Infant spaceborne creature clinging to the Starship Enterprise-D

Enterprise-D botanist Keiko O'Brien and her husband, Miles, conceive a child.

"Disaster" (TNG). Date is conjecture, but about eight months prior to the episode, given the suggestion that Molly's delivery was premature.

U.S.S. *Enterprise*-D at planet Malcor III to conduct covert sociological surveillance as prelude to possible first contact. Malcor III is currently under Prime Directive protection, but is believed to be on the verge of developing interstellar space-flight capability and may therefore be eligible shortly for first contact. Commander William Riker is transported to the planet's surface as part of the observation team.

Prior to "First Contact" (TNG).

"First Contact" (TNG). (No stardate given in episode.) Commander Riker is injured on the surface of planet Malcor III while participating in covert sociological surveillance. He is cared for in a local medical facility, but examination by indigenous persons uncovers evidence that he is an extraterrestrial and threatens the security of the surveillance operation. Local authorities are alerted of the Federation presence, and plead with *Enterprise*-D captain Picard that contact with the outworlders will cause serious cultural shock at this point in the planet's social development. Picard concurs, and orders the contact postponed indefinitely.

Malcorian science minister Mirasta Yale elects to remain on board the *Enterprise*-D.

Editors' Note: The bottle of Chateau Picard shared by the captain and Chancellor Durken was given to Picard by his brother, Robert, in "Family" (TNG).

Lieutenant Reginald Barclay joins Dr. Beverly Crusher's acting workshop aboard the *U.S.S. Enterprise*-D. Their first project is a performance of *Cyrano de Bergerac*.

"The Nth Degree" (TNG). Geordi notes that Barclay had been taking lessons for six weeks prior to the episode.

"Galaxy's Child" (TNG). Stardate 44614.6. *U.S.S. Enterprise*-D at Starbase 313 to pick up scientific equipment for a Federation outpost in the Guernica system, as well as a visitor, Dr. Leah Brahms, for an inspection tour. Brahms had earlier served on one of the design teams responsible for the propulsion system of the *U.S.S. Enterprise*-D at Utopia Planitia, and has since been promoted to senior design engineer of the Theoretical Propulsion Group.

Unusual energy readings from the unexplored Alpha Omicron system result in a diversion to that system for further research. An object is discovered orbiting planet Alpha Omicron VII, and is determined to be a spaceborne life-form. During the investigation, a low-level phaser burst is employed in an attempt to discourage a potentially hazardous radiation field from the creature, but the attempt proves lethal to the life-form. Later study of the creature's remains reveals an unborn child, which is delivered with the assistance of *Enterprise*-D personnel. The child appears to regard the *Enterprise*-D as a source of nurturing, drawing power from the ship's engines until a means can be found to urge it to join a school of its fellow creatures.

Starship *Enterprise*-D resumes its mission to the Guernica system.

Just after "Galaxy's Child" (TNG).

Captain Kathryn Janeway meets Lieutenant Tuvok.

"Phage" (VGR). Four years before the episode (2371).

"Night Terrors" (TNG). Stardate 44631.2. *U.S.S. Enterprise*-D, passing through an uncharted binary star system, discovers the derelict *U.S.S. Brattain*, reported missing 29 days ago. Investigation reveals only one survivor from the *Brattain* crew, the remaining 34 having died under violent but unexplained circumstances. During the investigation, the *Enterprise*-D becomes trapped in a Tyken's Rift, causing failure of ship's power systems. Cooperation with an unknown intelligence on the other side of the rift permits the *Enterprise*-D and the unknown intelligence to escape. Proximity to the alien intelligence is found to be responsible for severe dream deprivation of all *Enterprise*-D personnel, a side effect of a successful attempt to communicate by the aliens. This dream deprivation is believed to be the cause of the insanity that claimed the lives of most of the *Brattain* crew.

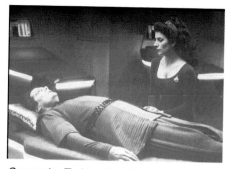

Counselor Troi tends to the sole survivor of the Brattain *crew*

U.S.S. Enterprise-D heads for Starbase 220.

Just after "Night Terrors" (TNG).

Emilita Mendez, a crew member aboard the *Starship Aries*, steals the *Shuttlepod Cousteau* and heads for planet Tarchannen III. Her crewmates later report that she was last seen an hour before her disappearance from the *Aries* and that she seemed completely normal at the time.

Prior to "Identity Crisis" (TNG).

Lieutenant Paul Hickman, missing in a stolen shuttlecraft, is reported sighted by a Federation supply ship en route to planet Tarchannen III.

A day before "Identity Crisis" (TNG).

Lieutenant Commander Susanna Leijten, formerly of the *U.S.S. Victory*, is assigned temporarily to the *Enterprise*-D to investigate aberrant behavior on the part of ex-*Victory* personnel who participated in an away mission to planet Tarchannen III in 2362. Among the former *Victory* crew members are Emilita Mendez, Paul Hickman, Ensign Brevelle, and Geordi La Forge.

Susanna Leijten

Prior to "Identity Crisis" (TNG), after Hickman is sighted near Tarchannen III.

"Identity Crisis" (TNG). Stardate 44664.5. *U.S.S. Enterprise*-D is at planet Tarchannen III investigating aberrant behavior by former *U.S.S. Victory* personnel, attempts to intercept a stolen shuttlecraft piloted by former *Victory* crew member Paul Hickman. The shuttle is incinerated on atmospheric entry before the *Enterprise*-D can reach tractor or transporter range.

Research of old *Victory* records and on-site investigation at the old Tarchannen III colony uncovers evidence of an indigenous life-form that reproduces by means of a viral parasite. This life-form is determined to have infected members of the *Victory* away team in 2362, compelling them to return to Tarchannen III, where their DNA is altered to match that of the parasite. The transformation is deemed irreversible for most of the ex-*Victory* personnel, but the parasite is successfully removed from Leijten and La Forge.

Former Victory *crew member, infested by the viral parasite*

Warning beacons are placed in orbit around planet Tarchannen III and on the planet's surface.

Just after "Identity Crisis" (TNG).

Distinguished Trill negotiator Curzon Dax falls gravely ill. Upon learning that he is dying, Jadzia, a young host candidate, requests that she be allowed to join with the Dax symbiont. Curzon had previously served as Jadzia's field docent and had helped her find the strength of will to complete the program.

"Playing God" (DS9). Shortly prior to Curzon's death.

Curzon Dax

Curzon Dax dies. The Dax symbiont is transplanted into Jadzia. She is the first female host that Dax has had in nearly eight decades. Prior to the joining, Jadzia had earned academic honors for her work in exobiology, zoology, astrophysics, and exoarchaeology.

"Dax" (DS9). Odo noted that Curzon died two years before the episode (2369). "Equilibrium" (DS9) establishes that Jadzia had been an initiate for three years before her joining, so she apparently enrolled in the initiate training program about three years prior to this point.

Cytherian

"The Nth Degree" (TNG). Stardate 44704.2. *U.S.S. Enterprise*-D at the edge of Federation space to investigate the apparent failure of the Argus Subspace Telescope Array. An alien space probe is discovered in the vicinity of the array. Initial studies of the alien probe are uninformative, although the probe is found to be emitting radiation that causes significant damage to computer systems of a shuttlecraft assigned to the investigation.

Lieutenant Reginald Barclay, part of the shuttlecraft crew, is discovered to have experienced unusual side effects from the probe radiation. His intellectual capacities are found to have dramatically increased by at least two orders of magnitude. This expanded intelligence is of significant value in saving the Argus Array from a series of critical malfunctions, and later allows Barclay to devise an extraordinary modification of the *Enterprise*-D warp drive system. Acting against direct orders from Captain Picard, Barclay pilots the *Enterprise*-D some 30,000 light-years toward the galactic core. This is learned to be due to the efforts of a previously undiscovered civilization called the Cytherians, who use such techniques to bring visitors to their world for cultural exchange. Picard agrees to such an exchange with the Cytherians, who then return the *Enterprise*-D to Federation space.

Worf, cast by Q into the role of Will Scarlet

"Qpid" (TNG). Stardate 44741.9. *Enterprise*-D at planet Tagus III to serve as host of the Federation Archaeology Council's annual symposium. *Enterprise*-D captain Picard delivers the keynote address on the ancient Tagus ruins.

The entity known as Q reappears, transporting Captain Picard, his staff, and Archaeology Council member Vash into an imaginary environment. Upon their return, Vash agrees to enter into a partnership with Q.

Klingon exobiologist J'Ddan, serving on board the *Enterprise*-D as part of an exchange program, accesses restricted technical information on the ship's dilithium chamber design. The incident is routinely recorded by the ship's computer system.

"The Drumhead" (TNG). A week before the Romulans got the technical data.

Stardate 44765.2. *U.S.S. Enterprise*-D is crippled by an explosion in the ship's dilithium chamber. No one is killed, but two members of the engineering staff are hospitalized with radiation burns. No apparent cause is immediately discovered, and sabotage is suspected.

Four days prior to "The Drumhead" (TNG).

Starfleet Command receives intelligence reports that schematic drawings of the *Galaxy*-class starship dilithium chamber have fallen into Romulan hands. Klingon exchange technician J'Ddan is implicated in the breach of security.

"The Drumhead" (TNG). About the same time as the Enterprise*-D dilithium chamber explosion.*

J'Ddan

"The Drumhead" (TNG). Stardate 44769.2. Admiral Norah Satie visits *Enterprise*-D for investigation of possible sabotage in the dilithium chamber explosion. Klingon exchange exobiologist J'Ddan is discovered to have been responsible for the transmission of technical schematics to the Romulans, but is found innocent of sabotaging the dilithium chamber. J'Ddan is arrested and referred to Klingon authorities on charges of espionage. Also implicated but found innocent is crewman First Class Simon Tarses, although Tarses is found to have falsified his Starfleet application in an attempt to conceal the fact that his grandfather is Romulan.

Admiral Satie continues to pursue her belief that a conspiracy is responsible for the *Enterprise*-D explosion despite evidence that the explosion was an accident. Admiral Thomas Henry rules Satie's investigation unconstitutional in the absence of evidence, and orders it discontinued.

Admiral Norah Satie

U.S.S. Enterprise-D security officer Jenna D'Sora breaks off a romantic relationship with fellow *Enterprise*-D crew member Jeff Arton.

"In Theory" (TNG). About six weeks prior to the episode.

Scientist Telek R'Mor, of the Romulan Astrophysical Academy, dies. In 2351, Telek had received a computer chip from the year 2371, containing messages from the crew of the *Starship Voyager*, lost in that future year. Telek had promised to store these messages until 2371 and to deliver them to the families of *Voyager*'s crew then.

"Eye of the Needle" (VGR). Telek's death in 2367 makes it quite uncertain whether the messages from Voyager*'s crew ever reached their families in 2371.*

Telek R'Mor

"Half a Life" (TNG). Stardate 44805.3. *U.S.S. Enterprise*-D at planet Kaelon II to assist in an experiment to demonstrate the practicality of a helium ignition process designed to extend the life of their star. Initial tests under the guidance of Kaelon scientist Timicin at the Praxillus system fail when unanticipated neutron migration causes Praxillus to explode. During post-mission analysis, further avenues of experimentation are uncovered, and Timicin decides to postpone his scheduled return to his homeworld so that he can pursue these developments. His failure to return, despite the Kaelon tradition of "Resolution" (voluntary suicide at age 60), threatens a diplomatic incident until Timicin reverses his decision. Lwaxana Troi accompanies Timicin to his home to join in the celebration of his Resolution.

Editors' Note: Timicin's daughter was played by actor Michelle Forbes, who would later portray the character of Ensign Ro.

Federation ambassador Odan is assigned diplomatic duty aboard the *U.S.S. Enterprise*-D to help mediate a dispute between the two moons of the Peliar Zel system.

Timicin

About ten days prior to "The Host" (TNG).

Wesley Crusher sends a letter from Starfleet Academy to his mother, Beverly Crusher, aboard the *U.S.S. Enterprise*-D. The younger Crusher reports he is doing well in exobiology, but that he is still having difficulties in his ancient philosophies class.

Just prior to "The Host" (TNG).

"The Host" (TNG). Stardate 44821.3. *U.S.S. Enterprise*-D en route to planet Peliar Zel, transporting Ambassador Odan to a diplomatic assignment there. Dr. Beverly Crusher works with Ambassador Odan to study effects of the controversial magnetic energy tap employed by the people of Peliar Zel Alpha, one of two moons in the system. En route to the conference, Odan's shuttlecraft is attacked by unknown forces, resulting in apparent-

Ambassador Odan occupying a Trill host body

Ambassador Odan occupying the body of Commander William Riker

ly fatal injuries to Odan. The ambassador is learned to be a member of a joined species, the Trill, and the symbiotic parasite living in Odan's body is discovered to be the actual intelligence known as Odan.

Commander William Riker volunteers to serve as temporary host to Odan until a new permanent Trill host body can arrive. The surgical procedure is accomplished by Dr. Beverly Crusher, a task made difficult by an emotional attachment she has developed for Odan. The ambassador, now in the new host body, is able to mediate the talks between Peliar Zel Alpha and Beta.

Kriosian rebels, seeking independence from the Klingon Empire, launch at least two attacks on neutral freighters, one Ferengi, the other Cardassian. The attacks are staged near the Ikalian asteroid belt, believed to be a hiding place for the rebels.

Sometime prior to "The Mind's Eye" (TNG).

An ice age ends on a Class-M planet in the Delta Quadrant. A few of the planet's humanoid inhabitants have survived the catastrophic change on their world by entering a state of artificial hibernation. The hibernation system is designed to automatically revive them now, since the ice age is over, but a malfunction keeps them asleep.

"The Thaw" (VGR). The ice age started 19 years before the episode (2372), and lasted for 15 years.

Governor Vagh

Governor Vagh of the Klingon Kriosian colonies charges the Federation with aiding rebel forces. Vagh cites Federation phaser rifles in rebel hands as evidence of such interference. Klingon special emissary Kell is assigned by the High Council to investigate these charges. Kell requests transport aboard the *Enterprise*-D to the Kriosian system and the assistance of *Enterprise*-D captain Jean-Luc Picard in the investigation.

Just before "The Mind's Eye."

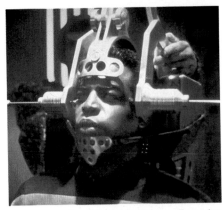

La Forge undergoes Romulan mental reprogramming

"The Mind's Eye" (TNG). Stardate 44885.5. *Enterprise*-D chief engineer Geordi La Forge transports via shuttlepod to planet Risa to attend an artificial-intelligence seminar. Unknown to the *Enterprise*-D crew, he is abducted en route by Romulan operatives, under the supervision of Sela, who employ sophisticated mental programming to plant commands in La Forge's brain.

Klingon special emissary Kell, aboard the *U.S.S. Enterprise*-D, meets with Kriosian governor Vagh to discuss allegations of Federation interference in Kriosian affairs. Close examination of purported Federation phaser rifles reveals the weapons to be of Romulan manufacture, suggesting the Kriosian rebel attacks to have been the result of Romulan hegemony. This theory is given further weight when Commander La Forge, acting under the influence of Romulan mental reprogramming, is apprehended in the act of attempting to assassinate Kriosian governor Vagh. Further investigation reveals Emissary Kell to be a Romulan collaborator responsible for triggering La Forge's implanted programming.

Editors' Note: The mysterious Romulan woman in the shadows during Geordi's brainwashing is, of course, later revealed to be Sela, the half-Romulan daughter of former Enterprise-D *security officer Tasha Yar. Her identity is not revealed until "Redemption, Part I" (TNG), two episodes later. The actor seen as Sela in "The Mind's Eye" (TNG) was not* Denise Crosby, *although Crosby did dub in Sela's voice during postproduction.*

Lieutenant Commander Data and Security Oficer Jenna D'Sora

Counselor Troi works with Geordi La Forge to help reconstruct his memories that were altered by the Romulan mental reprogramming.

After "The Mind's Eye" (TNG).

"In Theory" (TNG). Stardate 44932.3. The *Enterprise*-D enters Mar Oscura nebula on a scientific investigation mission. An unusual preponderance of dark matter in the nebula is found to result in small but dangerous subspace anomalies. These anomalies are found to threaten the structure of the *Enterprise*-D as well as the operation of its systems. A shuttle piloted by Captain Jean-Luc Picard is sent ahead of the ship as a scout to help navigate out of the region.

Lieutenant Commander Data, as part of his ongoing effort to experience humanity, attempts to establish a romantic relationship with security officer Jenna D'Sora.

Starship Enterprise-D heads for Starbase 260.

Just after "In Theory" (TNG).

Klingon attack cruiser Bortas

"Redemption, Part I" (TNG). Stardate 44995.3. *U.S.S. Enterprise*-D is en route to the Klingon Homeworld for the installation of Gowron as chancellor of the High Council. Prior to arrival at the Homeworld, the *Enterprise*-D is intercepted by Gowron aboard the Klingon attack cruiser *Bortas*. Gowron requests Starfleet assistance in preventing an anticipated ploy by the family of the late Duras to block Gowron's scheduled ascension to leadership of the Klingon High Council. *Enterprise*-D captain Picard declines, noting that such action would be beyond his role as arbiter of the succession. Additionally, Picard later orders Lieutenant Worf not to use his position as a Starfleet officer to influence the Klingon political process.

A challenge to Gowron's claim to the council is made by Toral, son of Duras. It is suspected and later confirmed that other Duras family members have been secretly working with Romulan operatives to assure Toral's ascendency. Captain Picard, as arbiter, rules Toral's claim inadmissible under Klingon law.

Goworn

Gowron, son of M'Rel, assumes leadership of the Klingon High Council and restores honor to the family of Mogh in exchange for the support of Worf and his brother, Kurn. Worf, seeking to avoid a conflict of interest, resigns his Starfleet commission and assumes the post of weapons officer aboard the Klingon attack cruiser *Bortas*.

6.5 STAR TREK: THE NEXT GENERATION—YEAR 5

Romulan operative Sela

2368

Gowron's forces are successful in destroying the Duras supply bases in the Mempa sector.

About three weeks prior to "Redemption, Part II" (TNG).

Tamarian captain Dathon

Three major engagements between forces loyal to Gowron and those of the Duras family result in significant losses to Gowron. Starfleet continues to resist involvement in what is principally an internal Klingon matter.

Within two weeks of "Redemption, Part II" (TNG).

A Tamarian spacecraft arrives at planet El-Adrel IV. The vessel transmits a subspace signal toward Federation space. The signal is determined to contain a standard mathematical progression, which Starfleet interprets as an attempt to start a dialog with the Federation.

"Darmok" (TNG). Picard noted the ship apparently arrived nearly three weeks prior to the episode.

Chancellor Gowron

"Redemption, Part II" (TNG). Stardate 45020.4. *U.S.S. Enterprise*-D at Starbase 234, where Fleet Admiral Shanthi authorizes Captain Jean-Luc Picard to lead an armada of 23 starships in an attempt to blockade a Romulan convoy suspected of being the source of supplies to forces loyal to the Duras family. Such Romulan interference is believed to threaten the stability of the Gowron regime.

Among the vessels assigned to the blockade are the *Enterprise*-D, *Excalibur*, and the *Sutherland*. Due to limited available personnel, *Enterprise*-D executive officer William Riker is assigned to temporary command of the *Excalibur*, and *Enterprise*-D operations manager Data is placed in charge of the *Sutherland*. Gowron's forces are reported in full retreat from the Mempa sector, this despite the fact that the Duras supply bases in that sector had been destroyed three weeks before.

Utilizing a tachyon network technique developed by Geordi La Forge, Picard's armada is successful in detecting a cloaked Romulan warbird, whose commander requests a meeting with Captain Picard. The commander identifies herself as Sela, the daughter of former *Enterprise*-D security officer Tasha Yar, claiming that Yar had been sent into the past and had been captured after the destruction of the *Enterprise*-C some 24 years ago. Sela further claims that she is the product of a union between Yar and a Romulan general, who spared the lives of the surviving *Enterprise*-C personnel when Yar agreed to become his consort. Later, La Forge's tachyon network is further successful in detecting additional Romulan spacecraft attempting to run the blockade line. The ships turn back after being located, and the Federation vessels also return to their home territory.

Worf

In the absence of Romulan support, the Duras family challenge to the leadership of the High Council fails, marking the end of the Klingon civil war. Although Toral, son of Duras, is convicted of treason, Worf, eldest son of Mogh, declines to exercise his right to take Toral's life for wrongfully having brought disgrace to Worf's family. Captain Jean-Luc Picard accepts Worf's request for reinstatement as a Starfleet officer.

Editors' Note: Other ships in Picard's armada included the U.S.S. Tian An Men (a remembrance of those who died for Chinese freedom, much as the U.S. Navy's Lexington *commemorated the first battle of the American Revolution), the* Endeavour *(named for James Cook's flagship, also for NASA's new space shuttle orbiter), the* Akagi *and the* Hornet *(two ships that fought against each other in the Battle of Midway, now serving side by side), and the* Sutherland *(named for the ship commanded by C. S. Forester's fictional Horatio Hornblower, one of Gene Roddenberry's inspirations for the character of Captain Kirk). These names were all selected by writer-producer Ron Moore.*

The Duras sisters

"Darmok" (TNG). Stardate 45047.2. *U.S.S. Enterprise*-D is en route to the uninhabited El-Adrel star system, near the territory of the enigmatic people known as the Children of Tama. Previous attempts at establishing communication with these people had been unsuccessful, and attempts by *Enterprise*-D personnel to communicate with the Tamarians are similarly unsuccessful, even with use of the universal translator.

Enterprise-D captain Picard is abducted by the Tamarians, and transported to the surface of planet El-Adrel IV, along with Tamarian captain Dathon. The abduction, initially believed to be a hostile act, is later learned to be an attempt at communication by Captain Dathon. The Tamarian gives his life in this attempt to bridge the communication gap between the Tamarians and the alien captain of the *Enterprise*-D. Because of Dathon's actions, it is learned that the Tamarian language is based on metaphors derived from Tamarian mythology, marking the first successful attempt at communication between the two dissimilar cultures.

Captain Dathon attempts to communicate through the use of metaphors from Tamarian mythology

A terrorist attack destroys the Federation settlement on planet Solarion IV. The attack is blamed on Bajoran terrorists seeking to involve the Federation in the Bajoran dispute with the Cardassian Empire.

Prior to "Ensign Ro" (TNG).

A Cardassian liaison meets with Starfleet Admiral Kennelly, requesting assistance in tracking down Bajoran terrorists, which the Cardassian describes as their "mutual enemy."

About a week prior to "Ensign Ro" (TNG), but after the Solarion IV attack. Kennelly said he'd met with the Cardassian liaison "last weekend."

Admiral Kennelly visits Ensign Ro Laren, in prison on Jaros II for the *Wellington* disaster at Garon II. He offers an administrative pardon in exchange for her agreement to undertake a special mission aboard the *Enterprise*-D to help resolve the Bajoran terrorist issue. It is later learned that Ro's orders from

Cardassian officer

Kennelly included the offering of illegal weapons to the Bajoran terrorists for use against the Cardassians.

Prior to "Ensign Ro" (TNG), after Kennelly's meeting with the Cardassian liaison.

Ensign Ro Laren

"Ensign Ro" (TNG). Stardate 45076.3. *U.S.S. Enterprise*-D at Lya Station Alpha with survivors from planet Solarion IV. Admiral Kennelly assigns *Enterprise*-D to seek out Bajoran terrorist leaders to dissuade them from further violence. Ensign Ro Laren is assigned as mission specialist because of her knowledge of Bajoran culture.

At the Valo star system, Ro assists in locating Bajoran leader Orta on the third moon of planet Valo I. Orta meets with Picard, presenting convincing evidence that the attack at Solarion IV was not the work of Bajoran terrorists. It is later learned that the Solarion attack had been staged by the Cardassians in an effort to gain Federation assistance in locating Bajoran leaders. It is further determined that Admiral Kennelly had acted improperly by permitting the Cardassians to destroy a Bajoran *Antares*-class sublight cruiser in an unsuccessful attempt to eliminate Orta.

Bajoran leader Orta

Ensign Ro elects to remain aboard the *Enterprise*-D as a crew member at the invitation of Captain Picard. She is assigned to the position of flight controller (conn).

Editors' Note: This episode marks the first appearance of Ensign Ro Laren. The class name of the Bajoran cruiser, Antares, *was suggested by writer Naren Shankar as an homage to the old freighter by the same name that was destroyed in "Charlie X" (TOS).*

U.S.S. Enterprise-D conducts survey assignment in sector 21305.

Just after "Ensign Ro" (TNG).

Editors' Note: The end of "Ensign Ro" suggests the Enterprise-D *will be returning to Lya Station Alpha in "a few weeks" after the survey in sector 21305, but it is not clear if this is before or after the next episode. It is possible that this is where the* Enterprise-D *went while the away team was assisting at Melona IV during "Silicon Avatar."*

Colonist Carmen Davila, killed by the Crystalline Entity

U.S.S. Enterprise-D drops off a contingent of personnel to assist with preparations for a colonization project on planet Melona IV, then departs from the area.

About a day before "Silicon Avatar" (TNG).

"Silicon Avatar" (TNG). Stardate 45122.3. At planet Melona IV, an *Enterprise*-D away team headed by Commander William Riker assists with survey preparations for construction of a colony. The planet's surface is devastated by an unprovoked attack by a powerful spaceborne life-form known as the Crystalline Entity. This is believed to be the same entity that destroyed the colony at Omicron Theta in 2336. Two colonists, including Carmen Davila, are killed in the attack before a secure shelter can be found.

Upon detecting the presence of the Crystalline Entity, Captain Picard orders the *Enterprise*-D to return to Melona IV ahead of schedule to rescue the survivors. Starfleet Command, notified of the incident, assigns xenologist Dr. Kila Marr to assist with the study of the entity. The mission is to locate and establish communication with the entity, but Marr, who lost her son in the attack at Omicron Theta, suggests that destruction of the entity would be a preferable course of action. Marr cites records suggesting the entity had been responsible for at least eleven attacks since 2338.

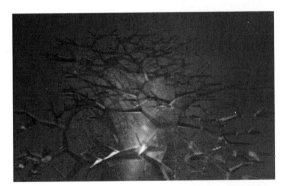

Crystalline Entity

During the investigation, it is learned that the transport ship *Kallisko* had been pursued and later destroyed by the Crystalline Entity, which has since departed Melona IV. Upon intercepting the entity near the Brechtian Cluster, *Enterprise*-D personnel attempt communication, using a modulated graviton beam. The attempt is interrupted by an unauthorized modification of the beam control program by Dr. Marr. This action, apparently motivated by Marr's desire for revenge for her son's death, creates a continuous graviton beam, resulting in the destruction of the Crystalline Entity.

Starship Enterprise-D completes a mission to planet Mudor V several days ahead of schedule, affording the crew a respite before their next assignment.

> *Prior to "Disaster" (TNG).*

Three children of *Enterprise*-D crew personnel, Jay Gordon, Marissa Flores, and Patterson Supra, win the ship's primary school science fair. Their prize is a tour of the ship to be personally conducted by Captain Picard.

> *Just prior to "Disaster" (TNG).*

Dr. Kila Marr

"Disaster" (TNG). Stardate 45156.1. *U.S.S. Enterprise*-D suffers major systems damage from collision with a quantum filament. The ship's main computer, warp drive, antimatter containment, and other key systems are affected. Counselor Deanna Troi, temporarily in command of the vessel, orders emergency procedure Alpha 2, bypassing computer control and placing key systems on manual. Indications are detected of a potential breach of the antimatter containment system, but Chief O'Brien and Ensign Ro Laren are successful in assisting engineering personnel in averting an explosion despite a major power failure in the engineering section.

Enterprise-D botanist Keiko O'Brien gives birth to a baby girl. Assisting with the delivery is security chief Worf. The child is named Molly.

> *Editors' Note: The name of the O'Brien child is not established until "The Game" (TNG), when Wesley asks how Molly is doing. Molly was named for Rick Berman's daughter and for former Star Trek staffer Molly Rennie. Molly, seen as a child in Star Trek: Deep Space Nine a year later, must have grown unusually quickly, although in "The Nagus" (DS9), Sisko said that Molly was three years old, which would put her birth in 2366, instead of 2368 (in which "Disaster" [TNG] is set).*

Keiko O'Brien and her newborn daughter Molly

Captain Picard takes the three winners of the *Enterprise*-D science fair on a tour of the ship that includes visits to the battle bridge and the torpedo bay. *U.S.S. Enterprise*-D proceeds to Starbase 67 for major systems repair.

> *After "Disaster" (TNG).*

After Counselor Troi's brief stint in command of the *Enterprise*-D, she realizes that she may want to pursue advancement within Starfleet so that she can experience the feeling of being in command, although she does not act on this for another two years.

> *After "Disaster" (TNG), as Troi mentioned in "Thine Own Self" (TNG).*

Ambassador Spock mysteriously disappears from his home on Vulcan. He has wrapped up his affairs very carefully, but has given little clue as to his plans.

> *"Unification, Part I" (TNG). Admiral Brackett said Spock had disappeared three weeks prior to the episode. Perrin implied that Spock's residence was on planet Vulcan.*

Enterprise-D science fair winners

Starship Enterprise-D on scientific mission to conduct studies at the previously uncharted Phoenix Cluster. Several science teams are transported from the *Starship Zhukov* to assist in the project. Although the exploration had been scheduled to last five weeks, a diplomatic mission to Oceanus IV has cut the available time to only two weeks.

> *Just prior to "The Game" (TNG).*

> *Editors' Note: Sensor scans of luminescent asteroids within the Phoenix cluster were apparently unsuccessful in locating the whereabouts of Lieutenant Talby.*

Ambassador Spock

Etana and Riker on Risa

"The Game" (TNG). Stardate 45208.2. Commander William Riker takes shore leave on planet Risa. He meets a woman named Etana, who is later learned to be a military operative for the Ktarians. Riker returns to the *Enterprise*-D with a small recreational device, which he replicates for distribution to his crewmates. It is later learned that these devices employ sophisticated neural-optical conditioning techniques to control the behavior of the *Enterprise*-D crew, part of a Ktarian attempt to gain control of the Federation Starfleet. Lieutenant Commander Data and Cadet Wesley Crusher, on leave from Starfleet Academy, are successful in developing an optical deprogramming technique to counteract the effects of the Ktarian devices. Mission specialist Robin Lefler is also credited with helping to identify the threat posed by the Ktarians.

U.S.S. Enterprise-D rendezvous with *U.S.S. Merrimack*, transferring Wesley Crusher for transport back to Starfleet Academy. *Enterprise*-D thereafter proceeds to Oceanus IV for diplomatic mission.

After "The Game" (TNG).

Cadet Wesley Crusher

A Ferengi cargo shuttle crashes in the Hanolin asteroid belt near Vulcan. Wreckage is recovered from over 100 square kilometers. Parts of a derelict Vulcan spacecraft, concealed in crates labeled as containing medical supplies, are found among the debris. The parts are sent to Vulcan for identification, and *U.S.S. Enterprise*-D personnel are later asked to assist.

Sometime prior to "Unification, Part I" (TNG).

Starfleet Intelligence reports Ambassador Spock, missing for nearly three weeks, has been sighted on Romulus. The unauthorized visit is of great concern to Starfleet Command because of the tremendous potential for damage to Federation security in the event that Spock has defected.

Two days prior to "Unification, Part I" (TNG).

Starship Enterprise-D terraforming mission to planet Doraf I is canceled, ship is recalled to Starbase 234 by Fleet Admiral Brackett.

Just prior to "Unification, Part I" (TNG).

Fleet Admiral Brackett

"Unification, Part I" (TNG). Stardate 45233.1. *U.S.S. Enterprise*-D is assigned by Fleet Admiral Brackett to investigate Spock's disappearance. At the suggestion of Ambassador Sarek, Captain Picard and Lieutenant Commander Data journey to Romulus to seek out Romulan senator Pardek. Despite initial reluctance by Klingon authorities, Klingon council leader Gowron agrees to the loan of a bird-of-prey for the purpose of a covert trip to Romulus. Picard later discovers that the Klingon reluctance to lend assistance was due to selective editing of the historical record by Gowron, intended to downplay the aid of the Federation in the recent Klingon civil war.

En route to Romulus, it is learned that Ambassador Sarek has died from Bendii syndrome, a degenerative brain disorder, at his home on Vulcan. He is survived by his wife, Perrin, and his son, Spock. Sarek was 203.

Enterprise-D personnel, assisting Vulcan authorities in investigating debris recovered from a recently crashed Ferengi shuttle, uncover evidence that unknown agents, possibly Ferengi, had been attempting to smuggle Vulcan spacecraft components to an unknown destination. The components are traced to a decommissioned Vulcan ship, the *T'Pau*, sent four years ago to the surplus depot at Qualor II. Investigation at the depot shows the *T'Pau* was removed under mysterious circumstances, probably by an unidentified spacecraft detected at Qualor II. The vehicle is reported to have self-destructed, apparently to avoid further investigation.

Ambassador Sarek

Picard and Data, working undercover on Romulus, are successful in making contact with Romulan senator Pardek and Federation ambassador Spock near the Krocton Segment.

Editors' Note: The death of Sarek is an important milestone in Star Trek *history, marking the first occasion when a major continuing character has died and not been resurrected. (Of course, it is possible that a younger Sarek might yet be seen in a feature film or other project set in* Star Trek's *earlier era.)*

The surplus depot at Qualor II used many wrecked ships originally built for the graveyard scene in "The Best of Both Worlds, Part II" (TNG). Some additional ships may be seen by those with a discerning eye and a good VCR or a laserdisk: Several study models, originally designed by Nilo Rodis, Bill George, and their colleagues at Industrial Light and Magic as possible designs for the U.S.S. Excelsior in Star Trek III: The Search for Spock, *are among the ships in the junkyard, as is a replica of the Klingon battle cruiser originally built for* Star Trek: The Motion Picture. *Even more intriguing are two study models for a proposed* Enterprise *redesign by Ralph McQuarrie. These models were made in the mid-'70s for a proposed* Star Trek *movie project that was never produced.*

Captain Picard in Romulan disguise near the Krocton Segment

"Unification, Part II" (TNG). Stardate 45245.8. Captain Picard is informed by Spock of his purpose on Romulus: to support the cause of reunification between the Vulcan and the Romulan peoples. Picard informs Spock of Federation objections to his presence on Romulus, but Spock cites the support of Romulan senator Pardek as evidence that such reunification may succeed.

U.S.S. Enterprise-D, still at Qualor II, continues to investigate the theft of a Vulcan ship. It is learned by Commander Riker that the *T'Pau* had been delivered to a Barolian freighter at Galorndon Core, near the Romulan Neutral Zone.

Romulan senator Pardek

Spock, meeting with Romulan proconsul Neral, is given assurances of support for the reunification movement. Later, Spock and Picard learn that this support, along with the support of Senator Pardek, had been part of a Romulan attempt to conquer Vulcan. This plan, under the direction of Romulan operative Sela, is discovered to involve use of the pretext of reunification to cover the movement of a Romulan invasion force to Vulcan. The invasion force is carried in three stolen Vulcan ships, including the *T'Pau*. Once discovered, the Vulcan ships are destroyed by Romulan forces to avoid their capture.

Despite the absence of official support in the Romulan government, Spock elects to remain on Romulus to continue his work for Vulcan/Romulan reunification.

Ullian telepathic researcher Jev, on a research project to two planets in the Nel system, commits two acts of telepathic rape, although the victims are mistakenly diagnosed as suffering from Iresine syndrome.

Capital city on Romulus

"Violations" (TNG). Geordi's research indicated Jev was in the Nel system between stardates 45321 and 45323, apparently between "Unification, Part II" (TNG), and "A Matter of Time" (TNG).

Hekaran scientist Rabal announces his support for the controversial theoretical models devised by his sister, Serova, suggesting that the continued use of warp drive is damaging the fabric of space.

"Force of Nature" (TNG). Two years before the episode (2370).

A Type-C asteroid impacts on planet Penthara IV. Although the asteroid has hit an unpopulated continent, scientists on the planet predict the resulting dust clouds may result in disastrous global cooling because of increased planetary albedo.

Just prior to "A Matter of Time" (TNG).

*Professor
Berlinghoff
Rasmussen*

"A Matter of Time" (TNG). Stardate 45349.1. *U.S.S. Enterprise*-D, proceeding to planet Penthara IV, encounters a time/space distortion, followed by the appearance of an individual identifying himself as Professor Berlinghoff Rasmussen, a researcher from the late 26th century.

Upon arrival at Penthara IV, *Enterprise*-D personnel attempt to counter global cooling by employing the ship's phasers to release massive underground pockets of volcanic carbon dioxide. It is hoped that the additional CO_2 will increase the amount of solar heat retained in the planet's atmosphere. Although initial results of the attempt are encouraging, seismic activity is much greater than anticipated, resulting in a massive release of volcanic dust, exacerbating the original problem. A second attempt successfully employs the *Enterprise*-D to trigger a massive electrostatic discharge to vaporize the dust particles, then directs the resulting energy surge harmlessly into space.

*Phaser beams release subterranean
carbon dioxide on Penthara IV*

Investigating reports of numerous small items discovered missing by *Enterprise*-D personnel, Lieutenant Commander Data searches Rasmussen's time-travel pod, and discovers Rasmussen to be the culprit. Upon questioning, Rasmussen confesses to being a time traveler not from the future, as previously claimed, but from the past. Rasmussen, who admits his goal was to return to the 22nd century with articles of 24th-century technology, is placed in custody.

Editors' Note: The incident with Rasmussen was mentioned by Odo in "Bar Association" (DS9).

U.S.S. Enterprise-D goes to Starbase 214 to turn Rasmussen over to authorities.

After "A Matter of Time" (TNG).

Helena Rozhenko, upon hearing that the *Enterprise*-D is in the sector, secures passage aboard the transport vessel *Milan* for herself and Worf's son, Alexander. The *Milan* will intercept the *Enterprise*-D.

Prior to "New Ground" (TNG).

*Alexander
Rozhenko,
son of Worf*

"New Ground" (TNG). Stardate 45376.3. *U.S.S. Enterprise*-D meets with transport ship *Milan* for transfer of passengers Helena Rozhenko and Alexander Rozhenko. Helena informs her adoptive son, Worf, that his son, Alexander, has been having difficulty adjusting to life on Earth. Worf agrees to take custody of his son aboard the *Enterprise*-D.

U.S.S. Enterprise-D at planet Bilana III to participate in an engineering test of the soliton wave development project. The test is initially successful in accelerating a test payload to warp 2.35, but subspace instabilities result in destruction of the payload. *Enterprise*-D is successful in overtaking the wavefront, and employs photon torpedoes to disperse the soliton wave.

Editors' Note: Solitons are real. They are nondispersing waves used in fiber-optic communications. Episode writer (and physicist) Naren Shanker observed the study of electromagnetic (but not subspace) soliton wave packets by Dr. C. R. Pollock while a graduate student at Cornell University.

Research vessel Vico, NAR-18834

Starbase 514 loses contact with research vessel *S.S. Vico*, on a mission to explore the interior of a black cluster. The *U.S.S. Enterprise*-D is assigned to investigate the disappearance.

Two days before "Hero Worship" (TNG).

"Hero Worship" (TNG). Stardate 45397.3. *U.S.S. Enterprise*-D locates the *Vico* inside the black cluster. The *Vico* is discovered to have been severely damaged, and an away team is able to rescue only a single survivor. The survivor, a young boy, Timothy, has been severely traumatized by the tragedy, but he is helped by Counselor Troi and Lieutenant Commander Data.

Data helps care for young Timothy

Immediately following the rescue mission, the *Enterprise*-D is buffeted by gravitational distortions within the black cluster. It is determined that a similar phenomenon caused the destruction of the *Vico*, and Timothy's recollection of the *Vico*'s final moments is instrumental in devising a means to avoid a similar fate for the *Enterprise*-D.

"Violations" (TNG). Stardate 45429.3. While on a mapping survey mission, *U.S.S. Enterprise*-D is assigned to transport a delegation of Ullians to planet Kaldra IV. The Ullians, conducting a research project to catalog telepathically retrieved memories from individuals on several planets, are linked to a series of unexplained neurological disorders resembling Iresine syndrome reported in several *Enterprise*-D crew members. Further investigation reveals one Ullian, Jev, to be responsible for the disorders. It is learned that Jev had been committing a form of rape involving memory invasion, and he is returned to Ullian authorities for prosecution and rehabilitation.

Jev

Enterprise-D stops at Starbase 440, where the Ullian delegation disembarks.

After "Violations" (TNG).

Professor Richard Galen visits the planet Loren III, a considerable distance outside of Federation space, while conducting micropaleontological research. While there, Galen visits the nearby planet Kurl, where he obtains a rare naiskos, a Kurlan artifact some 12,000 years old. Galen hopes to use the artifact to catch the interest of his former student, Jean-Luc Picard.

"The Chase" (TNG). In 2369, Galen said he had visited Kurl last summer.

Kurlan naiskos

A stellar core fragment, believed to be from a disintegrated neutron star, is detected in the Moab sector. *U.S.S. Enterprise*-D diverted to monitor possible disruption of planetary systems in the sector.

Just prior to "The Masterpiece Society" (TNG).

"The Masterpiece Society" (TNG). Stardate 45470.1. *U.S.S. Enterprise*-D, while tracking the stellar core fragment, discovers a previously unknown human colony on planet Moab IV, near the fragment's trajectory. Engineering analysis indicates the colony would be unable to withstand the resulting seismic disruption, although colony authorities decline assistance, citing an aversion to outside cultural influences. An agreement is later negotiated in which a limited number of *Enterprise*-D personnel are allowed within the colony to assist in structural reinforcement. Simultaneously, the *Enterprise*-D uses its tractor beam to partially deflect the core fragment, and thus reduce its seismic effect on Moab IV.

Scientist Hannah Bates

The effort is largely successful, although colony authorities express disapproval at the decision of 23 colonists, including scientist Hannah Bates, to leave their home and accept passage aboard the *Enterprise*-D. Colony authorities, explaining that their society had been planned as a sealed, self-contained biosphere, express further concern that *Enterprise*-D assistance may have thereby caused irreparable damage to the society.

Miles O'Brien's mother dies.

Two years prior to "Whispers" (TNG).

"Conundrum" (TNG). Stardate 45494.2. On a mission to investigate a series of subspace signals indicating possible intelligent life in the Epsilon Silar system, the *Starship Enterprise*-D is ambushed by what is later identified as a Satarran vessel. The attack employs a sophisticated energy weapon that disrupts *Enterprise*-D communication systems, selectively damages and alters *Enterprise*-D computer records, and erases the identities and short-term memories of all *Enterprise*-D personnel. The Satarran ship is believed to have self-destructed immediately after the attack.

Enterprise-D crew members are successful in retrieving information on their identities and their mission from the ship's computer. Unknown to the crew at

Captain Picard with Keiran MacDuff, a Satarran operative

Ro Laren and Worf

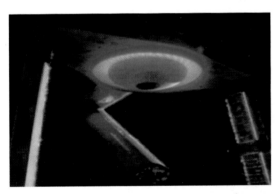

Lysian command center

U.S.S. Essex, *lost at Ma-Bu VI 200 years ago*

the time, this information includes deliberate disinformation planted by the Satarrans. The altered computer records falsely identify a Satarran, apparently from the destroyed ship, as *Enterprise*-D executive officer Keiran MacDuff. They also indicate that the Federation is currently at war with the Lysian Alliance and that the *Enterprise*-D's mission is to destroy the Lysian military command center.

Complying with the fraudulent Starfleet orders, *Enterprise*-D personnel engage and easily destroy a Lysian spacecraft, resulting in the deaths of approximately 53 Lysians. Tactical analysis of remaining Lysian forces indicates a weapons potential substantially inferior to that of the *Enterprise*-D.

Troubled by the extreme selectiveness of the damage to ship's records and crew memories and by the limited weapons technology of the Lysians, Captain Picard refuses to obey orders to destroy the command center. *Enterprise*-D personnel subsequently learn that the orders to act against the Lysians had been falsified by the Satarrans in an effort to use Federation weaponry against the Satarrans' enemies.

On the *Enterprise*-D's subsequent course to Starbase 301, crew memories are restored using a medical technique developed by Dr. Beverly Crusher in which the activity of the medial temporal region of the brain is artificially increased.

Editors' Note: This episode establishes significant biographical details about many of the ship's senior officers in the form of a computer display of the ship's crew manifest. A careful examination would reveal many personal facts like birth dates and years of graduation listed elsewhere in this chronology. In most cases, we're assuming that the display is accurate, except in cases where later episodes contradicted it, as with Geordi La Forge's mother, who was Alvera K. La Forge in the "Conundrum" (TNG) manifest, but was established as Silva La Forge in "Interface" (TNG).

This episode is also notable for introducing one of the few romantic liaisons between continuing characters, as Ensign Ro Laren successfully seduces Commander Will Riker.

Cadet Wesley Crusher and Cadet Joshua Albert participate in a ski trip to Calgary. Joshua forgets his sweater, so Wesley loans him one of his.

"The First Duty" (TNG). Wesley remembered that he and Josh had gone on the ski trip two months prior to the episode.

"Power Play" (TNG). Stardate 45571.2. *U.S.S. Enterprise*-D responds to a distress call originating from an unexplored Class-M moon of planet Mab-Bu VI. Due to electromagnetic disturbances in the moon's atmosphere, transporter use is not advised, and a shuttlepod piloted by Commander William Riker, along with Lieutenant Commander Data and Counselor Troi, is sent to investigate. Unexpectedly severe storms force the craft down on the surface, and a rescue mission effected by Chief O'Brien is successful in recovering the shuttle crew. Upon their return to the *Enterprise*-D, O'Brien, Data, and Troi exhibit severely aberrant behavior, blockading themselves in the Ten-Forward lounge and taking *Enterprise*-D crew personnel as hostages. The crew determines that this behavior is the result of control by alien life-forms, later learned to be convicted criminals, exiled to Mab-Bu VI some 500 years ago from the Ux-Mal system.

Enterprise-D captain Picard is successful in securing an agreement with the Ux-Mal terrorists to release *Enterprise*-D personnel and return to the Mab-Bu moon's surface.

Starfleet commissions the first runabout, a new type of short-range interstellar vessel.

"Paradise" (DS9). About two years before the episode.

"Ethics" (TNG). Stardate 45587.3. *U.S.S. Enterprise*-D is en route to Sector 37628 for survey mission, but is diverted upon receipt of a distress call from the transport ship *Denver*. The ship had struck a gravitic mine left over from the Cardassian war, resulting in heavy damage and many injuries. Responding at high warp speed, the *Enterprise*-D arrives at the accident site in under seven hours. All three *Enterprise*-D shuttlebays are converted to emergency triage and evac centers, allowing treatment of *Denver* crew and colonists.

Danube-calss runabout

Lieutenant Worf is seriously injured by an accident in the cargo bay, resulting in the shattering of seven vertebrae, and the crushing of his spinal cord. Although the prognosis suggests permanent paralysis, *Enterprise*-D chief medical officer Crusher consults Dr. Toby Russell, a neurogeneticist. Russell proposes an experimental genetronic replication technique that is successful in replacing Worf's spinal column and restoring virtually all of his muscular function. Crusher expresses objections to Russell's use of experimental procedures in a manner that Crusher characterizes as taking unnecessary and unethical risks with patients' lives.

Starship *Enterprise*-D drops off survivors from *Denver* accident, then proceeds to its survey mission at Sector 37628.

After "Ethics" (TNG).

Worf contemplates his life with his son

The Federation Medical Council announces the nominees for the 2368 Carrington Award. Dr. April Wade of the University of Nairobi is among those honored, although she does not win.

"Prophet Motive" (DS9). Three years prior to the episode (2371).

"The Outcast" (TNG). Stardate 45614.6. *U.S.S. Enterprise*-D is at the J'naii planet to help search for a missing J'naii spacecraft. A survey conducted by *Enterprise*-D commander William Riker and J'naii pilot Soren is able to map the anomalous null space pockets in the J'naii system. Shortly thereafter, a rescue attempt is successful in retrieving the crew of the J'naii shuttle.

The J'naii government expresses appreciation of the assistance lent by *Enterprise*-D personnel, but later accuses Soren of aberrant behavior, alleging a socially unacceptable sexual relationship with Commander Riker. *Enterprise*-D captain Picard, citing Prime Directive considerations, refuses to intervene with the J'naii judiciary in the Soren matter. Soren is found guilty of forbidden behavior and is rehabilitated, restoring one to social norms in accordance with local laws.

Dr. Toby Russeli attempts a risky surgical procedure on Worf

U.S.S. Enterprise-D proceeds to Phelan system to negotiate a trade agreement.

Just after "The Outcast" (TNG).

Lieutenant Dan Kwan and Ensign Maddy Calloway, both members of the *Enterprise*-D crew, meet for the first time. They are attracted to each other, but it is not for over a year that a romantic relationship begins to develop between them.

"Eye of the Beholder" (TNG). Two years before Kwan's suicide.

"Cause and Effect" (TNG). Stardate 45652.1. The *U.S.S. Bozeman*, a *Soyuz*-class Federation starship under the command of Captain Morgan Bateson, reported lost in 2278 near the Typhon Expanse, unexpectedly emerges from a rift in the space-time continuum, nearly colliding with the *U.S.S. Enterprise*-D.

Pilot Soren

Compelling evidence suggests a collision between the two ships did in fact occur, in which the *Bozeman* impacted the *Enterprise*-D's starboard warp nacelle, resulting in the destruction of the *Enterprise*-D, with loss of all hands.

Captain
Morgan Bateson
of the
U.S.S. Bozeman

U.S.S. Bozeman, NCC-1941

The magnitude of the explosion, however, appears to have thrown the *Enterprise*-D into a recursive causality loop in which the events leading up to the collision were repeatedly experienced by those aboard the ship. Verification with Federation Timebase Beacons indicate the outside universe had experienced the passage of 17.4 days while the *Enterprise*-D was trapped in several iterations of the causality loop. The *Bozeman* had apparently been caught in a similar causality loop for approximately 80 years.

The hypothesized disaster was apparently averted on the final cycle as the result of a message transmitted via dekyon field to Lieutenant Commander Data by the *Enterprise*-D crew on its penultimate cycle. During that final cycle, numerous crew members reported phenomena that appear to have been "echoes" of previous passes through the time loop.

Amanda Rogers begins to exhibit unusual telekinetic powers. Believing herself to be human, she does not realize that this is evidence that she is a member of the Q Continuum.

About six months prior to "True-Q" (TNG).

Ensign Wesley Crusher and four fellow cadets at Starfleet Academy are involved in a serious flight accident involving a collision of trainer spacecraft at the Academy range near Saturn. Cadet Joshua Albert is reported killed in the collision, and all five spacecraft are reported destroyed. The remaining cadets, all members of Nova Squadron, are able to transport safely to the emergency evac station on Mimas. No cause for the accident is immediately revealed.

Just prior to "The First Duty" (TNG).

"The First Duty" (TNG). Stardate 45703.9. *U.S.S. Enterprise*-D is en route to Earth, where Captain Jean-Luc Picard is scheduled to deliver the commencement address at Starfleet Academy. Just prior to arrival, Picard is notified of the accident involving Wesley Crusher.

Locarno testifies at Nova Squadron inquiry

At the academy, an investigation is convened by Superintendent Brand in an effort to determine the cause of the accident that claimed the life of Cadet Joshua Albert. Initial testimony by members of Nova Squadron suggests the collision was due to pilot error, but this is found to be inconsistent with telemetric data. A statement by Cadet Wesley Crusher reveals the cause of the crash to be an unauthorized attempt to perform a Kolvoord Starburst, a maneuver prohibited because of its extreme risk. The board of review expels Nova Squadron leader Nick Locarno for his role in the accident and for attempting to conceal information from the board. All three remaining Nova Squadron members, including Cadet Sito Jaxa, are reprimanded, and their academic credits for the year are voided.

The Traveler, living as a man named Lakanta among the Native American colonists at planet Dorvan V, has a vision of Wesley Crusher and his troubled spirit. The Traveler waits on Dorvan V, where he knows Wesley will join him.

Admirals Brand and Setlek preside at
Nova Squadron hearing

"Journey's End" (TNG). Two years before the episode. "Journey's End" was the 20th episode of the seventh season. An event that took place two years prior to this would therefore be set after the 19th episode of the fifth season, which was "The First Duty" (TNG). It's probably a coincidence, but Wesley's traumatic experiences in "The First Duty" might tend to explain why the Traveler had the vision of Wesley's troubled spirit that he described in "Journey's End."

Lieutenant Aquiel Uhnari is transferred from Deriben V to her new posting at subspace communications Relay Station 47.

Nine months prior to "Aquiel" (TNG).

Elim Garak, a member of Cardassia's powerful Obsidian Order, is politically disgraced with the Cardassian Central Command and is exiled to station Terok Nor. Garak finds life on the station difficult, but nevertheless opens a tailor shop and bides his time until he can seek political rehabilitation with his government. Prior to his fall from grace, Garak had been a protégé of Enabran Tain, the head of the Obsidian Order.

"Profit and Loss" (DS9). Two years prior to the episode (2370). His difficulties on the station, his first name, and his affiliation with the Obsidian Order from "The Wire" (DS9).

Elim Garak   Enabran Tain

"Cost of Living" (TNG). Stardate 45733.6. *U.S.S. Enterprise*-D destroys an asteroid to avoid a disastrous impact on planet Tessen III. Unknown to the crew, the asteroid had been rich in metallic nitrium, and that the nitrium had been a food source to parasitic nonsentient life-forms that had lived in the asteroid. The crew later discovers that these life-forms had settled on the *Enterprise*-D hull in the aftermath of the asteroid's destruction, resulting in significant damage to the ship's structure and systems.

U.S.S. Enterprise-D serves as the site for a wedding between Minister Campio of planet Kostolain and Ambassador Lwaxana Troi of planet Betazed. Just prior to the ceremony, Campio's protocol adviser, Erko, recommends cancellation of the wedding due to what he regards as irreconcilable differences between Kostolain and Betazoid customs.

U.S.S. Enterprise-D picks up a group of miners stranded at planet Harod IV, resulting in a slight delay in the ship's arrival at planet Krios.

Prior to "The Perfect Mate" (TNG).

Lwaxana Troi

"The Perfect Mate" (TNG). Stardate 45761.3. *U.S.S. Enterprise*-D arrives at planet Krios to pick up a Kriosian delegation for a critical Ceremony of Reconciliation between planets Krios and Valt Minor, in an effort to bring an end to a centuries-old war. En route to the ceremony site, *U.S.S. Enterprise*-D responds to a distress call from a Ferengi shuttle vehicle, successfully rescuing a crew of two before the shuttle explodes.

Preparations for the reconciliation ceremony are disrupted when a Kriosian gift to Chancellor Alrik of Valt is accidentally released from stasis. The "gift" is learned to be a humanoid female named Kamala, a Kriosian sexual "metamorph" intended as the mate of Alrick. Preparations for the ceremony are further complicated when Kriosian ambassador Briam is injured in an altercation with Ferengi personnel. *Enterprise*-D captain Picard is successful in finalizing preparations for the ceremony during Briam's convalescence. The Ceremony of Reconciliation is performed without incident, although Ambassador Briam would later express astonishment at Picard's ability to work so closely with Kamala without succumbing to her sexual attraction.

Kamala

Garak finds life in exile on station Terok Nor to be intolerable. In despair, he activates a neural implant device that had been placed in the postcentral gyrus of his brain by the Obsidian Order. The device, designed to allow Garak to artificially stimulate the pleasure centers of his brain, had been implanted to make it possible to resist torture if captured by enemies. In the absence of such torture, the implant serves as a powerfully addictive narcotic, one Garak uses to numb him to the pain of life in exile. Garak soon finds himself physically dependent on the endorphins generated by the implant.

"The Wire" (DS9). Two years before the episode, and presumably some time after Garak arrived on the station, which was two years before "Profit and Loss" (DS9).

"Imaginary Friend" (TNG). Stardate 45852.1. While on a scientific survey mission of nebula FGC-47, *U.S.S. Enterprise*-D accidentally encounters a previously undiscovered life-form. The entity materializes aboard the

Clara Sutter's imaginary friend

Enterprise-D in the form of a human child. The appearance of this entity on the ship is later found to correlate with an unexpectedly high drag coefficient encountered when passing through the nebula. It is eventually discovered that the entity is indigenous to the nebula and is attempting to evaluate the potential of the *Enterprise*-D as an energy source. The spaceborne entity, which has befriended young Clara Sutter, departs the ship when made aware of its negative impact on the child.

Bok buys his way out of Rog Prison, where he had been held by Ferengi authorities for being unstable and dangerous. Bok secretly vows to take vengeance on Jean-Luc Picard, who he still holds responsible for the death of his son in 2355 and the loss of his title of daimon in 2364.

"Bloodlines" (TNG). Two years prior to the episode (2370). Bok's history with Picard from "The Battle" (TNG).

A Borg scout craft crash-lands on a small moon in the Argolis cluster. Four of the five crew members on board the ship are killed in the impact.

Shortly prior to "I, Borg" (TNG).

Borg crash site in the Argolis cluster

"I, Borg" (TNG). Stardate 45854.2. *U.S.S. Enterprise*-D charts six star systems in the Argolis cluster as a possible prelude to colonization. A distress signal is detected from what investigation determines to be a Borg scout craft that had crashed on a small moon in the region. A single survivor, an adolescent Borg, is recovered from the wreckage.

Under the instructions of *Enterprise*-D captain Picard, analysis of the Borg survivor's biochip implants yields information on the Borg collective intelligence's command structure and interface protocols. This information is used to develop an invasive programming sequence believed capable of destroying the entire Borg race if introduced into the Borg system.

During the development of the invasive programming software, *Enterprise*-D personnel observe that the Borg, now cut off from access to the collective intelligence, exhibits behavioral characteristics of an individual. Deeming it unethical to use a sentient individual as a weapon of mass destruction, Picard orders the Borg, now known as Hugh, to be returned to the crash site for rescue by a second Borg scout craft. Engineer Geordi La Forge, observing Hugh's rescue at the crash site, later reports his belief that Hugh has retained his individuality despite reassimilation into the Borg collective.

Third of Five, aka Hugh

Captain Jean-Luc Picard files a report on the Argolis incident with Admiral Brooks of Starfleet Command.

"Descent, Part I" (TNG). Nechayev noted that Picard had filed the report after the events in "I, Borg" (TNG).

The Borg individual known as Hugh, having returned to the Borg collective, transfers his sense of individuality to his local group. This concept is totally alien to the Borg and nearly destroys them by leaving them lost, disoriented, and unable to function on their own. The local group is saved when the android Lore happens to discover them. Lore gives them a new sense of purpose by assuming the role of leader.

After "I, Borg" (TNG). It is not clear how long after "I, Borg" that Lore joined the group, although it had to be before "Descent, Part I" (TNG) in late 2369.

A Romulan scout ship experiences a serious malfunction of its propulsion system and issues a distress call. *U.S.S. Enterprise*-D responds to the signal.

Just prior to "The Next Phase" (TNG).

"The Next Phase" (TNG). Stardate 45892.4 *U.S.S. Enterprise*-D, on rescue mission to crippled Romulan ship, assists in safe ejection of malfunctioning engine core and provides temporary replacement components, permitting maintenance of life support and propulsion.

During the rescue operation, an apparent transporter malfunction results in the apparent loss of Lieutenant Commander Geordi La Forge and Ensign Ro Laren. Both La Forge and Ro are later found not to be dead, but rather suspended in an area of interspace rendering them effectively invisible. This interphase phenomenon is found to have been caused by an experimental Romulan cloaking device, and exposure to an anionic beam is successful in restoring both La Forge and Ro back to normal space.

U.S.S. Enterprise-D heads for planet Garadius IV for an urgent diplomatic mission.

Just after "The Next Phase" (TNG).

Starship Enterprise-D conducts a magnetic wave survey of the Parvenium sector, then proceeds to Starbase 218 for a scheduled meeting with Fleet Admiral Gustafson.

Prior to "The Inner Light" (TNG).

"The Inner Light" (TNG). Stardate 45944.1. En route to Starbase 218, *U.S.S. Enterprise*-D encounters a space probe of unknown origin. A low-level nucleonic particle beam from the probe is successful in penetrating the *Enterprise*-D's shields, interacts with Captain Picard, rendering him comatose. Upon regaining consciousness, Picard reports having experienced a lifetime of memories from a native of planet Kataan. The crew determines that the purpose of the probe was to transmit these memories from that long-dead civilization in hope of perpetuating a portion of the Kataan culture. Also discovered aboard the probe is an ancient Ressikan flute, an artifact of the people who once lived on Kataan.

Work crews excavating beneath the city of San Francisco on Earth discover artifacts suggesting an extraterrestrial presence in that city during the late 19th century. Among the artifacts discovered is an object identified as the head of Lieutenant Commander Data, decayed from having been buried for some 500 years.

Just prior to "Time's Arrow, Part I" (TNG).

"Time's Arrow, Part I" (TNG). Stardate 45959.1 *U.S.S. Enterprise*-D is recalled to Earth on a priority mission to investigate discovery of Data's severed head, found buried at the Presidio in San Francisco. Analysis of artifacts found at the dig site suggest origination from planet Devidia II in the Marrab sector.

Proceeding to Devidia II, *Enterprise*-D personnel discover humanoid life-forms existing on an asynchronous temporal plane, rendering the humanoids nearly undetectable. Evidence is uncovered that suggests these life-forms may have threatened 19th-century Earth. While investigating this possibility, Lieutenant Commander Data is accidentally entrapped in a temporal vortex, which transports him back to Earth in the 19th century. Recreating the vortex, an away team consisting of Picard, Riker, Data, Troi, Crusher, and La Forge follow Data into the past in an effort to prevent the Devidia II life-forms from threatening Earth, and in the hope of preventing Data's death.

Dr. Farallon begins activating an experimental particle fountain, a test of a radically new mining technology, from a station orbiting planet Tyrus VIIA. If successful, this will be the culmination of nearly six years of work.

"The Quality of Life" (TNG). Dr. Farallon said it had taken four months prior to the episode to get the flux level up.

Ro Laren in interspace

Enterprise-*D* encounters Kataan probe

Ressikan flute

Data seeks information from a 19th-century San Francisco native

Data's head, buried beneath the city of San Francisco

6.6 STAR TREK: THE NEXT GENERATION—YEAR 6
STAR TREK: DEEP SPACE NINE—YEAR 1

Earth writer Samuel Clemens looks into humanities future

2369

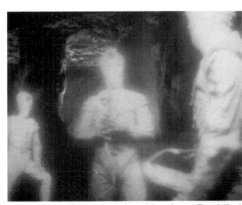

Extradimensional entities from Devidia II

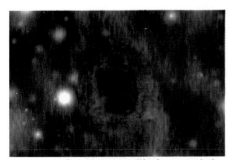

Quasi-energy life-forms existing in a transporte beam

"Time's Arrow, Part II" (TNG). Stardate 46001.3. *Starship Enterprise*-D personnel determine that the purpose of the Devidia II invasion of 19th-century San Francisco was to facilitate the theft of human neural energy from victims in Earth's past. An *Enterprise*-D away team is successful in destroying the Devidian time portal, thereby halting the Devidian attack. In the process, Data's body, severed from his head in 1893, is rejoined with his head, which had been discovered buried under the Presidio in San Francisco.

Nineteenth-century American writer Samuel Clemens is accidentally transported to the 24th century. Before he is returned to his proper time, he credits his glimpse of the future with restoring his faith in humanity.

The *Starship Yosemite*, studying the plasma streamer between a binary star pair in the Igo sector, is severely damaged when a sample container explodes.

Several days prior to "Realm of Fear" (TNG).

"Realm of Fear" (TNG). Stardate 46041.1. *U.S.S. Enterprise*-D assigned to investigate the disappearance of the *U.S.S. Yosemite*. It is learned that the *Yosemite*'s scientists had inadvertently captured several quasi-energy microbial life-forms that live in the plasma streamers in the Igo sector. These quasi-energy microbes, which infected several *Yosemite* crew members and the pattern buffers of both ships' transporter systems, were returned to their natural habitat.

The transport ship *Dorian* is attacked near planet Rekag-Seronia. The ship is carrying Lumerian ambassador Ves Alkar, on a mission to help mediate the armed hostilities on that planet, which had intensified recently, threatening a Federation trading route.

Prior to "Man of the People" (TNG).

"Man of the People" (TNG). Stardate 46071.6. *Starship Enterprise*-D assigned to transport Lumerian ambassador Ves Alkar to Rekag-Seronia. During the flight to Rekag-Seronia, Alkar's companion, a woman identified as his mother, dies of apparent old age. It is not learned until later that Alkar's companion was in fact a much younger woman, the victim of severe empathic abuse, who served as the "receptacle" for Alkar's negative emotions at the cost of her life. Alkar dies of his own psychic poisoning after being prevented from using *Enterprise*-D counselor Deanna Troi as his new receptacle.

Starfleet schedules an important diplomatic conference to be held on planet Atalia VII in six months. *Enterprise*-D captain Jean-Luc Picard is set to mediate the talks.

Six months prior to "The Chase" (TNG).

A Vulcan archaeological artifact, the only known surviving fragment of the ancient Stone of Gol, is stolen from a Vulcan museum, where it had been stored under heavy guard. According to myth, the Stone of Gol had been a telepathic weapon enabling its user to kill with a thought. Shortly after the theft, it is learned that mercenary ships have staged raids on archaeological sites across the quadrant.

A year prior to "Gambit, Part II" (TNG).

"Relics" (TNG). Stardate 46125.3. *U.S.S. Enterprise*-D, investigating a distress call, discovers an ancient Dyson Sphere. The distress call is found to have originated from the *U.S.S. Jenolen*, a transport vessel that crashed into the sphere in 2295 while en route to the Norpin V Colony. The only survivor is Captain Montgomery Scott, who had survived by suspending himself in a transporter beam for nearly 75 years. Scott is instrumental in freeing the *Enterprise*-D from the Dyson Sphere's interior, where it had become trapped. Scott is subsequently granted the indefinite loan of a shuttlecraft, in which he sets out, alone, to explore the cosmos.

Editors' Note: This episode featured the emergence of Scotty into the Star Trek: The Next Generation *era. We don't know what happened to Scotty after this episode, although we hope he is finally enjoying his retirement.*

A Jem'Hadar spacecraft crashes on planet Bopak III in the Gamma Quadrant. The only survivor is a soldier named Goran'Agar, who expects to live for only a few days because of a severely limited supply of ketracel-white. To his surprise, Goran'Agar survives without the drug, and is rescued 35 days later. Goran'Agar believes exposure to something in Bopak III's environment has cured him of his genetic addiction to ketracel-white.

"Hippocratic Oath" (DS9). Three years prior to the episode (2372). Some dialog in the episode suggests that the crash might have been four years before the episode.

"Schisms" (TNG). Stardate 46154.2. *U.S.S. Enterprise*-D, assigned to study the Amargosa Diaspora globular cluster, reports that several crew personnel have apparently disappeared from the vessel while asleep, only to be returned before awakening. Investigation reveals that these crew members have been abducted by solanagen-based life-forms from a previously undiscovered subspace domain. It is further learned that the incursion into our spatial domain had accidentally been made possible by a modification to the *Enterprise*-D's long-range sensors intended for study of the Amargosa Diaspora. Starfleet issues an advisory to prevent other ships from repeating the procedure.

The *Enterprise*-D arrives at Starbase 112 to onload relief supplies intended for planet Tagra IV, an ecologically devastated planet in the Argolis Cluster. Also joining the ship at Starbase 112 is young Amanda Rogers, a student intern.

Just prior to "True Q" (TNG).

Ambassador Ves Alkar

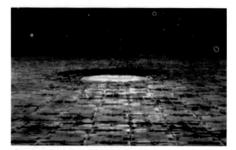

Surface of the Dyson Sphere

Montgomery Scott

Solanagen-based life-form

Amanda Rogers

Young Jean-Luc Picard

Ancient West holodeck program

"True Q" (TNG). Stardate 46192.3. The *U.S.S. Enterprise*-D is assigned to help install barystatic filters at Tagra IV in an effort to control pollution in that planet's atmosphere. Although serious technical difficulties threaten the mission, Amanda Rogers, who has just become aware of her powers as a member of the Q Continuum, uses her abilities to clean Tagra IV's air. Rogers had previously believed herself to be human. Rogers leaves the *Enterprise*-D, choosing to live as a Q, rather than as a human.

Several *Enterprise*-D personnel, including Captain Jean-Luc Picard, visit planet Marlonia via shuttlecraft.

Prior to "Rascals" (TNG).

Starfleet receives reports of theta-band subspace emissions from planet Celtris III in Cardassian space. Starfleet interprets this as evidence that the Cardassians are developing a metagenic weapons delivery system, in apparent violation of interstellar treaty.

A few weeks prior to "Chain of Command, Part I" (TNG), according to Picard.

"Rascals" (TNG). Stardate 46235.7. Upon returning to the *Enterprise*-D from planet Marlonia, the *Shuttlecraft Fermi* and all personnel onboard are exposed to an unusual energy field, resulting in the shuttle's flight crew being reverted to children when they are beamed back to the *Enterprise*-D. While studying the phenomenon, the *Enterprise*-D responds to a distress call from the Starfleet science team on planet Ligos VII. The rescue mission is threatened by an attempt by DaiMon Lurin to commandeer the *Enterprise*-D, but ship's personnel (including young Picard) are successful in repelling the offensive, and Chief O'Brien is able to use the ship's transporter to reverse the effects of the molecular inversion field. The Ferengi government later disavows the attack on the *Enterprise*-D as not having been authorized.

Editors' Note: Picard said that he'd spent 30 years of his life aboard starships, although he took command of the Stargazer in 2333, 36 years ago, and certainly served aboard starships prior to being promoted to captain. (Perhaps there were a few years after the loss of the Stargazer and before he commanded the Enterprise-D when he did not live on a starship?) The incident with DaiMon Lurin was mentioned by Odo in "Bar Association" (DS9).

Starfleet detects extensive Cardassian military activity, including the massing of troops in staging areas, assembly of strike forces, and reassignment of ships from normal patrol patterns.

Three weeks prior to "Chain of Command, Part I" (TNG), according to Captain Jellico.

The *Starship Enterprise*-D proceeds to planet Deinonychus VII for a rendezvous with the supply ship *Biko*, although the rendezvous is delayed.

At least two days prior to "A Fistful of Datas" (TNG).

"A Fistful of Datas" (TNG). Stardate 46271.5. During the wait for the *Biko* rendezvous, Commander La Forge and Commander Data conduct an experiment to interface Data's positronic brain with the *Enterprise*-D's computer system. During the test, a minor power surge in Data's neural net causes information from Data's personal files to appear in various recreational, library, and holodeck subsystems. Simultaneously, elements of a holodeck simulation program, "Ancient West," begin to appear in Data's behavioral patterns. Fortunately, both Data and the ship's computer systems are restored in time for the rendezvous with the *Biko*.

Cardassian forces begin to withdraw from the Bajoran sector and are redeployed along the Federation border. The Cardassians also conduct an elaborate program of disinformation designed to make Starfleet Intelligence believe that they are developing a metagenic weapons system on planet Celtris III.

Shortly before "Chain of Command, Part I" (TNG).

Editors' Note: This, of course, was part of the setup for the first episode of Star Trek: Deep Space Nine, which began airing shortly after "Chain of Command, Parts I and II" (TNG).

The Velos VII internment camp, used by the Cardassians for the imprisonment of Bajoran nationals, is closed on stardate 46302. Among the detainees released when the camp is closed is Dr. Surmak Ren, a former member of the Higa Metar sect of the Bajoran underground.

"Babel" (DS9). Stardate 46302 is apparently between "A Fistful of Datas" (TNG) and "The Quality of Life" (TNG).

Tyrus VIIA particle fountain

Starship Enterprise-D chief engineer Geordi La Forge begins to grow a beard. He doesn't keep it for long.

A few days prior to "The Quality of Life" (TNG).

"The Quality of Life" (TNG). Stardate 46307.2. *U.S.S. Enterprise-D* at planet Tyrus VIIA to monitor testing of a new particle fountain mining technology under the direction of Dr. Farallon. Although the particle fountain represents a potential breakthrough, the project to date has been plagued with setbacks. The tests are interrupted when evidence emerges that exocomp servomechanisms, modified by Farallon, have acquired sufficient computational power and complexity for them to be classified as bona fide life-forms. The exocomps also exhibit the ability for voluntary self-sacrifice, and do so when a serious malfunction of the particle fountain threatens the lives of several project scientists.

Dr. Farallon

Exocomp

U.S.S. Enterprise-D makes rendezvous with *Starship Cairo* for an urgent meeting of Vice-Admiral Alynna Nechayev with Captain Jean-Luc Picard regarding the Cardassian situation and Starfleet's fears that the Cardassians may be preparing for an attack on Federation space using metagenic weapons.

Just prior to "Chain of Command, Part I" (TNG).

"Chain of Command, Part I" (TNG). Stardate 46357.4. Captain Edward Jellico, formerly of the *Cairo*, assumes command of the *Starship Enterprise-D* and is assigned to conduct negotiations with Gul Lemec of the Cardassian ship *Reklar*. Captain Jean-Luc Picard, Lieutenant Worf, and Dr. Beverly Crusher conduct a special covert mission to planet Celtris III, investigating possible Cardassian metagenic weapons development. The mission is a failure, and Picard falls into Cardassian custody. It is later learned that there was no metagenic weapon, and that Starfleet and Picard were the victims of an elaborate Cardassian hoax designed to capture Picard in an effort to gain information on Starfleet's defenses at planet Minos Korva.

Captain Edward Jellico

The Cardassian Union, weary of decades of terrorist activity, relinquishes claim to the Bajoran system, leaving the planet Bajor in the hands of a provisional government. Over ten million Bajorans had been killed by Cardassian forces during the occupation. Prior to leaving Bajor, Cardassian troops poison much of the planet's farmlands.

Gul Dukat

Abandoned into Bajoran hands is the Cardassian mining station Terok Nor, orbiting the planet Bajor. The station had been commanded by Gul Dukat, prefect of the region. During the withdrawal, Cardassian forces vandalize much of the station, causing many station residents to flee. Retreating Cardassian troops also cause massive damage to cities on Bajor. Still in Cardassian possession are eight revered Bajoran religious artifacts known as Tears of the Prophets. The only Cardassian citizen left on Terok Nor is exiled former intelligence agent Elim Garak, who runs the tailor shop on the station's Promenade.

Kira Nerys

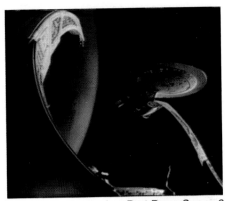

Enterprise-D at Deep Space 9

Miles O'Brien

Benjamin Sisko

Jake Sisko

Kai Opaka

During the withdrawal, Cardassian authorities inexplicably order numerous Cardassian war orphans to be abandoned. Many of these orphans are cared for in Bajoran orphanages, and some of them are adopted by Bajoran families.

About two weeks before "Emissary" (DS9). Dukat left his post at Deep Space 9 two weeks prior to the episode. "Cardassians" (DS9) establishes that the Cardassian name for the station was Terok Nor. Garak's presence established in "Past Prologue" (DS9). Bajoran death toll and the abandoned Cardassian war orphans established in "Cardassians" (DS9). Poisoning of farmlands established in "Shakaar" (DS9).

"Chain of Command, Part II" (TNG). Stardate 46360.8. Captain Jellico determines that the Cardassians have been staging spacecraft in the McAllister nebula in preparation for an attack on planet Minos Korva in Federation space. Jellico conducts a preemptive strike against the attack force, forcing the Cardassians to withdraw and to release Picard from Cardassian custody. Picard had been the victim of torture in violation of the Seldonis IV convention. Once returned to the *Enterprise*-D, Picard reassumes command of that starship.

The Bajoran provisional government asks Starfleet to establish a Federation presence in the Bajoran system following the withdrawal of Cardassian occupational forces. Commander Benjamin Sisko is assigned to command station Terok Nor, now designated by Starfleet as Deep Space 9. Sisko's assignment is at the recommendation of Admiral Leyton, who had been Sisko's commanding officer when they both served aboard the *Starship Okinawa*. At Sisko's request, a Bajoran national, Kira Nerys, is assigned to the station by the Bajoran government to serve as their liaison and as Sisko's second-in-command. Sisko had previously been assigned to Starfleet's Utopia Planitia Yards on Mars. The provisional government remains dangerously unstable, subject to violent dissent within the Bajoran people themselves; the First Minister is killed, apparently by Bajoran Kohn-Ma terrorists.

Prior to "Emissary" (DS9). The assassination of the First Minister was about a month before "Past Prologue" (DS9). Leyton's recommendation and the U.S.S. Okinawa established in "Homefront" (DS9).

While en route to his new posting at Deep Space 9, Commander Benjamin Sisko and his son, Jake, visit the planet known as Blue Horizon for a few hours. Blue Horizon is an extraordinary example of the art and science of terraforming.

"Second Sight" (DS9). Sisko said he and Jake visited Blue Horizon on their way to DS9.

The *Starship Enterprise*-D travels to the Bajoran system and docks at Deep Space 9. Miles O'Brien, newly transferred as chief operations office for the station, immediately begins work to restore systems stripped by the departing Cardassian forces. O'Brien is relocating to Deep Space 9 along with his wife, Keiko, and their daughter, Molly. Also transported to Deep Space 9 aboard the *Enterprise*-D are three runabouts, the *Rio Grande*, the *Yangtzee Kiang*, and the *Ganges*.

Two days before "Emissary" (DS9), according to Sisko's log.

"Emissary, Parts I and II" (DS9). Stardate 46379.1. Commander Benjamin Sisko arrives at Deep Space 9, finding the station in a shambles. Sisko pressures local business leaders to remain at the station in an effort to reverse the migration away from the station.

Sisko discovers a stable wormhole in the Denorios Belt in the Bajoran system, linking the Alpha Quadrant to the distant Gamma Quadrant. According to Bajoran spiritual leader Kai Opaka, alien life-forms discovered by Sisko in the wormhole are in fulfillment of Bajoran prophesy, casting Sisko into the role of what Bajorans call the Emissary. In the Bajoran religious faith, the emergence of the Emissary is a deeply significant event. The discovery of the wormhole has important economic implications for Bajor, since it means that Bajor will become a major center for interstellar commerce to the Gamma Quadrant.

Cardassian forces attempt to reclaim part of the Bajoran system, an effort made more urgent for both sides with the discovery of the stable wormhole, but they are thwarted when Deep Space 9 is relocated to the Denorios Belt, thus reinforcing Bajor's claim on the wormhole.

Dr. Julian Bashir and Lieutenant Jadzia Dax are assigned to Deep Space 9, arriving aboard the *Starship Cochrane*.

Inside the wormhole

Editors' Note: From this point in our chronology, episodes of Star Trek: The Next Generation *and* Star Trek: Deep Space Nine *are listed in (approximate) order of first national airing, based on "week of" air dates. Because the two shows followed different schedules, there were several weeks during this season when* Deep Space Nine *was airing first-run episodes, while* The Next Generation *was in reruns. For this reason, the two shows will tend to alternate in the chronology, but episodes of one series or the other are occasionally listed back-to-back. Note also that in some cities, the first run of* Deep Space Nine *episodes occurred before that week's episode of* The Next Generation, *but we're arbitrarily listing* The Next Generation *episodes first. Another peculiarity in this episode sequence is that stardates will occasionally run backwards when you compare an episode of one series to a later episode of the other show (even more frequently than they did before). Once again, we'll assume this is part of the ambiguities inherent in stardate calculation, since arranging the episodes in stardate order would entail even more inconsistencies, not the least of which is the fact that a significant number of episodes do not have stardates. (We are not going back and reordering earlier episodes on the grounds that we don't want to seriously obsolete earlier editions of the Chronology.)*

Jadzia Dax

We still assume that for episodes of the same series, the average time span from the beginning of one episode to the beginning of the next (including any unseen gap between episodes) is about two weeks. We also assume that the two shows happen nearly simultaneously, so that a period that includes two Star Trek: The Next Generation *episodes or two* Star Trek: Deep Space Nine *episodes would, on average, be approximately four weeks in length. On the other hand, a period that includes one episode from each series would, on average, be only about two weeks in length. In other words, the exact order of episodes should be taken with a grain of salt.*

The *Enterprise*-D departs Deep Space 9, traveling to the Detrian system for a scientific assignment.

After "Emissary" (DS9) and before "Ship in a Bottle" (TNG).

Space Station Deep Space 9

"Past Prologue" (DS9). (No stardate given in episode.) Bajoran Kohn-ma terrorist Tahna Los requests asylum from Cardassian pursuit at Deep Space 9. Cardassian authorities request his extradition for crimes allegedly committed against Cardassian forces, but station commander Benjamin Sisko grants Tahna's request. At the station, Tahna concludes a deal with Klingon outlaws Lursa and B'Etor to obtain powerful bilitrium explosives. Lursa and B'Etor are attempting to raise capital for another bid to gain control of the Klingon High Council, while Tahna attempts to use the bilitrium explosives to destroy the Bajoran wormhole. Although he is prevented from doing so, Tahna had expected to reduce Bajor's strategic importance in interstellar commerce in hopes of discouraging Cardassian and Federation interference in Bajoran affairs.

Tahna Los

Michael O'Brien, father to Miles O'Brien, remarries following the death of his wife last year. Miles is less than pleased that his father has married a woman he's never met.

Ibudan

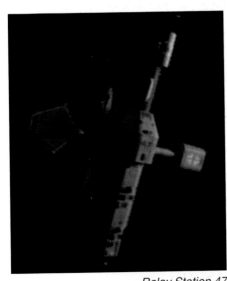

Gas giant planets in the Detrian system

Sentient holodeck program James Moriarty

Relay Station 47

"Whispers" (DS9). "Last Spring" prior to the episode. (If each production year is a calendar year, this point in the production year would probably be after Spring, but this is about as early in Deep Space Nine's year that O'Brien could have mentioned his discomfort over his father's wedding to Bashir.)

Ibudan arrives at Deep Space 9 aboard a Bajoran transport. Ibudan is believed to have enriched himself on the Bajoran black market during the Cardassian occupation.

Shortly before "A Man Alone" (DS9).

"A Man Alone" (DS9). Stardate 46421.5. Bajoran black marketer Ibudan is reported to have been murdered at Quark's bar on the Deep Space 9 promenade. Investigation by security chief Odo reveals Ibudan to have killed a clone of himself in order to frame Odo, who had successfully prosecuted Ibudan for murder several years ago.

Keiko O'Brien establishes a primary schoolroom on the Promenade of Deep Space 9. Although O'Brien is a botanist by trade, the lack of educational facilities on the station has concerned her.

"Ship in a Bottle" (TNG). Stardate 46424.1. Two gas giant planets in the Detrian system collide. The combined mass of the two planets is sufficient to cause nuclear fusion, resulting in the birth of a new star. *Starship Enterprise*-D personnel make observations of the event. The scientific mission is briefly delayed when a sentient holodeck program, a simulation of Sherlock Holmes character Dr. James Moriarty, attempts to seize control of the *Enterprise*-D. Ship's personnel are unable to meet Moriarty's demand of finding a way to grant physicality to Moriarty, but are successful in providing him and his companion with a virtual environment of sufficient realism for them to live out their lives.

A series of unexplained systems malfunctions plagues station Deep Space 9, including the navigational computer and the secondary phase modulator in the main power core.

A few days prior to "Babel" (DS9).

A freighter piloted by Captain Jarheel, docked at station Deep Space 9, suffers a malfunction, requiring repairs by the station's engineering staff.

Two days before "Babel" (DS9).

"Babel" (DS9). Stardate 46423.7. Deep Space 9 commander Benjamin Sisko orders the station placed under emergency quarantine when a virus of unknown origin causes station personnel to suffer from aphasia, making them unable to communicate. Investigation determines the virus to have been introduced through food produced by the station's replicator system. It is further learned that this is the work of Bajoran terrorists, who sabotaged the replicators eighteen years ago when the station was still under construction. Station personnel enlist the aid of Dr. Surmak Ren, a former Bajoran terrorist who helped develop the virus, to develop an effective treatment.

Lieutenant Keith Rocha arrives at Starfleet's subspace communications Relay Station 47. Rocha works with Lieutenant Aquiel Uhnari to perform a systems overhaul on the station. Uhnari later recalls finding Rocha to be arrogant and difficult to work with, despite his spotless Starfleet record.

A Klingon spacecraft, commanded by Morag, passes Relay Station 47 on routine patrol. He hails the station, located near the Klingon border, a regular practice that station personnel regard as harassment.

Lieutenant Aquiel Uhnari flees from Relay Station 47 after she is attacked by what she believes is her co-worker, Lieutenant Keith Rocha.

"Aquiel" (TNG). Rocha arrived five days before the episode. Aquiel fled about a day before the episode.

Ensign Stefan DeSeve, who gave up his Federation citizenship 20 years ago to live on Romulus, renounces the Romulan Empire, returning home aboard a Romulan scoutship.

Two weeks prior to "Face of the Enemy" (TNG).

Starship *Enterprise*-D arrives at Relay Station 47, near the Klingon border, to deliver supplies. Station personnel fail to respond to hails.

Just before "Aquiel" (TNG).

"Aquiel" (TNG). Stardate 46461.3. *Enterprise*-D personnel discover that Lieutenant Keith Rocha, assigned to Station 47, has been murdered. Preliminary evidence implicates Lieutenant Aquiel Uhnari in the death, but it is later learned that Rocha had been killed prior to his assignment to the station. The entity believed to have been Rocha was, in fact, a coalescent organism that formed a near-perfect replica of him.

Aquiel Uhnari

Lieutenant Aquiel Uhnari accepts a posting at Starbase 212.

After "Aquiel" (TNG).

Deanna Troi, attending a neuropsychology seminar on planet Borka VI, is abducted by Romulan underground operatives, surgically altered to appear Romulan, and held captive aboard the Imperial Romulan Warbird *Khazara*.

Before "Face of the Enemy" (TNG).

Tosk

"Captive Pursuit" (DS9). (No stardate in episode.) A spacecraft of unknown origin arrives at Deep Space 9 through the Bajoran wormhole, the first contact with a new life-form from the Gamma Quadrant. It is learned that the lone inhabitant of the vessel, identified as Tosk, is the subject of a ritual hunt. After rendering assistance to Tosk by repairing damage to his spacecraft, DS9 Operations officer Miles O'Brien permits Tosk to depart the station. Other individuals from Tosk's society, ritual Hunters, continue to pursue Tosk.

"Face of the Enemy" (TNG). Stardate 46519. *Enterprise*-D at Research Station 75 to pick up Ensign Stefan DeSeve, a Federation turncoat returning from the Romulan Star Empire. DeSeve, representing the dissident Romulan underground, conveys a message from Ambassador Spock, requesting assistance in smuggling Romulan vice proconsul M'ret to Federation space.

Deanna Troi, held captive aboard the Romulan warbird *K'hazara* by other Romulan underground operatives, is compelled to impersonate a member of the Tal Shiar intelligence service. In that capacity, she is successful in allowing the safe passage of M'ret and his top aides to the *Enterprise*-D. It is hoped that M'ret's defection to the Federation will make it possible for other Romulan dissidents to escape political persecution in the Romulan Empire.

Deanna Troi in Romulan guise

Deep Space 9 science officer Dax and Ensign Pauley conduct an exploratory mission into the Gamma Quadrant aboard the *Runabout Ganges*. They discover a human there, Vash, an archaeologist of questionable repute. Vash had been traveling in the company of Q, but the two had parted company. Q follows Vash to Deep Space 9.

Prior to "Q-Less" (DS9).

"Q-Less" (DS9). Stardate 46531.2. Archaeologist Vash, arrives at station Deep Space 9 from the Gamma Quadrant aboard the *Runabout Ganges*. Shortly after her arrival, the station experiences a severe power drain, threatening the safety of all inhabitants. Although Q is initially suspected as the cause, is learned that an artifact that Vash had brought back from the Gamma Quadrant is in fact an energy-based life-form and is causing the energy drain. Station operation returns to normal once the life-form is permitted to leave unhindered.

Vash

Vash leaves Deep Space 9 for Tartaras V.

After "Q-Less" (DS9).

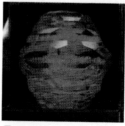

Energy-based life-form

Captain Silva La Forge accepts command of the *Starship Hera*. Just prior to departure on their mission, La Forge throws a party for her new crew. La Forge's son, *Enterprise*-D chief engineer Geordi La Forge, attends the party.

"Interface" (TNG). Seven months prior to the episode.

Captain Jean-Luc Picard, on an away mission, is attacked by Lenarians, who use a compressed tetryon beam. Energy from the beam causes failure of Picard's artificial heart.

Moments prior to "Tapestry" (TNG).

Enina Tandro, widow of General Ardelon Tandro

"Tapestry" (TNG). (No stardate in episode.) Picard is revived after a close brush with death following the Lenarian attack. Afterwards, Picard reports a near-death experience in which Q showed him what his life would have been like if he had changed certain key actions early in his career.

Miles and Keiko O'Brien take leave from Deep Space 9, traveling to Earth to celebrate Keiko's mother's 100th birthday.

Prior to "Dax" (DS9).

Starfleet lieutenant George Primmin embarks on a journey to Deep Space 9, his new posting.

"The Passenger" (DS9). Three weeks prior to the episode.

Jadzia Dax

"Dax" (DS9). Stardate 46910.1. Jadzia Dax is arrested by authorities from planet Klaestron IV, and she is accused of the 2339 murder of Klaestron general Ardelon Tandro. At an extradition hearing held on Deep Space 9, Benjamin Sisko, serving as Dax's defense attorney, argues that a Trill becomes a new person when joined with a new host, and that Jadzia Dax therefore cannot be held legally responsible for acts committed by Curzon Dax. The extradition is denied when Tandro's widow testifies that Curzon could not have committed the murder because he was having an affair with her, and that her husband was killed because he had betrayed his people. Jadzia Dax had refused to offer any defense against the charge because Curzon had sworn to protect the memory of General Tandro.

The *Starship Enterprise*-D returns to station Deep Space 9.

Just before "Birthright, Part I" (TNG).

"Birthright, Part I" (TNG). Stardate 46578.4. *Starship Enterprise*-D arrives at station Deep Space 9 to assist in the reconstruction of Bajoran aqueduct systems damaged during the Cardassian occupation. While at the station, Commander Data experiences a severe plasma shock during a test of an alien medical artifact. The shock activates a heretofore unsuspected subroutine in Data's positronic brain, allowing the android to dream during periods of cognitive inactivity, much as a human does. Data's dreams include visions of his father, noted cyberneticist Noonien Soong.

Lieutenant Worf uncovers evidence that his father may not have died in the Khitomer Massacre. Investigating this report, Worf travels to the Carraya system.

Data dreams of meeting his father, Noonien Soong

While at Deep Space 9, *Enterprise*-D executive officer William T. Riker distinguishes himself by being the only player ever to win triple down dabo at Quark's place. Quark claims not to have enough latinum to cover his winnings, and Riker is reluctantly forced to accept credit vouchers worth 12 bars of latinum.

"Firstborn" (TNG). The episode doesn't make clear when Riker won at dabo, but it seems fairly safe to assume that it was during the Enterprise-D's *visit in "Birthright, Part I" (TNG).*

A Vulcan expedition exploring the Gamma Quadrant makes contact with a species called the Wadi. The Wadi accept an invitation to send a delegation to the Alpha Quadrant.

Three weeks before "Move Along Home" (DS9).

Major Kira Nerys and Dr. Julian Bashir conduct a mercy mission aboard the *Runabout Rio Grande*. Bashir is successful in saving a woman's life, despite the fact that instrumentation showed her to be dead.

Prior to "The Passenger" (DS9).

"The Passenger" (DS9). (No stardate in episode.) Kobliad criminal Rao Vantika is apparently killed when a transport ship catches fire en route to station Deep Space 9. Vantika had been in custody of Kobliad law enforcement officer Ty Kajada. A series of unexplained malfunctions aboard the station are found to have been caused by Vantika, who is found to have survived the fire by means of synaptic pattern displacement, similar to a Vulcan mind-meld, through which Vantika placed his consciousness into the mind of Dr. Julian Bashir. With the assistance of station personnel, Kajada is successful in apprehending Vantika, and Kajada destroys Vantika's remaining consciousness.

Rao Vantika

"Birthright, Part II" (TNG). Stardate 46578.4. Lieutenant Worf reports that the rumors of a secret Romulan prison camp in the Carraya system are false, and that his father did die at Khitomer.

Editors' Note: Worf, of course, did indeed locate the secret Romulan prison camp at Carraya IV, where 73 Klingon warriors, survivors of the Khitomer Massacre and their children, lived. Because the Klingon warrior ethic which regards being taken prisoner to be a terrible disgrace, none of the Khitomer survivors wished to return to Klingon society. Although a few of their children did leave with Worf, all promised never to reveal the existence of the prison camp that they had come to regard as their home. (Picard presumably figured it out without Worf having to say anything.) Among those remaining behind was Ba'el, a young woman with whom Worf became romantically involved. "Rightful Heir" (TNG) establishes that the prison camp was on planet Carraya IV.

Romulan prison camp

"Move Along Home" (DS9). (No stardate in episode.) Station Deep Space 9 formally welcomes a Wadi delegation, the first formal first contact from the Gamma Quadrant. The Wadi delegation, led by Falow, Master Surchid, invite station personnel to participate in a traditional Wadi game as a form of cultural exchange.

Miles O'Brien returns to station Deep Space 9 from a visit to Earth, although his wife, Keiko, remains behind for another two weeks. Miles fills in as substitute teacher in Keiko's classroom in his wife's absence.

After "Move Along Home" (DS9), but before "The Nagus" (DS9).

Wadi delegate

"The Nagus" (DS9). (No stardate in episode.) Ferengi grand nagus Zek convenes a major business conference at station Deep Space 9 to discuss business opportunities in the Gamma Quadrant. During the conference, Zek makes the startling announcement that he is retiring and appointing Quark as his successor. Shortly thereafter, Zek is reported to have died, but it is later found that Zek had faked his death as a test for his son, Krax, to test Krax's suitability to serve as nagus. In this test, Zek finds Krax wanting, and therefore decides to postpone his retirement for long enough to establish a Ferengi presence in the Gamma Quadrant.

The annual Gratitude Festival is celebrated on planet Bajor.

The departure of the Cardassians also makes it possible for the Gratitude Festival to be celebrated on station Deep Space 9. Kira Nerys and Jadzia Dax set up the renewal scrolls in the station's Promenade.

Grand Nagus Zek

"Fascination" (DS9). The Gratitude Festival celebrated in "Fascination" was the third time the event was held on the station, which suggests that the event mentioned two years earlier, in "The Nagus" (DS9), was the first.

Arctus Baran

A group of mercenaries begins stealing ancient Romulan archaeological artifacts. The group, led by a mercenary named Arctus Baran, has been secretly employed by operatives for a Vulcan separatist group.

Six months prior to "Gambit, Part I" (TNG).

"Starship Mine" (TNG). Stardate 46682.4. The *Starship Enterprise*-D docks at the Remmler Array at Arkaria Base for routine decontamination of accumulated baryon particles. While the crew is evacuated during the decontamination procedure, a team of criminal intruders attempts to steal the highly explosive trilithium resin waste residue from the ship's warp drive. The criminals are thwarted, thanks to the efforts of Captain Jean-Luc Picard.

Enterprise-D at the Remmler Array

Starship Enterprise-D at Starbase 218. Lieutenant Commander Neela Daren is among the personnel joining the ship from Starbase 218. She is assigned to the ship's Stellar Sciences department.

Prior to "Lessons" (TNG).

"Lessons" (TNG). Stardate 46693.1. *Enterprise*-D responds to a request for assistance from the Federation outpost on planet Bersallis III, which is entering a period of firestorm activity. Subsequent forecasts from the Bersallis outpost indicate an unusually severe firestorm, and *Enterprise*-D personnel set up a series of thermal deflectors on the planet surface to protect the outpost, an extremely difficult and hazardous operation. Although the operation is successful in saving the lives of the 643 colonists, eight *Enterprise*-D crew members died while maintaining the operation of the deflectors during the storm. The captain's log notes that they gave their lives in the performance of their duty.

Bersallis III firestorm

Among the members of the thermal deflector team who survived the ordeal is Lieutenant Commander Neela Daren, who had become romantically involved with Captain Jean-Luc Picard. In the aftermath of the incident, both officers acknowledge the difficulty of a commanding officer placing the life of a loved one in jeopardy.

Lieutenant Commander Neela Daren accepts a transfer off the *Enterprise*-D.

After "Lessons" (TNG).

A Miradorn raider spacecraft docks at station Deep Space 9. Also arriving at the station is a Klingon vessel carrying a Rakhari fugitive named Croden, who was rescued in the Gamma Quadrant.

Prior to "Vortex" (DS9).

Neela Daren

"Vortex" (DS9). (No stardate in episode.) While at Deep Space 9 to sell a rare artifact, one member of a Miradorn pair is killed by an individual named Croden, a fugitive from the planet Rakhar in the Gamma Quadrant. The surviving Miradorn demands the death of Croden in vengeance, but Croden, who is wanted by Rakhari authorities, escapes while being returned to Rakhar.

Prior to his escape, Croden presented Odo with a small sample of shapeshifting material, evidence that Odo's species may have originated somewhere in the Gamma Quadrant.

Croden and his daughter, Yareth, travel to planet Vulcan aboard the Vulcan science vessel *T'Vran*.

After "Vortex" (DS9).

Croden

Professor Richard Galen visits planet Ruah IV in search of micropaleontological data. He also visits planet Indri VIII. Galen is gathering samples of genetic material from planets across the galaxy, looking for evidence that an ancient humanoid civilization had seeded the oceans of many planets some four billion years ago. Galen, who has been working in secrecy for a decade, has aroused the suspicions of many who believe his work might have military potential.

Before "The Chase" (TNG).

U.S.S. Enterprise-D arrives at the Volterra nebula for a three-week study of protostar development.

About two and a half weeks prior to "The Chase" (TNG).

Professor Galen, traveling by shuttlecraft, arrives at the *Enterprise*-D in the Volterra nebula for a brief visit.

An hour before "The Chase" (TNG).

Archaeologist Richard Galen

"The Chase" (TNG). Stardate 46731.5. Upon completion of the protostar study in the Volterra nebula, the *Enterprise*-D proceeds to a diplomatic conference on planet Atalia VII. While en route, the ship responds to a distress call from Professor Galen's shuttle, under attack by Yridian information dealers. Galen is killed in the attack. Captain Jean-Luc Picard, investigating Galen's death, learns that Galen had believed that the ancient humanoids who seeded the genetic material on numerous planets in the galaxy had encoded a message into the DNA patterns of those planets' life. Picard, an archaeologist in his own right, works to complete Galen's study, and is successful in reassembling the message from the past; a message of hope and friendship. It was in keeping with the wishes of those ancient humanoids that the message was completed by the cooperation of numerous different life-forms from around the galaxy.

A message from the distant past

Aamin Marritza, an instructor at the Cardassian military academy on planet Kora II, obtains information about Major Kira Nerys, learning that Kira had been a member of the Bajoran resistance group Shakaar, who helped liberate the notorious Gallitep labor camp in 2357.

Three months prior to "Duet" (DS9).

Residents of the settlement on planet Yadera II in the Gamma Quadrant begin to disappear mysteriously.

"Shadowplay" (DS9). "Last Fall" prior to the episode.

"Battle Lines" (DS9). (No stardate in episode.) Bajoran religious leader Kai Opaka, visiting station Deep Space 9, is the guest of Commander Sisko, Major Kira, and Dr. Bashir aboard the *Runabout Yangtzee Kiang* on an excursion through the wormhole into the Gamma Quadrant. While responding to a distress call, the *Yangtzee Kiang* crashes on a small Class-M moon in an uncharted binary star system, resulting in the apparent loss of life of the kai. The planetoid is found to be a penal colony where prisoners are kept alive by artificial microbes that repair damage on a cellular level, an unusually cruel means of prolonging their punishment through eternal war. These microbes repair Opaka's injuries and restore her to life. The result is that Opaka cannot leave the planetoid, since the microbes are designed to function only in that environment. When a rescue ship from Deep Space 9 arrives, Opaka willingly remains behind, believing that her destiny is to help the prisoners grow beyond their hatred.

Opaka visits Deep Space 9

The effective death of Kai Opaka leaves a vacuum in the power structure of Bajoran society, resulting in a bitter struggle to determine her successor.

After "Battle Lines" (DS9).

The prime minister of planet Tilonus IV is assassinated. A Starfleet research team on the planet is forced into hiding following the collapse of the planetary government.

Beverly Crusher's theatrical company aboard the *Starship Enterprise*-D begins rehearsal of a play entitled *Frame of Mind*, an original work written by Crusher.

Before "Frame of Mind" (TNG).

Enterprise-D theatrical director Beverly Crusher

"Frame of Mind" (TNG). Stardate 46778.1. While on an undercover mission to rescue the Starfleet research team on planet Tilonus IV, *Enterprise*-D executive officer William Riker is captured by one of the rival factions seeking control of the planet. Riker's captors subject him to neurosomatic techniques in an attempt to extract strategic information from his memory. After his rescue, Riker reports that the neurosomatic treatment caused him to experience unusually vivid and terrifying hallucinations derived from Crusher's play, *Frame of Mind*.

The leader of a small Bajoran village, anticipating his imminent death, allows his apprentice to conduct the ceremonial storytelling that serves to unite the villagers against a legendary enemy. Unfortunately, the apprentice fails to perform the ritual story with sufficient conviction, and he is rejected by the people.

Two days before "The Storyteller" (DS9).

The storyteller and his apprentice

"The Storyteller" (DS9). Stardate 46729.1. Deep Space 9 commander Benjamin Sisko successfully mediates talks between two rival Bajoran factions, the Paqu and the Navot. The two groups had been embroiled in a border dispute since the Cardassians diverted the river Glyrhond, which served as the boundary between the two.

Deep Space 9 personnel respond to a distress call from a small Bajoran village whose leader is on the verge of death. Upon arrival, Deep Space 9 operations officer Miles O'Brien is inexplicably appointed leader of the village, stirring resentment in the old leader's apprentice. It is later learned that the old leader had chosen O'Brien, who was blatantly unqualified, so that the disappointed villagers would give the apprentice another chance to prove himself.

Dr. Reyga

Dr. Beverly Crusher attends the Altine scientific conference. While there, she comes to respect Dr. Reyga, a physicist whose theories on subspace shielding technology are not widely accepted in the scientific community. After the conference, Crusher invites Reyga and several noted scientists to meet on the *Enterprise*-D in hopes of providing a forum at which to test the validity of Reyga's findings. The test involves equipping a shuttlecraft with a metaphasic shielding system based on Dr. Reyga's theories, then piloting the shuttle through a star's corona. Dr. Jo'Bril, a specialist in solar plasma reactions, volunteers to fly the shuttle, but is believed killed during an apparent failure of the metaphasic shield. Reyga himself is subsequently killed in an apparent laboratory accident.

While investigating the deaths, Crusher is accused of violating medical ethics by conducting an autopsy on Reyga's body against the expressed wishes of Reyga's family. She is relieved of duty pending an investigation.

Prior to "Suspicions" (TNG).

Jo'Bril

"Suspicions" (TNG). Stardate 46830.1. Further investigation into the death of Reyga and Jo'Bril reveals that Jo'Bril did not die aboard the shuttle, and that he had engineered both incidents in an effort to discredit Reyga's work. Jo'Bril is killed when he tries to cause Beverly Crusher's death in an attempt to cover up his murder of Reyga.

Former Starfleet Academy cadet Seska joins the Maquis, fighting against Cardassian forces. It is not realized by either Starfleet authorities or members of the Maquis that Seska is Cardassian, genetically altered to appear Bajoran.

"State of Flux" (VGR). Two years prior to the episode.

An employee of Quark's bar on station Deep Space 9 orders 5,000 wrappages of Cardassian *yamok* sauce, despite the fact that Cardassian patronage at Quark's establishment has declined sharply.

Morn asks Dax out for dinner. She declines, although she later remarks that she finds his forehead hairs kind of cute.

Prior to "Progress" (DS9).

Morn

"Progress" (DS9). Stardate 46844.3. The Bajoran government prepares to tap the molten core of Bajor's fifth moon, Jeraddo, in a project designed to transfer large amounts of power to cities on the surface of Bajor. Before the project can proceed, all forty-seven inhabitants of Jeraddo must be evacuated. The last person to leave is an old man named Mullibok, who had been a farmer on Jeraddo for 40 years. Mullibok's evacuation is assisted by Major Kira Nerys.

A company known as the Noh-Jay Consortium trades 5,000 wrappages of *yamok* sauce for a hundred gross of self-sealing stem bolts. The firm then exchanges the stem bolts for seven tessipates of land, before assigning interest to Quark, who sells it to the Bajoran government at what is assumed to be a healthy profit.

The tapping of the molten core of Jeraddo to provide energy for Bajor begins. The process releases sulfur and carbon compounds into Jeraddo's atmosphere, rendering it unbreathable.

About six days after "Progress" (DS9).

Mullibok of Jeraddo

U.S.S. *Enterprise*-D on course for the Gariman sector, conducting spectral studies of the Alwanir nebula.

Just prior to "Rightful Heir" (TNG).

"Rightful Heir" (TNG). Stardate 46852.2. U.S.S. *Enterprise*-D security chief Worf, experiencing a crisis of faith, is granted leave and travels via shuttlecraft to the sacred Klingon monastery on planet Boreth. At Boreth, Worf is greeted by a vision of Kahless the Unforgettable, but is shocked to learn that this image of the ancient Klingon leader is a living person, possibly the return of Kahless prophesied some fifteen centuries ago. Investigation reveals this person to be a clone of the original Kahless, created by the clerics of Boreth.

Boreth monastery

Klingon high council leader Gowron correctly interprets the emergence of the new Kahless as a challenge to his regime. Gowron denounces the new Kahless, but sees that many of his fellow Klingons hunger for the spiritual leadership that Kahless provides, and it becomes clear that to oppose this living legend would spark a new civil war. At the advice of Worf, son of Mogh, Gowron concedes that the clone is indeed the rightful heir to the throne. Under Worf's plan, Kahless becomes emperor, serving as spiritual leader of the empire, while political power remains in the hands of Gowron and the High Council.

The Klingon Empire celebrates the ascendance of the clone of Kahless as emperor. The new Kahless is the first emperor to reign in three centuries, although his role is largely symbolic.

After "Rightful Heir" (TNG).

Clone of Kahless

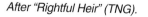

Rumplestiltskin

A Betazoid envoy arrives at station Deep Space 9, attracting the attention of chief medical officer Julian Bashir.

Prior to "If Wishes Were Horses" (DS9).

"If Wishes Were Horses" (DS9). Stardate 46853.2. A group of previously unknown life-forms from the Gamma Quadrant study the life-forms at station Deep Space 9. They are on a mission of exploration, and their method of study involves assuming the form of images discovered in the minds of various Deep Space 9 personnel. These images include Rumplestiltskin, baseball great Buck Bokai, and a version of Jadzia Dax that is highly attracted to Julian Bashir. These images initially prove to be disconcerting, but result in a small measure of understanding between the two cultures.

The Klingon vessel *Toh'Kaht* departs station Deep Space 9 to the Gamma Quadrant, by way of the Bajoran wormhole, on a routine bio-survey mission to evaluate planets for potential colonization. One planet, deemed unsuitable, was the home of a now-dead civilization that called themselves the Saltah'na.

At least 22 days prior to "Dramatis Personae" (DS9).

A duplicate of Riker

Ensign Taitt joins the crew of the *Starship Enterprise*-D. At the academy, she did her honors thesis on solar dynamics.

Six weeks prior to "Descent, Part II" (TNG).

"Second Chances" (TNG). Stardate 46915.2. *U.S.S. Enterprise*-D at planet Nervala IV, assigned to retrieve scientific data left behind when a research station on the planet's surface was abandoned eight years ago. At the station, a duplicate of executive officer William T. Riker is discovered, apparently formed during Riker's beam-out from the station eight years ago. The duplicate Riker, who adopts the name Thomas (their middle name), tries to rekindle his relationship with Deanna Troi, but the attempt fails when Thomas accepts a posting to the *Starship Gandhi*, once again separating the two.

Lieutenant Thomas Riker transfers to the *Starship Gandhi* for a terraforming mission in the Lagana sector.

After "Second Chances" (TNG).

Lieutenant Thomas Riker

A delegation of Federation ambassadors arrives at station Deep Space 9 on a fact-finding mission to study the Bajoran wormhole.

Prior to "The Forsaken" (DS9).

"The Forsaken" (DS9). Stardate 46925.1. A robotic space probe originating from the Gamma Quadrant arrives at station Deep Space 9. When station personnel downloaded information from the alien probe, a sophisticated software life-form was also downloaded into the station's computer system. This software life-form, which Operations Officer O'Brien nicknames "Pup," causes a series of system malfunctions until O'Brien recognizes that it simply wants attention. One of the malfunctions is a minor failure of the station's turbolift system that left security officer Odo and Ambassador Lwaxana Troi briefly trapped in a turboshaft.

Valerian spacecraft *Sherval Das* visits the Ultima Thule station en route to Deep Space 9. The ship had previously visited planet Mariah IV and Fahleena III.

One week prior to "Dramatis Personae" (DS9).

Aamin Marritza, who had served as an instructor at a Cardassian military academy on planet Kora II for the past five years, resigns his position, puts all of his affairs in order, provides for his housekeeper, then leaves Kora II aboard a freighter.

Two weeks prior to "Duet" (DS9).

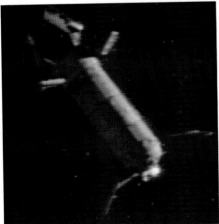

Probe from the Gamma Quadrant

Keiko O'Brien accompanies eleven Bajoran school children on a field trip to planet Bajor. They plan to visit the grain processing center at Lasuma.

Prior to "Dramatis Personae" (DS9).

Keiko O'Brien

"Dramatis Personae" (DS9). Stardate 46922.3. Klingon vessel *Toh'Kaht* returns a month ahead of schedule to the Alpha Quadrant by way of the Bajoran wormhole. Moments after emerging from the wormhole terminus, the ship explodes. Shortly thereafter, several key Deep Space 9 personnel begin exhibiting unusual behavior, becoming uncharacteristically combative and conspiratorial. Simultaneously, analysis of the Klingon ship's logs reveals that prior to its destruction, a mutiny had occurred. It is learned that the *Toh'Kaht* had been carrying telepathic archive devices, artifacts from a planet in the Gamma Quadrant. Evidently, telepathic energy from these devices had taken over the minds of the Klingon crew, causing them to reenact an ancient power struggle that destroyed a civilization of people that called themselves the Saltah'na, and the same telepathic energy is now affecting Deep Space 9 personnel. Once station personnel realize this, they force the Saltah'na telepathic energy to disperse harmlessly into open space.

Editors' Note: While under control of the Saltah'na telepathic matrix, Sisko built a Saltah'na mechanical clock that remained in his office as a display item in later episodes.

Neela joins the engineering staff at station Deep Space Nine. She serves as an assistant to Chief Miles O'Brien.

Neela

Prior to "Duet" (DS9), which was Neela's first appearance, but after "Dramatis Personae" (DS9), in which Anara was O'Brien's assistant.

Ensign Ro Laren departs the *Enterprise*-D to participate in Starfleet's Advanced Tactical Training program. The school is difficult; only half of each class generally graduates each year. During the year one of Ro's instructors, an officer holding the rank of lieutenant commander, resigns from Starfleet to join the Maquis resistance movement so that he can fight actively against the Cardassians.

A year before "Preemptive Strike" (TNG), assuming that the program is indeed one year long.

Ro Laren

Starship *Enterprise*-D senior staff members Jean-Luc Picard, Data, Geordi La Forge, and Deanna Troi attend a three-day conference on the psychological effects of long-term deep space assignments. During their absence, William Riker agrees to care for Spot, Data's pet cat.

Alien life-forms from another time-space continuum mistake the artificial quantum singularity in the engine system of a Romulan warbird for a naturally-occurring black hole. The aliens, which use black holes to incubate their young, lay eggs in the warbird's engine. The presence of the alien embryos causes a failure in the warbird's engine core.

Prior to "Timescape" (TNG).

Romulan warbird

"Timescape" (TNG). Stardate 46944.2. The Starship *Enterprise*-D responds to a distress call from a Romulan warbird that has experienced a serious power failure. *Enterprise*-D personnel attempt to render aid by establishing a power transfer beam between their ship and the crippled Romulan craft. During the power transfer, both ships experience a severe disruption of the time-space continuum.

Returning to the *Enterprise*-D via runabout, Captain Jean-Luc Picard and company observe that the *Enterprise*-D and the Romulan warbird appear to be "frozen" in time, with the *Enterprise*-D in the midst of a disastrous explosion. Investigating the phenomenon aboard both ships, it is learned that the power transfer provided by the *Enterprise*-D was threatening the lives of the alien embryos incubating in the warbird's engine core. Picard and crew are able to interrupt the power transfer beam, thereby permitting the aliens to rescue their young from the Romulan engine, and are successful in restoring the flow of time so that the *Enterprise*-D is not destroyed in the process.

The *Starship Enterprise*-D travels to the Romulan Neutral Zone, where it returns the crew of the Romulan warbird.

After "Timescape" (TNG).

Aamin Marritza

"Duet" (DS9). (No stardate given in episode.) A Cardassian national, believed to be Gul Darhe'el, the former commander of the infamous Gallitep forced labor camp, is detained at station Deep Space 9. Investigation by Major Kira Nerys determines, however, that the individual in question is in fact Aamin Marritza, who served under Darhe'el at Gallitep 12 years ago. Marritza had experienced tremendous sorrow and guilt over his inability to stop the atrocities at Gallitep, and so had devised an elaborate scheme whereby he would impersonate the now-dead Darhe'el, and confess to Darhe'el's crimes. Kira orders Marritza freed, but he is subsequently murdered by a Bajoran national. Marritza died at the hand of a man who hated him only because he was born Cardassian.

The Federation science outpost on planet Ohniaka III is attacked by an unknown force.

Prior to "Descent, Part I" (TNG).

Crosis of Borg

"Descent, Part I" (TNG). Stardate 46982.1. The *Starship Enterprise*-D, responds to the distress call from Ohniaka III, learns that the attack was made by a Borg spacecraft of previously unknown design. *Enterprise*-D personnel report that Borgs at the Ohniaka station are exhibiting uncharacteristic behavior and tactics.

After the encounter, Lieutenant Commander Data reports that at Ohniaka, he experienced a brief but powerful emotional outburst, this despite the fact that his systems and software do not have the capacity for human emotions. Data experiences a second unexplained emotional burst when interrogating a Borg individual named Crosis, captured after a Borg attack on another colony. Shortly thereafter, Crosis and Data flee from the *Enterprise*-D by stealing a shuttlecraft.

Pursuing Data and Crosis, the *Enterprise*-D follows the shuttle through a Borg transwarp conduit through subspace to a planet in the Delta Quadrant on which is located a major Borg stronghold. Data is found on the planet, in the company of his brother, Lore, who is the leader of these Borg.

Dr. Beverly Crusher, as senior officer aboard the *Enterprise*-D, commands the skeleton crew remaining on the ship while the majority of the crew engages in a planetside search for Data.

Borg installation

Ensign Aquino, a Starfleet engineer assigned to station Deep Space 9, is killed. His death is initially believed to be accidental, but it is later found that he had apparently been murdered because he had stumbled onto part of a plot to murder Vedek Bareil.

"In the Hands of the Prophets" (DS9). The night before Vedek Winn arrived.

Vedek Winn, a politically conservative contender to replace Bajoran religious leader Kai Opaka, arrives unannounced at station Deep Space 9.

Just prior to "In the Hands of the Prophets" (DS9).

"In the Hands of the Prophets" (DS9). (No stardate given in episode.) Vedek Winn, at station Deep Space 9, protests what she characterizes as "blasphemous" teachings of scientific theories at the station's primary classroom. Her protests trigger a controversy between the Bajoran and Federation population of the station. When another Bajoran religious leader, Vedek Bareil, arrives at Deep Space 9 to try to calm the situation, an unsuccessful assassination attempt is made on his life. Station engineering staff member Neela, a Bajoran national, is held in the attempt.

It is strongly suspected, although not proven, that the entire protest was engineered by Winn to set up the assassination attempt, an apparent effort to eliminate Bareil as a candidate to become Bajor's next kai, a position for which Winn is also a contender.

Vedek Winn

Vedek Bareil

6.7 STAR TREK: THE NEXT GENERATION —YEAR 7
STAR TREK: DEEP SPACE NINE — YEAR 2

*Borg leader
Lore*

2370

Sito Jaxa

U.S.S. Hera captain Silva La Forge sends a letter to her son, Geordi La Forge. Silva urges Geordi to visit her aboard the *Hera* so he can meet the new engineer, another effort by Silva to find a wife for Geordi.

"Interface" (TNG). Three weeks before the episode.

The Bajoran provisional government, factionalized since the loss of Kai Opaka, begins to suffer further infighting by political opportunists. There are reports of fighting in a half-dozen districts and religious riots throughout the southern islands. One particularly militant faction is the Alliance for Global Unity, also known as "The Circle."

Prior to "The Homecoming" (DS9), after "Battle Lines" (DS9).

Former Nova Squadron member Sito Jaxa is offered a post aboard the *Starship Enterprise*-D. Despite the serious blemish on her record following the death of Cadet Joshua Albert two years ago, Sito distinguished herself during her remaining time at Starfleet Academy, enough for Captain Jean-Luc Picard to take a chance on her.

"Lower Decks" (TNG). Seven months prior to the episode. The Joshua Albert story established in "The First Duty" (TNG).

Hugh

"Descent, Part II" (TNG). Stardate 47025.4. At Lore's Borg stronghold in the Delta Quadrant, it is learned that Lore has assumed the role of leader among a group of Borgs that gained a sense of individuality from contact with the Borg individual named Hugh. Lore's effectiveness as leader is made possible because of the emotion chip that he had stolen over two years ago from his creator, Dr. Soong, which enables him to manipulate the emotional inexperience of the Borg. Lore is also able to create powerful emotions in his brother, Data, and uses those emotions to control Data.

Lore hopes to use Data and the Borgs to embark on a campaign of conquest, but he is prevented from doing so when *Enterprise*-D personnel assist the Borg named Hugh in resisting Lore's destructive control. Shortly thereafter, Lore is dismantled, but Data manages to recover their father's emotion chip.

The *Starship Enterprise*-D and the *Starship Hera* are in the same sector and pass within shuttlecraft range.

"Interface" (TNG). A week after Silva La Forge's message to her son.

The *Starship Hera* passes near planet Marijne VII. A day later, the ship visits station Deep Space 3 before departing on routine courier mission.

Ten days prior to "Interface" (TNG). The Hera was at Deep Space 3 nine days before the episode.

"Liaisons" (TNG). (No stardate given in episode.) The *Starship Enterprise*-D hosts an Iyaaran delegation, the first cultural exchange between the Iyaaran people and the Federation. *Enterprise*-D personnel, serving as hosts for the seven-day exchange, initially find the Iyaarans' behavior puzzling, until it is learned that the Iyaarans' culture is dramatically different from many other humanoid species, and that the delegation has been attempting to learn about the concepts of eating and antagonism. *Enterprise*-D captain Jean-Luc Picard, on a shuttle flight to the Iyaaran homeworld, is apparently marooned after a crash landing, but this, too, is part of an Iyaaran study, this one into the concept of love.

Iyaaran delegation

Deep Space 9 security chief Odo arrests the first officer and two crew members from a Subytt freighter on charges of smuggling defective isolinear rods to Bajor.

A few days prior to "The Homecoming" (DS9).

A maintenance worker on Cardassia IV gives a Bajoran earring to a Boslic freighter captain, who promises to deliver it to Bajor. The earring bears the insignia of Bajoran resistance leader Li Nalas.

Prior to "The Homecoming" (DS9).

Jake Sisko asks Laira, a young lady residing on Deep Space 9, for a date. She accepts.

Prior to "The Homecoming" (DS9).

"The Homecoming" (DS9). (No stardate given in episode.) Major Kira Nerys is presented with evidence that Bajoran resistance leader Li Nalas, long thought to be dead, is in fact being held prisoner on Cardassia IV. Kira is successful in freeing the near-legendary Li, who is honored upon his return by the Bajoran assembly. Li is subsequently assigned as Bajoran liaison to Deep Space 9, replacing Kira. The reassignment has been ordered by Minister Jaro Essa.

Li Nalas

Contact is lost with the *Starship Hera*. The *Starships Excelsior* and *Nobel* are assigned to search for the *Hera*.

Four days prior to "Interface" (TNG). The Excelsior and Nobel were assigned 72 hours prior to the episode.

Enterprise-D officers Data and Geordi La Forge conduct tests on a new telepresence interface system that would allow Starfleet personnel to conduct work in hazardous situations by means of a robotic surrogate probe.

Just prior to "Interface" (TNG).

Testing the telepresence interface

"Interface" (TNG). Stardate 47215.5. *Starship Enterprise*-D responds to a distress call from the science vessel *Raman*, finding it in orbit around the planet Marijne VII. A rescue mission using the experimental interface probe reveals that crew of the *Raman* had been accidentally killed by subspace beings who live in orbit of Marijne VII. One of the beings, trapped aboard the *Raman*, communicates a message that it is trapped aboard the *Raman*. At significant risk to his personal safety, Geordi La Forge uses the interface probe to return the Marijne VII beings back to their home in low orbit.

Enterprise-D chief engineer Geordi La Forge learns that his mother, Captain Silva La Forge of the *Starship Hera*, has been lost, along with the rest of her crew.

Services for the *Hera* crew are held on planet Vulcan, homeworld to many *Hera* crew members. Private services are held by the La Forge family for Silva La Forge.

After "Interface" (TNG).

Captain Silva La Forge

Captain Jean-Luc Picard, investigating a series of recent raids on ancient Romulan archaeological sites, is captured by mercenaries at a bar on planet Dessica II. Eyewitnesses to the incident report that Picard was killed by a blast from an energy weapon.

Picard's captors were, in fact, the mercenaries who had been responsible for the raids on archaeological sites in the Taugan sector. Picard manages to convince them that he is a smuggler named Galen and offers his services to help appraise the stolen artifacts.

Several weeks before "Gambit, Part I" (TNG), but after "Interface" (TNG).

A minister of the Bajoran provisional government is reported to have been attacked and beaten. The attack is believed to be the work of the Circle, whose acts of violence in the streets of Bajor have increased dramatically.

Two days before "The Circle" (DS9).

Jaro Essa

"The Circle" (DS9). (No stardate given in episode.) Terrorist activity sponsored by the Circle continues to escalate on Bajor and on station Deep Space 9. Despite efforts by the provisional government to suppress the violence, the Circle appears to operate with impunity. Evidence is uncovered that the Circle is obtaining weapons from Kressari agents, and further investigation suggests that the Kressari are acting as intermediaries for Cardassian forces seeking to destabilize the Bajoran government.

Kira Nerys accepts an invitation to study at Vedek Bareil's temple and experiences the third orb, the orb of prophesy and change. She is kidnapped by Circle agents but later freed by Deep Space 9 personnel after learning that the Circle, under the covert leadership of Minister Jaro Essa, plans to attempt a coup d'état to depose the Bajoran provisional government.

Starfleet admiral Chekote, upon being informed of the deteriorating situation on Bajor, and citing Prime Directive prohibitions against involvement in what is essentially a local dispute, orders the withdrawal of all Starfleet personnel from Deep Space 9.

Enterprise-D personnel investigate the disappearance of Captain Jean-Luc Picard at planet Dessica II.

Shortly before "Gambit, Part I" (TNG).

Arctus Baran

"Gambit, Part I" (TNG). Stardate 47135.2. Evidence gathered at planet Dessica II suggests that Captain Picard had been killed by a blast from an energy weapon, and Commander William Riker receives authorization to place the *Enterprise*-D on detached duty to further investigate the incident. During the investigation, Riker is kidnapped by a mercenary group led by Arctus Baran. Aboard Baran's ship, he discovers Picard, who is posing as a smuggler named Galen.

"The Siege" (DS9). (No stardate given in episode.) Starfleet and other Federation personnel evacuate station Deep Space 9 as Circle forces arrive to take control of the facility, part of the Circle attempt to seize power from the Bajoran provisional government. A handful of Starfleet personnel remain aboard Deep Space 9 in violation of orders and are successful in retaking the station from Circle operatives, although Bajoran resistance leader Li Nalas is killed in the operation.

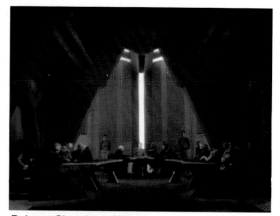

Bajoran Chamber of Ministers

Major Kira Nerys is successful in eluding Bajoran forces and presents evidence to the Bajoran Chamber of Ministers linking the Circle and Minister Jaro Essa to secret Cardassian weapons shipments, discrediting the Circle, and thwarting Jaro's attempted coup d'état. Kira is subsequently reassigned to Deep Space 9.

Starfleet personnel return to station Deep Space 9 as Starfleet reassumes administration of the facility.

After "The Siege" (DS9).

"Gambit, Part II" (TNG). Stardate 47160.1. Picard and Riker infiltrate Baran's crew in an effort to discover the reason for Baran's raids on Romulan archaeological sites. They learn that Baran has been employed by a militant Vulcan separatist group seeking to reassemble the pieces of the Stone of Gol. The ancient artifact, long thought to be mere myth, is found to be a functional psionic resonator weapon that enables the bearer to kill telepathically. Picard and Riker, with assistance from *Enterprise*-D personnel, are successful in apprehending Tallera, a member of the separatist group who had masterminded the operation. The psionic resonator is turned over to Vulcan security minister Satok, who promises that it will be destroyed.

Vulcan isolationist Tallera

Kes is born on the Ocampa homeworld in the Delta Quadrant.

"Elogium" (VGR). Kes said she was a little less than two years old at the time of the episode in early 2372. Date is conjecture from "Twisted" (VGR), in which she celebrated her second birthday.

Quark arranges for a Klingon operative named Yeto to visit station Deep Space 9 in order to purchase liquid data chains. In preparation for the transaction, Quark agrees to plant an illicit device to defeat station security sensors so that Yeto's arrival will not be detected.

Prior to "Invasive Procedures" (DS9).

Kes of Ocampa

A violent plasma storm in the Bajoran star system forces evacuation of station Deep Space 9, leaving behind only a skeleton crew aboard the station.

Just prior to "Invasive Procedures" (DS9).

"Invasive Procedures" (DS9). Stardate 47182.1. Deep Space 9 personnel render aid to the crew of the *Ekina*, a small space vessel reportedly damaged by the plasma storm. Their arrival is a ruse arranged by Quark for the sale of liquid data chains. The sale itself is quickly found to be a cover for Yeto's real objective: Yeto has delivered unsuccessful Trill initiate Verad to the station, where he intends to steal the Dax symbiont from Jadzia. Although Verad is successful in forcing the removal of the symbiont from Jadzia and its implantation into himself, Verad is thereafter overpowered, and the Dax symbiont is returned to its rightful host.

Verad and his accomplices are turned over to authorities.

After "Invasive Procedures" (DS9).

Verad

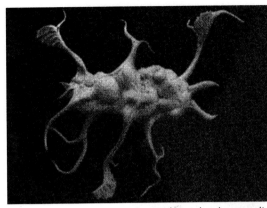

Interphasic parasite

Garak

Kotan Pa'Dar

Ambassador Troi

Ravinok crash survivor Lorit Akrem, working as a forced laborer in a Breen mine in the Dozaria system, is killed in a cave-in. Lorit had been a friend of Kira Nerys.

Two years before "Indiscretion" (DS9).

U.S.S. Enterprise-D travels to Starbase 84 for installation of a new warp core assembly. The core had been manufactured on planet Thantos VII using a new interphasic fusion process.

Commander William Riker gives Alexander Rozhenko a new music program. Young Alexander enjoys the music, an Earth form known as jazz, but his father, Worf, finds it unpleasant and is annoyed that Alexander plays it every night.

Prior to "Phantasms" (TNG).

"Phantasms" (TNG). Stardate 47225.7. Commander Data finds that his dream-inducing program is now generating nightmares, which he finds to be an unsettling experience. Shortly thereafter, Data finds himself having "waking dreams," in which he is unable to control his behavior. In one such waking dream, Data stabs and severely injures Counselor Deanna Troi. It is learned that the nightmares are caused by interphasic parasites that came aboard the ship in the new warp core, and that these life-forms are making operation of the warp drive system impossible. Once the nature of the parasites is understood, they are eradicated from the ship with a high-frequency interphasic sweep.

Enterprise-D captain Jean-Luc Picard is honored with an invitation from Admiral Nakamura to attend Starfleet's annual Admirals' banquet at Starbase 219. Unfortunately, the technical difficulties with the ship's new warp core make it impossible for Picard to attend.

A new warp conduit is replicated by the *Enterprise*-D engineering staff, replacing the parasite-infested unit installed at Starbase 84.

After "Phantasms" (TNG).

"Cardassians" (DS9). Stardate 47177.2. Cardassian citizen Elim Garak is assaulted by Rugal, a Cardassian youth whose adoptive Bajoran parents are passing through station Deep Space 9. Cardassian authorities suggest that the bizarre incident might have been the result of Bajoran foster parents teaching their adoptive Cardassian child to hate Cardassians. Investigation into the incident by station commander Benjamin Sisko reveals this to be true, but further reveals that Rugal's initial placement into a Bajoran orphanage eight years ago was a plot intended by Gul Dukat to embarrass Rugal's natural father, Kotan Pa'Dar. Despite the fact that Rugal's adoptive parents have cared for and loved Rugal, Sisko rules that the Cardassian youth has been the victim of Dukat's conspiracy, and orders Rugal returned to the custody of his birth father.

The *Enterprise*-D receives a delegation of Cairn representatives. These people communicate purely by telepathy and have no spoken language. The Cairn are accompanied by Ambassador Lwaxana Troi, whose telepathic abilities help the Cairn in what is to them, a very alien world. Troi's valet, Mr. Homn, remains on planet Betazed.

Prior to "Dark Page" (TNG).

"Dark Page" (TNG). Stardate 47254.1. Ambassador Lwaxana Troi is taken ill because of excessive use of her telepathic abilities in communicating with the Cairn delegation aboard the *Enterprise*-D. Treatment of Troi indicates her condition has been exacerbated by an old psychic trauma to her meta-conscious. The trauma is relieved when Ambassador Troi is able to acknowledge the source of her pain, the death many years ago of her older daughter, Kestra Troi. This is a significant revelation to Deanna Troi, who had not been aware that she had a sister.

A new restaurant opens on the Promenade at station Deep Space 9. The new eatery features traditional Klingon-style cuisine, prepared by a master Klingon chef, who even takes pride in serenading his customers with Klingon music.

Prior to "Melora" (DS9).

Master Klingon chef

Starfleet ensign Melora Pazlar is assigned to duty at station Deep Space 9 as a stellar cartographer. In preparation for her arrival, Chief Miles O'Brien and Dr. Julian Bashir modify a suite of living quarters to allow the artificial gravity to be shut off to approximate the low gravity conditions on her homeworld. They also fabricate a wheelchair to allow her mobility throughout the rest of the station.

Prior to "Melora" (DS9).

"Melora" (DS9). Stardate 47229.1. Ensign Melora Pazlar arrives at station Deep Space 9 aboard the *Starship Yellowstone*. Melora, an Elaysian, has initial difficulty adjusting to the one-gee gravity field on the station, but quickly demonstrates that she will not allow this challenge to compromise her performance as a Starfleet officer. She is befriended by Chief Medical Officer Julian Bashir, and the two become romantically involved.

Melora Pazlar

Fallit Kot, an old associate of Quark's, visits Deep Space 9, intending to exact revenge on Quark for a business deal that went bad eight years ago. Kot kidnaps Quark and takes other hostages, but is apprehended as he attempts to escape into the Gamma Quadrant.

Nurse Alyssa Ogawa becomes romantically involved with Ensign Markson, a fellow *Enterprise*-D crew member.

Prior to "Attached" (TNG). This is presumably before her involvement with Lieutenant Powell in "Lower Decks" (TNG).

Commander Will Riker visits station Deep Space 9, where he meets Jadzia Dax at Quark's bar. Riker earns a reputation as a good dabo player.

"Defiant" (DS9). Dax said she'd met Riker a year before the episode, the seventh of the third season.

Editors' Note: It seems possible that Dax may have been referring to the Enterprise-D's visit in "Birthright, Part I" (TNG), but that would have been about two years before "Defiant" (DS9).

Commander William Riker

The *U.S.S. Enterprise*-D travels to planet Kesprytt III in order to evaluate a request by the Kes government for associate membership in the United Federation of Planets. It is an unusual request in that Kesprytt III does not yet have a unified world government, normally a condition for membership in the Federation.

Prior to "Attached" (TNG).

"Attached" (TNG). Stardate 47304.2. *Enterprise*-D captain Jean-Luc Picard and Chief Medical Officer Beverly Crusher are abducted while beaming down on to Kesprytt III, apparently by the Prytt government. Initial diplomatic efforts by Executive Officer William Riker to work with both the Kes and the Prytt government to secure the release of both officers are unsuccessful, although their freedom is secured through covert means.

During their captivity, Picard and Crusher were both implanted with a neural control device that caused them physical discomfort if they became separated. A side effect of these devices was a sharing of their thoughts.

Picard and Riker both file reports to the Federation Council recommending against Federation membership for Kesprytt III because the planet's society is not yet advanced enough to solve its internal disputes.

After "Attached" (TNG).

Kes official   Prytt official

Pel

Pel, an ambitious young Ferengi entrepreneur, is hired as a waiter at Quark's bar on station Deep Space 9.

Prior to "Rules of Acquisition" (DS9).

Starship *Enterprise*-D executive officer William T. Riker and Counselor Deanna Troi complete their Crew Evaluation Report.

"Lower Decks" (TNG). Three months before the episode. This would seem to make the evaluation report a quarterly ritual.

Kira Nerys loses her springball racket. She last saw it in her quarters.

"Little Green Men" (DS9). Two years before the episode (2372).

Quark negotiates with Dosi representatives

"Rules of Acquisition" (DS9). (No stardate given in episode.) Ferengi Grand Nagus Zek returns to station Deep Space 9, offering Quark the opportunity to serve as his negotiator for Gamma Quadrant business. Quark learns that his first assignment, to negotiate the acquisition of tulaberry wine from the Dosi, is a ploy by Zek to learn about the Dominion at minimal risk to himself. The Dominion is believed to be a dominant power in the Gamma Quadrant. Quark suffers a setback in his standing with the Nagus when Quark's associate, Pel, reveals herself to be a female posing as a Ferengi male.

Editors' note: "Rules of Acquisition" (DS9) marks the first mention of the Dominion.

During Quark's absence in the Gamma Quadrant for Zek, Rom is forced to break into Quark's latinum floor vault in order to assure the safety of Quark's profits. Rom has also been opening Quark's storeroom using a desealing rod without Quark's knowledge.

"Necessary Evil" (DS9). Rom wasn't clear that his break-in occurred during "Rules of Acquisition" (DS9), but Quark did indeed visit the Gamma Quadrant during the episode.

Pel departs station Deep Space 9 aboard an Andorian transport.

After "Rules of Acquisition" (DS9).

Zek

Contact is lost with the Federation medical transport ship *U.S.S. Fleming*, last reported to be carrying a cargo of rare bio-mimetic gel through the Hekaras Corridor. A Ferengi trading vessel also passes through the region.

Four days before "Force of Nature" (TNG). The Ferengi ship passed through a week before the episode.

Geordi La Forge borrows Data's pet cat, Spot. La Forge told his friend, Data, that he was thinking of getting a pet cat for himself, and he wanted to experience the full range of feline behavior before making that decision. Spot is not happy in her temporary home, and Geordi proclaims the cat "untrainable."

A couple of days before "Force of Nature" (TNG). Geordi apparently did not get a pet cat of his own.

Spot

"Force of Nature" (TNG). Stardate 47310.2. Starship *Enterprise*-D investigates the disappearance of the *U.S.S. Fleming* somewhere in the Hekaras Corridor, a region of space characterized by unusually intense tetryon fields. It is learned that the *Fleming*, and other vehicles disabled in the area, were disabled by Hekaran scientists who sought to gain the attention of the Federation to their findings that the continued use of warp drive was causing serious damage to the fabric of space.

Hekaran scientist Serova sacrifices her life in a dramatic demonstration of how excessive use of warp drive in a region of space with subspace instabilities can cause a dangerous subspace rift. As a result, the Federation Council orders that all Federation spacecraft be limited to a maximum speed of warp factor 5, except in cases of extreme emergency, in order to limit further damage to the structure of space. Warp travel in areas found to be especially susceptible to damage is restricted to essential travel only.

Starfleet sets up a weather control matrix on Hekaras II to help maintain the planet's climate, since the subspace rift in the Hekaras Corridor has already caused a shift in the planet's orbit.

Editors' Note: The warp speed limit remained in effect for the remainder of Star Trek: The Next Generation.

Serova

Starfleet begins a program to develop a new warp engine design that will not cause damage to the fabric of space.

Conjecture, but they obviously succeeded in developing a new design or a modification to existing designs by the time the Voyager *was launched in 2371.*

Deep Space 9 commander Ben Sisko asks security chief Odo to record a daily log of law enforcement activities aboard the station.

Quark travels to planet Bajor at the request of a woman named Pallra.

Prior to "Necessary Evil" (DS9).

"Necessary Evil" (DS9). Stardate 47282.5. Ferengi entrepreneur Quark is severely injured while in the employ of a Bajoran woman named Pallra, seeking to obtain a list of Bajoran nationals who collaborated with the Cardassians during the occupation. Pallra had hoped to use the list for blackmail purposes, but is thwarted when her actions are discovered by security chief Odo. Also uncovered in the investigation is the fact that Kira Nerys had been responsible for the death of Pallra's husband, Vaatrik, five years earlier.

The Dominion invades and conquers the T-Rogorans in the Gamma Quadrant, making it possible for some three million Skrreeans, who had been enslaved by the T-Rogorans, to flee. The Skrreeans hope to make a new home on the other side of the Bajoran wormhole, which they call the "Eye of the Universe."

Several weeks prior to "Sanctuary" (DS9). Exact date is conjecture, but Skrreean refugees arrived at Deep Space 9 in the episode, several weeks hence.

Pallra

The *Starship Enterprise*-D travels to planet Atrea IV in response to a request for aid from the Atrean government to help prevent a natural disaster on their planet. Atrea IV's core is cooling at a very high rate, causing a dramatic increase in seismic activity.

Prior to "Inheritance" (TNG)

"Inheritance" (TNG). Stardate 47410.2. *Enterprise*-D personnel work with Atrean scientists to devise a means to infuse plasma energy into the core of Atrea IV so that stability can be restored to the planet. The plan is executed with only minimal problems.

One of the Atrean scientists working to solve the core cooling problem is Dr. Juliana Tainer, who was once married to Dr. Noonien Soong, when Soong constructed the android Data. Tainer, who was then known as Juliana Soong, is effectively Data's mother. When Tainer is injured during an accident on Atrea IV, Data learns that Juliana is in fact an android, built by Noonien Soong 34 years ago, in the image of his wife who was killed by the

Juliana Tainer

Gideon Seyetik

Fenna

Worf

Crystalline Entity. So sophisticated is Juliana that she is unaware that she is not human. Data chooses to accept his father's wishes in allowing Juliana to continue to believe she is human.

Benjamin Sisko has trouble sleeping on the fourth anniversary of the devastating battle of Wolf 359 in which his wife, Jennifer, died aboard the *Starship Saratoga*.

One day before "Second Sight" (DS9), according to Sisko's log.

Editors' note: The battle of Wolf 359 took place at the beginning of the fourth season of Star Trek: The Next Generation *(early 2367). Four years after that should be the beginning of the third season of* Star Trek: Deep Space Nine *(early 2371), so Sisko's remembrance here would seem to be a little early. These kinds of minor slippages in dating rarely introduce serious internal contradictions in the Star Trek* timeline, *but are one reason why we usually avoid trying to derive exact calendar dates for the episodes.*

Noted terraformer Gideon Seyetik arrives at station Deep Space 9 aboard the *Starship Prometheus*.

Prior to "Second Sight" (DS9).

"Second Sight" (DS9). Stardate 47329.4. Noted terraformer Gideon Seyetik is killed during an extraordinary experiment involving the use of protomatter to successfully reignite a dead star, Epsilon 119. He sacrificed himself on the altar of science.

During Seyetik's stay at Deep Space 9, Benjamin Sisko meets an attractive woman named Fenna. Investigation reveals that Fenna is not a physical life-form, but is an illusory projection created by Seyetik's wife, Nidell, who has psychoprojective telepathic abilities.

Nidell returns to her homeworld of New Halana, where she expects to spend the rest of her life.

After "Second Sight" (DS9).

Enterprise-D at the Argus Array

Worf takes personal leave to participate in a bat'leth competition on planet Forcas III aboard the *Shuttlecraft Curie*. He is honored with an award for Champion Standing. While Worf is gone, Deanna Troi cares for his son, Alexander, until Alexander departs from the *Enterprise*-D to visit his grandparents.

Prior to "Parallels" (TNG).

"Parallels" (TNG). Stardate 47391.2. Worf's birthday. *Starship Enterprise*-D is assigned to return to the Argus Array to investigate another apparent mal-function in the subspace telescope.

Upon Worf's return to the *Enterprise*-D, he becomes aware of a bizarre series of discontinuities in his sense of reality that he initially suspects may be due to a memory loss. It is later discovered that when returning from Forcas III, Worf's shuttlecraft passed near a quantum fissure in space, caus-ing a break in the barriers between quantum realities, so that Worf was thrown into a state of flux in which he traveled freely between those different realities.

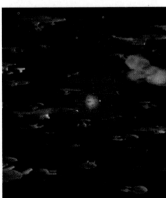

Starships Enterprise-D meet when quantum realities merge

Worf's state of quantum flux causes at least 285,000 alternate realities to merge. Elements of some of these alternate realities include: The marriage of Worf and Troi, the death of Captain Picard in the battle of Wolf 359, Riker's assumption of the *Enterprise*-D captaincy, Wesley Crusher's assignment to the *Enterprise*-D as a lieutenant, the conquering of the Cardassians by the Bajorans, Nurse Ogawa becoming a doctor, and the conquering of the Federation by the Borg. Worf is successful in using his shuttlecraft to create a broad-spectrum warp field to seal the quantum fissure, thereby returning himself to his original reality, and restoring the barriers between quantum states.

Editors' Note: In "Parallels" (TNG), Worf first began to consider the possibility of a romantic relationship with Deanna Troi. They shared dinner together (with champagne!) at the end of the episode.

Major Kira Nerys begins discussions with Bajoran minister Rozahn regarding an irrigation project for the Trilar Peninsula on Bajor that is behind schedule.

Two days before "Sanctuary" (DS9).

Varani

Noted Bajoran musician Varani begins performing at Quark's bar on Deep Space 9. Quark had promised Kira Nerys that he would try Varani for a month, but Quark is alarmed to note that Varani's music is so compelling that revenue from drinks and gaming is down.

Jake Sisko goes out on a date with Mardah, a young woman who works as a dabo game operator at Quark's bar. Jake is tutoring Mardah in entomology.

One day before "Sanctuary" (DS9).

"Sanctuary" (DS9). Stardate 47391.2. Large numbers of Skrreean refugees, fleeing from the Gamma Quadrant, arrive at Deep Space 9. After centuries of enslavement by the T-Rogorans, the Skrreeans seek sanctuary in a legendary place they call Kentanna. Skrreean leader Haneek believes planet Bajor to be their Kentanna, and requests that her people be permitted to settle on an uninhabited area of Bajor. The Bajoran provisional government refuses the request, and the Skrreean people depart Deep Space 9.

Skrreean leader Haneek

Editors' Note: Both "Sanctuary" (DS9) and "Parallels" (TNG) were set on stardate 47391.2.

A Bajoran science probe scans a planet designated LS-VI, about six light years from the wormhole terminus in the Gamma Quadrant. Data returned by the probe indicate DNA patterns resembling those of Deep Space 9 security chief Odo.

Date is conjecture, a few weeks before "The Alternate" (DS9).

An elderly couple from planet Pythro V files a complaint alleging that Martus Mazur has stolen their money through a confidence scam. Mazur flees to Deep Space 9, although station security chief Odo is alerted to his arrival.

Deep Space 9 operations chief Miles O'Brien builds a racquetball court on the station. He subsequently engages in a series of games with Julian Bashir, although a tournament sponsored by Quark is not completed due to a crisis on the station.

Martus Mazur

Prior to "Rivals" (DS9).

"Rivals" (DS9). (No stardate in episode.) A traveler visiting Deep Space 9 gives a small alien gambling device to entrepreneur Martus Mazur. It is not realized until later that the device actually affects the laws of probability, resulting in a number of extraordinarily improbable occurrences at the station. These include unexpected outcomes to sporting events, bizarre behavior of computer systems, unusual patterns of business activity, and an inexplicable distribution of solar neutrinos near the station.

Editors' Note: This episode first establishes the name of the El-Aurian people, the species to which both Martus and Guinan belong.

Starfleet Intelligence learns that the Romulan warbird *Terix* has found a piece of debris from the long-missing *Starship Pegasus* in the Devolin system.

Mazur with the gambling device

Admiral Erik Pressman

Starship Pegasus

Odo

Dr. Nikolai Rozhenko

Romulan high command subsequently orders the warbird to locate the rest of the ship. Starfleet's reaction is immediate: Admiral Erik Pressman is assigned to investigate the situation and attempt to retrieve a sensitive piece of hardware that had been thought lost when the *Pegasus* was believed destroyed in 2358. The plan has support at high levels in Starfleet Command, including Admiral Raner, the chief of Starfleet Security.

About two days prior to "The Pegasus*" (TNG).*

"The *Pegasus*" (TNG). Stardate 47457.1. The children aboard the *Starship Enterprise*-D celebrate "Captain Picard Day," to the acute embarrassment of the ship's commanding officer.

U.S.S. Enterprise-D conducting an energy output study of the Mekoria quasar, when diverted to rendezvous with the *Starship Crazy Horse* in sector 1607. At the Devolin system, Admiral Erik Pressman orders the *Enterprise*-D to search for the remains of the *U.S.S. Pegasus*, finding it deep within the body of an asteroid. Pressman is successful in recovering an experimental phase-cloaking device that had been covertly developed by Starfleet in 2358, in violation of the Treaty of Algeron. Pressman had sought to keep the cloaking device a secret, but *Enterprise*-D captain Jean-Luc Picard opts to reveal the existence of the device to the Romulans, and subsequently places Pressman under arrest.

Starship Enterprise-D travels to Starbase 247, where Admiral Erik Pressman and several others are charged in a general court-martial with violating the Treaty of Algeron.

After "The Pegasus*" (TNG).*

"The Alternate" (DS9). Stardate 47391.7. Deep Space 9 security chief Odo assists Dr. Mora Pol, studying planet LS-VI in the Gamma Quadrant, where evidence of life-forms chemically similar to Odo has been discovered. The expedition is cut short when members of the science party are exposed to noxious gases, apparently volcanic in origin. Upon returning to Deep Space 9, an unknown life-form assaults Dr. Julian Bashir and damages station science equipment. It is learned that the life-form is actually Odo, acting under the influence of the volcanic gas. Dr. Mora is successful in eliminating the gas from Odo's cellular structure. Years earlier, Mora had been the scientist who studied Odo when the shapeshifter first arrived on Bajor.

Dr. Mora returns home to Bajor. Jake Sisko and Nog take a test on Klingon opera.

The day after "The Alternate" (DS9).

The *U.S.S. Enterprise*-D responds to an emergency distress call from planet Boraal II. The call originated from Federation cultural observer Dr. Nikolai Rozhenko, Lieutenant Worf's foster brother.

Prior to "Homeward" (TNG).

"Homeward" (TNG). Stardate 47423.9. The *Starship Enterprise*-D, at planet Boraal II, finds intense plasmonic reactions about to destroy the planet's atmosphere within 38 hours. Federation cultural observer Rozhenko recommends that the *Enterprise*-D use its resources to rescue some of the indigenous humanoids from Boraal II, but Captain Jean-Luc Picard refuses on Prime Directive grounds. Rozhenko, acting against orders, surreptitiously beams one tribe to one of the ship's holodecks, where he has created a simulation of their planet's environment so that they are unaware that they have left their home. While the Boraals are in the holodeck, the *Enterprise*-D travels to Vacca VI, a Class-M planet in the Cabral sector, where they are transplanted to their new homes, still unaware that they had been aboard a starship. There is one Boraal casualty, the village chronicle, named Vorin, who accidentally left the holodeck and could not cope with his knowledge of the Federation's technology.

Dr. Rozhenko elects to remain on Vacca VI with the transplanted Boraals, where he intends to become the new village chronicle and to raise a family with a Boraal woman named Dobara.

Worf informs his adoptive parents, Sergey and Helena Rozhenko, that his step-brother has chosen to spend his life on Vacca VI. He tells them that his step-brother is happy there.

After "Homeward" (TNG).

Cardassia Prime

The United Federation of Planets concludes a long and difficult series of negotiations with the Cardassian Union. They agree to a pact formalizing the borders between the two powers, including the establishment of a Demilitarized Zone. The new border will require several established Federation and Cardassian colonies to be relocated.

"Journey's End" (TNG). Exact date is conjecture, but this is before the episode, and also before stardate 475542.9, mentioned in "Whispers" (DS9), since Sisko's log in that episode establishes that the Demilitarized Zone existed at that point, and therefore the treaty was presumably signed shortly before that.

Some Federation colonists living near the Cardassian border, dissatisfied with the new treaty with the Cardassian Union, organize into an underground terrorist group known as the Maquis. The Maquis view the ceding of Federation territory to the Cardassians to be evidence that their government has abandoned them.

Date is conjecture, but is presumably after the signing of the peace treaty established in "Journey's End" (TNG).

Felisa Howard dies at her home on planet Caldos. She was the grandmother of *Enterprise*-D chief medical officer Beverly Crusher, and had raised young Beverly after the death of her mother while Beverly was still a child. At Caldos, Felisa was widely respected as a healer.

Felisa Howard

Prior to "Sub Rosa" (TNG).

"Sub Rosa" (TNG). Stardate 47423.9. Following the funeral for her grandmother at the Caldos colony, Beverly Crusher learns that Felisa Howard had a mysterious lover named Ronin for much of her life. Beverly further finds that he is an anaphasic energy life-form, who, in the body of Ronin, had been the lover of Howard women for nearly eight centuries. So powerful is Ronin's attraction that Beverly initially chooses to resign from Starfleet so that she can be with him, but Beverly soon realizes that Ronin's love is a narcotic, and she is forced to destroy him.

Starfleet becomes aware of the existence of the Maquis and of the terrorists' activities against the Cardassians. Starfleet Academy newspaper editor Harry Kim writes an editorial on the subject, sparking debates, resulting in increased insight into the history of political rebellion for many cadets.

Memorial service for Howard

"Investigations" (VGR). Date is conjecture, but it is some time shortly after the first Maquis actions.

The T'Lani and Kellerun governments, finally at peace after centuries of war, request Federation aid in destroying stockpiles of deadly nanobiogenic weapons, called Harvesters. Deep Space 9 personnel are assigned to provide technical assistance aboard a T'Lani munitions ship.

"Armageddon Game" (DS9). Exact date is conjecture, but Bashir and O'Brien were aboard the T'Lani ship for at least a week prior to the episode, so the peace accord was presumably shortly before that.

Ronin

Harvesters in storage

Data's pet cat, Spot, becomes pregnant. Data does not know who the father is, but there are twelve male felines aboard the *Enterprise*-D.

"Genesis" (TNG). According to Data, nine weeks before the episode.

Editors' Note: Spot used to be a tomcat, but became a female when Star Trek's *producers wanted him, er, her, to have kittens. We maintain this is further evidence that Spot is either a shape-shifter or the victim of a transporter accident.*

Stardate 475542.9. Starfleet admiral Gupta arrives at Deep Space 9 to personally assess Cardassian movements across the border, in response to complaints by Federation colonists in the Demilitarized Zone.

"Whispers" (DS9). Stardate given in Sisko's log playback.

A former wife of the criminal known as the Albino dies at her home on planet Dayos IV. A week later, an amulet that she had worn is delivered by messenger to Klingon warrior Kang. Inside the amulet, Kang finds information revealing that the Albino's sanctuary is located in the Secarus system.

Kang travels to the Secarus system in an attempt to verify the information in the amulet. While Kang is at Secarus, the Albino contacts Kang and challenges him to one last battle. Kang subsequently summons his old comrades, Koloth, Kor, and Curzon Dax so that they may fulfill a blood oath that all four took some eighty years ago.

"Blood Oath" (DS9). Three months before the episode.

Runabout Ganges *attacked*

"Armageddon Game" (DS9). (No stardate given.) Dr. Julian Bashir and Miles O'Brien, assisting the T'Lani and Kellerun governments in destroying stockpiled Harvester nanobiogenic weapons, are believed killed by an old security booby trap aboard a T'Lani munitions ship. Investigation later reveals that this is not true; they are the target of a joint T'Lani and Kellerun effort to destroy all records of the Harvesters and to kill anyone with technical knowledge of their workings. Bashir and O'Brien are able to elude an initial attempt on their lives, and Deep Space 9 personnel are able to extract them from T'Lani territory before a second attempt is successful, although the runabout *Ganges* is destroyed in the process.

Miles O'Brien is released from the Deep Space 9 infirmary following treatment for exposure to a Harvester weapon.

A day after "Armageddon Game" (DS9).

Sito Jaxa

"Lower Decks" (TNG). Stardate 47566.2. *Starship Enterprise*-D executive officer William T. Riker and Counselor Deanna Troi prepare their Crew Evaluation Report, recommending promotions and new staff assignments.

The *Enterprise*-D retrieves an escape pod from Cardassian space carrying Joret Dal, a member of the Cardassian military. Joret, who is also a Federation operative, has brought valuable information about Cardassia's strategic plans. Afterwards, Ensign Sito Jaxa accompanies Joret back into Cardassian space, posing as his prisoner. Sito is believed to have given her life in the performance of her duty. Her sacrifice is credited with enhancing the security of the Federation and of her homeworld, Bajor.

Lieutenant Andrew Powell asks Nurse Alyssa Ogawa to marry him. She accepts.

Both sides in the Parada civil war indicate a willingness to participate in peace talks at Deep Space 9. Miles O'Brien travels to the Parada system to discuss technical issues relating to security for the talks.

Joret

"Whispers" (DS9). Nine days prior to the episode (assuming he left seven days before the fake O'Brien returned).

Among the crew members interviewed by Deanna Troi for the Crew Evaluation Report is Lieutenant Dan Kwan. Both Troi and Riker regard him positively, and Kwan is slated for assignment to one of the ship's nacelle control rooms.

"Eye of The Beholder" (TNG). Troi referred to the evaluation reports six weeks ago, coinciding with "Lower Decks" (TNG).

Current events at Deep Space 9 include the discovery of a new protozoic life-form, the loss of a shuttlepod somewhere in the vicinity of the third moon of Bajor VII, and a new request by the Bajoran Chamber of Ministers.

"Whispers" (DS9). All these things happened prior to stardate 47569.4, according to log playbacks.

Deep Space 9

Paradan authorities warn Commander Ben Sisko that one faction may have substituted a replica for the real Miles O'Brien.

"Whispers" (DS9). After stardate 47569.5, but before the episode.

A duplicate of Miles O'Brien returns to Deep Space 9. Station personnel, mindful of the Paradan warning, keep the duplicate under observation, although tests to determine whether or not he is a duplicate are inconclusive. The duplicate O'Brien, believing that he is in fact the original, grows suspicious of his coworkers, believing that they may have been tampered with or replaced.

Fifty-two hours prior to "Whispers" (DS9).

Miles O'Brien

"Whispers" (DS9). Stardate 47581.2. The duplicate Miles O'Brien returns to the Parada System, and is killed while attempting to learn what happened. Up until just before his death, the duplicate believed that he was the original, although it became clear to Deep Space 9 personnel and Paradan authorities that he had been programmed to disrupt the upcoming peace talks.

Peace talks are conducted aboard Deep Space 9 between the combatants in the Paradan civil war.

Dr. Julian Bashir and Miles O'Brien play a racquetball tournament against each other.

After "Whispers" (DS9). The racquetball tournament was set for the week after the episode.

Maquis terrorists capture a new Cardassian weapon near the border, a powerful missile equipped with a sentient guidance system. The Maquis refer to the missile, which had been targeted to a Maquis munitions base, as a "dreadnought." Maquis member B'Elanna Torres reprograms the dreadnought to destroy a Cardassian fuel depot on planet Aschelon V. The dreadnought disappears in the Badlands and never reaches Aschelon V. It is not realized at the time that the dreadnought had encountered the same type of displacement later responsible for the disappearance of the *Starship Voyager*.

"Dreadnought" (VGR). According to the dreadnought's computer, it had last encountered Torres on stardate 47582. Janeway noted that the Voyager *was not yet in service at this point.*

Automated Cardassian weapon

A Federation deep space probe goes off course and crashes on planet Barkon IV. Radioactive components in the automated probe's casing are deemed to pose a threat to Barkon IV's humanoid inhabitants. The *Starship Enterprise*-D is assigned to deal with the situation. Commander Data, whose android anatomy would not be adversely affected by the probe's radiation, is transported to the planet surface to recover the hazardous material.

Troi undergoes training

Inhabitants of Barkon IV

Alixus

Enterprise-D engine room transformed by archive, re-creating elements of D'Arsay mythology

While Data is working on the surface of Barkon IV, the *Enterprise*-D is briefly diverted to rendezvous with the *U.S.S. Lexington* to ferry some medical supplies to the Taranko colony.

Prior to "Thine Own Self" (TNG).

Counselor Deanna Troi departs the *Enterprise*-D via shuttlecraft to attend a three-day reunion of her Starfleet Academy class at Starbase 231, after which she returns to the *Enterprise*-D.

At least three days prior to "Thine Own Self" (TNG).

"Thine Own Self" (TNG). Stardate 47611.2. Commander Data, on the surface of Barkon IV, is damaged by exposure to a power surge from the remains of the deep space probe. Although the power surge causes a loss of memory in Data's positronic brain, Data is successful in protecting the inhabitants of Barkon IV from radiation from the probe's casing.

Counselor Deanna Troi undertakes the Starfleet training program for field promotion to the rank of commander. Her most difficult lesson is a holodeck simulation designed to test the candidate's ability to order a subordinate to his or her death in an appropriate situation. Troi is successful, and is promoted to commander.

Trill host candidate Arjin completes fifth-level flight training.

One month before "Playing God" (DS9).

Benjamin Sisko and Miles O'Brien embark upon a mission aboard the *Rio Grande* to survey planets for possible colonization.

Prior to "Paradise" (DS9).

"Paradise" (DS9). Stardate 47573.1. While surveying an M-class planet orbiting Orellius Minor, Sisko and O'Brien are captured by the inhabitants of a colony previously unknown to Federation authorities. It is learned that the colony's anonymity is by design: Colony leader Alixus had arranged for their transport vessel to make an unscheduled landing, and subsequently established a powerful duonetic electromagnetic damping field around the landing site, stranding the colonists and forcing them to live without any technological assistance. Sisko and O'Brien's arrival is unwelcome as they disrupt Alixus's authority over the surviving colonists. Upon arrival of a rescue team from Deep Space 9, Alixus is taken into custody for having caused the death of several colonists, but the remaining survivors elect to continue living in the community she established.

Starship *Enterprise*-D, in sector 1156, encounters a previously undiscovered rogue comet.

Prior to "Masks" (TNG).

"Masks" (TNG). Stardate 47615.2. Sensor scan of the rogue comet reveals an alien artifact in the nucleus, apparently originating in the D'Arsay system some 87 million years ago. During the scan, information from the artifact downloads itself into the *Enterprise*-D computers, causing the ship's systems to re-create elements of ancient D'Arsay mythology.

Starfleet sends an archaeological team to study the D'Arsan archive.

After "Masks" (TNG).

An unusual field of omicron particles is detected in the Gamma Quadrant. Deep Space 9 science officer Dax and security chief Odo, aboard the *Runabout Orinoco*, are dispatched to investigate the phenomenon.

Kono, cousin to Deep Space 9 entrepreneur Quark, arrives at the station. Kono, who is believed to have robbed a museum on Cardassia V, departs hastily when questioned by station authorities.

Prior to "Shadowplay" (DS9).

"Shadowplay" (DS9). Stardate 47603.3. Odo and Dax determine the omicron particle field to originate from a generator on the surface of planet Yadera II, in the middle of a village of humanoids. Further investigation reveals the village and most of its inhabitants to be holographic projections, but their holographic programs are found to be so sophisticated that the inhabitants qualify as bona fide life-forms. Odo and Dax assist in repairing a malfunction to the generator, thereby ensuring the survival of the sentient holographic life-forms.

Holographic inhabitants of Yadera II

Vedek Bareil arrives at station Deep Space 9 to speak at the station's shrine. He and Major Kira Nerys become romantically involved.

Kono, who has returned to DS9, is found to be in possession of bone carvings that had been reported stolen from the museum on Cardassia V.

Jake Sisko, at his father's suggestion, begins working as an assistant to Operations Officer Miles O'Brien. The assignment helps Jake realize that he does not want to pursue a Starfleet career.

*Starship Enterprise-*D engineering personnel conduct a refit of their warp drive nacelles. The procedure is supervised by Commander William T. Riker.

Prior to "Eye of the Beholder" (TNG).

"Eye of the Beholder" (TNG). Stardate 47623.2. *Enterprise-*D engineering staff member Dan Kwan commits suicide by jumping into the plasma stream in one of the ship's warp drive nacelles. Investigating the incident, Counselor Deanna Troi experiences a powerful empathic hallucination. It is learned that Kwan's suicide and Troi's hallucination were caused by exposure to an empathic pattern that had been imprinted onto a bulkhead in the nacelle interior. These patterns are determined to have been created eight years ago when three engineers at Starfleet's Utopia Planitia Fleet Yards were involved in a romantic triangle in which a jealous partner killed his lover and rival, then committed suicide by throwing himself into the nacelle's plasma stream.

Inside the warp nacelle

The *Enterprise-*D picks up medical supplies at Starbase 328 for transport to planet Barson II.

Editors' Note: Worf continues to exhibit an interest in Deanna Troi in this episode as he almost asks Riker for permission to date Deanna. In Deanna's hallucination, their relationship took a big step forward, but this was only in her imagination. This was the only episode in which we saw the interior of the ship's warp drive nacelles.

Dr. Julian Bashir and Trill initiate Arjin travel by transport ship from Starbase 41 to station Deep Space 9.

Voles begin infesting parts of Deep Space 9 that they had previously avoided. Unfortunately, these Cardassian rodents are attracted to electromagnetic fields, so they chew on power cables, wreaking havoc with station systems.

Vole

Prior to "Playing God" (DS9).

"Playing God" (DS9). (No stardate given in episode.) Jadzia Dax serves as field docent for Trill host candidate Arjin, who visits Deep Space 9 for his required field training experience. While on a science mission in the Gamma Quadrant, Dax and Arjin's runabout suffers an accidental impact with a subspace interphase pocket, after which an energy mass is discovered adher-

Protouniverse

Alyssa Ogawa

Worf reverted to a proto-Klingon

Natima Lang

ing to the ship. Upon returning to Deep Space 9, study of the energy mass reveals it to be a protouniverse in early stages of development. Although the expansion of the protouniverse poses a serious threat to the station and the Bajor system, sensor readings indicate the possibility that sentient life may exist in the microcosm. Accordingly, the protouniverse is returned to its original location in the Gamma Quadrant.

Jake Sisko, continuing to tutor Mardah in entomology, finds himself increasingly attracted to her, and is pleased to find that she returns the feelings.

Benjamin Sisko, uneasy that his son has fallen for a dabo game operator, urges Jake to invite Mardah over for dinner so that he can meet her. Jake doesn't, and Benjamin eventually invites her himself.

"The Abandoned" (DS9). Date is conjecture, but Sisko told Jake that he had spoken with Jake about Mardah "weeks" prior to the episode.

Nurse Alyssa Ogawa learns she is pregnant. Andrew Powell, the baby's father, is initially shocked, but gets over it.

Prior to "Genesis" (TNG).

Editors' Note: Andrew asked Alyssa to marry him four episodes ago in "Lower Decks" (TNG), but it is not clear if they were married at this point.

Tactical officer Rebecca Smith joins William Riker for a romantic walk in the *Enterprise*-D's arboretum. Unfortunately, as they get comfortable, Riker rolls over onto a Cypirion cactus, getting several painful thorns in his back, and requiring the care of sickbay personnel.

Just prior to "Genesis" (TNG).

"Genesis" (TNG). Stardate 47653.2. *U.S.S. Enterprise*-D personnel conducting field tests of new tactical systems and weapons upgrades. A series of minor problems, including a stray photon torpedo, plague the tests.

Enterprise-D systems engineer Reginald Barclay is treated for a minor case of Urodelan Flu. In treating Barclay's condition, Dr. Beverly Crusher introduces a synthetic T-cell into his body. A genetic anomaly in Barclay's biochemistry is responsible for mutating the synthetic T-cell into an organism that spreads like an airborne virus, causing crew members to genetically revert back to earlier forms of their species. The only crew member not affected is Commander Data, who develops a retrovirus that is successful in returning the other members of the crew to their original state. The malady is termed Barclay's Protomorphosis Syndrome.

Data's pet cat, Spot, gives birth to kittens, thereby ending once and for all the misconception that Spot is a male feline. The birth of Spot's kittens provides *Enterprise*-D personnel with an important clue to developing the retrovirus that cures Barclay's Protomorphosis Syndrome.

Deep Space 9 entrepreneur Quark somehow manages to obtain a small cloaking device. Despite the fact that possession of such a device is a violation of Bajoran law, Quark makes it quietly known that it is for sale.

Prior to "Profit and Loss" (DS9).

"Profit and Loss" (DS9). (No stardate given in episode.) Deep Space 9 personnel rescue a Cardassian shuttle that had reportedly suffered damage in a meteor storm. It is soon learned that the shuttle had been carrying Cardassian political dissidents Natima Lang, Rekelen, and Hogue, and that the damage to their ship had been inflicted by a pursuing Cardassian warship. The dissidents are wanted because they publicly oppose continued military dominance of the Cardassian government. The Cardassian Central

Command demands the extradition of the fugitives, but the trio escape, aided by Quark and Garak. Quark's assistance is motivated by his past romantic involvement with Lang. Garak later remarks enigmatically that his assistance in the matter was because of his love for Cardassia.

Cadet Wesley Crusher takes advantage of a school vacation and travels from Starfleet Academy to Starbase 310, so that he can spend some time with his mother and his former shipmates on the *Starship Enterprise*-D. Wesley has been experiencing serious doubts about his choice of a career in Starfleet. Academy superintendent Brand reports that his grades are falling.

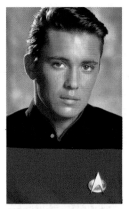

The *Starship Enterprise*-D arrives at Starbase 310 so that Captain Picard may be briefed by Fleet Admiral Nechayev on the repercussions of the new agreement with the Cardassians. Also boarding the ship at Starbase 310 is Cadet Wesley Crusher, on vacation from Starfleet Academy.

Prior to "Journey's End" (TNG).

Wesley Crusher

"Journey's End" (TNG). Stardate 47751.2. *U.S.S. Enterprise*-D travels to planet Dorvan V to carry out Admiral Nechayev's order of evacuating the Federation colonists, in compliance with the new border treaty with the Cardassians. *Enterprise*-D captain Picard meets with colony leaders in an attempt to negotiate their departure, but the colonists are adamant about remaining in their new homeworld. The situation is made more volatile when the Cardassian warship *Vetar*, under the command of Gul Evek, arrives early on a survey mission, further increasing the militant resolve of the colonists. Picard is successful in working with the colony leadership and the Cardassian government to develop a highly unorthodox solution. Under this new agreement, the Native American colonists of planet Dorvan V will relinquish their Federation citizenship and agree to live under Cardassian jurisdiction. Colony leader Anthwara indicates to Picard that his role in making it possible for Anthwara's people to remain on their chosen homeworld somehow atones for a crime against Native Americans committed by one of Picard's ancestors centuries ago.

Crusher and the Traveler at Dorvan V

Wesley Crusher spends time on Dorvan V with a colonist named Lakanta, who invokes Native American rituals to help Wesley resolve his inner turmoil about his future. Wesley's vision quest enables him to realize that he no longer wishes to follow his late father's footsteps, that he needs to make his own destiny. Freed from external expectations, Wesley resigns from Starfleet Academy. He begins to explore other possibilities, and, along with Lakanta, who reveals himself to be the Traveler, sets off on a voyage of discovery that will very likely transcend time and space.

Editor's Note: The Traveler's homeworld is mentioned in this episode as Tau Ceti, although previous episodes with the Traveler established him as coming from Tau Alpha C. We suspect Tau Alpha C is correct, since Tau Ceti is only a few light-years from Earth.

Klingon Dahar Master Kor arrives at station Deep Space 9. Also en route to the station are fellow warriors Koloth and Kang.

Prior to "Blood Oath" (DS9).

Dahar Master Kor

"Blood Oath" (DS9). (No stardate given in episode.) Klingon warriors Kor, Koloth, and Kang, along with Jadzia Dax, depart Deep Space 9 to planet Secarus IV, where they seek the criminal known as the Albino. The four fight the Albino and 40 of his troops for having murdered the firstborn children of Kor, Koloth, and Kang nearly eight decades ago. It is Kang who delivers the killing blow against the Albino. Kang and Koloth are both killed gloriously in battle, in a manner befitting a Klingon warrior.

Editors' Note: The three warriors, Kor, Koloth, and Kang were, of course, from episodes of the original Star Trek. *Kor first appeared in "Errand of Mercy" (TOS), while Koloth was featured in "The Trouble With Tribbles (TOS),*

The Albino

Koloth

Kang

Worf at the Kot'baval festival on Maranga IV

K'mtar

and Kang was seen in "Day of the Dove" (TOS). Kor later appeared in "The Sword of Kahless" (DS9), while Kang was seen briefly in "Flashback" (VGR).

Kang and Koloth are posthumously honored by the dedication of statues in their images in the Hall of Heroes on the Klingon Homeworld.

Dahar Master Kor is appointed ambassador to Vulcan for the Klingon Empire.

"The Sword of Kahless" (DS9). Dates for both events are conjecture, but they were after "Blood Oath" (DS9) and before Kor embarked on his quest to find the sword.

Klingon High Council member Kurn travels to the Hitora colony.

The *Starship Enterprise*-D prepares for a rendezvous with the *U.S.S. Kearsarge*.

Students in the science class aboard the *Starship Enterprise*-D make fullerines as a class project.

Prior to "Firstborn" (TNG).

"Firstborn" (TNG). Stardate 47779.4. The rendezvous with the *Kearsarge* is delayed for four days, making it possible for *Enterprise*-D to conduct additional studies of the Vodrey nebula while the ship travels to planet Maranga IV. Lieutenant Worf takes personal leave to take his son, Alexander, to the Klingon Kot'baval festival on Maranga IV, in hopes of kindling the boy's appreciation for his Klingon heritage. Also during the delay, Captain Jean-Luc Picard takes a side trip to the Hatarian system to view the ancient ruins being excavated there.

At Maranga IV, Worf and Alexander meet a stranger who identifies himself as K'mtar, who is *gin'tak* (advisor) to the house of Mogh. K'mtar informs Worf that he is there to protect Worf against a possible attempt against Worf's life from the house of Duras. Investigation reveals that there is no current Duras plot against Worf, and Worf learns that the stranger is not K'mtar, but is in fact Alexander Rozhenko, returned from the future in an effort to encourage his younger self to pursue the ways of a Klingon warrior. The future Alexander tells his father of the future, of Alexander becoming a great diplomat, and of Worf dying in Alexander's arms. Young Alexander continues to resist his elders' pressures to learn the fighting arts, but Worf now has a greater appreciation of the fact that his son must make his own destiny.

Captain Picard returns to the *Enterprise*-D, and the ship makes its rendezvous with the *Kearsarge*.

After "Firstborn" (TNG).

The Maquis, a small, but growing number of Federation citizens living near the Cardassian border who have banded together in self-defense against the Cardassians, begins to take a more militant posture. They acquire ships and weapons in increasing numbers, worrying both Federation and Cardassian authorities. The Maquis are resentful of Federation concessions to the Cardassians made in the recent border treaty, and feel the only way to protect themselves is to take matters into their own hands.

Prior to "The Maquis, Part I" (DS9) and "weeks" before "Preemptive Strike" (TNG).

Relationships between Federation and Cardassian citizens in the Demilitarized Zone continue to deteriorate. Two Federation colonists in Ropal City are stoned by a Cardassian mob. Reports suggest local Cardassian authorities may have encouraged the incident.

Three days before "The Maquis, Part I" (DS9).

"The Maquis, Part I" (DS9). (No stardate given in episode.) Cardassian freighter *Bok'Nor* explodes at station Deep Space 9. Cardassian authorities blame Maquis terrorists for the crime, accusing the Federation of being lax in policing its colonists in the Demilitarized Zone. As evidence that Federation citizens are responsible for Maquis activity, Cardassian authorities produce a recording of colonist William Samuels, in which Samuels admits responsibility for the explosion of the *Bok'Nor*. Unfortunately, Samuels dies of an apparent suicide while in Cardassian custody, making further interrogation impossible.

Bok'Nor at Deep Space 9

Gul Dukat, unofficially assisting with the investigation, is abducted by Maquis operatives and taken to an asteroid in the Badlands. Benjamin Sisko, hoping to avoid a more serious diplomatic incident, commands a rescue mission in pursuit of Dukat's abductors.

Gul Dukat

Starship Enterprise-D detects a small robotic probe in deep space.

Just prior to "Bloodlines" (TNG).

"Bloodlines" (TNG). Stardate 47829.1. The robotic probe delivers a personal message to *Enterprise*-D captain Jean-Luc Picard from former DaiMon Bok. It is a threat against a person named Jason Vigo, who Bok claims is Picard's son. Picard investigates the threat, finding evidence that Vigo is indeed Picard's son, but further investigation shows Vigo to be the victim of genetic tampering by Bok. Vigo is, in fact, not Picard's son, but the threat and the faked genetic evidence was an effort by Bok to win vengeance on Picard for having caused the death of Bok's son in the Battle of Maxia in 2355.

Former DaiMon Bok

Editors' Note: "Bloodlines" (TNG) takes place in the Xendi Kabu system, but for consistency's sake, we're arbitrarily changing it back to the Xendi Sabu system, which is where Bok met Picard in "The Battle" (TNG), since it seems clear that the writer intended the second story to have the same location.

"The Maquis, Part II" (DS9). (No stardate given in episode.) Sisko's attempt to negotiate Dukat's release from Maquis operatives is unsuccessful, and Sisko rescues Dukat by force. During the rescue, evidence is uncovered suggesting that Cardassian authorities had been secretly providing arms to Cardassian colonists in the Demilitarized Zone, in direct violation of the Federation-Cardassian treaty. Sisko and Dukat act decisively to prevent a Maquis strike against a Cardassian weapons depot, since such an offensive would result in many civilian Cardassian casualties, almost certainly leading to war.

Jason Vigo, victim of genetic tampering

Commander Data begins work on a holographic setting for a performance of Shakespeare's play, *The Tempest*. In this production, Data plays Prospero.

The *Starship Enterprise*-D, on assignment to survey sites for new Federation colonies in the Mekorda sector, encounters an unexpected magnascopic storm.

Prior to "Emergence" (TNG).

Data as Prospero

"Emergence" (TNG). Stardate 47869.2. *Starship Enterprise*-D experiences what initially appears to be a malfunction in its computer control systems. Diagnostic analysis of the malfunction reveals the presence of a number of abnormal circuit nodes imbedded into the ship's systems, apparently caused by the magnascopic storm in the Mekorda sector. These nodes transform the ship's computer systems into an emergent life-form that absorbs the programming of the ship's computers and uses its systems to give birth to a new space borne entity near the MacPherson nebula. While under control of the emergent life-form, the ship's holodeck programs appear to merge, providing a means by which the life-form attempts to communicate with the ship's crew.

Emergent life-form departs Enterprise-D

Data performs a scene from *The Tempest* in which Prospero's daughter, Miranda, first encounters other humans.

The evening after "Emergence" (TNG).

Keiko O'Brien departs station Deep Space 9 to attend a hydroponics conference on Rigel IV.

Prior to "The Wire" (DS9).

Dr. Julian Bashir stays up late reading the last few chapters of the epic Cardassian novel, *The Never-Ending Sacrifice.*

The evening before "The Wire" (DS9).

"The Wire" (DS9). (No stardate given in episode.) Deep Space 9 medical officer Julian Bashir observes that station resident Elim Garak appears to be in serious pain, although Garak refuses to be examined and declines offers of help. Investigation by Bashir reveals the fact that Garak had been using a neural implant device to subject himself to abnormally high concentrations of certain endorphins, producing a powerful narcotic effect. A malfunction of the neural implant is found to be causing severe withdrawal symptoms in Garak. Bashir is successful in obtaining Cardassian biomedical information from Garak's former associate in the Obsidian Order, Enabran Tain, to allow treatment of Garak.

Garak

Cardassian colonists living near the Demilitarized Zone attack and destroy a Juhrya freighter. The Cardassian government deplores the incident, but it is difficult to control because of similar attacks by Federation civilians who call themselves the Maquis. Both Cardassian and Federation authorities fear the situation may deteriorate into large-scale armed hostilities.

Less than a week before "Preemptive Strike" (TNG).

Keiko O'Brien returns to station Deep Space 9 after having attended a hydroponics conference on planet Rigel IV.

A week after "The Wire" (DS9).

Starfleet cadet Harry Kim graduates from Starfleet Academy. He requests assignment aboard the new *Starship Voyager.*

"Non Sequitur" (VGR). Kim's computer record indicated he graduated on stardate 47918.

Ro Laren

Lieutenant Ro Laren, having completed Starfleet's Advanced Tactical Training program, returns to duty aboard the *Starship Enterprise*-D.

Prior to "Preemptive Strike" (TNG).

On planet Bajor, the political scene heats up with the upcoming election to replace Kai Opaka. Among the leading candidates to become the next kai are Vedek Tolena, Vedek Winn, and Vedek Bareil.

A few weeks prior to "The Collaborator" (DS9).

Maquis leader

"Preemptive Strike" (TNG). Stardate 47941.7. Admiral Nechayev assigns Lieutenant Ro to a covert mission to infiltrate the Maquis near the Demilitarized Zone. Ro poses as a fugitive from Starfleet who is wanted for killing a Cardassian soldier and is subsequently invited to join a Maquis cell near the Demilitarized Zone. Ro learns of an impending Maquis preemptive strike against a rumored shipment of Cardassian biogenic weapons. Ro attempts to demonstrate her trustworthiness to her Maquis comrades by conducting a raid on the *Starship Enterprise*-D to secure badly needed medical supplies. The ploy is successful, and Ro is subsequently assigned to lure a Maquis force into a trap so that they can be captured. At the last moment, Ro feels remorse at betraying her new friends. She aborts the operation, escaping with her Maquis comrades, effectively ending her Starfleet career.

Deep Space 9 officers Kira and Bashir travel to the New Bajor colony in the Gamma Quadrant to assist with opening the colony's hospital.

Prior to "Crossover" (DS9).

"Crossover" (DS9). (No stardate given in episode.) Returning from the Gamma Quadrant, a runabout piloted by Kira and Bashir suffers a partially collapsed warp field while in the Bajoran wormhole. The malfunction transposes the ship into a mirror universe, the same alternate reality visited by Captain James Kirk and members of his crew a little over a century ago.

Kira meets her mirror counterpart

In the mirror universe, Kira and Bashir are captured by agents of the Alliance of the Cardassians and the Klingons that overthrew the Terran Empire many decades ago and enslaved humanity. They are taken to station Terok Nor, still orbiting Bajor in the mirror reality, where they escape with the aid of Terran slaves, the mirror versions of Benjamin Sisko and Miles O'Brien. Kira and Bashir's presence in the mirror universe helps the mirror Sisko and O'Brien realize that they can fight for human freedom.

Editors' Note: "Crossover" (DS9) was a sequel to "Mirror, Mirror" (TOS). The story of the mirror universe was later continued in "Through the Looking Glass" (DS9) and "Shattered Mirror" (DS9).

With the death of the mirror Quark during the visit of Benjamin Sisko to the mirror universe, Quark's brother, Rom, inherits the bar at Terok Nor.

"Shattered Mirror" (DS9). According to Nog.

An inverse tachyon beam triggers a catastrophic anti-time phenomenon

Lieutenant Worf and Counselor Deanna Troi spend an evening sharing a holodeck simulation of the Black Sea at night. It looks as if a romantic relationship may finally be blooming.

Moments prior to "All Good Things..." (TNG).

"All Good Things..." (TNG). Stardate 47988.1. *Enterprise*-D captain Jean-Luc Picard reports that he has experienced time shifts between the present day, seven years in the past, and twenty-five years in the future. According to Picard, the time shifts were caused by Q, who did so to give Picard the opportunity to stop a temporal anomaly from destroying all life on Earth. Picard further indicates that he had evidently been directly responsible for creating this anomaly, but this was in fact the work of the Q continuum, rendering a verdict in the trial begun seven years ago. Nevertheless, Picard credits Q with having lent a helping hand, making it possible to save humanity from total annihilation. Picard, believing that normal prohibitions against altering the timeline do not apply in this case, informs his friends of their possible futures, giving them an opportunity to shape their own destinies.

Q

Captain Jean-Luc Picard joins the ship's weekly poker game for the first time. Dealing to his friends, he observes that "The sky's the limit."

Editors' Note: "All Good Things..." (TNG) was the last television episode of Star Trek: The Next Generation, *although the adventures of Jean-Luc Picard and his crew continued the following year in the feature film* Star Trek Generations *and later in* Star Trek: First Contact.

Vedek Bareil, campaigning to become the next kai, takes three days off to visit Kira Nerys at station Deep Space 9. Although Bareil is favored to win, Vedek Winn continues to campaign hard.

Three days before "The Collaborator" (DS9).

"The sky's the limit...."

Vedek Winn

"The Collaborator" (DS9). (No stardate given in episode.) On the eve of Bajor's election to determine the next kai, Vedek Winn quietly reveals allegations that Vedek Bareil had, years ago, been a Cardassian collaborator. Winn accuses Bareil of having been the informer who caused the infamous Kendra Valley massacre in which 42 Bajorans were killed, including the son of then-Kai Opaka. Preliminary investigation supports these charges. Although Winn has publicized neither the accusations nor the investigation, Bareil withdraws from the election.

Winn is elected kai, becoming the new spiritual leader of the Bajoran people.

Editors' note: Bareil's appearance of guilt in "The Collaborator" (DS9) was because he was remaining silent to protect Kai Opaka, who had in fact allowed the massacre (and the death of her son), to save the lives of over a thousand other Bajorans. Only Bareil and Kira (and probably Winn) knew of Opaka's role in the tragedy, but they were likely to keep the secret, so it's likely that neither the Federation nor the Bajoran public learned the truth. The Kendra Valley massacre happened several years in the past, probably less than ten because Kubus was on the station at the same time as Dukat. Nevertheless, we don't really know enough to hazard a reliable guess as to when the massacre took place.

"Tribunal" (DS9). Stardate 47944.2. Miles and Keiko O'Brien depart station Deep Space 9 for a much-needed vacation. While en route via runabout, Miles O'Brien is abducted by a Cardassian patrol ship and taken to Cardassia to stand public trial for alleged involvement in illegal arms shipments to the Maquis. As is normal in the Cardassian system of justice, O'Brien's being brought to trial means that he has already been found guilty by the government; the trial merely serves as public confirmation of that guilt. Nevertheless, investigation by Deep Space 9 security chief Odo reveals that O'Brien had, in fact, been framed by Cardassian operatives seeking to link Starfleet with Maquis terrorist acts. Unwilling to permit public disclosure of this evidence, the Cardassian government, in an almost unprecedented move, sets aside the verdict and orders O'Brien released.

Miles and Keiko O'Brien finally get to take their vacation.

After "Tribunal" (DS9).

O'Brien on trial

Jake Sisko begins work on a science project to determine root growth of different Bajoran katterpod hybrids.

Prior to "The Jem'Hadar" (DS9).

"The Jem'Hadar" (DS9). (No stardate given in episode.) Commander Ben Sisko, Jake Sisko, Quark, and Quark's nephew, Nog, on a camping expedition to a planet in the Gamma Quadrant, are captured by Jem'Hadar soldiers, the first known direct Federation contact with members of the Dominion.

Shortly thereafter, a Jem'Hadar vessel arrives at station Deep Space 9, demanding an end to all traffic through the wormhole, threatening to destroy any Federation ship in the Gamma Quadrant. The threat is emphasized by the destruction of several Alpha Quadrant ships and the massacre of colonists at the New Bajor colony.

The *Starship Odyssey*, commanded by Captain Keogh, docks at station Deep Space 9 to confer with station personnel regarding the Jem'Hadar threat. Deep Space 9 runabouts *Mekong* and *Orinoco* accompany the *Odyssey* into the Gamma Quadrant to investigate the situation. Although the runabout crews are successful in rescuing Sisko and company, the *Odyssey* is destroyed in a Jem'Hadar attack, resulting in the loss of all hands. It is subsequently learned that the entire Jem'Hadar offensive had been an attempt to plant a spy in Federation territory, although the spy escapes upon being discovered.

Jem'Hadar soldier

Commander Benjamin Sisko files a request with Starfleet Command for additional equipment to protect Deep Space 9 and the Bajor Sector in the event of a Dominion incursion through the wormhole.

After "The Jem'Hadar" (DS9).

Kai Winn invites Vedek Bareil to become one of her principal advisors. Bareil accepts, believing that Winn's new responsibilities have changed her. Bareil works behind the scenes with Legate Turrel to pave the way for talks with the Cardassian Central Command that could lead to a peace settlement between Bajor and Cardassia.

Some time after "The Collaborator" (DS9), but before "Fascination" (DS9). Preliminary talks with Turrel established as having begun five months before "Life Support" (DS9).

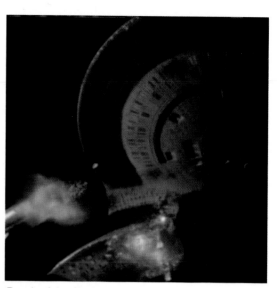

Death of the Odyssey

6.8 STAR TREK: DEEP SPACE NINE—YEAR 3
STAR TREK: VOYAGER—YEAR 1
STAR TREK GENERATIONS

Underground Ocampa city

2371

The godlike life-form known to the Ocampa people as the Caretaker falls ill and is near death. The Caretaker had created an underground city for the Ocampa and had provided it with power for the past millennium. Realizing that they cannot survive without him, he seeks to find a genetically compatible life-form with whom he can procreate so that his offspring can continue to care for the Ocampa. The Caretaker searches the galaxy, but is unsuccessful in his quest. In desperation, he begins to increase the power that he provides to the underground Ocampa city so that they may have a few years' worth of reserves after his death.

"Caretaker" (VGR). Several months prior to the episode.

El-Aurian scientist Dr. Tolian Soran engages the assistance of Lursa and B'Etor to steal quantities of trilithium compound from the Romulans. In exchange, Soran promises to provide technical information to the Duras sisters that will permit the construction of a trilithium-based weapon. Soran is currently working at the Amargosa solar observatory, where he has been secretly constructing a solar probe designed to deliver trilithium, a nuclear inhibitor, into the Amargosa star. Soran has also placed a second probe launcher on the surface of planet Veridian III.

Some time prior to Star Trek Generations.

Lursa and B'Etor

Commander Benjamin Sisko returns to Earth, where he spends several weeks debriefing Starfleet Command on the Dominion and Jem'Hadar situation. Sisko pleads for the means to defend the Bajor Sector in the event of a Jem'Hadar invasion. Another topic of discussion is Starfleet's discomfort with

Deep Space 9 security chief Odo. Although Sisko defends his officer, Odo's unorthodox style has been a source of irritation to headquarters, and Sisko is ordered to accept a Starfleet security officer on the station.

Sisko's son, Jake, accompanies him on the trip to Earth.

Two months before "The Search, Part I" (DS9).

Starfleet Command once again orders a change in the Starfleet emblem. The new design features a rounded rectangular bar behind the arrowhead.

Date is conjecture, but we saw the Next Generation-*style of communicator badges used through the end of the previous season, and the new version was introduced at the beginning of this season.*

Editors' Note: This version of the Starfleet emblem was first seen in "The Search, Part I" (DS9), although it was designed for the Enterprise-D *crew in* Star Trek Generations.

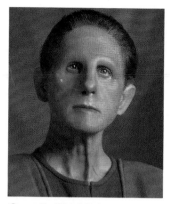

Security Chief Odo

The United Federation of Planets concludes an agreement with the Romulan Star Empire, under which the Romulans will provide a cloaking device to the Federation's Starfleet for the purpose of defending the Alpha Quadrant against the Jem'Hadar and the Dominion. The loaned cloaking device is installed into Starfleet's experimental *U.S.S. Defiant,* which is being assigned to Deep Space 9 at Sisko's request. This is the first treaty between Romulus and the Federation in many years.

Prior to "The Search, Part I" (DS9).

Ben Sisko, just prior to departing for Deep Space 9, has his personal belongings, including his prized African art collection, taken out of storage on Earth and shipped out to the station.

"Last Thursday" before "The Search, Part I" (DS9).

Redesigned Starfleet emblem

While en route from Earth to Deep Space 9, Benjamin Sisko meets with Ferengi grand nagus Zek. The nagus agrees that peaceful contact with the Founders of the Dominion is essential to maintaining business opportunities. Zek therefore agrees to grant Sisko the authority to order Quark to accompany Sisko on a mission into Dominion space for the purpose of making contact with the Founders.

Deep Space 9 personnel conduct simulations to determine defense strategies in the event of a Jem'Hadar attack of the Bajor Sector. The studies conclude that the station cannot last more than two hours without significant additional reinforcements.

Prior to "The Search, Part I" (DS9).

"The Search, Part I" (DS9). Stardate 47212.4. The *Starship Defiant,* newly assigned to defend the Bajor Sector, arrives at Deep Space 9, commanded by Benjamin Sisko. Also assigned to the *Defiant* is Subcommander T'Rul, a Romulan officer in charge of the cloaking device on loan from the Romulan government.

Grand Nagus Zek

The *Defiant's* first mission is to travel to the Karemma system in the Gamma Quadrant to locate the reclusive Founders of the Dominion. Based on information obtained from the Karemma, the *Defiant* then proceeds to Callinon VII, location of a subspace relay station used, indirectly, for messages from the Founders. While attempting to obtain information from the Callinon VII station, the *Defiant* and her crew are captured by the Jem'Hadar.

The only *Defiant* crew members to escape are Odo and Kira, who proceed by shuttlecraft to the Omarion nebula, where Odo believes his species may have originated. In the nebula, Odo finds a rogue Class-M planet, on which he locates a group of shape-shifters like himself.

Starship Defiant

A Jem'Hadar child is born. The infant is placed aboard a transport vessel.

About two weeks before "The Abandoned" (DS9).

Kolopak, a colonist living in a Native American settlement near the border between the Federation and the Cardassian Union, dies. He is survived by his son, Chakotay.

A year before "Initiations" (VGR).

Odo meets a Founder

"The Search, Part II" (DS9). (No stardate given in episode.) Odo, on the shape-shifters' homeworld in the Omarion Nebula, learns of his past. He finds that he was one of a hundred infants sent out into galaxy in hopes that he would one day return with new knowledge of the stars.

The *Defiant* command crew is subjected to an experiment that reveals the fact that life-forms in the Alpha Quadrant would vigorously defend against a direct incursion by the Dominion. This experiment is conducted by the Vorta for the Founders of the Dominion. It is learned that the shape-shifters hiding in the Omarion Nebula are, in fact, the reclusive Founders, and it is only through Odo's intervention that the *Defiant* personnel are permitted to leave unharmed.

Editors' Note: The shape-shifters revealed some of their history in "The Search, Part II" (DS9), of a past time when they freely roamed the stars, exploring the galaxy. They told of their persecution by non-shape-shifting "solids," of their retreat to the Omarion Nebula, of their founding the Dominion for self-preservation, and of their later efforts to explore the stars by sending a hundred infants into the galaxy. Unfortunately, they didn't give any significant clues as to when any of this happened, so these items don't appear in the main body of this Chronology.

Captain Kasidy Yates

Jake Sisko meets Kasidy Yates, a freighter captain. At Quark's bar on station Deep Space 9, Yates backs Jake in a high-stakes game of dom-jot. Jake is quite taken with Yates, and uses her as the basis of a character in a story he's writing. Jake also speculates about the possibility of a romantic relationship between Yates and his father, Benjamin Sisko.

Keiko O'Brien is impressed with Jake Sisko's finished story, and submits it on his behalf to the Pennington School on Earth.

"Explorers" (DS9). Date is conjecture, but we think it was before Keiko closed the school, prior to "House of Quark" (DS9).

Kozak

Traffic and commerce at station Deep Space 9 decline noticeably as word spreads throughout the Bajor Sector of the *Defiant* crew's confrontation with the Founders. Many Bajoran nationals, fearing for their safety in the event of a war with the Dominion, depart the station for their homeworld.

Keiko O'Brien closes her schoolroom at Deep Space 9 when enrollment drops to only two pupils.

Prior to "The House of Quark" (DS9).

"The House of Quark" (DS9). (No stardate given in episode.) Kozak, head of the Klingon House of Kozak, dies in an accident at Quark's bar on station Deep Space 9. Kozak's widow, Grilka, believing that Quark had caused her husband's death, invokes the Klingon *brek'tal* ritual, making Quark her new mate. Grilka's highly unusual move is intended to protect her House against the rival House of D'Ghor, which seeks to control the assets of the House of Kozak. The D'Ghor bid is rejected by Klingon High Council leader Gowron after D'Ghor demonstrates a lack of honor in his challenge against the Ferengi, Quark.

Grilka

Deep Space 9 personnel embark upon a major effort to upgrade the station's defensive and weapons systems in anticipation of a Dominion offensive.

"Way of the Warrior" (DS9). About a year prior to the episode (2372).

"Equilibrium" (DS9). (No stardate given in episode.) Deep Space 9 science officer Jadzia Dax experiences unexplained hallucinations, accompanied with a significant drop in her isoboramine levels. The condition is sufficiently troubling that Dax is returned to the Trill homeworld, where she is treated by specialists at the Trill Symbiosis Commission.

Dax at her homeworld

Editors' Note: On Trill, Deep Space 9 personnel learned that Jadzia Dax was suffering from flashbacks to an earlier host, one whose existence had been suppressed from the Dax symbiont's memory. They learned that records of the previous host had been erased because that host was an unsuitable candidate, but that he had survived in a joined state for several months. The Trill government feared that if this information became known to the Trill public, it would call into question the general belief that only one Trill in a thousand was suitable for joining. The government believed that such questions would undermine the commission's control over the selection of host candidates, and was willing to do virtually anything to maintain that control. Accordingly, the Symbiosis Commission was willing to let Jadzia Dax die, rather than reveal this information. After Ben Sisko and Julian Bashir uncovered these facts, Symbiosis Commission officials agreed to save Jadzia's life in exchange for their promise of silence. We therefore assume that outside of the Trill government, no one except for Sisko, Bashir, and Dax is aware that nearly half of the Trill population could be successfully joined, if only there were enough symbionts available.

The Emergency Medical Hologram program, EMH program AK-1 diagnostic and surgical subroutine Omega 323 is first activated aboard the *Starship Voyager*. The program generates a holographic physician intended to supplement ship's personnel in the event of a major medical disaster and was created by Lewis Zimmerman at Starfleet's Jupiter Station Holoprogramming Center.

Emergency Medical Hologram

"Projections" (VGR). According to the Doctor, he was activated on stardate 48308. Although many episodes in this season had no stardates, 48308 would normally be consistent with an event around the fourth or the fifth episode of a season.

A Jem'Hadar spacecraft crashes somewhere in the Gamma Quadrant. Wreckage is recovered by a Boslic ship, and taken to station Deep Space 9 for sale. The Boslic vessel's captain is unaware of the origin of the downed ship.

Prior to "The Abandoned" (DS9).

Keiko O'Brien and her daughter, Molly, depart station Deep Space 9 for an agrobiology expedition on planet Bajor.

About two months before "Fascination" (DS9), and about two weeks after "The House of Quark" (DS9). In "Accession" (DS9), Miles O'Brien notes that he spent the following year in virtual bachelorhood because of his wife's absence, although Keiko and Molly did visit the station during the year.

"The Abandoned" (DS9). (No stardate given in episode.) A Jem'Hadar infant is found among wreckage recovered from the Gamma Quadrant. In the care of Deep Space 9 personnel, the infant grows at an extraordinary rate. Starfleet Command expresses a strong interest in studying the youth, but security chief Odo objects. Odo, who spent much of his own life as a laboratory specimen, argues that this would be unfair to the child. The question becomes moot when the child, responding to his genetic programming, hijacks a station runabout and compels Odo to return him to the Gamma Quadrant.

Jem'Hadar infant

Dr. Julian Bashir's study of the Jem'Hadar youth reveals the child to be genetically engineered to have an addiction to an isogenic enzyme, apparently designed by the Founders to help maintain control over the Jem'Hadar soldiers.

Benjamin Sisko and Jake Sisko have dinner with Mardah, Jake's girlfriend.

Dr. Julian Bashir visits planet Klaestron IV, where he studies a new burn treatment technology developed there.

Prior to "Second Skin" (DS9).

Kira in Cardassian guise

"Second Skin" (DS9). (No stardate given in episode.) Major Kira Nerys is captured by operatives of the Obsidian Order. She is surgically altered to resemble a Cardassian intelligence agent, part of an elaborate plot to force the agent's father, Legate Ghemor, to expose members of the Cardassian underground. Kira and Ghemor escape the Obsidian Order with the aid of Deep Space 9 personnel and Elim Garak.

Legate Ghemor accepts political sanctuary with the Mathenite government.

Benaren dies on the Ocampa homeworld. He was the father of Kes.

"Resolutions" (VGR). Kes said she was one year old when her father died. This is one year before her second birthday, celebrated in "Twisted" (VGR).

"Civil Defense" (DS9). (No stardate given in episode.) While attempting to retrofit an old uridium ore processing unit on Deep Space 9, station personnel accidentally activate an automated Cardassian security program. This counterinsurgency program, left over from the days when the station was under Cardassian control, was designed to contain an uprising by Bajoran workers. The program is deactivated with the assistance of Gul Dukat, former commander of the station.

Ore-processing plant at Deep Space 9

Starfleet expresses serious concern over the continuing threat posed by the Dominion, but Benjamin Sisko convinces his superiors that exploration of the Gamma Quadrant should continue.

Prior to "Meridian" (DS9).

Major Kira Nerys meets Tiron, a business associate of Quark's, at Quark's bar on the Promenade of station Deep Space 9. Tiron is attracted to Kira, but she doesn't return the sentiment.

The evening before "Meridian" (DS9).

"Meridian" (DS9). (No stardate given in episode.) While exploring the Kylata system in the Gamma Quadrant, *Starship Defiant* personnel discover an unusual planet in the nearby Trialus system. This planet, whose humanoid inhabitants call it Meridian, exists on two intersecting dimensional planes. In this plane, the planet and its inhabitants have corporeal existence. In the other, the planet becomes noncorporeal and the inhabitants exist as pure consciousness. Scientists aboard the *Defiant* discover that the dimensional shifts are triggered by an imbalance of fusion reactants in the Trialus star, suggesting the possibility that a means may be found to stabilize the planet's dimensional shifts.

Meridian inhabitants celebrate corporeal existence

Tiron contracts Quark to produce a holosuite program featuring a holographic replica of Kira Nerys. Creation of such a program without permission of the person being copied is a highly unethical invasion of privacy. Upon learning of Quark's plan, Kira makes arrangements to modify the finished program to make it unsuitable for Quark's client.

Editors' Note: Dax fell in love with Deral of the planet Meridian. Although they were separated when Meridian lapsed back into its noncorporeal existence, Dax promised she'd be there for him when Meridian reemerges in 2431.

Robert Picard and his son, René Picard, are killed in a tragic fire.

Prior to Star Trek Generations.

Star Trek Generations. *Enterprise*-D security chief Worf is promoted to the rank of lieutenant commander in a ceremony aboard the ship's holodeck.

René Picard

Robert Picard

Data installs the emotion chip that was created for him by Dr. Noonien Soong. Although the device is successful in permitting Data to experience emotions, an unexpected overload fuses the chip into Data's neural net, making it difficult to remove. Later, Data adapts to the experience of emotions and elects to retain the chip in his positronic brain.

The Amargosa solar observatory is attacked by Romulan forces who correctly suspect that stolen trilithium may be hidden there. The *Starship Enterprise*-D responds to a distress call from the Amargosa Observatory, causing the Romulans to flee before they can locate the trilithium. While investigating the situation, Federation scientist Tolian Soran launches a trilithium-laden probe into the Amargosa star. The resulting quantum implosion destroys the star and the surrounding system. Further investigation by *Enterprise*-D personnel suggests that Soran's intent is to alter the trajectory of the temporal energy ribbon known as the nexus so that it will enter the Veridian star system. It is believed that Soran will also detonate the Veridian star so that the ribbon will intercept planet Veridian III. Such a detonation of the Veridian star would destroy the planets in the Veridian system.

Tolian Soran

Attempting to apprehend Soran, the *Enterprise*-D engages a Klingon bird-of-prey commanded by the Duras sisters. During the battle, the bird-of-prey is destroyed, with the loss of all hands. The *Starship Enterprise*-D suffers catastrophic damage to its stardrive section, necessitating an emergency saucer separation, causing the saucer section to enter the atmosphere of planet Veridian III. The crew of the *Enterprise*-D is successful in piloting the spacecraft to an emergency landing on the planet's surface. There are no fatalities in the crash, but the vehicle is deemed a total loss.

Enterprise-D saucer module crashed on Veridian III

Former *Enterprise* captain James T. Kirk is killed on planet Veridian III while working with *Enterprise*-D captain Jean-Luc Picard to prevent Soran from extinguishing the Veridian sun. The near-legendary Kirk, who had been thought killed in 2293, had been suspended in the temporal nexus encountered by the *Enterprise*-B on its maiden flight. Kirk emerged from the nexus to help save the millions of people living in the Veridian system. James T. Kirk is buried on a mountain top on Veridian III.

Former *Enterprise*-D security chief Worf goes on extended leave from Starfleet duty, visiting again the clerics at the monastery on planet Boreth. Worf finds the experience enlightening, and he even considers resigning his Starfleet commission.

After Star Trek Generations, *according to Worf in "Way of the Warrior" (DS9).*

Captain James Tiberius Kirk

Geordi La Forge undergoes surgery, receiving ocular implants that permit him to see without the use of his VISOR.

Date is conjecture. After Star Trek Generations, *but before* Star Trek: First Contact.

The Cardassian Obsidian Order and the Romulan Tal Shiar begin preparing for a preemptive first strike against the Founders' homeworld in the Omarion Nebula. Without the knowledge of their respective governments, the two agencies begin secretly assembling a fleet at the Orias system in Cardassian space. The plan is masterminded by former Obsidian Order head Enabran Tain. Although preparations for the attack are shrouded in secrecy, the Founders of the Dominion quickly learn of the plan. Word of activity in the Orias system also reaches Maquis agents, who mistakenly fear it is a prelude to a strike against Federation colonies.

Geordi La Forge after ocular implant surgery

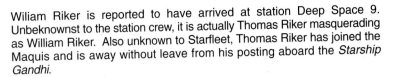

Wiliam Riker is reported to have arrived at station Deep Space 9. Unbeknownst to the station crew, it is actually Thomas Riker masquerading as William Riker. Also unknown to Starfleet, Thomas Riker has joined the Maquis and is away without leave from his posting aboard the *Starship Gandhi.*

Prior to "Defiant" (DS9). The secret base in the Orias system was established in "Defiant," but we didn't learn its purpose until "Improbable Cause" (DS9). Tain's role and the Dominion's knowledge was established in "The Die is Cast" (DS9).

The Founders of the Dominion quietly evacuate their homeworld in the Omarion Nebula. The move is in preparation for the anticipated attack by Romulan and Cardassian forces.

"The Die is Cast" (DS9). Soon after Tain began preparing his plan for attack.

"Defiant" (DS9). Stardate 48467.3. Lieutenant Thomas Riker, masquerading as William Riker, hijacks the *Starship Defiant* and proceeds to the Badlands. The hijacking is part of a Maquis plan to launch a preemptive strike against Cardassian forces.

Symbol of the Cardassian Empire

Deep Space 9 commander Benjamin Sisko fears that this Maquis action may threaten the Federation-Cardassian peace treaty. He travels with Gul Dukat to planet Cardassia Prime, where Sisko provides technical assistance to the Central Command in detecting and tracking the *Defiant.* Although Riker is successful in making strikes against several Cardassian installations, he is prevented from attacking a secret Obsidian Order base in the Orias system. Under the terms of an agreement negotiated by Sisko, Riker is surrendered to Cardassian custody, but Riker's Maquis accomplices are released to Federation authorities, and the *Defiant* itself is returned to Starfleet.

Lieutenant Thomas Riker stands trial in Cardassian court for crimes against the Cardassian people. Although the seriousness of these offenses would ordinarily warrant the death penalty, Riker is sentenced to life imprisonment at the Lazon II labor camp.

After "Defiant" (DS9).

Lieutenant Thomas Riker

Mardah is accepted at the science academy on planet Regulus III. She quits her job as a dabo game operator to attend the school, some 300 light-years from Deep Space 9.

Prior to "Fascination" (DS9).

"Fascination" (DS9). (No stardate given in episode.) The Gratitude Festival is celebrated on station Deep Space 9. The annual Bajoran holiday is marked with a carnival-like atmosphere and the ritual burning of slips of paper on which celebrants have written their problems. Participating in the festival on the station are Keiko O'Brien and her daughter, Molly, who are visiting Miles O'Brien from planet Bajor.

Betazoid ambassador Lwaxana Troi, representing her government at the festival, learns she has been suffering from Zanthi fever. The condition affects the empathic abilities of older Betazoids, causing them to project their own emotions onto others. Fortunately, Zanthi fever responds to a simple wide-spectrum antiviral treatment.

Keiko O'Brien and her daughter, Molly, return to planet Bajor via shuttle.

After "Fascination" (DS9).

The Federation colonists on planet Cestus III revive the ancient sport of baseball by forming their own league with six teams. The teams reject the designated hitter rule, and decide to use traditional wooden bats.

Bajoran Gratitude Festival

Six months prior to "Family Business."

Editors' Note: The fact that the a colony was established on planet Cestus III would seem to imply that the Federation ironed out its differences with the Gorns from "Arena" (TOS), set in 2267.

Molly, an Irish Setter belonging to *Voyager* captain Kathryn Janeway, becomes pregnant. Since Janeway is away on a mission, Mark, her significant other, takes care of the dog.

About two weeks before "Caretaker" (VGR).

Commander Benjamin Sisko and members of the Deep Space 9 senior staff depart for Earth aboard the *Starship Defiant* to attend a Starfleet symposium on the Gamma Quadrant.

Belongo, nephew to Ferengi grand nagus Zek, is held by Starfleet authorities on planet Aldebaran III.

Prior to "Past Tense, Part I" (DS9).

"Past Tense, Part I" (DS9). Stardate 48481.2. Arriving at Earth aboard the *Defiant*, Ben Sisko, Jadzia Dax, and Dr. Julian Bashir disappear while beaming down to San Francisco. Investigation suggests a transporter malfunction, caused by the interaction of chroniton particles with a microscopic singularity passing through the Solar System, may be responsible.

"Past Tense, Part II" (DS9). Shortly after the malfunction, *Defiant* personnel lose all contact with Starfleet, the result of a serious alteration in the timeline somewhere in the past. Miles O'Brien and Kira Nerys are successful in locating Sisko, Bashir, and Dax in Earth's twenty-first century, repairing the timeline.

The *Starship Defiant* returns to station Deep Space 9.

After "Past Tense, Part II" (DS9).

Starship Voyager security officer Tuvok is assigned to infiltrate a Maquis group near the Cardassian border.

Prior to "Caretaker" (VGR).

"Caretaker, Parts I and II" (VGR). Stardate 48315.6. Fleeing from a Cardassian warship, a Maquis raider spacecraft commanded by former Starfleet officer Chakotay attempts to seek refuge in the Badlands. While maneuvering through the plasma storms, the Maquis ship disappears when it is caught up in a massive displacement wave.

Starship Voyager departs station Deep Space 9 on a mission to investigate the disappearance of the Maquis ship. Joining *Voyager* at Deep Space 9 is former Starfleet officer Thomas Paris, assigned to *Voyager* as a mission observer because of his first-hand knowledge of Maquis activity, as well as Ensign Harry Kim, newly graduated from Starfleet Academy.

In the Badlands, the *Voyager* is swept up by a displacement wave identical to the one that hit the Maquis ship. The displacement wave transports the *Voyager* to the Delta Quadrant, some 70,000 light-years away.

Investigation by *Voyager* personnel reveals that they had been brought across the galaxy by a life-form calling itself the Caretaker, who provides all the necessities of life for a humanoid species called the Ocampa. The Caretaker, a sporocystian life-form, had been searching for a genetically compatible life-form with whom to procreate, in hopes of yielding an offspring who could continue to care for the Ocampa after his death. The abduction of the *Voyager* and the Maquis ship from the Alpha Quadrant had been his last attempt to find a compatible individual.

Kathryn Janeway's photo of Mark and Molly

Defiant *arrives at Earth*

Tuvok

Chakotay

Starship Voyager, *NCC-74656*

Displacement wave impacts Voyager

The Caretaker in human form

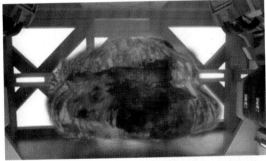

The Caretaker's demise

Harry Kim

Voyager *trapped in the event horizon*

Captain Kathryn Janeway, recognizing the need to protect the Ocampa after the Caretaker's death, destroys the Caretaker's spaceborne array in order to prevent Kazon-Ogla forces from using his machinery against the Ocampa after his death. Unfortunately, doing so precludes the *Voyager* from using the Caretaker's equipment to return home to the Alpha Quadrant. Although the Kazon are found to be formidable adversaries, their technology lags behind that of the Federation in several key areas, including the development of molecular replicators.

The surviving members of the Maquis vessel, commanded by Chakotay, agrees to join with the crew of the *Starship Voyager* as a single Starfleet crew. Captain Janeway appoints Chakotay as her second-in-command, and grants a field commission to Thomas Eugene Paris to serve as *Voyager*'s pilot. Janeway also grants de facto crew status to the ship's Emergency Medical Hologram, all three replacing crew members killed during the initial impact of the Caretaker's displacement wave. Also joining the *Voyager* crew are Kes, an Ocampa native, and Neelix, a Talaxian entrepreneur.

Voyager captain Kathryn Janeway orders a course set for return to the Alpha Quadrant.

Editors' Note: Under the editorial conventions we've used for much of the rest of this Chronology, Starfleet (and therefore this Chronology) probably shouldn't be aware of what happened to Voyager *in the Delta Quadrant. Nevertheless, we're taking the license of recording the adventures of the* Voyager'*s crew in this volume since they're such an important part of the Star Trek* saga. *"Cold Fire" (VGR) establishes the Caretaker to be a sporo-cystian life-form.*

Voyager operations officer Harry Kim attempts to link the ship's holodeck reactors into the power grid in hopes of providing more energy for ship's operations. Unfortunately the dedicated holodeck reactors are incompatible with the primary power grid, and the attempt overloads several relays.

Editors' Note: This incident was intended by the show's writers to explain why there wasn't enough power to use the ship's replicators, even though the Voyager'*s crew could still use the holodecks.*

Voyager crew member Carey is involved in an altercation with fellow crew member B'Elanna Torres. Since Carey is a part of the original *Voyager* crew, while Torres was a member of the Maquis, the incident serves to exacerbate tensions between the two groups.

Prior to "Parallax" (VGR).

"Parallax" (VGR). Stardate 48439.7. *Starship Voyager* captain Kathryn Janeway assigns Tom Paris to serve as a field medic to supplement the services of the Emergency Medical Hologram.

Voyager personnel discover a localized spatial disturbance near the Ilidaria system, apparently a quantum singularity. Closer scans also detect a distress signal from an unknown spacecraft trapped within the disturbance. Initial rescue attempts are unsuccessful, and further investigation reveals that the signal was a time-delayed reflection from *Voyager* itself, trapped in the singularity's event horizon. A dekyon beam is employed to enlarge a spatial rupture, making it possible for *Voyager* to escape.

Captain Janeway is sufficiently impressed with B'Elanna Torres's performance during the singularity crisis to assign her as chief engineer.

Kes begins a project to convert Cargo Bay 2 aboard the *Voyager* into a hydroponics bay to provide food for the ship's crew. She later incorporates airponics cultivation techniques, as well.

After "Parallax" (VGR), but before "Phage" (VGR). The use of airponics established in "Elogium" (VGR).

Tom Paris attempts to arrange a double-date for himself, Harry Kim, and the Delaney sisters of *Voyager*'s Stellar Cartography department.

Prior to "Time and Again" (VGR).

"Time and Again" (VGR). (No stardate given in episode.) *Starship Voyager* personnel detect a Class-M planet in a red dwarf system. Sensors reveal the planet to support a humanoid culture in a prewarp state, so Prime Directive considerations prohibit any attempt at contact.

B'Elanna Torres

Editors' Note: "Time and Again" (VGR) was a time-travel story in which the inhabitants of the planet were all wiped out by a polaric ion explosion. Our heroes investigated the aftermath, inadvertently transporting a day into the past, and learning that their presence in the past may have been what triggered the disastrous explosion. Once the Voyager crew was successful in setting things right, the explosion did not happen, and no one on the planet or the ship had any memory of that event. Only Kes had some faint sense that something unusual had happened.

Kai Winn and Vedek Bareil depart Bajor for a secret meeting with Legate Turrel of the Cardassian Central Command. Although prior to her election as kai, Winn had opposed reconciliation with the Cardassians, her new responsibilities have given her a broader perspective. The planned talks are the product of months of effort by Bareil who, ironically, has become one of Winn's most trusted advisors. The proposed treaty is strongly opposed by the Obsidian Order. Also opposing the treaty is Vedek Yarka, who is defrocked by the Vedek Assembly after leading a series of protests against the pact.

Kai Winn

An explosion aboard a Bajoran transport spacecraft critically injures Vedek Bareil. Radiation from the ship's plasma coil makes transporter use impossible, so ship proceeds to Deep Space 9 for emergency medical treatment.

Prior to "Life Support" (DS9). Objections by the Obsidian Order and Yarka established in "Destiny" (DS9).

"Life Support" (DS9). Stardate 48498.4. At Deep Space 9, Vedek Bareil is pronounced dead from injuries received in the transport ship explosion, but unusual radiation effects from the accident make it possible to revive him nearly an hour later. Bareil's condition remains grave, but he rejects an offer to place him in stasis until medical research can advance, so that he can continue to provide guidance to Kai Winn in the critical treaty negotiations with the Cardassians. Extraordinary efforts by Dr. Julian Bashir are, for a time, successful in keeping Bareil alive, but side effects of the treatment eventually become fatal.

Vedek Bareil

Kai Winn of Bajor and Legate Turrel of Cardassia sign a historic peace accord, ending decades of hostility between the two planets. The treaty is signed just before the death of Vedek Bareil, whom Winn privately credits with having made the agreement possible.

The Tholian ambassador visits station Deep Space 9.

Neelix removes the replicator terminals from the mess hall on the *Starship Voyager* and installs a makeshift kitchen to provide meals for the ship's crew. *Voyager* captain Janeway encourages her crew to accept natural food alternatives to replicator use to help preserve the ship's energy reserves. A system of ration credits is established to more fairly distribute available replicator resources among members of the crew.

Neelix

Prior to "Phage" (VGR). Rationing system first mentioned in "The Cloud" (VGR).

Vidiians

"Phage" (VGR). Stardate 48532.4. While prospecting on an asteroid for possible dilithium deposits, *Voyager* crew member Neelix is assaulted by humanoids who use a transporter to remove his lungs. *Voyager's* Emergency Medical Hologram is successful in resuscitating him by devising a computer program to create temporary holographic lungs in Neelix's body. The individuals who removed Neelix's lungs, identifying themselves as Vidiians, explain the attack on Neelix as a desperate effort necessary to help them survive the effects of a deadly virus they call the phage. The Vidiians lend technical assistance to *Voyager* personnel, making it possible to transplant a lung donated by Kes, an Ocampa, into Neelix, a Talaxian.

Kes agrees to undergo medical training to supplement or replace Tom Paris's role as field medic for the *Voyager* crew.

Editors' Note: This is the first appearance of the organ-stealing Vidiians on Star Trek: Voyager.

Major Kira Nerys and Odo travel to Prophet's Landing, the Bajoran colony closest to the Cardassian border. They review the colony's security procedures.

Prior to "Heart of Stone" (DS9).

"Heart of Stone" (DS9). Stardate 48521.5. While en route to Deep Space 9, Odo encounters a member of the Founders, who tests Odo to learn why he continues to live among the non-shape-shifting "Solids," even though he now knows where his people come from.

Nog

Nog, son of Rom, having undergone his Attainment Ceremony, expresses his desire to gain entry to Starfleet Academy as the first Ferengi member of Starfleet. Commander Benjamin Sisko submits a letter of recommendation to accompany Nog's application, a requirement since Nog is not a Federation citizen.

"The Cloud" (VGR). Stardate 48546.2. The *Starship Voyager* explores an unusual nebula that is discovered to be a spaceborne life-form. It is discovered that the *Voyager's* entry into the nebula has injured the life-form, but ship's personnel are successful in using a nucleonic beam to close the wound.

Voyager officer Thomas Paris compiles a holodeck program re-creating a bar named Sandrine's that he used to frequent in the French city of Marseilles on Earth.

Commander Chakotay assists Captain Janeway in performing an ancient Native American ritual, enabling her to find her spiritual animal guide.

Cardassian scientists work with Bajoran and Federation personnel to develop a subspace relay system. This joint venture is made possible by the peace treaty between the Bajorans and the Cardassians signed just a few weeks ago.

On planet Bajor, the Qui'al Dam is put back into operation, restoring the water supply to the city of Janir. Some Bajoran religious scholars interpret this as a partial fulfillment of Trakor's ancient prophesies. Former vedek Yarka seeks to suspend a Bajoran-Cardassian development project on the grounds that it will full the remainder of Trakor's dire predictions, but his plea is rejected by the Bajoran government.

Prior to "Destiny" (DS9).

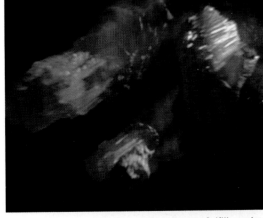

Cometary fragments fulfill ancient Bajoran prophecy

"Destiny" (DS9). Stardate 48543.2. A joint Bajoran-Cardassian science team at station Deep Space 9 tests a subspace relay system designed to permit communications with the Gamma Quadrant through the Bajoran wormhole. The test triggers an unanticipated gravitational surge, resulting in a rogue comet's being pulled toward the wormhole. Science team personnel from the *Starship Defiant* are successful in using a shuttlepod to prevent fragments of the comet from releasing dangerous silithium contamination into the wormhole itself. Sufficient contamination is released, however, to cause an unanticipated effect: The creation of a subspace filament inside the wormhole that allows subspace radio communications through the wormhole without the need for a relay station.

Bajoran theologian Yarka believes recent events are a fulfillment of Bajoran prophet Trakor prophesies of 3,000 years ago.

Voyager crew member Baxter injures her left wrist while working out in the ship's gym.

A couple of days before "Eye of the Needle" (VGR).

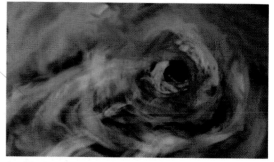

"Eye of the Needle" (VGR). Stardate 48579.4. *Starship Voyager* personnel discover a decaying wormhole. Although the wormhole has collapsed too far to permit transit of a starship, an instrumented probe is able to travel partway through the passage. Using the probe as a relay station, audio and visual contact is made with a Romulan science vessel in the Alpha Quadrant, and a way is even found to send a transporter beam through the relay. Unfortunately, it is discovered that the wormhole traverses not only 70,000 light-years of physical space, but some 20 years into the past as well. Starfleet prohibitions against altering timelines prevents *Voyager* captain Janeway from using the wormhole to facilitate the return of her crew to the Alpha Quadrant. Nevertheless, Romulan scientist Telek R'Mor accepts a computer chip containing messages from the *Voyager*'s crew members to their families. Telek, back in the year 2351, promises to store the chip for 20 years, then to deliver the messages to Starfleet in 2371.

Inside the wormhole

Voyager's Emergency Medical Hologram begins to accept his role as a member of the ship's crew, despite the fact that some of his shipmates are uncomfortable with a software-based holographic life-form. Kes, under the tutelage of *Voyager*'s Emergency Medical Hologram, supplements her field medic training with studies of anatomy and physiology.

Editors' Note: "Eye of the Needle" (VGR) establishes the current calendar year as 2371, which is consistent with a calendar year of 2364, established in "The Neutral Zone" (TNG) during the first season of Star Trek: The Next Generation. *The* Voyager*'s Doctor started his search for a name in this episode.*

Ferengi grand nagus Zek obtains a Bajoran Orb that had been stolen from the Bajoran people during the Cardassian occupation. Seeking to use the Orb to obtain future information from Bajor's Prophets, Zek travels through the Bajoran wormhole. The wormhole's inhabitants find Zek's aggressively acquisitive nature offensive, and cause Zek's personality to revert back to a time when Ferengi were kinder and more gentle. Upon Zek's departure from the wormhole, his new nature inspires him to write an entirely new version of the Ferengi Rules of Acquisition, one based on generosity and charity.

The Doctor

Nog travels to his homeworld, planet Ferenginar, to visit his grandmother.

The Federation Medical Council announces the nominees for this year's prestigious Carrington Award. Those honored include Dr. April Wade of the University of Nairobi, Healer Senva of the Vulcan Medical Institute, Dr. Henri Roget of the Central Hospital of Altair IV, Chirurgeon Ghee P'Trell of Andoria, and Dr. Julian Bashir of Starfleet station Deep Space 9. Bashir is the youngest nominee in the history of the Carrington Award.

Deep Space 9 entrepreneur Quark negotiates the sale of a hundred gross of self-sealing stem bolts.

Dr. Julian Bashir, Carrington Award nominee

Zek

Tolen Ren

Romulan official at Deep Space 9

Prior to "Prophet Motive" (DS9). Planet Altair IV is a reference to a planet of the same name from the classic MGM s-f film, Forbidden Planet.

"Prophet Motive" (DS9). (No stardate given in episode.) Ferengi Grand Nagus Zek makes an unexpected visit to station Deep Space 9, where he announces his new Rules of Acquisition, as well as the establishment of a new Ferengi Benevolent Association. Quark is horrified at this radical change in the master of Ferengi commerce and investigates the cause. Upon learning of the nagus's recent journey to meet the Bajoran prophets, Quark returns with Zek to the wormhole, and is successful in convincing the wormhole aliens to restore Zek's original personality.

The Federation Medical Council announces that Dr. Henri Roget is the winner of this year's Carrington Award.

The navigational array aboard the *U.S.S. Voyager* suffers a damaged collimator. While not immediately critical, the component requires repair.

"Ex Post Facto" (VGR). Prior to the ship's arrival at the Banean system.

Starship *Voyager* arrives at the Banean system, where technologically sophisticated natives offer to help repair the ship's collimator. In order to avoid involvement in an intrasystem dispute with a group called the Numiri, *Voyager* captain Janeway orders the ship to keep its distance from the planet. Instead, *Voyager* officers Paris and Kim travel to the Banean homeworld by shuttlecraft to discuss repairs with the planet's scientists.

"Ex Post Facto" (VGR). At least three days prior to Tolen Ren's murder.

Banean scientist Tolen Ren is murdered in his home. *Voyager* officer Tom Paris is accused of the crime.

Prior to "Ex Post Facto" (VGR).

"Ex Post Facto" (VGR). (No stardate given in episode.) Lieutenant Thomas Paris is found guilty of the murder of Tolen Ren. The conviction is based on memory information extracted from Ren's brain, identifying Paris as the killer. Investigation by *Voyager* personnel demonstrates that the evidence against Paris had been falsified by Numiri operatives, hoping to use Paris as a courier to smuggle Banean weapons information off the planet.

A Romulan delegation arrives at Deep Space 9 to study Starfleet intelligence reports on the Jem'Hadar and the Founders under the terms of the recent treaty under which the Romulans loaned a cloaking device to the Federation for the purpose of investigating the Dominion. It is not realized at the time that the Romulans have also positioned a cloaked warbird near the station, and that their true mission is to collapse the Bajoran wormhole to prevent a Dominion incursion through the wormhole and to destroy the station so that there are no witnesses.

A Klingon spacecraft traveling through the Bajor sector reportedly suffers damage to its main computer and puts in to station Deep Space 9 for repairs. It is not realized at the time that the ship is on a covert mission under the direct command of Klingon High Council leader Gowron to observe the Romulan delegation at the station.

Prior to "Visionary" (DS9).

Deep Space 9 operations officer Miles O'Brien suffers mild radiation poisoning when a plasma conduit in Ops bursts.

Just prior to "Visionary" (DS9).

"Visionary" (DS9). (No stardate given in episode.) Deep Space 9 commander Benjamin Sisko agrees to grant representatives of the Romulan government access to station records and *U.S.S. Defiant* logs relating to recent encounters with the Dominion. Sisko also authorizes the Romulans to debrief members of the *Defiant* crew.

Faint tetryon emissions from the cloaked Romulan warbird orbiting Deep Space 9 react with residual radiation in Miles O'Brien's body. These highly unusual reactions trigger a series of temporal shifts in which O'Brien jumps back and forth between "normal" time and about five hours in his future. Information gained by O'Brien during these time shifts enables Deep Space 9 personnel to learn of the cloaked Romulan ship and of a Romulan plan to destroy the station and the wormhole. With this advance warning, station commander Sisko is successful in preventing these events from occurring by activating the station's defenses.

While obtaining the information necessary to avoid Deep Space 9's destruction, Miles O'Brien receives a fatal radiation exposure. Another Miles O'Brien, his self from a reality three hours in his future, returns to the present to convey the information.

Editors' Note: Miles O'Brien died in this episode. From this point in the series, the character of Miles O'Brien is replaced with an (almost) identical person from the time continuum three hours in his future.

Miles O'Brien

"Emanations" (VGR). Stardate 48623.5. *Starship Voyager* personnel discover evidence of a 247th element in the ring system of a Class-D planet. Investigating deposits of this substance in an asteroid in the planet's ring system, *Voyager* personnel find that the deposits are byproducts of the decay of humanoid bodies. The asteroids, believed to be the burial ground for an unknown humanoid civilization, are found to be entirely composed of such decaying bodies. Ensign Harry Kim, part of the away team to the asteroid, vanishes into a subspace vacuole.

Kim finds himself on an unknown Class-M planet with people who call themselves Ktarians. Kim discovers that he has been transposed into another dimension, and that the ring of bodies discovered by *Voyager* is a result of a Ktarian death ritual, in which dying people are transported through a subspace vacuole into what the Ktarians call the Next Emanation. Kim participates in this death ritual in order to employ such a vacuole to return to his own dimension. *Voyager*'s Emergency Medical Hologram is subsequently successful in reviving Kim.

Voyager captain Janeway encourages Kim to take two days' leave in order to reflect on the enormity of his experience.

Ensign Harry Kim returns to duty.

Ring system on a Class-D planet, composed of dead bodies from another world

Two days after "Emanations" (VGR).

Tom Paris and Harry Kim go on a date with the Delaney sisters on *Voyager*'s holodeck. After only a brief time in a simulation of the Earth city of Venice, Harry Kim falls out of the gondola he'd been riding in with Jenny Delaney, to Harry's acute embarrassment.

Prior to "Prime Factors" (VGR).

"Prime Factors" (VGR). Stardate 48642.5. *Starship Voyager* encounters a planet called Sikaris, whose inhabitants possess a remarkable folded-space technology called a trajector that allows transporter-like conveyance across distances up to 40,000 light-years. Sikarian authorities refuse a request from *Voyager* captain Janeway for access to this technology to reduce the travel time for *Voyager*'s journey home. Janeway is bound by Starflect regulations

Sikarian official

Seska

Neelix

Altovar

Vole

to respect local laws in this matter. Nevertheless, *Voyager* personnel, acting without Janeway's authorization, made a clandestine exchange of Federation cultural information for technical specifications for the trajector. A subsequent attempt to use the ill-gotten data fails when it is learned that fundamental incompatibilities exist between Federation technology and the Sikarian trajector.

Voyager engineering technician Seska, believing Captain Janeway's policies to be inadequate to insure survival of the crew, forges an illicit alliance with the Kazon. She sends a covert message to a nearby Kazon-Nistrim ship, using a systems analysis test of *Voyager*'s dorsal emitters to conceal her transmission. Seska's message contains technical information intended to help the Kazon-Nistrim develop replicator technology, an area in which Kazon capabilities lag seriously behind that of the Federation.

A week before "State of Flux" (VGR).

Based on Neelix's recommendations, Starship *Voyager* stops at a Class-M planet, whose native fruits and vegetables may be of nutritional value.

Prior to "State of Flux" (VGR).

"State of Flux" (VGR). Stardate 48658.2. *Voyager* away teams assigned to gather fruits and vegetables from the Class-M planet are recalled when a Kazon-Nistrim spacecraft is detected in orbit. The Kazon-Nistrim ship suffers a disastrous explosion and issues a general distress call. Responding to the distress call, *Voyager* personnel discover that the Kazon had been testing an experimental replicator based on stolen Federation technology. Confronted with evidence that she had provided the technical information to the Kazon-Nistrim, Seska flees from *Voyager*, finding refuge with First Maje Jal Culluh aboard the Kazon ship.

After several former Maquis members of the *Voyager* crew break into the ship's food stores, first officer Chakotay orders replicator privileges revoked for two days for all persons involved, including himself.

"Distant Voices" (DS9). (No stardate given in episode.) Dr. Julian Bashir is assaulted by Altovar, a Lethean criminal seeking to transact an illegal purchase of bio-mimetic gel. Altovar employs a telepathic attack, usually fatal, that places Bashir into a deep coma for two days. During this time, Bashir experiences a series of vivid dreams in which his friends and acquaintances represent different aspects of his personality as Bashir fights to regain consciousness. Altovar is arrested by station security chief Odo.

Deep Space 9 chief medical officer Julian Bashir celebrates his 30th birthday.

In the mirror universe, members of the Terran rebellion, led by Captain Benjamin Sisko, make plans to prevent Professor Jennifer Sisko from creating a new transpectral sensor system for the Alliance of the Cardassians and the Klingons. If completed, this sensor array will make it impossible for the rebellion to operate undetected in the Badlands. Unfortunately, before the plan can be executed, Benjamin Sisko's ship is destroyed by Cardassian forces, killing Sisko and numerous other members of the rebellion.

Prior to "Through the Looking Glass" (DS9).

Quark and Morn prepare to stage a vole fight for gambling purposes. They are apprehended by Odo with some 27 voles in their possession in a storeroom aboard the station.

Just prior to "Through the Looking Glass" (DS9).

"Through the Looking Glass" (DS9). (No stardate given in episode.) Commander Benjamin Sisko is abducted by the Miles O'Brien from the mirror universe. The mirror O'Brien secures Sisko's aid in completing the mission to persuade the mirror Jennifer Sisko to abandon work on the transpectral sensor array. Jennifer Sisko not only agrees to cease work on the array, but joins the Terran rebellion to fight for human freedom in the mirror universe. Benjamin Sisko returns to his own continuum.

While the mirror O'Brien is in our universe, he downloads numerous computer files from the Deep Space 9 computer system, including complete plans for the *Starship Defiant*.

"Shattered Mirror" (DS9). The mirror O'Brien explained he did it when we weren't looking in "Through the Looking Glass" (DS9).

The mirror Rom is killed during the Terran uprising. Rom's son, Nog, inherits ownership of the bar at Terok Nor.

After "Shattered Mirror" (DS9), according to Nog.

Editors' Note: "Through the Looking Glass" (DS9) was actually filmed after "Improbable Cause" (DS9), but before "The Die is Cast" (DS9). The listings in this Chronology match the actual air sequence, which makes sense, since "The Die is Cast" is a direct continuation of "Improbable Cause." "Shattered Mirror" (DS9) was the continuation of the mirror universe's story.

Starship Voyager alters course to investigate unusually intense photonic activity in a nearby protostar.

Just prior to "Heroes and Demons" (VGR)

The mirror Jennifer Sisko

"Heroes and Demons" (VGR). Stardate 48693.2. Several *Starship Voyager* personnel disappear in a holodeck simulation based on the ancient epic poem *Beowulf*. Investigation suggests that photonic energy released during study of the protostar may have caused the crew members' accidental conversion into energy. *Voyager*'s Emergency Medical Hologram enters the holodeck and determines that the photonic energy is, in fact, a life-form trapped aboard *Voyager*. Releasing the photonic life-form causes that entity to restore the missing crew members to a solid form.

The Bajoran provisional government provides farmers in the Dahkur Province with the use of reclamation equipment intended to rid farmland of the toxic poisoning caused by Cardassian troops at the end of the occupation. The long-awaited reclamators represent a new hope for self-sufficiency for the people of Dahkur.

"Shakaar" (DS9). Two months before the episode.

The Cardassian Obsidian Order and the Romulan Tal Shiar intelligence agency begin final preparations for a massive attack against the Founders' homeworld in the Gamma Quadrant. Former Obsidian Order chief Enabran Tain, hoping for a major victory against the Dominion, makes plans for his return to power after the battle.

Holographic characters from Beowulf

Deep Space 9 personnel prepare for a visit by the Yalosian ambassador. Guest quarters are prepared for the ambassador, but Yalosian breathing mixture proves so corrosive it dissolves the carpet in the room.

Prior to "Improbable Cause" (DS9).

"Improbable Cause" (DS9). (No stardate given in episode.) Five former members of the Obsidian Order are reported to have died under a variety of circumstances. A sixth, Elim Garak, is nearly killed in an explosion at his tailor shop on the Promenade of station Deep Space 9. Investigation by security chief Odo reveals that all six had been associates of former Obsidian Order

Enabran Tain

Kes

head Enabran Tain, and had been targeted for elimination as part of Tain's plan to regain power. While conducting the investigation, Odo and Garak are captured and held aboard a Romulan warbird leading a fleet of twenty Romulan and Cardassian spacecraft for a sneak attack against the Founders' homeworld in the Omarion Nebula.

Kes's latent telepathic senses surface briefly, giving her the ability to sense the presence of *Voyager* crew member Hargrove in sickbay, even though he had left hours ago.

A week prior to "Cathexis" (VGR).

Commander Chakotay and Lieutenant Tuvok travel by shuttlecraft to conduct a trade mission with the Ilidarians. While proceeding to a rendezvous with *Voyager* after the mission, the shuttle passes through a dark matter nebula. At the nebula, the shuttle is apparently attacked by an alien spacecraft of unknown origin.

Prior to "Cathexis" (VGR).

"Cathexis" (VGR). Stardate 48734.2. Commander Chakotay, recovered from the shuttlecraft, is found to have suffered depletion of all his neural energy, and is declared brain-dead. In an attempt to learn more about the nature of Chakotay's injury, Voyager captain Janeway orders her ship to return to the dark matter nebula where the shuttle was attacked. A baffling series of apparent malfunctions, preventing *Voyager* from entering the nebula, is found to have been caused by Chakotay in a non-corporeal form. The most dramatic of his efforts is the ejection of *Voyager's* warp core. The *Voyager* crew learns that Chakotay is attempting to protect his ship from attack by the Komar, triolic-based energy beings living in the nebula. Finally, Chakotay uses his traditional Native American medicine wheel to provide navigational information to help the *Voyager* escape from the Komar. The ship's Emergency Medical Hologram is subsequently successful in reintegrating Chakotay's disembodied intellect with his body. *Voyager* personnel are successful in recovering and reinstalling the ship's warp core.

B'Elanna cares for Chakotay

Starship Voyager captain Kathryn Janeway begins spending a portion of her off-duty time in a role-playing holo-novel set in old England on Earth.

"The Die is Cast" (DS9). (No stardate given in episode.) The joint strike force of the Romulan Tal Shiar and the Cardassian Obsidian Order is ambushed at the Founders' homeworld in the Omarion Nebula. The Dominion had evidently learned of plans for the sneak attack, and had laid a trap to disable two powerful potential adversaries from the Alpha Quadrant. Former Obsidian Order chief Enabran Tain, architect of the failed offensive, is presumed to be among the many casualties. The only known survivors are Garak and Odo, rescued by the crew of the *Starship Defiant*.

Garak later reports that a number of Cardassian warships were still fighting when he was rescued by the *Defiant*, raising the possibility that some Cardassian citizens may have been captured by the Dominion.

"Broken Link" (DS9). According to Garak.

Ambush in the Omarion Nebula

In the aftermath of the failed offensive against the Dominion and the destruction of the Obsidian Order, tensions escalate on planet Cardassia Prime, with uprisings and civil disturbances adding to the unrest.

"Way of the Warrior" (DS9). Garak described the situation to Odo.

Starship Voyager conducts a survey of the Avery system. As part of the survey, officers Paris, Torres, and Durst conduct an away mission to survey magnesite formations on the surface of the third planet. *Voyager* personnel are unaware that a Vidiian force field masks the existence of a massive underground complex.

All three members of *Voyager*'s away team are captured by Vidiian scientists. B'Elanna Torres is genetically altered to isolate her Klingon genome structure from her human half. The genetronic process results in Torres being split into two near-duplicates; one who is entirely Klingon, the other completely human. This procedure, part of the Vidiian search for a cure to the disease they call the phage, is intended to determine whether Klingon physiology is resistant to the disease. The Vidiians also imprison Paris and Durst, holding them to serve as involuntary organ donors for Vidiian victims of the phage.

Prior to "Faces" (VGR).

B'Elanna in human form

"Faces" (VGR). Stardate 48784.2. After two days on the surface of planet Avery III, *Voyager*'s away team fails to report to the predesignated beam-out site for return to the ship. After a second away team reveals the Vidiian presence on the planet, Commander Chakotay undergoes cosmetic surgery to assume a Vidiian appearance in order to lead a rescue mission. Chakotay and his team are successful in recovering Paris and Torres from Vidiian custody, but Lieutenant Durst is found to have been killed as an involuntary organ donor. *Voyager* personnel are also successful in reconstituting B'Elanna Torres's original genetic structure to her human half, a remarkable feat made possible by her Klingon half's sacrifice of her life.

Deep Space 9 commander Benjamin Sisko attends the reopening of a library on planet Bajor. The library houses an extensive collection of Bajoran antiquities, including manuscripts dating back to before the fall of the First Republic. At the library, Sisko finds blueprints of an 800-year-old Bajoran spacecraft.

Prior to "Explorers" (DS9).

B'Elanna in Klingon form

"Explorers" (DS9). (No stardate given in episode.) Benjamin Sisko begins a recreational project to build a replica of an ancient Bajoran sailing spacecraft. Using only materials and tools available to the ancient Bajorans, Sisko, to the bemusement of his colleagues, builds an exact copy of a ship that might have been used to reach the Cardassian system some eight centuries ago. Once it is completed, Sisko and his son, Jake, embark upon a planned journey to the Denorios belt in hopes of demonstrating that the ancient Bajorans could have voyaged from Bajor to Cardassia. During the flight, the solar ship is caught in a tachyon current, accidentally demonstrating how a Bajor-to-Cardassia voyage could have been made, even with a small sublight craft.

The Cardassian government announces the discovery of an ancient crash site on Cardassia, at which the remains of a Bajoran solar sailing spacecraft were found. The announcement ends years of controversy over whether or not ancient Bajorans could have made the journey from Bajor to Cardassia in such primitive vessels, long before the development of interstellar travel by Cardassians.

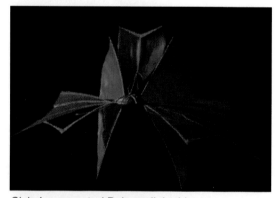

Sisko's re-created Bajoran lightship

The Pennington School in New Zealand on Earth offers Jake Sisko a writing scholarship on the strength of a story Jake had written. Jake declines the scholarship, but retains the option of accepting it next year.

The *Starship Lexington* docks at station Deep Space 9. *Lexington* chief medical officer Elizabeth Lense visits the station's Promenade, where she meets her former classmate, Dr. Julian Bashir.

A baseball game is held at the colony on planet Cestus III between the Pike City Pioneers and the Cestus Comets. One of the players transmits an audio recording of the game to his sister, Kasidy Yates, in the Bajor Sector.

Two weeks prior to the end of "Family Business" (DS9).

"Jetrel" (VGR). Stardate 48832.1. Haakonian scientist Ma'Bor Jetrel comes on board the *Starship Voyager*, requesting permission to perform a medical examination on Neelix. Jetrel's request angers and puzzles Neelix, consid-

Ma'Bor Jetrel

Ishka

Quark

Training exercise

ering Jetrel's key role in developing the devastating metreon cascade weapon that killed some 300,000 Talaxians in the war between the Haakonians and the Talaxians some 15 years ago. Jetrel later reveals his true purpose is to attempt to assuage his conscience by conducting a test of a process he calls regenerative fusion that could theoretically restore some of the people who were disintegrated by the metreon cascade. He explains that he is himself terminally ill from radiation effects of the metreon weapon, and that he has sought *Voyager*'s help because his own government has declined to fund his research. *Voyager* personnel agree to assist with Jetrel's test, but the degree of fragmentation suffered by the disassembled biomatter is found to be too great to permit reintegration. Just prior to Jetrel's death of metreon poisoning, Neelix indicates his gratitude and forgiveness to the man he had passionately hated for much of his life.

The Ferengi Commerce Authority learns that Ishka, daughter of Adred and wife of Keldar, has been earning profit in violation of Ferengi law prohibiting females from engaging in business activities.

A new runabout is delivered to station Deep Space 9, replacing the vehicle lost near the Founders' homeworld during the recent Cardassian and Romulan offensive against the Dominion. Station commander Benjamin Sisko later names the new runabout *Rubicon*.

A commercial freighter of Petarian registry, piloted by Captain Kasidy Yates, arrives at Deep Space 9.

Prior to "Family Business" (DS9).

"Family Business" (DS9). (No stardate given in episode.) Deep Space 9 entrepreneur Quark is served with a Writ of Accountability by the Ferengi Commerce Authority (FCA), charging him with improper supervision of a family member. The charge stems from the FCA investigation into the activities of Quark's mother, Ishka. Quark and Rom return to their homeworld of Ferenginar, where Quark is successful in persuading Ishka to plead guilty to having earned profit and to renounce her business activities.

Neither Quark nor the FCA is aware that Ishka has revealed only a third of her business holdings, and that she secretly retains control of her remaining assets.

At the urging of Jake Sisko, Benjamin Sisko meets Captain Kasidy Yates. Benjamin and Kasidy become friends when they learn that they have a common interest in the ancient sport of baseball.

Starship Voyager stops at planet Napinne, where ship's personnel acquire native foodstuffs, including varmeliate fiber, whole green putillos, and schplict. Neelix uses the schplict to make brill cheese in order to fulfill Ensign Ashmore's request for an Earth delicacy called macaroni and cheese.

A week before "Learning Curve" (VGR).

Voyager crew member Dalby is found to have tampered with the ship's systems to increase a friend's replicator rations. Dalby is later reported to have missed three of his last ten duty shifts.

Prior to "Learning Curve" (VGR).

"Learning Curve" (VGR). Stardate 48846.5. A malfunction in *Starship Voyager*'s bio-neural gel pack processing units is found to have been caused by a bacteria cultivated in some brill cheese prepared in Neelix's kitchen. An emergency plan to employ the ship's warp engines to generate sufficient heat to destroy the infectious bacteria is successful in restoring the gel packs to normal operating condition.

Captain Janeway, concerned that former Maquis members of her crew are having difficulty adapting to Starfleet discipline, orders Lieutenant Tuvok to conduct a class similar to those required for Starfleet cadets.

Editors' Note: "Learning Curve" (VGR) was the sixteenth and last episode aired during Star Trek: Voyager's *first season. Four additional episodes were produced during the first season (bringing the total to twenty episodes, counting "Caretaker, Parts I and II" [VGR] as two episodes), but these last four were held back to be aired at the beginning of* Voyager's *second season. This chronology follows Paramount's lead in regarding those four episodes as being part of the second season.*

Kalem Apren, First Minister of the Bajoran Provisional Government dies in his sleep of heart failure. Kai Winn is appointed to serve as his replacement until the next election.

Kai Winn

Acting First Minister Winn orders farmers in the Dahkur Province to return reclamation equipment that had been loaned to them to make their farmlands arable again. Winn cites the need for that equipment to develop the Rakantha Province to produce urgently needed cash crops for export. The Dahkur farmers, led by former resistance leader Shakaar Edon, refuse to return the equipment.

Prior to "Shakaar" (DS9).

"Shakaar" (DS9). (No stardate given in episode.) Bajoran leader Kai Winn enlists the assistance of Major Kira Nerys in persuading Shakaar Edon and other Dahkur farmers to return the loaned reclamators. Although Kira is successful in arranging a meeting between Winn and Shakaar, Winn chooses instead to send in the Bajoran militia, under the command of Colonel Lenris Holem, to retake the equipment by force. Winn continues to escalate the incident to the brink of civil war. The situation is defused when Shakaar and Lenaris agree on the futility of killing over a couple of pieces of farm equipment.

Standoff on Bajor

Former resistance leader Shakaar announces his candidacy for the office of First Minister. The elections are scheduled to be held in a month. Shakaar has strong popular support, and is favored to win. Shakaar and Lenaris urge Kai Winn to withdraw her bid for the office, threatening to publicize her mismanagement of the Dahkur incident.

Station operations chief Miles O'Brien enjoys a winning streak at the dart board in Quark's bar. The streak lasts until O'Brien unexpectedly injures his shoulder.

Shakaar Edon is elected to the office of First Minister.

"Crossfire" (DS9). After "Shakaar" (DS9).

Jadzia Dax

Nog begins a series of holosuite training sessions, hoping to improve his chances of gaining entry into Starfleet Academy. Quark continues to disapprove of his nephew's career choice.

Prior to "Facets" (DS9).

"Facets" (DS9). Jadzia Dax enlists the help of her friends to perform the Trill *zhi-an'tara* rite of closure, in which her friends temporarily embody her previous hosts. The ritual gives a Trill the chance to learn more about his or her previous lifetimes by actually meeting those hosts.

Editors' Note: "Facets" (DS9) provides much background on Dax's previous hosts. For a compilation of known data points, including a list of her hosts, see the entry on Jadzia Dax in Appendix C {Notes on Star Trek: Deep Space Nine *characters).*

Trill zhian'tara

Ambassador Krajensky

Odo kills a fellow changeling

Federation ambassador Krajensky, en route to planet Risa for an extended vacation, is kidnapped and possibly killed by an agent of the Dominion. A Founder assumes Krajensky's identity, and travels to station Deep Space 9.

Prior to "The Adversary" (DS9).

"The Adversary" (DS9). Stardate 48959.1. Benjamin Sisko is promoted to the rank of captain.

The *Starship Defiant* departs Deep Space 9 for a mission on the Tzenkethi border, in response to reports of a potentially destabilizing *coup d'état* on the Tzenkethi homeworld. While en route, the *Defiant* crew loses control of their ship. Investigation reveals that there has been no coup, but that a Founder, posing as Ambassador Krajensky, has planned the *Defiant's* mission in an unsuccessful attempt to trigger a new war between the Federation and the Tzenkethi. Control of the *Defiant* is regained and a war averted when Odo becomes the first Founder ever to kill another member of his race.

The incident is disquieting evidence that the Founders could already have infiltrated the highest levels of Starfleet Command and the Federation government, as well as other powers in the Alpha Quadrant.

Editors' Note: Sisko's log establishes that there had been a number of armed conflicts between the Federation and the Tzenkethi in the past. The last such conflict occurred at some point during Sisko's Starfleet career. "Homefront" (DS9) and "Paradise Lost" (DS9) establish that Sisko and Leyton battled the Tzenkethi while both served aboard the Starship Okinawa.

Odo files a full report on the Founders' activities, including his belief that a shapeshifter has already infiltrated the Federation itself. Shortly thereafter, Starfleet admiral Leyton and other high-ranking officers recommend sweeping security measures to protect Earth from a possible Dominion invasion. Federation president Jaresh-Inyo rejects the recommendations, calling them too extreme.

"Paradise Lost" (DS9). After the events of "The Adversary" (DS9).

6.9 STAR TREK: DEEP SPACE NINE—YEAR 4
STAR TREK: VOYAGER — YEAR 2

Starship Voyager
*lands to explore a planet
in the Delta Quadrant*

2371 (CONTINUED)

Science personnel aboard the *Starship Voyager* detect the anomalous presence of ferric oxide particles in a distant part of the Delta Quadrant.

Just prior to "The 37's" (VGR).

"The 37's" (VGR). Stardate 48975.1. Investigating the anomalous ferric oxide particles, *Voyager* personnel discover the existence of a human colony in the Delta Quadrant on a planet formerly controlled by a people known as the Briori. Also discovered at the colony are several humans held in cryostasis, among them noted aviator Amelia Earhart, who had disappeared from Earth in 1937.

Editors' Note: This episode marked the first occasion where a Federation starship was shown to land safely on the surface of a planet and then later return to space. Gene Roddenberry's format for the first Star Trek series was based in part on the fact that landing a huge starship on a planetary surface was impractical from a visual effects budget viewpoint. In the years since the first show, improvements in visual effects technology (and budgets) have made landing a starship something that is occasionally practical, although the transporter is still a lot cheaper.

As with virtually everything learned by the crew of Voyager *in the Delta Quadrant, the discovery of Amelia Earhart's fate presumably remained a mystery to the Federation, since the* Voyager *crew had no way of communicating this information back home. Nevertheless, this Chronology takes the license of including the* Voyager's *discoveries for the sake of completeness.*

"The 37's" was the twentieth and last episode produced during the first season of Star Trek: Voyager, *although it was not aired until the beginning of the*

Human descents

Amelia Earhart

Kolopak, father of Chakotay

show's second season. Unfortunately, not everyone on the Voyager production team was aware of this plan, so Janeway specifically notes in dialog that the year is 2371. Our general practice for this Chronology for Star Trek: The Next Generation-era shows has been to regard one season's worth of episodes as having taken place during a single calendar year, which puts Voyager's second season as being set in 2372, but we felt we could not ignore this particular data point. The seventeenth, eighteenth, and nineteenth episodes of Voyager's first season aired third, fourth, and fifth during the second year, and are presumed to be set in 2372, along with the rest of Voyager's second season.

2372

The senior staff of the *Starship Voyager* conduct a series of defense simulations in the ship's holodeck. Morale officer Neelix is not among the participants.

Prior to "Initiations" (VGR).

On the first anniversary of his father's death, Chakotay departs *Voyager* aboard a shuttlecraft so that he can perform the Pakra, a Native American ritual. Unbeknownst to Chakotay, his shuttle enters Kazon-Ogla space.

Just prior to "Initiations" (VGR).

"Initiations" (VGR). Stardate 49005.3. Commander Chakotay, away from *Voyager* on personal leave, accidentally becomes entangled in a young Kazon warrior's rite-of-passage ceremony. Chakotay's shuttlecraft is destroyed in the incident.

Kazon warrior

Editors' Note: "Initiations" (VGR) was the first episode produced for Star Trek: Voyager's second season, although it was the second episode aired.

The *Starship Voyager* encounters a subspace anomaly, producing a radiation surge in the ship's computer systems.

Shortly before "Projections" (VGR).

"Projections" (VGR). Stardate 48892.1. The *Starship Voyager*'s Emergency Medical Hologram experiences a series of program malfunctions and circuit degradations. The Doctor later reports that the malfunctions caused him to become delusional and caused him to wonder about the nature of his own existence.

"Projections" (VGR) was the seventeenth episode produced during Star Trek: Voyager's first season, although it was aired during the second season.

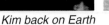

Kim back on Earth   *Extradimensional being*

"Elogium" (VGR). Stardate 48921.3. *Starship Voyager* personnel discover a swarm of spaceborne life-forms capable of free flight at speeds of one percent that of light. Several of the creatures are found to regard *Voyager* as a potential mate until a means is found to negate the ship's apparent attractiveness. Simultaneously, an electrophoretic field created by the spaceborne life-forms is found to have prematurely triggered the elogium, or sexual maturity, in Kes.

"Elogium" (VGR) was the eighteenth episode produced during Star Trek: Voyager's first season, although it was aired during the second season.

Spaceborne creatures swarm the Voyager

Voyager shuttlecraft *Drake*, piloted by Ensign Harry Kim, accidentally encounters a temporal inversion fold in the space-time matrix when the *Drake* suffers a catastrophic engine core breach. The incident transposes Kim into a parallel universe.

Just prior to "Non Sequitur" (VGR).

"Non Sequitur" (VGR). Stardate 49011. Kim is successful in returning from the alternate universe with the assistance of an extradimensional being and the self-sacrifice of an alternate Tom Paris. In this alternate universe, neither Kim nor Paris had been aboard the *Voyager* at the time it disappeared.

"Non Sequitur" (VGR) was the second episode filmed for Star Trek: Voyager's *second season.*

The Klingon Defense Force launches the starship *Negh'Var*, the first of a new class of attack cruiser, and the new flagship of the Klingon fleet.

"Way of the Warrior" (DS9). Prior to the episode. The Negh'Var *first appeared in the future scenes in "All Good Things..." (TNG).*

The Negh'Var

An uprising on the Cardassian homeworld results in the overthrow of the military Central Command and the transfer of governmental power to civilian authorities in the Detapa Council. Little information is forthcoming because the new government orders the Cardassian borders sealed. Some outside observers suspect the incident may have been engineered by the Dominion as a prelude to the feared invasion of the Alpha Quadrant.

Authorities throughout the Alpha and Beta Quadrants become increasingly concerned about the possibility of an imminent Dominion invasion. The Klingon High Council, led by Chancellor Gowron, orders secret preparation of a massive task force of more than a hundred ships to deal with the situation. Emperor Kahless opposes Gowron's military plans, but he is overruled. Also opposing Gowron's plans is council member Kurn.

Klingon High Council

Deep Space 9 personnel conclude nearly a year of work on major upgrades in the station's defensive systems in anticipation of a possible Dominion offensive. Station personnel also conduct extensive training exercises in the detection of shape-shifters.

Prior to "Way of the Warrior" (DS9). Kahless's opposition to Gowron's plans established in "The Sword of Kahless" (DS9). Kurn's opposition established in "The Sons of Mogh" (DS9).

Captain Kasidy Yates arrives at station Deep Space 9 aboard her *Antares*-class freighter, the *S.S. Xhosa*. Upon her departure, the *Xhosa* is briefly detained by a Klingon bird-of-prey, under orders to search for Dominion infiltrators.

Kasidy arrived the morning before "Way of the Warrior" (DS9).

S.S. Xhosa

"Way of the Warrior" (DS9). (No stardate given in episode.) The Klingon Empire, reportedly believing that the new civilian Cardassian government is controlled by the Dominion, launches a massive attack against the Cardassian homeworld. The Klingon government unilaterally dissolves the Khitomer accords when the United Federation of Planets refuses to participate in the invasion.

The Federation Council condemns the Klingon invasion, and in response, Chancellor Gowron orders all Federation citizens expelled from the Klingon Empire, and recalls all Klingon ambassadors from the Federation.

Chancellor Gowron

Starfleet personnel from station Deep Space 9 use the *U.S.S. Defiant* to render assistance to members of the civilian Detapa Council of the Cardassian Union, rescuing them from a battle zone. Fleeing Cardassian territory, the *Defiant* and Deep Space 9 come under heavy fire until Klingon forces are overpowered by the station's newly-upgraded defensive weapons systems.

Starfleet Command assigns Lieutenant Commander Worf to station Deep Space 9 to serve as a consultant in dealing with the Klingon presence. Worf subsequently accepts a posting as strategic operations officer aboard the station. Chancellor Gowron, viewing Worf's actions in the crisis as treaso-

Klingon fleet attacking

Cardassian fleet defeated

Janeway's arm caught in
the distortion wave

Lwaxana Troi

nous for a Klingon warrior, orders Worf's family lands seized, his titles stripped, and his brother expelled from the High Council.

In the aftermath of the unsuccessful Klingon invasion of Cardassia, Chancellor Gowron acts to protect his political position by declaring victory and recalling his forces. Gowron also orders his forces to reassert Klingon interests throughout the quadrant. This reassertion includes attacks on several outposts along the Romulan border.

"Hippocratic Oath" (DS9). According to Sisko's intelligence briefing.

While failing to conquer the Cardassian Union, the Klingon attack has destroyed the industrial base of literally dozens of Cardassian planets, with a disastrous effect on the Cardassian economy. What remains of the Cardassian military is primarily focused on defense against the Klingons. Few resources remain to fight the Maquis, so the terrorist group uses the opportunity to step up activity in the Demilitarized Zone.

"For the Cause" (DS9). In the aftermath of the invasion, according to Eddington.

"Twisted" (VGR). (No stardate given in episode.) *Voyager* crew member Kes celebrates her second birthday.

The *Starship Voyager* makes contact with a previously unknown life-form that exists as a ring-shaped spatial distortion wave. The crew's unfamiliarity with the characteristics of this life-form results in serious apprehension when the entity causes temporary disruption of the ship's spatial integrity. Nevertheless, the life-form communicates its desire to engage in an information exchange, and, with Captain Janeway's blessing, receives a copy of the ship's entire library computer database, leaving behind in exchange some 20 million gigaquads of information.

"Twisted" (VGR) was the nineteenth episode produced during Star Trek: Voyager's first season, although it was aired during the second season.

Ambassador Lwaxana Troi of Betazed, distraught over her inability to win Odo's affection, marries Jeyal, a Tavnian diplomat. Lwaxana subsequently becomes pregnant with Jeyal's child, a boy. Lwaxana becomes distressed to learn that in the Tavnian culture, women are not permitted to participate in the raising of male children, and soon begins to view her marriage as a trap.

"The Muse" (DS9). Date is conjecture. Lwaxana's pregnancy in the episode appeared to be close to full term, and "The Child" (TNG) establishes that full term for a Betazoid woman is about ten months. This suggests she became pregnant less than ten months before "The Muse."

"The Visitor" (DS9). (No stardate given in episode.) Crew members aboard the *Starship Defiant*, on a scientific mission to observe a subspace inversion in the Bajoran wormhole, narrowly avert a disaster when a surge in the wormhole's gravimetric field nearly causes a warp core breach.

Editors' Note: "The Visitor" (DS9) was the poignant story of Jake Sisko's life after his father's tragic death on the Defiant, and how old Jake's love for his father led him to sacrifice himself so that his father would have another chance at life. Because Jake was successful, Ben Sisko did not die on the Defiant, and the entire future timeline from the episode was excised. The main body of this Chronology therefore does not tell the story of that Jake's life and death. We might assume, however, that Sisko retains a memory of these events, although it seems unlikely he would tell them to his son. Some elements from the alternate Jake's future seem to be transpiring, however. "The Muse" (DS9) establishes the "real" Jake to be writing Anselem, one of the books mentioned in "The Visitor."

Jake Sisko

Ensign Harry Kim saves his food replicator rations for a week so that he can have the ship's replicators produce a clarinet for him.

Kes studies piloting under the tutelage of Tom Paris. The lessons include challenging holodeck shuttlecraft flight simulations.

Prior to "Parturition" (VGR).

"Parturition" (VGR). (No stardate given in episode.) *Starship Voyager* personnel, hopeful of finding a source for food supplies, conduct a survey of a Class-M planet believed to support extensive vegetation. The world, nicknamed "Planet Hell" by *Voyager* science staff, is found to have an atmosphere heavy in trigemic vapor, responsible for erroneous long-range sensor readings indicating plant life. During the survey, a shuttlecraft piloted by Tom Paris makes a forced landing on the planet's surface. A rescue mission by *Voyager* is delayed when an unknown spacecraft enters planetary space. Upon return from the planet, Paris reports discovery of an indigenous reptilian life-form whose young apparently hatch from eggs on the planet surface, but whose spacefaring adults were responsible for the unknown spacecraft.

Kim practices

Reptilian hatching

Dr. Julian Bashir and Chief Miles O'Brien, aboard the *Runabout Rubicon*, conduct a biosurvey of planet Merik III in the Gamma Quadrant.

Prior to "Hippocratic Oath" (DS9).

"Hippocratic Oath" (DS9). Stardate 49066.5. Deep Space 9 *Runabout Rubicon*, responding to evidence of a disabled ship, makes a forced landing on planet Bopak III, located some six weeks away from Dominion space in the Gamma Quadrant. On Bopak III, renegade Jem'Hadar soldiers enlist the aid of *Rubicon* crew members Julian Bashir and Miles O'Brien in an unsuccessful attempt to free the soldiers from their genetic addiction to the drug ketracel-white.

Kasidy Yates applies for a job with the Bajoran Ministry of Commerce to serve as captain of a Bajoran freighter. Yates hopes the job would allow her to spend more time at Deep Space 9 for the sake of her developing relationship with Ben Sisko.

Prior to "Indiscretion" (DS9).

"Indiscretion" (DS9). (No stardate given in episode.) Major Kira Nerys and Gul Dukat investigate a report that the long-missing Cardassian freighter *Ravinok* may have been found after six years. They find that the *Ravinok* had been attacked by Breen forces, and that the survivors had been forced to work in Breen dilithium mines on a planet in the Dozaria system. Among the survivors is Tora Ziyal, the daughter of Dukat and Tora Naprem, a Bajoran woman. Although Cardassian tradition demands that Dukat kill his illegitimate daughter to protect his family honor, Dukat instead brings Ziyal back with him to live with his family on Cardassia Prime.

Jem'Hadar leader

Kasidy Yates accepts the job with the Bajoran Ministry of Commerce, despite the fact that Ben Sisko seems somewhat nervous about their developing relationship.

Reaction to Dukat's return to Cardassia with an illegitimate half-Bajoran daughter is swift. Dukat's mother disowns him, and a week later, his wife takes their children and leaves him. He is stripped of his title as chief military advisor to the powerful Detapa Council, and is demoted to pilot a small Cardassian freighter, the *Groumall*. Ziyal, Dukat's daughter, also finds little acceptance in Cardassian society, and she is forced to live with her father on his freighter.

"Return to Grace" (DS9). After the events of "Indiscretion" (DS9).

Tora Ziyal

Kasidy Yates

Captain Kasidy Yates, now working for the Bajoran government, is assigned to cargo runs to outlying Bajoran colonies. One such regular run is between Bajor and the colony on Dreon VII. Yates now lives on station Deep Space 9, where she spends an increasing part of her free time with Captain Benjamin Sisko.

Deep Space 9 security chief Odo suspects that Yates may be secretly running weapons for the Maquis. Odo places her under surveillance, but fails to turn up hard evidence of any illegal activity.

"For the Cause" (DS9). After Kasidy took the job in "Indiscretion" (DS9).

Lenara Kahn

"Rejoined" (DS9). Stardate 49195.5. *Starship Defiant* personnel assist a Trill science team, led by Lenara Kahn, in an attempt to generate an artificial wormhole. Although initial tests are promising, significant additional work is found to be required before the technique can find practical application.

During the artificial wormhole tests, Lenara Kahn finds herself working with Jadzia Dax. Kahn and Dax, in previous Trill joinings, had once been married. Although the two briefly renew their relationship, Kahn ultimately chooses to respect Trill societal mores that prohibit reassociation of subsequent hosts.

Starship Voyager engineering personnel prepare the installation of holoemitters in key points of the ship. If successful, the emitters will permit the Emergency Medical Hologram to be transferred to those areas when necessary.

Prior to "Persistence of Vision" (VGR).

Bothan

"Persistence of Vision" (VGR). (No stardate given in episode.) Passing through Bothan space in the Delta Quadrant, *Voyager* personnel suffer severe disorientation when a Bothan individual causes the crew to experience disturbing hallucinations.

Kurn sends his last message to his brother, Worf. Kurn does not respond to his brother's subsequent attempts to contact him during the following weeks, causing Worf to become concerned.

"The Sons of Mogh" (DS9). Four months before the episode.

Nog

"Little Green Men" (DS9). (No stardate given in episode.) Nog, recently accepted to Starfleet Academy, conducts a sale of his childhood possessions in the Ferengi tradition of raising capital for him to begin his new life as an independent adult.

Gaila repays his debt to Quark by buying him a personal shuttle. Quark names his new ship *Quark's Treasure* and volunteers to use it to transport Rom and Nog to Earth. Quark does not reveal that his true purpose in traveling to Earth is for kemacite smuggling. En route, an apparent warp drive malfunction reacts with the kemacite, accidentally triggering a time warp. After a brief encounter with Earth natives in the year 1947, Quark and Rom are successful in returning *Quark's Treasure* to the 24th century by exposing the contraband kemacite to nuclear radiation. Quark is subsequently forced to sell his shuttle for salvage to pay for their return passage to Deep Space 9.

Nog remains on Earth, where he enrolls in Starfleet Academy.

Quark is charged with kemacite smuggling, but the charges are dismissed for lack of evidence.

After "Little Green Men" (DS9). It seems clear that the charges were dismissed because Quark was not in jail during "Starship Down" (DS9), the next episode. "Homefront" (DS9) establishes that Nog entered the academy about a month before that episode.

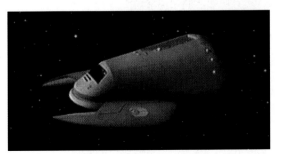

Quark's Treasure

The *Starship Voyager*'s warp coils are found to require servicing. *Voyager* personnel conduct a survey of a nearby Class-M planet in hopes of finding polyferranide deposits that can help seal the coils.

Prior to "Tattoo" (VGR).

"Tattoo" (VGR). (No stardate given in episode.) On a distant planet in the Delta Quadrant, *Starship Voyager* prepare to extract polyferranide deposits found below the planet's surface. On the planet, *Voyager* crew member Chakotay makes contact with members of a humanoid species that his ancestors once called the Sky Spirits. Respecting the wishes of the planet's inhabitants, *Voyager* departs without the needed polyferranide.

Sky Spirit

The Karemma Commerce Ministry requests a meeting with representatives of the Federation to discuss recent problems with their trade agreement. Captain Benjamin Sisko aboard the *Starship Defiant* is dispatched to the Gamma Quadrant to conduct talks.

Prior to "Starship Down" (DS9).

"Starship Down" (DS9). Stardate 49263.5. On planet Bajor, the annual Ha'mara celebration is observed, honoring the anniversary of the Emissary's arrival. The occasion is marked by fasting and a festival of lights in the Bajoran capital. The Emissary himself is not present at the festivities.

Starship Defiant, in the Gamma Quadrant for trade talks with the Karemma, is confronted by two Jem'Hadar warships. In order to escape destruction, the *Defiant* and a Karemma vessel seek refuge in the atmosphere of a Class-J gas giant planet. Although the *Defiant* suffers serious damage, *Defiant* personnel are successful in destroying the Jem'Hadar ships and rescuing the crew of the Karemma vessel.

The *Defiant and the Karemma vessel*

Ben Sisko and Kira Nerys share a baseball game program in a holosuite at Quark's bar.

Half an hour after "Starship Down" (DS9).

At the recommendation of Major Kira Nerys, Deep Space 9 commander Ben Sisko agrees to test a four-shift rotation for the station's personnel work schedule, replacing the former three-shift system. Kira believes the new system will improve performance due to less fatigue for station personnel.

Date is conjecture. This is presumably after "Starship Down" (DS9), in which Kira mentioned the idea to Sisko, but before "Accession" (DS9), in which Sisko adopted the system permanently.

Jem'Hadar vessels in pursuit

"Cold Fire" (VGR). (No stardate given in episode.) Tuvok tutors Kes in Vulcan mind control techniques in hopes of teaching her to harness her latent Ocampa telepathic abilities.

Voyager science personnel locate a sporocystian life-form, the female mate to the Caretaker who died last year at the Ocampa homeworld. This entity, who calls herself Suspiria, maintains a spaceborne array similar to that operated by the Caretaker, along with approximately 2,000 Ocampa individuals. One of these Ocampa, a man named Tanis, invites Kes to join her brethren on the array, promising to help develop her psychokinetic abilities to extraordinary levels. Kes, frightened at the undreamed-of powers latent in her mind, declines. Although Suspiria and Tanis attempt to force *Voyager* personnel to release Kes, Captain Janeway is successful in driving Suspiria and Tanis into a subspace domain that they call Exosia.

The opening narration for "Cold Fire" (VGR) establishes it to be set ten months after the events in "Caretaker" (VGR).

Tanis   *Suspiria*

Suspiria's true form

Toral

Tuvok continues to tutor Kes in the development of her latent psychokinetic and telepathic abilities, tempered by Vulcan disciplines.

After "Cold Fire" (VGR).

The Klingon High Council orders new internal security procedures to protect the empire against spies. These measures include the planting of false data in imperial computer systems.

"The Sons of Mogh" (DS9). Three months before the episode.

A Vulcan geological expedition conducting a mining survey on an uncharted planet in the Gamma Quadrant discovers what appears to be an ancient Hur'q artifact. The artifact, a tattered cloth, is taken back to Vulcan, where it is presented to Dahar Master Kor, the Klingon ambassador to Vulcan. The discovery of the cloth, which Kor believes to be the shroud of the Sword of Kahless, inspires Kor to embark on a great quest.

Kor returns to station Deep Space 9 where he seeks Dax's assistance on a search for the legendary Sword of Kahless, stolen from the Klingon Homeworld a millennium ago by the Hur'q. Despite Kor's efforts to keep his activities secret, others learn of his quest, including Toral, illegitimate son of Duras. The politically ambitious Toral employs Lethean agents to find out more about Kor's plans.

Prior to "The Sword of Kahless" (DS9).

The sword of Kahless

"The Sword of Kahless" (DS9). (No stardate given in episode.) Dahar Master Kor, along with Worf and Dax, depart Deep Space 9 aboard the *Runabout Rio Grande* on Kor's quest to find the Sword of Kahless. Although the three are successful in locating the artifact on a distant Hur'q planet, they also find the legendary stature of the sword to have the potential of causing terrible, divisive strife between factions vying for control of the Klingon Empire. Kor, Worf, and Dax conclude that it is in the best interests of the Klingon people that the sword remain lost, so they release the sword into deep space in a distant part of the Gamma Quadrant.

Culluh

"Maneuvers" (VGR). (No stardate given in episode.) *Starship Voyager* personnel detect a Federation-standard hailing signal from an automated beacon inside an ionized hydrogen cloud. While investigating the signal, a small team of Kazon warriors penetrates *Voyager*'s hull and steals a transporter control module. The device represents a significant security risk since the Kazon do not possess transporter technology. The daring raid was masterminded by First Maje Jal Culluh of the Kazon-Nistrim sect, under the guidance of former *Voyager* crew member Seska. Flushed with this victory, Culluh mounts an unsuccessful bid to unite several warring Kazon sects in an attempt to capture *Voyager* and its powerful technology.

Believing that his past relationship with Seska is responsible for the situation, Chakotay commandeers a *Voyager* shuttlecraft and makes an unauthorized attempt to recover the stolen hardware. Chakotay is subsequently captured by Culluh. Seska later claims to have a sample of Chakotay's DNA, with which she claims to have impregnated herself.

The *Starship Voyager* suffers a serious shortage of tellerium, critical to the ship's power generation systems.

Voyager arrives at an inhabited Class-M planet, the homeworld to people who call themselves the Mokra. Several *Voyager* crew members, including Captain Kathryn Janeway, beam down to the planet's surface in an effort to obtain the badly-needed tellerium from the planet's technologically sophisticated inhabitants. Because of the oppressive nature of the Mokra government, the *Voyager* away team is forced to operate covertly on the planet's surface.

Prior to "Resistance" (VGR).

"Resistance" (VGR). (No stardate given in episode.) While on an away mission to obtain tellerium on the Mokra homeworld, *Voyager* crew members are temporarily detained by government officials. During the away team's escape from Mokra custody, an Alsaurian resistance fighter named Caylem is killed. Caylem had been instrumental in helping the *Voyager* team deal with Mokra officials.

Caylem

The *Starship Enterprise*-E is launched under the command of Captain Jean-Luc Picard. The *Sovereign*-class vessel, the most advanced and most powerful in the Federation Starfleet, is the sixth starship to bear the illustrious name *Enterprise*. With the exception of Worf, who is currently assigned to Deep Space 9, all of Picard's senior staff from the *Enterprise*-D has been assigned to this new ship.

Star Trek: First Contact. *Almost a year prior to the film.*

Julian Bashir receives software for a new holosuite program, the adventures of a fictional agent of the British Secret Service on Earth in the late 20th century. Bashir, fascinated with the fantasy, spends much of his free time with the program.

Captain Jean-Luc Picard

Captain Benjamin Sisko and members of the Deep Space 9 command staff depart the station aboard the *Runabout Orinoco* to attend a conference. While at the conference, the *Orinoco* is sabotaged by members of a Cardassian terrorist group called the True Way, which blames the Federation for Cardassia's current problems.

Prior to "Our Man Bashir" (DS9).

"Our Man Bashir" (DS9). (No stardate given in episode.) Returning from a conference, the *Runabout Orinoco* is destroyed when its warp core overloads just prior to docking. Deep Space 9 personnel are successful in using station transporter systems to rescue the *Orinoco* crew and passengers, but a transporter malfunction causes a delay in completing the materialization sequence. During the delay, the transport patterns are temporarily stored in any available station computers. Portions of the transport patterns stored in the station's holosuite computers become temporarily intertwined with an active holosuite simulation program, although it is deemed inadvisable to terminate the simulation for fear of potential damage to the patterns.

Sovereign-class Starship Enterprise-E

A bomb blast disrupts a major conference between the Romulan and Federation governments at Antwerp on Earth. Some 27 people, including a Tholian observer, are killed in what is termed the worst crime of its kind on Earth in over a century. It is feared that agents of the Dominion may be responsible for the bombing. Federation president Jaresh-Inyo declares a planetwide day of mourning. Starfleet admiral Leyton and others believe the attack to be evidence that their worst fears of a Dominion invasion are about to come true.

Two days before "Homefront" (DS9). Leyton's reaction established in "Paradise Lost" (DS9).

Agent Bashir

Admiral Leyton begins personally reassigning over 400 Starfleet officers to key positions on Earth and on ships in Sector 001. Many of these officers are people who served under Leyton when he commanded the *Okinawa* against the Tzenkethi. The transfers are part of Leyton's covert efforts to prepare Starfleet for a possible Dominion invasion.

Three weeks before "Paradise Lost" (DS9), but after the Antwerp Conference bombing.

The Bajoran wormhole is observed to be opening and closing unexpectedly, apparently at random. Bajoran religious scholars interpret this as a message from the Prophets. Federation and Starfleet authorities fear this may be the passage of cloaked Dominion ships into the Alpha Quadrant.

Admiral Leyton

Sisko

Joseph Sisko

President Jaresh-Inyo

Voyager test shuttle Cochrane, *testbed for transwarp experiment*

Dax plays a practical joke on Odo, moving all the furniture in his quarters a few centimeters, just enough to disrupt his sense of order. It is the fourth time she's done this in the past year.

Prior to "Homefront" (DS9).

"Homefront" (DS9). (No stardate given in episode.) Evidence from the Antwerp conference bombing suggests the crime may have been committed by a shape-shifter, deepening concerns that the Founders of the Dominion may already have infiltrated Earth.

Captain Sisko, Commander Dax, and Odo are recalled to Earth to help Starfleet Command deal with the threat of Dominion infiltration. Sisko is appointed head of Starfleet security on Earth, working closely with Admiral Leyton. The Dominion threat is made clearer when Earth suffers a planetwide power failure, after which Federation president Jaresh-Inyo declares a planetwide state of emergency. Jaresh-Inyo thereafter authorizes the imposition of martial law under the command of Admiral Leyton.

During the crisis, Ben Sisko nonetheless finds the time to visit his father, Joseph, at the family restaurant in New Orleans.

A Klingon transport ship crashes in the mountains of planet Galorda Prime. Four hundred forty one people are reported killed in the accident.

Three months before "Rules of Engagement" (DS9).

"Paradise Lost" (DS9). (No stardate given in episode.) Captain Sisko, as Starfleet's temporary head of planetary security on Earth, uncovers evidence that both the power failure on Earth and the unexplained activity of the Bajoran wormhole had been engineered by Admiral Leyton. The admiral later acknowledges he had feared that President Jaresh-Inyo's leadership would be inadequate to face the Dominion threat, so he had manufactured the crisis in an effort to launch a coup d'etat. Leyton had planned to head a new military government on Earth, but faced with evidence of his activities, Leyton resigns his Starfleet commission.

Federation president Jaresh-Inyo orders the cancellation of martial law and the restoration of full civil liberties under the Federation Constitution.

After "Paradise Lost" (DS9).

Starship Voyager personnel, surveying an uncharted asteroid field, discover a new form of dilithium. Tests indicate this new dilithium is stable at a much higher warp frequency than the crystals normally used in Federation starships. Intrigued by the discovery, B'Elanna Torres and Tom Paris receive permission to test this mineral in a warp drive system. They believe the new dilithium may be the key to exceeding the warp 10 threshold, perhaps making it possible for a ship to attain transwarp speeds.

"Threshold" (VGR). A month before the episode.

Voyager personnel discover a robotic humanoid floating in free space in the Delta Quadrant.

Prior to "Prototype" (VGR).

"Prototype" (VGR). (No stardate given in episode.) *Voyager* personnel are successful in reactivating the robot found floating in space. They learn the robot is a sentient being that had been created by a now-extinct civilization called the Pralor. The robot itself, designated Pralor Automated Personnel Unit 3947, requests *Voyager* assistance in obtaining technology that would allow the robot to reproduce itself. Although *Voyager* captain Janeway denies the request on Prime Directive grounds, Unit 3947 abducts *Voyager* engineer B'Elanna Torres in an attempt to coerce her into providing assistance.

Although Torres initially supports the Pralor robot's request, she later changes her mind when she learns that the robots were originally constructed as weapons of war. Torres further learns that the robots in fact destroyed their builders decades ago when the Pralor attempted to conclude peace with their enemies, the Cravic, now also extinct.

Various Kazon sects launch a series of debilitating attacks on the *Starship Voyager*. Although Voyager has a significant technological advantage over Kazon weaponry, *Voyager's* lack of resupply capability proves a serious handicap.

Prior to "Alliances" (VGR). There were four attacks during the two weeks before the episode, but presumably after "Prototype" (VGR).

Mabus

"Alliances" (VGR). Stardate 49337.4. *Voyager* captain Janeway, faced with a serious deterioration of her ship's systems, agrees to talks with the Kazon-Nistrim sect in hopes of arriving at a truce. Although Janeway refuses to offer Federation technology in the talks, she is willing to participate in a mutual defense pact. When these talks collapse, a second attempt is made, this time with the Trabe, long-time enemies of the Kazon. At the urging of Trabe leader Mabus, Janeway's talks with the Trabe are expanded to include the leaders of several Kazon sects. Unfortunately, Mabus has engineered the talks as an opportunity to massacre the Kazon leadership. Although he is unsuccessful, Janeway concludes that an alliance is not possible at this time.

The Bajoran provisional government, under First Minister Shakaar Edon, allocates significant transit subsidies, expected to reduce the cost of interplanetary travel aboard Bajoran ships in the next few months. Shakaar is confident this move will help bolster his political support, but he still faces opposition because of recent tax increases.

First Minister Shakaar

Prior to "Crossfire" (DS9).

Botanist Keiko O'Brien conceives a child with her husband, Miles. The baby will be their second.

"Accession" (DS9). Two months before the episode, since Keiko said she was due in seven months.

"Crossfire" (DS9). (No stardate given in episode.) Bajoran first minister Shakaar visits station Deep Space 9 for talks with Federation representatives on the timetable for Bajor's admission to the Federation. The talks are disrupted by assassination attempts by the Cardassian terrorist group known as the True Way.

Deep Space 9 officer Kira Nerys becomes romantically involved with Minister Shakaar. The two had fought side-by-side for years during their days in the Bajoran resistance against the Cardassian occupation.

Kira

B'Elanna Torres and Tom Paris, continuing their transwarp development experiments aboard the *Starship Voyager*, make significant progress in their efforts to break the warp 10 barrier. Torres and Paris conduct extensive simulation tests in an effort to solve the remaining engineering problems.

Prior to "Threshold" (VGR).

"Threshold" (VGR). Stardate 49373.4. Lieutenant Thomas Eugene Paris becomes the first human to cross the warp 10 threshold and to fly a spacecraft at transwarp speeds. The feat is accomplished by using a new form of dilithium in the engines of the *Shuttlecraft Cochrane*. Postmission data analysis confirms that the vehicle did attain an infinite velocity, occupying every point in the universe, but no means is found for a transwarp vehicle to return to normal space at any particular predetermined point. Transwarp travel is found to have another complication: Life-forms that cross the threshold can experience dramatic mutations, apparently an accelerated evolutionary process, nearly killing Tom Paris. Captain Kathryn Janeway also

Thomas Eugene Paris, first human to cross the warp 10 threshold

Janeway

The offspring of an evolved Paris and Janeway

Bird-of-Prey

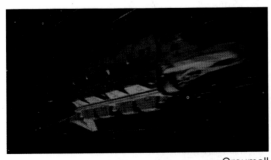

Groumall

experiences similar mutations when a deranged Paris abducts her and takes her across the transwarp threshold. Although *Voyager* personnel are successful in restoring the DNA patterns of both individuals, it is learned that while mutated, the two mated and produced a litter of amphibian-like offspring on a distant planet. *Voyager* first officer Chakotay elects to leave these offspring on the planet.

Voyager crew member Michael Jonas covertly provides technical information of the transwarp experiment to a Kazon operative.

Editors' Note: Once again, it's important to note that while Paris's flight is of great historical importance to the world of the 24th century, no one in the Federation will have any way of knowing about this feat until and unless Voyager *returns home, or finds a way of sending a message home.*

Captain Kathryn Janeway and Lieutenant Tom Paris complete their genetic therapy and return to their normal duties.

Three days after "Threshold" (VGR).

Voyager security chief Tuvok discovers evidence of Jonas's covert transmissions, but his investigations fail to determine the identify of the person sending the messages to the Kazon-Nistrim. With the approval of Captain Janeway, Tuvok devises an elaborate ruse intended to uncover the spy.

"Investigations" (VGR). Date is conjecture, but this is presumably shortly after Jonas first contacted the Kazon-Nistrim in "Threshold" (VGR).

Bajoran first minister Shakaar Edon takes Kira Nerys out to dinner at her favorite restaurant in Jalanda City on Bajor. She subsequently agrees to his request to attend a diplomatic conference for Bajoran and Cardassian officials to exchange intelligence information on the Klingons. The talks are scheduled to be held on an outpost on planet Korma.

Prior to "Return to Grace" (DS9).

"Return to Grace" (DS9). (No stardate given in episode.) Klingon forces destroy the outpost on Korma, killing numerous Cardassian and Bajoran officials there for a conference. Narrowly escaping death in the incident is Kira Nerys, who is en route aboard a Cardassian vessel commanded by Gul Dukat.

Dukat's ship, the freighter *Groumall*, is destroyed in an engagement with a Klingon bird-of-prey. During the battle, Dukat commandeers the Klingon vessel, claiming it as his own. Dukat subsequently embarks on a campaign against Klingon forces, despite orders to the contrary from the Detapa Council. Dukat asks Kira to join his quest, but she declines.

Dukat, realizing that his daughter, Tora Ziyal, has no place aboard a renegade Klingon warship, allows her to take up residence at station Deep Space 9.

Voyager staff engineer Frank Darwin is murdered in the ship's engine room. The only other person scheduled for duty in engineering at the time of his death is Lon Suder.

"Meld" (VGR). The Doctor placed the time of Darwin's death as 10:15 pm the evening before the episode.

"Meld" (VGR). (No stardate given in episode.) Lieutenant Tom Paris organizes a betting pool among the *Voyager* crew, collecting wagers for who can predict the radiogenic particle count measured by the ship's sensors. Upon learning of the operation, ship's executive officer Chakotay suspends the pool and puts Paris on report.

Investigation reveals former Maquis crew member Lon Suder to have committed the murder of Frank Darwin. Suder, conceding the charge, agrees to further the investigation by consenting to a mind-meld with security chief

Tuvok. As expected, Suder gains a temporary measure of Vulcan discipline from the meld, but Tuvok, inexperienced in melding with a Betazoid person, is briefly overcome with Suder's violent tendencies. Captain Janeway subsequently orders Suder incarcerated for the remainder of *Voyager*'s return home.

Tuvok tutors Suder in Vulcan meditation techniques in hopes of helping Suder control his violent tendencies. Still in confinement, Suder also spends his time raising orchids.

"Basics, Part I" (VGR). After "Meld" (VGR).

Lon Suder

Kurn, son of Mogh, despairs of his loss of status following his expulsion from the Klingon High Council, and contemplates the end of his life as the only means he can find to restore his honor. Kurn travels to station Deep Space 9 to request the *Mauk-to'Vor* rite of death from his brother, Worf.

Major Kira Nerys and Chief Miles O'Brien, aboard the *Runabout Yukon*, conduct an inspection tour of Bajoran colonies along the Cardassian border.

Prior to "The Sons of Mogh" (DS9).

Rom begins suffering from an infection in his ear. The condition is both painful and potentially life-threatening, although his job prevents him from seeking medical assistance in a timely fashion.

"Bar Association" (DS9). Three weeks prior to the episode.

Tuvok teaches Suder Vulcan meditation

"The Sons of Mogh" (DS9). Stardate 49556.2. Deep Space 9 personnel, investigating unusual Klingon spacecraft activity in Bajoran space, uncover evidence that the Klingons have placed cloaked subspace mines around the Bajoran system. Once discovered, station commander Benjamin Sisko orders the mines detonated to prevent their being used against Bajoran traffic.

Worf chooses to honor his brother's wish to die, but his attempt to kill Kurn in the Klingon ritual is blocked when station medical personnel intervene, resuscitating Kurn. Worf subsequently finds himself unable to kill his brother a second time, and with the assistance of Dr. Julian Bashir, instead consents to having Kurn's memory and identity erased. Kurn effectively no longer exists, and Worf provides a new identity for his brother, that of Rodek, son of Noggra. Kurn, now Rodek, is told that he had suffered amnesia after his ship was hit by a plasma discharge.

The Bajoran people observe what they call a Time of Cleansing, a month during which they abstain from worldly pleasures. Quark, operator of a bar at station Deep Space 9, notices a definite decline in his business.

Rodek

Prior to "Bar Association" (DS9), but apparently after "The Sons of Mogh" (DS9).

"Dreadnought" (VGR). Stardate 49447. *Starship Voyager* personnel discover an Cardassian weapon, a missile that was swept into the Delta Quadrant about two years ago by the Caretaker. The missile, which had been captured by the Maquis and reprogrammed by B'Elanna Torres, has targeted planet Rakosa V, an inhabited world. Initial efforts to disarm the weapon are unsuccessful, resulting in widespread panic on Rakosa V, and the evacuation of nearly the entire *Voyager* crew when ship's captain Janeway attempts to use her ship to stop the missile. Torres is later successful in forcing the missile, referred to as the dreadnought by the Maquis, to self-destruct.

Voyager crew member Michael Jonas continues to covertly provide information to a Kazon operative.

Dreadnought

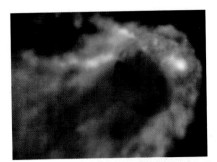

"Unusual comet"

On planet Vulcan, the Kal Rekk is observed. The Kal Rekk is a solemn day of atonement, solitude, and silence for the Vulcan people.

Two weeks after "Meld" (VGR).

Starship Voyager science personnel report the discovery of an anomalous object resembling a comet.

Just before "Death Wish" (VGR).

"Death Wish" (VGR). Stardate 49301.2. *Voyager* personnel accidentally release a life-form imprisoned in the comet. The entity, a member of the Q Continuum, is granted asylum by *Voyager* captain Janeway when Q appears and demands the prisoner's extradition. The prisoner, who later becomes known as Quinn, claims to be a philosopher from the Q Continuum who has come to regard immortality as an intolerable state, and that he wants to be allowed to die. Q, on behalf of the Continuum, argues that allowing a member of the Continuum to commit suicide would cause a serious disruption of their society. Janeway grants Quinn's request for asylum on the grounds that individual rights take precedence over the interests of the state. Janeway also pleads with Quinn to cherish his new mortal existence, but shortly thereafter, Quinn does choose to end his life.

Quinn

The *Starship Defiant* departs from station Deep Space 9 for a mission in the Gamma Quadrant. Their flight will take them through the asteroid belt in the Kar-telos system.

Five days before "Bar Association" (DS9).

"Bar Association" (DS9). (No stardate given in episode.) Quark informs the employees of his bar that he is arbitrarily cutting their pay by 33%. He cites sagging revenues during the month-long Bajoran Time of Cleansing as the reason for this move, but refuses to offer assurances that he will reinstate previous salary levels after the end of the month. Quark's employees, protesting the unfairness of Quark's management policies, are forced to organize into a labor union, the Guild of Restaurant and Casino Employees. When Quark refuses to meet with labor representatives, the union, led by Rom, declares a strike.

Q

The strike attracts the immediate attention of the Ferengi Commerce Authority, who sends Liquidator Brunt to Deep Space 9 to resolve the situation, since Ferengi culture finds labor unions to be abhorrent. Brunt attempts to use force to intimidate both sides, but union leader Rom refuses to capitulate to coercion. Quark, whose revenues fall dramatically during the strike, agrees to the union's demands, but secures from the union a promise to conceal his concessions from the FCA.

Rom resigns his job as a waiter at Quark's Bar and accepts a position as a junior grade diagnostic and repair technician for Deep Space 9's night shift.

Worf, finding living conditions on Deep Space 9 to be unsettling, moves his quarters to the *Starship Defiant.*

The Bajoran observance of the Time of Cleansing ends.

After "Bar Association" (DS9).

Despite Quark's efforts to keep the settlement with his employees secret, the FCA does learn of this gross violation of Ferengi principles.

"Body Parts" (DS9). After "Bar Association." (DS9).

Guild of Restaurant and Casino Employees

"Accession" (DS9). (No stardate given in episode.) Keiko O'Brien returns to Deep Space 9, along with her daughter, Molly, from an agrobiology expedition on planet Bajor. Keiko informs her husband, Miles, that she is pregnant with their child.

Keiko O'Brien

Noted Bajoran poet Akorem Laan emerges from the wormhole aboard an ancient solar-sailing lightship. Akorem was lost two centuries ago. In the wormhole, which Bajorans believe to be their celestial temple, Akorem encountered the life-forms known as the Prophets. As a result of this experience, Akorem believes that he is the Emissary to the Bajoran people. Benjamin Sisko agrees, relinquishing that title in Akorem's favor. Akorem subsequently imposes an orthodox interpretation of the Bajoran faith that threatens centuries of social progress. Sisko opposes Akorem's policies, and reclaims the title of Emissary, supported by a sign from the Prophets themselves. At Sisko's request, the Prophets return Akorem to his original time.

Vidiian physician Danara Pel, at planet Fina Prime to help treat an outbreak of the phage, begins the return trip to her homeworld.

Prior to "Lifesigns" (VGR).

Laan's solar lightship

Starship *Voyager* passes near an emission nebula. Pilot Tom Paris recommends that the ship fly through the nebula to save time, but Commander Chakotay instead orders the ship to take a course around the nebula.

About a week before "Lifesigns" (VGR).

"Lifesigns" (VGR). Stardate 49504.3. The *Starship Voyager* encounters a small Vidiian spacecraft carrying a lone occupant. Scans reveal the occupant to be in serious medical distress, so she is brought aboard *Voyager* for treatment. The patient, a Vidiian physician named Danara Pel, is so weakened by the phage that *Voyager*'s Doctor employs an extraordinary medical procedure, the creation of a holographic body to serve as a temporary repository for her consciousness. With the help of neural tissue donated by B'Elanna Torres, Pel's consciousness is successfully returned to her body. During her treatment, Pel grows professionally and emotionally close to *Voyager*'s holographic physician. The Doctor reports having fallen in love with Pel, an unexpected development, since his programming did not originally include the capacity for romance.

Akorem Laan

Commander Chakotay discusses the situation of Lieutenant Tom Paris with Captain Janeway. Chakotay has noted that he has been dissatisfied with Paris's attitude during the past few weeks.

Kazon operatives instruct *Voyager* crew member Michael Jonas to sabotage the ship's warp drive system, an apparent prelude to a Kazon attack on *Voyager*.

Pel's holo-image   *Pel*

The *Starship Voyager* arrives at Dr. Danara Pel's homeworld, where she disembarks to resume her work in caring for victims of the phage.

After "Lifesigns" (VGR).

Tom Paris, citing growing dissatisfaction with his life aboard *Voyager*, contacts a Talaxian convoy, offering to resign his Starfleet commission and to serve as a pilot with them.

Prior to "Investigations" (VGR).

"Investigations" (VGR). Stardate 49485.2. *Voyager* morale officer Neelix introduces a visual news program that he entitles *A Briefing with Neelix*. The report is a daily collection of news, crew information, and trivia.

A Briefing with Neelix

Jonas

U.S.S. Defiant

The Defiant

Worf on trial

Lieutenant Tom Paris resigns his Starfleet commission and leaves the *Voyager*, accepting a position as a pilot with a Talaxian convoy. Shortly after his departure from *Voyager*, Paris is abducted by Kazon-Nistrim operatives under the command of Maje Culluh and Seska. It is not revealed that Paris's actions are part of a ruse devised by security chief Tuvok, intended to help reveal the identify of a *Voyager* crew member who has been secretly providing information to the Kazon-Nistrim.

In the course of conducting research for his news program, Neelix inadvertently interferes with Tuvok's ongoing investigation, but is later instrumental in confirming that Michael Jonas is, in fact, the spy. Jonas is killed during an ensuing Kazon attack on *Voyager*, but Tom Paris is safely returned to the ship.

A Briefing with Neelix features fascinating information about the Bolian digestive system.

The day after "Investigations" (VGR).

Editors' Note: It is not clear if Neelix continued his news program after this point.

"Deadlock" (VGR). Stardate 49548.7. *Voyager* engineer Samantha Wildman gives birth to a baby girl. Unfortunately, the infant dies shortly after birth.

The *Starship Voyager*, while attempting to avoid several Vidiian spacecraft, encounters a spatial rift in which a near-duplicate *Voyager* is created in a parallel continuum. The original ship suffers severe damage when the duplicate begins to use powerful proton bursts in an effort to maintain the operation of its warp drive system. Other differences between the two ships is that on the duplicate *Voyager*, Ensign Wildman's baby girl did not die, but the original Harry Kim is killed when his ship suffers a hull breach. The crews of both ships soon assess the situation and work together to ensure their mutual survival. The task is made more difficult by a Vidiian attack on the second ship. The duplicate Kathryn Janeway, judging there to be no possibility of survival by both ships, orders her ship destroyed to prevent Vidiian forces from capturing both vessels.

Just prior to the destruction of the duplicate *Voyager*, the duplicate Janeway sends her Harry Kim and the surviving Wildman child to the original ship, replacing those individuals who died in the incident.

Editors' Note: Harry Kim and the Wildman baby died in this episode. From this point in the series, both are replaced by nearly identical individuals from the duplicate Voyager.

An outbreak of Rudellian plague strikes the Cardassian colony on planet Pentath III near the Klingon border. Numerous ships carrying medical supplies and relief workers are dispatched to the Pentath system, and the Cardassian government, concerned about possible Klingon attack, requests Starfleet protection.

Among the Federation starships assigned to protect the Cardassian convoys is the *U.S.S. Defiant*, commanded by Lieutenant Commander Worf. On stardate 49648, a Klingon spacecraft unexpectedly decloaks in the region of Worf's convoy. Fearing this to be a sneak attack, Worf orders the *Defiant* to fire on the decloaking ship, destroying the vessel. It is later reported that the ship was an unarmed transport, and that some 441 people were killed aboard the ship.

The Klingon government expresses outrage at the incident and demands that Lieutenant Commander Worf be extradited for trial on charges of murder. A hearing is scheduled to be held at station Deep Space 9.

Prior to "Rules of Engagement" (DS9).

"Rules of Engagement" (DS9). Stardate 49665.3. An extradition hearing for Lieutenant Commander Worf is convened at station Deep Space 9 by Starfleet admiral T'Lara at the request of the Klingon government. Klingon advocate Ch'Pok claims that Worf was acting as a Klingon warrior and should therefore be judged under Klingon law. T'Lara rules against extradition when evidence reveals the fact that there were no people aboard the destroyed Klingon transport, that the incident had been engineered by the Klingon government in hopes of ending Federation protection of Cardassian convoys.

Admiral T'Lara

A Drayan transport ship encounters severe electrodynamic turbulence, apparently caused by heavy solar flare activity. The vessel crashes on a small Class-M moon orbiting planet Drayan II in the Delta Quadrant. The ship's crew is killed, but they are successful in placing their five passengers into an escape pod. The passengers land safely on the surface of the moon.

A shuttlecraft attached to *Starship Voyager*, performing a survey mission in search of polyferranide, crashes on the same Class-M moon.

Prior to "Innocence" (VGR).

"Innocence" (VGR). (No stardate given in episode.) Lieutenant Tuvok, the only survivor of the shuttle crash on a moon of planet Drayan II, inadvertently interferes with the normal death ritual of several Drayan citizens. Tuvok does not realize that the Drayan people have an aging process that appears reversed in comparison to many humanoid species. In attempting to aid what appeared to be Drayan children, he actually impeded their return to what Drayans call the infinite energy at the natural conclusion of life.

Drayan "children"

The crew of the *Starship Voyager* makes formal first contact with the people of Drayan II. *Voyager* captain Kathryn Janeway invites First Prelate Alcia of Drayan II to be a guest aboard the *Voyager*, in hopes of establishing a trade agreement to obtain badly-needed polyferranide for the ship's warp drive system. Alcia, citing her people's reluctance to deal with outsiders, declines to conduct such talks.

Miles O'Brien, on a mission to the Argrathi homeworld in the Gamma Quadrant, is arrested by local authorities and convicted of espionage. O'Brien is subjected to the Argrathi system of punishment, which involves the implantation of artificial memories in the prisoner's mind, so that the prisoner has the experience of long-term incarceration without the expense to the Argrathi government. Upon his release a few hours after conviction, O'Brien believes he has experienced some 20 years of brutal imprisonment. In this memory, O'Brien shared a cell with an individual named Ee'Char, who befriends O'Brien, but who dies at O'Brien's hands. Ee'Char's death in the implanted memory is designed to cause severe guilt to O'Brien, part of the Argrathi punishment.

First Prelate

Prior to "Hard Time" (DS9).

"Hard Time" (DS9). (No stardate given in episode.) Miles O'Brien, returning home after punishment at the hands of the Argrathi government, suffers effects virtually identical to those he would have experienced after 20 years of actual imprisonment. After an initial period of denial, O'Brien agrees to a program of counseling and medication to help his readjustment.

Maquis terrorists, taking advantage of the recently crippled Cardassian military, steps up activity in the Demilitarized Zone. Starfleet Intelligence suspects the Maquis may have built several new bases in the Badlands.

"For the Cause" (DS9). A month before the episode, according to Eddington.

In the mirror universe, Terran rebels are successful in capturing station Terok Nor from the Alliance. Intendent Kira Nerys is imprisoned by the rebels. The only

Miles O'Brien

The mirror Jennifer Sisko

The Defiant *under construction in the mirror universe*

Regent Worf

Jeyal

Onaya   *First draft of* Anselem

surviving Cardassian is the mirror Garak, who flees the station and seeks refuge aboard a Klingon warship. Alliance authorities believe Kira to be responsible for this stunning defeat. The Alliance dispatches a task force of Klingon warships headed by Regent Worf to contain the situation.

Shortly thereafter, the mirror Miles O'Brien uses computer files obtained the previous year from our universe to construct a duplicate of the *Starship Defiant*. The rebels hope to use the ship to defend against an anticipated Alliance attack. Unfortunately, significant technical difficulties prevent the mirror *Defiant* from becoming operational.

The mirror Jennifer Sisko crosses over from the mirror universe to visit Benjamin Sisko at station Deep Space 9.

Prior to "Shattered Mirror" (DS9).

"Shattered Mirror" (DS9). (No stardate given in episode.) The mirror Jennifer Sisko meets Jake Sisko, and the two become friends. In her universe, Jennifer and the late, mirror Benjamin never had a son. Jennifer coerces Benjamin Sisko to return with her to the mirror universe by kidnapping Jake Sisko. In the mirror universe, he agrees to help the Terran rebels in making their version of the *Starship Defiant* operational. Upon completion of the task, Sisko pilots the mirror *Defiant* in defense of Terok Nor, successfully repelling the Klingon task force led by Regent Worf.

In the mirror universe, Intendent Kira escapes from rebel custody and flees station Terok Nor aboard a small Terran raider ship. During her escape, she kills Jennifer Sisko and the mirror Nog. Kira spares Jake Sisko's life, noting that she intends to collect this debt from his father.

The Cardassian government secretly contacts the Federation Council, admitting that it suffered far greater damage to its industrial base during the Klingon invasion than it had previously revealed. The Cardassians urgently request industrial replicators to assist in rebuilding. The Federation Council subsequently agrees to provide twelve class-4 industrial replicators to the Cardassian government.

"For the Cause" (DS9). Two weeks before the episode, according to Eddington.

Lwaxana Troi, increasingly upset that her Tavnian husband will not allow her to participate in the rearing of their soon-to-be born son, flees their home in defiance of Tavnian tradition. Her husband, Jeyal, sets out to find her.

Prior to "The Muse" (DS9).

"The Muse" (DS9). (No stardate given in episode.) Jake Sisko meets what appears to be a mysterious woman named Onaya, who encourages Jake's writing. Jake does not realize that Onaya is actually a noncorporeal life-form who literally thrives on creative energy. Under Onaya's influence, Jake writes the first draft of a semiautobiographical novel, *Anselem*, but the experience nearly costs him his life. Discovering the threat to his son, Benjamin Sisko drives Onaya away from the station.

Lwaxana Troi arrives at station Deep Space 9, asking security chief Odo to prevent her husband, Jeyal, from forcing her to return to his homeworld, where she will be forced to give up her son. Odo agrees to marry Troi so that her marriage to Jeyal is annulled under Tavnian law. The ceremony is performed at Deep Space 9.

Harry Kim and Susan Nicoletti, aboard the *Starship Voyager*, spend part of their free time rehearsing an orchestral performance for a new holodeck program of their devising.

Prior to "The Thaw" (VGR).

"The Thaw" (VGR). (No stardate given in episode.) *Starship Voyager* encounters a Class-M planet on which several humanoid survivors of an ice age have escaped death by placing themselves into a suspended animation system. Although the ice age has ended, the survivors have not been revived as programmed. Investigation by *Voyager* personnel indicates that while the survivors have been in hibernation, their minds have been active in a computer-generated synthetic reality. Unfortunately, the fears of the survivors have manifested themselves as a terrifying intelligent program that has prevented them from reviving as planned. *Voyager* captain Janeway is successful in neutralizing the fear program so that the survivors can be revived.

Suspended animation system

"For the Cause" (DS9). (No stardate given in episode.) Freighter captain Kasidy Yates is arrested for smuggling supplies to Maquis terrorists in the Badlands. Starfleet security officer Michael Eddington is also found to be a Maquis operative, although he eludes custody by fleeing station Deep Space 9 while stealing twelve industrial replicators intended for delivery to the Cardassians.

Tora Ziyal invites Elim Garak to share a holosuite program at Quark's Bar on Deep Space 9. In a very real sense, both are exiles on the station, since neither is welcome on Cardassia.

Eddington

"Tuvix" (VGR). Stardate 49655.2. While returning from a botanical survey mission, *Voyager* crew members Tuvok and Neelix are the victims of a bizarre transporter malfunction that somehow merges the two into a single person. This new individual possesses the DNA and the memories of both Tuvok and Neelix, but he has a distinctly separate, third identity. Extensive research yields a technique to tag the unique DNA segments of each part of the joined person so that the two original people can be separated. The joined person, now calling himself Tuvix, refuses to undergo the procedure, since it will effectively result in his death when Tuvok and Neelix are restored to individuality. *Voyager* captain Janeway orders Tuvix to undergo the separation, citing the rights of Tuvok and Neelix to live.

Tuvix

Voyager officers Janeway and Chakotay, surveying an uncharted Class-M planet in the Delta Quadrant, suffer nearly fatal viral poisoning from indigenous insect life-forms. *Voyager* medical personnel work to develop a treatment for the exotic insect virus.

"Resolutions" (VGR). A month before the episode, but after "Tuvix" (VGR).

New higher-resolution sensor systems are installed aboard the runabouts assigned to station Deep Space 9.

Quark surreptitiously programs computer systems on station Deep Space 9 to display an advertisement for his bar to all system users. Quark thoughtfully does not post this commercial on computers in the station's operations center. Quark also programs the food replicators aboard the *Starship Defiant* to serve beverages in mugs that bear an advertisement for his establishment.

Prior to "The Quickening" (DS9).

Quark's stationwide ad   *Quark's merchandise*

Starship Voyager medical personnel, still unable to develop a cure for the insect virus that threatens the lives of Captain Janeway and Commander Chakotay, place Janeway and Chakotay into stasis. Research continues, but the only clue is the discovery that some unknown agent in the planet's environment appears to protect them from the virus. This unknown agent is only effective when the patients are on the planet's surface.

Seventeen days prior to "Resolutions" (VGR).

"The Quickening" (DS9). (No stardate given in episode.) Responding to an ancient, recorded distress call, Deep Space 9 personnel discover a humanoid civilization in the Teplan system, near Dominion space in the Gamma Quadrant. Medical officer Julian Bashir, learning that the people of the planet suffer from a deadly disease known to the local population as the blight, attempts to develop a cure for the affliction. The blight had been introduced to the planet as a weapon some two centuries ago by the Jem'Hadar,

The remains of the Teplan civilization

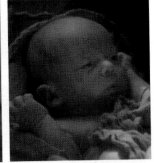

Blight stricken Teplan *Free of the blight*

Janeway and Chakotay

Vorta

Quark

Ferenginar

causing untold suffering since. Although Bashir's efforts to devise a treatment are unsuccessful, his experimental vaccine is found to be effective in inoculating unborn children, thereby offering the possibility that the next generation will be free of the disease.

Dr. Julian Bashir, having returned to station Deep Space 9, continues his research to develop a treatment for the Teplan blight.

After "The Quickening" (DS9).

"Resolutions" (VGR). Stardate 49690.1. *Voyager* medical personnel, after a month of exhaustive research, are unable to develop a cure for the viral toxin that threatens the lives of Captain Janeway and Commander Chakotay. Since their only option for survival is to remain on the planet's surface, Janeway orders the *Voyager* to leave them behind and to proceed on its course back to the Alpha Quadrant. Janeway and Chakotay, prepared to spend the rest of their lives on the planet, establish a home on the planet.

Acting *Voyager* captain Tuvok, acting in direct violation of Janeway's orders, contacts a Vidiian spacecraft, requesting medical assistance for Janeway and Chakotay, since the Vidiians have superior medical technology. Vidiian physician Denara Pel provides an anti-viral agent.

The *Starship Voyager* returns to recover Janeway and Chakotay from the planet that they have dubbed "New Earth," whereupon Pel's medication proves effective in treating the viral toxin, permitting Janeway and Chakotay to rejoin the *Voyager* crew.

Editors' Note: "Resolutions" (VGR) spanned approximately twelve weeks, and the beginning of this episode was set at least a month after the previous episode.

Dominion scientists discover the remains of an ancient Iconian gateway on Vandros IV, an outlying world in the Gamma Quadrant. Two hundred millennia ago, the Iconians used such gateways as sophisticated transporters to travel between star systems, allowing them to maintain control of a vast interstellar empire. The Dominion's scientists work to restore the Iconian gateway, but their efforts are disrupted when renegade Jem'Hadar soldiers seize control of the site.

The *Starship Defiant* embarks on a mission to protect Prophets' Haven, a Bajoran colony, from Breen privateers.

Renegade Jem'Hadar soldiers attack station Deep Space 9, seizing equipment to aid in rebuilding the Iconian gateway.

Prior to "To the Death" (DS9).

"To the Death" (DS9). Stardate 49904.2. Vorta agents of the Dominion enlist the aid of Captain Benjamin Sisko and the *Starship Defiant* on an urgent mission to destroy the newly discovered Iconian gateway on planet Vandros IV. Sisko agrees to the joint operation because of the grave threat that a functional Iconian gateway in renegade Jem'Hadar hands could pose to both the Dominion and the Federation.

Quark goes to planet Ferenginar, to negotiate a vole belly deal. He closes the sale in one day, making a respectable 15% profit margin. Quark remains on his homeworld for several days afterwards.

"Body Parts" (DS9). Two weeks before the episode, but after "To the Death" (DS9), since Quark appeared in the latter episode.

Seska, still aboard Maje Culluh's ship, gives birth to her child.

Prior to "Basics, Part I" (VGR).

Quark, still on his homeworld, has his annual insurance physical examination. Quark is diagnosed as having Dorek Syndrome and is expected to live only six or seven days. His insurance is accordingly canceled.

Major Kira Nerys, Dr. Julian Bashir, and Keiko O'Brien depart aboard the *Runabout Volga* for a three-day botanical survey mission to planet Tord V in the Gamma Quadrant. During the return flight, O'Brien is severely injured when an asteroid collides with the *Volga*. Dr. Bashir is successful in saving O'Brien's life, but is forced to surgically remove her unborn baby from her womb, and implants it in the body of Kira Nerys.

Before "Body Parts" (DS9).

Brunt

"Body Parts" (DS9). (No stardate given in episode.) Quark, returning to his bar on station Deep Space 9, attempts to raise capital to pay off his debts before his impending death by offering his remains on the Futures Exchange. He accepts an extraordinary offer of 500 bars of latinum from an unknown bidder, and is later surprised to learn that he has sold his remains to FCA liquidator Brunt. Quark is even more surprised shortly thereafter when he learns that he is not terminally ill. When Brunt nevertheless demands the fulfillment of the sales contract for his remains, Quark is forced to break the contract. Brunt accordingly revokes Quark's Ferengi business license, seizes his family assets, and orders that no Ferengi citizen may be employed at Quark's Bar, and that no Ferengi may patronize same. Although Brunt's intent was apparently to force the closure of Quark's Bar, Quark's friends contribute furniture and other goods to keep the bar in business.

Kira Nerys, as surrogate mother for the O'Brien child, accepts an invitation to move in with Miles and Keiko O'Brien for the term of her pregnancy.

The Federation Council calls upon the Klingon Empire to relinquish Cardassian territory seized during the recent invasion of Cardassian space.

Kira moves in with the O'Briens

A new restaurant called the Celestial Cafe opens on the Promenade at station Deep Space 9. The Celestial Cafe, which features a Bajoran menu, is owned by Chalan Aroya, a Bajoran national.

The Founders of the Dominion conclude months of debate on how to deal with Odo, who has violated his people's most sacred law, that no changeling may kill another. It is decided that Odo must return to the Founders' homeworld to face judgment.

Prior to "Broken Link" (DS9).

Chancellor Gowron, on behalf of the Klingon High Council, angrily rejects the Federation call to relinquish Cardassian territory. Gowron further demands that the Federation abandon all starbases and installations in the Archanis sector. The harsh, aggressive Klingon posture is a source of great concern to the Federation Council.

Chalan Aroya

Three days before "Broken Link" (DS9).

"Broken Link" (DS9). Stardate 49962.4. Odo becomes gravely ill, virtually losing his ability to maintain his form. All attempts at medical treatment are unsuccessful, and he is forced to travel to the Founders' homeworld aboard the *Starship Defiant* to plead for help. While en route, Odo learns that he is being compelled to return to his people so that he can face judgment for having killed another changeling. At the Founders' new homeworld, he joins the Great Link, where he is found guilty. His punishment is to be made human; his shape-shifting abilities are taken away from him and he is returned to the *Defiant*.

Garak is sentenced to six months' imprisonment for attempting to commandeer the *Defiant's* weapons systems in an attempt to destroy the Founders' Great Link.

Chancellor Gowron announces that he has suspended talks with the Federation and that he has dispatched a Klingon task force to retake the Archanis sector. Gowron gives the Federation ten days to withdraw from the sector.

Odo faces the judgment of the Great Link

Kazon Nistrim ship

Stranded, the crew looks on as Voyager *leaves*

Odo informs Captain Sisko that he retains some memories of the Great Link, and that one such memory from the Founders is a strong belief that Gowron has been replaced by a changeling.

"Basics, Part I" (VGR). (No stardate given in episode.) Using Chakotay's newborn son as bait, Culluh and Seska execute an elaborate plan to lure the *Starship Voyager* into a trap, leading to the capture of the Federation starship by Kazon Nistrim forces. Culluh strands the *Voyager* crew on a Class-M planet, then returns the ship to space under his control. The only *Voyager* crew member remaining on the ship is Lon Suder, whose presence is unknown to the Kazon.

Editors' Note: We arbitrarily moved "Basics, Part I" (VGR) to the end of this season, to allow enough time for the events in "Resolutions" (VGR). We realize that this violates our current rule of listing episodes in air sequence. In compiling this Chronology, we have generally resisted the temptation to shuffle episodes in this manner because doing so makes it more difficult to keep track of past events in relationship to other episodes. For this reason, we've generally assumed that episode durations, over the course of a season, will average out at two weeks, even though some individual episodes may be longer. (When an episode takes less than two weeks, we assume that there were several unseen days between episodes.) "Resolutions" clearly spanned at least twelve weeks (longer, if you count the month before the episode), so it seemed appropriate to move the next episode as far back as possible to make the time span work a little better.

"Basics, Part I" (VGR) was the season-ending cliffhanger for Star Trek: Voyager*'s second year. It was the twenty-second episode produced during the second season, but the twenty-sixth aired, because four episodes from the first season were aired as part of the second season. Four additional episodes, including "Basics, Part II" (VGR) were produced during* Voyager*'s second season, but were planned for airing during the third season.*

The human adventure is just beginning....

7.0 THE FAR FUTURE

Andromeda Galaxy, home of the Kelvan Empire

LATE 24TH CENTURY

Editors' Note: In the anti-time future visited by Picard in "All Good Things..." (TNG), we saw that after the end of Star Trek: The Next Generation, *quite a number of events transpired by the year 2395. There are significant questions of whether all (or any) of these events will "actually" happen in the "real"* Star Trek *timeline because our heroes indicated a desire to change some things. Also, the destruction of the* Enterprise-D *in* Star Trek Generations *has got to have some bearing on how the future will unfold. See Appendix H for more on alternate timelines.*

25TH CENTURY

Editors' Note: In the possible future from which Alexander returned in "Firstborn" (TNG), Alexander grew up to be a peacemaker who sought to end the destructive feuding between the great houses, tragically leading to Worf's murder on the floor of the High Council. Again, see Appendix H for more on alternate timelines.

Alexander, son of Worf

26TH CENTURY

A researcher from this century travels back to New Jersey, Earth, in the 22nd century, where his time pod is stolen by an individual named Berlinghoff Rasmussen. The unscrupulous Rasmussen uses the pod to travel to the 24th century.

"A Matter of Time" (TNG). Rasmussen confessed his past to Data.

27TH CENTURY

Scientist Kal Dano invents the *Tox Uthat,* a quantum phase inhibitor with enormous weapons potential because of its ability to halt all nuclear reactions within a star. An attempt is made to steal the *Uthat* by two Vorgon criminals,

Berlinghoff Rasmussen

Tox Uthat

Vogon criminals

so Dano travels back in time to the 22nd century, hiding the device on planet Risa. The device remains there until unearthed by archaeologist Vash, whereupon it is destroyed by *Enterprise*-D captain Picard in 2366.

"Captain's Holiday" (TNG). The Vorgons related the tale.

29TH CENTURY

A massive temporal explosion, inadvertently triggered by *Starship Voyager* personnel in Earth's 20th century, is narrowly averted by Captain Braxton of the Federation timeship *Aeon*.

"Future's End, Parts I and II" (VGR). According to Braxton.

123RD CENTURY

Radiation levels in the Andromeda galaxy are expected to reach intolerably high levels within ten millennia, according to scientists of the Kelvan Empire. Agents of the Kelvan Empire were dispatched aboard a multigenerational spacecraft to explore our Milky Way galaxy for possible colonization.

"By Any Other Name" (TOS). Rojan described the predicted radiation to Kirk. Note: The first edition of this Chronology mistakenly listed this as a 33rd-century event.

APPENDIX

About Appendices A through G. *There are a significant number of events in* Star Trek *history for which there are no reliable time references. In certain cases there were enough clues to narrow the range sufficiently that we felt we could suggest dates in the main body of this chronology. In others, however, the range of possible dates is too wide, or there is simply too little evidence to even hazard a guess. Appendices A through G are compilations of some of these undatable events, along with other interesting unknowns.*

Also incorporated into these appendices are timelines for the known dates associated with the various individual characters and other story elements. Inevitably, each timeline has gaps, and some of these gaps are discussed in the accompanying notes on undatable events. For more information on individual data points in these timelines, please refer to the main body of the Chronology.

New data. *The* Star Trek *timeline is constantly growing and evolving with the addition of each new episode and movie.* Star Trek: Deep Space Nine *and* Star Trek: Voyager *are still in production as this is being written, and Paramount is continuing to produce* Star Trek *feature films. Since the beginning of work on the first edition of this Chronology, it is interesting to note the number of items from these lists of undatable events that were deleted because they were in fact established. Most of these deleted items have since shown up in the main body of this book. Among these were the date for Earth's first official contact with extraterrestrial life (established in* Star Trek: First Contact*), incorporation of the United Federation of Planets (established in "The Outcast" [TNG] to have taken place in 2161), parts of the back story for Kahless the Unforgettable ("Rightful Heir" [TNG]), parts of the back story for the Vulcan reformation ("Gambit, Part II" [TNG]), and birth dates and academy graduation dates for several members of the* Enterprise-D *crew (established in "The First Duty" [TNG], "Conundrum" [TNG], and others). By the time you read this, it is entirely likely that other unknowns will have been addressed by the shows, although it seems certain that more questions will also be raised.*

APPENDIX A: NOTES ON STAR TREK: THE ORIGINAL SERIES CHARACTERS

James Tiberius Kirk. We believe that Kirk was born in 2233, and that he attended Starfleet Academy from 2250 to 2254. Sometime prior to "Where No Man Has Gone Before" (TOS), Kirk and Gary Mitchell were on planet Dimorus, where they encountered rodentlike life-forms who threw deadly poisoned darts. Gary took one of the darts intended for Kirk, and nearly died as a result. This would have happened sometime between Kirk's entry into the academy in 2250, and 2265, when the events in "Where No Man Has Gone Before" are set.

Kirk once suffered from a serious bout of Vegan chorimeningitis, a rare disease that can cause death in 24 hours if not treated. Although Kirk survived, his blood continued to carry the disease organisms, which the council of the planet Gideon attempted to use to control the overpopulation on their world ("The Mark of Gideon" [TOS]).

Kirk's relationships with women: James Kirk had several major romances during his life. Ruth (no last name given, seen in "Shore Leave" [TOS]) had apparently been close to Kirk during his days at Starfleet Academy. Endocrinologist Janet Wallace (seen in "The Deadly Years" [TOS]) eventually married Theodore Wallace because both she and Kirk were inflexible in their career choices. Areel Shaw served as Kirk's prosecutor when he was accused of causing Ben Finney's death ("Court Martial" [TOS]). Janice Lester and Kirk evidently shared a year together when Kirk was attending Starfleet Academy ("Turnabout Intruder" [TOS]). Carol Marcus and James Kirk conceived a child, David Marcus, in 2261 (*Star Trek II*, assumes that David was 24 at the time of the movie, 2285). There has been speculation that Carol Marcus may have been the "blond lab techni-

cian" that Kirk nearly married under Gary Mitchell's guidance while they attended Starfleet Academy (circa 2250, "Where No Man Has Gone Before" [TOS]). Of course, this lab technician just as easily could have been Janet Wallace, or some other woman we have not seen. Finally, a woman named Antonia left such a lasting impression that, when in the nexus and given the choice of being with any woman he'd ever known, he chose her. Little else was established about their past relationship, except for the fact that he later regretted not having asked her to marry him.

Kirk once visited the cloud city of Stratos prior to 2269 ("The Cloud Minders" [TOS]), but noted it was only a brief visit and he didn't have time to look around.

Kirk's retirement: *Star Trek Generations* establishes that Kirk retired from Starfleet sometime before 2282. We conjecture that he retired in 2281. We don't know much about this time, except that he met Antonia at his uncle's farm in 2282, and was living with her in his mountain cabin at the time he decided to return to Starfleet in 2284, nine years before the launch of the *Enterprise*-B. (Kirk apparently met Antonia during this time.) Kirk's second retirement was in 2293, just after *Star Trek VI*.

Kirk was believed killed shortly after the launch of the *Enterprise*-B in 2293 (*Star Trek Generations*), but it was later learned that he was alive in the nexus, where he remained until 2371. Kirk was killed shortly after emerging from the nexus, and he was buried on a mountaintop on planet Veridian III. Key data points from Kirk's life include:

2233: Born in Iowa on Earth (conjecture).
2250: Admitted to Starfleet Academy, serves aboard *U.S.S. Republic* (conjecture, "Court Martial" [TOS]).
2254: Graduated from Starfleet Academy, begins serving aboard *U.S.S. Farragut* (conjecture, "Obsession" [TOS]).
2261: Had son, David, with Carol Marcus (*Star Trek II: The Wrath of Khan*).
2263: Assumes command of *Enterprise* (conjecture).
2269: Returns from five-year mission, promoted to Admiral (*Star Trek: The Motion Picture*).
2271: Reassigned as *Enterprise* captain (*Star Trek: The Motion Picture*).
2281: Retires from Starfleet (*Star Trek Generations*).
2284: Returns to Starfleet, leaving Antonia (*Star Trek Generations*).
2286: Convicted of violating Starfleet orders (*Star Trek IV: The Voyage Home*).
2286: Assigned to command *Enterprise*-A (*Star Trek IV: The Voyage Home*).
2293: Retires again, believed killed at launch of *Enterprise*-B (*Star Trek Generations*).
2371: Emerges from nexus, killed at Veridian III (*Star Trek Generations*).

Spock. Computer records establish that as of 2267, Spock had earned the Vulcanian Scientific Legion of Honor, and had twice been decorated by Starfleet Command. ("Court Martial" [TOS]). We conjecture that Spock was born in 2230, and that he graduated from Starfleet Academy in 2253. We believe that Spock began serving aboard the original *Enterprise* in 2252, based on his statement that he had served under Captain Pike for over 11 years, and that Pike apparently concluded his stint on the *Enterprise* in 2263 ("The Menagerie" [TOS]). Accordingly, it seems that Spock served his first year on the *Enterprise* while still an academy cadet.

Spock apparently does have a first name. It has never been established, although he once told Leila Kalomi that "you couldn't pronounce it" ("This Side of Paradise" [TOS]). Amanda told Kirk that she could pronounce Sarek's family name after many years of practice ("Journey to Babel" [TOS]).

Spock's marriage: In "Sarek" (TNG), Picard mentioned that he attended the wedding of Sarek's son. There was no specific time reference to peg the date of this event, but Picard mentioned that he was a "young lieutenant" at the time. This would seem to suggest the wedding took place sometime between 2327 (when Picard graduated from the academy) and 2333 (when Picard took command of the *Stargazer*, and was therefore apparently a captain). Although the episode did not make clear if this son was Spock, Gene Roddenberry indicated that he was sure it was. This view is supported by Picard's mention in "Unification, Part I" (TNG) that he had met Spock once prior to that episode. It was not made clear if Spock was still married at the time of "Unification."

Spock was last seen as a Federation ambassador working undercover for Vulcan-Romulan reunification on Romulus in "Unification, Part II" (TNG), (2368). We do not know of his fate beyond that point. A summary of what we do know:

2230: Born on planet Vulcan (conjecture, "Journey to Babel" [TOS]).
2237: Betrothed to T'Pring ("Amok Time" [TOS]).
2249: Enters Starfleet Academy, alienating his father ("Journey to Babel" [TOS]).
2252: First serves aboard the *Enterprise* ("The Menagerie" [TOS]).
2253: Graduates from Starfleet Academy (conjecture).
2267: Experiences *pon farr*, but is rejected by T'Pring ("Amok Time" [TOS]).
2270: Retires from Starfleet (*Star Trek: The Motion Picture*).
2271: Returns to Starfleet (*Star Trek: The Motion Picture*).
2277: Promoted to captain, teaches at academy

(*Star Trek II: The Wrath of Khan*).
2285: Dies, but is reborn at Genesis Planet (*Star Trek II: The Wrath of Khan, Star Trek III: The Search for Spock*).
2368: Working undercover on Romulus for Vulcan/Romulan reunification ("Unification, Parts I and II" [TNG]).

Leonard H. McCoy. Based on McCoy's age of 137 in "Encounter at Farpoint" (TNG), (2364), we believe the good doctor was born in 2227. A large number of uncertainties exist regarding McCoy's early years, prior to his service aboard the first *Starship Enterprise*. We conjecture that he entered college or medical school in 2245 (assuming he was 18 at the time) and that he graduated in 2253 (assuming an eight-year medical program). Significant questions remain, however, as to whether or not those years were spent at Starfleet Academy or if he attended another school.

The main uncertainty surrounds a back story developed for McCoy by Dorothy Fontana and Gene Roddenberry in which McCoy had married, but that marriage ended in a bitter divorce. In this scenario, the emotional aftermath of this divorce was what drove McCoy to abandon a private medical practice and join Starfleet. This back story would have been described in an episode written by Fontana called "Joanna," which would have shown McCoy's grown daughter coming on board the *Enterprise*. (The episode was never produced, and was extensively rewritten, eventually becoming "The Way to Eden" [TOS].) Because none of this material was ever incorporated into any aired episodes, we have not included it in the

main body of this chronology. We mention it here because it offers some fascinating insight into the McCoy character, and because it does not significantly conflict with any aired material.

McCoy's father: *Star Trek V: The Final Frontier* established that sometime after McCoy had earned his medical degree, his father, David (name established in *Star Trek III: The Search for Spock*), suffered from a terminal disease that caused the elder McCoy terrible pain. Leonard "pulled the plug" on his father out of compassion, but was horrified when, shortly thereafter, a cure was discovered for the affliction.

McCoy had been briefly stationed on planet Capella IV apparently as part of a Starfleet mission sometime prior to his assignment to the *Enterprise* (2265). McCoy would later recall that the Capellans were totally uninterested in medical aid or hospitals because of a cultural belief that only the strong should survive ("Friday's Child" [TOS]). Sometime prior to "Court Martial" (TOS), (set in 2267), McCoy had earned the

Legion of Honor and had been decorated by Starfleet surgeons.

Dr. McCoy lived at least until the first season of *Star Trek: The Next Generation* (2364), since he made an inspection tour of the *Enterprise*-D in "Encounter at Farpoint" (TNG) at the age of 137.

2227: Born ("Encounter at Farpoint" [TNG]).
2245: Enters medical school (conjecture).
2253: Graduates medical school (conjecture).
2266: Assigned to *U.S.S. Enterprise* (conjecture).
2270: Retires from Starfleet *(Star Trek: The Motion Picture)*.
2271: Returns to Starfleet *(Star Trek: The Motion Picture)*.
2364: Conducts inspection tour of *Enterprise*-D at age 137 ("Encounter at Farpoint" [TNG]).

Montgomery Scott. We speculate that Scotty was born in 2222. This would make him 44, the same age as actor James Doohan during the first season of the original *Star Trek* series (2266). Scotty served as an engineering adviser on a couple of freighting runs to the miners in the asteroid belt of the Denevan system ("Operation: Annihilate!" [TOS]). This was apparently before his duty aboard the *Enterprise* (which began around 2265). "Relics" (TNG) suggests that Scotty disappeared around 2294, only to reappear in 2369. His disappearance had to occur after the launch of the *Enterprise*-B, since he was a guest on that ship's first flight *(Star Trek Generations)*. We don't know what happened to Scotty after he flew off into the sunset aboard the *Shuttlecraft Goddard* in 2369 ("Relics").

2222: Born ("Relics" [TNG]).
2240: Enters Starfleet Academy (conjecture).
2243: Begins serving as a Starfleet engineer ("Relics" [TNG]).
2244: Graduates Starfleet Academy (conjecture).
2293: Attends launch of *Enterprise*-B *(Star Trek Generations)*.
2294: Retires, is missing en route to Norpin V colony ("Relics" [TNG]).
2369: Discovered suspended in transporter beam ("Relics" [TNG]).

Uhura. Remarkably little has been established about Uhura's background (she doesn't even have a first name), although we speculate she was born in 2239, which would have made her 27 at the time of the original *Star Trek*'s first season. This, too, matches the age of the actor portraying the role. We last saw Uhura in 2293 in *Star Trek VI: The Undiscovered Country*.

2239: Born (conjecture).
2257: Enters Starfleet Academy (conjecture).
2261: Graduates Starfleet Academy (conjecture).

Hikaru Sulu. Almost as little is known about Sulu, although he did at least get a first name (Hikaru) in *Star Trek VI*, and his hometown was established as San Francisco in *Star Trek IV*. He had at least one child, Demora Sulu, who was a helm officer on the first voyage of the *Enterprise*-B in *Star Trek Generations*. In the 24th century, Sulu's portrait hung in Starfleet Headquarters, mentioned by Janeway in "Flashback" (VGR), although we don't know what specific thing he did to earn this recognition. It is possible that Hikaru Sulu recommended young Chakotay for admission to Starfleet Academy in 2350 ("Tattoo" [VGR]), although it is not clear if this was Hikaru or some other Captain Sulu. We speculate Sulu was 29 at the time of *Star Trek*'s first season, suggesting a birth date of 2237. Hikaru Sulu would have been 113 years old at the time Chakotay applied for the academy.

2237: Born in San Francisco on Earth (conjecture).
2255: Enters Starfleet Academy (conjecture).
2259: Graduates Starfleet Academy (conjecture).
2266: Transferred from physicist to helm officer aboard *Enterprise* ("The Corbomite Maneuver" [TOS]).
2271: Daughter, Demora Sulu, born *(Star Trek Generations)*.
2290: Assigned as captain of *U.S.S. Excelsior (Star Trek VI: The Undiscovered Country)*.

Pavel Andreievich Chekov. Prior to Chekov's assignment to the *Enterprise*, he was romantically involved with a woman named Irina Galliunin. At the time, both were apparently in Starfleet, although Irina subsequently resigned because she felt Starfleet was too regimented for her liking ("The Way to Eden" [TOS]). Chekov said he was 22 years old in "Who Mourns for Adonais" (TOS), (2267), suggesting a birthdate of 2245. As of this writing, the last data point we have for Chekov is 2293, at the launch of the *Starship Enterprise*-B *(Star Trek Generations)*.

2245: Born ("Who Mourns For Adonais?" [TOS]).
2263: Enters Starfleet Academy (conjecture).
2267: Graduates Starfleet Academy (conjecture).

2277: Assigned to *Starship Reliant* (*Star Trek II: The Wrath of Khan*).

2293: Attends launch of *Enterprise*-B (*Star Trek Generations*).

Janice Rand. Yeoman Janice Rand evidently left the original *Enterprise* crew in 2266, when Grace Lee Whitney's character was dropped from the show due to budgetary constraints. As a result, there are large gaps in Rand's career about which we know very little. We do know that she returned to the *Enterprise* around 2271, because she was seen aboard the refit ship as a transporter chief in *Star Trek: The Motion*

Picture. By 2285 she was no longer part of the *Enterprise* crew, because we saw her at Starfleet Headquarters in *Star Trek III*, and in Starfleet Command in *Star Trek IV*. She was evidently assigned to the *Starship Excelsior* in 2290 as Captain Sulu's communications officer as seen in *Star Trek VI* and "Flashback" (VGR).

Sarek. "Journey to Babel" (TOS) establishes Sarek's age at the time (2267) to be 102, suggesting a birth date of 2165. Among Sarek's many distinguished achievements are the Coridan admission to the Federation ("Journey to Babel" [TOS], 2268), the Klingon alliance (*Star Trek VI: The Undiscovered Country*, 2293), the Legaran conference ("Sarek" [TNG], 2367), as well as the treaty of Alpha Cygnus IX. This last item was not dated, nor were any other details established. The episode "Sarek" also refers to Spock's mother, Amanda, as having died sometime prior to the episode. This date is not established, nor is a date set for Sarek's marriage to Perrin.

Star Trek V: The Final Frontier establishes (perhaps apocryphally) that prior to his marriage to Amanda (conjecturally set in 2230), Sarek had been married to a Vulcan princess and that they had a son, Sybok. Spock noted that Sybok's mother died shortly after Sybok's birth, which may have taken place in 2224, seven years prior to Spock's birth. (For that matter, it is not made clear if he had one or more other marriages in the intervening years between Amanda and Perrin. On the other hand, Picard's log in "Sarek" (TNG) notes that Perrin, "like his first wife, is from Earth," which would appear to contradict the Vulcan princess back story.)

Sarek met a young Lieutenant Jean-Luc Picard once prior to the episode "Sarek" (TNG), at Sarek's son's wedding. This was apparently between 2327 and 2333. (See note

on Spock in this section.)

Sarek died at the age of 203 in "Unification, Part I" (TNG), (2368), making him one of the few major characters from the original *Star Trek* series whose fate we do know.

2165: Born ("Journey to Babel" [TOS]).

2229: Marries Amanda (conjecture).

2230: Son Spock born (conjecture).

2267: Babel Conference ("Journey to Babel" [TOS]).

2293: Khitomer Conference (*Star Trek VI: The Undiscovered Country*).

2366: Diagnosed with Bendii syndrome ("Sarek" [TNG]).

2368: Dies ("Unification, Part I" [TNG]).

Captain Christopher Pike. We know little about Kirk's predecessor other than the fact that he was born in Mojave, on Earth, and that he eventually went to live among the Talosians on Talos IV ("The Cage" [TOS]). Pike evidently commanded two five-year missions of exploration aboard the *Enterprise* and later served as fleet captain before being seriously injured in an explosion on a training ship in 2266.

Captain Garth of Izar. "Whom Gods Destroy" (TOS) establishes former Fleet Captain Garth to have been a major figure in Starfleet history. Garth led a major Federation victory at Axanar, and, in another battle, Garth used something called a Cochrane deceleration maneuver to defeat a Romulan vessel near Tau Ceti. It is unclear when any of this occurred (or who Garth was fighting at Axanar), but Kirk, noting that Garth was his hero, said that he had read all about Garth at the academy, suggesting some of this took place prior to Kirk's admission to the academy in 2250. Garth's Romulan encounter would have had to have happened after 2266 (when "Balance of Terror" [TOS] established the Neutral Zone had not been crossed for a century) and before 2269 (when "Whom Gods Destroy" [TOS] is set). One of Kirk's early missions as a cadet was a peace mission to Axanar, for which Kirk was awarded the Palm Leaf of the Axanar Peace Mission (as mentioned in "Court Martial" [TOS]). In later years Garth was seriously injured in an unknown accident, but he was treated by the inhabitants of planet Antos IV, who taught him the technique of cellular metamorphosis. Unfortunately, either the accident or the treatment left Garth mentally disturbed, and he tried to destroy the Antos people. Garth's starship crew refused to obey his orders, and Garth was eventually confined to the penal colony on Elba II for psychiatric treatment.

APPENDIX B: NOTES ON STAR TREK: THE NEXT GENERATION CHARACTERS

Jean-Luc Picard. We conjecture that Picard was born in 2305, which is consistent with an academy graduation date of 2327 ("The First Duty" [TNG]), assuming he tried unsuccessfully for admission at age 17 and was admitted a year later ("Coming of Age" [TNG]).

In "Where No One Has Gone Before" (TNG), Picard referred to his mother in the past tense, implying she was no longer alive in 2364. This is reinforced by "Family" (TNG), in which Picard returned to his family home in France, no longer occupied by his parents. In "Night Terrors" (TNG), Picard recalls that as a young man, he saw his "grandfather deteriorate . . . from a powerful, robust figure . . . to a frail wisp of a man, who couldn't even remember how to make his way home." Picard once recalled (in "Conspiracy" [TNG]) that his "oldest and closest friends were Jack Crusher, may he rest in peace, and Walker Keel." Keel was later killed when the alien parasites blew up the *Starship Horatio* in that episode.

In "Rascals" (TNG), Picard noted that he'd spent 30 years of his life on starships, although he took command of the *Stargazer* some 36 years prior to that point. (He clearly had at least a few years of starship duty prior to that point, as well.) Picard may simply have been rounding off the number, but it seems possible that there was a period of at least six years after the *Stargazer* disaster during which he was not aboard a starship.

2305: Born in LaBarre, France on Earth ("The First Duty" [TNG]).
2322: Applies to Starfleet Academy, but is rejected ("Coming of Age" [TNG]).

2323: Admitted to Starfleet Academy ("Coming of Age" [TNG]).
2327: Graduates Starfleet Academy ("The First Duty" [TNG]).
2333: Assumes command of *U.S.S. Stargazer* ("Tapestry" [TNG]).
2355: *Stargazer* nearly destroyed at Maxia Zeta ("The Battle" [TNG]).
2364: Assumes command of *Enterprise*-D ("All Good Things..." [TNG]).
2266: Captured by the Borg ("Best of Both Worlds, Parts I and II" [TNG]).
2371: *Enterprise*-D destroyed *(Star Trek Generations)*.
2372: Assigned to command *Starship Enterprise*-E *(Star Trek: First Contact)*.

William Thomas Riker. "The Icarus Factor" (TNG) establishes that Riker had not seen his father for 15 years prior to the episode (2365), and that he was 15 years old at the time his father left him, suggesting a birth date of 2335.

Riker served aboard the *Starship Hood* under the command of Captain Robert DeSoto prior to his assignment to the *Enterprise*-D ("Encounter at Farpoint" [TNG]). His service aboard the *Hood* would have been sometime after his graduation from Starfleet Academy, probably around 2357, and 2364, the date for "Farpoint." Prior to the *Hood*, he served aboard the *U.S.S. Potemkin* as a lieutenant ("Peak Performance" [TNG]), although little has been established to determine a date for this. Riker was also stationed on the planet Betazed prior to his *Enterprise*-D assignment ("Menage à Troi" [TNG]).

At some point during his service aboard the *Hood*, Riker, as first officer, refused to allow Captain DeSoto to beam down

to planet Altair III, citing the danger involved. While DeSoto apparently disagreed with Riker's judgment, Riker was acting in accordance with his duty to protect the life of his captain from unnecessary risk ("Encounter at Farpoint" [TNG]).

The relationship between Will Riker and Deanna Troi. Some years prior to *Star Trek: The Next Generation*'s first season, Riker served on Troi's home planet of Betazed. At that time they became romantically involved, and Troi still occasionally calls him *Imzadi*, which is Betazoid for "beloved," even though both Troi and Riker had subsequent relationships with other people. Neither the exact dates nor the specifics of this relationship have been given, although "Menage à Troi" (TNG) establishes that Riker was a junior lieutenant assigned to Betazed and that Troi was a psychology student at the time.

2335: Born in Valdez, Alaska on Earth ("The Icarus Factor" [TNG]).
2337: His mother dies ("The Icarus Factor" [TNG]).
2350: Abandoned by father ("The Icarus Factor" [TNG]).
2353: Enters Starfleet Academy ("Chain of Command, Part I" [TNG]).
2357: Graduates Starfleet Academy ("Chain of Command, Part I" [TNG]).
2357: Assigned to *Starship Pegasus* ("The *Pegasus*" [TNG]).
2358: *Starship Pegasus* believed destroyed ("The *Pegasus*" [TNG]).
2359: Becomes romantically involved with Deanna Troi ("Encounter at Farpoint" [TNG], "The *Pegasus*" [TNG]).
2359: Assigned to planet Betazed ("Second Chances" [TNG]).
2361: Assigned to *Starship Potemkin* "Second Chances" [TNG]).
2361: Duplicated during rescue mission at Nervala IV "Second Chances" [TNG]).
2361: Breaks up with Deanna Troi "Second Chances" [TNG]).
2364: Transferred from *Starship Hood* to *Enterprise*-D ("Encounter at Farpoint" [TNG]).
2372: Assigned to Starship *Enterprise*-E (*Star Trek: First Contact*).

Thomas Riker. A duplicate of Will Riker, created in a transporter accident at planet Nervala IV in 2361. The duplicate lived alone at the Nervala IV science outpost until rescued by the *Enterprise*-D in 2369. The duplicate adopted his middle name, Thomas, to distinguish himself from his identical twin, and served briefly aboard the *Starship Gandhi*, before joining the Maquis. ("Second Chances" [TNG]). Tom was arrested by Cardassian authorities in 2371 and sentenced to

life imprisonment for his Maquis activities. We don't know what happened to Tom after this point, although Kira Nerys vowed to free him ("Defiant" [DS9]). Note that "Second Chances" seems to imply that the two Rikers were absolutely identical at the time they were duplicated. One materialized on the ship, while the other was reflected back to the outpost. In that sense, Tom has just as valid a claim to being the "original" William T. Riker as does his twin.

Data. The crew of the *U.S.S. Tripoli* discovered Data 26 years prior to "Datalore" (TNG), (2364), suggesting a reactivation date of 2338. The computer record in "Measure of a Man" (TNG) establishes that Data had been honored with the Decoration for Gallantry, the Medal of Honor with Clusters, the Legion of Honor, and the Star Cross. No dates were associated with any of these awards, although they were presumably awarded prior to the episode's date of 2365.

We know little of Data's early days in Starfleet. He was once on the *Starship Trieste*, where he passed through an unstable wormhole. This event, mentioned in "Clues" (TNG), was apparently prior to 2367, but nothing else is known about it or about Data on the *Trieste*.

2335: Activated at Omicron Theta colony ("Inheritance" [TNG]).
2336: Abandoned at Omicron Theta when colony is destroyed ("Datalore" [TNG]).
2338: Discovered by *Starship Tripoli* personnel ("Datalore" [TNG]).
2341: Enters Starfleet Academy ("Conundrum" [TNG]).
2345: Graduates Starfleet Academy ("Conundrum" [TNG]).
2364: Assigned to *Enterprise*-D. ("Encounter at Farpoint" [TNG]).
2366: Builds daughter, Lal ("The Offspring" [TNG]).
2370: Obtains emotion chip from Lore. ("Descent, Part II" [TNG]).
2370: Meets "mother," Juliana Tainer ("Inheritance" [TNG]).
2371: Installs emotion chip (*Star Trek Generations*).
2372: Assigned to Starship *Enterprise*-E (*Star Trek: First Contact*).

Deanna Troi. The computer bio screen in "Conundrum" (TNG) suggests that Troi was born in 2336. We have established that Deanna Troi's father, Ian Andrew Troi, was a human Starfleet officer who married Deanna's Betazoid mother, Lwaxana. Troi's father is further established to be deceased ("Half a Life" [TNG], et al.), but the circumstances of his death have not been established. When Troi was studying psychology at the University of Betazed, Tam Elbrun, who later

became a Starfleet specialist in contact with alien life, was her patient ("Tin Man" [TNG]).

When Deanna was a child, she was genetically bonded with Wyatt Miller, a human, who is the son of Steven Miller, close friend of Deanna's father. The exact ages of Deanna and Wyatt were not established, but such bonding at childhood is still a common Betazoid custom, and generally results in marriage when both children reach adulthood. The marriage was never performed ("Haven" [TNG]).

The last few episodes of *Star Trek: The Next Generation* hinted very strongly at a budding romantic relationship with Worf, but neither of the *Star Trek* features produced since then has made clear what, if anything, developed between them. Worf's joining of the Deep Space 9 crew in 2372 might also seem to imply that any relationship was concluded by that point.

2336: Born on planet Betazed ("Conundrum" [TNG]).
2343: Ian Andrew Troi, her father, dies ("Dark Page" [TNG]).
2359: Becomes romantically involved with Will Riker ("Encounter at Farpoint" [TNG], "The *Pegasus*" [TNG]).
2361: Breaks up with Will Riker ("Second Chances" [TNG]).
2364: Assigned to *Enterprise*-D ("Encounter at Farpoint' [TNG]).
2370: Promoted to commander ("Thine Own Self" [TNG]).
2372: Assigned to Starship *Enterprise*-E (*Star Trek: First Contact*).

Beverly C. Crusher. The episode "Conspiracy" (TNG) establishes that *Horatio* captain Walker Keel was one of Picard's closest friends and that he introduced Beverly to Jack Crusher. No date is given for this, although this would have to had been sometime prior to Wesley Crusher's birth in 2349.

Beverly's biographical data screen in "Conundrum" (TNG) suggests her maiden name was Beverly Howard and that she was born in 2324. This is supported by the fact that her

grandmother's name was Felisia Howard ("Sub Rosa" [TNG]). At some point early in her life, Beverly was with her grandmother at the Arvada III colony, and helped care for the survivors of a terrible tragedy after the colony's medical supplies were exhausted ("The Arsenal of Freedom" [TNG]).

2324: Born Beverly Howard ("Conundrum" [TNG]).
2342: Enters Starfleet Academy medical school ("Conundrum" [TNG]).
2348: Marries Jack Crusher ("Family" [TNG]).
2349: Son Wesley Crusher born ("Evolution" [TNG]).
2350: Graduates medical school ("Conundrum" [TNG]).
2354: Husband killed serving on *U.S.S. Stargazer* ("True Q" [TNG]).
2364: Assigned to *U.S.S. Enterprise*-D ("Encounter at Farpoint" [TNG]).
2365: Serves as head of Starfleet Medical ("The Child" [TNG]).
2366: Returns to *U.S.S. Enterprise*-D ("Evolution" [TNG]).
2370: Grandmother, Felisia Howard, dies ("Sub Rosa" [TNG]).
2372: Assigned to Starship *Enterprise*-E (*Star Trek: First Contact*).

Geordi La Forge. "Imaginary Friend" (TNG) establishes Geordi's father to have been an exozoologist, and his mother to have been a command officer, both members of Starfleet. Geordi recalled that his parents were always on the move, sometimes living together, other times separately. As a child, Geordi spent time with his father, studying invertebrates in the Modean system. He also lived with his mother on an outpost near the Romulan Neutral Zone. Geordi's bio screen in "Cause and Effect" (TNG) suggests that he was born in 2335.

In "The Next Phase" (TNG), Picard mentioned that the first time he met La Forge was when Geordi was a young officer assigned to pilot Picard on an inspection tour. Picard recalled having made an offhanded remark about the engine, and Geordi stayed up all night that evening refitting the shuttle's fusion initiators. Picard was so impressed by this that he knew he wanted Geordi on his next command. This was presumably before Picard's assignment to the *Enterprise*-D in 2364.

2335: Born ("Cause and Effect" [TNG]).
2353: Enters Starfleet Academy ("Cause and Effect" [TNG]).
2357: Graduates Starfleet Academy ("Conundrum" [TNG]).
2362: Aboard *Starship Victory* ("Identity Crisis" [TNG]).

2364: Transferred to *Enterprise*-D ("Encounter at Farpoint" [TNG]).
2365: Promoted to chief engineer ("The Child" [TNG]).
2370: Mother killed in destruction of *Starship Hera* ("Interface" [TNG]).
2371: Undergoes surgery to receive ocular implants *(Star Trek: First Contact)*.
2372: Assigned to Starship *Enterprise*-E *(Star Trek: First Contact)*.

Worf. The first Klingon in Starfleet was six years old at the time of the Khitomer massacre (2346), suggesting a birth date of 2340. Much has been established about Worf's early years, but little is known about Nikolai Rozhenko, his adoptive human brother. Nikolai, the biological son of Sergey and Helena Rozhenko, was mentioned in "Heart of Glory" (TNG), but little has been established beyond the fact of his existence and the fact that they spent their formative years on the farm world of Gault, prior to moving to Earth, and that he dropped out of Starfleet Academy when he found it not to his liking. We actually saw Nikolai in "Homeward" (TNG), and he remained with the natives of Boraal on planet Vacca VI. Note that this is not the same person as Kurn, who is Worf's natural Klingon brother, seen in "Sins of the Father" (TNG) etc.

2340: Born on Klingon Homeworld ("The Bonding" [TNG]).
2346: Orphaned in Khitomer massacre; adopted by Starfleet officer Sergey Rozhenko ("Sins of the Father" [TNG]).
2357: First Klingon to enter Starfleet Academy ("Heart of Glory" [TNG]).
2361: Graduates Starfleet Academy ("Conundrum" [TNG]).
2364: Assigned to *Enterprise*-D ("Encounter at Farpoint" [TNG]).
2365: Promoted to security chief ("The Child" [TNG]).
2366: Son Alexander born ("Reunion" [TNG]).
2366: Sentenced to discommendation by Klingon High Council ("Sins of the Father" [TNG]).
2367: Resigns Starfleet commission ("Redemption, Part I" [TNG]).
2368: Gowron restores family name, returns to Starfleet ("Redemption, Part II" [TNG]).
2369: Involved with ascendance of second Kahless to the throne ("Rightful Heir" [TNG]).
2371: Promoted to Lieutenant Commander *(Star Trek Generations)*.
2371: Goes on extended leave to planet Boreth ("Way of the Warrior" [DS9]).

2372: Assigned to station Deep Space 9 ("Way of the Warrior" [DS9]).
2372: Opposes Gowron, stripped of family titles ("Way of the Warrior" [DS9]).
2372: Brother, Kurn, has memory wiped ("The Sons of Mogh" [DS9]).

Natasha Yar. Tasha said she was 15 years old at the time

she escaped from the failed colony at Turkana IV ("The Naked Now" [TNG]), and "Legacy" (TNG), (set in 2367) is 15 years after that escape, suggesting a birth date of 2337. Tasha, of course, died in 2364 ("Skin of Evil" [TNG]). Another Tasha, from an alternate timeline, ("Yesterday's Enterprise" [TNG]), had a half-Romulan daughter, Sela, who became a powerful Romulan operative, ("Redemption, Parts I and II" [TNG]), but we don't know what happened to Sela after the attempted Vulcan coup in 2368 ("Unification, Parts I and II" [TNG]).

2337: Born at colony on planet Turkana IV ("The Naked Now" [TNG]).
2342: Orphaned on Turkana IV ("The Naked Now" [TNG]).
2352: Flees Turkana IV and joins Starfleet ("Legacy" [TNG]).
2364: Assigned to Enterprise-D ("All Good Things..." [TNG]).
2364: Dies at planet Vagra II ("Skin of Evil" [TNG]).

Wesley Crusher. Wesley was 17 years old in "Evolution" (TNG), set in 2366, suggesting a birth date of 2349. As of this writing, we do not know what happened to Wesley after he went off with the Traveler in 2370 to explore time and space as seen in "Journey's End" (TNG).

2348: Born ("Evolution" [TNG]).

2364: Made acting ensign ("Where No One Has Gone Before" [TNG]).

2364: Fails to gain entrance to Starfleet Academy ("Coming of Age" [TNG]).

2367: Enters Starfleet Academy ("Final Mission" [TNG]).

2368: Admits to coverup in fatal accident, formally reprimanded ("The First Duty" [TNG]).

2370: Resigns Starfleet Academy to explore with the Traveler ("Journey's End" [TNG]).

Ro Laren. Ro served aboard the *U.S.S. Wellington* prior to her assignment to the *Enterprise*-D. She was court-martialed after a mission to Garon II in which she disobeyed orders and eight members of the *Wellington* away team were killed. Ro was released from prison on Jaros II after agreeing to duty aboard the *Enterprise*-D in 2368 on a crucial diplomatic mission with Bajoran terrorists ("Ensign Ro" [TNG]). No time frame has been established for her *Wellington* assignment or her subsequent court-martial. These events clearly had to take place prior to "Ensign Ro," but were apparently after 2364, since her computer bio screen in "Conundrum" (TNG) gave this as the date of her graduation from Starfleet Academy. Ro was last seen in "Preemptive Strike" (TNG), when she resigned Starfleet to join the Maquis.

Guinan. The mysterious hostess of Ten-Forward remains a significant unknown, although we know she is of El-Aurian descent, and is at least five hundred years old, since we saw her younger self on Earth in Samuel Clemens's era ("Time's Arrow, Parts I and II" [TNG]). She was less than seven hundred years old, since that's how old she said her father was in "Rascals" (TNG). Guinan said she'd been in serious trouble once, and had extricated herself only because she'd trusted Captain Picard. This was presumably before her joining the *Enterprise*-D, per-

haps even before her travels aboard the *Stargazer* with Picard. Guinan once mentioned she had several children and an uncle named Terkim, her mother's brother ("Hollow Pursuits" [TNG]). We don't know what happened to Guinan after the crash of the *Enterprise*-D in 2370 *(Star Trek Generations)*.

Katherine Pulaski. The former *Enterprise*-D chief medical officer was married three times prior to her *Enterprise*-D tour of duty ("The Icarus Factor" [TNG], 2365). She noted that she remains good friends with all three exes. Prior to 2365, Pulaski wrote a ground-breaking scientific paper entitled "Linear Models of Viral Propagation" ("Unnatural Selection" [TNG]). We don't know what happened to Pulaski after she left the *Enterprise*-D at the end of that year.

Boothby. The wise old groundskeeper at Starfleet Academy, mentioned in "Final Mission" (TNG) and "The Game" (TNG), was reunited with Picard in "The First Duty" (TNG). Boothby alluded to some incident during Picard's academy days in which Picard was involved in a fight and thereafter nearly resigned from Starfleet. This was probably not the incident with the Nausicaans from "Samaritan Snare" (TNG), because "Tapestry" (TNG) clearly puts the fight after Picard's graduation from the academy. Boothby said he was then about as old as Picard was at the time of "The First Duty," suggesting Boothby was around 105 years old at that point (2368).

APPENDIX C: NOTES ON STAR TREK: DEEP SPACE NINE CHARACTERS

Editors' note: Because Star Trek: Deep Space Nine *and* Star Trek: Voyager *are still in weekly production at this writing, we have indulged in relatively little conjecture about these characters' past, since it is still very likely that upcoming episodes will reveal more details about their backgrounds.*

Benjamin Lafayette Sisko. We conjecture that Sisko was born in 2332. He was married to Jennifer Sisko, who was killed in 2368 aboard the *U.S.S. Saratoga* in the battle of Wolf 359. Benjamin survived the battle with his son, Jake. ("Emissary" [DS9]). Prior to Sisko's tour of duty aboard the *U.S.S. Saratoga*, Sisko served as executive officer under Captain Leyton aboard the *Starship Okinawa* (established in "Homefront" [DS9]). We don't know anything else about Sisko's time on the *Okinawa*, except that Leyton was highly impressed with him. Sisko's timeline:

2332: Born in New Orleans on Earth ("Emissary" [DS9]).
2350: Enters Starfleet Academy ("Emissary" [DS9]).
2354: Graduates Starfleet Academy, meets future wife, Jennifer ("Emissary" [DS9]).
2355: Son Jake Sisko born ("Move Along Home" [DS9]).
2367: Wife killed in battle of Wolf 359 ("Emissary" [DS9]).
2367: Assigned to Utopia Planitia Fleet Yards ("Emissary" [DS9]).
2369: Assigned to command station Deep Space 9 ("Emissary" [DS9]).
2371: Becomes romantically involved with Kasidy Yates ("Family Business" [DS9]).
2371: Promoted to captain ("The Adversary" [DS9]).

Kira Nerys. Kira was born during the Cardassian occupation of Bajor, and the occupation shaped her life. She joined the Bajoran underground at age 12, and fought for her people's freedom until 2369, when the Cardassians withdrew from her homeworld.

2343: Born on planet Bajor ("The Maquis, Part I" [DS9]).
2346: Mother dies at refugee camp ("Second Skin" [DS9]).
2355: Joins Bajoran underground ("The Circle" [DS9]).
2369: Assigned to station Deep Space 9 as second-in-command. ("Emissary" [DS9]).
2370: Romantically involved with Vedek Bareil ("Shadowplay" [DS9]).
2371: Bareil dies ("Life Support" [DS9]).
2372: Romantically involved with Shakaar ("Crossfire" [DS9]).

Jadzia Dax. The Dax symbiont has had eight different hosts to date (not counting Verad, who stole the Dax symbiont for a few hours in 2370 as seen in "Invasive Procedures" [DS9]). We know very little about Dax's early hosts, although "Facets" (DS9) gave us a list of all of the hosts, as well as some personal information about them. Note that we don't have even conjectural dates prior to Audrid's death, so those earlier hosts do not appear in the main body of the Chronology.

Lela was Dax's first host. Lela Dax was one of the first women ever to serve as a council member on Trill. "To the Death" (DS9) establishes that Lela had a son named Ahjess. We do not know when the Dax symbiont was born, nor when Lela was joined. Jadzia Dax noted on occasion that she was over 300 years old, which would seem to put Lela's joining around the mid-21st century. (If Lela, Tobin, Emony, and Audrid all had joined lives that averaged 72 years each, Dax's joining with Lela would have taken place around 1996!)

Tobin Dax was a shy, technically knowledgeable man who was proud of the fact that he'd worked on developing another remarkable proof of Fermat's last theorem. Jadzia Dax inherited her love of science and mathematics from Tobin. "Rejoined" (DS9) establishes that Tobin enjoyed dabbling in slight-of-hand magic tricks. We do not know when Tobin was joined, nor when he died.

Emony Dax was a professional gymnast. Jadzia Dax's interest in Klingon martial arts probably came from her. We do not have dates for Emony's joining or death.

Audrid was Dax's fourth host. She was a member of the Symbiosis Commission and a mother who had at least two children. "Babel" (DS9) establishes that Dax had not had a female host for 80 years before that episode, suggesting that Audrid died around 2289. We're arbitrarily assuming that she actually died in 2284, five years earlier, since "Equilibrium" (DS9) establishes that Torias died in 2285, and "Blood Oath" (DS9) establishes that by 2289, Curzon Dax was already a well-known Federation mediator.

Torias Dax was a test pilot who lived a brief joined life before dying in a shuttle accident. He was joined in 2284 (based on Audrid's assumed death date) and married a scientist named Nilani Kahn, who was also a joined Trill. Torias died in 2285 ("Equilibrium" [DS9], "Rejoined" [DS9]). We met Nilani in "Rejoined."

Joran Dax was a musician and a violent criminal. Joran hosted the Dax symbiont for only six months in 2285, as revealed in "Equilibrium" [DS9]). Trill authorities have attempted to eradicate all record of Joran Dax's joining, and our people promised to keep the secret.

Curzon, Dax's most recent past host, rejected Jadzia as a host candidate ("Playing God" [DS9]), but in "Facets" (DS9) we learned that it was because he was in love with Jadzia. Later, Curzon felt guilty over having been unfair to Jadzia, so he allowed her to return to the initiate program. Curzon was joined from 2285 until his death in 2367 ("Dax" [DS9]). We saw Curzon briefly in "Emissary" (DS9).

Jadzia was Dax's eighth host, and was joined in 2367. (She was generally regarded as Dax's seventh host, since the Trill authorities were largely successful in suppressing knowledge of Joran Dax. "Equilibrium" [DS9]). Jadzia Dax joined the Federation Starfleet and served as a science officer on station Deep Space 9. Prior to her joining, Jadzia had earned academic honors for her work in exobiology, zoology, astrophysics, and exoarchaeology ("Dax" [DS9]). (The Dax symbiont was briefly stolen from Jadzia by Verad in 2370 ["Invasive Procedures' (DS9)], but he apparently wasn't considered to have been a "real" host.)

Once again, we know very little about Dax's first few hosts. We don't have dates for Lela, Tobin, or Emony. The first reasonably firm host date is for the death of Audrid, Dax's fourth host. To summarize known data points:

2284: Audrid dies, Torias joined ("Babel" [DS9]).
2285: Torias joined ("Equilibrium" [DS9]; "Rejoined" [DS9]).
2285: Torias dies, Joran joined and dies ("Equilibrium" [DS9]).
2285: Curzon joined ("Equilibrium" [DS9]).
2341: Jadzia is born ("Emissary" [DS9]).
2367: Curzon dies; Jadzia joined ("Dax" [DS9]).
2369: Jadzia Dax assigned to station Deep Space 9 ("Emissary" [DS9]).
2370: Verad briefly steals Dax symbiont ("Invasive Procedures" [DS9]).

Dr. Julian Subatoi Bashir. The son of a diplomat, Julian Bashir fancied himself an adventurer, so he volunteered for duty at station Deep Space 9, a distant and dangerous outpost on the frontier of Federation space.

2341: Born ("Distant Voices" [DS9]).
2359: Enters Starfleet medical school (conjecture).
2367: Graduates medical school (conjecture).
2369: Assigned to station Deep Space 9 ("Emissary" [DS9]).
2371: Nominated for Carrington Award ("Prophet Motive" [DS9]).

Miles Edward O'Brien. Unfortunately, there is much about O'Brien's background that appears to be confusing. In some episodes of *Star Trek: The Next Generation*, O'Brien appeared to be a Starfleet officer of various ranks, while "Family" (TNG) and "Starship Down" (DS9), seem to make clear that he did not attend the academy and was not an officer. (While Starfleet is modeled after the present-day Navy, there are areas in which Starfleet seems significantly different than the Navy. This might be one, although it is not clear what changes would account for O'Brien's apparent variations in rank.)

The terrible Setlik III massacre (first mentioned in "The Wounded" [TNG]), appears to have taken place in 2347, since "Realm of Fear" (TNG) establishes that he had been working with transporters for 22 years prior to the episode (2369), and in "Paradise" [DS9], he says he had worked a transporter for the first time at Setlik III. This would put O'Brien's Starfleet enlistment at some time prior to 2347. If O'Brien was 19 years old at the time of Setlik III, this would seem to put his birth at 2328. (This would make O'Brien 44 years old during *Star Trek: Deep Space Nine's* fourth season, set in 2372).

However, "Tribunal" (DS9) seems to imply that Setlik III took place around 2362, eight years before that episode (2370). This is because *Rutledge* crew mem-

ber Raymond Boone, captured by the Cardassians at Setlik III, was released eight years before that episode. If we accept that data point, O'Brien's birth could have been as late as 2343 (which would make him 29 years old during the fourth season), even though this seems to contradict information from other episodes. Until another episode clears matters up, we will use the 2347 date for the Setlik III massacre, but we will refrain from speculating on O'Brien's birth in the main body of the Chronology. We will rationalize that Boone was captured in 2347, and that he was held until 2362. Note that "Tribunal" suggests O'Brien was still serving on the *Rutledge* at the time of Boone's release.

2347: Serves aboard *U.S.S. Rutledge*; Setlik III massacre ("The Wounded" [TNG]).

2364: Assigned to *U.S.S. Enterprise*-D ("Encounter at Farpoint" [TNG]).

2266: Marries Keiko Ishikawa ("Data's Day" [TNG]).

2368: Daughter Molly born ("Disaster" [TNG]).

2368: Mother dies ("Whispers" [DS9]).

2369: Transferred to station Deep Space 9 ("Emissary" [DS9]).

2369: Father, Michael O'Brien, remarries ("Whispers" [DS9]).

2371: Dies. Replaced by Miles O'Brien from alternate timeline ("Visionary" [DS9]).

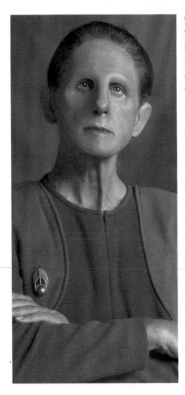

Odo. We have learned that Odo was one of a hundred changeling infants sent off into the galaxy by the Founders of the Dominion. A powerful urge to return home was implanted into these children, so that they would help the reclusive Founders explore the galaxy without leaving their homeworld. ("The Search, Part II" [DS9]). We don't know when Odo was sent to the Alpha Quadrant, nor do we know when he was discovered in the Denorios Belt in the Bajoran system, nor when he was studied by Dr. Mora Pol at the Bajoran Institute of Science. Some of the data points we do know are:

2363: Meets Gul Dukat ("Necessary Evil" [DS9]).

2365: Begins working as security chief at Terok Nor ("Necessary Evil" [DS9]).

2369: Works for Starfleet when Federation takes over station ("Emissary" [DS9]).

2371: Travels to Founders' homeworld to meet his peo-

ple ("The Search, Part I" [DS9]).

2371: Kills a fellow changeling ("The Adversary" [DS9]).

2372: Shape-shifting powers removed by the Founders ("Broken Link" [DS9]).

Quark. We don't really have a basis on which to conjecture Quark's age, and we know little about his timeline prior to the point when he reached his Age of Ascension and left home in 2351.

2351: Leaves home to seek his fortune ("Family Business" [DS9]).

2363: Romantically involved with Natima Lang ("Profit and Loss" [DS9]).

2365: Arrives at Terok Nor, opens bar ("Emissary" [DS9]).

2369: Serves as grand nagus for a week ("The Nagus" [DS9]).

2371: Mother accused of earning a profit ("Family Business" [DS9]).

2372: Negotiates with labor union ("Bar Association" [DS9]).

2372: Ferengi business license revoked by FCA ("Body Parts" [DS9]).

Jake Sisko. "The Visitor" (DS9) suggests that Jake will continue to pursue his writing and that he may become a highly-respected author. Even though Jake's future will undoubtedly unfold on a somewhat different path from that seen in "The Visitor," we have already seen (in "The Muse" [DS9]) that he has written the first draft for *Anselem*.

2355: Born ("Move Along Home" [DS9]).

2357: Mother killed in Battle of Wolf 359 ("Emissary" [DS9]).

2369: Moves to Deep Space 9 with his father ("Emissary" [DS9]).

2371: Declines scholarship to Pennington School ("Explorers" [DS9]).

2372: Writes first draft of *Anselem*, his first novel ("The Muse" [DS9]).

Elim Garak. The back story for Garak should probably be taken with a considerable grain of salt, since Garak frequently intimated that many of his stories were lies. We believe that Garak was once a member of Cardassia's elite Obsidian Order intelligence agency, serving under Enabran

Tain. While part of the Obsidian Order, Garak was apparently responsible for the downfall and execution of Gul Dukat's father, alluded to in "Civil Defense" (DS9), et al. Garak also hinted that he once served as a gardener in the Cardassian embassy on Romulus, where he may have played a part in the assassination of several prominent Romulan officials. ("Broken Link" [DS9]). Even if these stories are true, we don't have dates for them.
Garak was apparently forced out of the Obsidian Order in 2368, at which time Tain had him exiled to station Terok Nor, which later became known as Deep Space 9 ("The Wire" [DS9]). The events to which we do have dates are:

2368: Exiled to station Terok Nor ("Profit and Loss" [DS9]).
2371: Attempts comeback with Enabran Tain ("Improbable Cause" [DS9]).

APPENDIX D: NOTES ON STAR TREK: VOYAGER CHARACTERS

Editors' note: Star Trek: Voyager, *like* Star Trek: Deep Space Nine, *is still in weekly production as of this writing. We have therefore refrained from extensive conjecture about these characters' backgrounds, since future episodes will undoubtedly reveal more information.*

Kathryn Janeway. The commander of the *U.S.S. Voyager* once served as science officer aboard the *Starship Al-Batani* under Tom Paris's father. We don't know a time frame for this assignment, except that it was before the *Voyager* was lost in the Delta Quadrant.

2371. ("Caretaker" [VGR]). At the time this edition of the Chronology was compiled, we knew little about her past, and did not even have conjectural dates for her academy years. The only major events we have are:

2371. Assumes command of *Starship Voyager* ("Caretaker'" [VGR]).

2371. Lost in the Delta Quadrant ("Caretaker'" [VGR]).

Chakotay. Although he attended Starfleet Academy, Chakotay resigned from the service in order to join the Maquis and fight in defense of his homeworld against the Cardassians. We don't know exactly when he quit Starfleet, although it was after he graduated from the academy, but before *Voyager* was lost in 2371. (It was probably after the signing of the Cardassian peace treaty of 2370, first mentioned in "Journey's End" [TNG]).

2335. Born ("Tattoo" [VGR]).

2350: Enters Starfleet Academy ("Tattoo" [VGR]).

2354: Graduates Starfleet Academy ("Tattoo" [VGR]).

2371: Father, Kolopak, dies ("Initiations" [VGR]).

2371: Lost in Delta Quadrant aboard a Maquis ship; joins *Voyager* crew ("Caretaker" [VGR]).

Thomas Eugene Paris. Prior to his expulsion from Starfleet and prior to his service aboard the *Voyager*, Tom Paris once served aboard the *Starship Exeter*, as briefly mentioned in "Non Sequitur" (VGR). We don't know many specifics (including date) of Paris's crime (and subsequent confession) established in "Caretaker" (VGR) that led to his expulsion and prison sentence. In 2372, Paris became the first pilot to break the warp 10 barrier, putting him in the same league as Orville Wright, Chuck Yaegar, and Zefram Cochrane. ("Threshold" [VGR]). Ironically, no one in the Federation knows about this momentous event.

2371: Paroled from Federation prison, joins *Voyager* crew; lost in the Delta Quadrant ("Caretaker" [VGR]).

2372: First pilot to break warp 10 barrier ("Threshold" [VGR]).

Tuvok. "Flashback" (VGR) establishes that Tuvok served aboard the *Excelsior* under Captain Sulu from 2293 to 2298, at which time he resigned from the service. He subsequently attempted to undergo the *Kohlinar* discipline, but abandoned this after six years when he underwent *pon farr* and married T'Pel. They raised a family, and Tuvok later returned to Starfleet, some five decades after his resignation. At some undetermined point prior to *Voyager*, Tuvok once served as Janeway's tactical officer. "Flashback" also establishes that at the time of Tuvok's service aboard the *Excelsior* in 2293, his parents were both aboard the *U.S.S. Yorktown*.

2264: Born ("Flashback" [VGR]).

2289: Enters Starfleet Academy ("Flashback" [VGR]).

2293: Graduates Starfleet Academy; assigned to *U.S.S. Excelsior* ("Flashback" [VGR]).

2298: Resigns from Starfleet, attempts *Kohlinar*

("Flashback" [VGR]).
2304: Marries T'Pel ("Ex Post Facto" [VGR]).
2349: Returns to Starfleet, serves aboard *U.S.S. Wyoming.* ("Flashback" [VGR]).
2371: Lost in Delta Quadrant aboard *Starship Voyager* ("Caretaker" [VGR]).

B'Elanna Torres. We know few specifics about B'Elanna's past except that her father was human and her mother was Klingon. B'Elanna spent her early years at the Federation colony on Kessik IV. After her father abandoned her at age five, B'Elanna and her mother moved to the Klingon Homeworld. B'Elanna enrolled in Starfleet Academy, but dropped out after her second year because she couldn't take the discipline. She subsequently joined the Maquis. Because we don't have a conjectural birth date for Torres, we can't determine dates for these data points. All we know is:

2371: Joins *Voyager* crew ("Caretaker" [VGR]).
2371: Assigned as *Voyager* chief engineer ("Parallax" [VGR]).

Harry Kim. Kim was born in 2349, the same year as Wesley Crusher. Kim was an only child. He completed the academy in 2371 ("Eye of the Needle" [VGR]) and the *U.S.S. Voyager* was his first posting. ("Caretaker" [VGR]). At the time *Voyager* was lost in the Delta Quadrant, he had a serious relationship with a woman named Libby, who lived in San Francisco ("Non Sequitur" [VGR]).

2349: Born ("Eye of the Needle" [VGR]).
2370: Graduates Starfleet Academy ("Non Sequitur" [VGR]).

2371: Assigned to *Starship Voyager*, lost in the Delta Quadrant ("Caretaker" [VGR]).
2372: Dies. Replaced by counterpart from alternate continuum ("Deadlock" [VGR]).

Kes. Even though Kes was only a year old at the time she joined

the *Voyager* crew, she was nearly fully grown. This is because her people, the Ocampa, have a life span of about nine years, so Kes was essentially an adult in 2371. We therefore assume that her year prior to joining the *Voyager* crew was as rich as any human childhood, even though we don't know any specifics.

2370: Born ("Elogium" [VGR]).
2371: Father, Benaren dies ("Resolutions" [VGR]).
2371: Joins *Voyager* crew ("Caretaker" [VGR]).
2372: Undergoes premature elogium ("Elogium" [VGR]).

Neelix. As an independent trader, Neelix had considerable experience dealing with many cultures in the Delta Quadrant. This knowledge made him a valuable asset to the *Voyager* crew, although Neelix quickly found other ways, including his service as ship's cook, to make himself indispensable. We don't know when Neelix was born, but it was before his family was killed when the terrible metreon cascade killed everyone on Rinax. At the time, Neelix may have already been considered an adult, since he was living away from his family on planet Talax.

2356: Family killed by metreon cascade ("Jetrel" [VGR]).
2371: Joins *Voyager* crew ("Caretaker" [VGR]).

Emergency Medical Hologram (The Doctor). By contrast, *Voyager's* Emergency Hologram Program was installed only shortly before the ship's launch in 2371, so it is unlikely that many biographical data points remain to be discovered. On the other hand, the Doctor's program was extremely large and complex, so it seems likely that there are many aspects to his personality and capabilities that have not yet been explored. It does appear that the Emergency Medical Hologram was standard equipment on recent Starfleet vessels, since another version of the Doctor was seen briefly aboard the *Enterprise*-E in *Star Trek: First Contact.*

2371: Installed aboard *Starship Voyager.* ("Projections" [VGR]).
2371: Activated upon death of *Voyager's* chief medical officer ("Caretaker" [VGR]).
2373: Program reinitialized ("The Swarm" [VGR]).
2373: Gains ability to exist outside of sickbay ("Future's End, Part II" [VGR]).

APPENDIX E: NOTES ON STARFLEET AND THE STARSHIPS ENTERPRISE

Editors' note: Despite the fact that we've seen literally hundreds of hours of film aboard the various Starships Enterprise, *we know remarkably little about most of the ships, and even less about the Starfleet as a whole. Part of this is the effective use of a trick of drama: The episodes and movies show relatively little of the ships and the fleet, but the viewers' imaginations fills in much more than the studio could ever afford to build. (Paramount spends a lot of money making these shows, but nowhere near what even one starship would cost!)*

The spaceship ***Enterprise.*** In *Star Trek: The Motion Picture,* Decker showed Ilia a display in the recreation room of various ships called *Enterprise.* Besides a wooden frigate, the aircraft carrier, the space shuttle, and the original television series starship, there was another spaceship *Enterprise* that appears to predate the starship. One can probably assume that this vessel was not designated as a starship, because the *Enterprise*-D has been established as the fifth starship to bear the name, and the previous four starships have all been accounted for. Nothing else has been officially established for this vessel, although we understand the design had actually been developed for a proposed Gene Roddenberry television project that never reached the production stage.

The original ***Starship Enterprise.*** This ship was apparently commissioned in 2245, a date derived from working backward from the 2266 date for the first season of the original series, taking into account such past events as Spock's tenure with Pike ("The Cage" [TOS] and "The Menagerie" [TOS]) as well as a conjectural five-year mission under the command of Captain Robert April. The ship was extensively refitted prior to *Star Trek: The Motion Picture,* which we con-

jecture took place in 2271. (In fact, the movie establishes that it takes place after the *Enterprise* has undergone 18 months of refitting in drydock. We assume that those 18 months began after Kirk's five-year mission, but it is possible that the ship might have had other assignments after the five-year mission, and before the ship returned to drydock.) This ship served Starfleet for many years during which it was refitted several times until it was destroyed in 2285 at the Genesis Planet *(Star Trek III: The Search for Spock).* Key dates for this ship include:

2245: Launched from San Francisco Yards under command of Robert April (conjecture).
2250: Christopher Pike assumes command (conjecture).
2252: Spock first serves aboard *Enterprise* ("The Menagerie" [TOS]).
2254: "The Cage" (TOS).
2256: Pike completes first five-year mission (conjecture).
2261: Pike completes second five-year mission (conjecture).
2264: Kirk assumes command, embarks on five-year mission (conjecture).
2265: "Where No Man Has Gone Before" (TOS).
2266-2269: Original *Star Trek* series.
2269: Major refit begins *(Star Trek: The Motion Picture).*
2271: *Star Trek: The Motion Picture.*
2277: Retired from exploratory service, assigned to Starfleet Academy *(Star Trek II: The Wrath of Khan).*
2285: *Star Trek II: The Wrath of Khan.*
2285: Destroyed at Genesis Planet *(Star Trek III: The Search for Spock).*

The *Enterprise*-A. The second starship to bear the name. (The first was, of course, the ship seen in the original *Star Trek* series and the first three movies.) This second ship was launched in 2286 *(Star Trek IV: The Voyage Home)* under the command of Captain Kirk. Kirk retired as commander, and the ship was apparently decommissioned in 2293 *(Star Trek VI: The Undiscovered Country).* The fact that the ship was apparently retired, not destroyed in action, might seem to suggest the possibility that this ship was later scrapped or that she became a museum piece. It is something of an puzzle why the ship was retired so soon after it had been launched. It has been speculated elsewhere that when the ship was launched in 2286, it had previously been in service under another name (possibly *Yorktown),* and that the ship was therefore quite a bit more than seven years old at the time it was retired.

> 2286: Launched under command of James T. Kirk *(Star Trek IV: The Voyage Home).*
> 2287: *Star Trek V: The Final Frontier.*
> 2293: Retired *(Star Trek VI: The Undiscovered Country.)*

The *Enterprise*-B. The third *Starship Enterprise,* an *Excelsior*-class vessel, remains a significant unknown. We saw the launch of this ship in 2293 *(Star Trek Generations)* under the command of Captain John Harriman, but know virtually nothing else about its history, except that Captain James Kirk was believed killed on its first voyage. The *Enterprise*-B would have to have been decommissioned or destroyed some

time prior to 2344, when its successor, the *Enterprise*-C, was nearly destroyed ("Yesterday's *Enterprise*" [TNG]).

> 2294: Launched under command of Captain John Harriman *(Star Trek Generations).*
> 2294: James T. Kirk believed killed on first flight *(Star Trek Generations).*

The *Enterprise*-C. Little is known, either, about the fourth *Enterprise*. This ship was an *Ambassador*-class vessel, and was established to have been virtually destroyed in 2344 while defending the Klingon outpost at Narendra III ("Yesterday's *Enterprise*" [TNG]). It was apparently launched after the decommissioning or destruction of the *Enterprise*-B, but there is nothing further to establish the date. Just prior to its destruction, the *Enterprise*-C was commanded by Captain Rachel Garrett.

> 2344: Presumed destroyed at Narendra III outpost ("Yesterday's Enterprise" [TNG]).
> 2366: Briefly emerges into the future before returning to 2344 ("Yesterday's Enterprise" [TNG]).

The *Enterprise*-D. We know more about this ship than any other Federation starship, since seven years of its adventures were chronicled in *Star Trek: The Next Generation.*

> 2363: Launched ("Lonely Among Us" [TNG]).
> 2364: Picard assumes command ("All Good Things..." [TNG]).
> 2364-2370: *Star Trek: The Next Generation.*
> 2371: Destroyed at planet Veridian III *(Star Trek Generations.)*

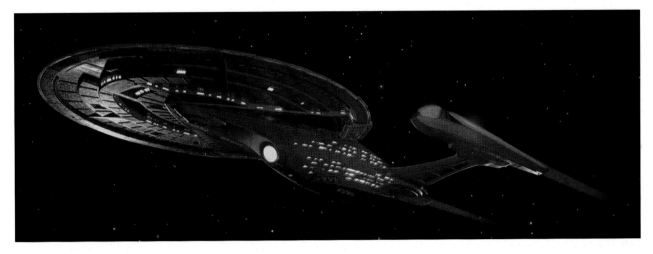

The *Enterprise*-E. The sixth and most recent *Starship Enterprise* is a *Sovereign*-class vessel, launched in 2372 under the command of Captain Jean-Luc Picard, with most of his senior staff from *Star Trek: The Next Generation*. Beyond its single appearance (as of this writing) in *Star Trek: First Contact*, we don't yet know much about this latest *Enterprise*.

    2372: Launched *(Star Trek: First Contact)*.
    2373: *Star Trek: First Contact*.

Station Deep Space 9. While technically not a Starfleet facility, Deep Space 9 was operated by Starfleet officers. We know little about the station's early years, when it was known as Terok Nor, a Cardassian mining station orbiting planet Bajor.

    2351: Built by Cardassian forces as mining station Terok Nor ("Babel" [DS9]).
    2369: Cardassians withdraw from Bajor, station now under Federation control ("Emissary" [DS9]).
    2371: *Starship Defiant* assigned to Deep Space 9 ("The Search, Part I" [DS9]).

The *Starship Voyager*. Starfleet probably assumes that the *Voyager* was destroyed in 2371 while searching for the missing Maquis ship. Starfleet had no way of knowing that the *Voyager* was swept into the Delta Quadrant by the Caretaker. ("Caretaker" [VGR]). There is a slight possibility that some messages, sent into the past through a microwormhole, were somehow delivered by Romulan scientist R'Mor. Although R'Mor died in 2367, it is possible that he made arrangements for the messages from *Voyager's* crew to be delivered in 2371. ("Eye of the Needle" [VGR]).

    2371: Launched ("Caretaker" [VGR]).
    2371: Lost in the Badlands, presumed destroyed ("Caretaker" [VGR]).

Establishment of the Prime Directive. One of the most important principles of the Federation's Starfleet is the Prime Directive, which prohibits interference in the normal development of any society. This rule, also known as Starfleet General Order Number One, was apparently instituted before Kirk took command of the *Enterprise* in 2264, but it is unclear exactly when this happened, or what events led to the adoption of the directive. "A Piece of the Action" (TOS) establishes that the Prime Directive had not yet been instituted in 2168, when the *U.S.S. Horizon* made contact with planet Iotia.

U.S.S. Hera. The science starship that was commanded by Geordi LaForge's mother was lost and presumed destroyed in 2370. What really happened to the ship was never revealed, although the entire crew was believed killed in the incident. ("Interface" [TNG]).

Starfleet cloaking device. Starfleet captain Erik Pressman was part of a conspiracy in 2358 to develop and test a Starfleet cloaking device in direct violation of the Treaty of Algeron. It was never revealed just how extensive this conspiracy was. Also, it was not clear what happened to Pressman and the others involved after the conspiracy was uncovered in 2370, and what was the Romulans' response to the revelation. "The *Pegasus*" (TNG).

APPENDIX F: NOTES ON SCIENCE AND TECHNOLOGY

Although the Star Trek *scenario is remarkably well detailed in the areas of science and technology, there are significant gaps in the backstory of how (and when) many of these things were developed.*

Return to the moon. At the time the original *Star Trek* series was made in the 1960s, it seemed perfectly logical that space projects like Apollo would continue, leading to ships that would travel to other planets and, eventually, to the stars. Few suspected that we would drastically curtail our space program after only a handful of moon landings. While today's space shuttle, the Mir space station, and robotic exploration projects continue to make important progress, there is a serious question as to when we will return to the moon, and when we will reach beyond to put humans on other planets. By *Star Trek's* 24th century, Earth's moon had been dramatically transformed and was home to some 50 million people. Lake Armstrong and New Berlin city were large enough to be clearly visible from Earth. Assuming that Lake Armstrong is, in fact, a large body of water (large enough to be visible from Earth), one might conclude that the Moon has been given an Earth-like atmosphere in *Star Trek's* time. *(Star Trek: First Contact).*

Invention of warp drive and first contact. Zefram Cochrane's historic invention of the space warp, first alluded to in "Metamorphosis" (TOS), was actually depicted in the motion picture *Star Trek: First Contact.* Based on information in "Metamorphosis," the first edition of this Chronology conjectured that Cochrane's first warp flight had taken place in 2061, although the film reveals that the actual date was 2063. The invention of faster-than-light travel led directly to Earth's first official contact with extraterrestrial life, and was the key to a renaissance of Earth's society in the late twenty-first century.

The invention of the transporter. We don't know when the transporter was invented. In "Masterpiece Society" [TNG], Geordi suggested that the transporter had been invented "over a century" prior to the episode, set in 2368. On the other hand, the transporter would have had to have been invented prior to "The Cage" (TOS), set in 2254, because we saw Captain Pike and company beam down to planet Talos IV. "Realm of Fear" (TNG) established that transporter psychosis was first diagnosed in 2209, which suggests that the transporter was invented prior to that date.

Invention of subspace radio. Although faster-than-light warp drive was developed by Zefram Cochrane in 2063, the invention of subspace radio had not occurred as late as 2168, when the *Starship Horizon* made contact with planet Sigma Iotia II. As a result, a message from that ship was not received by Starfleet for a century. ("A Piece of the Action" [TOS]). This would seem to imply that there was a significant period in history when warp-drive starships (and perhaps automated message drones) were the fastest means of interstellar communication, since radio was limited by the speed of light prior to the invention of subspace radio. On the other hand, "Balance of Terror" (TOS) establishes that the Romulan wars, which we conjecture ended around 2160, were ended by negotiations conducted entirely by subspace radio. Since this Chronology assumes that the *Star Trek* timeline is internally consistent, then one or more of our assumptions in dating the above events may be a little off, but there appears to be no clear way to determine which it might be until an episode or movie addresses the issue.

Invention of the replicator. We don't know when the replicator was invented or when it came into general use. It was definitely in existence during the first season of *Star Trek: The Next Generation* (2364). "Flashback" (VGR) establishes that replicators were *not* in use aboard Federation starships in 2293, suggesting that the original *Starship Enterprise* (circa 2266) did not have those handy devices. That ship had "food slots" that dispensed fully-prepared meals. In "Charlie X" (TOS), we heard the voice of the *Enterprise* chef (the voice of Gene Roddenberry!) suggesting that the crew's meals were prepared, synthetic food. This would seem to support the notion that replicators weren't used at this point and that the food slots were part of some kind of a delivery system.

Invention of the holodeck. Since the holodeck incorporates some measure of matter replication, it probably could not have been developed before the replicator. "Flashback" (VGR) establishes that starships in Captain Kirk's day did not have holodecks. On the other hand, the holodeck (and the holosuite), like present-day television, was probably large group of diverse inventions and refinements that were developed over a period of many years. It would therefore seem to be possible that more limited forms of holographic simulation or virtual reality could have been in use before the holodeck as we know it.

Recalibration of the warp scale. Starfleet used a different warp factor scale during the original *Star Trek* series (set in 2266-2269) than was in use during the time of *Star Trek: The Next Generation* (2364). The older warp scale was generally believed to designate speeds at the cube of the warp factor, so that a warp factor of two would indicate a speed of two to the third power, or eight times the speed of light. By the time of Captain Picard's *Starship Enterprise*-D, a different mathematical formula was in use that established warp factor 10 to be an infinite value at the absolute top of the scale. ("Threshold" [VGR] establishes warp factor 10 to be the mysterious transwarp phenomenon first mentioned in *Star Trek III: The Search For Spock*.) It is not known why the warp scale was recalibrated, or when this happened.

The warp scale recalibration had actually been suggested by *Star Trek: The Next Generation* story consultant David Gerrold, who proposed an absolute warp 10 speed limit for story reasons. He felt that some original *Star Trek* series episodes relied too heavily on scenes in which artificial danger was created by having Scotty worried that the *Enterprise* might blow up because of a high warp speed. Gerrold wanted to prevent episodes of the new show from having the *Enterprise*-D crew endangered by ever-increasing warp speeds. Putting warp 10 at the absolute top of the scale accomplished this goal, and making the scale asymptotic made it possible for the occasional god-like entity to cross the galaxy in the space of a commercial break.

A second recalibration of the warp scale apparently occurred in Q's anti-time future seen in "All Good Things..." (TNG), since we saw ships traveling at warp 13 in 2395. We know even less about this second recalibration, and frankly, we don't even know if it will come to pass in the "real" *Star Trek* timeline.

Development of hyronalin. According to Dr. McCoy in "The Deadly Years" (TOS), adrenaline-based treatments had been used for radiation sickness early in the atomic age. Although early research had been highly promising, adrenaline was abandoned shortly after the invention of hyronalin. Hyronalin was the treatment of choice by the year 2267, and was still in use by Starfleet in the 24th century, as evidenced by Dr. Crusher's treatment of *Enterprise*-D personnel in "Final Mission" (TNG).

Emergent intelligence entity. The entity brought into being in 2370 by the temporarily sentient *Enterprise*-D computer left the starship and has not been heard from since. Will this being grow and then later return to further interact with humankind? ("Emergence" [TNG]).

Ilia and Decker. Similarly, the joint life-form created when Ilia and Decker merged with the V'Ger entity has not been seen since the end of *Star Trek: The Motion Picture*. We know nothing of what became of them, nor anything further of the machine planet that intercepted the Voyager VI space probe.

The Guardian of Forever. Little was revealed about the Guardian of Forever's origin in "City On the Edge of Forever" (TOS), except that it was probably billions of years old. Neither have we learned anything about the Federation's later

handling of this remarkable artifact. It seems reasonable that something of such immense power would warrant extraordinary precautions to prevent misuse.

Vulcan development of spaceflight. *Star Trek: First Contact* establishes that the Vulcans had warp travel capability before Earth did. The Vulcans, in fact, had to have had interstellar spaceflight capability at least 2,000 years ago, since this was when dissidents left their Vulcan homeworld to found what became the Romulan Star Empire ("Gambit, Part II" [TNG]). The time frame and the circumstances of their first voyages into space are unknown, except that they probably occurred prior to that point.

APPENDIX G: NOTES ON PLANETS AND SOCIETIES

As with the preceding few appendices, this is primarily a collection of notes on what we don't *know about these elements of the* Star Trek *universe.*

Earth. In the *Star Trek* universe, the last decade of Earth's 20th century was marred by the Eugenics Wars, in which Khan Noonien Singh rose to power. (Oddly enough, Los Angeles, as seen in "Future's End, Parts I and II" [VGR], seems to have been spared the effects of this conflict). World War III, in the mid-21st century, was a nuclear conflict that cost millions of lives and wrought terrible environmental damage to the Earth. *Star Trek: First Contact* establishes that the nuclear holocaust took place prior to 2063. Colonel Green, seen in "The Savage Curtain" (TOS), was described as having led a genocidal war on Earth during the twenty-first century, which would seem to refer to the same event. We conjecture that the actual nuclear exchange took place about ten years prior to Cochrane's flight, since the problems of contaminated fallout and nuclear winter seemed to have subsided by 2063. (The nuclear winter was mentioned in "A Matter of Time" [TNG]). Even though Cochrane's flight in that year was the beginning of a renaissance of human civilization, that rebirth did not happen overnight. In "Encounter at Farpoint" (TNG), Q told of a barbaric period on Earth during the "post atomic horror" during which all the lawyers were killed sometime before 2079, at which time "all 'united Earth' nonsense [had been] abolished. World War III was apparently a distinctly different event than the Eugenics Wars ("Space Seed" [TOS]), which started around 1992 and were over by 1996. ("Space Seed" also had Spock describing the third world war as having taken place during the mid-1990s, although he admits that records from that period are "fragmentary.")

It is not clear exactly when Earth's people finally were united under a single government, although based on *Star Trek: First Contact*, we conjecture that it occurred around 2113, which is 50 years after Cochrane's first warp flight. It was not as far back as the mid-21st century, when the planet was devastated by World War III, but was presumably before 2161, when the United Federation of Planets was incorporat-

ed. In "Up the Long Ladder" (TNG) Data noted that the establishment of a political entity called the European Hegemony was a step toward the establishment of a world government on Earth in the 22nd century. "Attached" (TNG) established that Australia joined Earth's world government in 2150. These might seem to suggest that Earth's world government came into being between 2150 and 2161. On the other hand, it is possible that a world government came about sooner than 2150, if one assumes that not all the nations of Earth joined at once (meaning that Australia would have been a latecomer). This conjecture would be consistent with *Star Trek: First Contact*, which suggested that Earth had some kind of world government within 50 years after Cochrane's first warp flight in 2063.

> 1961: Space age begins (contemporary accounts).
> 1992: Eugenics Wars start ("Space Seed" [TOS]).
> 1996: Eugenics Wars end ("Space Seed" [TOS]).
> 2050: World War III (conjecture).
> 2063: Invention of warp drive; first contact with Vulcan *(Star Trek: First Contact)*.
> 2103: Mars colonized ("The 37's" [VGR]).
> 2113: World government established *(Star Trek: First Contact)*.
> 2160: Romulan Wars ended ("Balance of Terror" [TOS]).
> 2161: Federation founded ("The Outcast" [TNG]).

Mars. Samuel T. Cogley cited the Fundamental Declarations of the Martian Colonies, along with the Bible, the Code of Hammurabi, and the Constitution of the United States as a historic milestone in the evolution of legal systems that

protect individual rights. Also cited were the Tribunals of Alpha III. No date was given for either document ("Court Martial" [TOS]), but we do know that humans first colonized Mars in 2103, so the declaration was presumably some time after this point ("The 37's" [VGR]). The Martian Colonies were presumably home to the Utopia Planitia Fleet Yards, where the *Enterprise*-D was built. Benjamin Sisko served at the Utopia Planitia yards following the battle of Wolf 359 ("Emissary" [DS9]).

The Klingon Empire. We know quite a bit about the Klingon Empire, but virtually nothing about the Klingon people prior to the ascendance of Kahless the Unforgettable some 15 centuries ago.

We know that prior to the emergence of the second Kahless in 2369, the Klingon Empire had not been ruled by an

emperor for three centuries ("Rightful Heir" [TNG]). We do not know what extraordinary events transpired around that last emperor's death in 2069 that prevented the ascendance of a new emperor and allowed the High Council to rule the empire for the next 300 years. Major known data points from Klingon history include:

c.600: Kahless the Unforgettable unites the empire ("The Savage Curtain" [TOS]).

1372: The Hur'q invade Klingon Homeworld; steal sword of Kahless ("The Sword of Kahless" [DS9]).

2069: Klingon emperor dies, but no successor ascends the throne ("Rightful Heir" [TNG]).

2218: First contact between Federation and Klingon Empire ("Day of the Dove" [TOS]).

2242: Battle of Donatu V ("The Trouble With Tribbles" [TOS]).

2267: War with Federation narrowly avoided by Organian Peace Treaty ("Errand of Mercy" [TOS]).

2267: Klingons lose claim to Sherman's Planet ("The Trouble With Tribbles" [TOS]).

2268: Enters alliance with Romulans ("The *Enterprise* Incident" [TOS]).

2292: Alliance with Romulans collapses ("Reunion" [TNG]).

2293: Praxis explodes; Khitomer peace accords (*Star Trek VI: The Undiscovered Country*).

2344: *Starship Enterprise*-C defends Klingon outpost at Narendra III ("Yesterday's *Enterprise*" [TNG]).

2346: Khitomer massacre ("Sins of the Father" [TNG]).

2367: Chancellor K'mpec murdered; succeeded by Gowron ("Reunion" [TNG]).

2368: House of Duras makes unsuccessful bid to unseat Gowron ("Redemption, Parts I and II" [TNG]).

2369: Second Kahless ascends the throne ("Rightful Heir" [TNG]).

2372: Gowron declares war on Cardassia; withdraws from Khitomer accords ("Way of the Warrior" [DS9]).

The Organian peace treaty. When we first met the Klingons in "Errand of Mercy" (TOS), a major war between the Klingons and the Federation was prevented by the noncorporeal Organians, who made it impossible for the two sides to fight. "The Trouble With Tribbles" (TOS) establishes that this was formalized into a peace treaty. In later episodes and movies, however, it became clear that hostilities between the two powers did indeed flare up, occasionally quite seriously. It is not clear what happened to the Organian peace treaty, or if anything happened to the Organians. It is possible that they simply adopted a hands-off attitude toward these two primitive cultures, or perhaps something happened to them.

The Romulan Star Empire. Two millennia ago, a group of dissident Vulcans who opposed Surak's philosophy of logic and peace, left their homeworld and founded what became the Romulan Star Empire. The Romulans fought a war with Earth in the mid-22nd century, just prior to the founding of the Federation. Although we estimate that the Romulan wars were concluded around the year 2160, we have no information to suggest the events that led to the beginning of this conflict, or for first contact with the Romulan Star Empire itself ("Balance of Terror" [TOS]).

We do know that between the end of the Romulan wars (2160) and the episode "Balance of Terror" (2266), the Neutral Zone treaty remained unbroken. We also know that there was no contact between the Federation and the Romulans between the Tomed Incident (2311) and the events of "The Neutral Zone" (TNG), (2364). "Homefront" (DS9) seems to

imply that the Romulan wars reached Earth, since Sisko commented that a Founder invasion of Earth would involve "the kind of war Earth hasn't seen since the founding of the Federation."

One of the most significant recent events between the Federation and the Romulans was the Tomed Incident, mentioned in "The Neutral Zone" (TNG) as having taken place in 2311. We know that thousands of Federation lives were lost in the incident, that the Treaty of Algeron was signed afterward, and that the Romulans subsequently went into an extended period of isolationism. Unfortunately, we don't actually know what happened in the Tomed Incident. Major data points include:

c.369: Vulcan dissidents leave their homeworld and establish the Romulan Empire ("Balance of Terror" [TOS]; "Unification, Parts I and II" [TNG]).

2156: War with Earth ("Balance of Terror" [TOS]).

2160: War with Earth ended; Neutral Zone established ("Balance of Terror" [TOS]).

2266: Neutral Zone first violated ("Balance of Terror" [TOS]).

2268: Enters alliance with Klingons ("The *Enterprise* Incident" [TOS]).

2271: Battle of Klach D'kel Brakt.

2292: Alliance with Klingons collapses ("Reunion" [TNG]).

2311: The Tomed Incident; Treaty of Algeron ("The Neutral Zone" [TNG]).

2344: Romulans attack Klingon outpost on Narendra III ("Yesterday's *Enterprise*" [TNG]).

2346: Romulans attack Khitomer Outpost ("Sins of the Father" [TNG]).

2364: End of isolationism with Federation ("The Neutral Zone" [TNG]).

2367: Romulan operatives attempt to overthrow Klingon government ("The Mind's Eye" [TNG] et al.).

2368: Romulan operatives attempt coup of Vulcan government ("Unification, Parts I and II" [TNG]).

2371: Agrees to permit *Starship Defiant* to use a cloaking device ("The Search, Part I" [DS9]).

2371: Tal Shiar intelligence agency decimated in disastrous attack on Founders' homeworld ("The Die is Cast" [DS9]).

Romulan-Vulcan war. In "Death Wish" (VGR), we learned that a member of the Q Continuum once did something that triggered a hundred-year-long war between the Romulans and the Vulcans. This could presumably have taken place at almost any point after the Vulcan-Romulan schism of 2,000 years ago, since they both had to have had interstellar spaceflight capability at that point. It started well before 2072, since this was when Quinn was imprisoned.

Romulan alliance with dissident Klingons. "The *Enterprise* Incident" (TOS) establishes that some measure of cooperation existed between the two empires during the third season of the original *Star Trek* series, c. 2268. At this point, the two powers were allied against the United Federation of Planets. However, by 2292 (just prior to *Star Trek VI*), relations between the Romulans and Klingons had deteriorated significantly (from Geordi's line in "Reunion" (TNG) that suggested the two powers had become "blood enemies" 75 years prior to that episode). The Romulans attacked the Klingon outpost at Narendra III in 2344 ("Yesterday's *Enterprise*" [TNG]), and in

2346 the Romulans also attacked the Khitomer Outpost near the Romulan border, killing thousands of Klingons. "Sins of the Father" (TNG) and "Redemption, Part II" (TNG) show, however, that the Romulans had been working with at least some factions of the Klingon government in an effort to overthrow K'mpec's regime. The dates and circumstances of this Romulan alliance with dissident Klingons are unclear.

"Conspiracy" parasites. Starfleet Command was infiltrated by extragalactic parasites in late 2364 as seen in "Conspiracy" (TNG). Although Picard and company were successful in eradicating them, the parasites did send a mysterious radio signal, presumably to others of their kind. At the time the episode was written, this was apparently intended to lead to the introduction of the Borg in *Star Trek: The Next Generation's* second season. The Borg connection was dropped before "Q Who?" (TNG) was written, and the truth about the parasites remains a mystery.

The mirror universe. This is the alternate reality first visited in "Mirror, Mirror" (TOS). Although parts of the mirror universe history are close parallels to the "real" *Star Trek* history, many specific details are significantly different, and there are many large gaps in our knowledge about this reality. Rather than a Federation, the mirror universe was dominated, in 2267, by the Terran Empire. In "Mirror, Mirror," the James Kirk from our dimension urged the mirror Spock to become the force of change to reform the repressive empire. In "Crossover" (DS9), we learn that Spock was indeed successful in ending the empire's barbaric ways, but that this paved the way for an alliance of Klingon and Cardassian forces to conquer the Terrans. We don't know many specifics about this downfall. Neither do we know how Spock brought about this extraordinary revolution, or what led to its unintended consequences. We do know that in 2370, the Cardassian mining station Terok Nor (still orbiting Bajor in this universe), became a hotbed of Terran resistance, inspired by visits by Benjamin Sisko ("Crossover" and "Through the Looking Glass" [DS9]). By 2372, the resistance had driven Alliance forces off of Terok Nor. ("Shattered Mirror" [DS9]). These mirror universe episode dates are interesting in that they give a range of dates for these various events, but rarely do we know exactly when anything happened, since most major events happened at unspecified times between the episodes.

2267: "Mirror, Mirror" (TOS).

2370: "Crossover" (DS9).

2371: "Through the Looking Glass" (DS9).

2372: "Shattered Mirror" (DS9).

Diplomatic relations with the Gorns. A state of hostility (but apparently not armed conflict) existed between the Federation and the Gorns in 2267, as seen in "Arena" (TOS). Although the Metrons prevented an actual war from breaking out, there was no indication that the two powers would establish diplomatic relations. Yet "Family Business" (DS9) establishes that a Federation colony was thriving on planet Cestus III, in territory previously disputed by the Gorns, by 2371. This would seem to suggest that a significant easing of tensions occurred at some point between the two episodes.

Diplomatic relations with the Tholians. Similarly, various episodes of *Star Trek: Deep Space Nine* have included offhanded references to visits by a Tholian ambassador, or trade in such goods as Tholian silk. This would seem to suggest a substantial improvement in relations between "The Tholian Web" (TOS), set in 2268, and "Life Support" (DS9), set in 2371. "The Icarus Factor" (TNG) establishes that at some point early in Kyle Riker's career, a Tholian attack nearly destroyed a Federation starbase. We haven't actually seen a Tholian since "The Tholian Web," so we don't know if the crystalline shape we saw on the bridge viewer was actually Commander Loskene's head, or if he/she was simply wearing a helmet. Similarly, we don't know what a Tholian's body looks like below the head.

The Borg. "The Best of Both Worlds, Part II" (TNG) and "Emissary" (DS9) both showed parts of this terrible battle in which forty Federation starships made a costly and futile attempt to prevent a Borg ship from reaching Earth. "The Drumhead" (TNG) establishes that of the 40 starships there, 39 were destroyed. We do not yet know the name of the surviving ship, nor the circumstances of its escape.

Although Starfleet believed that the first Borg incursion into the Alpha Quadrant was in 2367 ("The Best of Both Worlds, Parts I and II" [TNG]), the Borg did attack Guinan's homeworld around 2265 ("Q Who?" [TNG]). This would seem to suggest that the Borg did approach Federation space at that point, although it appears that they only destroyed the El-Aurian homeworld. (It is not clear if the El-Aurians were part of the Federation, although there had apparently already been contact between the two groups, since the crew of the *Enterprise*-B seemed familiar with the El-Aurian refugee ships in *Star Trek Generations*.) A second early Borg incursion may have occurred in 2364, when there was evidence of massive surface excavations on planets near Romulan space ("The Neutral Zone" [TNG]). To summarize what we do know:

- 2265: Borg destroy El-Aurian homeworld (*Star Trek Generations*).
- 2364: Possible Borg incursion near Romulan space ("The Neutral Zone" [TNG]).
- 2365: First known Federation contact with the Borg ("Q Who?" [TNG]).
- 2367: Battle of Wolf 359 ("The Best of Both Worlds, Part II" [TNG]).
- 2369: Renegade Borg offensive, led by Lore ("Descent, Parts I and II" [TNG]).
- 2373: Borg attack on Earth (*Star Trek: First Contact*).

Cardassian wars. "The Wounded" (TNG) establishes that an uneasy truce between the Cardassians and the Federation was signed sometime in 2367, and that hostilities had existed for at least several years prior. "The Wounded" also establishes that Chief Miles O'Brien had served under Captain Ben Maxwell on the *Starship Rutledge* in 2347 during the massacre at planet Setlik III. Maxwell's family, along with about a hundred other civilians, were killed in the incident. The *Rutledge* arrived at Setlik a day later. (Glinn Daro admitted in "The Wounded" [TNG] that the Setlik massacre had been a terrible mistake on the part of the Cardassians, who believed the outpost was to be used as a launching point for a

massive attack by the Federation.) "Unification, Part I" (TNG) establishes that Ambassador Sarek had been involved in negotiations with the Cardassians, although Spock publicly opposed his position. Hostilities with the Cardassians extend at least as far back as 2347 (the time of the Setlik III massacre, established in "Tribunal [DS9]). In 2355, Picard, commanding the *U.S.S. Stargazer*, was assigned to make preliminary overtures for a truce, but the gestures were rejected and the *Stargazer* was forced to flee at warp speed ("The Wounded" [TNG]).

Tholian wars. Relations between the Federation and the Tholian Assembly are shown to be less than friendly during "The Tholian Web" (TOS), set in 2268. "Peak Performance" (TNG) establishes that Riker, during an academy simulation, calculated a sensory blind spot on a Tholian vessel, suggesting that relations between the Federation and the Tholians were at least somewhat strained during Riker's academy days. Riker's father, Kyle, was injured in 2353 (the same year that William entered Starfleet Academy) during a Tholian attack on a starbase ("The Icarus Factor" [TNG]). This suggests that there were open hostilities at that point. In "Reunion" (set in 2367), K'Ehleyr expressed fear that internal Klingon conflicts could escalate to involve other powers, including the Tholians. By the time of *Star Trek: Deep Space Nine*, there were several references to a Tholian ambassador and mentions of trade with the Tholians, suggesting that there were diplomatic relations between the Federation and the Tholian Assembly by that point. A Tholian ambassador visited Deep Space 9 in "Life Support" (DS9). A Tholian observer was reported killed in a terrorist bombing in Antwerp in 2372 in "Homefront" (DS9). Except for the viewscreen shots in "The Tholian Web" (TOS), we still haven't seen what a Tholian looks like.

Altarian conflict. Admiral Komack, in his communiqué to the *Enterprise* in 2267, explained that the Altair system was in the process of putting itself together after a long interplanetary conflict. The inauguration of a new president just after that episode was expected to stabilize the entire system, demonstrating friendship and strength, and causing ripples clear to the Klingon Empire ("Amok Time" [TOS]).

APPENDIX H: ALTERNATE TIMELINES

involved time travel and alternate timelines. In many cases, these stories have involved the efforts of our heroes to repair the damage that caused the alternate (and presumably improper) timelines, thus restoring the flow of history to "normality." Because of this, some of the following story lines are not entirely incorporated into the main body of this chronology, since many of the alternate timelines never "really" happened.

"Tomorrow Is Yesterday" (TOS). This episode involved the *Enterprise*, under the command of Captain Kirk, accidentally thrown into the past, to Earth in the year 1969. While attempting to avoid detection by the U.S. Air Force, *Enterprise* personnel accidentally destroyed an Air Force fighter aircraft and were forced to bring the pilot, Captain John Christopher, to the starship. These events created an alternate timeline in which the U.S. Air Force made a confirmed, documented UFO sighting in 1969. Additionally, the capture of Captain Christopher would have prevented Christopher from fathering a child. According to historical records, that child, Shaun Geoffrey Christopher, commanded the first Earth-Saturn probe. The history of space exploration in this timeline would presumably have followed a significantly different course from the one described in this chronology. This alternate timeline was eliminated when the *Enterprise* returned to the 23rd century, restoring John Christopher and an Air Force security guard to their original coordinates before they were beamed to the *Enterprise*. It is not clear if, in the "repaired" timeline, either Christopher or the guard retain memory of their stay aboard the *Enterprise*.

"City on the Edge of Forever" (TOS). Traveling into Earth's past through the Guardian of Forever, Dr. McCoy prevented a fatal traffic accident involving social worker Edith Keeler in 1930. This created an alternate timeline in which Keeler became a factor in American politics, delaying that nation's entry into the Second World War long enough for

Adolf Hitler's scientists to develop the atomic bomb. In this alternate timeline, Nazi Germany won the Second World War, becoming Earth's dominant power in the 20th century. This alternate timeline was excised when Kirk and Spock followed McCoy into the past, preventing McCoy from saving Keeler in that critical traffic accident.

"Mirror, Mirror" (TOS), et al. The mirror universe is arguably an alternate timeline, parallel to the "real" *Star Trek* universe. Unlike many alternate timelines, it did not disappear when the phenomenon causing it ended. When Kirk and company returned home, the mirror Spock headed a revolution that led to the downfall of the repressive Terran Empire. By 2370, the Empire had been conquered by an alliance of the

Klingon and Cardassian empires ("Crossover" [DS9]), but Ben Sisko was successful in inspiring a rebirth of human resistance in the mirror universe ("Through the Looking Glass" [DS9]; "Shattered Mirror" [DS9]). It appears that the mirror universe saga will continue.

"Assignment: Earth" (TOS). This episode does not exactly involve an alternate timeline, but deals with Kirk and Spock on Earth in 1968 working to prevent what they fear is interference from future aliens. In fact, the alien "interference" was from an individual named Gary Seven, who was found to be part of the "normal" events in that day. Thus, it appears that no alternate timeline was created in the episode.

Star Trek IV: The Voyage Home. An alternate timeline was apparently created in this film in 1986 when Kirk and company visited San Francisco to find two humpback whales. In this timeline, two humpback whales disappeared near San Francisco, a mysterious stranger was captured on the Navy aircraft carrier *U.S.S. Enterprise* and later disappeared, Dr. Nichols of Plexicorp invented transparent aluminum, and Dr. Gillian Taylor disappeared, never to be seen again. This alternate timeline was not "corrected," and we might therefore conclude that the entirety of *Star Trek* history from that point is in that continuum. It is also possible, therefore, that an "original" timeline exists in a parallel continuum in which neither the humpbacks nor Taylor disappeared.

It is interesting to note that an early draft of the *Star Trek IV* script had one of the questions in Spock's memory test establish that Dr. Nichols had invented transparent aluminum back in 1986. Since this was "prior" to our heroes traveling back in time, this would have implied that an alternate timeline was not created, but that Kirk and his crew were simply part of "proper" past history.

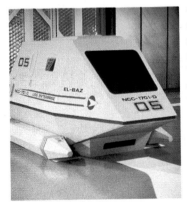

"Time Squared" (TNG). Captain Picard evidently made a decision that resulted in the destruction of the *Enterprise*-D. Just before the ship was destroyed, however, Picard departed the vessel aboard a shuttle. The force of the starship's explosion threw the shuttle back in time by several hours. As a result, an alternate timeline was created in which the *Enterprise*-D was not destroyed. All subsequent *Star Trek* episodes have apparently been set in this alternate timeline.

"Yesterday's *Enterprise*" (TNG). This is one of the strangest and most complicated alternate timeline stories in *Star Trek* history. The triggering event here was a photon torpedo explosion back in 2344, fired by the *Enterprise*-C, which accidentally opened a temporal rift, sending that ship into the future. Once removed from its "proper" time, an alternate timeline was created in which the *Enterprise*-C did not attempt to help defend the Klingon outpost at Narendra III. Later, tensions between the Federation and the Klingons escalated, and an extended war ensued. The *Enterprise*-C emerged from the temporal rift in the year 2366, by which time the Federation was on the verge of defeat. The crew of the *Enterprise*-C, once made aware of the impact of their removal from the original timeline, returned back in time to 2344, where they were nearly destroyed rendering assistance to the Klingons at Narendra III. Although this act restored the timeline to its original form, or nearly so, *Enterprise*-D security chief Tasha Yar — who in the alternate timeline did not die at Vagra II — elected to join the crew of the *Enterprise*-C when it returned to the past.

"Captain's Holiday" (TNG). This is another complicated one. Vorgon criminals from the 27th century traveled back to Picard's time in an effort to locate a valuable artifact, the *Tox Uthat*. The Vorgons knew from historical records that Picard would be involved with the discovery of the *Uthat*, and also that Picard would later destroy the artifact. The criminals from the future therefore tried to steal the *Uthat* before Picard was able to destroy it. Although they were unsuccessful, the Vorgons traveled back in time again to make another attempt to acquire the object.

It may be that no significant alternate timelines were created in this episode, although it seems possible that the Vorgons could continue nearly *ad infinitum* to steal the *Uthat*, and that they would be eventually successful. If this is the case, then each attempt might be considered a different alternate timeline. (In fact, the script as originally written ended with a repeat of the first scene! Had the episode been shown in that form, viewers could have concluded that the Vorgons would eventually succeed in their effort.)

"Redemption, Parts I and II" (TNG). In these episodes, we learn that the alternate Tasha did not die in the battle at Narendra III. Instead, she and her crewmates were captured by Romulans, and Tasha won the lives of her crewmates by agreeing to become the consort of a Romulan official. A year later, Yar gave birth to a daughter, Sela, who later became a powerful Romulan operative. According to Sela, Yar was killed trying to escape when Sela was four years old.

Even though this version of Yar originated in an alternate timeline, she returned to the past with the *Enterprise*-C, and thus continued to exist, even after the timeline was restored. This raises the question of whether this past Tasha had existed prior to the creation of the alternate timeline. In other words, it would have been interesting if the *Enterprise*-D, prior to "Yesterday's *Enterprise*" (TNG), had traveled into the past to Romulus. Would they have met Yar and Sela? If not, one might reasonably argue that the entire *Star Trek* scenario since "Yesterday's *Enterprise*" (TNG) is an alternate (or at least an altered) timeline.

"A Matter of Time" (TNG). A researcher from the 26th century went back to the 22nd century, where he or she had the misfortune of encountering Professor Berlinghoff Rasmussen. The unethical professor stole the researcher's time machine and attempted to use it for his own gain. An alternate timeline was apparently created here when the 26th-century researcher met Rasmussen in the past.

"Time's Arrow, Parts I and II" (TNG). Life-forms from planet Devidia II traveled back in time to Earth's 19th century to steal neural energy from humans suffering from a cholera epidemic. Even though several

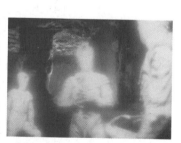

Enterprise-D people followed them into the past, it appears that no significant change in the timeline resulted, although Samuel Clemens got a brief glimpse into humanity's future.

"Tapestry" (TNG). Q transported Jean-Luc Picard back in time to 2327, just after Picard's graduation from Starfleet Academy, giving Picard the opportunity to live his life differently. Picard did do things differently, but was stunned to learn that the results were not what he had expected. By not making the terrible "mistake" of getting into a near-fatal fight with some Nausicaans, Picard found that his career path led not to starship command, but to a boring job as a junior officer on the *Enterprise*-D. Q obligingly restored the original timeline for Picard, so it appears that any alternate timeline created here was also excised. (It is, of course, possible that Q simply created an illusion for Picard, and that no alternate timeline was created at all.)

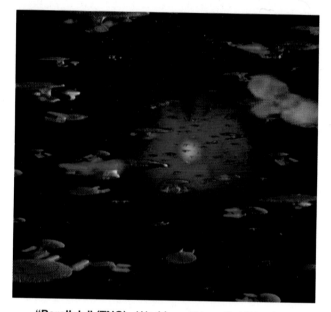

"Parallels" (TNG). Worf found himself shifting between different quantum realities. "Parallels" was based on the theory that there exists somewhere an infinite number of possible universes, and we encountered some 285,000 of them in this episode. Although those different realities apparently ceased to exist at the end of the episode, if the theory of quantum realities is true, those universes must still exist on different planes of reality.

"Firstborn" (TNG). Several decades in the future, Worf's grown son, Alexander, who had refused to become a warrior, instead became a peacemaker who sought to end the destructive feuding between the great houses. But Klingon society was not ready for Alexander's reforms. His father, Worf, was murdered on the floor of the High Council chambers. Alexander blamed himself for Worf's death, and traveled back in time to 2370 to try to persuade his younger self to follow the path of a Klingon warrior. The episode does not indicate if

Alexander succeeded in changing his own destiny, so we don't really know if the "actual" future will unfold in this manner or not. If the future Alexander was successful, then an alternate timeline was created in this episode.

"All Good Things..." (TNG). Three alternate timelines were apparently created by Q in this episode, in which Picard bounces between the past (the beginning of *Star Trek: The Next Generation's* first season), the present (the end of the seventh season), and the future (some 25 years after the end of the series). These were all a puzzle devised by Q to see if Picard could understand the nature of anti-time, and in doing so, save humanity. All three alternate timelines were apparently excised when Picard figured out Q's puzzle. (Once again, we are assuming that these are not just illusions created by Q.)

In the anti-time past (2364), Picard experienced a different version of the events in "Encounter at Farpoint" (TNG). Instead of encountering Q and traveling to Farpoint Station, the *Enterprise*-D investigated the anti-time phenomenon and was destroyed.

In the anti-time present (2370), Picard also investigated the anti-time phenomenon, with disastrous results.

The anti-time future, set around the year 2395, also had Picard investigating the anti-time phenomenon. We learned quite a bit about this alternate future, although it appears unlikely that the "actual" *Star Trek* timeline will follow this exact course.

In this future, the Klingon Empire conquered the Romulans, and the neutral zone between the Romulan Star Empire and the United Federation of Planets ceased to exist by 2395. Relations between the Klingons and the Federation deteriorated as well. The Klingons had a new, larger, much more powerful class of attack cruiser in service.

Captain Jean-Luc Picard married Dr. Beverly Crusher, but the two later divorced. Picard resigned Starfleet to become a Federation ambassador, and later went to live on his family farm in France. By 2395, Jean-Luc Picard had advanced Irumodic Syndrome, a degenerative disorder that causes irreversible deterioration of the nervous system. Dr. Beverly Picard became captain of the *Starship Pasteur.* Her ship was destroyed in 2395 when the

Pasteur was attacked by Klingons in the Devron system.

Data left Starfleet to become a professor of physics at Cambridge University. He accepted an appointment to the Lucasian Chair, an honor previously bestowed on such luminaries as Sir Isaac Newton and Dr. Stephen Hawking.

Geordi La Forge also left Starfleet, married the former Leah Brahms, moved to Rigel III, and had three children, Bret, Illandra, and Sydney. Leah became director of the Daystrom Institute, Bret applied to Starfleet Academy in 2394, and Geordi, who no longer needed his VISOR to see, became a novelist.

Deanna Troi died unexpectedly in 2375, about five years after the end of *Star Trek: The Next Generation's* seventh season.

Worf never pursued a romantic relationship with Deanna Troi because of Will Riker's unspoken disapproval. After Troi's death, Worf and Riker became enemies. Worf served for a time as a member of the Klingon High Council, and by 2395 he was governor of a Klingon colony. (This appears to be reasonably consistent with Alexander's future from "Firstborn" [TNG]).

The *Starship Enterprise*-D was nearly decommissioned by Starfleet in 2390, but Admiral William Riker took a persoal

interest in his old ship, ordered it upgraded, and took personal command of the *Galaxy*-class vessel. The ship was destroyed in 2395 while trying to collapse Picard's subspace anomaly.

Starfleet recalibrated the warp scale for some reason, so in 2395, it was not uncommon for a starship to be traveling at warp 13.

Finally, remember that Picard made a point of telling his friends in 2370 about the future that he saw in 2395 for the express purpose of giving them the chance to understand and perhaps change their destinies. We expect that some of them did so. Some of these future events probably show possible directions for the future, but it is difficult to tell which these might be. For example, in "The Way of the Warrior" (DS9), we saw the new, large Klingon battle cruiser that was first seen in Picard's anti-time future, suggesting that at least that one element of that future has already come to pass. In "The Visitor" (DS9), we saw in Jake's future that Starfleet had adopted the same future uniforms and insignia as seen in "All Good Things..." (TNG). And in *Star Trek: First Contact*, Geordi has already undergone surgery to replace his VISOR. On the other hand, the destruction of the *Enterprise*-D in 2371 *(Star Trek Generations)* would seem to indicate that at least some things will be different.

"Past Tense, Part I and II" (DS9). Sisko, Bashir, and Dax traveled back in time to a pivotal point in Earth's twenty-first century, where Sisko accidentally caused the death of a historic figure, Gabriel Bell, just before the critical Bell Riots of 2024. In order to maintain the integrity of the timeline, Sisko assumed Bell's identity, and was apparently successful in preserving the overall flow of time. Nevertheless, an alternate future was created, one in which history's records of Gabriel Bell bear a remarkable resemblance to Ben Sisko. It is also possible that O'Brien and Kira also altered the timeline at each point in the past where they visited to search for Sisko and company, although this seems unlikely since they were only in each period for a few seconds.

"Time and Again" (VGR). A catastrophic polaric ion explosion on a planet in the Delta Quadrant destroyed that planet's inhabitants in 2371. The resulting subspace fractures transported Janeway and Paris back a day in time, where they learned that they had caused the disaster, and so worked to prevent it from happening again. It appears that the alternate timeline here is one in which our people unwittingly triggered the polaric ion disaster, and that this timeline was excised

when our heroes returned. Like all such alternate timelines, it is unclear if the alternate timeline disappeared, or if there still exists somewhere a parallel universe in which the planet's population was wiped out in a terrible explosion triggered by the *Voyager* people.

Star Trek Generations. When Picard was unable to stop Soran at Veridian III, he traveled back in time through the nexus to get a second chance with the aid of James T. Kirk, thereby creating an alternate timeline. It would also appear that the nexus itself is an alternate reality and timeline, one that we don't pretend to understand.

"Visionary" (DS9). Miles O'Brien dies, but another Miles O'Brien, from an alternate timeline three hours in the future, crossed over into our universe, becoming a "replacement" O'Brien. In that alternate universe, Miles O'Brien presumably disappeared and was never heard from again.

"Non Sequitur" (VGR). When Harry Kim's shuttle accidentally collided with a time stream from some extremely advanced civilization, history and events were "scrambled a little," sending Kim into an alternate timeline in which he did not join the *Voyager* crew and was therefore not lost in the Delta Quadrant. The mysterious shopkeeper hinted that this alternate timeline was created by Harry's shuttle collision, so perhaps this alternate timeline also disappeared when Kim returned to his original time.

"The Visitor" (DS9). Ben Sisko died in 2372 aboard the *Defiant.* His son, Jake, devoted much of his life to studying the bizarre accident that took his father's life, and to studying why his father kept reappearing. Old Jake sacrificed himself so that his still-young father could have a second chance at life, and so that his younger self need not grow up without a father. The timeline was changed when Ben returned to the moment of his death, but with Jake's warning, dodged the deadly energy bolt. Although the timeline in which Ben died was apparently excised, certain elements of that timeline still seem to be playing themselves out: Jake is still pursuing his writing, and he has (as of "The Muse" [DS9]) already completed the first draft of his first novel, *Anselem.*

"Little Green Men" (DS9). In this episode, we learn that the United States Army did indeed capture an extraterrestrial spacecraft near Roswell, New Mexico, in 1947. It was a small Ferengi ship, carrying Quark, Nog, Rom, and Odo. The ship and its crew escaped from Hangar 18 at Wright Field, and the Army subsequently denied the entire affair. It does not appear that an alternate timeline was created here. On the other hand, if an alternate timeline was created, it seems possible that our present 20th century could, in fact, be that alternate timeline, if the Army did indeed capture some aliens at Roswell in 1947.

"Death Wish" (VGR). When the member of the Q Continuum known as Quinn went back to the beginning of the universe to hide himself and the *Starship Voyager* in the Big Bang, it seems very likely that the course of the universe could have been altered quite dramatically. On the other hand, since the universe seemed pretty much unchanged when they returned to the 24th century, it appears that they either caused no changes, or they were part of what was "supposed" to have happened during the Big Bang. In the episode, we also learn that Quinn visited several points in Earth's past, but it also appears that he was part of what was "supposed" to have happened at those points in time.

"Accession" (DS9). The Bajoran prophets saved the life of Bajoran poet Akorem Laan, who was lost aboard his traditional Bajoran solar-sailing lightship around the year 2172. The Prophets, unfamiliar with the human concept of linear time, returned Akorem to normal space in the year 2372, where Akorem believed he was chosen by the Prophets to be the Emissary. The Prophets, upon informing Akorem that he was not the Emissary, granted Ben Sisko's request to return Akorem to 2172, where he could live out the remainder of his life with his family. In doing so, an alternate timeline was created. In the original timeline, Akorem disappeared in the year 2172 and was not heard from again until 2372. In disappearing, Akorem left behind a legacy of classic poems, including the unfinished "Call of the Prophets." In the altered timeline, Akorem reappeared in 2172, almost immediately after his disappearance. He presumably lived the remainder of his life with his family, and he did finish "Call of the Prophets." One of the Prophets said that once returned, Akorem would not remember his trip into the future. Oddly enough, even in the altered timeline, Kira Nerys remembered that Akorem had not finished the poem, and she was surprised when she read the "revised" version in that alternate timeline. No explanation was offered for this, but Ben Sisko noted that the "Prophets move in mysterious ways."

"Deadlock" (VGR). A parallel timeline was created when a nearly-identical copy of *Voyager* appeared in a spatial rift. Both *Voyagers* experienced a variety of problems, including the death of Harry Kim and of Samantha Wildman's baby on the original ship. Eventually, the duplicate Janeway sacrificed her *Voyager* so that the original could survive. Just before the destruction of the duplicate *Voyager*, the duplicate Harry Kim and Samantha Wildman's baby crossed over to the original, so that they replaced the originals killed aboard the first *Voyager*.

Star Trek: First Contact. In the eighth *Star Trek* feature film, a Borg ship traveled in time from the 24th century, back to the middle of the 21st century, in an attempt to prevent Zefram Cochrane from making his historic first warp flight. In the past, the Borg prevented Zefram Cochrane from making his first warp spaceflight, and were successful in altering history. In this altered timeline, by the 24th century, Earth was a Borg planet. The *Enterprise*-E followed the Borg ship back in time to correct history to its "normal" flow. In this restored history, Cochrane had some help from *Enterprise*-E personnel in making that first faster-than-light flight. It appears that in this film, two alternate timelines were created. The first was the future in which the Borg did conquer Earth. This timeline was apparently excised when the second alternate timeline, in which the *Enterprise*-E people helped Cochrane, was created.

"Future's End, Parts I and II" (VGR). This episode, in preproduction as this Chronology was being completed, suggests that a Federation time traveler from the 29th century became stranded in the 20th century. When an unscrupulous 20th-century entrepreneur began using future technology as the basis of our present-day microcomputer revolution, an altered timeline was created. The implication here seems to be that we have, in fact, been living in that alternate timeline for the past three decades. It has been speculated that this alternate timeline may be the reason why we saw no evidence of the Eugenics Wars in that episode, although we prefer to assume that the city of Los Angeles was fortunate enough to have escaped destruction in that conflict. (In "Space Seed" [TOS], Spock admitted that records of that period were "fragmentary.") "Future's End" also establishes that by the 29th century, the Federation operated small "timeships" that appar-

ently explored time in the same way that starships explored space. The timeline of the 29th century was apparently disrupted by a massive temporal explosion inadvertently triggered by the *Voyager* crew, but this was averted by the crew's actions back in the 20th century.

"The Trouble With Tribbles" (TOS). Another episode in preproduction just before our publication deadline was an episode of *Star Trek: Deep Space Nine* in which our heroes revisited the events from "The Trouble With Tribbles." An older Arne Darvin, living in disgrace after the diplomatic disaster at Station K-7, managed to travel back in time to 2267, where he tried to prevent Kirk from discovering the poisoned quadrotriticale. In doing so, he hoped to create an alternate timeline in which the Klingons were successful in claiming Sherman's Planet. Since Sisko and company were able to prevent him from doing so, history remained pretty much intact. Nevertheless, there were probably minor changes in the timeline since certain key events at K-7 now had a few people present who weren't there in the original timeline. (The *Star Trek: Deep Space Nine* episode did not have a final title at this writing.)

Other episodes: Time travel elements were also part of such episodes as "The Naked Time" (TOS) and "Cause and Effect" (TNG). In most of these cases, the time travel was either a one-way trip forward, or a recursive loop, which did not appear to create an alternate timeline.

It's about time: The question of whether or not the time continuum is ultimately fixed or mutable in the *Star Trek* universe has never been definitively addressed. Almost every time a significant change occurs, our people have been pretty much able to restore the "proper" flow of history, suggesting that both the change and the restoration were "normal." Nearly every time a change is not restored, we are often left with the possibility that the change is simply what was "supposed" to have happened.

If these suppositions are true, we may be left with the conclusion that very few of the items listed here are in fact truly alternate timelines. However, if time is truly changeable, each of the events here may have created a completely independent, parallel universe. On the other hand, if time is changeable, but parallel timelines cannot exist, we are faced with the possibility that the continuum may have been altered an infinite number of times, and that there is no way that we can know what the "original" timeline was like.

It is the authors' opinion that time travel stories almost never stand up under close scrutiny. Questions such as those posed here ultimately become questions about the nature and mechanics of time travel, and therefore become questions about the rules of time travel in the *Star Trek* universe. One might suppose that those rules might vary with the specific time-travel method used in a particular story ("slingshot" effect, temporal rift, Guardian of Forever, et cetera.)

Those interested in further examination of the mechanics of time travel and its ramifications may enjoy the novel *The Man Who Folded Himself* by David Gerrold (Bantam Books). Also highly recommended for the same reasons is the classic short story "All You Zombies" by Robert Heinlein.

APPENDIX I : REGARDING STARDATES

Gene Roddenberry said he invented stardates primarily as a means to remind us that the show was set in the future. We thought about trying to derive a formula to convert stardates to our present Gregorian calendar, but we quickly discovered that several different methods have been used to determine stardates over the history of the show. It became clear that stardates were never intended to be examined too closely, and that many errors have crept into the system over the years. (Naturally, we *did* examine them too closely, but at least now you've been warned.)

Much of the first *Star Trek* series seemed to advance the stardate an average of about 57 units each episode, from 1512 in "The Corbomite Maneuver" (TOS) to 5928 in "Turnabout Intruder" (TOS). Within a given episode, an increase of one unit (i.e., 1312 to 1313) seemed to correspond to about 24 hours. Additionally, there were a few episodes in which stardates apparently went backward from the previous week's show. The real reason for this is that the *Star Trek* production staff didn't always know which order the network would air the episodes. Dorothy Fontana also notes that some episodes were filmed out of intended order when writers were late in completing their scripts. (Ms. Fontana was diplomatic enough to avoid naming any names.)

Nevertheless, enough people asked about these apparent "errors" so that Gene Roddenberry came up with an explanation in Stephen Whitfield's *The Making of Star Trek,* which explains that stardates "adjust for shifts in relative time which occur due to the vessel's speed and space warp capability." Roddenberry added that "the stardate specified in the log entry must be computed against the speed of the vessel, the space warp, and its position within our galaxy in order to get a meaningful reading." (Gene also admitted that he wasn't quite sure what that explanation meant, and that he was glad that a lot of people seemed to think it made sense.)

The *Star Trek* feature films showed a gradual increase in stardates in each succeeding film. The numbers seem to have been arbitrarily determined, since the apparent value of stardate units seemed to vary widely in the gaps between movies. *Star Trek VI: The Undiscovered Country* was an even stranger case. This picture was set about four years after *Star Trek V* (stardate 8454). We've seen from the original *Star Trek* series that a span of three years can correspond to an increase of 4416 units, which could easily have put *Star Trek VI* into the five-digit range. A five-digit stardate seemed inappropriate for a *Star Trek* movie with the original *Enterprise* crew, since the longer stardates have been the province of the *Next Generation.* For this reason, the stardate for *Star Trek VI* was arbitrarily set at 9523, since this was near the upper limit of four-digit numbers. (We have a bit of insight into this selection process as *Star Trek VI* cowriter Denny Martin Flinn consulted with chronology coauthor Mike Okuda on this matter.)

Yet another method for stardate computation was employed for episodes of the *Star Trek: The Next Generation*-era spinoff shows. Gene Roddenberry made *Next Generation* stardates five-digit numbers, apparently to underscore the years that theoretically elapsed since the first *Star Trek* series. He arbitrarily chose 4 as the first digit (supposedly because this show is set in the 24th century, although we expect stardates to cross the 50000 mark at the beginning of the 1996-1997 season), and designated the second digit as the number of the show's current season. The last three digits increase unevenly from 000 at the beginning of a season, to 999 at the end. This means that a stardate of 43999 would be the last day of the third season of *Star Trek: The Next Generation.* (Of course, given this setup, the last four digits of a stardate do not contain enough information to account for an entire century.) As with the original series, an increase of a single unit within an episode corresponds to about 24 hours, even though this is inconsistent with a 365-day year. (We rationalize that relativistic time dilation makes up the difference.) *Star Trek: The Next Generation* script coordinator Eric Stillwell served as the show's keeper of stardates during the first five seasons. Every year, Eric issued a memo listing suggested stardate ranges for each upcoming episode. This memo served as a guide to help our writers keep their stardates in order. Still, as we noted earlier, stardates were never intended to stand up under close scrutiny.

Several methods of deriving stardates from calendar dates have been developed by *Star Trek* fans. One of the most popular systems arranges the year, month, and date so that a Gregorian calendar date of July 20, 1969, corresponds to a "stardate" of 6907.20. Although this does not correspond to the stardates used on the show, many fans enjoy using them anyway.

Another conjectural theory espoused by some fans theorizes that stardates relate only to the length of the ship's current voyage. For example, a stardate of 1312 (as in "Where No Man Has Gone Before" [TOS]) would indicate that the log entry was made thirteen months, twelve days since the ship left port. By coincidence or design, stardate 5928, given in "Turnabout Intruder" (TOS), the last episode of the original series, would correspond under this system to the sixtieth month or the end of the fifth year of the *Enterprise*'s mission.

APPENDIX J: WRITING CREDITS

The authors of this book wish to acknowledge the writers of the Star Trek television episodes and motion pictures, from whose work this volume has been compiled.

STAR TREK: THE ORIGINAL SERIES
YEAR 1 (ORIGINALLY AIRED 1966-67)

"The Cage." Written by Gene Roddenberry.

"Where No Man Has Gone Before." Written by Samuel A. Peeples.

"The Corbomite Maneuver." Written by Jerry Sohl.

"Mudd's Women." Teleplay by Stephen Kandel. Story by Gene Roddenberry.

"The Enemy Within." Written by Richard Matheson.

"The Man Trap." Written by George Clayton Johnson.

"The Naked Time." Written by John D. F. Black.

"Charlie X." Teleplay by D. C. Fontana. Story by Gene Roddenberry.

"Balance of Terror." Written by Paul Schneider.

"What Are Little Girls Made Of?" Written by Robert Bloch.

"Dagger of the Mind." Written by S. Bar-David.

"Miri." Written by Adrian Spies.

"The Conscience of the King." Written by Barry Trivers.

"The Galileo Seven." Teleplay by Oliver Crawford and S. Bar-David. Story by Oliver Crawford.

"Court Martial." Teleplay by Don M. Mankiewicz and Steven W. Carabatsos. Story by Don M. Mankiewicz.

"The Menagerie, Part I." Written by Gene Roddenberry.

"The Menagerie, Part II." Written by Gene Roddenberry.

"The Squire of Gothos." Written by Paul Schneider.

"Arena." Teleplay by Gene L. Coon. From a story by Fredric Brown.

"The Alternative Factor." Written by Don Ingalls.

"Tomorrow Is Yesterday." Written by D. C. Fontana.

"The Return of the Archons." Teleplay by Boris Sobelman. Story by Gene Roddenberry.

"A Taste of Armageddon." Teleplay by Robert Hamner and Gene L. Coon. Story by Robert Hamner.

"Space Seed." Teleplay by Gene L. Coon and Carey Wilber. Story by Carey Wilber.

"This Side of Paradise." Teleplay by D. C. Fontana. Story by Nathan Butler and D. C. Fontana.

"The Devil in the Dark." Written by Gene L. Coon.

"Errand of Mercy." Written by Gene L. Coon.

"The City on the Edge of Forever." Written by Harlan Ellison.

"Operation: Annihilate!" Written by Steven W. Carabatsos.

STAR TREK: THE ORIGINAL SERIES
YEAR 2 (ORIGINALLY AIRED 1967-68)

"Catspaw." Written by Robert Bloch.

"Metamorphosis." Written by Gene L. Coon.

"Friday's Child." Written by D. C. Fontana.

"Who Mourns for Adonais?" Written by Gilbert Ralston.

"Amok Time." Written by Theodore Sturgeon.

"The Doomsday Machine." Written By Norman Spinrad.

"Wolf in the Fold." Written by Robert Bloch.

"The Changeling." Written by John Meredyth Lucas.

"The Apple." Written by Max Ehrlich.

"Mirror, Mirror." Written by Jerome Bixby.

"The Deadly Years." Written by David P. Harmon.

"I, Mudd." Written by Stephen Kandel.

"The Trouble with Tribbles." Written by David Gerrold.

"Bread and Circuses." Written by Gene Roddenberry and Gene L. Coon.

"Journey to Babel." Written by D. C. Fontana.

"A Private Little War." Teleplay by Gene Roddenberry. Story by Jud Crucis.

"The Gamesters of Triskelion." Written by Margaret Armen.

"Obsession." Written by Art Wallace.

"The Immunity Syndrome." Written by Robert Sabaroff.

"A Piece of the Action." Teleplay by David P. Harmon and Gene L. Coon. Story by David P. Harmon.

"By Any Other Name." Teleplay by D. C. Fontana and Jerome Bixby. Story by Jerome Bixby.

"Return to Tomorrow." Written by John Kingsbridge.

"Patterns of Force." Written by John Meredyth Lucas.

"The Ultimate Computer." Teleplay by D. C. Fontana. Story by Laurence N. Wolfe.

"The Omega Glory." Written by Gene Roddenberry.

"Assignment Earth." Teleplay by Art Wallace. Story by Gene Roddenberry and Art Wallace.

STAR TREK: THE ORIGINAL SERIES
YEAR 3 (ORIGINALLY AIRED 1968-69)

"Spectre of the Gun." Written by Lee Cronin.

"Elaan of Troyius." Written by John Meredyth Lucas.

"The Paradise Syndrome." Written by Margaret Armen.

"The *Enterprise* Incident." Written by D. C. Fontana.

"And the Children Shall Lead." Written by Edward J. Lakso.

"Spock's Brain." Written by Lee Cronin.

"Is There in Truth No Beauty?" Written by Jean Lisette Aroeste.

"The Empath." Written by Joyce Muskat.

"The Tholian Web." Written by Judy Burns and Chet Richards.

"For the World Is Hollow and I Have Touched the Sky." Written by Rik Vollaerts.

"Day of the Dove." Written by Jerome Bixby.

"Plato's Stepchildren." Written by Meyer Dolinsky.

"Wink of an Eye." Teleplay by Arthur Heinemann. Story by Lee Cronin.

"That Which Survives." Teleplay by John Meredyth Lucas. Story by Michael Richards.

"Let That Be Your Last Battlefield." Teleplay by Oliver Crawford. Story by Lee Cronin.

"Whom Gods Destroy." Teleplay by Lee Erwin. Story by Lee Erwin and Jerry Sohl.

"The Mark of Gideon." Written by George F. Slavin and Stanley Adams.

"The Lights of Zetar." Written by Jeremy Tarcher and Shari Lewis.

"The Cloud Minders." Teleplay by Margaret Armen. Story by David Gerrold and Oliver Crawford.

"The Way to Eden." Teleplay by Arthur Heinemann. Story by Michael Richards and Arthur Heinemann.

"Requiem for Methuselah." Written by Jerome Bixby.

"The Savage Curtain." Teleplay by Gene Roddenberry and Arthur Heinemann. Story by Gene Roddenberry.

"All Our Yesterdays." Written by Jean Lisette Aroeste.

"Turnabout Intruder." Teleplay by Arthur H. Singer. Story by Gene Roddenberry.

STAR TREK MOVIES
(ORIGINALLY RELEASED 1979-94)

Star Trek: The Motion Picture. Screenplay by Harold Livingston. Story by Alan Dean Foster.

Star Trek II: The Wrath of Khan. Screenplay by Jack B. Sowards. Story by Harve Bennett and Jack B. Sowards.

Star Trek III: The Search for Spock. Written by Harve Bennett.

Star Trek IV: The Voyage Home. Story by Leonard Nimoy and Harve Bennett. Screenplay by Steve Meerson & Peter Krikes and Harve Bennett & Nicholas Meyer.

Star Trek V: The Final Frontier. Story by William Shatner & Harve Bennett & David Loughery. Screenplay by David Loughery.

Star Trek VI: The Undiscovered Country. Story by Leonard Nimoy and Lawrence Konner & Mark Rosenthal. Screenplay by Nicholas Meyer & Denny Martin Flinn.

Star Trek Generations. Story by Rick Berman & Ronald D. Moore & Brannon Braga. Screenplay by Ronald D. Moore & Brannon Braga.

STAR TREK: THE NEXT GENERATION
YEAR 1 (FIRST AIRED 1987-88)

"Encounter at Farpoint, Part I." Written by D. C. Fontana and Gene Roddenberry.

"Encounter at Farpoint, Part II." Written by D. C. Fontana and Gene Roddenberry.

"The Naked Now." Teleplay by J. Michael Bingham. Story by John D. F. Black and J. Michael Bingham.

"Code of Honor." Written by Katharyn Powers & Michael Baron.

"Haven." Teleplay by Tracy Tormé. Story by Tracy Tormé & Lan Okun.

"Where No One Has Gone Before." Written by Diane Duane & Michael Reaves.

"The Last Outpost." Teleplay by Herbert Wright. Story by Richard Krzemien.

"Lonely Among Us." Teleplay by D. C. Fontana. Story by Michael Halperin.

"Justice." Teleplay by Worley Thorne. Story by Ralph Wills and Worley Thorne.

"The Battle." Teleplay by Herbert Wright. Story by Larry Forrester.

"Hide and Q." Teleplay by C. J. Holland and Gene Roddenberry. Story by C. J. Holland.

"Too Short a Season." Teleplay by Michael Michaelian and D. C. Fontana. Story by Michael Michaelian.

"The Big Goodbye." Written by Tracy Tormé.

"Datalore." Teleplay by Robert Lewin and Gene Roddenberry. Story by Robert Lewin and Maurice Hurley.

"Angel One." Written by Patrick Barry.

"11001001." Written by Maurice Hurley & Robert Lewin.

"Home Soil." Teleplay by Robert Sabaroff. Story by Karl Guers & Ralph Sanchez and Robert Sabaroff.

"When the Bough Breaks." Written by Hannah Louise Shearer.

"Coming of Age." Written by Sandy Fries.

"Heart of Glory." Teleplay by Maurice Hurley. Story by Maurice Hurley and Herbert Wright & D. C. Fontana.

"The Arsenal of Freedom." Teleplay by Richard Manning & Hans Beimler. Story by Maurice Hurley & Robert Lewin.

"Skin of Evil." Teleplay by Joseph Stefano and Hannah Louise Shearer. Story by Joseph Stefano.

"Symbiosis." Teleplay by Robert Lewin and Richard Manning and Hans Beimler. Story by Robert Lewin.

"We'll Always Have Paris." Written by Deborah Dean Davis and Hannah Louise Shearer.

"Conspiracy." Teleplay by Tracy Tormé. Story by Robert Sabaroff.

"The Neutral Zone." Television story & teleplay by Maurice Hurley. From a story by Deborah McIntyre & Mona Glee.

STAR TREK: THE NEXT GENERATION
YEAR 2 (FIRST AIRED 1988-89)

"The Child." Written by Jaron Summers & Jon Povill and Maurice Hurley.

"Where Silence Has Lease." Written by Jack B. Sowards.

"Elementary, Dear Data." Written by Brian Alan Lane.

"The Outrageous Okona." Teleplay by Burton Armus. Story by Les Menchen & Lance Dickson and David Landsberg.

"The Schizoid Man." Teleplay by Tracy Tormé. Story by Richard Manning & Hans Beimler.

"Loud as a Whisper." Written by Jacqueline Zambrano.

"Unnatural Selection." Written by John Mason & Mike Gray.

"A Matter of Honor." Teleplay by Burton Armus. Story by Wanda M. Haight & Gregory Amos and Burton Armus.

"The Measure of a Man." Written by Melinda M. Snodgrass.

"The Dauphin." Written by Scott Rubenstein & Leonard Mlodinow.

"Contagion." Written by Steve Gerber & Beth Woods.

"The Royale." Written by Keith Mills.

"Time Squared." Teleplay by Maurice Hurley. Story by Kurt Michael Bensmiller.

"The Icarus Factor." Teleplay by David Assael and Robert L. McCullough. Story by David Assael.

"Pen Pals." Teleplay by Melinda M. Snodgrass. Story by Hannah Louise Shearer.

"Q Who?" Written by Maurice Hurley.

"Samaritan Snare." Written by Robert L. McCullough.

"Up the Long Ladder." Written by Melinda M. Snodgrass.

"Manhunt." Written by Terry Devereaux.

"The Emissary." Television story and teleplay by Richard Manning & Hans Beimler. Based on an unpublished story by Thomas H. Calder.

"Peak Performance." Written by David Kemper.

"Shades of Gray." Teleplay by Maurice Hurley and Richard Manning & Hans Beimler. Story by Maurice Hurley.

STAR TREK: THE NEXT GENERATION YEAR 3 (FIRST AIRED 1989-90)

"The Ensigns of Command." Written by Melinda M. Snodgrass.

"Evolution." Teleplay by Michael Piller. Story by Michael Piller and Michael Wagner.

"The Survivors." Written by Michael Wagner.

"Who Watches the Watchers?" Written by Richard Manning & Hans Beimler.

"The Bonding." Written by Ronald D. Moore.

"Booby Trap." Teleplay by Ron Roman and Michael Piller & Richard Danus. Story by Michael Wagner & Ron Roman.

"The Enemy." Written by David Kemper and Michael Piller

"The Price." Written by Hannah Louise Shearer.

"The Vengeance Factor." Written by Sam Rolfe.

"The Defector." Written by Ronald D. Moore.

"The Hunted." Written by Robin Bernheim.

"The High Ground." Written by Melinda M. Snodgrass.

"Deja Q." Written by Richard Danus.

"A Matter of Perspective." Written by Ed Zuckerman.

"Yesterday's *Enterprise*." Teleplay by Ira Steven Behr & Richard Manning & Hans Beimler & Ronald D. Moore. From a story by Trent Christopher Ganino & Eric A. Stillwell.

"The Offspring." Written by Rene Echevarria.

"Sins of the Father." Teleplay by Ronald D. Moore & W. Reed Moran. Based on a teleplay by Drew Deighan.

"Allegiance." Written by Richard Manning & Hans Beimler.

"Captain's Holiday." Written by Ira Steven Behr.

"Tin Man." Written by Dennis Putman Bailey & David Bischoff.

"Hollow Pursuits." Written by Sally Caves.

"The Most Toys." Written by Shari Goodhartz.

"Sarek." Television story and teleplay by Peter S. Beagle. From an unpublished story by Marc Cushman & Jake Jacobs.

"Menage à Troi." Written by Fred Bronson & Susan Sackett.

"Transfigurations." Written by René Echevarria.

"The Best of Both Worlds, Part I." Written by Michael Piller.

STAR TREK: THE NEXT GENERATION YEAR 4 (FIRST AIRED 1990-91)

"The Best of Both Worlds, Part II." Written by Michael Piller.

"Suddenly Human." Teleplay by John Whelpley & Jeri Taylor. Story by Ralph Phillips.

"Brothers." Written by Rick Berman.

"Family." Written by Ronald D. Moore.

"Remember Me." Written by Lee Sheldon.

"Legacy." Written by Joe Menosky.

"Reunion." Teleplay by Thomas Perry & Jo Perry and Ronald D. Moore & Brannon Braga. Story by Drew Deighan and Thomas Perry & Jo Perry.

"Future Imperfect." Written by J. Larry Carroll & David Bennett Carren.

"Final Mission." Teleplay by Kasey Arnold-Ince and Jeri Taylor. Story by Kasey Arnold-Ince.

"The Loss." Teleplay by Hilary J. Bader and Alan J. Alder & Vanessa Greene. Story by Hilary J. Bader.

"Data's Day." Teleplay by Harold Apter and Ronald D. Moore. Story by Harold Apter.

"The Wounded." Teleplay by Jeri Taylor. Story by Stuart Charno & Sara Charno and Cy Chermax.

"Devil's Due." Teleplay by Philip Lazebnik. Story by Philip Lazebnik and Willian Douglas Lansford.

"Clues." Teleplay by Bruce D. Arthurs and Joe Menosky. Story by Bruce D. Arthurs.

"First Contact." Teleplay by Dennis Russell Bailey & David Bischoff and Joe Menosky & Ronald D. Moore and Michael Piller. Story by Marc Scott Zicree.

"Galaxy's Child." Teleplay by Maurice Hurley. Story by Thomas Kartozlan.

"Night Terrors." Teleplay by Pamela Douglas and Jeri Taylor. Story by Sheri Goodhartz.

"Identity Crisis." Teleplay by Brannon Braga. Based on a story by Timothy DeHaas.

"The Nth Degree." Written by Joe Menosky.

"QPid." Teleplay by Ira Steven Behr. Story by Randee Russell and Ira Steven Behr.

"The Drumhead." Written by Jeri Taylor.

"Half a Life." Teleplay by Peter Allan Fields. Story by Ted Roberts and Peter Allan Fields.

"The Host." Written by Michel Horvat.

"The Mind's Eye." Teleplay by René Echevarria. Story by Ken Schafer and René Echevarria.

"In Theory." Written by Joe Menosky & Ronald D. Moore.

"Redemption, Part I." Written by Ronald D. Moore.

STAR TREK: THE NEXT GENERATION
YEAR 5 (FIRST AIRED 1991-92)

"Redemption, Part II." Written by Ronald D. Moore.

"Darmok." Teleplay by Joe Menosky. Story by Philip Lazebnik and Joe Menosky.

"Ensign Ro." Teleplay by Michael Piller. Story by Rick Berman and Michael Piller.

"Silicon Avatar." Teleplay by Jeri Taylor. From a story by Lawrence V. Conley.

"Disaster." Teleplay by Ronald D. Moore. Story by Ron Jarvis and Philip A. Scorza.

"The Game." Teleplay by Brannon Braga. Story by Susan Sackett & Fred Bronson and Brannon Braga.

"Unification, Part I." Teleplay by Jeri Taylor. Story by Rick Berman and Michael Piller.

"Unification, Part II." Teleplay by Michael Piller. Story by Rick Berman and Michael Piller.

"A Matter of Time." Written by Rick Berman.

"New Ground." Teleplay by Grant Rosenberg. Story by Sara Charno and Stuart Charno.

"Hero Worship." Teleplay by Joe Menosky. Story by Hilary J. Bader.

"Violations." Teleplay by Pamela Gray and Jeri Taylor. Story by Shari Goodhartz and T. Michael and Pamela Gray.

"The Masterpiece Society." Teleplay by Adam Belanoff and Michael Piller. Story by James Kahn and Adam Belanoff.

"Conundrum." Teleplay by Barry Schkolnick. Story by Paul Schiffer.

"Power Play." Teleplay by Rene Balcer and Herbert J. Wright & Brannon Braga. Story by Paul Ruben and Maurice Hurley.

"Ethics." Teleplay by Ronald D. Moore. Story by Sara Charno & Stuart Charno.

"The Outcast." Written by Jeri Taylor.

"Cause and Effect." Written by Brannon Braga.

"The First Duty." Written by Ronald D. Moore & Naren Shankar.

"Cost of Living." Written by Peter Allan Fields.

"The Perfect Mate." Teleplay by Gary Perconte and Michael Piller. Story by René Echevarria and Gary Perconte.

"Imaginary Friend." Teleplay by Edithe Swensen and Brannon Braga. Story by Jean Louise Matthias & Ronald Wilkerson and Richard Fliegel.

"I, Borg." Written by René Echevarria.

"The Next Phase." Written by Ronald D. Moore.

"The Inner Light." Teleplay by Morgan Gendel and Peter Allan Fields. Story by Morgan Gendel.

"Time's Arrow, Part I." Teleplay by Joe Menosky and Michael Piller. Story by Joe Menosky.

STAR TREK: THE NEXT GENERATION
YEAR 6 (FIRST AIRED 1992-93)

"Time's Arrow, Part II." Teleplay by Jeri Taylor. Story by Joe Menosky.

"Realm of Fear." Written by Brannon Braga.

"Man of the People." Written by Frank Abatemarco.

"Relics." Written by Ronald D. Moore.

"Schisms." Teleplay by Brannon Braga. Story by Jean Louise Matthias & Ron Wilkerson.

"True-Q." Written by René Echevarria.

"Rascals." Teleplay by Allison Hock. Story by Ward Botsford & Diana Dru Botsford and Michael Piller.

"A Fistful of Datas." Teleplay by Robert Hewitt Wolfe and Brannon Braga. Story by Robert Hewitt Wolfe.

"The Quality of Life." Written by Naren Shankar.

"Chain of Command, Part I." Teleplay by Ronald D. Moore. Story by Frank Abatemarco.

"Chain of Command, Part II." Written by Frank Abatemarco.

"Ship in a Bottle." Written by René Echevarria.

"Aquiel." Teleplay by Brannon Braga & Ronald D. Moore. Story by Jeri Taylor.

"Face of the Enemy." Teleplay by Naren Shankar. Story by René Echevarria.

"Tapestry." Written by Ronald D. Moore.

"Birthright, Part I." Written by Brannon Braga.

"Birthright, Part II." Written by René Echevarria.

"Starship Mine." Written by Morgan Gendel.

"Lessons." Written by Ronald Wilkerson & Jean Louise Matthias.

"The Chase." Story by Ronald D. Moore & Joe Menosky. Teleplay by Joe Menosky.

"Frame of Mind." Written Brannon Braga.

"Suspicions." Written by Joe Menosky and Naren Shankar.

"Rightful Heir." Teleplay by Ronadl D. Moore. Story by James E. Brooks.

"Second Chances." Story by Mike Medlock. Teleplay by René Echevarria.

"Timescape." Written by Brannon Braga.

"Descent, Part I." Story by Jeri Taylor. Teleplay by Ronald D. Moore.

STAR TREK: DEEP SPACE NINE
YEAR 1 (FIRST AIRED 1993)

"Emissary, Parts I and II." Teleplay by Michael Piller. Story by Rick Berman and Michael Piller.

"A Man Alone." Teleplay by Michael Piller. Story by Gerald Sanford and Michael Piller.

"Past Prologue." Written by Kathryn Powers.

"Babel." Teleplay by Michael McGreevey and Naren

Shankar. Story by Sally Caves and Ira Steven Behr.

"Captive Pursuit." Teleplay by Jill Sherman Donner and Michael Piller. Story by Jill Sherman Donner.

"Q-Less." Teleplay by Robert Hewitt Wolfe. Story by Hannah Louise Shearer.

"Dax." Teleplay by D.C. Fontana and Peter Allan Fields. Story by Peter Allan Fields.

"The Passenger." Teleplay by Morgan Gendel and Robert Hewitt Wolfe & Michael Piller. Story by Morgan Gendel.

"Move Along Home." Teleplay by Frederick Rappaport and Lisa Rich & Jeanne Carrigan-Fauci. Story by Michael Piller.

"The Nagus." Teleplay by Ira Steven Behr. Story by David Livingston.

"Vortex." Written by Sam Rolfe.

"Battle Lines." Teleplay by Richard Danus and Evan Carlos Somers. Story by Hilary Bader.

"The Storyteller." Teleplay by Kurt Michael Bensmiller and Ira Steven Behr. Story by Kurt Michael Bensmiller.

"Progress." Written by Peter Allan Fields.

"If Wishes Were Horses." Teleplay by Neil McCue Crawford & William L. Crawford and Michael Piller. Story by Neil McCue Crawford & William L. Crawford.

"The Forsaken." Teleplay by Don Carlos Dunaway and Michael Piller. Story by Jim Trombetta.

"Dramatis Personae." Written by Joe Menosky.

"Duet" Teleplay by Peter Allan Fields. Story by Lisa Rich & Jeanne Carrigan-Fauci.

"In the Hands of the Prophets." Written by Robert Hewitt Wolfe.

STAR TREK: THE NEXT GENERATION
YEAR 7 (FIRST AIRED 1993-94)

"Descent, Part II." Written by René Echevarria.

"Liaisons." Teleplay by Jeanne Carrigan Fauci & Lisa Rich. Story by Roger Eschbacher & Jaq Greenspan.

"Interface." Written by Joe Menosky.

"Gambit, Part I." Teleplay by Naren Shankar. Story by Christopher Hatton and Naren Shankar.

"Gambit, Part II." Teleplay by Ronald D. Moore. Story by Naren Shankar.

"Phantasms." Written by Brannon Braga.

"Dark Page." Written by Hilary J. Bader.

"Attached." Written by Nicholas Sagan.

"Force of Nature." Written by Naren Shankar.

"Inheritance." Teleplay by Dan Koeppel and René Echevarria. Story by Dan Koeppel.

"Parallels." Written by Brannon Braga.

"The Pegasus." Written by Ronald D. Moore.

"Homeward." Teleplay by Naren Shankar. Television story by Spike Steingasser. Based on material by William N. Stape.

"Sub Rosa." Teleplay by Brannon Braga. Television story by Jeri Taylor. Based upon material by Jeanna F. Gallo.

"Lower Decks." Teleplay by René Echevarria. Story by Ronald Wilkerson & Jean Louise Matthias.

"Thine Own Self." Teleplay by Ronald D. Moore. Story by Christopher Hatton.

"Masks." Written by Joe Menosky.

"Eye of the Beholder." Teleplay by René Echevarria. Story by Brannon Braga.

"Genesis." Written by Brannon Braga.

"Journey's End." Written by Ronald D. Moore.

"Firstborn." Story by Mark Kalbfeld. Teleplay by René Echevarria.

"Bloodlines." Written by Nicholas Sagan.

"Emergence." Teleplay by Joe Menosky. Story by Brannon Braga.

"Preemptive Strike." Teleplay by René Echevarria. Story by Naren Shankar.

"All Good Things..." Written by Ronald D. Moore & Brannon Braga.

STAR TREK: DEEP SPACE NINE
YEAR 2 (FIRST AIRED 1993-94)

"The Homecoming." Teleplay by Ira Steven Behr. Story by Jeri Taylor and Ira Steven Behr.

"The Circle." Written by Peter Allan Fields.

"The Siege." Written by Michael Piller.

"Invasive Procedures." Teleplay by John Whelpley and Robert Hewitt Wolfe. Story by John Whelpley.

"Cardassians." Teleplay by James Crocker. Story by Gene Wolande & John Wright.

"Melora." Teleplay by Evan Carlos Somers and Steven Baum and Michael Piller & James Crocker. Story by Evan Carlos Somers.

"Rules of Acquisition." Teleplay by Ira Steven Behr. Story by Hilary Bader.

"Necessary Evil." Written by Peter Allan Fields.

"Second Sight" Teleplay by Mark Gehred-O'Connell and Ira Steven Behr & Robert Hewitt Wolfe. Story by Mark Gehred-O'connell.

"Sanctuary." Teleplay by Frederick Rappaport. Story by Gabe Essoe & Kelley Miles.

"Rivals." Teleplay by Joe Menosky. Story by Jim Trombetta and Michael Piller.

"The Alternate." Teleplay by Bill Dial. Story by Jim Trombetta and Bill Dial.

"Armageddon Game." Written by Morgan Gendel.

"Whispers." Written by Paul Robert Coyle.

"Paradise." Teleplay by Jeff King and Richard Manning & Hans Beimler. Story by Jim Trombetta and James Crocker.

"Shadowplay." Written by Robert Hewitt Wolfe.

"Playing God." Story by Jim Trombetta. Teleplay by Jim Trombetta and Michael Piller.

"Profit and Loss." Written by Flip Kobler & Cindy Marcus.

"Blood Oath." Television story and teleplay by Peter Allan Fields.

"The Maquis, Part I." Teleplay by James Crocker. Story by Rick Berman & Michael Piller & Jeri Taylor and James Crocker.

"The Maquis, Part II." Teleplay by Ira Steven Behr. Story by Rick Berman & Michael Piller & Jeri Taylor and Ira Steven Behr.

"The Wire." Written by Robert Hewitt Wolfe.

"Crossover." Teleplay by Peter Allan Fields & Michael Piller. Story by Peter Allan Fields.

"The Collaborator." Teleplay by Gary Holland and Ira Steven Behr & Robert Hewitt Wolfe. Story by Gary Holland.

"Tribunal." Written by Bill Dial.

"The Jem'Hadar." Written by Ira Steven Behr.

STAR TREK: DEEP SPACE NINE
YEAR 3 (FIRST AIRED 1994-95)

"The Search, Part I." Teleplay by Ronald D. Moore. Story by Ira Steven Behr & Robert Hewitt Wolfe.

"The Search, Part II." Teleplay by Ira Steven Behr. Story by Ira Steven Behr & Robert Hewitt Wolfe.

"The House of Quark." Story by Tom Benko. Teleplay by Ronald D. Moore.

"Equilibrium." Story by Christopher Teague. Teleplay by René Echevarria.

"Second Skin." Written by Robert Hewitt Wolfe.

"The Abandoned." Written by D. Thomas Maio & Steve Warnek.

"Civil Defense." Written by Mike Krohn.

"Meridian." Teleplay by Mark Gehred-O'Connel. Story by Hilary Bader and Evan Carlos Somers.

"Defiant." Written by Ronald D. Moore. Directed by Cliff Bole.

"Fascination." Teleplay by Philip LaZebnik. Story by Ira Steven Behr & James Crocker.

"Past Tense, Part I." Teleplay by Robert Hewitt Wolfe. Story by Ira Steven Behr & Robert Hewitt Wolfe.

"Past Tense, Part II." Teleplay by Ira Steven Behr & René Echevarria. Story by Ira Steven Behr & Robert Hewitt Wolfe.

"Life Support." Teleplay by Ronald D. Moore. Story by Christian Ford & Rober Soffer

"Heart of Stone." Written by Ira Steven Behr & Robert Hewitt Wolfe.

"Destiny." Written by David S. Cohen & Martin A. Winer.

"Prophet Motive." Written by Ira Steven Behr & Robert Hewitt Wolfe.

"Visionary." Teleplay by John Shirley. Story by Ethan H. Calk.

"Distant Voices." Teleplay by Ira Steven Behr & Robert Hewitt Wolfe. Story by Joe Menosky.

"Improbable Cause." Teleplay by René Echevarria. Story by Robert Lederman & David R. Long.

"Throught the Looking Glass." Written by Ira Steven Behr & Robert Hewitt Wolfe.

"The Die is Cast." Written by Ronald D. Moore.

"Explorers." Written by René Echevarria. Story by Hilary Bader.

"Family Business." Written by Ira Steven Behr & Robert Hewitt Wolfe.

"Shakaar." Written by Gordon Dawson.

"Facets." Written by Rene Echevarria.

"The Adversary." Written by Ira Steven Behr & Robert Hewitt Wolfe.

STAR TREK: VOYAGER
YEAR 1 (FIRST AIRED IN 1995)

"Caretaker." Teleplay by Michael Piller & Jeri Taylor. Story by Rick Berman & Michael Piller & Jeri Taylor.

"Parallax." Teleplay by Brannon Braga. Story by Jim Trombetta.

"Time and Again." Teleplay by David Kemper and Michael Piller. Story by David Kemper.

"Phage." Teleplay by Skye Dent and Brannon Braga. Story by Timothy DeHaas.

"The Cloud." Teleplay by Tom Szollosi and Michael Piller. Story by Brannon Braga.

"Eye of the Needle." Teleplay by Bill Dial and Jeri Taylor. Story by Hilary Bader.

"Ex Post Facto." Teleplay by Evan Carlos Somers and Michael Piller. Story by Evan Carlos Somers.

"Emanations." Written by Brannon Braga.

"Prime Factors." Teleplay by Michael Perricone and Greg Elliot. Story by David R. George III & Eric Stillwell.

"State of Flux." Teleplay by Chris Abbott. Story by Paul Robert Coyle.

"Heroes and Demons." Written by Naren Shankar.

"Cathexis." Teleplay by Brannon Braga. Story by Brannon Braga & Joe Menosky.

"Faces." Teleplay by Kenneth Biller. Story by Jonathan Glassner and Kenneth Biller.

"Jetrel." Teleplay by Jack Klein & Karen Klein and Kenneth Biller. Story by James Thomton & Scott Nimerfro.

"Learning Curve." Written by Ronald Wilkerson & Jean Louise Matthias.

STAR TREK: DEEP SPACE NINE
YEAR 4 (FIRST AIRED 1995-96)

"The Way of the Warrior." Written by Ira Steven Behr & Robert Hewitt Wolfe.

"Hippocratic Oath." Teleplay by Lisa Klink. Story by Nicholas Corea and Lisa Klink.

"The Visitor." Written by Michael Taylor.

"Indiscretion." Teleplay by Nicholas Corea. Story by Toni Marberry & Jack Treviño.

"Rejoined." Teleplay by Ronald D. Moore & René Echevarria. Story by René Echeverria.

"Starship Down." Written by David Mack & John J. Ordover.

"Little Green Men." Teleplay by Ira Steven Behr & Robert Hewitt Wolfe. Story by Toni Marberry & Jack Treviño.

"The Sword of Kahless." Teleplay by Hans Beimler. Story by Richard Danus.

"Our Man Bashir." Teleplay by Ronald D. Moore. Story by Robert Gillian.

"Homefront." Written by Ira Steven Behr & Robert Hewitt Wolfe.

"Paradise Lost." Teleplay by Ira Steven Behr & Robert Hewitt Wolfe. Story by Ronald D. Moore.

"Crossfire." Written by René Echevarria.

"Return to Grace." Teleplay by Hans Beimler. Story by Tom Benko.

"Sons of Mogh." Written by Ronald D. Moore.

"The Bar Association." Teleplay by Robert Hewitt Wolfe and Ira Steven Behr. Story by Barbara J. Lee & Jenifer A. Lee.

"Accession." Written by Jane Espenson.

"Rules of Engagement." Story by Bradley Thompson & David Weddle. Teleplay by Ronald D. Moore.

"Hard Time." Story by Daniel Keys Moran & Lynn Barker. Teleplay by Robert Hewitt Wolfe.

"Shattered Mirror." Written by Ira Steven Behr & Hans Beimler.

"The Muse." Teleplay by René Echevarria. Story by René Echevarria & Majel Barrett Roddenberry.

"For the Cause." Teleplay by Ronald D. Moore. Story by Mark Gehred-O'Connell.

"The Quickening." Written by Naren Shankar.

"To the Death." Written by Ira Steven Behr & Robert Hewitt Wolfe.

"Body Parts." Teleplay by Hans Beimler. Story by Louis P. DeSantis & Robert J. Bolivar.

"Broken Link." Teleplay by Robert Hewitt Wolfe & Ira Steven Behr. Story by George Brozak.

STAR TREK: VOYAGER
YEAR 2 (FIRST AIRED 1995-96)

"Projections." Written by Brannon Braga.

"Elogium." Teleplay by Kenneth Biller and Jeri Taylor. Story by Jimmy Diggs & Steve J. Kay.

"Twisted." Teleplay by Kenneth Biller. Story by Arnold Rudnick & Rich Hosek.

"The 37's." Written by Jeri Taylor & Brannon Braga.

"Initiations." Written by Kenneth Biller.

"Non Sequitur." Written by Brannon Braga.

"Parturition." Written by Tom Szollosi.

"Persistence of Vision." Written by Jeri Taylor.

"Tattoo." Teleplay by Michael Piller. Story by Larry Brody.

"Cold Fire." Teleplay by Brannon Braga. Story by Anthony Williams.

"Maneuvers." Written by Kenneth Biller.

"Resistance." Teleplay by Lisa Klink. Story by Michael Jan Friedman & Kevin J. Ryan.

"Prototype." Written by Nickolas Corea.

"Death Wish." Teleplay by Michael Piller. Story by Shawn Piller.

"Alliances." Written by Jeri Taylor.

"Threshold." Teleplay by Brannon Braga. Story by Michael DeLuca.

"Meld." Teleplay by Michael Piller. Story by Michael Sussman.

"Dreadnought." Written by Gary Holland.

"Investigations." Teleplay by Jeri Taylor. Story by Jeff Schnaufer & Ed Bond.

"Lifesigns." Written by Kenneth Biller.

"Deadlock." Written by Brannon Braga.

"Innocence." Teleplay by Lisa Klink. Story by Anthony Williams.

"The Thaw." Teleplay by Joe Menosky. Story by Richard Gadas.

"Tuvix." Teleplay by Kenneth Biller. Story by Andrew Shepard Price & Mark Gaberman.

"Resolutions." Written by Jeri Taylor.

"Basics, Part I." Written by Michael Piller.

INDEX

F

Fabrina (people); 73
Fabrina system (in which sun goes nova),
6, 73
"Faces" (VGR), 136; **238**
"Face of the Enemy" (TNG); 108, **186**
"Facets" (DS9), 13, 22, 83, **240**
Fajo, Kivas (Zibalian trader), 149
fal-tor-pan (Vulcan ceremony), 34, 86
Falow (Master Surchid), 188
"Family" (TNG), 105, 106, 107, 110, **153**,
159
"Family Business" (DS9), 27, 110, 118,
227, 238, **239**
Famous Spock Nerve Pinch (FSNP); SEE:
Vulcan nerve pinch
Farallon, Dr. (inventor of particle fountain),
120, 182
Farpoint Station, 121, 122, 295
Farragut, U.S.S. (NCC-1647):
conjecture regarding Kirk's *Republic*
assignment, 43;
and Kirk's rank at the academy, 44;
Kirk assigned to, 45, 268;
Garrovick commands, 45;
visits Tyree's planet, 46;
encounters vampire cloud, 47;
Kirk feels responsible for deaths on,
67
"Fascination" (DS9), 189, 220, 224, **227**
Fearless, U.S.S.; Kosinski performs warp
upgrades on, 124
Federation. SEE: United Federation of
Planets
Fek'lhri (Klingons defeated by Kahless), 9
felicium (addictive drug used to halt plague
on Ornara), 34, 129
Fenna (wife of Seyetik, Gideon), 205
Ferengi (people):
begin following path of capitalism, 6;
Gint is first Grand Nagus, 6;
ship crashes near Roswell, 18;
homeworld is called Ferenginar, 110;
ship attacks *Stargazer*, 112:
steal an energy converter, 124;
first contact with Federation, 125;
authorities relieve Bok of command,
126;
attempt to buy Barzan wormhole, 143;
at Trade Agreements Conference,
150;
release Bok, 177;
disavows attack on *Enterprise*-D, 181;
Grand Nagus Zek convenes
conference, 188;
attempt to open trade in Gamma
Quadrant, 203;
Nog is first Ferengi in Starfleet, 231;
Zek rewrites Rules of Acquisition,
232,233;
authorities charge Ishka, 239;
ritual of adulthood, 247;
consider labor unions to be abhorrent,
255,
revoke Quark's business licence, 262
Ferenginar (planet, Ferengi homeworld):
Quark leaves, 110;
Rom leaves, 118;
Nog visits, 232;
Quark and Rom return to, 239;

Quark visits, 261
Fermat, Pierre de (Earth mathematician);
dies, 12
Fermat's last theorem (mathematical
puzzle):
formulated, 12-13;
validated in 1993, 22;
Dax, Tobin attempts to solve, 277
Fesarius (ship of the First Federation), 51
Ficus Sector (location of Bringloid V and
Mariposa), 32
"Final Mission" (TNG), 29, **155,** 276, 287
Finn, Marla (Starfleet engineer); body
thrown in plasma stream, 120
Finnegan (friend of Kirk from the acade-
my), 44
Finney, Benjamin;
befriends Kirk, James T., 43;
names daughter after Kirk, 43;
makes error on *Republic*, 43;
believed killed, 55;
Kirk accused of his death, 55-56, 268
Finney, Jamie (daughter of Finney,
Benjamin), 43
First Contact, Star Trek: SEE *Star Trek:
First Contact*
"First Contact" (TNG), 38, 106, **159**;
"First Duty, The" (TNG), 33, 45, 66, 93, 95,
96, 98, 104, 111, 121, **175**, 197
"Firstborn" (TNG); 9, 187, **215,** 264, 267
"Fistful of Datas, A" (TNG); **181**
"Flashback" (VGR); 49, 89, 90, 91, 92,
107, 215, 270, 271, 281, 282, 286
Fleming, U.S.S. (Federation Starship),
203
Flint (nearly immortal human):
born in Mesopotamia, 7;
identities of, 40, 76-78
"Force of Nature"(TNG); 170, **203-204**
"Forsaken, The" (DS9), **193**
Fontana, Dorothy C. (Star Trek story editor,
associate producer):
predicts day of moon launch, 20;
chooses name for Christopher, John's
son, 24;
discusses UESPA, 34;
discusses Spock's age, 39;
writes "Yesteryear," 40;
discusses Kirk's middle name, 50;
discusses dilithium crystals; 50
discusses "Naked Time" (TOS) and
"Tomorrow Is Yesterday" (TOS),
53;
comments on Klingons and
Romulans, 60; and "Joanna", 76,
269;
discusses animated episodes, 78;
discusses McCoy's marriage and
divorce, 269;
discusses episodes being filmed out
of order, 299
"For the Cause"(DS9), 258, 259, **260**
"For the World is Hollow and I Have
Touched the Sky" (TOS), 6, **73**, 78
Fox, Ambassador (Federation official); 58,
59
Founders (of the Dominion);
founded Dominion, 9;
controlled other races, 9;
Zek wants peaceful contact with, 222;
Defiant, U.S.S. attempts to locate,

222;
conduct experiment on *Defiant* crew,
223;
fear of causes decline in trade at
Deep Space 9, 223;
use drugs to control Jem'Hadar
soldiers, 180, 225;
Romulan and Cardassian attack
against, 226-227, 236-237;
evacuate homeworld, 227;
Odo is a, 223;
Alpha Quadrant concerns about, 223,
241, 250, 251, 262, 263;
Romulan/Cardassian fleet ambushed
by, 237;
Odo judged by, 262
"Frame of Mind" (TNG), 111, **191**
Frame of Mind (play written and directed
by Crusher, Beverly), 191
France, Earth:
life begins in, 2;
Sandrine's bar opens in, 14;
student unrest, 25;
Picard, Jean-Luc born in, 92, 272;
Picard visits, 107, 153, 272;
"Friday's Child" (TOS); **62**
FSNP (Famous Spock Nerve Pinch),SEE:
Vulcan nerve pinch
"Future's End, Part I" (VGR), 22, 265, 298
"Future's End, Part II" (VGR), 22, 265, 298
"Future Imperfect" (TNG), 98, **155**, 157

G

Gagarin, Yuri (first human to travel in
space), 19
Gagarin IV (planet, site of Darwin research
station), 111, 134
Gaila (Quark's cousin), 118
Galaxy class Starship development project,
102
"Galaxy's Child" (TNG), 115, **159**
Galen IV (planet with Federation colony),
111, 114
Galen, Richard (archaeologist), 100, 116,
172, 190
Galileo (scientist, built first astronomical
telescope), 12
"Galileo Seven, The" (TOS), **55**
Galileo, Shuttlecraft;
crashes on Taurus II, 55;
crashes on planetoid, 62;
transports Picard to *Enterprise*-D, 112
Gallitep, Butcher of, 114, 195
Gallitep labor camp, 114
Galliulin, Irina (Chekov's love interest), 270
Galorndon Core (planet):
near Federation space, 142;
Enterprise-D responds to distress call
from, 142;
Vulcan ship sent to, 170
"Gambit, Part I"(TNG), **199-200**
"Gambit, Part II"(TNG), 9, **200**
"Game, The" (TNG), 168; **169**
Gamelan V (planet); radioactive freighter
orbits, 29, 155
"Gamesters of Triskelion, The" (TOS), **67**
Gamma Arigulon system; *Enterprise*-D
investigates radiation anomalies in,

gateway found by the Dominion, 261

"Identity Crisis" (TNG), 14, 113, **160**

"If Wishes Were Horses" (DS9), 26, 27, 32, 43, **193**

Ilia, Lieutenant (*Enterprise* navigator);
reported missing in action, 80;
would have appeared in second TV series, 81;
and rec room display, 283;
whereabouts still a mystery, 287

"Imaginary Friend" (TNG), **176-177**

"I, Mudd" (TOS), **65**

"Immunity Syndrome, The" (TOS), **67-68**

"Improbable Cause"(DS9), 102, 227, **236-237**

impulse engine (spacecraft propulsion system); new type developed, 35; Torias Dax's shuttle not ready for full test of, 84

Imzadi (Betazoid term for "beloved," 118, 273

"Indiscretion" (DS9), 111, 201, **246**

Indri VIII (planet); seeded with genetic material, 2

Ingraham B (planet); suffered mass insanity, 13, 50

"Inheritance" (TNG), 97, 98, 99, **204-205**

Inheritors (name given indigenous hunters in Earth's Siberian Peninsula by extraterrestrials), 5, 44

"Initiations" (VGR), 104, 223, **243**

"Inner Light, The" (TNG), 11, **178**

Innis, Valeda (Electorine of Haven), 124

"Innocence" (VGR), 81, **258**

interdimensional gateways; 4, 261

interdimensional transport device; Ansata separatists begin using, 142

"Interface" (TNG), 98, 187, 197, 198, **199**

interphase (subspace phenomenon);
causes loss of *Defiant* and Kirk, 72;
basis for experimental Romulan cloaking device, 178
and protouniverse, 213

interphasic parasites, 201

"In Theory" (TNG); 162, **164**, 164

"In the Hands of the Prophets" (DS9); **196**

Intrepid, U.S.S. (*Constitution*-class Starship, NCC-1631); has all-Vulcan crew, 68; destroyed, 67

Intrepid, U.S.S. (*Excelsior*-class Starship, NCC-38907):
renders aid at Khitomer, 105;
rescues young Worf, 105;
Sergey Rozhenko is warp field specialist on, 104;
Donald Kaplan serves aboard, 111;
Enterprise-D compares data logs from, 147

"Invasive Procedures" (DS9), **200**

"Investigations" (VGR), 208, 253, **256-257**

invidium (chemical contaminant); aboard the *Enterprise*-D, 148, 149

Iowa, Earth; birthplace of Kirk, 39

Ireland, reunification of, 26

Irina. SEE: Gallilun, Irina

Ishka (mother of Quark), 239

Ishikawa, Keiko; SEE: O'Brien, Keiko

"Is There in Truth No Beauty?" (TOS), 41, **72**

Iyaaran (people), 198

J

Jadzia, SEE: Dax, Jadzia

Jarheel (spaceship captain), 185

Jameson, Admiral Mark;
born, 82;
commands *Gettysburg*, 82;
marries, 94;
solves hostage situation, 94;
actions exacerbated civil war on Mordan IV, 116;
Karnas requests assistance of, 126;
returns to Mordan IV and dies, 126

Jameson, Ann; marries Jameson, Admiral Mark, 94;

Janeway, Kathryn (*Voyager* commanding officer);
meets Tuvok, 159;
dog Molly is pregnant, 228;
protects Ocampa, 229;
orders *Voyager* to return to Earth, 229;
promotes B'Elanna Torres to chief engineer, 229;
encourages energy conservation, 230;
performs Native American ritual, 231;
refuses to use trajector technology, 234;
enjoys holodeck program of old England, on Earth, 237;
concerned with integration of Maquis crew members, 240;
her dialog establishes year of early second season, 243;
cultural exchange with subspace distortion wave life-form, 245;
has mutated baby with Tom Paris, 253;
undergoes genetic therapy, 253;
orders Suder incarcerated, 254;
grants asylum to Quinn, 255;
duplicate version sacrifices her life and ship, 257;
orders Tuvix to death, 260;
suffers nearly fatal virus poisoning, 260;
put in stasis, 260;
orders *Voyager* to leave her behind, 261;
personal timeline and notes, 281

Janus VI (planet), home of the Horta, 4

Jarada (people contacted by *Enterprise*-D); last contact with prior to 2364; 103

Jared (leader of Ventax II), 10

Jaresh-Inyo (Federation president);
begins political career, 92;
rejects security clampdown on Earth, 251;
declares planetwide day of mourning, 250;
authorizes planetwide state of emergency, 251;
restores civil liberties to Federation citizen, 251

Ja'rod (Klingon politician):
suspected of treason by Klingon High Council member, 105;
father of Duras, 105;
discovered to have plotted with

Romulans, 105

Jaro Essa (Bajoran minister);
assigns Li Nalas to station Deep Space 9, 198;
attempts coup to depose Bajoran government, 199;
linked to secret Cardassian weapons shipment, 200

Jarok, Admiral Alidar (Romulan officer);
and Battle of Cheron, 33;
censured by Romulan High Command, 141;
defects to Federation and commits suicide, 144

J'Ddan (Klingon exobiologist), 161-162

Jellico, Captain Edward (Starfleet officer);
takes temporary command of *Enterprise*-D, 182, 183

Jem'Hadar; enforcers for the Founders, 9, 36, 180, 219, 221, 223, 224, 246

Jenolen (transport), 91, 180

Jeraddo (Bajoran moon); 110, 192

"Jetrel" (VGR), 106, 113, **238-239**

Jetrel, Ma'Bor (Haakonian scientist), 238, 239

Jev; commits telepathic rapes, 170, 172

Jo'Bril (scientist), 191

J'naii (androgynous species), 174

"Joanna," earlier verson of "Way to Eden, The" (TOS), 76, 269

joint strike force (of Romulan and Cardassian attack forces), 236, 237

Jonas, Michael (*Voyager* crew member);
provides technical information to Kazon operative, 253;
evidence of his transmissions found, 253;
continues to send technical information, 254;
instructed to sabotoge *Voyager*, 256;
killed during Kazon attack, 256

Jones, Dr. Miranda; links minds with Kollos, 72

Jono, aka Rossa, Jeremiah, 111

"Journey to Babel" (TOS); 34, 38, 40, 42, 45, 48, **66**, 71

"Journey's End" (TNG), 13, 35, 108, 109, 175, 208, **214**

July 4, 2033; Fifty-second state admitted to United States, 26

Jung, Carl, (psychiatrist), 17

"Justice" (TNG); **125**

Justman, Robert; his gag about Roddenberry, Gene became "May the Great Bird of the Galaxy," 52

K

Kaelon II (planet); adopted custom of Resolution, 10

Kahless the Unforgettable (early Klingon leader):
united Klingon Homeworld, 9;
fought brother Morath, 9;
being calling itself found on Excalbia, 77;
clone of becomes emperor, 192

Kahlest (Worf's nursemaid); survives

Rugal (son of Pa'Dar), 119, 201
Ruk (android built by the Old Ones), 3
"Rules of Aquisition" (DS9), **203**
Rules of Aquisition (Ferengi wisdom);
    written by Gint, 6; revised by Zek,
    232, 233
"Rules of Engagement" (DS9); 106, 251,
    258
Rumarie (ancient Vulcan pagan festival),
    11
Rurigan (Yaderan person); creates
    holographic village, 101, 116
Rura Penthe (dilithium mines); Kirk and
    McCoy are sentenced to, 89
Rushton infection (disease); Aster,
    Jeremy's father dies of, 117
Russell, Dr. Toby (physician); attempts to
    cure Worf with experimental
    procedure, 174
Ruth; romantically involved with Kirk, 45
Rutia IV (planet); Ansata separatists are
    located on, 91, 139
Rutledge, U.S.S. (Federation Starship);
    at Setlik III massacre, 106, 279, 291;
    O'Brien, Miles Edward serves on,
        106;
    former crewmember apparently
        moves to Volan III, 119, 278;
    commanded by Ben Maxwell, 106,
        291
R'uustai ceremony (Klingon ceremony of
    bonding); Worf and Aster, Jeremy par-
    ticipate in, 142
ryetalyn (drug needed to cure Rigelian
    fever), 77

S

Saavik, Lieutenant (Starfleet officer):
    enters Starfleet Academy, 83;
    promoted to lieutenant while at
        Starfleet Academy, 85;
    takes *Kobayashi Maru* test, 85;
    assigned to *Grissom*; investigates
        Genesis Planet, 85;
    survives destruction of *Grissom*, 86
Sahndara star system (original home of the
    Platonians), 8, 73
Sakuro's disease; Hedford contracts, 62
Salia (head of state of Daled IV), 135
Saltah'na (Gamma Quadrant civilization),
    193, 194
"Samaritan Snare" (TNG), **137**
Samuels, William (Federation colonist);
    born, 96;
    settles on Volan II, 109;
    apparently admits crime, 216;
    apparently commits suicide, 216
Sanction (Ornaran freighter ship); T'Jon
    assumes command of the, 114;
    destroyed, 129
"Sanctuary" (DS9); 12, 204, **206**
Sanctuary Districts (American internment
    camps);
    established, 25;
    site of Bell Riots, 25;
    abolished, 26
Sandoval, Elias (Omicron Ceti III colony
    leader), 48, 49

Sandrine (bar owner), 14
Sandrine's (bar); opened, 14; re-created in
    holodeck program, 231
San Francisco, Earth (city by the bay);
    Guinan lives in, 15;
    invaded by Devidians, 15;
    Data visits, 15;
    Clemens, Samuel in, 15;
    O'Brien, Miles and Kira Nerys in, 17,
        19, 27;
    Kirk, et al. visit in 1986, 21, 293;
    Sanctuary Districts located in, 25;
    Bell Riots in, 25;
    United Federation of Planets
        Council located in, 33;
    Hikaru Sulu born in, 40, 270;
    Uhura stationed in, 40;
    Starship Enterprise launched
        from, 41, 283;
    orbital drydock, *Enterprise* undergoes
        refitting at the, 79;
    Enterprise assigned to academy
        duty in, 82;
    Excelsior commissioned at, 84;
    Kirk has apartment in, 84;
    Data's head is found beneath,
        15, 178, 179;
    Kim, Harry has relationship with
        woman in, 282
Sankur, Jal (Kazon), 104
Saratoga, U.S.S. (Federation Starship,
    NCC-1937); first female captain
    commanded the, 78
Saratoga, U.S.S. (Federation Starship,
    NCC-31911); destroyed at Wolf 359,
    152; Sisko, Benjamin is survivor of,
    152, 277;
    anniversary of destruction of, 205
"Sarek" (TNG), 52, 66, 81, **149**, 269, 271
Sarek (Vulcan ambassador, Spock's
    father);
    born, 34;
    has son, Sybok, with Vulcan
        princess, 38;
    marries Grayson, Amanda, 38;
    Spock's father, 39;
    and Spock's childhood, 40;
    disapproves of Spock's career choice,
        42, 48;
    has heart attacks, 66;
    attends Babel Conference, 66;
    works on Legaran treaty, 81;
    asks Spock to serve as envoy to
        the Klingons, 89;
    discusses meeting of Spock and
        Pardek, 90;
    suffers from Bendii Syndrome, 149;
    mind melds with Picard, 149;
    secures agreement with Legarans,
        149;
    suggests that Picard meet Pardek,
        169;
    dies, 169, 170;
    family name of, 269;
    son's wedding, 269;
    achievements of, 271;
    personal notes and timeline, 271
Sargon (citizen of an ancient civilization);
    his people explore the galaxy, 3;
    discusses the destruction of his
        planet, 3;

    departs into oblivion, 68
Sarpeidon (planet, homeworld to
    Zarabeth);
    experiences an ice age, 7;
    Zarabeth exiled to past 7,
    atavachron on, 77;
    sun of explodes, 77
Satie, Admiral Norah (Starfleet official);
    posts Picard to command
        Enterprise-D, 122;
    investigates conspiracy, 130;
    investigates possible sabotage of
        Enterprise-D, 162;
    investigation of found unconstitutional,
        162
Satok (Vulcan security minister), 200
"Savage Curtain, The" (TOS), 9, 28. **77**,
    288
Scalos (planet), 74
Scalosians, SEE: Scalos
"Schisms" (TNG), **180**
"Schizoid Man, The" (TNG), **134**
Scott, Montgomery (*Enterprise* chief
    engineer);
    born, 38;
    enters Starfleet Academy, 40;
    begins career as engineer, 41;
    graduates Starfleet Academy, 41;
    injured in explosion, 63;
    supervises refit of *Enterprise*, 79;
    supervises testing of *Enterprise*-A,
        87;
    buys a boat, 89;
    attends launch of *Enterprise*-B, 90;
    retires and disappears, 91;
    inconsistencies between "Relics"
        (TNG) and *Star Trek
        Generations* discussed, 91;
    found aboard *U.S.S. Jenolan*, 180;
    flies off into the unknown, 180;
    notes and timeline, 270
Scott, Tryla (Starfleet officer); present on
    Dytallix B, 130; Satie enlists aid of,
    130
"Search, The, Part I" (DS9), 140, **222**
"Search, The, Part II" (DS9), **223**
"Second Chances" (TNG), 115, 117, 118,
    193
"Second Sight" (DS9); 183, **205**
"Second Skin" (DS9); 103, 104, 225
Second World War; SEE: World War II
sehlat (Spock's childhood pet), 40
"Seige, The" (DS9), 116, **200**
Sela (offspring of Yar, Tasha and a
    Romulan general);
    born, 104, 146, 275;
    Yar, Tasha tries to escape with, 108,
        294;
    supervises La Forge's brainwashing,
        163;
    not played by Denise Crosby in
        "The Mind's Eye" (TNG), 163;
    in Klingon civil war, 166;
    directs Romulan force to conquer
        Vulcan, 170;
    describes fate of Yar, Tasha, 103;
    questions about alternate time line,
        294
Selar, Dr. (*Enterprise*-D staff physician);
    discovers Graves to be ill, 134;
    other mentions of, 134

born, 94;
involved with Jean-Luc Picard, 105;
son, Jason, is born, 106;
settles on Camor V, 115;
dies, 119
Vigo, Jason (son of Miranda):
born, 94;
moves to Camor V, 115;
appears to be son of Picard,
Jean-Luc, 216
Viking I; lands on Mars, 20
Vilmor II (planet); seeded with genetic
material, 2
Vina (last survivor of *Columbia*);
discusses Talosians with Pike, 4;
survives *Columbia* crash, 39;
cared for by Talosians, 39;
"Violations"(TNG), 103, 170, **172**
virus, alien, 52
"Visionary" (DS9), 233, **234**
"Visitor, The" (DS9), 95, **245**
VISOR (gizmo that lets Geordi see),
84, 101, 226
Volan II (planet); near Cardassian
border, 109
voles (Cardassian rodents);
infest Deep Space 9, 212;
Quark and Morn prepare to stage
fight of, 235;
Quark negotiates deal for bellies
of, 261
Volterra nebula (site of protostar
development), 190
Vorta (administrators for the Founders), 9,
223, 261
"Vortex" (DS9), **189**
Vostok I (first Earth manned spacecraft),
19
Voyager VI (early interplanetary robotic
science probe); is launched from
Earth, 23; later becomes V'Ger, 80
Voyager, U.S.S. (Federation Starship);
at Big Bang, 1;
departs Deep Space 9, 228;
caught in displacment wave,
transported 70,000 light years,
228;
unable to use replicators, 229;
caught in spatial disturbance, 229;
finds unusable wormhole, 232;
warp core ejected, 237;
launches rescue mission, 238;
lands, 242, 262;
Kazon steal transporter module,
249;
encounters spatial rift, 257;
encounters humanoids in suspended
animation, 260;
stolen by Seska and Culluh, 263;
vrietalyn, SEE: ryetalyn
Vulcan (planet, homeworld to Spock and
Tuvok);
seeded with genetic material, 2;
pre-history of exploration by Sargon's
people, 3;
suffers terrible wars, 8;
Surak leads toward logic and peace,
8;
schism with Romulans, 8;
Spock undergoes retraining on, 86;
ship *T'Pau* is stolen as part of plot

against 169;
Vulcan nerve pinch; first use of, 52
Vulcan princess; is Sybok's mother, 38
Vulcans (people):
entire crew of *Intrepid* are, 68;
dissidents depart planet, 8;
interstellar flight capabilities, 9;
mind-melding ability of, 54
Vulcan Science Academy, 42, 112

W

Wade, Dr. April (researcher); born on
Earth, 49; nominated for Carrington
Award, 174
Wadi (people from Gamma Quadrant),
188
Wallace, Dr. Janet (endocrinologist); Kirk
has romantic liaison with, 48
Wallace, Theodore (husband to Janet
Wallace), 48
warp core assembly, 201
warp drive, 26, 28, 46, 70, 143; causing
serious damage to fabric of space,
203
warp factors; discussed, 57
warp field; low level, used in attempt to
fix the orbit of the Bre'el IV moon,
145
warp drive nacelles, 212
warp speed limit, 204
"Way of the Warrior" (DS9), 110, 152; 224,
226, 237, **244**
"Way to Eden, The" (TOS), **76**, 269, 270
"We'll Always Have Paris" (TNG), 102,
107, **129-130**
Wellington, U.S.S. (Federation Starship);
Ro Laren serves on the, 101, 166,
276
Wesley, Commodore Bob (Starfleet
official); task force commander, 69;
named for Roddenberry, Gene's
pseudonym, 69
"What Are Little Girls Made Of?" (TOS),
3, 39, 48, **54**, 61
"When the Bough Breaks"(TNG), 7, **128**
"Where No Man Has Gone Before" (TOS),
23, 28, 37, 40, 41, 43, 44, 49, **50**,
90
"Where No One Has Gone Before" (TNG),
124, 272, 275
"Where Silence Has Lease" (TNG); **133**
"Whispers" (DS9), 115, 172, 209, **210**
"Whom Gods Destroy" (TOS); 42, 43, 73,
75
"Who Mourns for Adonais" (TOS), 7, 42,
63
"Who Watches the Watchers?" (TNG), **141-
142**
Wiles, Andrew (mathematician), 22
"Wink of an Eye" (TOS), **74**
Winn (Bajoran leader):
contender to become kai, 196, 217;
suspected of assassination attempt,
196;
campaigns hard, 218;
forces Bareil to withdraw from
election, 219;
elected kai, 219;

asks Bareil to become advisor,
220;
conducts secret peace talks with
Cardassians, 230;
signs peace accord, 230;
becomes acting first minister, 240;
mishandles Dahkur Province
farm equipment incident,
240;
withdraws bid to become first minister,
240
Winter, Captain James (early draft name
for *Enterprise* captain), 42
"Wire, The" (DS9), 102, 176, **217**
Wise Ones; name for the Preservers, 13
"Wolf in the Fold" (TOS), 17, 20, 29, 31,
32, 51, 63, **64**
Wolf 359 (star near Sol);
armada assembled at, 151;
thirty-nine ships lost in battle of, 152;
Picard's death in battle of in
alternate quantum reality,
205;
Sisko in, 152, 277
Woodstock, New York, Earth; musical
festival, 20
Worf (first Klingon warrior in Starfleet);
born on Qo'noS, 101;
brother Kurn is born, 104;
goes to Khitomer with his parents,
104;
is rescued by Rozhenko, Sergey, 105;
moves to Earth, 110;
reaches Age of Ascension, 113;
beats up some teenaged boys, 106;
bonds with Aster, Jeremy in *R'uustai*
ceremony, 142;
poses as captain of the *Enterprise*-D,
138;
resumes relationship with
K'Ehleyr, conceives a child, 138;
promoted to full Lieutenant, 132;
visited by foster parents, 153;
learns of son, 154;
kills Duras, 154;
resigns Starfleet commission, 164;
joins Klingon defense forces, 164;
honor is restored to family of by
Gowron, 164;
is reinstated into Starfleet, 166;
assists with O'Brien, Molly's birth,
168;
is seriously injured, 174;
has crisis of faith; 192;
thrown into state of flux, 205;
promoted to lieutenant commander,
226;
visits Boreth again, 226;
assigned to Deep Space 9, 244;
tries to kill Kurn as requested, 254;
moves his quarters to *Starship
Defiant*, 255;
fires on decloaking Klingon ship,
257;
murdered in future Klingon High
Council, 264
World Series (Earth baseball game);
Cardinals win, 19; Kings win the last,
27
World War II; Keeler, Edith's work delays
American entry into, 16; Hitler wins in

BIBLIOGRAPHY

Alexander, David: *Star Trek Creator, the Authorized Biography of Gene Roddenberry* (Roc Books, 1994). In-depth biography of *Star Trek*'s creator.

Asherman, Allan: *The Making of Star Trek II* (Pocket Books, 1982). Interviews with key production personnel and the cast of the second feature film.

Asherman, Allan: *The Star Trek Compendium* (Pocket Books, rev. ed. 1993). Episode-by-episode guide to the original *Star Trek* series and feature films.

Asherman, Allan: *The Star Trek Interview Book* (Pocket Books, 1988). Interviews with cast and key creative personnel from the original *Star Trek* television series and feature films.

Clarke, Arthur C.: *Profiles of the Future* (Bantam Books, 1958). Clarke's classic exploration into the limits of technology; arguably the source of inspiration for some of *Star Trek*'s future science.

Dillard, J.M.: *Star Trek: Where No One Has Gone Before, A History in Pictures* (Pocket Books, rev. ed. 1996). A photographic history of *Star Trek* from the original series to *Star Trek: Voyager*. Introduction by William Shatner.

Fern, Yvonne: *Gene Roddenberry: The Last Conversation, A Dialogue With the Creator of Star Trek* (Pocket Books, rev. ed. 1996). The last in-depth interview with Roddenberry, conducted shortly before his death.

Gerrold, David: *The Trouble with Tribbles* (Ballantine Books, 1974). Gerrold's experiences in the writing and production of the classic Original Series episode.

Gerrold, David: *The World of Star Trek* (Ballantine Books, 1974; rev. ed. Bluejay Books, 1984). Overview of the original *Star Trek* phenomenon by one of the writers of the original *Star Trek* series.

Koenig, Walter: *Chekov's Enterprise: A Personal Journal of the Making of Star Trek: The Motion Picture* (Pocket Books, 1980; Intergalactic Press, 1991). Anecdotes from the actor's personal diary.

Krauss, Lawrence M.: *The Physics of Star Trek* (Basic Books, 1995). Real science as seen through the *Star Trek* universe. Introduction by Stephen W. Hawking.

Nemecek, Larry: *Star Trek: The Next Generation Companion* (Pocket Books, rev. ed. 1995). Episode-by-episode guide to the series.

Okrand, Marc: *The Klingon Dictionary* (Pocket Books, 1985). Authentic reference to the spoken Klingon language by the linguist who invented it for the films and show.

Okuda, Michael and Okuda, Denise and Mirek, Debbie: *The Star Trek Encyclopedia: A Reference Guide to the Future* (Pocket Books, 1994). An A-to-Z listing of virtually everything in the *Star Trek* universe.

Reeves-Stevens, Judith and Garfield: *The Art of Star Trek* (Pocket Books, 1995). An extensive collection of art from all incarnations of *Star Trek*. Introduction by Herman Zimmerman.

Reeves-Stevens, Judith and Garfield: *The Making of Star Trek: Deep Space Nine* (Pocket Books, 1994). Behind the scenes of *Star Trek: Deep Space Nine*.

Sackett, Susan and Roddenberry, Gene: *The Making of Star Trek: The Motion Picture* (Pocket Books, 1980). Behind the scenes of the first feature film.

Shatner, William with Kreski, Chris: *Star Trek Memories* (Harper Collins, 1993). Anecdotes from the making of the original series.

Shatner, William with Kreski, Chris: *Star Trek Movie Memories* (Harper Collins, 1994). Anecdotes from the making of the *Star Trek* feature films.

Solow, Herbert F. and Justman, Robert H: *Inside Star Trek, The Real Story* (Pocket Books, 1996). Insightful, authoritative history of the original *Star Trek* series by two of the key figures who made it happen.

Sternbach, Rick and Okuda, Michael: *Star Trek: The Next Generation Technical Manual* (Pocket Books, 1991). Just about everything you ever wanted to know about the inner workings of the *Starship Enterprise*-D, in far more technical detail than you *ever* wanted to know it. Introduction by Gene Roddenberry.

Sternbach, Rick: *Star Trek: The Next Generation U.S.S. Enterprise NCC-1701-D Blueprints* (Pocket Books, 1996). Detailed deck plans of the *Galaxy*-class *U.S.S. Enterprise*-D. Introduction by Robert H. Justman.

Toffler, Alvin: *Future Shock* (Random House, 1970). Toffler's classic treatise on the impact of technology and accelerating change on our society.

Trimble, Bjo: *On the Good Ship Enterprise, My 15 Years With Star Trek* (Donning Company, 1982). Trimble's adventures in and around *Star Trek* production, fandom, and conventions.

Trimble, Bjo: *The Star Trek Concordance* (Citadel Press, rev. ed., 1995). Trimble's updated reference to the first *Star Trek* series, the movies, and the animated *Star Trek*.

Whitfield, Stephen E. and Roddenberry, Gene: *The Making of Star Trek* (Ballantine Books, 1968). Behind the scenes of the first *Star Trek* television series.

Denise Okuda's credits include *Star Trek: First Contact, Star Trek Generations, Star Trek VI: The Undiscovered Country,* and promotional work for 20th-Century Fox's cult classic, *The Adventures of Buckaroo Banzai: Across the Eighth Dimension.* Taking advantage of her degree in nursing, Denise has occasionally served as a medical consultant to the writing staff of *Star Trek.* Her hobbies include tropical fish and frequent trips to Yosemite National Park. She is active in supporting environmental causes.

Denise currently works as a scenic artist and video playback coordinator for *Star Trek: Deep Space Nine* and as video coordinator for *Star Trek: Voyager.* Along with her husband, Michael, Denise is a coauthor of *The Star Trek Encyclopedia* and was an associate producer on Simon and Schuster Interactive's *Star Trek Omnipedia* CD-ROM. Denise lives in Los Angeles, California, with her husband and their dogs, Molly and Tranya.

Michael Okuda is the scenic art supervisor for *Star Trek: Voyager* and *Star Trek: Deep Space Nine.* He is responsible for those shows' control panels, signage, alien written languages, computer readout animation, and other strange things. Michael worked on all seven years of *Star Trek: The Next Generation,* during which he was recognized with three Emmy nominations for Best Visual Effects. His other credits include five *Star Trek* feature films, The *Flash, The Human Target,* and *The Osiris Chronicles.*

Along with Rick Sternbach, Michael serves as a technical consultant to the writing staff of *Star Trek* and is coauthor of the *Star Trek: The Next Generation Technical Manual* book and CD-ROM. Michael grew up in Hawai'i, where he graduated from Roosevelt High School and earned a BA in communications from the University of Hawai'i at Manoa. He is a member of IATSE Local 816 (Scenic, Title and Graphic Artists) and wants to be the first graphic artist in space.